In the Cold Light of Day

Also by Pauline Barclay

Magnolia House
Satchfield Hall
Sometimes It Happens…
Storm Clouds Gathering

Available in Kindle and Paperback

Next Christmas Will Be Different – a 20 minute read

Available only in Kindle & e-copy

In the Cold Light of Day

Pauline Barclay

www.paulinebarclay.co.uk

In the Cold Light of Day

Copyright © Pauline Barclay 2016

Cover design by Cathy Helms, Avalon Graphics
www.avalongraphics.org
Copyright © Pauline Barclay 2016

The author or authors assert their moral right under the Copyright, Designs and Patents Act, 1988, to be identified as the author or authors of this work.

All rights reserved. No part of this publication may be reproduced, stored in a retrieval system, or transmitted in any form or by any means, electronic, mechanical, photocopy, recording or otherwise, without prior written permission of the copyright owner. Nor can it be circulated in any form of binding or cover other than that in which it is published and without similar condition including this condition being imposed on a subsequent purchaser.

The characters in this novel and their actions are imaginary.
Their names and experiences have no relation to those of actual people, living or dead, except by coincidence.

ISBN-13: 978-1530377923

Acknowledgements

A special thank you to Cathy Helms at Avalon Graphics, whose wonderful skills has produced another beautiful and stunning cover.

To my wonderful editor, Jo Field who ensures my books are polished so they shine as bright as any star in our galaxy.

Thank you to everyone at Famous Five Plus for all your support. You are all amazing and successful authors.

A grateful thank you to you the reader for downloading, In the Cold Light of Day, I hope you enjoyed the book and that you ended up loving Bertie Costain as much as I did. Hugs to you x

And last but not least, a HUGE hug to my fabulous husband for just being the best.

Chapter One

Pressing the palms of his hands down on the table top, Bertie Costain nudged his chair back and pushed himself to a standing position. His legs felt like India rubber and as he stepped back his knees buckled. Grabbing the chair arms for support he inhaled deeply, filling his lungs with the stale tobacco-laden air. Waiting for the sudden dizziness to subside, he gazed around the room and took in the scene: the subdued lighting; tables surrounded by men in dark suits; roulette wheels spinning; faces taut with hope and fear watching in anticipation, greedy eyes feasting on stacks of coloured chips. The occasional shout of joy or cry of despair.

Bertie knew he had to get out of here as quickly as possible, and not just for fresh air. He also knew that to leave hastily would attract attention, and right now the last thing he needed was to betray the alarm that was coursing through him like an electric current, making his skin crawl. Already one or two heads were turning in his direction, eyebrows raised, eyes glaring through the fug, faces expressing a mixture of pity and irritation. Or was it stupidity? He did not know, nor at this moment could he have cared less, for panic was beginning to grip tightly around every nerve in his body, squeezing his chest so it was hard to breathe. Part of him wondered if it was possible to die of nerves being crushed by panic, because if so, he was on the verge of imminent demise. And that might be no bad thing, he reflected.

Pulling himself up straight, he willed his legs to move, transferred his sweaty grip to the back of the heavy oak chair and stepped round it, forcing down another deep breath of fetid air. It shuddered into his lungs seeming to burn his air passages on its way down. He coughed, blinking several times before he could focus clearly, aware that several more pairs of eyes were now casting their curious gaze at him. Ignoring them he let go of the chair, moulded his features into a deadpan expression and with studied nonchalance made his way unsteadily towards the exit door. The illuminated sign, 'Raffles', the club where he had arrived when it was still daylight, was now shining out in the darkness, bathing the foyer in a bright red glow. Bertie knew he had been here for hours; he had lost all track of the time.

He had taken no more than half a dozen steps when two men stepped forward to block his path: Brian Smith and his sidekick, Kevin Bryant. Smith was the club's owner, six foot tall and heavily built; jet black hair slicked back; ebony eyes dark as molasses, and a neatly trimmed moustache above thick lips that now parted to smile at Bertie. Even a blind man would know the smile was as false as a sunrise at midnight.

Bryant wasn't smiling. 'A touch of bad luck there Mr Costain,' he said, yet his tone was not commiserating, nor did it reveal that Bertie had been taken to the cleaners. In build the man was a double of Smith, but in all other respects they were as different as chalk and cheese. Bryant's features were softer, his hair Scandinavian blond, his powder-blue eyes deceptively amiable. He looked like a muscle man who, beneath the bulky exterior, was a gentle giant. Both men were smartly dressed in dark tailored lounge suits and crisp white shirts, their matching blood-red ties peeping over their waistcoats.

Bryant placed his huge hand on Bertie's shoulder, 'Mr Costain, before you go, we'd appreciate you accompanying us to the office, we have a few details to settle.'

The under-statement of the year, thought Bertie as he squared up against the two heavies, knowing he had no choice. It was not a request.

With long steps, Brian Smith led the way in silence. Bertie followed, aware that Kevin Bryant was snapping at his heels. It was a short walk to Smith's office, but to

Bertie it felt like the long walk to the gallows. The summons to Raffles' inner sanctum was worse than being sent to the headmaster's office back in his schooldays. At least then it had been only a caning that awaited him. Now it was punishment of a different kind. Retribution for a crass lack of judgement that was going to cost him dear. Shock had set his every nerve-end jangling, but if he was to survive this encounter he needed to be careful; keep his wits about him.

Smith pushed the office door open and strode ahead into the spacious room, which in Bertie's view was less like an office than the opulent lounge of some up-market bordello: a vision of flocked wallpaper, padded chaise longues, gilded mirrors and elegant Louis Quinze side tables. Up-lit Lautrec-style paintings graced three walls. *Christ, they might even be originals!* thought Bertie. The vulgar display of wealth smacked him squarely in the face as he walked in behind Smith and came to a standstill. So this was how the owner of Raffles spent all the punters' losses. *My own contribution must be in here somewhere*, he thought, clenching his jaw.

With a mixture of apprehension and sickening disdain he watched Smith cross to the other side of the office, his handmade leather shoes sinking into the Axminster's thick pile, richly patterned in deep maroon and gold. With practised precision Smith placed himself squarely behind his oversized, carved mahogany desk. Making no attempt to sit, he leant forward, rested his hands on the green leather top and looked down, as if the words he needed to say were written on the piece of hide beneath his balled fists.

Bertie was keenly aware of Bryant closing the door behind him and standing in front of it, arms folded over his massive chest. A lull filled the room. After what seemed like an eternity, Bertie opened his mouth to say something, anything to break the unpleasant hush, but before he could get a word out, Smith focused his eyes on him and without preamble, in a voice that matched the flatness of Bryant's tone earlier, he spelt out the terms of payment.

'It's business Costain, you know the rules, settle up by the deadline and you return as a fully paid up member of Raffles and will, of course, be welcomed back with open arms into our exclusive club.' He paused, flicked a non-existent speck of ash off his lapel, added, 'As of now the deadline is forty-eight hours.'

Jaw-dropped, at first unable to take in what he had heard, Bertie stared with unblinking eyes at the owner of Raffles. As the implication of those words seeped into his brain he wanted to yell in protest; to bang his fist down hard on the ostentatious leather-topped desk or better still, smash it into Smith's smug face, but he was too numb to flex a muscle. Long seconds passed before the power of movement returned and he was able to lift his hand. He took a deep breath, was about to speak, when Smith raised his own hand, palm outwards, effectively silencing whatever Bertie had intended to say. Stepping out from behind his desk, a broad smile on his thick lips, Smith now extended his hand and walked over to where Bertie stood stunned into silence.

'We're all gentlemen here,' Smith said, 'and we pride ourselves on who we are. I'm looking forward to putting all this behind us, aren't you?' He took hold of Bertie's hand in a vice like grip and shook it vigorously.

Bertie was starkly aware that to voice any kind of protest at the impossible deadline Smith had imposed would be a waste of time. Not only that, it would doubtless add a further nail to his already assembled coffin. Gentleman or no gentleman, he'd been stuffed and trussed like an overfed fowl ready for the oven. So instead, he nodded his head as if in agreement. Feeling welcome release from the powerful handshake, which to his mind conveyed more words than Smith probably had in his vocabulary, he turned away and forced his legs to propel him forward, thankful that Bryant had pulled open the door for him. The meeting, it seemed, was over.

Grinding his teeth together in an attempt to keep a lid on his anger and frustration, Bertie reluctantly accepted that now was not the time to lose face. Were he to cause a scene he would likely end up in Casualty. With all the dignity he could muster and with a control he had not thought he possessed, he held his head high and marched out of Smith's office without saying a word.

Stepping out of Raffles into a balmy night, Bertie was in a state of shock. He made it only as far as the bank of *Rugosa* roses growing in profusion along the edge of the car park, before he threw up. He retched several times, heaving up the contents of his stomach and wondering how he came to be in this situation; one that he never wanted to repeat. Nothing short of a miracle was going to sort this one out. And the clock was already ticking. Bertie groaned, pulled a handkerchief from his pocket and wiping his face walked over to his car. His prized possession: an E-type Jaguar.

Breathing in the warm summer air, his senses assaulted by the heady scent of roses, a fragrance so sickly sweet he almost threw up again, Bertie leaned against the car, his mouth filled with the bitter taste of bile. He shut his eyes and let the evening's fiasco sink into his tired brain. Forty-eight hours? His shock turned into indignation and quickly progressed to anger. The bastards knew what they were doing alright; they'd screwed him good and proper this time. Risking another deep breath he wondered if it might be his last. Was his heart going to give out? It was hammering in his chest like a hundred drummers on parade.

No matter what happened, Bertie knew he somehow *had* to meet the deadline. Failure to do so would mean the loss of much more than his reputation. The thought of it made him shudder; more than ever before he needed the quick thinking and cunning mind of his old friend, Howard Silvershoes, to dig him out of this hole.

Opening his eyes, Bertie reached in his trouser pocket for his car key and slipped it into the door lock, at the same time contemplating the wisdom of driving. If he got behind the wheel he just might end up wrapping himself and his precious Jag round a lamp post. He was angry and in a panic over his loss, but he certainly was not suicidal. He decided to walk the five miles back to Wentworth Place. Smith and Bryant would not be troubled by his E-type sitting in the car park until morning. The car was certainly valuable, but its worth paled to insignificance against what he had lost on the tables that evening. No, they didn't want his Jag; it was his blood they wanted… or something close!

Setting off down the deserted road, Bertie's mind reeled as he tried to work out a plan to pay his debt. He did not hear the voices of the two youths until they were almost on him. He looked up startled, taking in the denim jeans and dark leather jackets. The taller of the two deliberately pushed into him. 'Oi, mister, watch were you're goin',' he sneered.

All of Bertie's recently suppressed anger and distress bunched into his fist. He was about to lash out at the ignorant lout when he saw the approaching panda car. It slowed, the window wound down and a policeman called out, 'What's going on here?'

'Nothing Officer,' Bertie responded and at the same time stuck his left foot out, gratified to see the shorter of the two lads trip over it. 'Looks like these two have had a skin full,' he called. 'Three sheets to the wind, seems to me,' he added as the youth lost his balance and went sprawling into his mate. Righting themselves, swearing under their breath, the lads ran off mumbling obscenities. The officer grinned, raised his hand at Bertie and the patrol car pulled away.

Watching its tail lights disappear, Bertie relaxed. It seemed his luck was in on the street if not on the roulette wheel. These days London was turning wild.

With the distraction over, his mind raced back to the losses he had accumulated. It crossed his mind that he might have been better off if he had been mugged after all.

Then at least he would be tucked up safely in a hospital bed with a pretty nurse fussing over him. Instead he was walking the streets in the hope of a miracle and not a sign of Florence Nightingale.

Spying a telephone box, Bertie fumbled in his jacket pocket for a handful of coins. Relieved he had enough to make a call and oblivious of the late hour he decided to ring Howard Silvershoes. Good old Howard; always there to help and advice. He still kept the books for Bertie's building company. They went back years. If anyone could get him out of the dire straits into which he had plunged himself, Howard would. And if ever there was a time he needed his old friend's help and advice it was right now.

The phone box stunk. It took six rings before the call was answered, every ring adding further tension to his already strained nerves. Hearing Howard's sleepy voice, Bertie launched into a diatribe against Raffles, describing the outcome of the evening and emphasising the pay back deadline. Then he waited for Howard's response. None came. A silence hung between them until Bertie's impatience and agitation got the better of him and he snapped, 'Well?'

'Well what? I warned you, but—'

'Look Howard, right this minute I don't need a lecture, I need help to get it sorted. I'm standing in the street and I'm desperate.' Bertie grimaced. He didn't want to think about the many warnings Howard had dished out over the years. The man was quite probably right, but now wasn't the time to be reminded.

'Have you any idea what time it is Bertie?' Howard grumbled. 'How the hell am I expected to sort out your mess when everyone but you is tucked up in bed sleeping? Just go home and get some sleep. We can talk again in the morning – in my office and not in the street! And be warned, Bertie, you have overstepped the mark this time on all counts.'

The abrupt click on the line told Bertie the call had ended and he guessed Howard had slammed the phone down, he didn't care; he had said what he wanted. Howard would work something out, he always did. Pushing the heavy door open Bertie stepped out of the phone box, relieved to exchange the stench of stale sweat and urine for rose-laden air. He was exhausted, but sleep was the last thing he would be capable of. He needed a cigarette. Rooting in his jacket pockets, Bertie swore: he had left the packet at Raffles. Remembering there was another in his car, he almost ran back to the club.

As he walked into the car park, he saw that the Raffles sign had been switched off. Instead, the security light flashed on, lighting up the Jaguar. Feeling conspicuous, Bertie unlocked the car, almost pulling the door handle off in his haste to get it open and take the weight off his feet. Dropping into the driver's seat, he reached over to the dashboard and grabbed the half-full packet of Benson and Hedges, felt for his lighter and lit up a cigarette. Letting the smoke fill his lungs Bertie leaned back against the leather seat, feeling instant relief as the nicotine entered his bloodstream. The security light clicked off; the streets were still and quiet; the silence heavy. Bertie thought about Howard's words, '*Go home and get some sleep.*' Ludicrous, he smirked and almost laughed out loud, but ended up spluttering and coughing. There would be no sleep for him and before he could go home he needed to have a watertight story for Kitty. The last thing he needed was for his wife to know where he had spent the evening and what he had been up to. There were parts of his life that were private and roulette was one part that was very private indeed.

Chapter Two

Kitty Costain yawned. Rolling onto her side, she reached across the king-size bed and let her hand move across the cool, crisp cotton sheets. Her hand stilled, her eyes snapped open. Kitty sat up and stared down at the empty space beside her. 'Bertie,' she whispered. From the smooth sheets and fluffed up pillow, it was obvious her husband had not slept in their bed last night. In the eight months since they had married she had not once slept alone. Glaring at Bertie's side of the bed as if the answer was sewn in the bed linen, a wave of disquiet swept over her. Had Bertie realised his mistake in marrying an older woman, she wondered, one ten years his senior? Kitty grimaced as this flight of fancy took hold. Pushing the covers back she realised she was being neurotic. This kind of thinking would get her nowhere. Hadn't Bertie told her he was attending a building contract meeting that included dinner? Of course he had. He had not arrived home by eleven o'clock and her eyes had struggled to stay open. Mrs Watson, their housekeeper had long since retired down to her apartment, leaving Kitty alone. Knowing she would fall asleep in front of the television she had made her way to bed with the intention of reading until Bertie turned in, but as soon as her head had touched the pillow she was asleep. None of which answered the question as to why Bertie had not come to bed. Swinging her legs over the edge of the mattress she let her feet settle on the soft carpet, her toes sinking into the thick pile as she puzzled over her husband's absence.

    A shaft of sunlight pushed its way through the narrow opening of the lightweight summer curtains. Kitty guessed the time to be around seven o'clock. Leaning forward she plucked the alarm clock from the top of the bedside cabinet. The sudden movement made the little hammer on top tremble as it vibrated against the two bells on either side, giving out a hollow ring. Staring at the cream clock face she saw it was later than she had believed. Seven-thirty and no sign of Bertie: so where was he?

Leaving her question hanging in the warm morning air and suppressing a qualm of anxiety, she flipped the clock over and wound it up. With every turn of the key she was reminded that she was past the first flush of youth. If she was brutally honest, past the second one too! At the age of fifty-five, she had succumbed not only to marrying again, but to marrying a younger man. A mischievous smile curved her lips as she remembered how eyebrows had risen and tongues wagged with tittle tattle at her 'scandalous behaviour'. The ladies at the tennis club had twittered behind their glasses of sherry wondering if she had lost her marbles or worse and all the while she had revelled in the attention of a younger man. It had even crossed her mind that some of them might be jealous.

It had been a whirlwind romance and within two months of meeting they had married. Two months! Looking back, Kitty could not believe she had done something so rash and yet it had seemed perfectly normal at the time. Now, though, she wondered if Bertie's attention had strayed elsewhere. Was she about to get her comeuppance? Surely not? Nonetheless, she was disappointed Bertie had not telephoned to say he was staying out all night. Kitty frowned; she could not allow herself to think that something awful might have happened to him. There had to be a simple explanation.

Pushing herself out of bed, she slipped her bare feet into a pair of dusky pink mules and padded over to the Regency-upholstered chair in front of the kidney-shaped dressing table. She looked into the mirror: two almond-shaped emerald eyes stared back at her; a cloud of strawberry blonde hair framing her face. Not bad for fifty-five years, she thought, though the lines were beginning to show. Plucking a light dressing gown from the seat, she slipped her arms into the silk robe and was poised to tie the belt around her waist when the bedroom door flew open, the sudden draught making the soft curtains swish gently against the open window. Swinging round, Kitty watched as Bertie swept into their bedroom, the tails of his white cotton shirt hanging loosely over his underwear. His head was down as he fiddled with a cufflink, his expensive aftershave wafting in the air. In an instant Kitty took in that her husband was freshly bathed and shaved and was in the process of dressing for a day at the office.

Relief warred with bewilderment. 'Bertie! Where have you been all night?' she asked, tying the belt of her dressing gown tightly around her waist as she spoke then biting her lip. She had not meant to sound so querulous.

'What?' Bertie cried, his head snapping up as he stopped in his tracks, a startled expression making his face appear oddly like that of a child woken from a bad dream.

Kitty met his gaze and an icy shiver ran down her spine. The look Bertie threw her was akin to that of a rabbit caught in the headlights: startled, frightened and for the briefest of moments it seemed he had no idea where he was.

'Kitty it's you!' Bertie's voice, strained, carried across the room.

'Who else would it be in our bedroom?' She smiled, made an effort to keep her voice even, but the sight of him worried her. 'Where have you been? You didn't come to bed last night.' Padding across the room she took in his appearance and frowned. 'Why are you dressed already? You look like you're about to dash off. It's only seven-thirty, Bertie. You should have some breakfast before you go.'

A weak smile flashed across his face as she neared him. She was sad to note it did not reach his eyes. Opening her mouth to say more, her words stayed hanging between her tongue and lips as Bertie turned his back on her. It was as if he didn't want to speak to her. Still fiddling with his left cufflink, he hissed through clenched teeth, 'Damned things won't fasten.'

Having never seen this side of Bertie, Kitty was taken aback. In the months since they had met he had only ever displayed kindness, affection and a penchant for enjoying life with her.

'Come here and let me help.' She reached out and taking hold of Bertie's hand found to her surprise that it was shaking. What had her husband been up to, she wondered, gently squeezing his trembling hand. Letting it go, she deftly linked the small gold studs together. 'There you are. It just needed two hands.' She looked into his face, 'Are you going to tell me what happened that kept you from coming home last night or is it none of my business?'

Bertie combed his fingers through his thick dark hair making it stand on end. 'I'm sorry Kitty, but something unexpected turned up regarding the contract meeting. It went on for ages and it was the early hours of the morning when I eventually got home.' He looked into her eyes, 'I should have phoned you last night, but by the time everything had been discussed it was late.' He rubbed his chin as if to think, 'I'm not sure what time I eventually got back, but the last thing I wanted was to disturb you, so I slept on one of the sofas in the drawing room.' He nodded his head as if confirming his actions.

Kitty placed her hand on his arm, no wonder he looked pale and drained. 'If the meeting went on to the early hours of the morning, why are you in such a rush to go out so soon? Surely it was all dealt with last night?' She had some experience of running a business, knew about the stresses and strains involved. For years her late father had owned Maddisons, an exclusive country hotel. It had demanded much of his time. Late meetings, usually concerning staffing or marketing, were not unknown, but they were nothing compared to the scale of her husband's business, nor had there been the tension created by architects, building regulations and planning approvals with which Bertie had to deal, not to mention difficulties with fluctuating cash flow.

Bertie shrugged her hand away, anger flashing in his eyes. 'Kitty, please don't fuss. I might have been up half the night trying to square things, but in the end nothing went to plan. It was a shambles. I would not be rushing around to leave this early if I didn't think it was important, believe you me.'

Hurt, taken aback at Bertie's outburst, Kitty glared at him. 'Whatever it is, surely it can't be so bad? And knowing you, it will all be sorted and the contract will be in your hands by the end of the day.' How many times had he come home saying he had won this or won that and always after a period of worry?

However, this time her words of reassurance appeared to land on deaf ears. Bertie turned his back on her and in his stockinged feet strode over to his wardrobe, but not before Kitty saw fear flicker in his eyes. What had he got involved with? She did not ask, for as much as she wanted to know, with him in this attitude it was not the time to press for details. She watched in silence as he pulled the wardrobe door open, the door swinging back with a bang, almost wrenched from its hinges. She knew other contracts had been important, but this one seemed to be taking its toll even before a signature had been penned on the legal documents. Whatever had transpired the previous night had turned the normal cavalier, fun-loving Bertie Costain into Jekyll and Hyde. Kitty didn't like what she saw.

Rifling through the contents on the rail, Bertie grabbed a hanger holding a dark brown suit. As if reading Kitty's mind, he said over his shoulder, 'This morning we all meet again and I cannot afford to be late.' He whipped the trousers off the hanger. 'And as for things being bad, believe you me, bad is not the word.' He hooked the hanger, with jacket, onto the door knob then slipped into a pair of impeccably pressed trousers. Snatching a silk tie from the rack he deftly tucked it under his shirt collar before tying a Cambridge knot. 'So don't talk to me about bad, Kitty. You have no idea what you're talking about.'

As he slipped the perfect knot into position, Kitty, stung into silence, accepted that her presence, like her questions, was unwelcome. Any further words would only fuel Bertie's frustration and right now she needed a hot drink. Mrs Watson would be downstairs in the kitchen. At least she would give her a warm 'Good morning', as well as a hot cup of tea. Soothed by the prospect of amenable company Kitty turned away from her irritable husband and made her way to the door.

'Kitty, wait, please.' Bertie called as he slipped his feet into a pair of dark brown brogues. Hastily he fastened the laces then strode after her, reaching out to grasp her arm. 'I'm so sorry, it was unforgivable of me to snap at you. I didn't mean to. It's been a trying few days and I'm tired.'

Hearing the strain in his voice, Kitty turned to stare at him. Today he most certainly *was* Jekyll and Hyde, his mood turning on a sixpence.

'Come here,' he said softly, pulling her close to him and wrapping his arms around her. 'I am sorry, darling. Unfortunately some contracts demand blood, and this appears to be one of them.'

He sounded more positive than he had moments earlier and he dropped a kiss on the top of her head. The gesture was enough to lessen Kitty's unease. Smiling she looked into the china-blue eyes that held her gaze without flinching.

'Bertie Costain, you're like a bear with a sore head this morning, yet I still love you. If there is anything I can do to help, tell me. Do you need a little financial help to get the contract started? You know you only have to ask. I'm positive you'll win this one; it will be yours by the end of the day, you'll see. And I'm always here for you, especially when you hold me close and look at me like that.' She didn't miss the flicker of a sparkle in Bertie's eyes at her words.

'I will always hold you close and keep looking at you like this, Kitty. You are so beautiful. Who said age does nothing to improve a woman? Whoever they were, they're wrong. Clearly they never met Kitty Costain,' he smiled down at her.

'Flattery will get you everything,' she said, raising her eyebrow and returning his smile. 'So stay and have breakfast with me?' She had hoped to stall him long enough for him to calm down, but Bertie let her go and stepped back. Checking his watch, he scowled.

'Sorry darling, it's tempting, but I really must get a move on. Seriously, I cannot be late.' As he spoke he grabbed his jacket off the hanger and hurried across the room to the door. Kitty saw his knuckles turn white as he grasped the brass door knob and pulled the door open with unnecessary force. Shrugging into his jacket he strode to the landing and without looking back, called, 'I promise I'll make it up to you just as soon as I have this all sorted and buttoned down. See you later.'

Listening to the hurried foot fall as her husband thundered down the stairs, Kitty was enveloped by a feeling of foreboding. Bertie's odd behaviour was hardly the enthusiasm of a man about to win a large building contract.

Chapter Three

Taking them two at a time, Bertie sprinted down the front steps outside Six, Wentworth Place, the palatial townhouse he still could hardly believe he had managed to own. Reaching the pavement he felt the heat in the early morning sun and was painfully aware it was going to be a stifling hot day – in more ways than one. He snorted derisively and wondered how he was going to get through the next few hours. Over the years he had been in a few tight corners, but what he had got himself into last night made a tight corner look like a fire escape. Right now he needed a miracle or an act of God to stave off his execution. He snorted again, both seemed as likely as Brian Smith telling him it was all a mistake and he had not lost his shirt last night in Raffles.

Bertie stared at his elegant car parked at the kerbside, glad he had changed his mind and driven it home last night. He wondered if this morning would be the last time he would sit behind the wheel. Not wanting to believe they would take his E-type as a donation to his debt, he shook his head and dismissed the very idea, then immediately regretted it. His head ached from too much whisky, too little sleep and too much panic. He had thrown up twice more since arriving home. Thankfully, the housekeeper was tucked up in her bed in the basement flat when he had lurched to the cloakroom. The old woman's disapproving glare would have finished him off after such a disastrous night. After wiping down his mess and liberally squirting magnolia air freshener from the can Mrs Watson kept on the window ledge, he had stretched out on the sofa, knowing sleep was impossible. The moment he heard the bustle of the housekeeper in the hall signalling it was morning, he pulled himself off the sofa and made his way upstairs to the bathroom. A hot soak was what he'd needed. Barely had he shuffled up two stairs when he heard Mrs Watson call after him. He had no idea what she had said, but he ignored her anyway. No doubt the woman would be regaling the state of him to Kitty over the breakfast table. At that moment he cared not a jot. He was exhausted and whatever energy he had left must be reserved for his meeting with Silvershoes. His heart missed a beat as he thought about the mess he was embroiled in, and yet no matter which way he looked at how the evening had played out, he could not come to terms with what had happened. Not even in his wildest dreams could he have imagined how one turn of the wheel could be such a disaster. Over the years he had been in a few uncomfortable situations, but he had never strayed too far out of his comfort zone; always backed off when he could see the edge of the cliff. Of course there had been occasions when he had misjudged and ended up teetering on the brink, but never had he gone over it feet first like he had yesterday. In the past there had always been those who had hauled him back onto *terra firma* and he had never forgotten to reward them. More often than not it had been Howard. He hoped and prayed his old friend could do it again, help get him back on his feet, find a solution in the time he had left, even if it meant calling in a few favours.

He slipped the key into the driver's door lock, which took one turn to click free. With his hand on the Jag's chrome handle, he pulled open the door. A mental image of Kitty in her silk robe flashed into his mind. It was not how alluring she looked that had arrested his attention when he walked into the bedroom, more the surprise on her face at his appearance, which had spoken a thousand words. After his long soak in the bath he had felt half human again. Assuming Kitty was still asleep and not wanting to disturb her – not wanting to face her if he was honest – he had taken a clean shirt from the cupboard where Mrs Watson hung the ironed laundry to air before placing it in his wardrobe. The woman was too fussy by half in his book, but so long as he had clean clothes he couldn't care less how she did things and as it turned out it was useful, for he had found underpants and socks on the shelf too. Preoccupied, he had been startled at the sound of Kitty's voice when, half-dressed, he had blundered into their bedroom, thinking he could retrieve a newly pressed suit without waking her. He hadn't missed the anxious enquiry on her face. Her right eyebrow arching into the thin lines of her forehead was a sure sign that she was looking for answers; honest answers! Instantly he saw she had other ideas on her mind as to his whereabouts last night, but as much as it hurt to have Kitty thinking he was having an affair, for now he preferred her to think that than have her discover the truth. She would never forgive him.

Pushing his hands through his hair, he tried to block out thoughts of Kitty, but the E-type's odour of newness drifting through the open door and filling his nostrils was a sharp reminder that this expensive car had been a gift from his wife. She had presented it to him six months ago after he had announced he had won the contract to build a multi-storey car park in Redhill. 'It's not every day you win a prestigious contract,' she had enthused as he had swept her off her feet with the news. Recalling the conversation now, Bertie swallowed hard. Like this morning's episode, that too had been a lie. He had not won a prestigious contract to build a car park, multi-storey or otherwise. In reality he had won a small contract to build six two-bedroomed semi-detached council houses on the edge of a large estate. The returns were abysmal; the profit not enough to purchase a decent runabout, let alone a brand new E-type Jaguar. The truth was that he had won an enormous amount on the roulette table and had wanted to flash the cash and celebrate. Even more importantly, he wanted Kitty to see him as a successful businessman, which of course he was. Though these days the real money he made was not from his company, B.C. Builders, but from a source Kitty never needed to know about, and that was gambling. This morning's charade had tested his ability to lie to breaking point. Even to his own ears he was appalled at how convincing he had sounded. It did nothing to cheer him. If he was honest he was disgusted with himself, even more so as it had been effortless to lie through his teeth. But on the other hand he could hardly trot out what had really happened. It hurt him to speak to Kitty the way he had. She did not deserve his outburst or the deceit, but he had no choice, the lies were an evil necessity. Quite simply, he could not allow her to discover his predilection for gambling even if it meant letting her think he was an adulterer. She would never in a thousand years lend him money if she knew what he did with it. No harm done. He'd pay it all back eventually if it killed him – which at this rate it might! He sniffed and wondered if, after this morning's performance, he might have greater success on the stage; be an actor instead of a builder or gambler. He knew he had the looks for it, though he was getting a bit ragged round the edges these days. He gave a bark of self-mocking laugh at this flight of fancy. Spotting a thumbprint on the door of the sleek, dark blue car he rubbed at it with his elbow and the laugh died in his throat. For the briefest of moments, the guilt of all the lies weighed him down, threatening to sap his already depleted mental energy. This beautiful E-type Jaguar came from the love of a beautiful woman, and he deserved neither.

Slipping into the soft leather driver's seat, Bertie reminded himself that now was not the time to let sentiment get in the way, better to concentrate on saving his skin and what he still owned. He tugged on the door handle and pulled the door towards him before slamming it shut. Staring down at the flashy key fob, another stab of anxiety took his breath away. Beads of perspiration trickled from his brow down his freshly shaved cheeks. Feeling the wetness he lifted his shaking hand and brushed the sweat away acutely aware that his unnatural hot state was nothing to do with the heat of the summer morning, but more to do with the meeting he must attend. 'Who in their right mind would come up with such a ridiculous deadline of forty-eight hours?' he cried out loud, knowing that only a greedy bastard would.

His hand still shaking, he tried to slot the key into the ignition. It took two attempts before he was successful. The car roared into life on the first turn of the key. Slotting the gear lever into first he released the handbrake then pushed with his right foot on the accelerator pedal. He added too much pressure and the wheels spun, the tyres screeching loudly as the E-type shot away from the kerb and into the road.

Gasping at his hasty get away, Bertie gripped the leather-clad steering wheel firmly with both hands, more in an attempt to steady his anxiety than to control the beast of a car. The last thing he needed was to arrive in a lather at Howard's office. There was no doubt in his mind that Silvershoes would take advantage of the situation. Seeing him frothing at the mouth in agitation would only have the man leaping back up on his pedestal lecturing him on the foolishness of gambling. Howard had no idea how it hooked you, gripped you tight, made your pulses race and your eyes water with success and failure. And Bertie Costain wasn't always a loser, oh no! He'd hit the big time on more occasions that he could count. These days his lifestyle was underpinned by his success on the tables. He smiled at the memories of his great wins.

Dwelling on more prosperous times he became aware of a loud blare from a car horn. Startled out of his preoccupation he jerked his head and glared into the rear view mirror. Exasperated, he spied a green Morris Minor close to his rear. Taking in the blue-rinsed hair of the driver peering through the steering wheel, he cursed loudly, 'Bloody hell,' he snapped, realising it was the rotund cleaner from the house next door. If only the bossy little woman would drop her glasses on her nose instead of admiring her brightly coloured hair in the vanity mirror, she might have seen him pull out, he cried silently.

A second blast from the Minor's horn screamed out.

'Shit,' he hissed and as tempted as he was to wind down the window, stick his hand out and put two fingers up in the air, he resisted. Instead he slammed his right foot hard on the accelerator and roared off down the road leaving the cleaner holding up the traffic and honking her horn like someone demented.

'Bloody woman,' he snarled, swinging the car round the corner. Had he not enough on his plate right now without Mrs Mop hooting and tooting at him first thing in the morning?

Changing up a gear, Bertie reminded himself once again he needed to calm down, if not he would be having a heart attack. Christ, my blood pressure must be sky high, he worried and at the same time took a deep breath in a vain hope it would return his vital organ to a more even keel. Holding the air deep in his lungs, he exhaled slowly. Hell's bells, that would put the tin lid on everything if he ended up as a stretcher case in Casualty, he mused. On the other hand, as he had thought last night after those two thugs had tried to do him over, at least in hospital he would be safe for a while. Or would he? An image came into his head of a crowd around his bed: Smith and Bryant, threatening to pull out his saline drip and demanding he pay up before popping his clogs. Howard Silvershoes, a murderous look on his face, leaning over the bed and giving him another one of his, *'I warned you about gambling'* lectures. And not a bunch of grapes between them, Bertie scoffed to himself.

Joking apart, he recalled Howard's abrupt, sanctimonious attitude on the phone last night and gave a derisory snort. His old friend was hardly the saint he made himself out to be. Like most successful people, Silvershoes had not got where he was today by being Mr Nice Guy to the rich and needy. He was an opportunist, out to make money and rarely did he miss a trick. Well educated, with a voice that smacked of public school, he dressed well in tailored suits from Saville Row and handmade leather shoes from Jermyn Street. Even had his hair cut and styled like he was a girl! Without a doubt, up front Howard Silvershoes was a vision of well-heeled respectability, yet behind the scenes he had in the past been as shady as the next man, as Bertie had cause to know, hence why he liked him. Between them they had enough contacts and friends in high places to get what they wanted much of the time and hopefully that would be the case today. He was pinning his hopes on that miracle.

The thought of what had happened last night in Raffles, the awfulness of his loss and the humiliation of being taken to Smith's office, brought Bertie out in a fresh rush of sweat. He could feel it soaking into his shirt. He was painfully aware that whichever way he cut it, today someone would have him by the short and curlies; of that he was certain. Wincing, Bertie tried to think of something positive to lift his spirits. Nothing came to mind.

Chapter Four

Walking round the corner into Wentworth Place Mark Dufton tucked his folded newspaper under his left arm and slowed his step sufficiently to admire the smart row of Georgian town houses. It was not his usual route to work and he knew it would add twenty minutes to his journey, but he had set aside the extra time to enable him to check out an address he had been given.

He gazed surreptitiously around and hoped he did not look too out of place. Wentworth Place was where the wealthy lived. No matter how many years he worked he would never earn enough to live in one of the basements, let alone a house in a road like this. Should he win the pools then he might have a chance, but he knew the chances of that happening were about as likely as him flying to the moon. 'Millionaires Row' his father had once called this part of town and as a top solicitor who'd had dealings with people of this kind, dad would have known. It was the thought of his father that had Mark going out of his way on a sunny summer's morning, walking down a road that had meant nothing to him until a few months ago.

Now, as he took in the row of elegant town houses with their short flights of tiled steps leading to columned portico entrances where heavy, carved wood doors shut out the world, he wondered who lived in these palatial homes. He observed that most had three storeys, although judging by the dormer windows that peeked out of red-tiled roofs, one or two had been extended to add an additional floor. From curtained windows below the short flight of steps it was clear most had a basement, no doubt for keeping the expensive wine they quaffed each night over candlelit dinners, or maybe converted to accommodate staff, he daydreamed. The basements in Wentworth Place would be a far cry from the cellar his grandparents had in their terraced house. That underground cave had no windows, though his granddad had painted the brick walls white to help reflect the light from the sixty-watt bulb swinging from the long cord dangling down from the ceiling. Of course that cellar was not used for vintage wines, Mark doubted his grandparents had heard of vintage wine let alone tasted a drop. Their basement was where they kept the coal; their only source of essential warmth. He remembered there had been a hatch in the pavement outside the living room window. The coalman would pull it open before emptying his sacks of wet slack down into the cellar. He recalled how the water ran off the coal and pooled in the middle of the floor. It would take days, sometimes weeks, before it dried out sufficient to burn on the fire. Staring at the elegant terraced houses, Mark smiled at the memory and realised it was a long time ago.

As his gaze travelled down the exclusive road, his attention was caught by the sight of a dark blue E-type Jaguar parked against the kerb, but before he could get close enough to admire the sleek sports car, it shot away from the kerb, tyres squealing loudly.

As he slowed his pace almost to a standstill a green Morris Minor screeched to a halt at his side, the driver blasting the horn. The shrill, blaring sound in these genteel environs was so unexpected that Mark almost jumped out of his skin. As if rooted to the spot he stared down the road as the E-type sped off on the opposite side, leaving the Morris Minor stationary in the middle.

Feasting his eyes on the driver, who was insistent on hooting the Morris's horn, disturbing the peace of this classy part of town, Mark was surprised to see it was not a man, but an elderly blue-haired woman. Dwarfed behind the large steering wheel she was peering through the windscreen at the rapidly departing sports car. So much for demur old ladies, thought Mark with a smirk, shaking his head.

To his chagrin the driver suddenly turned and as their eyes met she threw him a look of utter contempt. Taken aback at such hostility, he dropped his gaze and carried on walking. The old lady honked her horn again, shook her fist at him, then crunched the gears and with too much throttle kangarooed the car down the road. He watched in amusement as the Morris Minor jolted out of view and wondered why it had never occurred to him that the well-heeled had crazy people in their neighbourhood and problems like everyone else. As his mother always used to say, 'Money doesn't buy happiness, son.' He grinned remembering his rejoinder, 'But it sure as hell helps, Ma!'

With these thoughts slipping through his mind, Mark almost missed the twitch of a curtain on the second floor of number six. Staring longer than was polite at a woman looking down onto the street he wondered if she had heard the commotion. She could hardly have failed to, of course. He was tempted to smile up at the face that gazed down at him, but thought better of it. He was already out of his comfort zone without making an exhibition of himself.

He checked his watch and saw if he did not get a move on he would be late at the bank. He could do without that, particularly as the new office manager was to be announced before the end of the week. Mark had it on good authority that his name was at the top of the promotion list. The increase in salary would be useful now he and Susan planned to expand their family. He had everything crossed that they would be celebrating by the end of the week.

After a further surreptitious glace at the upstairs window of number six, Mark's lips curved in a satisfied smile. He had achieved what he had set out to do. So far so good. With purposeful steps and his right hand swinging at his side, he strode down Wentworth Place. From the communal, gated, beautifully manicured garden the rasp from a motorised lawn mower broke the peacefulness of the area.

Chapter Five

As the front door slammed shut, the sound reverberating through the silent house, Kitty shook her head in an attempt to fathom out what was going on with Bertie, because, from where she was standing, it was as clear as the nose on her face that all was not well. What puzzled her was why he was so agitated about the Town Hall contract. He had been like a cat on a hot tin roof these last couple of days. 'God alone knows what's got into him,' she muttered to herself.

The squeal of screeching tyres filling the peace of Wentworth Place had Kitty hurrying to the bedroom window. Flicking back the soft net curtains, she watched her husband's E-type Jaguar shoot away from the kerb. A hiss escaped her lips, 'Oh my God!' she cried, her hand going involuntarily to her throat as she saw Mrs Jenkins' Morris Minor just miss Bertie's expensive sports car. A flash of brake lights brought the little green car to a shuddering halt. A blast from the horn followed; the sound slicing through the early morning tranquillity of the neighbourhood. Standing stock still, Kitty held her breath knowing there would be a few choice words flying out of the fat little cleaner's surly mouth as she sat fuming in the middle of the road.

A sly grin crossed Kitty's face: in her husband's car too, the language would be as blue as Mrs' Jenkins's hair, particularly given the mood he was in. She smirked at how Bertie was inclined to swear when under pressure, especially if he was cut up at the traffic lights or a roundabout. She smiled, sure that the language in either car would make a trooper blush.

She watched as the Jaguar sped off down the road, Bertie clearly ignoring the hooting and tooting from behind. She was in no doubt that her husband's mind was somewhere else and certainly not on his driving. 'Men,' she murmured, 'what would you do with them? They live on another planet most of the time and right now my Bertie is behaving like his mind is somewhere out of this orbit!' Doubtless the near miss was his fault, but Kitty did wonder how Mrs Jenkins held onto her licence. The Morris Minor was stationary in the middle of the road. Already two cars were waiting behind to drive on, while the elderly cleaner, one hand still pressed on the horn, was attempting to engage first gear. Hearing the gearbox screech in protest, Kitty winced. *'Has she even got her foot on the clutch?'* she wondered.

Bored with the drama below, she was about to turn away when she spotted a young man on the other side of the street staring up at her window. To her discomfort he appeared to be regarding her. Even from this distance she sensed he was watching her. 'The audacity of some people,' she muttered flicking the net curtains back into place. What has happened to manners? More importantly, what was so fascinating about her?

Stepping back far enough to appear invisible, she continued to observe. She had not seen the young man before and from her vantage point guessed he felt uncomfortable; he certainly looked out of place. Even from this distance she could see he jerked his right leg as if he was nervous. She noted he held something under his arm, perhaps a folded newspaper, but there was no stationer's in the immediate vicinity, and anyway, Wentworth Place was not the kind of road that attracted casual pedestrians. So who was he? And more importantly, why was he staring up at her? An unexpected chill ran through Kitty's body as if someone had walked over her grave. His scrutiny was making her feel uncomfortable. She did not like his interest in Wentworth Place, especially number six. There was something slightly furtive about him. '*You can never be too careful,*' she thought, taking a careful mental note of his appearance. She guessed his age at around mid-twenties. Similar in height to her husband, but thinner, he was smartly dressed in a light grey suit, his dark hair combed forward to form a short fringe. He looked a bit like a sales rep or perhaps an estate agent. Confident that should anything untoward happen in the near future she would have enough details for the police to identify and question the young man, Kitty stepped away from the window and filed him to the back of her mind.

More now than ever, she needed her morning cup of tea. Crossing the carpeted floor she caught sight of her silhouette. Her long shadow stretching across the floor revealed nothing more than her willowy shape; everything else about her was missing. She had no features and no personality. It occurred to her that this was how, from time to time, she felt about Bertie, even more so after this morning. Their whirlwind romance and hasty marriage had left her little time to find out more about the man, ten years her junior, who had swept her off her feet. A smile played across her face at the memory of the night she had been introduced to the charismatic Bertie Costain.

Judy Brown, her one-time neighbour in the tranquil village of Wimbledon, who had lived in the apartment below hers in elegant Camden House, had telephoned and asked if she would make up the numbers at one of her Saturday dinner parties. 'A do that is always filled with fun, if I say so myself,' Judy's excitable voice had rung out, a ripple of laughter tinkling down the line as if to encourage a positive response, she continued to expand on her dilemma about odd numbers until Kitty had finally agreed. Judy's cooking was reputed to be out of this world and it certainly was, but 'fun' Ms Brown's dinner party turned out *not* to be, for while the ingredients had been in abundance in the culinary delights, they were sadly lacking in all other respects. Kitty had struggled to keep abreast of the heated discussion on golf, ranging from the quality of the greens and the fees, to the need for Pings. This train of conversation had been followed by tedious arguments about etiquette in the game of Bridge, and if that was not enough to have Kitty drowning in her Rioja, the overdressed and overfed prattled on endlessly about the government. A false smile had moulded itself onto Kitty's face as the excited voices assaulted her ears. She had stifled a yawn and looked across the table at the dapper man opposite. To her surprise he not only smiled at her, but had the audacity to play footsie under the table! Hastily pulling her feet back out of his reach she had treated him to a withering stare before dropping her gaze.

After the cognacs had been poured and gulped down, Kitty had ostentatiously looked at her watch and offered her apologies, saying that she was expecting a call from her son in Australia and would have to leave. 'The time difference makes it so awkward,' she had added, thinking, *'That much at least is true.'*

Judy had simply nodded, announcing in slurred words, 'Kitty my dear, you have been a life saver, thank you. We will be doing all this again very soon…'

Thankfully, at this point their somewhat piddled host had been drawn into yet another unintelligible conversation, this one about the welfare system, and Kitty had been free to make her escape.

Standing in the soft lighting of the carpeted communal hall she had drawn a deep breath of relief. She hadn't exactly lied to Judy, she had simply told a little fib. Simon did indeed live down under, but she was not expecting a call from him tonight. Stepping away from Judy's front door, Kitty had kicked off her shoes to free her aching feet from the bounds of her stiletto heels, almost leaping out of her skin when she heard a soft chuckle behind her.

'My recollection is that Cinders placed a glass slipper *on* her delicate foot, while this Cinderella appears to *remove* her footwear.'

Swinging round, Kitty had come face to face with the same man who, beneath the impeccably laid dinner table, had played fast and loose with her patent leather-shod feet. The china-blue eyes, which had repeatedly attempted to catch her gaze throughout the evening, were sparkling with merriment.

'And I suppose you see yourself as Prince Charming?' she had responded tartly, surprising herself. The wine and cognac had given her more confidence than she would normally have with someone she had met only three hours before.

'Allow me,' he said in a silvery voice, bending to retrieve her shoes and handing them to her. 'Kitty – I hope you don't mind me calling you Kitty? – I think Prince Charming is quite apt in the circumstances. Until you jumped up to leave the party I was working on a plan for our mutual escape. I could see you were every bit as excited by the company as I was.'

Taking the shoes and thanking him, Kitty could not help but laugh; he did indeed look like a charmer.

'How on earth do you come to mix with that lot?' he had asked, nodding his head towards the closed door of Judy's flat.

'Good heavens! 'I'm not one of them,' she had exclaimed, taken aback that he believed her to be in Judy's boring set. 'I was only making the numbers up, but what about you?'

'The same, I was asked to fill in when a guest had dropped out.'

'Wise guest,' she had said, and they had both laughed like schoolchildren sent out of the classroom for bad behaviour.

'Well we can't stand out here or we will be heard and heaven forbid we could be asked to return,' she had said, moving towards the staircase that led up to her own apartment. Stopping on the bottom step, she had called over her shoulder, 'You are welcome to a nightcap if you have time.'

'What about your phone call?'
'There never was one.'

'Really? Well in that case I will take you up on your offer, thank you', he replied. Then, raising an eyebrow, had added with a smile, 'You're a minx.'

Like a couple of teenagers they had run up the stairs to her apartment. At fifty-five, a widow with two grownup children, Kitty had felt like a youngster again. It had been a long while since she'd had such a fun-filled time with a handsome man so obviously flirting with her; it was a heady experience.

The fun had continued. After Judy's party, the following six weeks had been a whirlwind for Kitty. Bertie Costain had wined and dined her. Spoiling her or showing her off to business colleagues and friends. She could not remember ever in her life having such a wonderful time. They had spent a weekend in a luxurious suite at the Ritz; three nights in Paris; they had even spent a weekend on a narrowboat on the Norfolk Broads. And after six weeks of living a lifestyle that belonged to the super rich or superstars, Kitty, breathless with it all and hardly able to believe it was really happening, had accepted Bertie's proposal of marriage. They had tied the knot at Chelsea Registry Office. Afterwards, Bertie had whisked her off for three weeks in a sumptuous hotel in the South of Spain, before bringing her back to live in his elegant town house in Wentworth Place.

Looking back, Kitty knew he had captivated her from the moment they had met and yet, after eight months of marriage, if asked what she knew about Bertie Costain what could she say? Postage stamp and large print came to mind! He owned this splendid property in an exclusive area – he had revelled in telling her how that had come about. The story was fanciful, not unlike him and she still wondered which part of it was true. One thing she had learnt about her husband was that he had an imaginative way of making the normal appear exciting and sensual. As much as she loved this particular aspect of him, it was just one facet. She had also discovered that Bertie had several layers to his personality and this morning he had revealed one she had not seen before: a dark side; one that was agitated and clearly troubled. She had not missed the damp circles of perspiration under the arms of his impeccable white shirt; the slight tremor of his hands. His dapper appearance had done nothing to mask that mysterious, and dare she think, dangerous glint in his eyes that had flashed at her before he had left the house. Whatever meeting Bertie was in a tearing rush to go to, it surely had more implications than the simple award of a building contract. Kitty hoped that whatever it was, Bertie walked away with what he felt he needed or deserved.

Now, as she traced her shadow with the tip of her big toe, she wondered what other surprises she could expect to discover in the coming days, months and years. Flicking a strand of hair from her face, her thoughts melted away at the sound of a firm knock on her bedroom door. Spinning round, she watched as the door swung open and an elderly, rotund woman appeared, a wide smile filling her face.

'Morning Kitty, I see himself's gone rushing off and not even stopped for breakfast.'

'Good morning Mrs Watson, how are you today?' Kitty said, not missing Flo Watson's tone of disapproval at the mention of Bertie.

'I'm fine, though not too sure about the master racing out like the place was on fire,' her old housekeeper tutted. Turning to leave, she added, 'If you're on your way down, I'll get the kettle on.'

'Give me ten minutes to wash and dress and I'll be down,' Kitty replied. It saddened her that Mrs Watson had such little time for Bertie, it made the atmosphere between them awkward, which Kitty found unsettling. But right now she needed to put her own disturbing thoughts about Bertie away and concentrate on the busy day ahead. If she didn't get a move on, she'd be late opening up her shop and she was expecting a big consignment of mixed summer flowers from Holland to arrive at Rosebuds this morning. Then there would be bouquets to make up ready for a wedding at the weekend. With these thoughts driving

Bertie out of her head, Kitty started to sing, *'Where have all the flowers gone…'* as she hurried to the bathroom.

Chapter Six

With laboured steps, Flo Watson made her way down the wide, carpeted stairs, gripping the polished oak banister to steady herself. Behind her she heard Kitty's dulcet tones singing as she headed across the landing to the bathroom. Flo smiled to herself, even in her mid-fifties Kitty had a beautiful voice. What the neighbours made of it all Flo had no idea. The walls were thick, though not totally soundproof, yet nobody ever complained. And why would they? For herself she liked to hear Kitty singing.

Entering the kitchen, Flo took in the expensive modern units and worktops in the bright, well-lit room, so in keeping with the fashionable style of this elegant house. Goodness knows what it had all cost! Until arriving at Wentworth Place Flo had never seen a kitchen like it. Set into the worktop was a stainless steel gas hob. The large electric oven was at eye-level, housed in one of the matching handmade cabinets. Fancy and futuristic she thought, though the oven had the advantage of saving her back as she didn't need to bend down to slot dishes in and out. The fridge too was encased in a cabinet, again saving her back, but the appliance that fascinated her most was the Kelvinator Foodarama. She'd never seen or heard of one of these contraptions before. From what she could make of it, it was a fancy pantry that kept everything stone cold. It too, like the fridge and oven, was set in a large cabinet. More money than sense that Bertie Costain, and where he got his ideas and money from Flo didn't like to think about. Mind you, when it came to Mr Costain there were a few other things she didn't want to think about either, this morning being one of them.

She had been washed, dressed and her hair tied back when she had ambled up the narrow staircase from her flat to the house around six o'clock this morning. As usual, she had gone through to the hall and headed for the front door to collect the milk from the step. Before she could reach the entrance, Mr Costain had shuffled out of the drawing room and into the hall, dishevelled and reeking of stale tobacco and alcohol. He had stood gawping at her like someone who'd lost a pound and found a penny. She had looked him over with disdain, barely able to believe he was the same man who normally strutted around the house like the lord of the manor. This morning it was clear to Flo that he'd had more than a good night on the tiles; wrecked was the word that came to her mind. His cold blue eyes had glared at her and he'd muttered something, but she didn't catch what. Out of the goodness of her heart she'd been about to offer him a cup of strong tea, but he had slunk upstairs, leaving her thinking it was a good thing she hadn't got the milk in yet because it would have turned sour at the sight of him! By the time she had wandered back through the hall, clutching two bottles of fresh milk, the sound of water running told her Mr Costain was soaking his sins in a hot bath. It had been well over an hour before she had heard him cross the landing to the master bedroom. Obviously he had a lot of scrubbing to do, but what was it he needed to wash away, she wondered, as if she couldn't guess.

Now, as Flo walked over the blue ceramic-tiled floor and made her way to where the carving board and bread bin sat on the Formica top, Kitty's husband continued to nag at her mind. There was something about the man she found disturbing. Living under his roof in this modern, expensively furnished house did not make her happy, but what could she do? Leaving Kitty wasn't an option. Shrugging away disquieting thoughts, Flo pushed up the lid on the roll-top stainless steel bread bin. She knew she ought to be thanking her lucky stars that she lived in this fashionable townhouse where, seemingly, no expense had been spared.

She recalled the first time she had seen it, picturing the wrought iron railings and the flight of dark red ceramic-tiled steps leading from the pavement to the front door. At the time it had troubled her that there was no front garden to keep the street from the letter box and the road dust from the steps. Be that as it may, Bertie Costain had gone to great pains to explain that everything in the kitchen and bathrooms, of which she had counted three, had been bought from Heal's in Tottenham Court Road, no less. She had sniffed, assuming he wanted to impress, and so he had, but not in the way he might have expected. From then onwards, she had silently referred to him as 'Mr B' – Mr Braggart!

Lifting out a fresh white loaf from the bin, Flo placed it on the board, pulled open the cutlery draw and slid out a bread knife. With years of practice, she cut four even slices, pushed what was left of the loaf back into the bread bin and left the knife on the board to wash later. That done, she tilted her head and stared up at the ceiling, hearing Kitty's footfall scurrying around upstairs and knowing it would be another ten minutes before she appeared. Flo sidled over to the sink, reached across to the window and pulled on the thin cords to adjust the slats on the Venetian blinds. Flicking them to horizontal, she clicked her tongue as the slats swished to the desired position. She loathed them; they needed a constant wipe down to keep them clean. Why Mr B couldn't have curtains on the kitchen window like everyone else, she had no idea. Spotting a few water marks on the lower slats she gave a deep sigh and reached out her index finger to wipe the tiny stains away, not satisfied until they vanished.

Placing her elbows on the side of the stainless steel sink, Flo rested her chin in her upturned palms and stared out of the window. These days she felt not so much under the weather as thoroughly out of sorts. Right now, instead of feeling sorry for herself she should be filling the kettle and making a pot of tea, but she just couldn't get going this morning. Peering out at the back garden she saw a

43

couple of sparrows were splashing around in the ornamental bird bath. Old and covered with moss, it sat in the middle of a small lawn. She smiled as the little birds flapped their wings in the stone bowl sending rivulets of water trickling over the side to run down the weather-pitted pedestal and pool at the base.

Watching their antics, Flo felt a lump gathering in her throat. She stifled a sob and to her dismay felt tears slipping from her eyes. Keeping her misty gaze on the frolicking sparrows, she pulled a linen handkerchief from her overall pocket and dabbed at her wet face. What had got into her? Was it watching the little birdies that had brought her unhappiness into focus? She so missed living in the sticks. No matter how hard she tried to embrace the city life and tell herself this was home, London was not for her. A fish out of water wouldn't feel as much out of its depth as she did right now. If she was honest, she felt like a foreigner in her own country. Nothing and nobody behaved anything like normal. Only the other day she'd had to make her way through a gaggle of giggling teenage girls, all with flowers in their hair and brass cow bells dangling from their necks. She had tried to see the funny side of it, but being a country girl born and bred, in her book flowers lived in the garden or in a vase on the kitchen table. As for brass bells, in her home they had been confined to the mantle shelf with the rest of the ornaments. Had she reached an age where change was not so much hard as impossible, she wondered. Was she just a silly old woman? Thinking of herself in that way brought a fleeting smile to Flo's lips and catching sight of her reflection in the window she saw her ruddy complexion light up, her smile smoothing away the lines and creases around her eyes and mouth. She didn't like to see herself as old, not yet, but at sixty-five she was no spring chicken. The grey-haired woman with a face full of wrinkles reminded her of that every time she glanced in the mirror.

Watching the sparrows splashing in the water, like children in a paddling pool, reminded Flo of the countryside where she yearned to be, and as she thought about it, her mind's eye took her there. She went racing away down the road, along country lanes and across streams, until all she could see were rolling hills and empty spaces, and instead of the deafening noise of a busy city, all she could hear was peaceful silence. Not total silence, for there you could always hear the birds singing. It was music to her ears, like an orchestra playing a melody of tranquillity that was not drowned out by the constant hum of traffic. The only thing likely to knock you off your feet in the countryside was the wind, she thought, a fresh wave of homesickness threatened to set her off blubbing again. Why was she here, living in London, in a house she didn't feel at home in, and worse, in close proximity to a man she didn't trust?

Flo counted back to when she had arrived at Wentworth Place. Seven long months ago. How could she forget? Until the call that had got her packing her bags, she had lived in 'The Wells', her sister's cottage outside Epsom. She had not spoken to Kitty for a couple of months, so the call had come as a surprise, but it had been a welcome one. Kitty, buoyant and happy, had chattered amiably before she had got to the crux of the matter. There was always a crux of the matter where Kitty was concerned. That particular one was to ask if Flo would consider moving to London and doing a little housekeeping.

'It would only be temporary,' Kitty had said. 'You see Mrs Watson, I have remarried and it would be wonderful if you would consider coming to live with me again, if only for a few months until I am settled in. Please say yes, it would be like old times,' she had enthused, adding that annexed to their house was a beautiful little flat for her to live in, which Kitty had proceeded to describe in great detail.

At the time, Flo had thought it would be nice to have a place of her own again. On the other hand, she had asked herself, could she bear to live in London? Yet she was tempted; she had always liked Kitty. Back then, of course, she'd had no idea about Bertie Costain, and if she was honest, she missed looking after people. It was second nature to her and she was good at it. She had no husband of her own to worry about, him having run off years earlier with the tart from the baker's in Epsom. Her two children now long grown up had their own lives to lead. And although living with her sister was fine, it was not perfect. They were like chalk and cheese. Funnily enough, only the week before Kitty's call Flo had enquired about the cottage down the lane from her sisters – Primrose Cottage it was called – but was told that a new tenant was due in at the end of the month. With no chance of renting the cottage she had set her heart on, it had seemed that a move to London was meant to be.

Sighing, Flo remembered how much the hustle and bustle of the city had taken her aback; she had not counted on that. Nor had she anticipated how uncomfortable Kitty's husband made her feel. Some people you took to and some you didn't, thought Flo, and in his case she hadn't. Quite simply, she did not like him, nor did she trust him. Naturally she couldn't say as much to Kitty, who was quite clearly besotted with the man, though God alone knew why!

Sniffing, Flo wiped her nose on her damp hanky and counted back the years. She had been sixteen when she had started working for Kitty's parents at 'Maddisons', their small fashionable hotel nestling on the edge of Epsom Downs. That had been in the autumn of 1922 and she had begun work as a chamber maid. Maddisons had been a genteel place, its clientele the kind who wore twinsets and pearls or three-piece suits and silk ties, and drank sherry and cocktails. On more than one occasion Flo had glimpsed minor royalty and once an American film star had stayed there too. Such excitement!

After four years of cleaning beautiful hotel rooms, Flo's job had changed. Kitty's mother, increasingly frail having suffered several miscarriages, had asked her if she would consider taking up the position of cleaner-cum-housekeeper in the Maddisons' home, a big house called 'The Rookeries'. By then Flo was engaged to Albert Watson. The work had been lighter than in the hotel; a large part of her duties had been to supervise Miss Kitty, who was then just ten.

Throughout the years the Maddisons had been kindness itself to Flo. After she had married Albert, Mr Maddison had allowed them to live in the gatehouse in exchange for Albert's gardening services at the weekend. Years later, when Albert had upped and gone and their two children left school, Flo had changed jobs again, moving into Kitty's household as housekeeper-cum-nanny, Kitty having married by then and with two young children of her own. Thinking about it, it was hardly surprising she still felt a sense of responsibility towards Kitty, thought Flo, never mind that they were both in their middle years now – well, in her own case quite a bit past them. The Maddisons had been like family to her and she had grieved for Kitty's parents when both had died within a few months of each other. The hotel had been sold some years before when it all got too much for Mr Maddison. Sadly, today there was no hint of the lovely old hotel; in its place stood four large detached houses. How times had changed. The Maddisons had left Kitty very well off; not just the proceeds of the hotel, but The Rookeries as well, and a very nice house it was too, Flo reflected.

Startled out of her reverie by the noise of a car backfiring, Flo blinked. That would likely be Mrs Jenkins coming back in her Morris Minor. It was high time the old biddy stopped driving, Flo thought, giving a disdainful sniff. What was wrong with catching the bus? The sparrows she had been watching, equally startled, flew up out of the bird bath and away over the garden. She watched them go, a pall of sadness hanging over her. It did no good thinking back, yet she could not help it.

Death had seemed to be in the air the year the Maddisons passed on. Barely five months later, Kitty's husband had joined them. He had sat down one evening to have his usual nightcap tipple, a large brandy, and unfortunately never got to finish it. Heart attack, they said, and him only in his fifties poor chap. After he had gone to his maker and the two children had flown the nest, Kitty had sold The Rookeries; it was much too big for her to rattle around in on her own, she had said. But then she had bought a flower shop and an apartment in Wimbledon Village. Quite why a wealthy woman like Kitty had wanted a flower shop still mystified Flo. It wasn't as if she needed to work. By then Flo had turned sixty and was ready to retire, so she refused Kitty's invitation to join her in her spacious apartment. It hadn't seemed right at the time. Besides, she had already agreed to move in with her recently widowed sister.

Just thinking about her sister's cottage brought a fresh bout of tears. 'My word', Flo muttered; she was seriously out of sorts to be blubbing like this. It was not at all like her to be feeling so sorry for herself. 'Pull yourself together,' she hissed, knowing it was easier said than done. It wasn't as if she hadn't tried to make Wentworth Place her home, but no matter which way she cut it, it never would be. London was dirty and everyone was in a perpetual rush: people with tight jaws, steely purpose written all over their faces, jostling for space on the busy pavements, pushing past and knocking into you. The noise of cars, buses and lorries thundering past, oblivious to pedestrians and spewing out noxious fumes, produced a cacophony of sound that did nothing to create peace. '*The smoke*' they called London, and for good reason!

As for Bertie Costain, Flo knew little about him, but there was something that alerted all her senses when she was in his company. There were secrets and whispers down the phone and she was convinced Kitty was unaware of them. Flo also wondered how much of Kitty's inheritance was being frittered away on smart new appliances, not to mention sports cars! Yet as much as she wanted to pack her bags and head for the hills, Flo accepted that she needed to stay here a little longer, if only to see if she was wrong about Kitty's new husband. She hoped she was, because if not, Kitty would be heartbroken, but if she was right then someone needed to be here to pick up the pieces. And she had always been there for Kitty. *'Old habits die hard,'* Flo thought.

Her attention was caught by movement in the garden. A trio of squabbling starlings had alighted in the bird bath. Even the birds need to bathe regularly, thought Flo, smiling through her tears. They didn't stay long. Watching them flap away over the hedge into next door's garden Flo gave herself a mental shake. She needed to pull herself together. Slipping down memory lane and getting herself all upset would get her nowhere. For now she would try to concentrate on looking after Kitty. And goodness me, look at the time and she had not yet made the tea!

At the sound of footsteps on the stairs Flo reached out for the hand towel hanging over the oven door handle and surreptitiously wiped her face, then plastering on a thin smile she turned to see Kitty enter the kitchen.

Chapter Seven

Tapping his fingers in agitation on the steering wheel, his left foot lifting on the clutch and his heart racing, Bertie waited impatiently for the traffic lights to change. Monitoring the lights, his thoughts swung back to the previous evening.

'God was it only last night,' he groaned out loud, feeling as if he had travelled down a long road on a wild horse for what seemed an eternity. His head ached, but he guessed that was as much down to the whisky as the shock of his bad luck.

Balling his right hand into a fist, he thumped it down hard on the steering wheel, anger and frustration oozing out of every pore. He had believed it couldn't happen to him and now hours later he still could not take it in. Until Monday he had been on a roll of amazing luck. Gone had the helter-skelter days when he would win and then lose. So good had been his luck that he had begun to believe he was untouchable. He scoffed at how he had convinced himself he had been born under a lucky star, but on Monday everything had changed. The lucky star that shone over him had disappeared from the heavens and without it he had lost. His loss had not been particularly significant, but it was enough to encourage him back to the tables. He had needed to prove to himself that this was just a blip; that his loss of luck was only temporary, and so, drawn like a moth to a candle flame, back he had gone.

At the end of the afternoon, ignoring the mountain of paperwork that cluttered his desk, most of which was screaming demands for payment, he had hurried home to change into fresh clothes. Told Kitty, just back from her shop, that he'd forgotten he had a business dinner that evening and not to wait up as he might be late, making out that he'd infinitely rather be spending it with her. There was also the problem with her car he'd had to sort out. That done, he had gone to Raffles, convinced he would not only enjoy the game but walk away the victor. Monday's loss would be inconsequential to the winnings he would pocket. He was Bertie Costain; he could not lose! Adrenalin had pumped round his veins giving him a high and a welcome boost of confidence. But as it turned out, his confidence had been misplaced. Neither the stars nor the gods had shone down on him; it had been an unmitigated disaster. Sweat trickled down his face at the memory. He swiped the dampness away with the back of his hand. No matter how many times he revisited last night he could not get his head round how the wheel of fortune had swung against him. How on earth had he miscalculated so badly?

Seeing the amber light flash on, Bertie let the events of the disastrous night fade as he pushed the gear lever into first with a sickening crunch. Checking his rear view mirror he noted an Austin 1100 too close to his rear, a bespectacled man sat behind the wheel, was he a debt collector? *'Am I being followed?'* Bertie thought, panic making him sweat even more. The Austin indicated left and Bertie groaned. *'Christ, get a grip Costain, you're becoming paranoid''* The lights turned to green and with his foot hard down on the throttle he gunned the sports car and sped across the junction. Howard's office was less than five miles away the other side of town and right now Bertie could not care less if he broke the speed limit, just so long as he got there swiftly and alone.

Ahead, he spied the turning he needed to take. Without indicating, he stabbed at the brakes and at the same time pulled the car to the left. As the speeding sports car squealed round the corner, the steering wheel snatched out of his hands and the low profile tyres clipped the kerb. Momentarily Bertie lost it. Holding his breath, he grabbed at the steering wheel and brought the powerful car back under his control thankful that no one was in his path. A trickle of sweat dripped off the end of his nose and fell off his chin onto his knife-creased trousers. He slowed down to a crawl until his breathing steadied then nudged the speed up to forty. Glancing at the car clock, he saw it was coming up nine. He made a quick mental calculation: there were still enough hours to meet the deadline. Though no matter how many minutes there were in an hour, in his book the next few hours would be the shortest time ever recorded. The terms of his gambling debt were simple: if he did not produce the full amount with interest by the deadline, he could kiss goodbye to a considerable portion of his possessions – almost all of them, in fact. He did not like the thought of losing his home, the three-storey town house that had started his change of fortune. Though, of course, there was his building company too. If he was not careful that could be snatched instead of his precious house. Or as well as! 'Christ!' he muttered on a sigh, it would not be so much another brick in the wall, but no sodding bricks at all. Feeling his heart rate pick up again, all Bertie could think was that the day could turn not so much into a nightmare as into a bloody circus.

Spying a pack of Benson and Hedges sitting on the dashboard shelf, he realised how desperate he was for a smoke. When he had collected his precious car he had vowed never to smoke in it, but he had broken that vow last night and now, having nearly wrapped himself round a lamp post, he decided he was again in desperate need of nicotine. Pushing in the car lighter, he reached over and picked up the packet, shook out a cigarette and stuffed it between his lips. The lighter clicked out. He pulled it from its holder and held the glowing end to his Benson and Hedges, drawing the smoke deep into his lungs. The calming effect was almost immediate. As blue tobacco smoke filled the car interior, Bertie wrinkled his nose and rolled down the driver's window hoping to minimise the smell that he knew would linger, overlaying the pleasing scent of newness and leather. With the cigarette sitting in the corner of his mouth, he stared ahead and saw the next set of traffic lights turn red at the junction.

'Dammit! It's like an obstacle course out here this morning,' he spluttered, the stub of his cigarette bouncing precariously on his lower lip. Checking the rear view mirror, to his chagrin he saw yet another elderly bespectacled man, this one clutching the steering wheel of a green Morris 1100 and driving far too close for comfort. What was happening on the roads these days, Bertie wondered? He had driven barely a couple of miles and in that time all he had seen was old fogies who could hardly see through the windscreen, let alone make out what was ahead as they pootled along on the Queen's highways. What was the place turning into?

Taking one last drag on his cigarette, Bertie plucked the stub out of his mouth and flicked it out through the open window. As it rolled onto the tarmac he wound up the window then sat waiting at the lights, tapping his fingers on the steering wheel and silently praying that the old codger behind was not into kangaroo starts. It would sure as hell put the kybosh on the day if he smacked into the arse of the E-type! Turning his attention back to the road ahead, Bertie raised his wrist and checked his watch. 'Christ, lights!' he cried out, fuming with impatience. 'Bloody get a move on and turn green won't you? Time is ticking on and so is the deadline.'

Chapter Eight

Wearing light green trousers, a cream silk blouse and soft leather shoes, Kitty strolled into the kitchen. The room was unusually quiet. It was not like Mrs Watson not to be listening to the news and weather on the radio. Normally, the minute Kitty entered the kitchen she was assailed by the latest headlines and Mrs Watson's view on what should or should not be done with the country. This morning the only noise that filled the room was the kettle coming to boil.

'Why are you not listening to the news?' she asked and at the same time turned the knob on the transistor sitting on the corner of the surface top. Immediately the voice of John Dunn floated into the air. She liked his soothing tones this time of the morning.

Flo Watson glanced over her shoulder, 'Sometimes the stillness of the house is more peaceful first thing,' she announced and at the same time the kettle's whistle let out a loud shrill announcing the water was boiling. Flo turned her attention back to tea making.

'Is everything alright?' Kitty asked, noticing Mrs Watson's eyes looked puffy as if she had been weeping, but it was the subdued expression on the housekeeper's face that worried her the most. She had seen that careworn expression before and knew it was an indicator that her dear old friend was unhappy. She had not settled into Wentworth Place nor had she taken to Bertie and although she had never said it in so many words, Kitty was sure Flo suspected him of being a gold digger, only after her money. It wasn't true, of course. Admittedly there had been the odd loan when his business let him down, but he had assured her he would repay it and now, with this Town Hall contract in the offing, she was certain he would hold to his word. Seeing Mrs Watson's gloomy face Kitty frowned, almost wishing she had never asked her to come here. *'Have I been selfish digging the old dear out of retirement?'* she wondered. *'But she could have said no, couldn't she?'*

'You look miles away, anything wrong?' Kitty persisted, eyeing the heavily creased hand towel clutched in her housekeeper's hand.

'Just thinking... as you do,' Flo answered, a wistful clip to her voice. 'Sit yourself down and I'll pour the tea,' she added and at the same time shook out the creases in the towel, folded the crumpled linen into a small square and distractedly patted it flat on the draining board. 'You look smart,' she said, a false bravado lifting her tone, 'that shade of green suits you, though I expect I've told you that before.'

'You have, but thank you all the same,' Kitty smiled, watching Flo fussing with the tea and toast; another sure sign she had something to get off her chest. 'You know you can talk to me anytime... about anything,' she reminded her, moving to the table and pulling out a chair.

'I know and thank you. Anyway, the toast should be popping up any minute, so sit yourself down and I'll bring the teapot over.'

Kitty did as she was told, but she was not fooled by all the bustling around, far more fuss than was warranted by a pot of tea and a couple of slices of toast. Flo Watson had a habit of behaving as if all was perfect on the surface, yet underneath she would be paddling on full steam to maintain normality. The thought that her dear old housekeeper was sufficiently upset about something to cry disturbed Kitty. She made a mental note that when she arrived home from Rosebuds later she would make time to sit down with her and get her to talk about whatever was worrying her.

'If this glorious weather stays, maybe we could sit in the garden this afternoon with a drink,' Kitty suggested, putting her thought into words as Flo placed tea and toast in front of her and patted her on the arm.

'That would be nice,' she agreed. 'You don't need to be worrying about me though,' she added, as if she knew what Kitty was thinking.

'You need to stop reading my mind Mrs Watson, it is a dangerous place and you never know what you might see there,' Kitty teased.

At Kitty's tone of mock disapproval, a smile lit up Flo's face. 'I take it you're off to that shop of yours?' she asked, changing the subject.

Kitty nodded, inwardly grimacing at the housekeeper's disparaging tone. Rosebuds was another thing Mrs Watson did not approve of: 'Why would someone like you with all your money want to spend time in a shop selling flowers?' she had asked on more occasions than Kitty cared to count. And as many times she had tried to explain, but either it had fallen on deaf ears or the woman did not want to understand. 'Yes, I've a delivery at nine-thirty and as you know, Julie does not get in until around ten.'

'Dog and tail comes to mind,' Flo said, rolling her eyes to look at the ceiling. 'That young woman should be doing all the running around, not you,' she added, pushing the butter dish towards Kitty. 'Even more so when you are so soft with her, she's the one that takes *your* van home at night.'

'She hasn't got a car of her own and I can't drive two vehicles at once.' Kitty pressed her lips together realising there was no point in arguing. Thinking it best to eat her breakfast rather than get tangled up with Mrs Watson's thoughts and innuendos, especially the mood she was in, Kitty took hold of a knife and spread butter onto the overdone toast. Biting into it she heard the grandfather clock in the hall chime out nine loud dongs as it announced the hour. Hastily swallowing a mouthful of toast, she groaned. 'Thanks to Bertie and his mad dash out to a meeting, I'm going to be late. Oh, and by the way, he slept in the drawing room last night so there are probably a of couple blankets that need putting away.'

The housekeeper shot her a piercing look, 'I know. No need to worry, it's sorted.'

Her tone warned Kitty to ignore the response. Mrs Watson's dislike of Bertie would only encourage her to say more and add her thoughts on why he had not slept in the marital bed. Not giving her a chance to voice them, Kitty smiled, said, 'Thank you for doing that, now I must be on my way.' Picking up her cup, she took several mouthfuls of tea then wished she hadn't as it scalded her mouth. 'I'll leave the other slice of toast, I really do need to be heading down the road,' she said, thinking her mouth would be in ribbons if she attempted to eat the crisp, scorched bread. Getting to her feet she hurried through to the hall leaving Mrs Watson frowning after her.

Pulling a lightweight jacket from the coat rack Kitty grabbed her handbag from the floor, reached across the hall table and hunted for her car keys. She pushed the telephone to one side and searched around the large vase of flowers; lifted the phone and looked underneath it. There were no keys to be seen. 'This is crazy,' she hissed, dropping her bag down on a chair next to the table and rooting through the contents. 'Damn! Where are you?' she cried out, her frustration growing. Picking up her bag, she turned it upside down and emptied it onto the leather seat of the chair. 'Damn and blast,' she cursed. It was only then she remembered Bertie had mentioned something about having had her car towed to the garage. Before he went out yesterday evening he had offered to fill it with petrol for her just after she had arrived home from Rosebuds. Evidently, on the way to the petrol station the car had broken down. It had never broken down before. '*But these thing can happen*,' Bertie had explained in an apologetic tone. Had she not been so distracted with his behaviour first thing, she would have remembered. And of course, when he had told her about what had happened he had promised he would drive her to Rosebuds this morning.

Obviously there was no chance of that now. Clearly he had forgotten.

Annoyed she stuffed everything back into her bag. If only she had not let Julie have the van she could have used that. Taking a deep breath she told herself not to panic. Hopefully, the delivery man would wait until someone arrived. In the meantime she would call Julie. Picking up the slim handset from the newly installed Trim Phone, she dialled her assistant's home number and waited, tapping her fingers impatiently on the glass top table and sending tiny particles of dust into the air. 'Come on Julie,' she cried agitated. She was about to put the phone down when a voice gasped out, '65521.'

'Oh Julie thank goodness you're there,' Kitty trilled down the phone, relieved to hear her assistant's cheerful voice.

'Oh, it's you Mrs C, are you alright?'

'Yes and no. The thing is—'

Before she could continue, Julie waded in. 'I heard the phone ringing as I got out of the van. You see I've just taken the twins to school and at the sound of the phone I legged it to the front door, but then the Yale key jammed in the lock, thankfully it released and I managed to get in and grab the phone before it stopped ringing. Then I heard it was you on the phone,' she paused for breath. 'What is it, Mrs C? Nothing wrong I hope?'

Not sure whether to scream or laugh, Kitty wondered where Julie found so much to say. The words hind leg and donkey came to mind, as Mrs Watson would say! 'I'll explain later, but for now I need you to open up this morning.'

Her breathing returned to normal, Julie bounced back, a hint of a smile in her voice, 'No problem, the twins are safely in school I can go straight away.'

'That would be perfect,' Kitty said, relief making her voice rise. 'We have a delivery from Saxons due around half nine, but they sometimes turn up early—'

'Consider it done,' Julie interrupted.

'And the other thing is, my car is in the garage so I'll just find out what's going on and then I'll be on my way. I'll see you soon.'

'Oh, but...'

Anxious for Julie to be on her way, Kitty ended the call before her assistant found a lot more inconsequential things to say. She would apologise later, though knowing Julie she would not have noticed the abrupt end to the call. As much as the young woman could drive her to distraction with her constant chatter, Kitty was very fond of her. From the moment the bubbly twenty-seven-year-old with bleached blonde hair had waltzed into her shop eighteen months earlier asking for work, they had hit it off straight away. Julie practically ran the shop now. '*If I'm honest,*' thought Kitty, '*I hardly need to be there at all, certainly not as much as I am, but I do love my little Rosebuds so.*' She sighed, it seemed that nobody but Julie really understood that, least of all Flo Watson.

Now the shop opening was sorted, it was time to find out what was happening with her car. Sliding the phone book towards her, Kitty flicked it open. Running her finger down the index she stopped on F, pushed the tab button, the page sprang open. Casting her gaze down the list she spied the number she needed for Farraday's Garage and picking up the phone she dialled.

Five minutes later, Kitty replaced the phone. Frowning, she went over the conversation in her mind and was no less puzzled. What was going on and why did they know nothing about her car? Tempted as she was to track down Bertie and ask to speak with him, she decided against it. With the mood he had been in this morning, fretting over being late, his meeting was clearly important. She would hardly be endearing herself to him if she interrupted it to ask about her car. As concerned as she was, Kitty felt she had no alternative but to call a taxi.

The loud sound of the doorbell rang out interrupting her thoughts.

'Are you still here?' Mrs Watson called, bustling from the kitchen down the hall towards the front door.

'I was just about to order a taxi when the bell went,' Kitty said. 'No need for you to answer the door, I'll see who it is,' she added, wondering if she would ever get out of the house.

Taking her frustration out on the door, she wrenched it open and stared out. There was no one on the doorstep. Instantly she remembered the young man who had earlier stood on the opposite side of the street staring up at her. Had he returned and this time decided he would call on her? If so, he must have changed his mind. She shrugged, was about to close the door when a man in a smart dark suit appeared as if from nowhere. He ran up the short flight of steps and stood smiling at her. Relieved to see it was not the same man, Kitty looked him up and down and wondered why anyone would be coming to her door without an appointment.

'Mrs Kitty Costain?' The suited gentleman spoke politely, a smile as wide as the River Thames filling his face as his dark brown eyes scrutinized every inch of her.

Chapter Nine

Long before it pulled up outside his office Howard Silvershoes heard the deep-throated roar of the Jaguar as it travelled down the road. At the same time he registered the imminent arrival of Bertie Costain, curled beneath Howard's desk, his black cocker spaniel pricked up his ears and sat up. Deaf as he was, he too had heard the car approaching. 'It's alright, Mr Boy, it's only Bertie,' Howard murmured, bending to pat the silky head.

With the slowness of the old, Mr Boy stumbled to his feet, stretched first on his front paws then a long stretch on his back ones. After an almost rotating shake that nearly knocked him off his feet, he ambled on stiff legs over to the door, his tail stub wriggling left to right. Sniffing noisily at the bottom of the door, the spaniel flopped down and lay in wait for their visitor.

Howard watched his faithful old dog and smiled. He loved his furry friend beyond words and wondered how he would cope when the day arrived for them to part. These days he was sadly aware that Mr Boy, now twelve, had stiff joints and moved around like a wooden soldier at times. Even the warmth of the summer sun did little to ease his gait. The old dog enjoyed nothing more than sleeping as close to his master's feet as he could get or next to him when Howard sat in an easy chair. Now, Mr Boy waited at the door, keen to be the first to greet Bertie. Smiling at him, Howard sometimes wished he too was a dog; life would be so much less complicated when all one had to worry about was eating and sleeping. Instead, he was dead on his feet after a disturbed night and wondering if there was any easy way to let Bertie know the full price of his visit to Raffles last evening.

After the panicked call, which had roused Howard from a deep sleep sometime after two a.m., he had thrown on his dressing gown, slipped his feet into leather slippers and taken himself blearily down to the kitchen for a cup of strong coffee. As he had opened the kitchen door and switched on the light, Mr Boy had raised his head and wiggled the stub of his tail, but had not left the comfort of his blanket-covered basket. Howard had felt a spark of envy watching the dog snuggle back down and resume his slumber. 'Lucky Mr Boy,' he had murmured, knowing that for himself sleep was now impossible.

The panic in Bertie's voice trilling down the phone had continued to vibrate in Howard's head as he filled and switched on the kettle, spooned instant coffee into his mug and waited for the kettle to boil. He had pinched himself to check he was awake and not sleepwalking, because what Bertie had told him was of nightmare proportions. Forty-eight hours to pay such a vast amount of money was by anyone's standards verging on impossible. And as much as he believed what Costain had said, Howard had needed to find out for himself exactly what the *real* terms of payment were. And so, after he had taken several large mouthfuls of coffee, strong and black to fortify him, he had called Raffles. His call had been picked up almost immediately with a terse 'Yes?' He had instantly recognised the voice of Kevin Bryant, but neither of them had acknowledged the other. Howard had asked for Brian Smith and to his relief had been connected without any questions.

As far as Howard could see, Smith, a man he neither liked nor trusted, had his podgy fingers in more pies than the factory in Melton Mowbray could produce in a month. He constantly appeared to have a hidden agenda and the fact that the bastard had given Bertie an unimaginable time to pay his debt had told Howard there was something Smith wanted far more than Bertie's money. It hadn't taken a rocket scientist to work out what that something was, and by the time he had replaced the receiver his gut feeling had not only been confirmed, but rubber stamped.

Even now, as he waited for Bertie to pull into the courtyard, he continued to tell himself that this time he should leave the silly sod to pull himself out of the mire he had so foolishly got himself into, but they had known each other too long. Howard grimaced at the number of warnings he had given; all the breath he had wasted encouraging Bertie to stop gambling before it was too late. In truth he had lost count of the times he had advised him that if he could not stop altogether, he should at least walk away before he lost his shirt. Howard sighed, if only it *was* just his shirt! Now he realised it had all been futile: Bertie Costain thought himself invincible. 'Born under a lucky star,' he was always saying. 'It'll all come out right, Howard, you'll see,' was another oft repeated phrase. There was no sense in talking to the man, he had myopic vision when the red lights of warning began to flash, and his hearing was muted when alarm bells started ringing, even when they rang out loud enough to deafen the hard of hearing.

After last night's phone call, Howard was convinced that Bertie Costain was either out of control or out of his mind – and right now he would not want to place a bet on either. A derisive snort escaped his lips at his own pun, but there was no mirth in it. He did a quick calculation on the years he had known Bertie. It didn't take many seconds. They had worked together for over twenty years. An old associate, Archie Sanford, having done a spot of business with Bertie, had introduced them. 'You and Costain would be good for each other, Silvershoes,' he had said. Even now, all these years later, Howard was still not sure what the old boy had meant by that, but on Archie's recommendation he had taken Bertie on as a client. Since which time he had looked after Bertie's accounts, taken care of the tax man, given up trying to explain the difference between avoidance and evasion, and from time to time advised on the running of the building company, B.C. Builders.

The company's reputation had gone from strength to strength through several Council contracts. A rueful smile twisted Howard's lips as he recalled how Archie had got Bertie's measure all those years ago and had used it to his own ends. The old boy had been wily even then. Spotting that young Bertie Costain was both greedy and ambitious Archie had known exactly how to play him. Not much had changed, Howard thought ruefully, rubbing a hand over his chin. The old boy had played a blinder and in the end it had benefited both parties. Archie had been as good as his word and made sure Bertie not only had all the right contacts, but eventually got his hands on Wentworth Place. The award of the first Council building contract to B. C. Builders had been down to Archie. More had followed, along with a list of the councillors Bertie needed to keep sweet. This had set the scene on how Bertie would operate in the future. New housing estates were springing up everywhere and plenty of them had fallen like ripe plums into the pockets of B.C. Builders.

What neither Howard nor Archie – not that he would have cared – had foreseen was that as Bertie became increasingly well off, he had looked for other ways to stimulate his appetite for living dangerously. First it was the dogs, then the horses and then, with money burning a hole in his pocket, he had turned away from the odd bet on the racetracks to greater risks and gains; those that could be made in a fraction of the time. He had bragged that on one occasion he had made more money in a single night than the profit from a small building contract. Even with such a win, it seemed until now his habit had been kept under control. Of course, there had been the odd occasion when it had been necessary to grease a few hands: the odd new car turning up on a drive; a week or two in the Costas bought and paid for. Such inducements were petty cash by comparison and all manageable, nothing that could not be sorted without too much pain for all concerned. Looking back, Howard had to admit that overall Costain had in reality gained more than he had lost, not that he would admit this to Bertie. But lately the idiot had taken to playing the stakes too high and last night had shown what can happen when greed and stupidity join forces.

'It's a right bloody mess!' He spoke out loud and at the sound of his master's voice, Mr Boy turned his head and made a small whimper as if in agreement. 'And what would you know about it old fella, eh?' A rueful smile flitted across Howard's features as the spaniel settled back to resume his vigil at the door, his ears cocked like a schoolgirl's bunches. 'If only humans were more like dogs we wouldn't be in such a mess, isn't that right old chap.'

Howard knew full well that as ridiculous as the situation was, if he did not help Bertie out of this particular mess, he too stood to lose. Maybe not everything, but if the heavies came to claim what they believed they were owed, a good deal more than he needed to. At the end of the day he had a reputation to maintain; a business and a lifestyle, all of which he intended to keep.

After his call to Smith in the early hours and their subsequent conversation, he had secured a solution for Bertie. It was not one he would be pleased about, but it would dispense with the impossible deadline and get him out of this enormous hole. Satisfied he had some good news, Howard reached across his leather-topped desk for the pack of cigarettes. Shaking one out, he put it to his lips and slid the flashy desk lighter towards him. Made from a block of solid jade, it was satisfyingly heavy. A lot less satisfying was the weight that now sat on his shoulders, he thought grimly, pushing down on the lighter's stiff button and leaning forward to light the cigarette. The flame shot up instantly, so high it almost singed his eyebrows. 'Bloody hell!' he exclaimed, starting back while making a mental note to trim the wick lest next time he found himself hairless. He took a deep pull, letting the much needed fix of nicotine fill his lungs in a vain hope it would give him the patience to deal with his imminent visitor.

With the cigarette nipped between his lips he crossed the room to the small table beside a tall filing cabinet, where his new Braun coffee machine, together with a set of smoked glass coffee cups, stood ready and waiting. He flicked the switch to 'on'; the light glowed red and the machine instantly gurgled, emitting the pungent aroma of freshly ground coffee. Satisfied, Howard pulled the cigarette from his mouth and flicked the ash into the waste bin under the table. Seeing the first drips of dark liquid drop into the glass jug, he was conscious that he and Bertie would need rather more than caffeine before the day was out, but much as he was inclined to risk a stiff brandy, strong coffee was all that was on offer at this hour of the morning.

Sighing heavily, Howard strolled over to the window and looked out onto the small cobbled courtyard just as the long nose of Bertie's sports car nudged through the gates.

Chapter Ten

'Mrs Kitty Costain?' the caller asked again, standing on the top step smiling at her.

'Depends who's asking?' Kitty retorted, scrutinizing his face to be absolutely sure he was not the young man who had stared up at her bedroom window earlier. Of course he wasn't: this man was older, she decided, holding onto the brass door knob. Not in the mood to be well-mannered, she glared at the stranger's face convinced he was a salesman. Only the other day a rep had ventured to her door and she had lost no time in dealing with him. As no doubt other Wentworth Place homeowners or their staff had also done. She gave a sly grin imagining that he had probably never made it to the end of the road alive – at the very least his ears would have been hopping with fleas! She was still entertaining this thought when the man flapped a stiff white card in front of her face.

'Michael Middleton from Middleton Autos,' he announced; his broad, River Thames smile and confident tone bringing Kitty out of her amusing thoughts.

Leaving the safety of the door knob, she plucked the card from his light hold, a knowing smirk twisting her lips as she read the details. She was spot on with this one. She was about to shoo him away, none too politely, when Michael Middleton continued. 'It was requested that I deliver the car to you in person.' He slipped his hand into his jacket pocket and pulled out a silver key fob with a car manufacturing logo emblazoned in bright red. A set of car keys dangled from the ring. As the keys jangled against each other, Michael Middleton turned, extended his left arm and pointed at a bright red Mini Cooper S parked at the kerbside in front of number six.

'As much fun as these little cars are said to be, I've neither the time nor the patience this morning to be talking with salesmen on my doorstep,' Kitty snapped. What with Bertie's strange behaviour, Mrs Watson's emotional state and the apparent disappearance of her veteran MG, her patience had worn thinner than a Crêpe Suzette! Right now she just wanted to get to Rosebuds, not have some smartarse salesman delivering a car to the wrong address. 'It seems to me the information you have been given is incorrect. I have a perfectly good little runabout thank you very much,' she said tersely. Shouldering her front door wider, a signal for the man to leave, Kitty stepped back, but Michael Middleton stepped forward.

'Mrs Costain,' he said anxiously, 'I am here to deliver *your* new car.' The keys still dangled from his hand. He held them up for Kitty's inspection.

'I've not ordered a new car. I know nothing about you or your garage. There must be some mistake.' Though this was part lie, she had seen the flashy showrooms of Middleton´s Cars and admired the new vehicles sitting on the forecourt.

A puzzled expression flashed across his face, 'I can assure you, Mrs Costain, this car has *your* name on the log book and I am here so that you can take delivery.'

Unblinking, Kitty stared at him, 'But I know nothing about a new car.'

'You were not meant to, it is a surprise from your husband,' Michael Middleton explained, still holding the keys in front of her, his fatuous smile returning.

'My *husband*?' she said weakly.

'Mr Costain, yes, it has all been dealt with by him. Please come and take a look and then I will explain everything to you.' Middleton stood to one side and extended his arm with a flourish to indicate the new car.

Confused, Kitty took the keys.

'Your husband was quite insistent that I deliver the car to you personally today and said that it had to be early this morning. So here I am,' he beamed.

Tightening her fingers around the key fob, Kitty was bemused. Why would Bertie order a new car for her? She already had a perfectly good little car, even if at the moment she had no idea where it was. She looked blankly at the well-dressed car dealer unsure what to say. Her head filled with more unanswered questions as she watched Michael Middleton skip down the steps and with another theatrical flourish open the driver's door. She took a deep breath and wondered what else awaited her around the corner.

'Please,' Michael Middleton called.

Hearing the pleading in the voice of the man she belatedly realised was probably the garage's owner rather than a lowly salesman, for Bertie would not deal with less, Kitty wondered what her husband would do next to surprise her. With neither a smile nor a frown, merely nodding her head to acknowledge she had heard him, she pulled the front door closed and made her way down the short flight of steps to where the new car awaited.

Standing at the suited man's side, Kitty raised her left eyebrow, 'Call me fanciful, but I have really no idea know who you are. Oh, I know who you *say* you are,' she said quickly, seeing his bewilderment, 'but apart from a white calling card –and let's be honest, anyone can have those printed these days – I've never seen you before, and here you are asking me to get inside a new car that you say my husband has ordered. For all I know you could be a kidnapper enticing decent women from their homes and holding them to ransom until their poor families pay up for their safe return.'

Michael Middleton's face lit up and his eyes sparkled reflecting his amusement. 'Mrs Costain, believe you me, I have neither the time nor the inclination – or even the imagination – to consider what you suggest. Surprising as it may seem to you, I am a humble car dealer delivering a new vehicle to the wife of my client. Of course, now you are holding the keys you can be said to have taken possession of the vehicle, so I can simply walk away and leave your husband to explain. On the other hand, perhaps you would like to telephone him to reassure yourself that this is all above board? I am happy to wait.'

Kitty noted the amusement in his tone. She couldn't disturb Bertie, but all she had to do was telephone the garage to confirm who Middleton was – assuming the whole business was not an elaborate scam. Inwardly she laughed at the wild flight of her imagination. She was getting as bad as Mrs Watson! Men did not go around delivering cars with a view to kidnapping hostages. Well, at least she'd never heard of such a thing happening, and especially not in Wentworth Place. Maybe she had been unsettled by the young man watching her earlier. Right now she wanted to get to the shop and the car would certainly be useful for that. As for Bertie, she hoped he had answers to the list of questions that was growing by the minute.

For the first time since she had answered the door, Kitty smiled. Dangling the key ring in front of her she said, 'I will give you the benefit of the doubt Mr Middleton. I think it best you show me what I am supposed to be taking possession of.'

'I'd be delighted to do so, and I'm relieved you have changed your mind. Now, if you would be so good as to step inside…?' he again pulled on the driver's door.

Kitty stepped forward and gripping the top of the door, lowered herself into the bucket seat. Immediately the newness of the car assailed her nostrils. She took in the pristine interior and the compact cream and red colour scheme. It was smart, the clean lines very different from her racing green sports car. She bit her bottom lip and wished she hadn't thought about her little MG Midget. She was so attached to that car. Where was it and why now was she sitting in this new Mini? More questions! But before she could think further, Michael Middleton slipped into the passenger seat, leaving the door open.

'Now we are comfortable, let me give you the owner's papers' he said, his Thames smile returning as he handed over a brown envelope. 'You will find everything is in order. Signatures all completed,' he added, as Kitty took the envelope.

She looked down at the small package, but did not open it, instead placed it on the tiny shelf in front of her.

'Now then, what would you like me to explain to you?' Michael asked, his voice filled with enthusiasm.

She looked at the minimalistic dashboard and the various switches and turned to her passenger, 'It all looks pretty simple not much to get to know, but it is rather nice,' she said and this time she meant it. 'There is one thing though, I do need to get to my shop sooner rather than later.'

Crestfallen, Michael Middleton's smile changed from a full-blown river to a mere tributary. 'I had planned to explain everything in detail, but if you are sure you are happy to drive without me going through everything, then I will leave you to enjoy your new car. You'll find a handbook on the shelf under the dash,' he said, twisting round towards the open door. 'I'm sure you'll have fun driving this smart little motor, but please do not hesitate to call me if you need anything.'

Halfway out of his seat, one foot on the pavement, he was about to pull himself out of the car when his action was arrested by Kitty's peremptory call.

'Where are you going Mr Middleton?'

Startled, he slipped back into the seat and swung round to face her, 'Back to my garage.'

'But how will you get there?'

He raised his eyebrows at the question and answered lightly, 'It is just round the corner, a few long strides and I'll be there. I'm sure you will be much happier driving alone for the first time.'

'Nonsense,' she replied as she felt for the little catch on the window. Locating it, she slid her window open. 'I'll give you a lift.'

Michael Middleton ran a hand over his face, 'That's very kind of you Mrs Costain, but it is not necessary, my premises are no more than a stone's throw away.'

'I insist. It is really no problem. Aside from the fact that it will save your legs and shoe leather, it will give you the opportunity to ensure I know where everything is and how it works. Now please close your door, we don't want the new paintwork to get scratched,' she commanded, wanting to leave.

Michael Middleton, hesitated, 'There is really no need I can—'

'Kindly pull the door to,' Kitty interrupted, hearing a hint of panic in the garage owner's voice. It occurred to her that Middleton was not comfortable unless he was behind the wheel, many men were like that. He was probably not a fan of women drivers. Her first husband had been just the same. It had always been a bone of contention between them. Fiddling with her seat to adjust it to a comfortable driving position, Kitty tried not to show her amusement. What had happened to the confident man who had been so keen to show her the car?

Positioning the rear view mirror while, from the corner of her eye, she checked her passenger, she almost giggled. He looked positively crestfallen and very ill at ease, his weak smile shrunk to a grimace. It seemed Michael Middleton was not too good with surprises any more than she was! Slotting the key in the ignition she started the engine. The little car roared into life at the first turn.

'Now, let's see. Where is first gear,' she said, pushing her foot on the clutch and pushing the gear stick forward. She did not miss Michael Middleton's sharp intake of breath as he gripped the sides of the seat, his knuckles white.

'Don't look so nervous Mr Middleton, I've been driving for years and we are only going round the corner,' she said to reassure him.

Ignoring the mumble of a reply, Kitty bit the inside of her bottom lip. Checking her mirrors, she swung out into the road. The Mini Cooper S did a perfect kangaroo impression before she got to grips with the new snatching clutch, then with breathtaking speed she zigzagged down the short little streets. Within moments Kitty brought the car to a shuddering halt outside Middleton's large, modern, all glass showroom.

'Here we are Mr Middleton, safe and in one piece,' she cried triumphantly, knocking the gear stick into neutral. 'I'll soon get the hang of this.'

Michael Middleton remained silent.

Twisting round in the leather seat she took in the liverish tones of the man's taut face. Green about the gills was what Mrs Watson would call it. He really did not enjoy being a passenger, she mused. What a shame if he vomited up his breakfast all over her new car! Keen to return colour to his pallid cheeks Kitty flashed him her sweetest smile and putting on her simpering voice, tongue firmly in cheek, trilled, 'Thank you *so* much for delivering my little surprise Mr Middleton. I have to say, it is a lively little minx and *so* easy to drive. I'm going to *really* enjoy spinning around town in this.'

Without a word, Michael Middleton pulled at the window and slid it open. Reaching out he tugged on the door handle, opened the door and with ungainly speed jumped out. Standing up straight on the pavement, he retrieved from his trouser pocket a somewhat crumpled handkerchief and wiped it across his forehead. Stuffing the handkerchief back in his pocket he bent down to peer through the open door.

'Mrs Costain, I am delighted you are pleased with your new car, though I fear the roads of this town will never be quite the same again,' he said, a slight tremble to his voice. Pushing the door shut, he placed a hand on the roof and leaning towards the open window, added, 'Any problems do not hesitate to call me and we will sort it forthwith. In the meantime, do enjoy your new car.' With that he stepped back as if to distance himself from the new owner.

'I will and thank you again for delivering me such a *wonderful* surprise,' Kitty called, leaning over the passenger seat and stifling the amusement in her voice.

Leaving Michael Middleton standing in the middle of his forecourt, she checked the road was clear then stepped on the accelerator and shot off down the road. '*This little car really is nippy*,' she thought, thrust into the back of her seat by the sudden turn of speed. Checking her rear view mirror she saw the fading image of the garage owner shaking his head. The word 'surprise' echoed round and round in her head and for the hundredth time that morning she asked herself, 'What is Bertie up to?' She did not want or need a new car and anyway, where was her Midget?

Chapter Eleven

Staring out of his office window, Howard noted a couple of cars parked at the far side of the courtyard, one had its boot open. Two men, each wearing a brown coat, took out several boxes and began lugging them through the open door on the opposite side of the yard. He wondered what the cartons contained. The company had taken the lease a couple of weeks ago and he had yet to be introduced. It was good the vacant office had not stayed unoccupied for more than a few days, thought Howard. The previous company had moved to a large purpose-built office block in Watford leaving him as the only original tenant left in this small development of five office units. It had been converted from the stables of an old brewery, which had long since been pulled down, although the stables and courtyard remained. The brick walls, the rough, concreted floors and the stalls had disappeared and it was hard now to imagine that they had once been filled with straw. The past had been erased and replaced with smooth plastered walls, central heating, large windows and thick piled carpets. Expensive desks, busy telephones and heavy ledgers now occupied the areas where shire horses had rested with their nosebags after a long day hauling drays filled with ale barrels. Yet the yard, now a small car park, still retained the original cobblestones, which in Howard's mind added a touch of nostalgia from a bygone age. Some days he imagined he could hear the heavy clip clop of those working dray horses and hear their deep snorts as the barrels were loaded onto flatbed carts. And every now and then, more so when it rained, he caught the whiff of the building's former life. It was as if the redolence of malt, hops and sweating horses still lingered in the fabric of yesterday. The brewery owner's name remained, though it too had been modernised, today it was known as 'Hopkinson's Mews'.

Mr Boy's excited barking brought Howard's thoughts back to the present. Eyeing the E-type that had come to a stop outside his office entrance, he wondered what Mr Hopkinson, should he be able to look down from above, would have to say about his brewery now. He would certainly not recognise the horsepower under that sleek bonnet. Trying to calculate exactly how many shire horses it represented, Howard turned to his dog, 'Be quiet Mr Boy!' he commanded. The spaniel's frenzied barking subsided into a loud whimper of protest.

Watching as Bertie stepped out of his car, Howard wondered how much longer the man would be in possession of this latest ego booster, because from where he was standing, Bertie Costain was well on the road to ruin if he did not curtail his behaviour. Last night he had stepped over the line. It was a wakeup call for him to stop before it was too late. Howard hoped that what he had to tell him this morning might take the wind out of his sails, bring him up sharp and remind him of all he had worked to achieve.

Struggling to his feet Mr Boy's whining continued. Howard moved back to his desk and stubbed his cigarette out in the ashtray. Striding over to the door, he bent down and patted Mr Boy. Wincing at the raucous noise he leaned over the dog and reached for the door handle. The moment he began to open the door, Mr Boy pushed through the gap and with his whole rear end wagging furiously, ambled out to greet their visitor.

Stopping short of the entrance, Bertie reached down and fussed the dog. 'Anyone would think you were pleased to see me,' he chuckled, fondling the spaniel's silky ears. 'Come on then Mr Boy, let's get in.'

Standing to one side, Howard waited for Bertie and the dog to enter. 'Morning,' he said, closing the door behind them.

Staring at Howard Bertie did not respond. Mr Boy continued to snuffle around his legs depositing a smear of black hairs and wet nose on his immaculately pressed trousers. Leaving his dog to take in the measure of Bertie, Howard walked back to his desk, pulled out the green, leather-button chair and sat down. Seeing Bertie attempting to brush off the dog hairs, Howard snapped his fingers and called out, 'Enough Mr Boy, come back under here.' As his dog dutifully obeyed, Howard found himself wishing it could be that easy with Bertie Costain.

'I take it you've not lost the power of speech along with everything else?' he asked, moving his legs so Mr Boy could flop down under the desk once more. As the words left Howard's lips all thoughts of castigating Bertie for his reckless behaviour melted away. Instead he took in the state of his old friend and colleague. Bertie's pristine attire and clean-shaven appearance did not deceive. His pallor was a pale shade of grey. Eyes that were normally alert were today sunken in dark shadows and puffy underneath. A man who habitually stood up straight, as if he needed to be seen as taller than his five feet ten inches, was hunched forward as if his shoulders carried the weight of the world. In short, Bertie Costain looked shattered. The tragedy was he had brought it all on himself. But knowing this did not stop Howard from experiencing a sliver of compassion, even if he was not about to reveal, either in tone or manner, how distressed he was himself at what had happened.

'Christ man, what did you do after you phoned me last night?' Howard asked his tone harsher than he had intended it to be, but pussyfooting round Bertie would not get them anywhere. They had some ground to cover before the end of the day.

Plucking the last of the dog hairs from the sleeve of his jacket, Bertie slumped down into the sofa adjacent to the desk – a buttoned Chesterfield in maroon leather – and with a withering look snapped back, 'I threw a party. What do you think I did?'

'If I didn't know better, I'd believe you. Though downing a bottle of whisky to numb the pain will not do.' Howard was fairly sure that was exactly what Bertie had done. No wonder he looked like death warmed up. 'It would have been more prudent to work out how you plan to pay your little debt back, Bertie. Sitting there feeling sorry for yourself is not on.'

'That's uncalled for,' Bertie said, all the spirit of a successful man missing from his voice. 'Ok, I did have a drink or two. I needed to calm the old ticker down. But I've not come here for another lecture, I'll concede you have been right, and yes, I've made a mess of things,' he had the grace to bow his head as if ashamed. Then, making eye contact with Howard, he added, 'And yes, I drank too much in the hope it would help me see a way forward, and as I might have expected, it hasn't. I am here to see what can be salvaged with your help.'

'I'm assuming you think I can sort something out?'

Bertie threw a look of desperation at Howard. 'I'm counting on it.'

'Then let me get us a coffee. We both need a strong fix before we struggle into the murky waters of your latest escapade.'

Seeing Mr Boy settled down, Howard carefully moved his feet and pushed his chair back then headed over to the coffee machine, the jug now three parts full of steaming murky liquid. He poured them each a mug of strong coffee, the aroma adding a false conviviality to the tense atmosphere of the office. Spooning two heaped teaspoons of sugar into Bertie's mug he added a drop of milk from the open bottle and stirred vigorously. Placing the spoon on an empty saucer he picked up the two filled mugs, walked over to the sofa and handed the sweet one to Bertie. 'I'm sure you'd prefer something stronger, but I need you to be listening with your full attention. And maybe what I have to say will wipe away that "*I've lost a pound and found a penny*" look on your face. Figuratively speaking, of course,' he added.

Grabbing hold of the coffee mug, Bertie winced, 'Jesus Christ, Howard, I'm sweating enough as it is without you having a joke at my expense.'

The words that came out of Bertie's mouth were edged with frustration, but there was no fight in his tone and Howard was not sure if that was a good or bad thing. He did know it was in poor taste to goad the man, but could not help grinning at the aptness of his words given the hangdog expression on Bertie's face. In the circumstances, though, it was unfair to tease him, particularly since Howard was under no illusion that by the end of the day his friend would be wishing that a pound was all he *had* lost.

Heading back to his desk, Howard took a sip of his own black coffee then put his mug down on the ink blotter. Bertie, having placed his on the square, onyx coffee table in front of him, was pulling a pack of Benson and Hedges from his jacket pocket.

About to pass him the desk lighter, Howard changed his mind – he had yet to adjust the wick, and burning eyebrows was the last thing Bertie needed. Retrieving his pocket lighter, he slid it across the desk, noting as Bertie picked it up how badly the man's hands were shaking. It was clear to Howard that his friend was all too well aware of exactly how far and how deep he had gone this time. Maybe the price for this lapse, which he was about to have revealed to him, would be enough to stop him in his tracks. Howard could only hope this would be the case, for everyone's sake.

Bertie lit up, his head wreathed in a blue haze of cigarette smoke. Howard took another sip of coffee to delay the inevitable. Not sure what his reaction would be to the news, he wondered what was going on in Bertie's head. He knew the man liked to play his cards close to his chest, now though, was not the time to hold anything back.

Pulling himself to his feet Bertie paced over to the window and stared out onto the cobbled yard. At the sound of movement, Mr Boy opened his eyes and peered out from under the desk. He looked no less hangdog than the object of his affections, but seeing Bertie was not about to leave, the spaniel closed his eyes again and settled back with a sigh.

'You'll not find any answers out there,' Howard said.

Turning and shrugging his shoulders, Bertie met his gaze. 'The question is will I find them in here?' He spoke almost in a whisper as he returned to the Chesterfield. Taking a long pull on his cigarette, he coughed several times before stubbing out what was left in the glass ashtray on the table. Leaping up again, he paced back to the window, combing his fingers through his hair. Slick with Brylcreem It stood up on end as if he had been plugged into the mains.

'You have told me everything, haven't you?' Howard asked. 'There are no more surprises you need to share?'

'Don't you think last night's was enough?' Snorting loudly Bertie strode away from the window, but he did not look at Howard, instead he kept his eyes focused on his shoes.

Barely able to keep the edge of impatience out of his voice, Howard frowned. 'Stop pacing Bertie, sit down and drink your coffee and then we can get down to business.'

As if he had been kicked up the backside, Bertie stopped in his tracks, looked up, his eyes wild with despair. He focused on a picture that hung on the wall behind Howard's head: a hand-painted portrait of Mr Boy when he was young and spry. 'I'm ashamed of what I've done and I can tell you I'm not afraid to admit it. I still can't believe what happened and how much I lost. I'll be honest with you Howard, I never thought I'd hear myself say this, but you are right, gambling is a mug's game and I'm never going to do it again. Whatever happens today, I don't want Kitty to know anything about it. I'll do whatever is necessary to pay this debt, but it remains between us, is that clear?'

Momentarily, Howard was knocked back. He had never believed he would hear Bertie admit to shame or that he had made a mistake. Maybe all was not lost in the end. Relief flooded through him. There was hope after all. Could this be the turning point when Bertie returned to what he had always been good at: running a reputable building company? '*It may be that my concerns about him marrying Kitty were unfounded after all,*' thought Howard. It seemed that for once Bertie was concerned about someone other than himself. That had to be a first!

'Clear as a bell,' Howard nodded. Keeping his voice even, not wanting to show his pleasure at what he had just heard, he said, 'I'm glad to hear this, Bertie. I won't say any more about your lack of judgement, you've said it all. So what I am going to tell you now is that I think I may have a solution, but I'm afraid it has a cost that you may find hard to take.'

Dropping himself down on the sofa, Bertie perched on the edge. Wiping the palms of his hands on his knees he now looked straight at Howard. 'When you say cost, how big and please tell me it's not Wentworth Place?'

The pleading in Bertie's eyes at mention of his home reflected his concern, but Howard ignored it. Who would not be anxious at the thought of losing his home, especially one such as Wentworth Place? It had personal history. Howard made no reply. Sipping on his coffee whilst peering over the rim of his mug, he saw fear in Bertie's blue eyes. Even though the man had bared his soul moments earlier, Howard wanted to keep him on the edge; he still needed to make sure Bertie was listening and sweating. The man needed to be frightened enough to keep to his word and stop gambling.

Leaning forward, Howard rested his elbows on the leather top of his desk and steepling his fingers, cleared his throat. His voice measured and steady he said, 'I hope you don't think that finding an answer has been easy because it hasn't—'

He was not so much lying as expanding on what he wanted to say, but before he could continue, Bertie slammed his hands onto his knees and burst out, 'Jesus

Christ, Howard, why didn't you tell me you had an answer as soon as I walked in instead of making me sweat?'

Howard glared at him and with a steely look stared him down, but not before, to his chagrin, he caught the hint of relief flash in Bertie's eyes.

'I'm sorry,' Bertie said, a slight flush staining the pallor of his cheeks. 'That was uncalled for.'

Swallowing down his anger, Howard continued, 'Why didn't I tell you when you arrived? Why do you think? But you are right I did want to see you sweat. I've sweated buckets all night for you and I want you to understand this can *never* happen again. But if it should, you will be on your own. This is it, Bertie. Believe you me I will never help you out again. I spent half the night on the phone to Smith trying to work out a deal while you drank yourself into a stupor. A thank you might not come amiss!' Howard stopped speaking abruptly, aware that his anger was making him shout, which in turn was making Mr Boy whimper.

A loud expulsion of air escaped from Bertie's open mouth, 'I've said I'm sorry and I've already said this is the last time. What more do you want, blood?'

Howard wanted to believe him. Why couldn't he? Was it the sudden sparkle in Bertie's eyes; the eagerness with which he leant forward. The man's whole demeanour seemed to have turned on a sixpence – but he hadn't heard the worst of it yet.

'And the deadline…?' Bertie asked.

'We can meet that too. You are a lucky bastard, Costain. You have what is needed to pay in full within the drop dead time.'

Frowning, Bertie looked taken aback. If it's not Wentworth Place what is it? Not B. C. Builders?'

Howard shook his head, 'Your home and business are safe.'

'There are two stipulations, both have to be agreed. You cannot have one without the other. First is that a brand new red Triumph Spitfire must be delivered by the end of next week to Brian Smith's home; a present for his missus. It seems she likes the idea of a car that sums up her personality and red is her favourite colour!'

'A Triumph?' Bertie spat, jumping to his feet. 'You mean to tell me all this agony is about a new car?' Striding over to the desk he leaned his hands on it and faced Howard. 'We can manage that, but I can't believe a car is the real deal because something tells me Smith wants to hang me out to dry.'

Howard said nothing.

'I take it Smith wants something close to priceless?'

Howard could almost hear Bertie's cogs whirring on what else he possessed that he could use to pay his gambling debt. 'You're getting ahead of the game here, Bertie.' Howard saw a fresh wave of panic flash in his friend's eyes and knew that what he was about to impart would knock Bertie off his feet.

Pushing his chair back, Howard walked round his desk and took up a position on the Chesterfield. 'Sit down, Bertie,' he said, his hand reaching automatically to pat Mr Boy's head as the dog bestirred himself and followed, plonking down at his feet.

Bertie moved back from the desk and sank down at the other end of the sofa, 'So tell me,' he said, his voice flat with resignation.

His gaze never leaving Bertie's, Howard nodded. 'The price of last night is not so much about the car, though it will put a smile on Smith's good lady's face. But what will put an even bigger smile on Smith's face is something far more important and valuable. The only payment that will satisfy him and draw a line under what took place last night is the building contract for the New Town Hall.'

A heartbeat passed as Bertie's face paled. Stunned he stared at Howard. 'No, he croaked. 'No way; no, Howard, that contract is worth several times what I lost. It's preposterous! No, no, and no!' Then, as if realisation hit him, he roared, 'My God, if he took Wentworth Place he'd be robbing me of thousands, but that contract's worth…'

his voice trailed away, the unspoken word dying in his throat.

A hush hung in the air broken only by the dog's little snores. The sudden striking of the hour from the brass carriage clock on the windowsill shattered the silence. The ten tinny chimes seemed louder than the deep tones of Big Ben. As the clock ended its announcement, the rasp from a car horn in the yard filled the vacuum it had left.

Wiping his hands across his face, Howard was reminded he had not shaved before coming to his office. The last few hours had been taken up with more pressing matters. He sighed. 'Of course you can say no, my friend, but I can tell you now, Smith does not want anything else you have. It's the Town Hall or cash. But there lies another problem: with interest that means finding four times what you lost. You don't have that sort of money, not that you can get your hands on in the time, and nor can I.' Howard's voice sliced through the peace of the room.

Bertie raised his hands to cover his face. 'He can't do this,' he said. 'It's not legal… is it?' The mixture of anger and shock in his broken, muffled voice made Howard think of a wounded animal caught in a gin trap.

'Try telling Smith that,' Howard snapped, speaking to the top of Bertie's head, all that was visible beneath his shaking hands. 'And when did that ever matter anyway? I don't need to spell out what happens when a debt – particularly one of this size – is not paid. If the boot was on the other foot, you'd be expecting Smith to pay you.'

Bertie snorted with contempt, 'But not in forty-eight hours!'

Lack of sleep and the fact that he had worked so hard to find a solution had left Howard short of patience. He had done the best he could. In truth, he had moved mountains to get Costain out of this mess; one of the stupid man's own making. 'Can I take it you are in agreement?' he said coldly.

Lowering his hands, his eyes red-rimmed, Bertie shook his head, 'This is ridiculous. I've no intentions of stepping out of the frame for the Town Hall contract. It's mine for the taking.'

'Then, Bertie, you had better find another answer to your problem, because I don't have one.' Howard pushed himself off the sofa. 'I have a busy day, so if you don't mind, from my point of view our meeting is over.' Ignoring the hunched form of Bertie, he stepped over Mr Boy and headed for the exit. Placing his hand on the handle he pulled the door open, a gust of warm summer heat wafted into the frigid atmosphere of the office.

'It is theft on a grand scale,' Bertie cried, jumping to his feet. Pointing at Howard, he pleaded, 'Surely there is another solution?'

Pushing the door too, Howard spun round. 'If there is one I don't know of it. You, Bertie, must decide. Accept what you have done and pay up, or leave. I'm not going to lose any more sleep for you.' Again he snatched at the handle, this time he yanked the door wide open.

A mutinous look filled Bertie's face as he marched to the door and pushed past Howard. Without a second glance he strode out into the courtyard. Strutting round his car, his fists clenched, Howard could see he was cursing under his breath.

Counting to ten, Howard closed the door, went straight to his desk and picked up the phone. As he did so, the door flew open.

'It's wrong and totally illegal,' Bertie's voice bellowed across the room, the door slamming in his wake as he tore across the office.

Dropping the phone, his face like thunder, Howard asked in a matter of fact voice, 'I take it you mean to accept Smith's offer?'

'What choice have I got?' Bertie flung back.

Ignoring the tantrum, Howard thought of several choices. He wanted to say, '*For a start, stop gambling, it's dirty, dangerous and a disastrous way to live,*' but he said nothing. All he could hope was that Bertie would keep to his word, otherwise there would be nothing left to barter.

The house and business would be next; the car, of course. Any other bits of capital he had salted away – a few antiques that he could sell. And when everything had gone he'd somehow get his sticky paws on Kitty's money – if he hadn't already – and his marriage would go down the plughole. What would Bertie turn to then? Drink? Sleeping rough? Shuffling along the pavement with a begging bowl? Howard had seen it all before: it was a downward spiral; a slippery slope. But he said none of those things. Thoroughly depressed, he felt a measure of relief that Bertie had at least come to his senses over Smith's offer. Maybe now he could get on with the day.

'From where I'm standing, Bertie, you have no choice. You'd better sit down again. I've organised for Marcus to be here later this morning.'

Bertie looked up, 'Whatever for?'

'The paperwork needs to be done, for a number of reasons, mainly to ensure there is no further call on your debt after today. Marcus will sort out the wording to remove you from the Town Hall bidding list. He will endeavour also to ensure your exit is covered well enough for you to be able to bid for future building developments.' He didn't add that the chances of him bidding for council work again would be slim after today.

'I take it you've spoken to Marcus already?'

'Clearly.' Stuffing his hands in his trouser pockets, Howard looked over at Bertie, 'I had to; Smith is not prepared to accept your word that you'll pull out of the bidding. The notification to withdraw has to be official; witnessed by your solicitor. For speed, I asked Marcus to come to my office. I was about to put him off. The irony, Bertie, is that you set yourself up for one hell of a fall. We all knew Smith's brother-in-law was gunning for that contract. With you out of the frame he'll be the number one. The job was yours to lose and you just did.'

'You think I don't know that?' Bertie snapped. Then, all the bluster going out of his voice, he asked, 'Do you think I was set up, Howard?'

'I have no idea,' he replied. It was true; he had no idea, but Bertie losing like he had at Raffles last night raised questions, though none that he could ever answer or prove.

Sitting back down on the sofa, Bertie leaned forward and rested his chin on his hands. For several minutes he remained silent then raising his head, his eyes moist, all the fight extinguished, he stared up at Howard. 'I'm sorry, Howard, I am truly sorry. I never dreamt it would be like this. I can't believe they'd go to such lengths to get that building contract. Is it legal?'

'You tell me, Bertie. All I know is that you have not lost everything.'

'As good as,' Bertie said. 'There is no way Smith is going to get away with this.'

Howard winced at the thinness of Bertie's voice, the bleakness of his gaze. 'My advice for what it's worth is to let it go, my friend. Forget Smith; forget Raffles and above all, forget anything to do with gambling. Remember what you told me when you arrived. Importantly, remember that you gave me your word.'

Hoping this reminder would sink in, Howard smiled and held his hand out for Bertie's empty mug. 'In the meantime, I'll pour us another coffee. I've made it extra strong. You'll need your wits about you when Marcus arrives.'

Chapter Twelve

Seeing a green van pull away from outside the front of Rosebuds, Kitty deftly manoeuvred her mini into the vacant parking space. She was still chuckling at the sight of Michael Middleton's face when she drove him back to his saleroom. 'Silly man,' she muttered, 'that'll teach him to turn his mouth down when a woman offers him a lift!'

Thankful for the temporary distraction of her new car, which had given Kitty a few moments' respite from fretting over Bertie, her MG Midget and Mrs Watson, she switched off the engine and twisted in her seat to take in the interior of the little car. It was compact and yet stylish in a minimalistic sense. It was also a nippy little number and she would have to watch her speed. 'Zippy,' she said out loud, that's what I will call you. We'll make a good team, I'll steer and you can race.' Self-consciously aware that she was talking to a mechanical object and was clearly going doolally, she chuckled loudly and pulled on the door handle. There was no doubt in her mind that most women would be over the moon if their husband had arranged for a surprise like this to be delivered to their home. Under normal circumstances so would she be, but the little question about the whereabouts of her little green sports car niggled away at the back of her mind.

'What's all this?'

Kitty swung round at the sound of Julie's voice and saw her peering through the driver's window.

'Now it all makes sense,' Julie cried, stepping back as Kitty opened the car door and frowning, levered her tall, willowy frame out of the tight bucket seat.

'Well I'm glad someone can make sense of it, because believe you me Julie, nothing is making sense to me today.

Anyway, before you put me right on it all, have Saxons delivered the flowers?'

'Yes, all present and correct and I've already started preparing the roses,' Julie replied, not taking her gaze from the car, 'How on earth did you keep this a secret, Mrs C? I'd be shouting from the roof tops if I was getting one of these. It is so fabulous,' she gushed, stroking the Mini's shiny new paintwork.

'I bet you would,' Kitty said affably, knowing how excitable Julie always was, 'but there was no secret to keep. I knew nothing about it until this morning when the car salesman rang the doorbell and presented me with the keys. A Mr Middleton; know him? He's paranoid about women drivers,' she laughed.

'Oh my goodness, I bet it's from your Bertie,' Julie cried, still cooing over the car.

'Well of course it is,' Kitty said, pushing the door closed, the young woman's enthusiasm making her feel guilty. In Julie's world you took everything with a pinch of salt or with grateful thanks. 'Anyway, I thought you were going to tell me something.'

'Oh that,' Julie shrugged, 'it'll keep. That gorgeous husband of yours is one for surprises isn't he,' she crooned, peering through the windscreen.

'You could say that,' Kitty remarked drily, but if Julie noticed her scepticism she made no comment, still too intent on examining the Mini. 'Here, Kitty held out the keys, have a sit in it, I'll go and put the kettle on and take a look at what Saxons have delivered.'

'Oh can I?' Julie squealed plucking the keys from Kitty's outstretched hand.

'Of course you can,' Kitty smiled, turning away.

The moment she entered her shop the strong scent of cut flowers caught in her nostrils and she sneezed. It always happened when she first walked into Rosebuds in the morning. Fortunately it never lasted: one sneeze and it was over for the day. Just as well she did not have a serious allergy, she thought, pulling a handkerchief from her pocket and wiping her nose. She loved the fragrance of her shop. In fact she loved everything about her little enterprise. Becoming a florist was a dream she had harboured all her life. It had taken the death of her husband, the shock of finding herself alone at fifty and the sale of her parents' house to realise that with the children flown the nest she could do whatever she wanted, and all she had ever wanted was to work in a flower shop.

As far back as she could remember Kitty had been fascinated by flowers, a fascination that had become an obsession when, as a teenager, she had walked into Mrs Spencer's florist shop, the 'Ivy Leaf' and watched that gifted lady turn a simple bunch of flowers into a spectacular display. Immediately Kitty had wanted to see how it was done and Mrs Spencer had been happy to show her. Kitty had spent more hours than she could count, after school and at weekends, helping out in the Ivy Leaf. In return Mrs Spencer had taught her everything there was to know about flower arranging until Kitty was sufficiently accomplished to make up displays for the shop and bouquets for its customers. But her parents did not approve and once Kitty had left school at the age of sixteen, it had not been easy to sneak away from her duties at the family hotel. As her father had constantly reminded her, Maddisons would one day be hers and she needed to know the business inside and out. Under sustained parental pressure, Kitty's dreams of a career working with fragrant blooms had wilted away and until she had married John Moore, a bank manager, and their first child was born, she had worked at Maddisons, immersing herself in the hotel trade. If nothing else, it had given her a reasonably good head for business.

Hanging her jacket up in the back room of Rosebuds and dumping her shoulder bag on the side, Kitty cast her gaze over the various blooms that stood waiting in buckets of water for her attention, and mentally ticked off those she had ordered from Saxons. Yet for some reason this morning, her thoughts were continually being drawn back down memory lane. As she filled the kettle and switched it on, in her mind's eye she could see the Georgian-columned entrance of the hotel, the brilliant red of the Virginia creeper clambering over its façade. She could hear the crunch of tyres on the gravelled drive, the genteel hum of conversation and tinkle of laughter from the guests. Some parts of it she had enjoyed: welcoming the VIPs who came to stay had been fun; arranging the floral displays best of all.

As the years ticked slowly by Kitty had done her best to become the hotelier her parents wanted her to be, but her heart was never in it and relations between them had become increasingly strained. The birth of her firstborn, a son, had kept her more than occupied and thereafter Kitty had never returned to Maddisons to work. She had been ridden with guilt when years later, her disappointed father had finally given up waiting for her to take over the reins and had sold the hotel to a developer.

The sound of the kettle coming up to the boil brought Kitty back to the present. Spooning tea into the stainless steel teapot, she reflected with considerable satisfaction on her success as a florist. Rosebuds was one of eight shops on the prestigious Kimberly Estate, a mixture of bungalows and modestly sized houses. The pretty homes and shops had been built by B.C. Builders and Morgan Homes. It gave Kitty a warm feeling knowing her new husband had been one of the builders. Who would have thought she would be married to someone who had built her dream? Life was full of surprises, she thought. It had taken her nearly forty years to do what she had wanted to do all those years ago. Maybe if she'd had the courage she might have done it sooner, but then, of course, there had been John and their children to consider. When he had succumbed to cancer Kitty, who had not allowed herself to believe it would happen, had been floored by grief. Caring for her children was all that had saved her from sinking into deep depression. Flo Watson's brisk sympathy had helped. 'Life must go on,' she had often said. And so it had – and goodness, how her life had changed in the last few years, most especially since she had met Bertie.

'You're miles away come back,' Julie called, striding through the shop, zigzagging to avoid knocking over water-filled pails of flowers, the Mini's car keys dangling from her right hand. 'I just love that little car and oh my word, what a surprise. I think I'd faint if my husband gave me a present like that.' With a dreamy look on her face Julie dropped the keys next to the teapot.

'I thought somehow you might.' Kitty laughed, imagining the emotional scene that would ensue. A truer romantic than Julie had yet to be born, hence why she thought the sun shone out of Bertie's backside!

As if picking up on Kitty's thoughts, Julie crooned, 'Mr C is such a romantic man; you never know what he will do next. You know Mrs C, I think you have such a perfect husband. I bet he made you close your eyes as he led you to the car,' she said, no doubt picturing the scene behind her eyelids. 'Do you think he will ever stop showering you with surprises?'

Now that was a good question, Kitty mused trying not to think too much about the state Bertie had been in as he raced out of the house this morning. 'Bertie had already left for work, Julie. As I said, Michael Middleton delivered the new car to the house not long after I phoned you. And the word "surprise" doesn't cover it,' she grinned, 'but my surprise was nothing compared to his when I drove him back to his showroom.'

'You drove Mr Middleton?'

'Yes, like I told you. I think you must be away with the fairies this morning, Julie. He wasn't what I'd call a willing passenger. He was going to walk back to his showrooms, but since he was sitting in the passenger seat I put my foot down and there was nothing much he could do except hang on in there.' Kitty's tinkling laughter filled the shop, 'You should have seen his face. I thought he was going to lose his breakfast.'

'Honestly, Mrs C,' Julie giggled, 'you are some lady at times.'

'Is that so,' Kitty arched her eyebrows in amusement. 'Here, take this,' she said, pouring the tea and handing Julie a steaming mug, 'and then you can tell me what you meant by "*now* it all makes sense".'

'Oh that,' Julie cried, clasping the mug between her palms. 'After I'd dropped the twins off at school and was heading back home I saw your Midget. I'd just turned into Rowan Way. Naturally, I thought it was you, so I tooted my horn and raised my hand to wave. Imagine my surprise when the car came alongside and I saw it wasn't you at the wheel after all. It was a woman I've not seen before. She had the Marilyn Munroe look, you know, peroxide blonde and bright red lipstick....' Julie frowned, 'Now I think of it, though, it's funny you should say the Midget was in the garage.'

'That can't be right, Julie. You must have been mistaken.'

Julie shook her head. 'Absolutely not, Mrs C; the thing is I know the registration number. It definitely *was* your green Midget.'

'Are you sure?' Kitty asked, not wanting to doubt Julie but knowing how absent minded her dreamy assistant could be.

'Of course I'm sure. Like I said, it was a woman with bleached blonde hair and yes, it *was* your car. 4232 LG,' Julie recited the number as if it were her date of birth.

'Really?' Kitty murmured, her mug of tea close to her lips. What kind of garage employed a brassy blonde as a mechanic, she wondered, and more to the point, which garage had Bertie taken her car to, because Farraday's had known nothing about it.

Chapter Thirteen

Bertie's feet felt like lead walking out of Howard's office. The heavy steps that had taken him in there several hours earlier felt no lighter as he crossed the cobbled courtyard to his car. Raising his strained, pale face to the sun, he felt the heat beat down. It dried the sheen of cold sweat on his forehead, making his skin itch. He rubbed at it, but his fists had been tightly clenched for so long that he could no longer feel his fingers. Bertie shivered, rubbing his hands together in an attempt to bring back the circulation. They tingled painfully as the blood rushed into his fingertips. Was it the coolness of Silvershoes' office or the shock of the meeting's outcome that had rendered him feeling like a block of ice, he wondered? It might be summer, but right now everything around him had a definite frosty touch. And why was he finding it so hard to breathe? He tugged at his tie, pulled the knot loose and wrestled with the top buttons of his shirt, drawing in a lungful of fresh air as his collar loosened. *Will I ever feel normal again?* he thought, raking his fingers through his hair.

Gazing down the long cobbled yard of Hopkinson's Mews Bertie glanced around at the smart offices. According to Howard, the one at the end had a new business. He wondered idly what it was, not that he cared; he was too numb to think about anything at the moment. He should be feeling relieved, even euphoric, that Howard had somehow pulled the rabbit out of the hat, even if it was less of a rabbit and more of a stoat, but instead, all he felt was a sharp angry pain in the pit of his stomach. And all the time his head throbbed, nagging with a beat that said he had been set up. Of course he had. The Town Hall contract had been his: his for losing, not winning. And he had lost it. The whole situation stunk to high heaven, but it would be difficult if not impossible to prove. Bertie gritted his teeth: if those toe-rags thought they were going to outsmart him, they had better think again. He would bide his time, but eventually they would pay; he'd make sure of it. Damn them, he'd get even if it took him the rest of his days. One day Brian Smith was going to wake up regretting what he had done, the bastard.

Reflecting on the meeting, Bertie knew that Howard had done more than his best. His swift intervention and thinking had saved them from a blood bath, for that is what it would have been, quite literally. Marcus, too, had gone the extra mile, producing a set of documents that were word perfect. Typical of the man, he had spent ages going through the finest detail as if looking for a needle in a haystack. Picking up on Bertie's impatience, Marcus had peered over the top of his half-moon reading glasses and in a voice edged with annoyance, had said, 'Bear with me Mr Costain. Dotting the i's and crossing the t's is critically important, and never more so than when one is dealing with the likes of Smith and his ilk, believe you me. You might be in bed with some of those Councillors down at the Town Hall, but you can take my word for it that Smith will be in there too.'

The solicitor's quietly delivered admonishment had served to remind Bertie exactly why Marcus was having to nit-pick with the words. At that moment he had felt like a worm crawling out from under a stone. Apologising, he had agreed with everything Marcus had suggested, signing where indicated on the relevant dotted lines. He was not proud of himself.

Bertie knew the ache of pain at his loss and the price he now had to pay would fester like a cancer; eating away at him because he had been cheated. There were no two ways about it. It was this knowledge as much as anything else that stuck in his craw. The contract for the new Town Hall was worth a fortune and he had needed that for B.C. Builders and to pay off some of his loans. He was going through a rough patch and the contract had meant survival – in more ways than one.

'Damnation,' he hissed as he bent to unlock his car, the tension in his shoulders like a stabbing pain. Slotting the key into the lock, he pulled open the door, slipped into the driver's seat and checked his watch. It was just after one o'clock; he had been sitting in Howard's office for the best part of four hours. No wonder he felt like death warmed up. Closing the door he turned the key in the ignition and wound down the window to enjoy the throaty roar reverberating in the courtyard from the Jaguar's twin exhaust. As warm air filtered into the car an involuntary shudder shook Bertie's body, the enormity of what he'd just given away hitting him once again. He felt like a punch bag. He still could not take it in. How could he have lost such a vast sum at the tables and how could it have happened so fast? A year of hard work greasing palms, all blown away by the turn of the wheel and Smith's perfidy.

Manoeuvring round Howard's Porsche 911, Bertie nudged the long bonnet of the E-type out into the road, pausing as a red Triumph Spitfire raced past. He sneered at the sight of it. What a pile of crap! Smith had no taste. *In his position*, thought Bertie, *I'd have demanded something far more stylish, like one of the new Jenson Interceptors.* Now there was a car and a half. He had not seen one out on the road yet, but he had read enough about the beast to know he wanted one. Maybe when his luck changed, he mused, the new Jenson might be something to consider as a replacement for the E-type. As if! Bertie's lips twisted in a sardonic smile of self-mockery at his pipe dream. Already he was spending money he did not have and nor was he likely to have, the way things were going. 'Christ, Bertie, get real,' he said, an image of Marcus's steely gaze drilling into his head. But dammit, his luck *would* change for the better, he just *knew* it would.

A spark of determination lit up Bertie's china-blue eyes as he pulled out into the traffic. Sooner or later he'd get round this. He'd made things happen before; he could do it again. Nobody could hold Bertie Costain down for long. 'And then watch out Brian Smith,' he muttered, 'because next time it'll be me gunning for you!'

Chapter Fourteen

'Thanks again, Marcus,' Howard said, leaving his office, Mr Boy following close at his heels. Chatting amiably, the two men walked, side by side, over the ancient cobbles to where Marcus had left his Mercedes-Benz.

'My pleasure, Howard,' though I can't help thinking there is something smelly about the whole business. The timing was just too perfect. Costain losing so much and then the ridiculous timeframe in which to pay it back. There's nothing we can do about it of course. Our thoughts are pure supposition,' Marcus added in a deep, gravelly voice brought on by years of heavy smoking. Gripping his briefcase in his left hand, he swung it in time with his step and continued. 'Of his own free will Bertie entered Raffle's and happily played for very high stakes. Indeed, unusually high stakes I would say. On the face of it pure coincidence, but nonetheless it makes you wonder.' Marcus stopped and looked up into Howard's face. 'However, let us hope that Bertie Costain has learnt a valuable lesson, if not such a very expensive one,' Marcus said in a resigned tone. 'That is to say, not as expensive as it might have been had Smith not wanted that contract.' Taking a deep breath of warm air into his tobacco-clogged lungs, he wheezed, 'I think they played him, Howard. Cast the fly, waited till he bit and then reeled him in like a greedy trout. But like I say, there's no proof. Trouble with Costain is he doesn't know when to stop and he needs to learn, Howard, otherwise much more than a building contract will be lost.'

Looking at his friend as they stopped at Marcus' car, Howard saw a successful lawyer, a man who knew both the good and the seedy side of business, but he also saw a weary man. He placed his hand on the solicitor's shoulder and nodded in agreement. 'I'm hoping this business will have taught him that lesson and he'll take it to heart, Marcus. Bertie found himself out of his depth today. He's had a serious wake up call. He's always looked for an opportunity to go that extra mile and until now he's always come out the other end if not the winner, never the loser. What's happened has changed the colour of everything.'

Marcus nodded, 'What I say is between you and me, Howard, but my real concern is Kitty. I have known her and her family for most of my career and she is—' A bout of coughing forced Marcus to pause in what he was saying. Spluttering, he drew a snowy white handkerchief from his pocket and wiped his mouth. 'Got a bit of a cold,' he mumbled, wheezing, 'always goes to my chest.'

Not buying it, Howard grinned. 'You should cut down on the fags, Marcus.'

Shoving the handkerchief back in his pocket, the solicitor raised an eyebrow, but made no comment. 'Anyway,' he continued, 'I was saying that Kitty is a wealthy woman. She inherited a substantial amount of capital from her parents and added to it after John's death, what with the sale of the family home, plus insurances and other investments. Even with death duty and capital gains, she was left very well off. It came as something of a shock to learn she had married Bertie Costain. Needless to say, I was perturbed. Of course, I'm just the family solicitor. It is not my place to warn Kitty about her husband's gambling habit. But she has approached me about signing over half her shop and apartment to him. For the moment I've stalled her, suggesting she waits until Bertie signs half of B. C. Builders and Wentworth Place over to her. I have to say that I fear for her future, Howard. The way Bertie is going she could end up destitute.'

Knitting his brows together, Howard rubbed at his chin. He too had been taken aback at Bertie's marriage, but he had known the man for many years and did not believe he would stoop so low as to marry only for money.

'Bertie is suffering today, Marcus, not just because he lost such a vast sum at Raffles last night, but the shame of what his gambling has done. The Town Hall contract was critical to keeping his head above water, keeping BCB's afloat. Even if he was set up, as we believe likely, it is his predilection for playing with high stakes that made it possible in the first place. He's not stupid, he knows that. It will take some time for him to get back his dignity. Bertie has a good reputation and he can be a man about town, a charmer, but taking a wife just because she is rich is not his way. I've seen him with other women in the past, but none would he consider marrying. Bedding them yes, but Kitty was different from the start. She is special, Marcus, not just beautiful but intelligent. On the rare occasions I have met her, she seemed more than capable of handling Bertie. Actually, that's what I believe he loves about her. I think your fears for her are groundless.

Patting Howard's arm, Marcus nodded, 'I hope you are right.'

So did Howard, though he did not miss the doubt etched on the solicitor's face.

Placing his brief case on the roof of his car, Marcus extended his hand. Howard reached out and held the firm grip, adding, 'Costain is a good builder and not without reputation. If my dealings with Stephen Woolly are anything to go by—'

'Isn't he the big honcho in the Planning Office?'

Marcus nodded, 'The same. I suspect that Bertie will not lose out in the end. Stephen let slip that there are a number of prestigious, high profile developments in the pipeline. Bertie Costain is a lucky bastard most of the time. He'll come up smelling of roses eventually. I hope so anyway. What he's signed away today is close to suicidal as far as the Council is concerned right now, but these things tend to get buried over time – give it a year or so – as long as Bertie keeps his nose clean in the meantime, of course.' Marcus pulled the car keys out of his jacket pocket and letting go of Howard's hand, smiled, 'Let us have a drink sometime before I throw in the towel.'

Howard's eyebrows shot up in surprise, 'You're not thinking of doing that just yet are you?' Somehow he could not imagine Marcus not being there to turn to. They had known each other for more years than he could count; their friendship one of liking as well as respect for each other's judgement.

'Probably not just yet, but it is tempting to call it a day sooner rather than later. It's all change these days, as you know only too well: endless paperwork and then more paperwork.'

Howard nodded, murmured, 'Tell me about it.'

'The legal profession has always immersed itself in vats of ink, bolts of pink ribbon and mountains of paper,' Marcus went on, 'but these days it seems a hundred times worse. And even more tiresome are some of the folk I'm expected to deal with. The Law Society has a strict code of behaviour, of course, but of late I question the very definition of some people's understanding of ethics. Ah well, never mind, I'll keep soldiering on till the end of the year at least and then we wait and see.'

'I'd be lost without you, Marcus,' Howard said.

'I'm sure you'll manage,' the solicitor smiled. Wheezing with the exertion of all the talking, he pulled open the driver's door and slumped into the Mercedes' plush leather seat.

'Don't forget your briefcase,' Howard grinned. Flipping it off the roof and reaching inside, he dropped it on the passenger seat then closed the driver's door.

'Thanks,' Marcus mouthed, rolling his eyes and grinning back.

As the Mercedes-Benz pulled away, Howard bent down and patted Mr Boy's head. 'I'm worried about our friend, Mr Boy.' Tail stub waggling, the panting spaniel leaned his head against his master's legs.

'Come on then old chap, let's go back inside, it's getting hot out here,' Howard said, turning to stroll back across the cobbled yard. He wondered how anyone else but Marcus would have dealt with Bertie's dilemma so well and at such speed. Watching the stocky man puffing and panting, struggling to make himself comfortable in his expensive car, Howard was concerned. Yet despite the heavy, laboured breathing and the slowness of his movements, a sure sign of emphysema, Howard knew that Marcus could still run rings round most people, particularly when it came to the intricacies of law. Five feet, seven inches tall, always impeccably dressed, a silver-grey moustache perfectly trimmed under his long, arched nose, dark grey eyes and hair that had long since receded to baldness, Marcus Greengrass not only appeared distinguished, but oozed authority: that *je ne sais quoi* that demanded respect. He was by repute one of the best legal minds of his day and was held in high regard by everyone who had connections with the world of Lincoln's Inn. The day he hung up his hat and bowed out would be a dark day for many. 'Including me,' Howard muttered. He could only hope that when that day arrived, he would no longer be requiring Marcus's services to sort out the messes left behind by Bertie Costain!

Hearing his phone ring out, Howard picked up his pace, 'Come on Mr Boy, he called over his shoulder as he headed to his office door.

Leaning over his desk, he picked up the receiver. A puzzled look creased his features as he listened, seizing a pen to scribble down the caller's name on his blotter. Saying little, he nodded from time to time, a deep frown cleaving his brow.

Five minutes later, Howard replaced the receiver and with his fountain pen, circled the name he had written down: *Dufton.*

Chapter Fifteen

Negotiating the new roundabout, Bertie steered his car out of town, his head still reeling from the shock of the last twenty-four hours. As much as he told himself he should get back to the office and yard, deal with an avalanche of paperwork and sort out the various building jobs, he could not get his head round any of it. He needed some time to come up for air and draw breath.

Checking his rear view mirror, he indicated to take the second exit off the roundabout, but no sooner had his front wheels crossed into the outside lane than a flash of blue had him stabbing at his brakes. The E-type came to a stop so suddenly that Bertie was jolted forward into the steering wheel and bit his tongue. A clapped out dark blue van cut him up, roaring past him and continuing on round the roundabout in the outside lane, leaving a cloud of black fumes in its wake.

'God dammit!' Bertie yelled, letting out a string of choice expletives and blasting his horn at the maverick driver. 'The town has turned into something akin to a slapstick comedy film,' he muttered. 'It's like being in "*The Great Race*". It'd be safer behind the wheel of a dodgem car at the fair!'

Relieved that he had missed the van and the Jaguar was unscathed, Bertie shifted into second gear and pulled off the roundabout, coming up behind a white Mini. 'Jesus Christ!' Bertie cried, feeling another jolt, this time a mental one. What with one thing and another he had completely forgotten about the new car. 'Oh my God, she'll kill me!' he said, remembering that he had also forgotten to sort out the garage. If Kitty phoned asking about the MG they'd not have a clue what she was talking about. He needed to get his head round everything and come up with yet another plausible excuse. His brain working overtime, he tried to think what he would say to his wife. He had to make sure she was unaware of what he had been through these last few days. It was not that he wanted to hurt her, nor lie to her, quite the contrary, but it was better for Kitty that she did not know. A few tall tales would do no harm. '*At the end of the day*,' thought Bertie, '*it'll all turn out good, I'm certain of it.*' But today his normal optimism was more than a little shaky.

He drove past a row of shops, his eye caught by a group of young women standing talking and laughing in the middle of the wide pavement, all of them hanging onto pushchairs. '*Nice life*,' he thought, with a fleeting stab of regret, wishing briefly that he had not missed out on fatherhood. '*A bit late to worry about that now!*' he snorted, returning his attention to the road. At which point the reason for his dilemma with the MG Midget manifested itself. Wincing at the memory, Bertie's mind flashed back to four nights ago. He had left a stack of unpaid invoices on his desk, told Cynthia, the receptionist, to lock up, and then headed out to Raffles. He had been on a winning streak lately, it had seemed he could do nothing wrong. That night the dice, the cards, everything he touched appeared to have his name on it and his winnings had been substantial.

Afterwards, he was sat at the bar feeling life was more than good, when Brian Gott appeared at his side. 'Evening Bertie Boy,' Gott had chirped, 'you are the very man I need to talk to.' His sly grin had made him look even more unsavoury than usual and Bertie had inwardly groaned, wanting to sneer, but forcing a smile instead. Brian Gott was short, wiry and of such slight stature that it seemed a puff of wind could easily blow him over. Bertie was tempted to blow hard, but he knew Gott's fragile appearance was deceptive. The little man did not suffer fools; he had a sharp mind and was short on patience. It was no coincidence that out of earshot he was referred to as the 'Poison Dwarf'.

Recalling what happened next, Bertie's mood took a dive into deep anger. In a show of camaraderie, Gott had slapped him on the shoulder and given him an over-friendly smile. Warned by past experience that when Gott wanted something, his behaviour was full of bonhomie, alarm bells had rung out in Bertie's head. However, still on a high from his win, he simply raised an eyebrow and waited to hear what the little runt wanted. Even the Poison Dwarf could not upset him that night.

He did not have to wait long. In a matter of seconds Brian Gott cut to the chase. It transpired that on this occasion what he wanted was Kitty's MG Midget. Snapping his fingers at the barman to top up both their glasses, Gott squinted up at Bertie from behind expensive horn-rimmed glasses. 'I'd like to make you an offer on that nice little sporty runabout your new wife races around in,' he said, going on to explain that Lizzie, his wife, was born on 4th February 1932. The Midget's number plate was 4232 LG – perfect for his little lady.

Bertie, his eyebrows disappearing beneath his hairline, was rendered speechless by the man's gall. Catching sight of the look on the barman's face, he wondered just what would be refilled into their glasses; watched with satisfaction as the barman upturned two fresh whisky glasses and filled each with expensive single malt whisky.

Looking down into Gott's steely grey eyes Bertie let the little man prattled on. 'I want the car for my missus, I owe her big time due to a slip up, and without going into any detail,' he had winked, 'that little motor would be the answer to a maiden's prayer, so to speak. What I mean is, it would put some of the harm I've done back to rights, if you know what I mean.'

Taking an appreciative gulp of the ten-year-old Glenmorangie, Bertie smiled. The smile did not reach his eyes. 'Thanks for the drink Brian, but as for the car, sorry, no can do, it's not for sale. And more importantly, it's not mine to sell, so you'll have to find some other way to treat your good lady. Kitty's little run around, as you put it, might get *you* out of the shit, but it'd drop me right in it!'

Instead of appearing crestfallen, Gott had flashed a winning smile revealing his set of perfect white teeth. 'I thought you might say that, so I've come prepared.' He fished inside the inner pocket of his tailored jacket and yanked out a wad of banknotes. Gripping them tightly in his small hand, he continued, 'I'm about to make you an offer, a very generous offer. Much more than the car is worth,' he smirked, waving the bundle under Bertie's nose. 'Let's say that little lot should go a long way to replacing your wife's motor with one of those new Mini Coopers. Cheeky little cars they are; right up your Kitty's street I'd say. You'll not have to wait if you call my mate, Michael Middleton. He'll sort one out for you pronto.' This information imparted, he slapped down an obscene amount of cash on the polished bar top.

Despite himself, Bertie's eyes had feasted on it. 'If you've so much cash to splash, Brian, why don't you buy one for Lizzie? These days you can order your own number plate into the bargain, for a price. Problem solved.'

Fixing Bertie with the steely gaze that was at odds with the wide, perfect smile, Gott said, 'My dear Bertie, I don't think you've heard me. I don't want to buy a new car or faff around looking for a number plate. I want your missus' car. So why not take the cash and we will all be happy, eh?'

Staring at the wad of notes, Bertie was sorely tempted, but rather than walk away with the money, he knew he could do much better. He sucked in his cheeks and felt his heart flutter. As so often in the past, faced with an opportunity to gamble he was unable to resist. Play his cards right and he could walk away with a large, unlooked for bonus to top off what had been a hugely successful evening. He grinned. His luck had lasted so long he was convinced he was untouchable. He would take what he desired, same as he always did. Ignoring the small voice in his head that told him what he *ought* to do, Bertie decided to challenge the sarcastic little sod, teach him a lesson. Tearing his gaze away from the wad of notes, which Gott had scooped up in his fat little fingers and now held tight against his chest, Bertie's heart beat faster.

'I'll tell you what, Brian. I'll toss you for it. I'll put up the MG Midget against that wad of notes. You win it's yours; I win, I keep the car and your money.' Raising his glass, Bertie added, 'Cheers,' and taking a nonchalant slurp of malt, he waited.

A brittle laugh escaped the Poison Dwarf's thin lips as he returned the salutation and took a noisy gulp of his whisky, his Adam's apple rising up and down like a roller blind. The glint of excitement in Gott's eyes told Bertie that the man had bitten. The wait had been no more than a split second.

'I was hoping you would say that,' Gott crooned, dropping his tumbler onto the bar top, all the time keeping a tight grip on his money. 'It's no secret that you've had a run of luck, Bertie, but so have I, so one of us is about to have that run broken. Reckon that'll be you.' His lips had curled into an evil grin.

All Bertie could think of was removing the smirk from the nasty little squirt's face, and the sooner the better. He fished a half-crown out of his trouser pocket and slapping it down on the polished bar top, suggested, 'Best of three?'

Eyeing the coin, Gott nodded and called out, 'Heads.'

And that was the moment Bertie's luck ran out.

As the Queen's head flipped down for a second time, Gott, his eyes glinting with triumph, stuffed the pile of notes back into his jacket pocket. 'Nice for me to win and take something from you, hey, Bertie Boy,' he had preened.

Now, drumming his hands on the Jag's steering wheel, Bertie yelled out, 'Damn the man!' He felt sick to the pit of his stomach as he relived the moment he had gambled away Kitty's beloved little car. If only he had

107

simply accepted Gott's deal and taken his money, or better still, walked away. What had he been thinking of?

When he had been walking away from Raffles, he had thought of trying to replace the old MG with another similar, but finding one in the time would be tricky. Besides, the new Mini was all the rage. He had managed to convince himself that Kitty would love to have one, so the next day he had gone into Middleton Motors and spoken to the owner, bandying Gott's name. Fortunately there was a Mini Cooper S in the showroom and Middleton, after agreeing payment terms, had promised delivery in three days. Yesterday, lying to Kitty that he'd go to the petrol station and fill up the Midget for her, he had in fact handed it over to Gott. The lie about it having broken down was pure genius, except that he had forgotten to tip Farraday's the wink

Now, remembering that delivery of the new car had been scheduled for this morning and he had planned to be at the house when it arrived, Bertie sighed in frustration. It was too late to worry about that now. He just hoped Kitty would accept the car as the gift it was meant to be. 'Shit!' Bertie spat, glancing down at the dashboard and noting he was well over the speed limit. Easing his foot off the accelerator, his thoughts about Kitty's car and the Poison Dwarf took his mind on another journey, back to this morning's meeting. He wondered if there was to be any end to the bloody mess he now found himself in, because it was as clear as the nose on his face that he had let everything get out of hand this last week. He needed to put everything back on track or he would end up with nothing. 'Get a grip, Bertie!' he muttered.

As the road veered round to the right he spied a large pub sign ahead. *"The Angry Bear"*, it read as it swung lazily in the breeze. The sign was suspended on two heavy chains from a large wooden frame that to Bertie's jaundiced eye looked more like a gallows. The grizzly brown bear loomed menacingly on its hind legs, teeth bared, claws extended, its greedy eyes seemed to bore into

Bertie as he swung the E-type into the car park. 'I know how you feel mate,' he snorted.

What he needed was a drink. The office and yard could wait for a moment.

Chapter Sixteen

With a large whisky in his hand, Bertie took a seat at a small square table near the window, which looked out onto a gravelled area serving as the *Angry Bear's* car park. Gazing out of the window, he counted four cars that did not include his own. At the far side he noted a wide strip of grass that was home to half a dozen wooden benches and tables. Two of them were taken; he imagined they would be in demand at the weekend if the weather held. Everyone liked to sit out when the sun was shining, but he had seen enough of the weather when he had done his apprenticeship, working all hours outside, rain or shine. These days he was happy to be dry and warm. He shrugged his shoulders; it was good to take in a different scene, take his mind off the eye-watering cost of his loss – as if he could. Only a few days ago he had been in the big league, raking it in, his sights set on becoming a millionaire. It had seemed a real enough goal at the time. Not anymore. Bertie was sharply aware that he had learnt a hard lesson. Common sense told him he must keep well away from places like Raffles, if he did not he would end up bankrupt.

Turning away from the window and placing his tumbler down on the ring-marked wooden table, he pulled out a packet of cigarettes and felt for his lighter. Pushing his hand back into his pocket, to his dismay he could not locate it. He manoeuvred his way round the table and was about to head to the bar to ask for a light when a dark shadow fell over him.

'Well well! I never had you down for this kind of place,' Brian Gott chirped, flicking at his lighter and letting the flame dance in front of Bertie's face.

Ignoring the sarcastic remark, Bertie leaned forward, pushed the cigarette end into the light and inhaled deeply, letting the tobacco smoke curl out of his mouth, all the while keeping his sights on Brian Gott.

'*Christ,*' he thought, wincing, '*when bad luck pays a visit it has no manners, instead of dropping by for a quick hello then buggering off, it lingers following your every step whilst inviting low life to join you.*' As tempted as he was to blow cigarette smoke straight into Gott's ugly face, he resisted and instead tilted his head back and blew a grey plume towards the yellow stained ceiling. Licking his lips to remove traces of tobacco, he rested his gaze on the Poison Dwarf. 'What have I done to deserve seeing you again?' he sneered.

Ignoring the question, Gott pulled out one of the three chairs from under the table and sank down onto the hard seat banging his glass down on the table top. Bertie glared down at the top of Gott's ginger head, his thoughts anything but Christian as he too sat down. He needed this bloke's company like a bullet in the head. He groaned inwardly as he took in Gott's supercilious smile and puffed out cheeks. What did the man want now?

'I take it your missus is pleased? Nice little motors those Minis, even more so with the extra bite under the bonnet. The Cooper S I heard you'd taken. Mind you, my missus is over the moon with her little gift, not only am I back in her good books, but we're back on form too. If you know what I mean.' Gott winked and a salacious grin split across his face as he alluded to his antics in the marital bed.

Grabbing his glass, Bertie masked his distaste by taking a swig of whisky, followed closely by a drag on his cigarette. Throwing up was not something he did often, but it was a close call. Why the hell had he stopped at this shabby pub? he thought, wishing he had driven on by. All he wanted was a quiet drink, alone. He had enough going on in his head right now. The last thing he needed was twenty questions and suggestive innuendos from this nasty little man. Taking another swig Bertie slammed his glass down on the table. 'Whatever it is you want this time, before you ask, the answer is no.'

'Sometimes Bertie Costain you don't know who your mates are. If you will play with the big boys, sometimes it can get nasty, if you get my drift.'

Christ, what was this man on, Bertie wondered tiredly, his lip curling with disdain, 'You, a big boy? Behave yourself and stop threatening me or you'll live to regret it, believe you me.'

'Grow up Bertie Boy. It's *your* time to behave yourself, not mine. Gambling is a mug's game, but if you want to be in the big league you've got to expect bad luck from time to time, and that is when your friends come to the fore. I'm not your enemy, Bertie. I'm like you: an opportunist. We've both made serious gains and sometimes it goes the other way, but we always come back and you will too if you have the stomach for it. Talking of which, I heard on the grapevine that Howard Silvershoes saved your bacon this morning. See what I mean about friends?'

Bertie's jaw dropped. How the *hell* did Gott know about that almost before he knew it himself? Surely Howard hadn't advertised it – and certainly not Marcus? Christ, what was going on? Was there no end to this weasel's claptrap? Sliding the overflowing metal ashtray towards him from the middle of the table, Bertie viciously stubbed out his cigarette. 'It seems the jungle drums have been busy. Have you lot got nothing better to do than spy on me?' He shoved the ashtray away, scattering ash on the table. 'Look Gott, I don't care what you think you know. If you're here to gloat, or anything else come to that, you're wasting your time.'

'Not at all,' Gott shot back. He emptied his glass and reached for Bertie's, 'I'll get these recharged,' he said, getting to his feet.

'Not for me thanks, I've a business to run and people to see.' he swiped his glass clear of Gott's reach and downed the remains.

'Haven't we all.'

What would Gott know about business? Bertie wondered. He was a chancer; at best, a crook. If it was legal the man would be suspicious!

'Seeing as you've had a spot of bother Bertie Boy, I wanted to give you a bit of advice, because from time to time we all need some help. What I'm saying is if you're ever in a tight spot, I can recommend Bernie Palmer. Not only has he contacts, but he can produce any paper or papers, legal or otherwise, that you might need.' He tapped his nose as if to add weight to the privileged information he was giving out.

Bertie's eyes narrowed, 'Why would a bloke like you want to help me?'

'Believe it or not, taking the car from you for free was not what I'd planned, but that's life,' he shrugged, 'well, gambling life that is. Take it as my way of giving something back.'

For a minute Bertie thought the Poison Dwarf was having a laugh, and yet he both looked and sounded sincere. Dropping his glass back down on the table with a thud, he jumped to his feet. 'I'm down but not out, but thanks for the thought,' he grinned, 'it was heart-warming.'

As his words registered, Bertie saw an answering glint of amusement in Gott's grey eyes. The tow rag was having a laugh at his expense and one day he would get his comeuppance. *'I may be in trouble at the moment,'* thought Bertie, *'but not for long. All I've got to do is stay calm and then I'll take this squirt for every penny he has.'* Despite his bravado, the mini fiasco with Gott, though insignificant compared to what he had just been through with Howard and Marcus, nonetheless pained him.

Pulling his car keys out of his pocket, he headed for the door as Gott's voice travelled behind him, 'See you soon Bertie Boy. Until then stay out of trouble.'

Bertie did not look back, but muttered, 'Not if I spy your first.' Pulling the door open, he was assaulted by a gust of fresh air as the summer's day collided with the pub's smoky atmosphere. Above his head the Angry Bear sign creaked on its heavy chains. Lengthening his stride, he headed across the car park to his Jag. He had to get his stories sorted before he headed home. Questions would be asked and he needed the right answers.

Chapter Seventeen

Pulling off her apron, Kitty dropped it on the surface top next to a pair of scissors and a large yellow bow. What a strange day it's been, she thought, pulling her summer jacket from the hook behind the door of the cloakroom. Draping the jacket over her arm, she slipped her handbag over her shoulder, dipped her hand into the cavernous bag and plucked out her car keys. Holding them in the palm of her hand, Kitty stared down at them. 'Yes it certainly has been an extraordinary day,' she said to her silent audience of fragrant blooms. How many people had a new car delivered to them as a surprise, only to learn later that a blonde woman appeared to be driving her old MG Midget around town? Most women would be over the moon at their husbands being so attentive. She was too, of course, but she did not like shocks.

    Stepping out into the balmy afternoon and locking the door to Rosebuds behind her, Kitty asked herself for the thousandth time, '*What is Bertie up to?*' She had heard nothing from him despite leaving several messages with Cynthia at the office. The receptionist had told her he would be at the yard in the afternoon, yet still he did not call back. Surely he could not still be ensconced in the meeting? She sighed; Bertie had been in a terrible state before he'd left. Goodness knows what he'll be like if it all went against him, she thought with a shudder, feeling suddenly cold despite the warm day. Pulling on her jacket she raised her head to look at the azure blue sky. She did not want to think about a negative result. The sun burnt down on her face and she smiled. Who would dare not to give the contract to Bertie on such a beautiful day, she mused, laughing at herself as she headed over to her new Mini.

Ten minutes later Kitty pulled up outside Wentworth Place. Gathering up her bag and tucking it under her arm, she pushed the door open. For a moment she stood at the kerbside, running her hand over the shiny new paintwork of the Mini's roof. All the years she had been married to John, he had never once given her surprises, the odd shock, from time to time. She grimaced at the memory of her late husband. Their marriage had been a happy one, but John had not set her world on fire, barely a flicker when she looked back. Not that she had realised it then. He had loved her and she had loved him and he had been a good father to their two children. When he died she had felt his loss keenly, but it had taken Bertie to show her what she had been missing all those years. Now here she was, married barely five minutes and Bertie had organised a new car for her.

Kitty glared down at the red Mini Cooper S, 'Zippy,' she said. 'You and me both!' She had certainly lived life in the fast lane these last few months. Bertie didn't seem so much intent on setting her world on fire as creating an inferno! So far he had not failed to take her breath away on several occasions. As the thought of his generosity washed over her, she crossed her fingers that their evening would be a time to celebrate. Bertie had put a great deal of energy into preparing for and putting together the Town Hall proposal; he deserved to be rewarded with the contract.

Locking the car door, Kitty headed up the short flight of steps to number six. Her feet felt as if they were encased in lead boots as opposed to soft shoes. The heat and being on her feet for hours had made them ache and the excitement of the day had also caught up with her. She was exhausted. A cup of tea with Mrs Watson would revive her, she told herself, an unsettling feeling stirring in her stomach at the thought of her beloved housekeeper. Mrs Watson was not her usual self. Kitty had a few suspicions as to what might be the cause, but it was good to talk over a cuppa and hopefully Flo would open up and feel better when they sat down together.

Unlocking the door, she stepped over the threshold into the coolness of the high-ceilinged hall. Immediately she was conscious of the unusual quietness. No radio playing or Mrs Watson bustling around the place. Pushing the door closed, Kitty called out. 'I'm home.' Waiting for a reply, she dropped her handbag on the floor next to the telephone table and hooking her jacket onto the coat rack, called out again. Her voice echoed back at her, the deep tone of the grandfather clock the only other sound resonating through the house, ticking the seconds of life away.

'Where has Flo got to?' Kitty muttered, looking down the wide hallway at the clock. Almost five-thirty. Mrs Watson always meandered through to the hall to greet her at this time, announcing she was about to make a fresh brew. Kitty strode down the hall towards the kitchen, calling out for a third time, 'Hello? Mrs Watson?' No response. There was no sign of her housekeeper in the kitchen. The place was spick and span, the cream-coloured Formica tops sparkling in the late afternoon sunshine.

She must have gone out for a walk with the weather being so beautiful, Kitty guessed. Or maybe she was having a lie down in her flat. That would be unusual, but not unheard of. Whatever she was doing, Kitty hoped it was having a good effect. It had disturbed her to see Flo so down and tired this morning. She was very fond of the old lady and wanted her to be happy. *'Perhaps we can chat later over a glass of sherry,'* thought Kitty, *'then maybe I'll find out what it's all about.'*

Picking up the kettle and taking it over to the tap, Kitty stopped. It was not a cup of tea she needed, but a glass of chilled white wine. She placed the kettle back down on the surface top and moving over to the fridge pulled open the door. A bottle of Chablis was chilling on the shelf; next to it a large prepared salad and a smaller bowl covered with a cloth. Lifting the cloth, Kitty saw fresh prawns peeled and ready to eat. She shook her head, whatever, Mrs Watson was up to, it was evident she had not forgotten to prepare something for the evening. Things could not be as bad as she feared.

She pulled out the Chablis and nudging the fridge door closed with her elbow rummaged in the cutlery draw for the corkscrew. The cork came out of the bottle with a resounding pop. From one of the wall cupboards she plucked down a large wine glass and filled it almost to the brim, enjoying the glugging sound as the golden liquid swirled into the glass and misted the sides. Pushing the cork back into the bottle Kitty returned it to the fridge. Time to sit down, she signed with relief, making her way to the French windows. It was too beautiful to be parked indoors, a day like today meant sitting out on the terrace.

As Kitty stepped outside, the warm breeze brushing against her face, she heard the subdued chatter of voices punctuated with the sound of clinking glasses drifting over the hedge. It seemed her neighbours were also enjoying the summer afternoon's heat.

With the moisture from the cold wine glass trickling down her fingers, Kitty ambled down the wide stone steps to the semi-circular crazy-paved patio. The air heavy with fragrance from a honeysuckle that meandered along a trellis attached to the wall of the boundary to number four. Kitty inhaled the cloying fragrance – as if she'd not inhaled enough perfumes at Rosebuds! – but in her mind flowers were to be enjoyed not only for the way they looked but for their fragrance too. Reaching the round wrought iron table set in the middle of the terrace, Kitty placed her glass down and pulled out one of the four chairs. The iron legs gave out a high-pitched screech as they scraped across the dark grey flagstones putting her teeth on edge.

Dropping onto the cushioned seat, Kitty kicked off her shoes and rested her bare feet on the chair opposite. 'Cheers,' she said to an invisible guest, taking a mouthful of the cool crisp wine and letting it slip down her dry throat. Placing the glass back down on the table, she leaned her head against the chair's high back and closed her eyes, trying not to think about anything. It was impossible. Straight away the questions that had been plaguing her all day surged back into her mind, jostling for attention: the Town Hall contract; Bertie's foul mood; her MG and the new Mini. Contemplating Bertie's extravagant ways she wondered how he managed to maintain it all. He clearly had means, not that he ever discussed the financial side of his life. 'A gritty subject,' he had said on the one occasion she had ventured into such territory. Though evidently not so gritty when it came to asking for a loan! 'Asset rich but cash poor this month,' he had confessed, adding that it was important he greased a few influential people's palms. If she could possibly help him out he would, needless to say, pay her back with interest, he had said.

In the short time they had been married this had happened more than once. And of course she had helped him, and of course she had told him to forget it; he was her husband and she loved him to distraction. It was not the loans that troubled her but the company her husband was apparently keeping. In Kitty's book people who worked on backhanders were unethical and there was no doubt in her mind that this was contributing to the stress Bertie had lately been under.

The slamming of the front door, echoed through the house.

Kitty snapped her eyes open at the sound, her thoughts melting away.

'It's me, Kitty,' Bertie called out, the rich timbre of his voice drifting out to the terrace. Kitty swung her feet from the chair and stood up on the sun-warmed flagstones.

'Are, there you are,' Bertie's crooned standing on the top step, his tie and jacket discarded. In one hand he was clutching to his chest a large box wrapped in gold paper, a deep red ribbon tied in a bow across the middle. The other hand was held mysteriously behind his back.

'Oh my goodness, what have you got there?' Kitty cried, laughing.

Bertie sprinted down the short flight of steps. He stopped in front of Kitty and feigning a hangdog look, he peered above the chocolate box. 'I'm seeking forgiveness for my appalling behaviour this morning,' he said in a humble tone, handing the box over to her and narrowly missing knocking over the wine glass. 'And to show you just how sorry I am, this is also for tonight,' he added, drawing his left hand from behind his back and producing a bottle of Moet and Chandon. 'I would have brought you flowers too, but… well, coals to Newcastle…' he grinned. Beads of moisture slipped down the misted bottle as he placed the champagne carefully on the patio table. 'Come here,' he said softly, opening his arms to her.

'Oh Bertie, thank you, but you didn't to need to do all this. One way or another, it's been a day of surprises,' she cried, her voice wobbling as she swallowed a lump that had suddenly found its way into her throat. What was Bertie going to do next? Kitty was not one for tears, but the events of the day had her emotions running close to the surface.

'Oh goodness, my darling, I didn't mean to upset you, anything but that,' Bertie said softly, wrapping his arms around her. 'I love you Kitty and I am truly sorry about this morning. I just wanted to say sorry in the only way I know,' he kissed her gently on her lips.

Feeling the softness of his mouth on hers, Kitty's anxieties of the day fell away and she was reminded why she had fallen in love with the handsome Bertie Costain. Nothing got him down for long, he was unique.

Pulling away from her, Bertie stared into her face. 'You're so beautiful,' he whispered. 'With those green almond eyes of yours you remind me of Audrey Hepburn.'

She laughed, 'You mean aside from the fact that she's a brunette and her eyes are brown?'

'Don't tease,' he smiled. 'What a day it's been. If you can find it in your heart to forgive my outburst this morning then this will not have been in vain.'

'There's nothing to forgive, my love. I could see you were under terrible pressure. I take it your brightness is down to everything going to plan?' Kitty had not forgotten about the car, but she did not want to spoil this moment. She would deal with it later.

Bertie stiffened, withdrew his arms and stepping back reached for the bottle of champagne and box of chocolates. A muscle twitched nervously in his left temple and the brightness faded from his eyes.

'Oh no!' thought Kitty, dismayed. In assuming his breezy countenance meant he had won the contract she had stupidly touched a raw nerve. Before she could think what to say to put it right, Bertie had swung away from her and sprinted back across the patio. Racing up the steps two at a time, he stopped on the top one, turned and called down, 'I'm about to open this and then I'll tell you.'

Seeing his roguish grin back in place and the sparkle restored to his blue eyes, Kitty was perplexed. Had she been mistaken?

Chapter Eighteen

Stripping off the foil from the bottle of champagne, Bertie's hands trembled, the words that had innocently floated out of Kitty's mouth rattling round in his head, jangling his nerves further: '*It's been a day of surprises*'. A day of surprises, he silently repeated, if only it had been that, but from where he stood the day had been full of shocks. His mind was reeling with all that had happened and, more importantly, how he was going to sort it out. Though one thing he now knew: whatever he did would be between himself and whoever he was doing business with. After the disaster this morning, the least Howard Silvershoes knew about what he was up to, the better chance he had of survival. He was still smarting at the lash up with the Town Hall contract. Something stank and it stank to high heaven.

Balling the foil between his fingers, Bertie snorted. His winnings along with that contract were to have been his saviour, until the fickle finger of fate had stepped in. Now his plans for getting his financing sorted had gone down the drain. Never in a million years could he have imagined he would lose so badly. And worse, when he had turned to Silvershoes for help, he could never have imagined that his erstwhile friend would pander to Smith's ridiculous demands. It was becoming painfully clear to Bertie that in persuading him the only way to save his skin was to acquiesce and bow out of the Town Hall contract, Howard had sold him down the river. To his detriment, Silvershoes was not the man he used to be. He'd gone soft of late: instead of fighting Bertie's corner, he'd allowed that toe rag Smith to gain the upper hand.

Untwisting the wire and carefully removing it from the bottle's neck, Bertie's thoughts drifted back to the

Angry Bear. The day had not been a total black out. Inadvertently bumping into the Poison Dwarf might actually prove useful. Maybe the dwarf was not so poisonous after all! Something the little squirt had said had got him thinking. Now, thanks to Gott, he had the bones of an idea to help his haemorrhaging finances and keep B.C. Builders afloat until the other contracts he had greased palms for came in. All was not totally lost. He just needed to think it through and wait a few days. The ghost of a smile flitted across Bertie's face as a hint of his natural optimism reasserted itself. Timing was crucial, but he was confident his idea could work. It was the only glimmer of light in an otherwise colourless day.

Placing his left hand over the top of the cork to prevent it flying out before he had released it, Bertie gently twisted. Standing poised for the cork to let rip, he heard the soft padding of Kitty's bare feet crossing the kitchen tiled floor. Glancing over his shoulder, it saddened him to see how tired she looked. The last thing he wanted was for her to be affected by his dark mood. For once he was reminded that she was ten years older than him: most of the time it was impossible to take in that she was in her mid-fifties. Beautiful, intelligent and articulate, she was a tad eccentric and a fun person to be with. There was no denying he was extremely fond of her, but he was no longer sure he loved her as much as he told her he did – or as much as he had thought in those heady days of their whirlwind romance. Had it been love or lust? He wasn't sure he could tell the difference. He told her often enough that she was his sun, moon and stars and it was certainly true that she had made a huge difference to his life – in more ways than one! If he was honest, he knew that part of her attraction had been her bank balance. Maybe he should feel guilty for marrying her, but right now all he felt was numb.

It suddenly hit Bertie how exhausted he was. Stress had a greedy appetite and it had feasted on him for too long. But no matter how weary he felt, he needed to keep it together long enough to come up with plausible answers to all the questions he could see building in his wife's lovely eyes. The chocolates and champagne were a start to camouflaging the mire he was in. On top of the Raffles nightmare, he had yet to explain the car. With his head pounding, all Bertie could hope was that Kitty would be taken in and that the bones of the plan simmering away at the back of his mind would come together and work, because if it did not, his debtors would be fuming at his door and B. C. would stand for Buggered and Closed!

Not wanting to believe he was that close to the wire, subconsciously Bertie pushed down on the champagne cork with unnecessary pressure. Not for one minute did he entertain the disturbing thought that what had happened might all be down to him. His lifestyle and B. C. Builders had been borne out of his own hard work and, like most things in his adult life, luck! He had left school at fifteen having no idea what he wanted to do, although working out in all weathers was certainly not on any list he might have made, but his father had other plans. 'Shift your arse son, we can't keep you forever. It seems you don't go much on school, well we don't go much on you idling around chewing your nails and doing nowt.' Before he had been able to argue back, a scrap of paper had been thrust into his hand and he had been told to report to Jim Fairclough's for work the next day.

Bertie had learnt the hard way that his father was not a man to defy. At seven-thirty the next morning he had presented himself at the shabby lean-to that served as the office for Fairclough Builders. He had hardly wiped his feet before he was given a biro and told to sign a pile of papers. He was signing up to do an apprenticeship in bricklaying. 'Right son,' Jim Fairclough had said in a friendly tone, 'get yourself down the yard and ask for Nobby. He'll show you what needs doing.' As the weeks ran into months, the rain pissing down most of the time, Bertie had wondered how anyone could lay bricks in such weather. He had soon found out and to his surprise, once his muscles had developed and his hands hardened to leather, he had enjoyed working for Jim Fairclough. The firm had a decent reputation and soaked up most of the best contracts in the area. In the years he worked to get his papers, Bertie had watched and listened and had learned how building contracts were won or lost. He'd never been a fool; he knew as well anyone that from time to time palms were greased and from what he had observed, Fairclough had not been averse to scratching someone's back in return for a favour. When Jim had dropped down dead with a massive heart attack in the *Pig and Whistle*, the company had gone downhill rapidly. His sons, not interested in working in the cold and wet, had shut the doors on Fairclough's yard and moved to Spain to build villas for rich ex-pats. As the dust settled from their dash to sunny climes, Bertie had picked up a few jobs on his own. A stroke of luck with a town house in Wentworth Place had provided the opportunity to set up his own building firm: B C Builders. The company was now well established with several high profile builds – and as from today, a bloody large hole in its funds!

'Are you all right?'

Kitty's anxious voice broke into Bertie's reminiscences. At the sound of her voice he blinked and shook his head as if to clear his thoughts.

'What's wrong?' she asked.

'Nothing's wrong. I'm just about to pour us a glass to celebrate. Come and hold the glasses whilst I pour.' He nodded to the two champagne flutes he had placed on the counter top before he had begun opening the Moet and Chandon. He let the cork fly out of the bottle and as the champagne foamed over the top into the glasses held in Kitty's hands, he once again silently rehearsed the answers he needed to offer. The explanation he was about to give for the car could have been true under different circumstance. If only he could turn the clock back a week. But he couldn't. Deep inside himself, Bertie was gripped by a feeling of frenzy at the thought that all his chickens were coming home to roost. Suddenly he burst out laughing; even to his ears, his laughter sounded like hysteria.

Apparently not to Kitty's, though. 'Laughter, that sounds promising, so?' Kitty gazed up at him as the bubbles rose to the top of the glass.

'So what?'

'Oh Bertie, you are impossible. Where do I start? Importantly, did you get the contract? I rang the office, but they said you were still out.'

Checking the glasses were sufficiently filled Bertie placed the bottle down. Cynthia had informed him of Kitty's call the moment he had marched into the office. He had not returned the call, needing to calm down before he could actually speak to his wife.

'What do you think?' Taking hold of one of the glasses, he answered in a steady, measured tone and watched as Kitty's lips twisted into a smile, a sparkle flashing in her tired eyes. She had faith in him, how could he bring himself to destroy it? He couldn't. 'Yes, of course we got the contract. I knew it was in the bag, though as you saw, they had me sweating and dangling on a string for a moment; paperwork and all that nonsense. It seems these civil servants have nothing better to do than insist on a programme of form filling.' Bertie knew he was gushing, the words tripping over each other in his haste to sound convincing.

'That is wonderful news,' she beamed. 'I know how important that contract is to you and the company. You deserve it, darling, all the hours you've put in.' Raising her glass she clinked against Bertie's, adding, 'I never thought there was any other answer. Cheers Bertie, to you and B. C. Builders. I'm proud of you.'

'Yes, cheers,' Bertie responded, trying to sound animated, but he felt sick to the pit of his stomach for lying to her. He hated himself for such deceit, but for now he had no choice. '*Oh what a tangled web we weave when first we practice to deceive...*' he thought to himself. Sir

Walter Scott got that right! One lie led to another and another, until the web of lies was impossible to untangle.

Taking a sip of the crisp champagne, Kitty held on to her glass and with a look of admiration asked, 'So my wonder boy, how does winning a prestigious contract fit in with the surprise of my new car delivered today and now parked outside our house?'

Not missing a beat, Bertie responded with a wide smile, 'The Mini Cooper S? No need to thank me, darling, I knew that would be a wonderful surprise. You have no idea how hard it was for me to not say a word to you about it this morning, but you see, the other day when I took your Midget to Farraday's to have it seen to, Mick told me it needed so much doing it would take at least a week to get it back on the road. I knew you had to have wheels this morning and I had not forgotten your van is with that crazy assistant of yours. So, knowing the Town Hall contract was as good as in the bag, I went straight round to Michael Middleton's and ordered a Mini Cooper S to be delivered to you today. I wanted so much to be here to see your face when it arrived and I would have been, had it not been for the rigmarole over the contract.' He took a deep breath and a shameless gulp of champagne. God, he was gabbling like a demented lunatic, but he needed to get it all out before he slipped and tripped himself up. Christ, who would be a liar by choice?

'But I phoned Farraday's and they said they knew nothing about the car.'

'Really? It seems I'm not the only one having a mad day then.' Placing his hand on Kitty's, 'My darling don't you worry, I'll deal with this. Garages! You wonder how they keep customers when it seems they can't keep basic records. Rest assured I've everything under control, I promise!' Wondering what was coming next and in an attempt to steer the conversation away from her old car, he put on an exaggerated downcast expression and asked, 'I hope you like it? It's a racy little number. It is you to a tee Kitty, full of energy and life.' He wanted to add, '*and a little crazy'*, but decided not to push his luck. Though in marrying him she had to be mad!

Gulping down his drink in one swallow, Bertie felt his world crushing him. It was hard to keep alert when he felt so exhausted. Reaching over, he grabbed the bottle and topped up his glass. He could see Kitty was pondering what he had told her, 'Here let me fill you up, we have so much to celebrate,' he said, trying to distract any more talk about the MG Midget and cars in general. He hadn't expected her to phone Farraday's. Hell, he'd planned to give Mick a handout to play along, but with the fiasco in Raffles it had slipped his mind.

'The Mini is a super little car, Bertie, and your generosity is overwhelming, but what about my MG? When exactly will I get it back?'

'Kitty, please let us just enjoy our day, we've plenty to be thankful for,' he said, refilling their flutes. 'I've asked the garage to repair whatever is broken and let me know when it is ready. Then you can decide which car you prefer,' he lied. What a mess; he wished he'd never got into the ludicrous bet with the Poison Dwarf.

Kitty smiled at him and leaning forward placed a chaste kiss on his cheek, 'Bertie Costain, you are one for secrets. I never know what you are going to do next. New car, Town Hall contract, chocolates and this,' Kitty raised her glass. 'How can I not love a man who is so amazing?'

'Oh, hello you two; sounds to me like there is celebration in the air?' Mrs Watson's voice filled the kitchen as she ambled into the room, a carrier bag in one hand and her wicker basket in the other.

Bertie swung round, almost spilling his champagne. He had thought the old woman was in the flat below watching the television. *'Calm down,'* he told himself, he didn't need to sweat; he had everything under control now.

'Mrs Watson, I wondered where you were. Please come and join us, Bertie has brought champagne to celebrate the announcement of the Town Hall contract,'

Kitty cried, her face showing her pleasure at seeing her housekeeper.

'Is that so,' Flo Watson replied, shooting a dark look at Bertie.

Seeing the scorn on Mrs Watson's face, Bertie wished there was some way he could encourage her to pack her bags and leave. The woman was trouble. Nosy and with too much to say, but he would sort her in time. 'Yes, you are most welcome to join us. Please let me pour you a glass.' His tone of false camaraderie almost choked him as he gave her his most winning smile.

'Not for me, thanks. If you don't mind, I'll leave this bag here, it's just a few bits that need putting in the refrigerator and I'll get back to my flat. I've got a humdinger of a headache, must be all the hot air,' Flo said, handing the carrier bag to Kitty. With a sly sideways glance at Bertie she turned on her heals.

'Thank you, Mrs Watson. I'll pop in and see you later,' Kitty called to the housekeeper's receding back. 'I'm concerned about her, Bertie; she's not been herself at all today. I think something's wrong, but she won't tell me what. I mean to get to the bottom of it, though.' She smiled up at him, 'Shall we take this back out to the terrace, darling?'

'Good idea.' Taking a gulp of champagne, Bertie hid a smile. At least the conversation had steered away from cars and Town Hall contracts. '*Thanks Mrs W*, he said under his breath, '*the old biddy is a saviour after all!*'

Chapter Nineteen

It had been over a week since Bertie had arrived home, his arms filled with chocolates and champagne. As the days passed, Kitty saw that instead of her husband being jubilant over winning a prestigious contract he seemed distracted and on edge. He was short on patience and no amount of special treatment from her appeared to make a difference. When she asked him what was troubling him, he either snapped at her that he was tired or mumbled that it was nothing, just pressure of work. The sad effect of this meant they had not made love in over a week. Not that Kitty especially wanted to have sex as such, but she missed the intimacy and the closeness and began to worry that Bertie no longer found her attractive, so she too had become edgy. Each night since the celebration, he had come to bed late and after a peck on the cheek had fallen soundly asleep. At the shrilling of the morning alarm, he pushed the covers back, jumped out of bed and headed to the bathroom to wash and shave. She tried to entice him back, but all her efforts were in vain. It was as if he needed to distance himself from her, but why? Kitty racked her brains trying to think what she might have said or done to upset him, but nothing came to mind. Bertie appeared to be constantly distracted and it was clear to her that he had too much on his mind. The fun side of his personality, which was one of the aspects she so loved about him, had taken a holiday. It saddened Kitty that he did not want to talk to her about his work or turn to her for support. If she tried to initiate a conversation he would flare up and say he'd had enough of work at the office and didn't want to bring it home as well.

Kitty began to feel as if she was walking on eggshells. This new, sombre Bertie was a long way from the man she had married eight months earlier: the man who had swept her off her feet and shown her the extravagant life as they travelled together down the fast lane. Until lately he had been full of energy, brimming with ideas, always coming up with surprises to delight her. That was the Bertie she had fallen in love with. She revelled in the memories of that time: nights in the Ritz; shopping in Harrods like there was no tomorrow; taking in shows and late night films. Those early months had her catching her breath and wondering how the once quiet wife and mother, happily looking after her family and home for years, had turned into a middle-aged diva, seduced by a younger man and embracing the celebrity lifestyle. Bertie had made her forget that in five years she would be an OAP! Kitty felt young again; she was all done with the menopause and could enjoy life to the full. She was a new woman and she liked this new self. Except that of late, her self-confidence seemed to have taken a holiday with Bertie's sense of fun! Searching for a reason why he had become so distant, she had begun to notice her encroaching grey hairs; the lines on her face and neck; her inability to see the small print without reading glasses. Was that it? Did Bertie resent saddling himself with a woman ten or more years too old for him?

Now, as she walked into the kitchen to be greeted by the wonderful smell of frying bacon, she saw to her amazement that Bertie was tucking into a cooked breakfast. 'That's not like you,' she commented, eyeing the three rashers of bacon, two eggs, sausages and tomatoes. Thinking back, she could not recall Bertie having any breakfast at all this last week, never mind a full English! She made her way to the chair opposite him where a place had been laid for her.

Bertie grinned, 'Good news always makes me hungry.' With a nod towards Mrs Watson's stiff back and a slight shake of his head, he flashed Kitty a secretive smile and continued wolfing his food down as if he had not eaten for weeks.

Raising an eyebrow at him, Kitty called across the kitchen to where the housekeeper was busily turning bacon rashers over in the frying pan, 'Good morning Mrs Watson.'

'Morning Kitty,' Flo glanced over her shoulder. 'I take it you'd like the same? I've a larder full of bacon, thanks to that daft butcher. Stupid man got carried away yesterday when I asked for a half a pound of best back and a pound of sausages, seems he thought I was feeding the five thousand and not genteel folk watching their waistlines,' she went on.

Kitty did not miss the housekeeper's surreptitious glance of contempt towards Bertie, but decided to ignore it. She felt guilty having not had the opportunity to find out why Mrs Watson had been so obviously distressed lately. Kitty had tried to engage her in conversation, but it seemed Flo wanted to avoid discussing her troubles. There was always something else needed doing whenever Kitty had suggested they sit down with a cup of tea or glass of sherry. The sight of her old housekeeper wiping tears from her eyes the other morning had upset Kitty and she was determined to get to the bottom of it. She would try again later today when she got back from Rosebuds.

'The smell of bacon frying always makes me hungry, so yes I'd loved a couple of rashers,' Kitty smiled, reaching across the table for the teapot and pouring the strong tea into her cup. Still holding the teapot she looked over to Bertie. 'And what good news has got you eating like a horse?' Her relief at seeing her husband more like his old self lifted her mood like nothing else could. 'I heard the postman push letters through the letterbox. I presume he brought the good news?' She placed the teapot down on the table and stared at the two envelopes beside Bertie's plate. 'Anything for me?' she asked, adding milk to her cup.

'No. Both for me and both look like bills,' he said in between mouthfuls of breakfast. She noted the envelopes where upside down so the name and any bank or company stamp was not visible.

'So where did the news come from? You never mentioned anything last night and I don't recall the phone ringing.'

With a half a sausage speared on his fork, Bertie held it between his plate and mouth, 'You're not keeping tabs on me are you?' he asked, raising an eyebrow.

'Don't be silly, I'm far too occupied to play Miss Marple,' she joked, but did not miss the flash of unease in his eyes. What was he up to now, she wondered? Did he not have enough on his plate with his building company and now the Town Hall, without adding more?

Swallowing down the last piece of sausage, Bertie picked up a white linen napkin, pulled it from its ring and wiped his mouth, his roughish smile returning as he dropped the napkin back on the table. He looked across to where Mrs Watson was cooking and winked. 'The good news that's had me devouring one of Mrs W's excellent breakfasts did not come in the post, Kitty, and what I have to tell you I wanted to save until now.' He pushed his plate away and reaching across the table placed his hand on Kitty's and lightly stroked her fingers, the secretive smile once again flitting across his face.

A shiver ran down her spine. It was the first time he had touched her in that way since the day Zippy had been delivered and in that moment she saw the Bertie she had first met. 'It must be very good news,' she smiled. 'Are you going to keep me sitting here all day before you share whatever is making you smile like the Cheshire Cat?' she asked, placing her other hand over the top of his.

'You are so impatient Mrs Costain,' he said jovially, 'it is quite simple. Do you prefer your new car to the MG Midget?'

'What a strange question,' she said, a frown puckering her forehead. He had led her to believe it was good news that had him ploughing through a huge breakfast not the talk of her car. Unsure where this was going, she decided to humour him. After all it was good to see her husband relaxed and smiling again. 'Well...' she began, and hesitated.

'It's important for me to know, so do you or don't you?' Bertie insisted, removing his hand from between hers.

'It has its qualities...' she answered, picking up her cup and bringing it to her lips, 'but why are you asking?' She took a mouthful of the cooling tea.

'Mick phoned me late yesterday to say your MG Midget has all its new parts fitted and will be ready for collection later today.'

That was the last thing Kitty had expected to hear. 'Really!' she shrilled, plonking her cup down on the saucer. She'd had an uncomfortable feeling that she would never see her MG again, even more so after Julie had told her about the mysterious blonde woman driving it the day her Mini was delivered. Kitty had almost convinced herself Julie had been mistaken, but had not dared mention it to Bertie knowing that in his present mood he would bite her head off. She had stood by while he phoned Mick at the garage to sort out the mix up, but he had sounded strained, almost as if he was speaking lines, and despite his call, Kitty's doubts about the whereabouts of her Midget had continued to nag her. Pushing them away, she beamed at him.

'That is such good news. I know it's silly, but you know how sentimental I am about that little car. I thought it was past being repaired, but then, what do I know about cars?' Kitty laughed and recapturing Bertie's hand gave it a squeeze, at the same time wondering how she could have harboured such negative thoughts. Mentally castigating herself for doubting Bertie, she reminded herself that he was everything a gentleman could be and he cared about her. How many husbands would have bought their wife a new car at the drop of a hat just because their old one needed major repair? She didn't answer her own question, she didn't need to.

'I said I would get it sorted. Why would I lie to you?' he said, looking down at her hand and not at her face, but making no attempt to pull away.

'I can't imagine you would,' she said with conviction. 'Thank you Bertie.' As she spoke he turned his eyes to her. They laughed back at her making her catch her breath. She had never seen such blue eyes on a man before.

Lifting his tea cup to his mouth, Bertie downed the remains in one gulp and dropped the cup down with a clatter in its saucer. 'We do have a little problem though, darling, we can't drive three cars. So it would be helpful if you could decide which car it is you want to steam around town in.'

Kitty, suddenly aware that Mrs Watson's ears were flapping, hoped what she was hearing would change her mind about Bertie. She must see now that he was every inch an honourable man and not worthy of her mistrust. Revisiting her earlier mental note to speak to her housekeeper, Kitty added an asterisk to signal it was important they had a chat about that too, the air needed clearing.

'Well?' Bertie pressed, slicing once more into her thoughts.

Aware he was growing impatient, Kitty replied, 'It should be a tough answer, but it isn't. 'The Mini is wonderful and I loved it that you bought it for me like you did, darling, but what will happen to it if I say I want to keep my MG?' As the words slipped from her lips Kitty was certain she detected a flicker of panic in Bertie's eyes, but it vanished before she could consider it further.

'It would go back to Middleton's, no problem. Middleton knew there was a chance you would prefer to keep your MG Midget once it was back from the garage and we had a special arrangement,' he answered confidently, though a tic twitched in his left temple. 'However, if you would prefer to keep your Zippy, as you call it, then Mick has a buyer who would be prepared to pay a good price for the Midget. Of course, you must make the decision; after all, both cars are technically yours.' Bertie picked up his tea cup and brought it to his mouth, he looked over the top at her then remembering the cup was empty, frowned and put it back down.

Mrs Watson placed a plate of egg and bacon silently in front of Kitty. Wiping her hands on her apron she leaned over the table, picked up Bertie's empty plate and without a word, headed back to the sink and switched on the radio. The chinking of dishes being washed echoed above the muted sound of John Dunn's dulcet tones.

Ignoring the domestic arrangements going on around him, Bertie pushed back his chair and stepped round the table to Kitty's side, leaning forward to place a soft kiss on the side of her cheek. 'Don't worry Kitty. If you would prefer to keep your MG, I fully understand and there is no pressure.'

A pang of guilt made the heat rush up Kitty's neck. Ashamed, she tilted her head and looked up into Bertie's handsome face. His eyes seemed to search into her soul and all she saw in them was trust and kindness. What had got into her, she wondered? At her age she should know better. In some ways Bertie was like a little boy seeking reassurance. How could she put her love for her little MG before his need to feel she preferred what he had chosen for her? 'I'm fond of both the cars,' she answered as Bertie pulled out the chair next to her and turning it round, straddled the seat. Resting his arms on the back, he kept his gaze on her.

'I'm a hopeless sentimentalist at heart, darling,' Kitty said, 'so parting with anything, no matter how long it has been in my possession, is always difficult.' As she spoke she was aware of Bertie holding his breath. '*Zippy* is special to me because you chose it for me. I've never had such a wonderful surprise in my life. And as difficult and sad as it will be to say goodbye to my MG, you are right, I can't drive two cars. So yes, I will keep the Mini. Please let Mick know that I'll sell to his buyer.'

Bertie Jumped up from the chair, almost tipping it over in his enthusiasm. 'Rightyho, you eat your breakfast and I'll give him a call straight away. I promise you I won't accept anything less than the top price and more since we've had to pay for all the repairs.' The relief in his voice was palpable.

His reaction was so over the top that Kitty's appetite vanished. She felt a renewed surge of doubt: something was decidedly odd about this whole business with the car. But what could it possibly be? Maybe she was just being over-sensitive. As Bertie bolted out of the kitchen and into the hall, she pushed the plate of untouched breakfast away. 'I'm sorry Mrs Watson, but I don't think I can eat this after all.' She got up from her chair and walked over to the older woman, 'But thank you, it was a lovely thought.'

Mrs Watson picked up the hand towel from the side of the sink and wiped her hands dry. She looked so weary that Kitty, feeling suddenly guilty, wrapped her arms around her and gave her a quick hug. 'I know you only have my best interest at heart Mrs Watson, but it would just make things easier if you could bring yourself to like him a little. He's not bad you know. He just does things differently. There is no need to worry. He won't hurt me if that is what is going through your head.'

The housekeeper nodded her head as if in agreement. 'If you say so and I'll try my best, but he's not good enough for you. I admit what he had to say this morning made me think. Maybe after all I have been a little hasty,' she admitted, stroking Kitty's arm.

Wistfully Kitty looked over at the table and her untouched food. 'You know, we still haven't had that chat, Mrs Watson. Perhaps when I get back from Rosebuds later, you and I can sit down with a decent glass of something potent and put the world to rights.'

''Why not? Mrs Watson gave Kitty a wan smile, 'And after all these years, my dear, can't you call me 'Flo'?

'Of course I can, Flo, bless you. It's just that I always think of you as Mrs Watson,' Kitty smiled back. 'I'm already looking forward to our chat, it will be like old times,' she said, moving away. 'I'd better get myself washed and dressed or else the day will be over before we know it.'

Meandering through to the hall she was almost knocked over by Bertie as he raced down the stairs two at a time. 'Did you talk to the garage? Kitty asked, negotiating her way round him.

'Indeed I did. All is in place. We just need to hand over the log book,' he said, breathlessly.

'Goodness, I'd better get my skates on,' she cried, continuing up the stairs.

'Why?' Bertie shouted, striding to catch up with her.

Feeling his hand on her shoulder, Kitty swung round, 'Because I need to take the log book to the garage and collect the bits and bobs left in my old car, why else?'

'No need,' Bertie responded, hastily moving in front and stopping her from going up the stairs. 'I've said I'll drop by with the documents later today. I can clear out the MG for you at the same time.' He stroked her hair, 'Kitty, by your own admission you said how sad you were at parting with things. Leave me to deal with it all then you won't have to face saying goodbye to your old car. All I need is for you to sign the log book and I'll do the rest, it's the least I can do.' He kissed the tip of her nose.'

Kitty hesitated, a few seconds ticked by punctuated by the grandfather clock then she laughed and wrapped her arms around his neck, 'Yes, of course, you are right. I would only get all sentimental and want to drive it back home then where would that leave the Mini?'

'My thoughts exactly,' he grinned. Gently he removed Kitty's hands from around his neck, kissing the back of each hand before releasing them.

'I'll go and get the log book then,' she said.

Filling up with happiness at Bertie's romantic gesture, Kitty ran up the stairs to her study. Pulling down the lid of the rosewood writing bureau, she slid open the small drawer where she kept the papers for her car and lifted out the log book. Sinking down onto the writing chair, she flipped open the folded pages. Her lips curved up as she read the details. She had loved that little car. Her MG had been one of the first things she had bought after John's death, her first step into a world of independence. 'Bye-bye little car,' she muttered under her breath. Then pushing sentiment away she reached for her fountain pen, pulled off the top and with bold handwriting filled in the relevant details, finishing with the flourish of her signature.

Seeing Bertie leaning on the door jamb, she blotted the ink then folded the pages. 'Here you are,' she said, holding out her hand.

'Thanks.' Bertie took the document and pushed it into his inside breast pocket. 'If it means anything, Kitty, you and Zippy make a striking addition to the roads of London.' For a moment he gazed down at her and then he smiled. 'I feel as if I have been neglecting my ravishing wife just lately…. And talking of ravishing, maybe we can get an early night tonight?' He raised his eyebrow so suggestively that Kitty burst out laughing.

Chapter Twenty

'There you are,' Bertie said, flinging a scorching look at the Poison Dwarf as he threw the log book for Kitty's MG Midget across the Formica-topped table.

Sitting in Vera Porter's coffee shop, at one of the tables next to the large window overlooking the busy shopping street, Gott looked up from his cup of coffee and leered at Bertie. 'I was beginning to wonder if I'd ever see this,' he snarled and grabbed at the folded green card as it skidded towards him. With his eyes fixed on the log book, he pulled the folded document open. 'Not that it would make any difference if you'd kept the book, getting forgeries is not that difficult if you know the right people,' Gott snorted, tapping the side of his nose to add validation to his knowledge. 'Though the genuine article is best and I see Mrs Costain has done the necessary too. How did you manage that?' A smirk twisted Gott's thin lips as he squinted up at Bertie.

'If I see that man tap his nose just once more, I will not be held responsible for my actions,' Bertie cursed under his breath. His lip curling with distaste he ignored Gott's inane question and watched the little man screw up his eyes in an attempt to decipher the almost illegible writing that filled much of the log book,

'That's disappointing; seems your good lady was not the original owner.'

'Who cares,' Bertie shrugged, standing in front of the table. 'Your missus is now one of them.'

'Indeed that is true and of course she is one happy bunny.' Staring through lenses thick as milk bottle bottoms, Gott raised his shifty eyes to Bertie and smiled, 'I take it yours is too, with that flashy little motor. I told you those Cooper S's were shit hot.' Winking at Bertie, Gott added, 'I don't suppose you fancy another flutter?'

Balling his fists, Bertie took a step closer to Gott's chair.

'Okay,' Gott cried, raising his hands, palms forward, as if to ward off an attack, the smug smile slipping from his face. 'I was only joking. Where's your sense of humour?' Lowering his hands he fumbled to fold up the log book, stuffed it into a card wallet sitting next to his coffee cup then tapped the folder as if to confirm he had stowed the precious book away safely.

'Drink up and you can have this one as well,' Bertie said, shoving the full cup, which had been waiting for him on his arrival, across the table to Gott, the contents slopping into the saucer. 'I don't have time to chew the fat with the likes of you.'

Ignoring Bertie's barbed comment, Gott said mildly, 'Surely we can part as friends, Bertie Boy? A cup of coffee won't hurt you. Sit down, life's too short to be charging around like a blue-arsed fly.'

'Friends?' Bertie almost choked on the word and wished he had not arranged to meet the obnoxious man here. The idea of stopping at the little café was, metaphorically speaking, killing two birds with one stone. He had meant to hand over the log book on Kitty's MG before popping round the corner to Bernie Palmer's grubby office. Under the present circumstances Bertie felt his principal investments might benefit from having two owners; importantly it would be an insurance against any financial difficulties he may encounter in the future. These days he needed to keep one step ahead of the fickle finger of fate. To that end he had decided to transfer half of Wentworth House to Kitty's name. Rather than going to Marcus Greengrass, who would insist on pawing over every detail, the last thing he needed right now, he had gone to Palmer – a shady character if ever there was one – and asked him to deal with the paperwork, arranging to pick it up this morning. He had deliberately kept Howard out of the loop on this one. Silvershoes would only muddy the water. Bertie wanted to do something on his own for once and what he chose to do within the confines of his marriage was nobody's business but his own. He was still smarting and licking his wounds from the disaster of two weeks ago, but he had to put that behind him and get on with making money *his* way. Thankfully, he was back on a roll and meant to stay that way.

Now, as Bertie took in Gott's face, he could see the man was a shilling well short of a pound. Nobody in their right mind would want to win a used sports car with two previous owners, yet somehow this halfwit had. Clearly his dumb blonde wife led him by the nose; not as dumb as she looked then. Bertie knew she had been driving round the town like Boadicea in her chariot, causing mayhem with her dangerous driving. The woman was such a pain on the road that she attracted attention wherever she went and although Kitty had said nothing, Bertie knew she must by now have heard about it, if only from that dippy assistant of hers. It no longer mattered. Whatever Kitty had suspected, it was done and dusted now. He had sorted it.

A warm feeling coursed through Bertie's veins at how everything had worked out perfectly in the end. He also counted his blessings that Kitty was more than happy with the new car. As soon as she had told him she had called it *Zippy*, he knew she had fallen in love with the little hell raiser. Thankfully, not only had his lies about the MG been convincing, but he had managed to feign exactly the right little-boy-anxious-to-please-and-fearing-disappointment look. He had not had to feign the anxiety! It had been hairy for a while, but she had fallen for it. Yet, when she had handed him the log book and said, *'I know why I married you, Bertie, and not a day has passed that I regret it,'* instead of feeling euphoric he had felt disloyal and ashamed. Starkly aware that he'd had no choice, however, Bertie had soon shrugged off the guilt. And anyway, now that his luck had at last returned he would be able to make up for what he had done. He sent up a swift prayer to whoever was listening that good fortune continued to stalk him, because now more than ever, he needed things to go right.

Bringing his attention back to the Poison Dwarf, Bertie said, 'Now you've got what you wanted – though God alone knows why you wanted it – I'll make sure I keep a wide berth from you in future.' Turning on his heels, he strode to the door.

Behind him Gott called out, 'I take it you didn't take up my advice regarding Bernie Palmer?'

Bertie glanced over his shoulder and closed his eyes at the revolting sight and sound of Gott slurping coffee. If only he could close his ears too! He glared back at the Poison Dwarf and sneered, 'Who?' He did not wait for a response. The bell above the door tinkled loudly as he wrenched the door open and stalked out of Vera Porter's coffee shop.

Chapter Twenty-One

Less than five minutes after leaving the coffee shop Bertie arrived at Palmer's office, an Edwardian terraced property situated in West Street. He had walked only a short distance, but at least it was enough to put a decent gap between him and the insufferable Gott. He was, however, pleased to know the wretched little man had not heard of his visit to Palmer. It seemed the legal beagle could be trusted not to blab, which was good news.

Standing outside the office entrance he noted the peeling paintwork and the door handle hanging drunkenly on one screw. A plaque on the wall listed the names of several businesses occupying the building and Bertie, re-reading them, snorted. Among them was a bookkeeper, A. C. Accountants, and a private detective called "Findus" – he'd bet it was not pronounced the same way as the frozen food company! "Bernie Palmer LLB" was given the spurious title of 'legal advisor'. To Bertie's certain knowledge, Bernie Palmer no more had a law degree than did Bertie Costain, but whatever the man purported his qualifications to be, he was never found wanting. Amused, Bertie shook his head at how people hoodwinked themselves as well as others.

Pushing on the peeled paintwork, the door groaning loudly on its hinges as it opened, Bertie stepped over the threshold into a dingy hall. A light bulb hanging from a long cord attached to the mottled ceiling gave off a dim glow. He elbowed the door closed unable to believe how low he had sunk that he now had to deal with someone working in a dive like this. The place stank of tom cats and other indefinable odours. Trying not to breathe too heavily, he cautiously crossed the narrow hall to the brown and cream patterned linoleum that covered the stairs and made his way to the first floor. Reaching the landing he took in the three doors, to his amazement noting that each one was newly varnished, the smell going some way to masking the cat pee downstairs. A dazzling polished brass plate on the first door announced the office of Bernie Palmer. Grinning at the man's pretentiousness Bertie knocked gingerly on the door. The varnish still felt soft and sticky beneath his knuckles. Not waiting for an answer he twisted the brass knob and walked in.

Filtered sun rays shone through strategically angled slats from white venetian blinds. Swiftly taking in Palmer's office, Bertie saw that it was a contradiction to the motley looking building in which it was housed. Since his last visit it had changed out of recognition. Gone was the stained grubby carpet, in its place was rich, dark parquet flooring. He could see from the sheen that it had been polished to within an inch of its life. Perhaps he ought to get the name of the cleaner; it seemed she would put Mrs Watson to shame. Bertie sniffed at the thought of the old bag, wishing Kitty would find a reason to send her packing. The woman unnerved him and had done since at Kitty's insistence she had joined them as housekeeper. He chewed on the inside of his mouth, now was not the time to sweat over some old Mrs Mop. Pushing unsettling thoughts of the cleaner out of his mind he gazed around in admiration at the moderately-sized, refurbished office. It had been vastly improved since the week before last when he had first stepped inside. Even the chipped old school desk had been replaced by a large walnut affair. Along one wall was a glazed mahogany bookcase stuffed with reference books and on the opposite wall hung a series of framed Punch cartoons. Bertie was impressed by the speed with which the changes had taken place: legal advisors must be making a mint these days, he thought, staring at Bernie Palmer's smart three-piece, pin-striped suit and what looked like a silk tie. The man sat behind the desk, a grey cloud of cigar smoke hovering above his head.

'Bertie Costain as I live and breathe,' Palmer enthused rising to his feet and extending a chubby hand across the desk, a fat Havana poking from the side of his mouth.

Bertie shook Palmer's hand, saying amicably, 'My my, things have changed since I last visited you.'

'All completed over a weekend. Couldn't have the office disrupted during the working day,' Palmer said with pride. 'Believe you me, there's plenty of work out there and thankfully much of it's been heading my way.' Leaving go of Bertie's hand, Palmer indicated one of two brown leather armchairs in front of the desk. 'Sit yourself down and I'll hand over all the papers. Everything's straightforward, you need to sign and get Mrs Costain to sign in front of a witness. That's all there is to it.' Palmer said in a positive tone, placing his cigar into an oversized cut glass ashtray. Wheezing with the effort, he reached across to the far side of his desk and pulled a buff-coloured folder towards him. Flicking it open he pulled out several sheets of paper. Without taking his gaze from the file, he picked up a pair of half-moon spectacles lying on an open reference tome and slipped them onto his nose to inspect the papers. 'Yes, as I said earlier, everything is in order and awaiting your witnessed signatures.' He smiled, picked up the papers and handed them to Bertie.

Something about Palmer's supercilious smile reminded Bertie of the Poison Dwarf. God forbid there could be two such creatures on the planet! Flicking through what had been handed to him, he nodded. 'I think what I am doing is the best thing for the future, don't you?'

'Indeed.' Again that disdainful smile.

Disquieted, Bertie stood up, moved to the side of the chair he had vacated and shuffled the papers back into order. 'Thank you Bernie, it's good doing business with you.'

'Pop them in this,' Palmer advised, flicking a large brown envelope across his desk.

Slipping the documents into the envelope, Bertie was again assailed with the positive feeling that everything was about to improve. His luck was on the turn; that familiar tingle of adrenalin rushing through his system was back. A sensation he had experienced many times, but not lately. Buoyed up with confidence, he nodded to Palmer. 'Thanks again,' he tapped at the envelope as he spoke.

'You've got what you paid for and I hope it all goes to plan.' Not moving from his chair Palmer picked up his cigar and re-lit it from a swanky, quartz-cased desk lighter. 'I hope we will do business again?'

'I'm sure we will,' Bertie said, thinking that the stench of the stale, billowing cigar smoke was almost as bad as a tom cat's piss. He felt Palmer's gaze on his back as he left, still wondering at the rapid transformation of the scruffy den of a couple of weeks ago into a palatial office that wouldn't look out of place in Lincoln's Inn. Whatever 'legal advice' Bernie Palmer was offering, Bertie would lay odds that the term '*legal*' was wide of the mark. The man was nothing more than a jumped-up spiv! Clutching the envelope to his chest, Bertie grinned. He didn't have to like him and he couldn't care less how the man made his money, so long as he delivered the goods.

Chapter Twenty-Two

Sliding into his car, Bertie dropped the envelope onto the passenger's seat and slipped the key into the ignition, but all he could think of was the papers he'd had Palmer draw up. He glanced at the envelope, decided he was in no rush to drive off and reached across to pick it up. Flipping it open he pulled out the sheaf of documents, fingering the pages as if they were a precious metal and in some ways they were almost as priceless, he thought. Frowning slightly at the formal style of the wording he started to read the first page. As his brain absorbed the content, Bertie's eyes lit up and he flicked to the next page.

It took several minutes for him to read all four documents, but he was satisfied the details were correct. On the last page he saw the crosses Bernie Palmer had pencilled indicating the place for his, Kitty's and a witness's signatures to be added along with the date. In normal circumstances he would have asked Howard to be the witness, but he was keeping Howard out of the loop. Marcus too; he did not trust the man. Not that he'd had a lot to do with him. Howard was the one who had a penchant for using Marcus. Bertie had always preferred the senile old goat, Jim Dawson. These legal beagles might have a code of ethics, but now he thought of it, he didn't trust one of them. And, of course, he could not forget that Marcus Greengrass was Kitty's solicitor too. Who was to say what he and Kitty chatted about, drinking tea in fine bone china cups and discussing her wealth and Bertie's business? Keeping his affairs close to his chest was the only way. In his book, Greengrass was old school and Bertie did not fit into that select membership.

Returning the papers to the envelope he dropped it back on the passenger's seat. Bertie was confident he was back on form. It was business as usual. His unfortunate loss had only been a glitch. He had panicked. On reflection, his reaction had been down to the shock of losing such a vast sum and the heart-stopping forty-eight hours Smith had given him to pay it all back before sending in the heavies to beat it out of him. Alright, so he'd lost the Town Hall contract. If he was honest that had hurt his pride as much as it had damaged his finances, but there was more than one way to kill a cat than by skinning it, and he would find the perfect way to kill this particular cat, and restore his self-esteem in the process. The other unfortunate business with Kitty's car was all sorted and now water under the bridge. And of course, in his hand he had the papers he needed from Bernie Palmer, once Kitty's signature was witnessed, the safety net he needed would be in place.

Smiling with satisfaction, Bertie started the car and headed for his office, preoccupied with the knowledge that he'd had a turnaround in luck and could use it to his advantage in bringing his plans to fruition. To that end he spent several hours at B.C. Builders getting to grips with the paperwork, the mountain of unpaid invoices, and listening to the constant griping of his workforce. By mid-afternoon he'd had enough. He needed an adrenalin fix and he needed to quench his thirst. The only place that would satisfy these needs was Raffles. He had thought of finding another club, but he wanted Smith and Bryant to see he was not beaten. The thought of returning to the club lifted his mood even further and with a wide, satisfied smile, he turned the E-type's nose towards Raffles.

Nudging into the club's car park he found there was only one space left. Knowing the place was heaving sent adrenalin pumping through his veins, giving him renewed confidence. He had not come to lose. 'Lose?' he murmured. 'Wash your mouth out, Costain,' he quipped, deciding that the evil word should be banished from his vocabulary. This afternoon all he needed to do was keep his wits about him and watch. That would ensure he left in a healthy position and several hundred pounds, if not thousands, the richer. The heat of the afternoon and what lay ahead had him breaking out into a sweat. He would enjoy nothing more than removing his jacket, but the rules of the club were strict. Dress code was paramount. Formal was all that was allowed. Even loosening his tie could find him being asked to leave. Today was not a day for breaking the rules and drawing unnecessary attention to himself. The fact that Smith and Bryant would be keeping an eye on him was more than enough to put him in the spotlight.

With the gravel crunching under his shoes, Bertie made his way to the Edwardian portico, the sun lighting up the pale-coloured brickwork. At the top of the short flight of steps to the entrance Raffles' doorman stood waiting to receive him.

'Good afternoon, Mr Costain, nice to have you back, sir.' The doorman smiled a greeting and with a white-gloved hand touched the side of his forehead in a casual salute.

Bertie nodded an acknowledgement and stepped through the opened door into the palatial foyer, his polished, handcrafted, classic Oxford brogues sinking into the thick dark carpet. Shifting his weight he cast his gaze around the ornately decorated room, which to Bertie's eyes looked as much like a Toulouse-Lautrec painting of a brothel as did Smith's office. The entire place had all the hallmarks of Brian Smith and Kevin Bryant: vulgar solid furniture, heavy red velvet drapes, flocked wallpaper and gilded cut-glass chandeliers. The room screamed money and tasteless imagination. It was suffocating, yet Bertie drank it all in as if his eyes had never feasted on the garish interior or his feet had not trodden the hallowed halls of Raffles. He snorted, it was a mixture of derision and pleasure, the place might be ostentatious and gaudy with outdated rules, but he was glad to be back. He belonged here.

Breathing in cigar smoke, which permeated the building, he couldn't believe it had been just over a fortnight since he had left on the verge of a breakdown, worrying how he would meet the payment of his debt. He tugged on his left shirt cuff to reveal his gold link. That part of his life was history, he told himself. From now on all he needed to do was concentrate and he would be rewarded with the heart-stopping thrill of winning.

'Mr Costain, welcome back,' Brian Smith's voice boomed loudly, slicing into Bertie's positive thinking. Approaching Bertie he extended his right hand.

Startled, Bertie swung round, but not without noting the formal salutation. 'It's good to be back,' he replied, keeping his voice even and trying not to wince as, with a vice like grip, the owner of Raffles pumped his hand. Smith looked him in the eye, but Bertie could detect nothing there other than affability.

'Before you get down to business, let me offer you a drink,' Smith said, releasing Bertie's hand and applying gentle pressure to his shoulder, encouraging him to head towards the bar. 'Glad there are no hard feelings between us.' Indicating a small, round table and chairs he snapped his fingers at a waiter, who scurried to do his bidding.

'None at all,' Bertie lied, knowing it would be pointless. No way was he going to give Smith the satisfaction of seeing a visible sign that he bore a grudge. He intended to enjoy the ambience of the club whilst making sure he emptied Raffles' coffers. He had made enquires about the Town Hall contract and what had happened on that black night. Bertie was still convinced he had been set up. But no amount of asking and poking around had given him a hint that anything had been or was out of place. Even so, he refused to accept it was a coincidence, never mind that evidence said it was. Time would tell, he thought grimly, sipping the double whisky in his hand as Smith left him to enjoy his afternoon at the tables.

Three hours later, eyes shining, a satisfied grin on his lips, Bertie walked out of Raffles. His return to the fold had eventually gone well, though half way through his early session he had come close to losing his shirt. Refusing to panic he'd fortified himself with a large whisky and then another, and kept his cool. As he expected, the tables had turned and once again he was filled with the euphoria of winning. There was no feeling like it – even an orgasm didn't come close!

Buoyed up with his success, before leaving the club Bertie stopped at one of the private telephone booths and booked a table at *Pierre's*. He had two reasons to enjoy a fine meal with his wife: the fact that he was back in the saddle and the surprise he had for Kitty, both were perfect reasons for a celebration.

Chapter Twenty-Three

Kitty pushed the door open to Rosebuds and immediately her nostrils filled with the heady fragrance of flowers and foliage. Sneezing twice, she pulled a handkerchief from her jacket pocket and wiped at her nose. 'It must be the lilies,' she mumbled, striding across the threshold and almost stepping on a couple of letters delivered earlier by the postman. Balancing on one foot to avoid standing on them, she bent down and picked up the two envelopes, 'No doubt more bills,' she moaned to a shop where the only sound to be heard was the distinct hum of an insect. Kitty looked around and saw the yellow stripped bee hovering round the bucket filled with the fragrant lilies. Smiling, she turned over the envelopes: it was clear the brown one was a bill, but she had no idea about the white one. *'Interesting,'* she thought, pulling the key out of the lock and dropping the bunch into her bag. Leaving the door open to allow fresh air to filter in, she turned the small envelope over, ran her thumb through the sealed flap and pulled out a sheet of paper.

Unfolding the letter, Kitty smiled. Judging by the poor English, it was from Mrs Goodie. Rosebuds had supplied the bouquets for her daughter's wedding a couple of weeks ago. Reading the words scribbled on the lined blue paper, courtesy of Basildon Bond, Kitty knew her day had just got off to a flying start.

"Dear Mrs Costain,
I am not much good with words but me and the family thought you done us proud. I was going to come in the shop and tell you to your face but I did too much twisting at the ~~receepsh~~ reception and me backs gone!

Anyway thanks again. The bookays and them little posys for the bridesmades was lovely.
Yours sincerely,
Edith Goodie.

Kitty chuckled at the spelling, but the words warmed her heart. Not many customers bothered to send her a letter of thanks. What an unlooked for surprise. Mrs Goodie might not have the full command of the Queen's English, but clearly she had the manners and kindness to show how appreciative the family were with the arrangements.

Folding the letter, Kitty pushed it back into the envelope. She would make sure Julie saw it; her assistance had been invaluable in getting everything sorted and delivered. Thinking about that Kitty was reminded how lucky she was to have the young woman working for her. No doubt Julie would squeal loudly when she heard the explanation of what had happened with the MG. Over-excitable she may be, but she was dependable too. Oh to be Julie's age with all the opportunities these modern times offered, she reflected. Holding Mrs Goodie's letter to her chest, Kitty realised she had made two mistakes in judging people lately. In future she would be more careful and look beyond the obvious.

Half an hour later, Kitty having regaled the story of the garage and her car, she gave Julie the letter to read. Predictably there were more happy squeals and Kitty listened with amusement as Julie laughed out loud. 'Wow! Fancy that old biddy getting up on the dance floor to do the twist.'

'She's not that old,' Kitty said, feigning disapproval, 'she's not much older than me.'

'Oops, sorry Mrs C. Anyway, I thought the twist was old-fashioned now.' Handing the letter back to Kitty she picked up a pair of scissors and began snipping the stalks of some deep pink lilies.

Watching her, Kitty frowned. She had not missed the knowing look slipping across Julie's face at the suggestion that a blonde couldn't possibly have been driving the

Midget on the day Zippy was delivered. Pondering it for a while, Kitty then dismissed it with a shrug; Julie must have been confused, it was the only explanation.

The rest of the day passed in a blur of sprays and bouquets and Kitty was relieved when, after wiping down the preparation area, Julie slipped her bag over her shoulder, trilling as she headed for the door, 'It's time to pick up the kids from school already; where has the day gone?'

'Have a good evening,' Kitty responded with a smile. She would follow shortly as she needed to get home to talk to Flo. Hopefully, at last, she would find out what was upsetting her old housekeeper. They had still not managed to have a chat, though not for the want of trying on Kitty's part.

'Thanks. You too. See you tomorrow Mrs C,' Julie called, 'and as always, thank you for letting me take the van home. You're the best.' This said, Julie swept out of Rosebuds pulling the door closed, her cheerful voice ringing out above the tinkling doorbell as she bumped into someone she knew.

A couple of minutes later the bell tinkled again. Expecting to see Julie dashing back having forgotten something, she called out, 'Honestly, Julie, you'd forget your head if it was not screwed on!'

'I beg your pardon?' a voice replied. It was not Julie.

Startled at who had entered her shop, Kitty did a double-take, instantly recognising the young man who, with a newspaper tucked under his arm, had stood on the pavement outside Wentworth Place and stared up at her on that awful morning. Was it only two weeks ago? No, three, surely. At closer proximity he looked a little older than she had at first thought. This time it was her turn to stand and stare, the hairs on the back of her neck prickling. There was something about him that unsettled her and as rude as it was to stare, she could not take her eyes off him. Thankfully, he seemed oblivious to her interest, too busy scanning the buckets filled with colourful perfumed blooms.

Wiping her hands down the side of her apron, Kitty took a deep breath to steady herself. 'Good afternoon, can I help you?' she asked politely, moving to his side.

An alarmed expression crossed his face as he whirled round to face her. 'Yes, good afternoon,' he replied, his voice catching in his throat.

Not missing the uncertainty in his eyes, Kitty wondered why he was in her shop and more importantly, why he had stood outside the house watching her window. Contemplating whether or not to ask these questions, she remembered Rosebuds was a shop and people came in to buy flowers. As for the window gazing, maybe she had been mistaken and he had been looking at her neighbour's house or just admiring the Georgian architecture. She wasn't wholly convinced, but nonetheless remained silent.

'I'm sorry,' he spoke more firmly this time. He enunciated clearly in a cultured tone, as if he had been educated at an expensive school. Pointing to the lilies Julie had prepared earlier, which now sat regally in a bucket of water, he said, 'I would like five of those, please; the deep pink ones.'

'Yes of course. Would you like them with a little greenery?' Kitty asked, still wondering why he had walked into her shop. He didn't look the type to buy flowers. Who was he and why did she have the feeling he was looking for her and the lilies were just an excuse? Dressed expensively, he was a handsome man with dark brown hair and pale skin. The eyes that smiled at her were a soft blue. He looked innocent enough, but looks could be deceptive. Strange she should remember his face so well, even though he had been standing on the other side of the street that morning. She had never seen him before and yet she could not push away the feeling there was something familiar about him.

'No,' he shook his head to her question, 'just the lilies.'

'Rightyho,' Kitty said, plucking five long-stemmed blooms from the bucket. Gently she shook off the excess water before wrapping them in green soft paper and handing them to her customer. 'Be careful of the pollen,' she warned, 'it stains. Is there anything else?'

'No thank you.' Taking the blooms he sniffed them and wrinkled his nose.

'Rather fragrant aren't they?' Kitty chuckled, seeing him wipe the back of his hand over the tip of his nose to remove the trace of orange pollen.

He made no comment, simply handed over a five-pound note.

Opening the till, Kitty took out two shillings and sixpence and gave it to him. Without further words, he dropped the change into his trouser pocket, nodded to her and clutching the green parcel of blooms, left the shop.

Walking to the open door, her gaze followed him as he crossed the road. She kept watching him until he was out of sight, wondering who would be the lucky recipient of those expensive lilies. More importantly, who was he and why did she get the feeling he was keeping tabs on her?

Chapter Twenty-Four

Rinsing the soap suds from her hands, having finished the washing up, Flo Watson turned the tap off and plucked the hand towel from the side of the draining board. She wiped her hands on the soft cloth and wondered if she had got everything wrong. She kept coming back to the things she had overheard Mr Costain saying to Kitty about the car. For days they had been going round and round in her head like a fairground ride as she had gone about her daily chores. The last thing she had expected to hear was that Kitty's car had been repaired. There was nothing she could put a finger on, but she'd had a feeling in her water that Mr Costain had been telling porkies about the MG. She tried to remember if it was his tone of voice or the fact that his pupils were noticeably dilated when he told Kitty her car had needed a lot doing to it. Funny that it had never broken down before – not that Flo knew much about cars and she supposed there was always a first time, but it had seemed odd to her that he'd straight away bought Kitty a new one. Why would he do that if he had expected to get the MG back? Something didn't add up, but whatever it was, it now seemed to have sorted itself out.

As the days passed and domestic harmony returned to number six Wentworth Place, she grudgingly admitted that to Bertie Costain's credit he had at least not left Kitty without a car. She had the van, of course. Flo clicked her tongue at the thought of Kitty's commercial vehicle. It was hardly fitting that Kitty should be seen driving a white van, even if it was decorated with flowers on the side. Thank goodness she let the young woman at Rosebuds run around in it. Gripping the hand towel, Flo wondered what had got into Kitty these days; she used to be so sensible.

The more Flo had thought about Mr Costain's kindness in letting Kitty choose for herself which car she wanted, the more Flo acknowledged that maybe her harsh opinion of him had been a tad hasty. She had always reckoned to be a good judge of character, but of late her judgement seemed to have been distorted. She put it down to feeling her age and her dislike of city living, accepting that she was turning into a crotchety old woman. Be that as it may, she was an old woman who needed a break. More importantly, she needed to pack her bags and leave Wentworth Place. The more she thought about her circumstances the more she knew she had to do something about it. If she could just convince herself all was well here then she would take steps to leave. Flo sighed, wringing the hand towel in her hands as if the answer was in hidden in the stripes of the fabric and a squeeze would reveal what she needed to do. As she twisted the towel, her thoughts cascaded down through the years to the first day she had met Kitty Maddison.

It had been a bitter cold day, but although her hands were red raw she had not noticed the weather. The state of her extremities had nothing to do with the climate so much as with her job as chambermaid. Her hands were constantly plunged in water, washing or scrubbing down. She never had time to dry them properly and they chapped in the cold wind. The day she had met Kitty Maddison, she had been helping out in the hotel kitchen because two of the kitchen maids had been off sick with influenza. Flo had just finished peeling and cutting a mountain of spuds when she had heard voices approaching in the corridor. Wiping her hands down the pinny she wore to protect her uniform, she had swung round to see Mr Maddison with a young girl at his side coming through the door. Flo's breath had caught in her throat at the sight of the hotel's owner in the kitchen. Reliving that moment now she recalled with a smile that he had been an incredibly handsome man. When he had addressed her she had blushed all the way to the tips of her ears, so overcome with a mixture of nerves and shyness that she had almost curtseyed.

'Good morning Florence, where is everyone else?' Mr Maddison had asked, his deep voice ringing out as he cast his gaze around the kitchen.

'They are about somewhere, sir,' she had said, her words tripping over each other. 'I'll go and get Mrs Hetherington if you like, sir.'

Mr Maddison had waved a hand and carried on addressing her. 'Florence, this is my daughter Kitty, I don't think you two have met before, you being new here, but Kitty needs to stay here until I return from my meeting. Please let Mrs Hetherington know. I'll leave you two to get to know each other,' he had smiled at her and even after all these years Flo could still remember the heat that had swept up her neck in the wake of that smile. 'Maybe Kitty can help you,' he had said, adding, 'my daughter is a very practical young lady.' With that he had marched out of the kitchen, his heels clicking loudly on the linoleum floor as he headed back down the corridor. After he had gone, Kitty had set to peeling spuds with a will; nothing had seemed to faze her and although Flo could never quite bring herself to forget the difference in their status, the two of them had become firm friends.

Of course, at the time Flo had no idea their first meeting would be the catalyst that changed her life. All the Maddisons had been kind to her and she never forgot what a huge debt she owed to the family. It was because of that perceived debt that she wanted to be sure Kitty was happy and not being used. Her wealth had not changed her one bit; inside she was still the girl who trusted without question and helped anyone she could. This made her especially vulnerable and Flo, knowing this, worried about her constantly. It would break Kitty's heart were she to discover Bertie Costain had married her for her money. Until the business with the cars, Flo had been sure of it, but his subsequent words and actions had not been those of a man who was out for money. He appeared genuinely to care a great deal about Kitty, and despite her earlier misgivings, Flo was immeasurably relieved.

The shrilling of the telephone startled her making her jump. 'Goodness me!' she exclaimed, wiping her hand across her face. Throwing the screwed up towel onto the draining board, she bustled out of the kitchen and into the hall where the phone continued stridently to demand attention.

Snatching the receiver to silence the noise, Flo held it to her ear and in a purposeful voice sang out the number. She listened to the voice on the other end, her face breaking into a smile. 'Oh, it's you. No problem Mr Costain and thank you for letting me know.' Carefully replacing the receiver on its cradle, Flo glared down at the two-tone blue Trim Phone. 'What a flimsy thing you are, even if your ring *is* loud enough to wake the dead,' she snorted.

Staring into the mirror above the telephone table Flo wondered who the tired stranger was glaring back at her. Thankfully she didn't have to cook dinner tonight. His lordship was taking Kitty out. Flicking at a loose strand of hair and nipping it back into place under a hairgrip, she acknowledged that it was good of Mr Costain to let her know. It seemed he planned to give Kitty a special surprise tonight. Funny he should think to call her, now she thought of it. It was most unlike him to be so considerate. Of course he had asked her to keep his secret. That was the trouble with Mr Costain: he was full of secrets and surprises, he should have been a magician, always pulling rabbits out of hats, she thought, chuckling at her analogy of the man who owned this posh house in Wentworth Place, as well as a flashy, big sports car. Thinking about it, she admitted to feeling honoured that he had shared his latest surprise with her. Now she was even more convinced that she had been a little harsh on him, especially when she added in her misunderstanding about Kitty's car.

Suddenly, Flo felt her eyes filling up with tears. 'My word, what has got into me?' she muttered, mopping her face with her pinny. Why was she so sensitive and emotional just now? What had become of the Flo Watson who coped with everything and everybody? These days the person that inhabited her body was a stranger. It was as if she'd had a personality change. This other Flo saw doubt and fault everywhere, and worse, she was so weepy all the time. It was not like her at all. It was as clear as the nose on her face that she needed a tonic, maybe she should go and see the doctor and ask for one. She had meant to do that before now, but had not got around to making an appointment. She had never been one to go crying to the doctor every time she felt unwell. She just had to shake herself out of this silly mood she was in. Lily-livered her mother would have called it.

Sinking onto the straight-backed chair beside the telephone table, Flo continued to stare at her reflection. It seemed that her loyalty and fondness for Kitty had blinkered her to everything. She imagined danger round every corner and mistrusted everyone who came near. Yet Kitty was a grown woman who could look after herself. There might have been good reason to feel this urge to protect her if Kitty had been her daughter, thought Flo, but she wasn't. *'I am just the housekeeper; what am I thinking of? I've been on a fool's mission; she doesn't need me. She's got him now.'* That thought had fresh tears coursing down her face and a sob rose in her throat. Swallowing it down she wagged a finger at her reflection. 'Behaving like this is no way to carry on,' she said sternly, her voice echoing around the hall. It was high time she pushed the demons away. To all intents and purposes it seemed Mr Costain was a loving, caring husband and that was all that mattered.

Flo stuck her tongue out at her reflection. 'It's past time for you to move on, Florence Watson,' she said. 'You should never have come here in the first place. You might have known it could never be like old times. What are you? A stupid old woman, that's what!'

Determined that tomorrow she would ring the letting agent and enquire about Primrose Cottage, as she had meant to do three weeks ago, Flo wandered back into the kitchen and put the kettle on to make herself a nice strong cup of tea. Then she'd go and watch Coronation Street on the master's big television. The folk in the *Rovers Return* were so much worse off than she was it always made her feel better!

Chapter Twenty-Five

Watching as the sommelier expertly poured the chilled Bollinger into flutes, Bertie, with his arm resting across the table, held Kitty's hand.

'What is so special about today?' she asked, looking around the private booth they had been brought to. Their table was on the first floor of Pierre Duval's restaurant, one of the most fashionable eating houses in the capital. From their table was a splendid view across the river. It was still daylight and they could see several small vessels on the calm water enjoying the summer evening.

A half-filled flute of vintage champagne was placed at Kitty's side and a similar glass for Bertie. The sommelier slipped the bottle into an ice bucket, covered the top with a crisp white linen cloth, bowed his head towards Bertie then stepped away from the table and soundlessly left the booth.

Bertie's mind raced with all the plans he had formulated as he removed his hand from Kitty's. Maintaining eye contact, he reached down and fingered the large brown envelope that rested against the front leg of his chair. 'It's been an eventful couple of weeks in more ways than one,' he said, the ghost of a smile lighting his face. 'The stress of dealing with officials in the council and wondering if any of my debtors would pay up on time, and of course, the Town Hall contract, all of this has meant I have not given enough time to you.' He hesitated to add conviction to his words. 'Tonight I wanted to make up for being preoccupied and short of patience.' Glancing at Kitty's glass of champagne, he continued, 'This special restaurant, the meal we will shortly enjoy…' Again he hesitated, picking up his glass and holding it in front of him, 'And the champers, is my way of saying thank you to you for your patience. I've not been an attentive new husband these last few weeks and I apologise.' As he spoke he saw how Kitty looked at him. Her eyes filled with love and something he had not expected, respect. Guilt stabbed at him and he wondered if he could go through with his plan.

'Bertie, there is no need to apologise, I understand.' She gave a tinkle of laughter, 'My little shop challenges me enough, never mind having a multi-million-pound building company to run like you do. I'm not surprised you are sometimes distracted. I just wish I could help.'

'You help just by being there my darling. I didn't marry you to be at meetings day and night. Especially at night,' he raised his eyebrows suggestively and grinned. Picking up the envelope he flapped it over the table. 'Tonight I have a special gift for you.' He saw the look of interest flash in Kitty's eyes making them sparkle like emeralds. There were no two ways about it, he thought, his wife was very attractive. She may be a woman of mature years, but there was an aura about her; she retained the spirit of youth. He supressed a chuckle remembering the story Michael Middleton had relayed to him of how Kitty had scared him witless driving him back to the showrooms. How she had passed a driving test beggared believe! Watching her, Bertie felt his pulses quicken. Meeting this gorgeous, wealthy lady had been a stroke of luck.

Looking at the envelope in his hand, Kitty raised a curious eyebrow. 'You've showered me with gifts ever since we met, Bertie. I'm thoroughly spoilt and I love it, but you don't have to do it all the time.'

Hearing the happiness in her voice, Bertie prayed he would not hurt her. No matter what he planned or schemed, it was to improve their life not destroy it. 'One of the chief pleasures in life for us married men is spoiling our wives,' he grinned. 'So, my darling, please take a look at this.' Bertie handed over the foolscap envelope. 'If you agree with everything, all it needs is your signature.'

'What is it?'

'Have a look and see.'

As Kitty took the envelope their hands brushed together and a frisson of anticipation raced through his veins. 'You are a very special lady and I love you very much. Let's toast our future,' he said, raising his glass.

With her free hand, Kitty picked up her glass and clicked it against Bertie's. 'Cheers,' she said, taking a sip of champagne.

'To us,' Bertie added.

Putting down her wine, Kitty proceeded to open the envelope. Bertie held onto his champagne flute, the condensation trickling down the glass and dripping onto the white linen tablecloth. He took a large mouthful and savoured the crisp dry taste, the bubbles fizzing on his tongue. Watching Kitty open the flap and pull out the documents with unnecessary haste, he smiled at her eagerness. She was always like that; her enthusiasm never let him down. It was one of the things he loved about her.

With her eyebrows knitting together, Kitty let out a low cry, 'Bertie, what is this? I don't understand. It looks like a legal document,' she frowned.

'Legal is precisely what it is, my darling. How else am I able to add your name to the deeds of Wentworth House unless the papers are drawn up?'

'But why?' Kitty asked, laying the documents down and staring across at him, clearly mystified.

Seeing her confusion, the corners of Bertie's mouth lifted in a thoughtful smile. He wondered what she was thinking and hoped she would accept what he offered without too many questions.

'Well?' she asked, an impish smile making her look flirtatious. 'I can't plough through all this legalese, Bertie, can't you just tell me what it's about? Why have you done this?'

'You're an impatient little minx aren't you,' he grinned, 'and why not? I love that about you. But to answer your question, there are a number of reasons. One being you're my wife. Also, you have recently loaned me two sizeable amounts of money. Money that was vital for my business and I have not yet been able to repay you.'

'I told you not to worry about that,' she said.

'I know, but—' Bertie stopped speaking as an impeccably dressed waiter appeared at their table and handed them each a gold-embossed menu. Swiftly removing the champagne bottle from the ice bucket he refreshed their glasses then backed away and left them alone again.

'I wanted to give you something that means a great deal to me,' Bertie said. 'Something I can share with you. Six Wentworth Place is not only a lovely property, it's special to me. It was the springboard for my success. The papers you are holding give you ownership of half the house.' He observed Kitty's face as he spoke, expecting to see joy at his gift, but she simply stared back at him blankly. Momentarily disconcerted, all he could think was that she saw it not as a gift but as payment for the loans. Thinking on his feet, he said, 'Kitty, this is to demonstrate to you what you mean to me and how grateful I am that you consented to be my wife. Whatever you say, once the new building contract payments start to fly in I intend to repay every penny of the money you lent me.' Aware that he was speaking too fast, Bertie drew breath. '*Slow down*,' he thought, '*give her time*.'

Abandoning his chair, he made his way to the other side of the table and dropped a soft kiss on Kitty's cheek. To his dismay her cheek felt damp. Hunkering down, he took her hand in his, 'I hope you can accept my gift to you. It would mean a great deal to me. I have not forgotten you were there when I needed support, it is my way of showing how much that meant to me.' Rising to his feet, he plucked a folded white handkerchief from his trouser pocket, shook it out then tenderly dusted her face with the edge. 'Don't cry, my love, it is not meant to be an emotional evening, it's meant to be a celebration.' Pressing the handkerchief back into his pocket he picked up the documents and crossed the space to his chair. About to sit down, his movement was arrested by the waiter who with swift and silent footsteps appeared in the booth. Placing himself behind Bertie's chair, with practised precision he positioned it squarely to the table, enabling Bertie to settle back into his seat.

'Are you ready to order, sir?'

'No. Give us a few minutes, will you?'

'Of course, sir,' the waiter said, once more disappearing from the booth.

Bertie laid the papers down, his heartbeat increasing as he thought about their importance. He needed Kitty to sign, no questions asked. He leant his elbows on the table and said softly, 'Have I got it wrong?'

'Heavens no, Bertie, you've got nothing wrong, it's just that I'm overwhelmed by your generosity. It's really too much. I know how much Wentworth Place means to you, all the years of hard work you put in to make it a beautiful home. I'm truly grateful for your gift. It is worth many times more than the money I lent you. I don't need the surety of half your house, Bertie. It has never once crossed my mind that you won't repay me when you can. Please tell me this is not about any doubt you think I might have?'

It saddened Bertie to see the hurt in his wife's eyes. 'The papers have nothing to do with the loans, Kitty,' he said, needing her to understand. 'Don't you see? I wanted to give you something tangible to show I'm a man of my word. Things have been tough this year due to poor payers and other factors that I'll not bore you with, but I *will* pay you back that money. I promise. Good God, woman,' he grinned, 'I can't have Mrs Watson telling you I only married you for your money.'

'*Bertie*!' she shrieked, 'Don't even *think* it, never mind say it. I *know* that's not true.'

In promising to pay her back, Bertie was not deluding himself; he had every intention of doing so, with interest. His luck was changing. If it continued – and he saw no reason why that should not be the case – he would not only be able to pay Kitty back, he'd be able to carry out some serious investment for BCB's. He was filled with optimism. *'Money makes money,'* he thought. On the other hand, in the unlikely event that things went pear-shaped again, then having half the house in his wife's name would be a saviour.

'Seriously, Bertie, I have more than enough funds in my account from my inheritance and as you know, Marcus is canny when it comes to looking after my investments. By comparison, Rosebuds is inconsequential, but it too is doing really well. So you see, I can afford to help you out and there really is no need for you to worry about paying me back, however long it takes. I meant what I said. Just forget about it. As much as I appreciate the thought, I can't accept your gift. Like I said, it's too much and there's no need.'

'Let me try again,' he said, wanting to take hold of her hands, but afraid he might end up squeezing them too hard in his enthusiasm to have her understand. 'Call me old-fashioned, Kitty, but I'm the man in this partnership. I'm the one who should provide for *you*, not the other way round. I'm not having you bailing me out when things get tough. I should be able to manage my own affairs.' Bertie dropped his gaze and allowing his voice to break, added, 'I feel unworthy of you, darling, and less of a man. Please try to understand that. On all sorts of levels it's important to me that you sign these papers. *And that's not a lie,'* he thought. *'Christ, they'll be offering me an Oscar at this rate!'* Looking up at her from under his lashes and seeing the glisten of unshed tears in her eyes Bertie knew he'd won.

'I do understand, really I do,' Kitty protested. 'It is far too generous, but then, that is you, Bertie. You're the most generous person I have ever met. Thank you, I accept, but there is a small condition.'

Bertie's heart sank. '*What now*?' he thought, meeting her gaze and waiting.

'If I accept half of number six, then you have to accept half of Rosebuds and my Wimbledon penthouse. I'll get it sorted out and sign them over to you. I spoke to Marcus about this very thing some time ago. I'll give him a call and ask him to get on with it.'

Right now that was the last thing Bertie wanted. He did not want Marcus Greengrass poking his nose in, but he caught the steely sting in Kitty's voice and knew there would be no arguing. Importantly, for now he had the agreement he needed. He would deal with Kitty's generosity when he was in a stronger position.

'My darling, there is no need, but if it will make you feel better about having half of Wentworth Place then I will humbly accept, thank you.' Relief and a feeling of triumph surged through him. He wanted to gulp down the champagne and order a whisky chaser, but forcing himself to remain calm he recharged their glasses and raising his own, said, 'To us: the best partners in everything,' Stretching across the table he waited for Kitty to raise her glass to his, adding, 'Thank you Mrs Costain, you have made this middle-aged man feel worthy again. Now I think we should order or our waiter is going to burst a blood vessel!'

Having selected their food and wine and handed the menus back to the waiter, Bertie returned to the subject of the documents. 'I hope you won't mind, but in case you accepted my gift, I asked Pierre if he would witness our signatures when we've finished dinner. His reputation is second to none.'

A baffled shadow slipped across Kitty's face. 'I know that, but surely Marcus needs to see them and check all is in order first? Not that I doubt you have used a reputable solicitor,' she said hastily, 'but I've never signed anything legal without passing it by Marcus first. He's looked after me since before John died. I'm sure you understand?'

Bertie did not understand. Why the hell did Kitty want that blasted man to check everything? But in fact he was prepared. He had expected this would be a sticking point and had second-guessed it would happen. Good God, all he needed was her signature. Why did she have to make such a fuss? Keeping his voice soft to avoid any detection of his irritation, he said, 'Really there is no need to involve your solicitor, darling. I have every confidence in my man. Everything has been drawn up by him and he is satisfied for Pierre Duval to witness our signatures. It's a simple enough document. It will be attached to the deeds specifying that you are an equal owner.'

'Yes, I see that, but something as important as this needs Marcus to witness my hand,' Kitty insisted.

'Ok, ok, I give in.' Bertie held his hands up, a mischievous grin hiding his exasperation and disappointment. 'I'll explain to Pierre that his services are not required after all. Seriously, I don't want you to sign anything without feeling comfortable about it. I do understand. Have Marcus check it out first. I can tell that you don't trust me,' he teased, 'and I really don't mind.' He was lying through his teeth, hoping she wouldn't call his bluff. It was like the car saga all over again. She had to feel she was free to choose. Picking up the documents, he slid them back into the envelope, reminding himself he needed to keep calm.

The appearance of the sommelier stopped further conversation. Bertie breathed a sigh of relief for the interruption and checked the proffered bottle, nodding in affirmation that it was what he had ordered. To avoid eye contact with Kitty he fixed his gaze on the waiter as the man opened the wine. A feeling of defeat washed over him. The evening had not gone to plan: Marcus would be pawing over his personal business after all. Damn it! He needed to rethink, he told himself, as he watched the expensive liquid glugging into a wine glass the size of a small goldfish bowl.

Taking hold of the long-stemmed glass handed to him Bertie swirled it around, in his frustration almost spilling the rich, velvety wine over the rim. Steadying his hand he raised the glass to his nose and sniffed deeply.

Without tasting it, he looked up at the waiter and nodded. 'That's fine,' he said, but the odour of panic overlaid the bouquet of the special reserve Rioja that lingered in his nostrils.

Chapter Twenty-Six

Bertie had chronic indigestion and had he not been at the exclusive restaurant he would have taken great satisfaction in belching out loud, instead he suffered in silence. His discomfort had nothing to do with the exquisite food served from a world class master chef, but from Kitty digging her heels in regarding the papers he had asked her to sign. He rubbed at his chest as he made his way down the wide curving stairs, disappointed that a first class evening had been blighted by Kitty's need for everything on paper to be sniffed at by her solicitor. The thought of Marcus Greengrass added further irritation to his suffering. Throughout the meal he had kept his voice even and his face fixed in a permanent smile. He had also kept silent on the papers drawn up by Bernie Palmer. Now, while Kitty powdered her nose in the ladies cloakroom, he made his way to Pierre Duval's office and tapped on the door. Not waiting for a response he pushed the door open and stepped into the small office, nudging the door closed with his elbow.

At the sight of Bertie, Pierre crossed the room, a wide smile stretched across his tanned face, his outstretched hand welcoming him. 'Bertie, I've been expecting you, come and join me in a decent drop of cognac.' He spoke like a dyed-in-the-wool Londoner, all trace of the heavy French accent that was familiar to his clientele dropping from his soft voice.

Bertie took hold of the proffered hand and smiled back at the tall, broad-shouldered man with luxuriant, dark wavy hair, who dwarfed him by three inches. Pierre was wearing a formal dinner jacket and looked every inch the successful restaurateur he undoubtedly was. The two men shook hands. 'That sounds perfect,' Bertie replied, deciding to enjoy Pierre's fine cognac before mentioning he would not need his signature after all. The drink would help ease his annoyance at Kitty's decision.

'Sit down,' Pierre indicated one of the two cream leather sofas separated by a stylish smoked glass coffee table. At the same time he looked towards the door. 'Where is your good lady?'

Crossing the room, which was lit by two shaded wall lights that lent a soft ambiance to the well-appointed surroundings, Bertie settled into the soft leather and rested his elbow on the arm. 'Powdering her nose,' he answered, crossing his legs. 'She will join us in a moment,' he added, dropping the envelope with the papers at his side.

Pierre sat down on the matching sofa opposite. Perching on the edge, he reached across the low table for the crystal decanter, which rested on a silver tray next to four matching brandy balloons. Upturning two of the glasses, he pulled out the stopper from the decanter. A whiff of the contents floated through the opening, the fiery redolence making Bertie's nose twitch and his mouth water in anticipation. Lifting the heavy decanter, a smile playing on his lips, Pierre poured two large cognacs and handed one of the glasses to Bertie. 'I hope you were well looked after by my staff?' he asked.

'Need you ask? You not only run a tight ship, but serve the finest food and wine this side of the Channel.'

'I'll take that as a compliment,' Pierre said and picked up his glass.

Bertie swirled his brandy and took an appreciative sniff of its bouquet, aware that a Jacquiot XO, one of the finest cognacs in the world, was about to slip past his lips. Intoxicated by the rich aroma, he raised his glass to the man sitting opposite him, whose real name, as his birth certificate would attest, was Peter Dudley. Bertie smiled; not only did he like the man, he admired his shrewd business acumen. Peter was no more French than he was himself, although he had trained as a chef in Paris, acquiring new skills and a new name along the way. They had been friends for years and whilst each had embarked on a different road to employment and wealth, it had been a roulette table in the now defunct *Spinning Wheel* that had brought them together. Years ago 'the Wheel' had been the place to be, but the club had eventually gone out of business. Bertie was not surprised: too many of its punters had been lucky and its huge losses had proved unsustainable. Peter, now a famous restaurateur, had been one of the lucky ones, collecting in a single night enough money for a deposit on a small restaurant. Since then he had gone from strength to strength.

Unlike Bertie, who could not resist the pull of gambling, Peter had never chanced his arm again and yet Lady Luck had continued to shadow him. Today he owned one of the top restaurants in the country and was patronized by the rich and famous, peers of the realm and royalty among them. Yet wealth and fame had not gone to his head, he was still the same decent chap for whom Bertie had felt instant rapport when they first met. Sipping cognac that had the texture of silk, Bertie wondered if he too was unchanged by what fate had thrown at him. Was he the same Bertie Costain who had worked in all weathers laying bricks and trudging around in mud up to his knees? Probably not, he mused. His luck had not been as reliable as Peter's and pressure had played a part in adding demands to his life.

'What can I do for you, Bertie? Delighted as I was to receive your call, I'm guessing it means you want something?' Pierre's question, accompanied by a teasing grin, broke into Bertie's thoughts.

'I was just thinking that you haven't changed,' Bertie responded with a rueful smile. 'A prestigious restaurant and a foreign name have not altered your suspicious mind, Peter.'

'Dealing with you Bertie what would you expect? Behind every façade is the real person and I've known you long enough to see right through you,' Pierre batted back with humour.

'Like you, I'll take that as a compliment,' Bertie retorted, cupping the glass with his hands and savouring the golden liquid that slipped far too easily down his throat.

'What is it you want me to witness? You sounded garbled on the phone.'

'Yes, well I was about to—' A gentle knock on the door stopped Bertie in mid-sentence.

Pierre sprang to his feet, strode to the door and swung it open. A smile lit up his dark brown eyes, 'Kitty, *comment tu es belle comme toujours.* How wonderful to see you, please do come in and join us,' he said, switching to English but maintaining a suave French accent. 'Your husband is about to explain what he wants from me.' Pierre winked at Kitty as she squeezed past him and taking her fingers in his, dropped a kiss on her outstretched hand.

'Merci Monsieur Duval, I don't feel as beautiful as you tell me I always look, but it's kind of you to say so,' she smiled, her voice low and brimming with laughter.

As Pierre, with his hand on the small of Kitty's back, ushered her to the sofa, Bertie got to his feet. 'Darling, come and sit down. Your timing is perfect. I was about to explain to Pierre the change of plan,' he said, masking his irritation with a beaming smile. Taking hold of her elbow, he guided her to sit at his side. He had hoped to explain things to Pierre before Kitty appeared. Now he'd have to be honest. Thank God the expensive cognac helped blur the lines!

'Would you like a nightcap, sweetheart?' Pierre asked, discarding his accent. Not waiting for a response, he poured a small measure into a brandy balloon and took it over to her.

'Thank you,' she said, raising her glass to him, a mischievous glint in her eye. 'Much as I adore your accent Peter, I feel more at ease when you drop the pretence.' Taking a cautious sip, she rested her glass on her knees. 'So, Bertie has not explained why we are here?'

'Not yet,' Pierre replied, returning to his seat on the other side of the coffee table. 'He was about to when you arrived.'

'Thank goodness, I was afraid... never mind.' Turning to Bertie, she smiled, 'You're right darling, what we do as husband and wife is between ourselves. Forgive me, I was being silly and over-cautions for no reason whatsoever. There is no need to involve Marcus. Let's just stick to your plan.'

With the utterance of each syllable Bertie felt the heat rise to his face. His heart skipped an extra beat at his wife's change of mind. Inclining towards her he dropped a chaste peck on her freshly powdered cheek. 'Thank you darling,' he said, wanting to say more, but decided discretion was more appropriate.

Twisting to face Pierre, Bertie casually explained the reason for their visit.

'I hope it's legit,' Pierre retorted sceptically, looking from Bertie back to Kitty, one eyebrow raised.

'And there was me thinking you hadn't changed. You've turned into an old cynic,' Bertie volleyed back. 'As a matter of fact I'm signing over half my house to my lovely new wife and since we are here enjoying your fine restaurant, it made sense to ask if you would oblige by witnessing our signatures.'

Pierre's face broke into a smile as he nodded his agreement.

Taking hold of the envelope Bertie pulled out the sheet of paper he knew needed their signatures. Handing it to Kitty he watched as she scanned the document again and at the same time he slipped his hand into the inside pocket of his jacket and produced a fat gold fountain pen. Twisting the top before removing it, he offered the heavy pen to Kitty.

'Darling, if you would just sign here.' With his index finger he pointed to the pencilled 'X' added earlier by Bernie Palmer. 'Then I will sign and Pierre will witness our signatures.'

Biting her lip, Kitty looked from Bertie to Pierre and back again to Bertie. 'I can't help feeling I'm about to rob you of your precious home by signing this.'

'Nonsense,' Bertie said, taking a deep breath. 'We've been through it all and you said you understood my reasons. So please just add your signature with its usual flourish. That is all it takes to call six Wentworth Place our *joint* home.'

Taking hold of the pen, Kitty signed and blowing on the ink, passed the document to Bertie. Adding his spider-like signature, he laid his pen on the table and waited for Pierre to witness the two signatures.

Leaning forward, Pierre took hold of the pen and twisted the paper to face him, quickly scanning what was written before signing with his true name and adding his address. Handing the pen and document back to Bertie, he took a long look at Kitty. 'You must be a special lady if you don't mind me saying so. Not many people get close to Bertie and no one has ever stolen his heart enough for him to sign away anything he owns, let alone his precious town house.'

Kitty blushed and looked down at her hands.

'She most certainly is,' Bertie endorsed as he took hold of the document and pushed it back into the envelope with the rest of the papers, which neither Kitty nor Pierre had bothered to read. As Bertie fiddled with the flap, Pierre reached across the table and picked up the cognac decanter. 'A small celebration is in order,' he insisted, recharging all three glasses.

'Cheers to you Kitty, the first lady to turn Bertie into a gentleman,' he grinned. Raising his glass he again reached over the table, this time to chink his brandy balloon against Kitty's and Bertie's.

Smiling at his friend's teasing comment and murmuring, 'Here's to you my darling,' Bertie toasted his wife. It had been a long day and he was not so much tired as exhausted, but he was happy; very happy.

Chapter Twenty-Seven

Flo Watson stood in the middle of her cosy lounge. She had spent much of yesterday spring cleaning her basement flat and now, having walked through the bedroom, checked the bathroom and then the tiny kitchen, making sure it was all spotless and sparkling, she had ended up in the lounge. It was the last room to check to see that everything was as she wanted it to be.

Glancing at the two green Moquette fireside chairs in front of the gas fire, her gaze roamed to the black and white television set perched on top of a four-drawer dark oak cabinet in the corner of the room. She shook her head thinking about what Mr Costain had told her the other day. It seemed he had ordered a colour television for upstairs, which should be delivered in time for Christmas. Another surprise for Kitty.

'Colour television indeed, whatever next?' she muttered under her breath. It was clear to her the man had more money than sense. Then she chuckled. 'If he had a penny he would still have too much brass.' No matter how kind and polite he was to her and even though her feelings towards him had mellowed a little, she still could not bring herself to like the man.

Watching the sun filter through the top corner of the window, creating coloured prisms on the ceiling as the rays reflected off the small crystal light fitting, Flo satisfied herself that there was not a speck of dust on the glass pendants. It had taken her hours to clean the thing, but seeing the glass reflecting the morning sun in all its glory, she knew it had been worth the extra effort.

Flat 6B had been her home for the last nine months and as relieved as she was to be leaving, sadness still swept over her. Plopping down on the arm of one of the fireside chairs, Flo sniffed. She didn't want to cry, but a lump rose in her throat and tears pricked at the back of her eyes. 'Come on Flo, take a deep breath and pull yourself together,' she scolded, after all wasn't this what she had wanted since the day she arrived? Retrieving the hanky tucked in her sleeve, she blew her nose, reminding herself how much she looked forward to seeing Primrose Cottage again. But the picture in her mind's eye did nothing to stop the tears slipping down her wrinkled face. She needed to get away from London. The fresh air and being close to her sister would bring back the old sparkle and of course she was doing the right thing. Kitty was fine and happy and all wrapped up with her little shop or out gallivanting with her husband. She didn't need her old housekeeper, and no matter how much she insisted she wanted Flo to stay, her words had sounded hollow to Flo's ears. Even himself had seemed disappointed to hear she was heading back to the sticks, but Flo was not taken in by that. If he wanted to, Bertie Costain could charm the birds out of the trees, but she was no bird, she thought with a grim smile.

The weeks had slipped by since July, when she had enquired about Primrose Cottage and been told it was not available for the foreseeable future. Her disappointment had been such that she had confided in Kitty one sunny evening, when they had eventually sat out on the terrace for a chat over a glass or two of sherry. It was no doubt down to the second glass – any alcohol had the habit of loosening her tongue – that for once Flo had not held back her feelings but had confessed how unhappy she was living in the city.

A couple of weeks after she had bared her soul, she had received a call from the agent asking if she was still interested in taking Primrose Cottage. It transpired that the previous tenant had unexpectedly moved on. Flo had wondered why, but of course she had said yes straight away. Like everything these days, nothing was quite as straightforward as it should be. For a start, Kitty had wanted to purchase the cottage for her outright. 'What on earth would I do with a house of my own at my age?' Flo had said. Kitty being Kitty had gone on to explain her motives in an effort to persuade her, but Flo did not want Kitty's money, nor did she want the responsibility of ownership. Thankfully, Kitty had accepted this eventually and both of them had shed tears. Kitty had never been one for being overly demonstrative, even with her children, yet Flo had never had so many hugs as she'd had in the last few weeks as her departure from Wentworth Place drew nearer. All of this had added to her discomfort at leaving. Bitter sweet was all she could think, like taking a boiled sweet and finding it was an acid drop. She had always known the hardest part would be actually leaving, closing the door for the last time. Of course, once she was on her way she would be fine. She would settle in her little cottage in the knowledge that Kitty was happy in her new life and she could get on with hers.

Now, standing in the sitting room her boxes and battered old suitcase in the hall, Flo felt a sense of peace that the moment of departure had arrived.

'Are you ready Mrs W?' Bertie called, poking his head round the door. 'All set then?' He looked down at all her worldly goods contained in the few meagre boxes that needed to be taken to Primrose Cottage.

'As I'll ever be,' Flo said, taking in her erstwhile employer's immaculate appearance in his dark blue pin-stripe suit. She noted he had on the pale blue shirt she had starched the collar and ironed yesterday: *Rael Brook*, that one. She didn't think he owned a shirt that did not have a designer label in it; his suits were Saville Row and his shoes handmade. Where he got his wealth from she had no idea. She had suspicions, of course, but Flo decided she didn't want to travel down the road of speculation any more, she had done that enough these last few months and where had it got her? Nowhere! Though it did seem bricks and mortar were in the same league as gold: expensive and very profitable!

She eyed him from top to toe and even though she saw him most days of the week, thought he looked thinner. He might be smiling, but there was no sparkle in his eyes and his face was drawn. Even his expensive clothes appeared a little on the loose side. One thing she did know, it had nothing to do with not eating. He had a good appetite; she had seen him eat enough of her dinners to prove that. Whatever it was, she hoped he was not sickening for something, she did not care too much about him, but for Kitty's sake she would not wish him a day's harm. Well, not as long as he looked after Kitty properly, which he seemed to be doing.

'Well, I'm glad I caught you before Kitty whisks you out of London and back to the countryside,' Bertie said, cutting into her thoughts. 'I know I am not your favourite person, Mrs W, but speaking for myself, I will miss you bustling around keeping our home in order.' He looked down and focused on what he held in his hands. 'I've not been one for words, but I would like to thank you for all you have done. You've made Wentworth Place a real home and you've helped Kitty settle in, and for that I am grateful.' He raised his eyes to hers and smiled, 'I want you to have these.' He handed her an envelope and a small box, gift-wrapped and tied with a blue satin bow. 'The envelope is from both of us, but the box is from me in appreciation of everything you have done for me and Kitty.' He stepped forward.

Flo gingerly took the gifts from his outstretched hands. 'You shouldn't have, there was no need,' she said.

'Nonsense, it's the least we could do. Anyway, I know you and Kitty will keep in touch with each other, you must let us know how you are getting on,' he said, his fingers plucking nervously at his jacket buttons as if he did not know quite what to do with his hands. As he spoke Flo did not miss the tick pulsing in his left temple and wondered how many times she had seen that of late. It was funny how someone so wealthy and self-contained could be such a bag of nerves underneath. Maybe London had got to him too, she thought, as he stepped away from her.

'Thank you again Mrs W, and be happy. Have a safe journey back to Epsom.' He hovered awkwardly in the doorway for a few seconds and Flo feared he was about to kiss her, but to her relief he turned on his heels, picked up two boxes and slotted her suitcase under one arm before disappearing up the stairs, his footsteps resounding through the flat. She wondered what he was thinking about because there was no doubt Bertie Costain's mind was elsewhere. Oddly enough, she had never heard him utter so many words to her and such kind ones at that. Again she felt the prickle of tears and the unwelcome lump creep into her throat. Not wanting to give in to her emotions, she swallowed hard and feeling as if her legs no longer wanted to hold her up, she dropped into the chair next to where she stood and stared down at the beautifully wrapped box and its label, which was simply addressed, *Mrs W*. Her head should be filled with a thousand thoughts, but for now she was numb. She was still gazing at the unopened gifts when Kitty burst into the room.

'Flo, are you all right? I've got the van outside. What is it? What's wrong?' she cried, hunkering down beside Flo's chair.

Peering down at her through teary eyes, Flo held up the gifts. 'These,' she said softly. 'Your Bertie just handed these to me. Funny, in all the months I've been here, I've never heard him have so much to say. He even thanked me for making the house a home,' she sniffed loudly. 'Talk about making you feel guilty about leaving. And I do, you know, feel guilty. I've told you all my reasons for going and I know you said I'm a silly old goose for feeling that way, but I can't help thinking I'm selfish to be leaving you in the lurch.'

Fingering the blue bow Flo wondered what Bertie had bought her. For a moment she felt her heart miss a beat. 'What's he got me, Kitty?' Raising her eyebrows she summoned a weak smile, 'And what's in the envelope? Do I need to be worried or even embarrassed?'

Kitty chuckled, but Flo did not miss the glint in her eyes. 'You will only know if you open them and see what's inside,' she said, moving to sit on the chair next to Flo's and leaning her elbow on the arm. 'Well?'

'Well what?'

'Are you going to open them or save them until you get to Primrose Cottage?'

Sighing heavily and once again pushing down a lump that was determined to have a go at choking her, Flo fiddled with the envelope, pulled at the flap and slid out a sheet of heavy notepaper. She recognised Kitty's neat, flowing hand, the letters slanting to the left. Holding the letter in trembling fingers she gasped. The tight lump she had so far managed to keep under control broke free and she choked back a sob. 'Heaven's, what are you thinking! I can't accept this,' she cried, waving the letter like a flag.

Kitty reached over, placed her hand on Flo's arm and squeezed it gently, 'Yes you can. It was Bertie's idea after you wouldn't let me buy the cottage. At least for the next five years you don't need to worry about your rent, it's paid for. Call it a bonus for all your hard work, and when all is said and done, it's no more than you deserve. You've been looking after me and mine for forty years give or take.'

'But…' Flo tried to speak, tears streaming down her face. *'Why does nothing seem as it is?'* she asked herself.

Getting up to perch on Flo's chair arm, Kitty wrapped her arms around her. 'Hush, there are no buts,' she said, her voice strained. 'And if you don't stop crying you'll set me off too and where will that leave us? I have to drive, remember,' Kitty added, wiping the back of her hand over her eyes.

Slowly shaking her head from side to side, Flo dabbed at her eyes with her now damp handkerchief. Nothing in her wildest imagination would have had her thinking Mr Costain and Kitty would give her such a generous gift. If she had won the pools she would not be any better off. Their generosity made her head ache. 'I'm sorry Kitty. I don't know what to say. You know that at first I was worried about your new husband, but I've seen of late how much he loves you. Like you kept telling me, only I couldn't see it, he *is* a good man,' she sniffed, gripping the letter in her left hand. 'I was so afraid he was a gold digger it clouded my opinion. I should have realised he was a wealthy man and didn't need your money. I've turned into a silly old woman these days and I'm sorry for allowing my anxiety to make things awkward for you. I should have known better.'

'I knew what you were thinking,' Kitty stroked her hand over Flo's face wiping away her tears, 'and you have no idea how it felt knowing it was only because you were looking out for me. Even at my age, it's reassuring. But you must put your fears to rest. I don't believe Bertie is a saint, but he's shown me nothing but kindness and love.' As if wanting to lift the mood, she suddenly grinned. 'Tell you what though, Flo, I can certainly recommend having a younger man in your life,' she winked.

'I'll stick to having a cat in my bed when I get settled, if you don't mind,' Flo said tartly, arching her eyebrow, but she spoke with affection and although she was not one for risqué comments as a rule, it did them both good to laugh. Actually, now she thought about it, she probably would re-home an unwanted pet and she was fond of cats.

'Come on then, let's get you back to fresh air and birdsong,' Kitty said, pushing herself up from the chair and walking to the door, 'sitting here will only make us maudlin.'

Flo struggled to her feet and followed, but at the door she stopped to look over her shoulder. Clutching the little box unopened in her hand, she nodded, smiled and whispered, 'Goodbye little flat. I'm going home.'

Chapter Twenty-Eight

Four months had passed since Flo Watson had left Wentworth Place. Kitty missed her more than she could have imagined, the house was not the same without her bustling around and sharing a glass of sherry and a chat. The only consolation was the knowledge that her old housekeeper was settled and happy in her cottage. Since that tearful day when Kitty had driven Flo to Epsom and carried her belongings into Primrose Cottage, she had visited her several times. On every visit she had seen a change in her old friend: Flo seemed always to be smiling and colour had returned to her cheeks.

From time to time she asked after Bertie, but Kitty knew it was simply Flo's way of checking all was well at Wentworth Place and ensuring Bertie was looking after her properly. Kitty was always able to reassure her, regaling the way he continued to spoil and surprise, the latest had been the appearance of a colour television for Christmas. 'Always full of surprises that man of yours,' Flo Watson had said light-heartedly. 'I mean, look at the expensive watch he bought me, Kitty. It's very nice, but it frightens me to death to wear it just in case I lose it.' It amused Kitty to see the watch, still resting in its opened box, taking pride of place on the mantelpiece, the blue ribbon rolled up neatly beside it.

Flo was right, Bertie never ceased to amaze Kitty with his surprises. Nearly a year after marrying him, she loved him more than ever. This thought brought a warm feeling at how life had a way of giving you a second chance. If there was a dark cloud in her perfect blue sky, it was that Bertie worked too hard. As B.C. Builders won more and more building projects he regularly arrived home late and drained, complaining the building industry was out of control and he was drowning in a sea of endless paperwork. Increasingly concerned about him, Kitty had suggested that she ask Julie to run *Rosebuds* without her for a while so she could to help him in the office. She took a dim view of Cynthia, who seemed to be letting him down all the time. As well as that, it appeared from the various disparaging remarks Bertie let slip about Howard Silvershoes that their working relationship was under a strain too. Kitty hadn't found out why that should be and Bertie refused to discuss it with her, but whatever it was, it put yet more pressure on her husband.

Kitty had been disappointed that Bertie apparently did not want her help. When she had suggested it, he had flung his arms around her and scooped her up into a bear hug. Laughing, he had said, 'My darling Kittycat, what will you think of next?' I'll tell you what; if you're bored with Rosebuds I'll buy you another shop instead, a bigger one in a more up-market area.' Her protests that she could never be bored with Rosebuds and he was completely missing the point had fallen on deaf ears. He had carted her off to bed and that night they had made love several times, both falling asleep sated and exhausted. But that was nearly a month ago and since then Bertie had slipped back into putting in long hours at work so she scarcely saw him, and when she did, he seemed more and more distracted.

Driving Zippy to work that damp morning, Kitty parked the Mini outside Rosebuds and delving in her handbag for the door key hurried across the pavement to get out of the drizzle. Preoccupied with concerns about Bertie she slotted the key into the lock. Maybe she should again approach the idea of helping out in BCB's office. It wasn't as if the shop was particularly busy just now; Julie would be able to manage without her. Kitty was pushing the door open when she became aware that someone had come up behind her holding an open umbrella.

'Mrs Costain?' a deep voiced enquired.

Her thoughts dissolving, Kitty swung round and came face to face with a tall, heavily built gentleman of mature years. His dark hair had been combed back to reveal a large forehead and pallid skin. A five o'clock shadow indicated he had not shaved that morning, which made him look scruffy, yet he was well turned out: the black overcoat he wore screamed hand-tailored. Two top buttons were unfastened revealing a dark grey tie against an impeccable white shirt. Under his left arm he clutched a dark brown document wallet. She guessed he was around fifty; his sombre, funereal appearance gave the impression that he carried the weight of the world on his broad shoulders.

Staring at him, Kitty wondered if he was the new funeral director from Rivet's whose premises were down the road. She had heard on the grapevine they were taking on a new partner. Maybe he needed some flowers for the funeral parlour. No problem; she always kept Arum lilies in stock. Whatever his business, there was strain in his pale face and uncertainty in the pair of ebony eyes that stared back at her from beneath the umbrella. A thin line of perspiration on his top lip did not escape her scrutiny. Tilting her head, Kitty looked up at the cloudy grey sky. The fine drizzle wet her face and a cool breeze brushing against her cheeks made her shiver. Why, on such a dismal, chilly day, would a man be perspiring, she wondered.

'Yes, I'm Mrs Costain,' she said, the hint of a smile curving her lips. 'If it is flowers you are looking for, I'm about to open the shop.' Crossing the threshold and entering Rosebuds she looked over her shoulder and called out, 'It is rather unpleasant out so please step inside. I'll go and put the lights on to make the place feel brighter,' she added, flicking the door sign from "Closed" to "Open".

Without responding the pale-faced man shook the excess rain drops from his brolly before deftly furling and securing it. Gripping it tightly he followed Kitty into the shop. Then stepping back as if he had forgotten something, he reached out an arm and pushed the door closed, the bell above tinkling loudly. Still sneezing, Kitty watched him move further into the shop, his nose wrinkling at the pungent perfumes that permeated the air. He took several steps across the green linoleum floor, stopped in front of a bucket of flowers and bending down fingered one of the blooms.

Wiping her nose, Kitty shrugged out of her coat. She did not get many gentlemen in the shop so it was nice to see a man interested in buying flowers. Usually it was red roses for someone special, but this man seemed more interested in the dahlias. Leaving him to browse, she pulled open the cloakroom door, hung up her coat and taking her poppy print apron from the hook, put it on. Automatically she ran her hands down the apron's front as if to iron out the red flowers printed in the material. Satisfied, she closed the back room door and turned to her customer.

'Now sir, what can I do for you?' At the sound of her voice he started, as if he had forgotten she was there. He had propped his umbrella against a large terracotta jardinière filled with bright yellow chrysanthemums. For a moment he regarded her without speaking, his dark eyes appearing to consider her as though checking her out, much as he had the dahlias. Kitty felt suddenly uncomfortable, a fleeting rush of apprehension coursing through her body.

Eventually he spoke, his voice sounded flat with no discernible emotion. 'Mrs Costain, I'm not here to purchase flowers, I am here on another business...' His eyes watering, he dragged from his coat pocket a large white handkerchief and sneezed into it loudly.

'Bless you,' Kitty said automatically. 'They make me sneeze too,' she added, feeling sorry for him, even more so if he was, as she suspected, the new funeral director. Normally she could smell the balming fluid a mile off; it lingered around undertakers like a personal cloud. She opened her mouth to speak and introduce herself properly, but before a word could pass her lips he raised his hand, still clutching the handkerchief, and stopped her.

'Mrs Costain, my visit to your shop is not of the most pleasant nature. The business I need to discuss with you is due to the lack of contact from your husband, who appears to be a very elusive man if I might say so.' His dark gaze never left her as he spoke.

So he wasn't the new Funeral Director after all, she thought, ignoring the uneasiness that uncurled in the pit of her stomach. 'Why ever do you imagine my husband might be here?' she asked, clasping her hands together and giving a soft peal of laughter. 'My goodness, you haven't tried hard enough, I said goodbye to him this morning as he left for his office and I'll be dining with him this evening; that hardly makes him elusive! If you are not the new Funeral Director from Rivets and you are not here to buy flowers, what exactly is your business?'

A confused look flashed across his face, 'A funeral director? No, definitely not. My name is William Walker and generally speaking my business is with the living.'

Did she see a hint of amusement? Kitty wondered, but if she had, it had vanished. Before she could respond, he continued.

'As I said, we are trying to speak to Mr Costain and despite leaving messages with the receptionist at B. C. Builders, notwithstanding the letters sent to your home address, we have heard nothing from your husband. Oddly enough, I called at Wentworth Place this morning and your cleaner said you had both left for work.' Pursing his lips, he added, 'She gave me your shop address.'

'So if it is my husband you want to speak to, then why are you standing in my shop? Surely it would make sense for you to go to his office. Believe you me, Mr Walker, this is the last place you will find my husband. He's a builder not a florist.'

A weak smile turned up the corners of his mouth. 'Oh, Mrs Costain, I have visited your husband's company on several occasions and like today he is never there, hence why I am here.' Circling a large cheese plant as he was speaking, he said, 'Nice plants you have here.' His smile grew broader, 'What made you think I was a funeral director?' The attempt to soften his tone did nothing to make Mr Walker appear less formidable.

Kitty shook her head; she could hardly tell him he looked like one or alternatively, that he could easily pass for Count Dracula! Leaning against the work surface on which she prepared bouquets and flower arrangements, she tried to take in what this tall, sombre man was implying. Nothing he had said so far made any sense: her husband was no more elusive than Santa Clause at Christmas. Bertie had left the house that morning, a little earlier than usual. 'I'll be at the office all day,' he had said, downing a piece of toast. 'A mountain of paper work; contracts to sign and a never ending list of people to pay. And there was me thinking I was a brickie. These days it seems I'm nothing but a pen pusher.' Exaggerating a moan he had dropped a gentle kiss on her lips. Recalling the moment, Kitty smiled. She had told him she loved him. 'I know,' he had smiled, adding that he would bust a gut to get home in time to take her out for dinner. It had been a while since they'd had an evening out.

Frowning, Kitty now wondered if this Mr Walker had in fact been to Bertie's office at all. Maybe he'd got the wrong address. And what about the letters he purported to have sent: what reason would Bertie have for ignoring them? She could think of none.

'Might you have got the wrong office, Mr Walker? If you had been to B.C. Builders as you say, you would have spoken with my husband, though I think you can accept that like all successful businessmen, he's a busy man and in much demand. I would advise that you make an appointment.'

Stepping back from the cheese plant, Mr Walker fingered the dark green leaves of the sweetly scented lilies of the valley, which sat bunched in a shallow tray filled with water. 'In demand you say. Mm, I guess he would be.' His dry tone implied the opposite. Kitty did not miss the sarcasm. Tempted as she was to say more, she bit her tongue. Whoever this stranger was he was making her feel uneasy and if he did not explain soon why he was in her shop she would call the police.

'I can assure you, Mrs Costain, that I got the right office, but Mr Costain was not there, nor was his expensive E-type Jaguar anywhere to be seen.'

'He is a builder, Mr Walker with a very successful company. He could be called out to any number of situations. Again, I suggest you make an appointment and by doing so you will guarantee my husband's full attention. Now if there is nothing else, please forgive me but I must get on.' Her patience slipping, she tried to navigate round him to usher him to the door. Seeing no clear route through, she stepped back, positioned herself behind the counter and silently began counting to ten, her hand straying to the telephone, ready to dial 999.

Making no move to leave, Mr Walker rubbed his thumb and forefinger together in an attempt to remove the greasy residue left from the leaf. His amusement manifested in his voice as he spoke in a lighter tone. 'I can see my presence is inconvenient, Mrs Costain, but please would you let me explain?' Not waiting for a response, he pulled the document wallet from under his arm and tugged on the zip. After two jerks on the zipper, the wallet sprang open. 'I really do need to speak to you,' he said, pulling out several documents.

Her annoyance turning to curiosity, Kitty gazed at the wad of papers in Mr Walker's hand as he stepped towards the counter. 'May I?' he said, dropping the wallet and documents on the surface. Without making eye contact with Kitty, he fumbled through the papers then flicked one sheet to the top of the pile. Keeping his attention on the paper, he said, 'Mrs Costain, I am here because the rent on Primrose Cottage has not been paid and it is now three months in arrears.'

'Excuse me!' Kitty cried out, 'That cannot be true. What are you talking about?' Grabbing hold of the top sheet of paper, she scanned it, her face turning puce as she neared the bottom. Dropping the paper back on the surface top, Kitty rounded on him, 'Mr Walker, I assume that it is your real name? You strut into my shop causing me consternation by accusing my husband of not answering your calls or letters and expecting me to believe you have visited his work place but have failed to speak with him. And as if that were not enough, you have the gall to tell me a pack of lies about Primrose Cottage.'

Taking a deep breath to steady her voice and her anger, Kitty stabbed her index finger at the documents. 'For your information, my husband paid the rent for five years in advance. *Five years*, you understand. How *dare* you come in here and spout these false allegations!' Her face flushed with annoyance Kitty pushed her hands in her apron pocket and balling them into fists waited for an answer. None came; he simply gazed at her in silence as though she were some recalcitrant child having a tantrum. Exasperated, she continued, 'I have no idea what these or any other papers you might have filed away have to do with me or my husband. And furthermore I would like you to leave. Please go!'

Apparently unruffled, the man smoothed the palm of his hand over his slicked-back hair and said calmly, 'I am truly sorry if I have upset you, but I am here to clear up this business. I cannot leave until I have it sorted.' He raised his eyes to gaze into hers and added, 'I am sure you understand my position. I assure you these are not false allegations. The rent has not been paid no matter what you are telling me. Our books clearly show three months to be outstanding.' His voice was crisp as he enunciated each word. Bringing himself up to his full height, he handed Kitty the pile of paper. 'Just look more closely, Mrs Costain. As you can see, you and your husband's names are on the tenancy agreement. You both signed and had your signatures witnessed. Therefore it is your husband or you who need to resolve this issue. We have written to you both but neither you nor your husband have answered our letters and since I am unable to speak with Mr Costain, I must now deal with you.'

As he spoke, Kitty's stomach clenched with anxiety. What was going on here? Checking the document, to her upset she saw it was indeed the tenancy agreement she and Bertie had signed four months ago. Her mind racing, she thought through everything Mr Walker had said: letters sent, calls to Bertie, visits to his office, and yet, as she regurgitated these facts, nothing made any sense. 'There must be some mistake,' she said at last, her voice barely audible. 'The rent for Primrose Cottage was a joint gift from my husband and me to my retired housekeeper, Florence Watson, who lives there. We paid up front for the next five years.' She could see from the way Mr Walker looked at her that he did not believe her. Her mind did somersaults: why was this Count Dracula insisting it had not been paid?

Kitty cast her mind back to when they had dealt with this back in the summer; paying that substantial sum of rent was not something one easily forgot. She had initially approached Mr Foreman, the owner of Brightlands Lettings. Bertie had been tied up with meetings all day so she had gone on her own. Pointing out that it was highly unusual to pay so far in advance, Mr Foreman had stressed that aside from anything else, it was not in her best interest; the lease might well change in that time and he could not promise that over five years the rent would stay the same. A bi-annual review was more normal. Allowances would have to be made. But Kitty had insisted and Mr Foreman had eventually agreed to consider her proposition. A few days later he had telephoned to inform her he had come up with the ideal solution. The money would be placed in a special account and the rent would be taken out each month. Interest would accumulate on the balance. Should the rent increase, adjustments would be made at the time. It was a perfect plan and straightforward. If she or Mr Costain would like to call in with a cheque for the deposit, he would set it all in motion and then all that was left to do was for them to sign the agreement.

Satisfied that everything was in order, Kitty had handed Bertie not only fifty percent of the total amount, but a large sum to cover the deposit. He had taken the cheque from her and slipped it into his wallet explaining he would transfer the full amount to Brightlands Lettings direct from his bank account the following morning. 'It would be safer as a bank transfer than handing over two separate cheques and as I have to go to the bank anyway, it makes sense I pay the full amount,' he had said.

The following day she had asked him if the transfer had gone through. Without hesitation, Bertie had assured her the money was winging its way to Brightlands Lettings. To reassure her all was in order he had fished into his wallet for the bank receipt, but without looking at it, she had told him to place it in the safe with other important items. Knowing all of this, Kitty could not now understand why Mr Walker was insisting the rent was not paid, and who the hell was he anyway? Had he come from Brightlands? But why would he? It occurred to her that she should have asked to see some identification. Concern replaced her belligerence; she needed to think, but not before ensuring this man knew he was making a terrible mistake.

'The thing is, Mr Walker, I converse with Mrs Watson on a regular basis, sometimes on a daily basis and there has never been a hint regarding anything untoward from Brightlands Lettings. On the contrary, she loves the cottage and feels very much at home there. I can assure you that my husband and I jointly paid the rent up until July, 1972 and you are making a mistake – a *slanderous* mistake! I think you should go back to where you came from and sort it out. I meanwhile, will be getting in touch with my solicitor.' Handing the documents back to him Kitty burned with anger, unable to believe that their integrity was being questioned.

'So far Mrs Watson has not been involved,' he said calmly, ignoring her threat. The tenancy agreement is in yours and Mr Costain's name. Our first enquires, as I explained, were sent to you and your husband, but as we have not received any response I now must deal with you. I know I am repeating myself, but I need to proceed.'

It was clear to Kitty that nothing she had said had this creepy man budging from his quest to be in her shop and sort out what he mistakenly believed to be rent arrears. The whole situation was ludicrous and if she hadn't been so wound up she would have laughed.

William Walker checked his watch as if time was of the essence then fished in his jacket pocket. Alarmed, Kitty wondered what he was going to produce this time. From the corner of her eye she spotted the scissors, she could just about reach them if necessary. She began to edge that way then snorted. *What was she thinking!* Even so, she breathed out with relief as he produced nothing more ominous than a small blue notebook. He shot her a look of amusement as he opened the book and flicked through the pages.

'Mr Walker,' Kitty said, trying to speak calmly, 'before anything further is said, I need to talk to your office. The situation I find myself in is untenable. Therefore it is important I speak to Mr Foreman. He will clarify the situation.' Casting her gaze to the signed paper, she read and memorized the office number.

'Please do. You will learn nothing new, but if it makes you feel happier, I am a patient man.' He folded his arms, hugging the notebook.

Ignoring his words, Kitty scurried to the door and with a flick of her wrist twisted the sign to "Closed". Feeling she was in a nightmare, she turned and hurried to the telephone extension on a shelf at the back of the shop. With trembling fingers, she dialled the number to Brightlands Lettings. Hearing the connection tone, she wondered if she should have called Bertie first, then argued that if he had been in his office, Mr Walker would hardly have beaten a path to her shop. That was assuming the man was telling the truth….

'Good morning, Brightlands Lettings, can I help you,' a young voice trilled down the line.

'Yes you can, my name is Kitty Costain and I would like to speak to Mr Foreman please. It is a matter of some urgency,' she said abrasively.

'I'll connect you straight away, Mrs Costain,' the cheerful voice replied. Two clicks sounded before Kitty heard the pleasant voice of Mr Foreman.

'Hello Mrs Costain, I am delighted that you have contacted the office. I confess to being concerned about the silence, which has meant we have had to take unusual action. An unfortunate business.'

Kitty froze at Mr Foreman's words.

'Mrs Costain…?'

'I'm here Mr Foreman are you suggesting what I think you are?'

'I'm not suggesting anything, though I am hoping your call is to clear this matter up.'

Trying to keep her voice steady because she did not want to believe she was being told Mrs Watson's rent had not been paid, Kitty said in a firm voice. 'As far as I can see there is no matter to clear up.' She heard, what she thought was a sniff down the line.

'Indeed there is, Mrs Costain.'

This time she remained silent and listened. As Mr Foreman continued speaking, the colour drained from Kitty's face. Feeling her legs weaken, she sank down on the tall stool next to where she stood. When he stopped speaking she responded unsteadily, 'Thank you Mr Foreman, indeed, as you say, perfect timing.' Ending the call, she dialled Bertie's office. She needed to know if he was there. Waiting for the call to connect, she was aware Mr Walker had paid full attention to her conversation with his office. Standing with his hands folded across his broad chest, clutching the blue book as if it were a matter of life and death, he kept his gaze fixed on Kitty.

Hearing a voice on the other end of the phone, she spoke anxiously, 'Hello Cynthia, please put me through to my husband.'

'I'm sorry Mrs Costain, but he's not here. I've not seen him this morning. He's always got a list of meetings to go to these days, so I can't say when he'll be back.'

'I see, thank you.'

Kitty dropped the phone back onto its cradle. Bertie had told her he would be in the office all day, so why would Cynthia say he wasn't there. Raising her hand to her forehead, she rubbed her temples. Even after speaking to Mr Foreman she was convinced Brightlands Lettings had made a terrible blunder. It had to be a clerical error. The money had been paid. What they did not appreciate was that she could easily prove the mistake was theirs. All she had to do was produce the transfer receipt from the bank, which was in the safe in Wentworth Place.

Peering at Mr Walker from the corner of her eye, she didn't think he would wait for this piece of evidence, especially since it would take some time. She would need to plough through piles of paper that always seemed to materialize whenever the safety box was opened. On top of this, she needed a key, Bertie always kept the safe key on his key ring. For now she would have to come up with a temporary solution, the last thing she wanted was for Mrs Watson to be troubled. The sudden awful image of her dear old friend being evicted from her home because of some ridiculous clerical error, made Kitty shiver.

With her mind made up to tackle the problem and later provide the evidence of payment, she turned her focus back to Mr Walker. He had not moved from the spot. It seemed he had rooted himself there, like one of her potted house plants. Considering what Mr Foreman had told her, she needed to be careful how she handled what she did now. If only she could get hold of Bertie, she could prove to this man loitering menacingly in her shop that he was wasting his time.

Accepting she had to do something to get rid of him, Kitty steeled herself and asked. 'What is it exactly that you want from me?'

As if Kitty's words had flicked a switch, Mr Walker flashed a pleasant smile revealing a set of tombstone teeth, unfolded his arms and stepped towards her. In a voice that hinted at victory, he spoke. 'Thank you, Mrs Costain. Since I am unable to speak to Mr Costain, I need your co-operation. As I mentioned, there are three months arrears to be met and if the present occupant... a Mrs Watson, you said?'

Tight-lipped, Kitty nodded.

'Yes, well If she is to remain in Primrose Cottage we need to establish who will be paying the rent in future,' he finished, looking at her expectantly.

It was clear to Kitty that the man wanted money before he would leave. Thankfully she had her cheque book with her. Biting her lip, she checked her watch. Julie would be here any minute. It was embarrassing enough having someone coming into her shop to discuss such a delicate matter. The last thing she wanted was for her young assistant to witness this debacle.

'Mr Walker, here is not the most comfortable of places to discuss this confidential matter any further. I would prefer we go elsewhere before my assistant arrives. Would you be prepared to accompany me to the tea shop just down the road?'

'That's fine by me, Mrs Costain, I would be obliged.'

Pulling off her apron, Kitty scribbled a note to Julie explaining she had been called away and would be back later. As she turned to fetch her coat, she heard the rustle of papers as he gathered them up and stuffed them back in his wallet. The rasp of the zip being pulled told her Mr Walker was ready to leave.

Scurrying out of Rosebuds and locking the door behind them, Kitty led the way to Betty's tea rooms round the corner. It was early yet and there were few customers. Selecting an isolated corner table, Kitty ordered a pot of tea for two and sat opposite Mr Walker, resting her elbows on the blue gingham table cloth. 'So what exactly do you want from me?'

'Three months arrears of rent, an additional month in advance and arrangements made for future payments, preferably by standing order,' he said succinctly.

'I see,' Kitty said, lowering her gaze to her hands. She was still convinced a mistake had been made, but until she had spoken with Bertie and found the proof of the bank transfer, she needed to sort out a temporary solution: one that would get rid of this wretched man.

As one of Betty's waitresses, having placed a laden tray on the table, scuttled back to the counter, Kitty poured two cups of steaming tea and pushed one towards her nemesis. Reaching for her handbag she pulled out her cheque book and fountain pen. 'I take it a cheque is acceptable?' she asked, dropping the dark blue book onto the table.

'As long as it's not made of rubber,' he answered glibly, helping himself to four sugar cubes and stirring his tea vigorously.

Ignoring his attempt at humour, Kitty shot him a look of contempt. ''I'll make it out to Brightlands Lettings. The cheque will be for the arrears and a further two month's rent. I expect to receive a full refund along with an apology when it is proved your company has made a gross mistake. In my view it is tantamount to slander.'

Leaning forward, amused, Mr Walker raised an eyebrow, 'There is no mistake Mrs Costain, I can assure you. I would not be here were that the case.'

Tempted as she was to point her pen at the man and poke it in his eye, she gripped it tightly to restrain herself from committing assault. He wasn't worth it. 'Let us agree to disagree for now,' Kitty said, forcibly removing her gaze from his smug face.

Unscrewing her fountain pen, she opened the book to a new cheque and mentally calculating five months' rent, wrote out the cheque. Once signed and dated, she handed it over and to her disgust saw a triumphant glint in Mr Walker's cold, dark eyes as he reached out and removed the cheque from her outstretched hand, waggling it back and forth to dry.

'Thank you Mrs Costain, I am sorry it had to come to this,' he said, his tone now agreeable as he inspected what had been handed to him.

'Are you? I somehow doubt it. It is your job after all. However, for now I want no trouble for Mrs Watson. As far as a standing order is concerned, that will, of course, not be necessary, as I shall prove in due course. You might inform Mr Foreman that I will be speaking to my solicitor about compensation for the trouble and distress Brightlands' error has caused me.'

He nodded, 'As you wish, Mrs Costain. I'm simply the debt collector. It is my job to make sure people honour what they agree to pay, especially when they are enjoying the goods. I'm sure you wouldn't want people taking your flowers without paying, now would you?'

Not waiting for a response Mr Walker folded the cheque in half and placed it in the inside pocket of his jacket then pushed back his chair, the legs sliding on the linoleum floor. 'Thank you Mrs Costain,' he said, standing up. 'I wish all the calls I have to make were as easy as this one, but if you don't mind, I'll leave the tea. You'd be surprised how many cups I have to get through in a day.'

With a wry smile he stood and reached out his hand to her. Remaining seated, Kitty reluctantly took it, knowing it would be churlish not to.

'Good day to you,' he said. Then releasing her hand he stepped round the table and marched out of Betty's tearooms without a backward glance, his umbrella swinging at his side.

Unsure what could have happened that had a debt collector looking for her, Kitty watched as the tall, heavy-set man left the stuffy café, no doubt off to his next victim. She clicked her tongue. An error had been made, a gross error, and as soon as she returned home she would find that bank receipt and stop the cheque she had just made out. Looking down at the table where her tea sat going cold, she bent down and picked up her bag. By the time she had finished with Brightlands Lettings, Mr Foreman and his henchman would wish they had never heard of the Costains. Marcus Greengrass would see to that! Pulling out her purse, she drew out a ten-shilling note to pay and called over a waitress, aware her silent threats did nothing to ease her troubled and increasingly suspicious mind. An insidious little phrase insisted on going round in her head, no matter how much she attempted to stamp on it: *'But what if...?'*

Chapter Twenty-Nine

Slumped in the cream leather chair in the drawing room of his home, Bertie swigged on the generous measure of whisky he held in a cut glass tumbler. He had already downed a large one, but he needed more.

He raked his hand through his hair. No matter which way he turned these days, it seemed everything he touched turned sour. One minute he was on a high and filling his pockets with his winnings and then he was plummeting down, falling at an alarming speed until he hit the bottom. The bottom he had hit this time was a pit of pythons, hissing and spitting, wrapping their muscular skin around him as if to squeeze every drop of blood from his body

Of late the highs had not only been less enjoyable, but further apart. He could trace the moment his fortune changed. It had all begun to spiral out of control after the loss of the Town Hall contract. Since that black day his life had been nothing short of a roller coaster. One moment he was breaking out in a confident smile, the next he was breaking out in a sweat. He gripped on tight as he rode the white knuckle ride of gambling. It had started as a pleasurable way to pass the time; then it had become a habit. Now, however, Bertie knew it had turned into an addiction. He needed it like his lungs needed air. And always there was the anticipation that *this time* luck would come to sit on his shoulder and he would be able to turn things around. And sometimes it did, but more often it did not. It was a constant tease and far from turning things around, he was spinning deeper and deeper into the mire.

Savouring the malt whisky on his tongue, he drew a du Maurier cigarette from its square red pack, put it to his lips and lit it, inhaling deeply and tilting his head to blow a cloud of smoke towards the ceiling. Whisky and smoke;

the mingled taste of them was the taste of gambling. A derisive snort escaped the thin line of his lips, yet the remembered surge of adrenalin when the wheel spun in his favour almost took his breath away. It was a sensation that tingled in his fingers and flooded his body, making him believe he was invincible. At those moments there was *nothing* he could not achieve. It was electrifying and nothing he had ever experienced could touch that feeling. He wanted it more and more and wanted to keep it for as long as possible. And the only way to do that was to return again and again to the club and play the game of chance. Except the highs never lasted and these days were replaced with a desperate state of foreboding when the game went against him as so often it did.

Flicking away a speck of cigarette ash from his immaculately pressed trousers, he sank into a deep gloom, still stinging from the trouncing at Raffles earlier. Of course it was not the end of the world, though Smith and his honcho had indicated it was. More than anything Bertie had wanted to show how successful he was and at the same time teach them a lesson, especially after the Town Hall fiasco. He had wanted to win a haul of money so vast it would wipe the smug smiles from their faces. It had not worked out like that so far. Instead, Smith had once again invited him into the office – invited! He scoffed at their use of that word. It had been delivered with a menacing glare and Bertie, sandwiched between the two burly men, had been frogmarched into the ostentatious office. Once there, his feet sinking into the luxurious carpet, he had not been asked to sit on one of the sumptuous leather chairs but left standing in the middle of the room like an errant schoolboy.

Smith, speaking in a soft, amiable tone that belied his body language, had proceeded to spell out to Bertie what the disastrous couple of hours in the exclusive club had cost him. He remembered flinching as if Smith had punched him in the face: the amount of his losses made his eyes water; they read like a telephone number. Yet as high as they were, Bertie was confident it would be sorted in an instant. All he needed was more time at the tables and he would be back on his feet in the blink of an eye. Then the only people smarting would be Smith and Bryant. In less than one hour his fortune would change.

'Next time it will be different,' he had insisted.

'It always is,' Smith had said dryly. Bryant had chuckled and Bertie had found himself signing an IOU. 'No more gaming till it's paid, Costain,' Smith had said, pointing to the door.

Bertie recalled that he had been in a similar situation a few months earlier and it had all been sorted out, even if he had been robbed blind in the process. This time the losses were considerable and with no hope of going back to the tables and playing to win, he had to come up with a plan and fast. He needed a strategy that would keep Smith, along with everyone else, off his back long enough for him to return to winning. He knew that as soon as word was out about his latest performance at Raffles, the vultures would be circling above his head; the dogs snapping at his heels, demanding payments or worse, his blood!

Taking another slug of whisky he cried out, 'What had happened to patience and trust?' Of late it seemed to Bertie that everyone was demanding or threatening. His desk was littered with pieces of paper, all filled with scrawled, handwritten messages that Cynthia had scribbled down from phone calls or from visitors asking to see him or requesting payment. These 'requests' often came with intimidation or warnings of imminent legal proceedings. Bertie sighed in exasperation. There were enough scraps of paper to cover the office walls and a few rooms in the houses BCB's were supposed to be building. Thankfully, so far he had managed to avoid everyone, including that insistent bugger, Bill Walker. Not that the bloke had any chance of seeing the money he demanded. He would have to join the increasingly lengthy queue forming up outside the office. Christ, these days half the bloody country wanted to speak to Bertie Costain! Fortunately, that morning he had parked the Jag round the corner and hearing Cynthia repeat Walker's name, he had beat a hasty retreat via the rear exit.

Running his hands again through his tousled hair Bertie's mind raced. Of course he would try and settle with everyone, just as soon as he could get his luck back, but not today. And unless a miracle happened, it wouldn't be tomorrow either.

As the list of debts scrolled through his head Bertie tried to focus on the positive and, importantly, what he had achieved. It was the only way to keep sane. If he was a loser he wouldn't be here living in this splendour, he'd be a hod carrier humping bricks up scaffolding. He had been in the brown smelly stuff before – perhaps not quite this deep – but he had always pulled himself up and come out smelling of roses. There was no question about it he had the ability to succeed.

Sitting up, the blood pounding though his veins, Bertie took in the opulence of the drawing room. It was a million miles away from the parlour in 16, Union Terrace, the two-up-two-down artisan cottage where he was raised and where his parents still lived. Here in Wentworth Place the floors were parquet, a scattering of oriental rugs on dark polished wood, not linoleum and cheap carpets. Here were no lumpy fustian armchairs, no sagging settee, but Italian leather sofas and chairs made from the softest buttoned hide. Expensive, made-to-measure, drapes hung from tall Georgian windows, and half a dozen paintings by lesser known artists adorned the walls. It could have come straight out of the pages of *Homes and Gardens*, and it had all cost a bomb. Every extravagance of his home and lifestyle had, in the main, been paid for by the same means. And if he did not gather his wits together he was about to lose it all.

Comparing all this luxury to his childhood home reminded Bertie of his mother and his heart skipped a beat. If he lost everything she would be mortified. Nothing had given her more pleasure than bragging about how her

Bertie had made good. Even his old man had found the odd word to congratulate him. Throughout the years he had made sure they wanted for little. He had looked after them. He had even bought their house so they would never have to worry about rent. The opportunity to acquire the tiny terrace had arisen when the shameless, lazy, greedy landlord had found himself in trouble with the authorities. These days they cracked down on backstreet landlords – a legacy of the notorious Peter Rachman – and quite right too.

The landlord's downfall had been Bertie's windfall: he had ended up owning the house without any money changing hands. Back in those days his skills had been with his building tools, though even then he had never missed an opportunity to take risks. In exchange for the deeds of 16 Union Place he had agreed to renovate a handful of the dilapidated dwellings in the same terrace. It had been a gamble, but the cost of tidying up the houses was nothing compared to the real value of the deal. It had been a steal, even more so as no matter how ramshackle the terrace had become, the houses had steadily increased in value. Not that his parents had any intention of moving out. 'It's home son and hopefully you'll understand that one day. I can tell you now, the only way I'll be leaving 16 Union Terrace is feet first,' his father had said every time Bertie had suggested they move to a better neighbourhood and house.

Despite the material support he had given his parents, as a family they had never been close. 'Distant' was the way he would describe them, but this had not stopped him from making sure they lived relatively comfortably and now, as he tried to come to terms with his latest disaster, he breathed a sigh of relief that the deeds of Union Place were safe. Thankfully, he had insisted at the time that they be made out in his parents' joint names. So nobody could grab the property if things got nasty and there was every chance they would if he didn't find the money to pay for his latest losses very soon.

His head crowded with all these gloomy thoughts, Bertie had a sudden flash of inspiration that gave him a jolt. It was as if someone had flicked on a light bulb and lit up a dark room. He jumped to his feet, punched his fist in the air and cried out, 'Yes! Why the hell didn't I think of this earlier?'

Dropping back into the soft cream leather, he thought things through. It was as clear as the nose on his face that he needed to get the hell out of here for a few days, leave all the attitudes and threats and take some breathing space to calm down. He would return when he had the wherewithal to deal with all those bastards baying for his blood. A slow grin crept across his anxious face, bringing a malevolent glint to his blue eyes. Oh yes, he would give them all a heart attack thinking he'd done a runner. Then, just when they thought they'd never see him or their money again, like in all the best Hollywood films he would gallop into town on his silver stallion and show them Bertie Costain was not only a winner, but a gentleman who always paid his debts. True, he paid them a tad late these days, but as his headmaster had spouted out from the stage each day in Assembly, hands behind his back, a superior look on his ruddy face, "Whatever you want to do in life make sure you go for it and if you can't do it straight away, do it later. And remember boys, better late than never!" For the first time in his life, Bertie had to agree with the old codger's homily.

Satisfied he had the perfect plan, still smiling, he gripped his empty glass as if it were a life line and stood up. Right now he felt a weight had been lifted from his shoulders. He needed another drink to help think where he would go. With purposeful steps he strode over to the drinks cabinet, a walnut affair with a flip-top pull-down bar. Carelessly he tugged it open so that the top dropped down with a clatter revealing several bottles of spirits, along with two bottles of fizz.

Bertie's gaze roved over the array of bottles, but he did not see what each contained, his mind was too busy working on his escape plan. Automatically he reached for the whisky decanter. He was now more than convinced the only solution was to get away from London. Taking a deep breath he wondered why he hadn't thought of it earlier, it would have saved a lot of sweating. He would head for the North, the greater the distance he could put between himself and London the better. Leeds would be a good place to bury himself away for a few days and while there he would look up Mike Bedingfield. He may not have seen the scoundrel for years, but the man owed him. Years ago, not that Bertie could recall exactly how many, Bedingfield had lost at poker and was unable to pay. Flush at the time, Bertie had got him out of sticky situation, sorted out the debt and in return taken ownership of Bedingfield's Triumph Vitesse. Good as it looked, however, the car had turned out to be knackered. Bertie had sold it on and still smarted at how he had lost out on that little deal. So, he told himself, this was a convenient moment to call in the favour. He had heard on the grapevine that Bedingfield now owned a night club; he must have got lucky. It was likely a flea pit, a long way from the plushness of Raffles. Nonetheless, it sounded as if it had all the ingredients Bertie needed. It would be a distraction, give him space to think and a chance to stop panicking.

Adrenalin was pumping round Bertie's body, he could feel his heart beating faster than a cook's whisk whipping up an omelette. Placing his right hand across his chest, he felt the rapid thumping, 'Christ,' he spat. He needed to bring the situation under control and slow the old ticker down before he keeled over with a coronary. Realising then that dropping down dead would solve a few problems, Bertie guffawed. Be that as it may, right now he needed to concentrate on staying alive and a temporary disappearance could only help. Meeting his maker was not on the cards just yet, thought Bertie, seized with euphoria as he contemplated his imminent escape.

Aware that he was now some way beyond tipsy, he gazed down at his shaking hand clutching the decanter, his knuckles turning white as he gripped it more tightly. Bringing it level with his eyes he squinted then let out a loud groan. For a split second his euphoria evaporated; the decanter was almost empty. Shrugging his shoulders he tipped it up and poured the remains of the expensive malt into his glass. A few drops sloshed over the top and dribbled onto his hand. 'Waste not, want not,' he muttered with a smirk, bending to lick them off. With a shattering clunk Bertie dropped the stopper back into the decanter and raising his glass he toasted himself. He was not beaten yet. Now all he had to do was tell Kitty he had an urgent meeting he needed to attend tomorrow morning. As the glass touched his lips, Bertie lifted it away. On second thoughts he could leave immediately. It would save him having to tell any more lies.

Returning the glass to his lips he strolled with an alcohol-induced swagger over to the window that overlooked the quiet road and gated community garden. Peering through the net curtains he turned his gaze first to the left and then to the right, a sigh of relief shuddering through him as he took in the silent road. No one to be seen lurking behind the plane trees or pretending to read a newspaper while keeping an eye on his home. Wentworth Place was deserted. Even his shadow, the young man who always seemed to appear on every corner and follow him, was not there. *'Who the hell is he and why is he so interested in my movements,'* thought Bertie. Another debt-collector, he assumed, though he didn't look much like one. 'Sod them all,' he muttered with a shrug. Suddenly he burst out laughing. It was not a sound of mirth, more akin to the cry of a wounded animal.

'Good God, Costain,' he groaned, 'you are one paranoid bastard these days. Get a grip or else the only ones following you will be wearing white coats. And stop talking to yourself or they really *will* be carting you off to the loony bin!' But even has he scoffed at himself, Bertie was under no illusion. He knew he was at the end of his tether and on the brink of both mental and financial collapse.

The sight of Kitty's red Mini Cooper S pulling up at the kerb, its throaty engine filtering into the silence of the room, wound up Bertie's panic still further. 'Damn and blast!' he exploded. The opportunity to slip away before his wife arrived home had disappeared. Continuing to swear under his breath, he downed the last drops of his whisky and dropped the empty glass on the bar.

Chapter Thirty

'I'm home,' Kitty called, dropping her bags on the floor and throwing her car keys onto the telephone table. In an attempt to keep her mind off Mr Walker she had bought herself a couple of pairs of slacks from the boutique two doors down from Rosebuds. She hoped she would still like them when she wore them later in the week. Julie had insisted they were perfect for her figure. She cleared her throat as the fragrance of lavender polish permeated the air and her nostrils. Kitty sneezed and cursed silently. The new cleaner was a stickler for polishing, if it didn't move, it was polished and buffed to a lustre that would put a shoe shiner to shame. Kitty knew she should be happy that Mrs Dobbs had the house shining like a new pin, but right now she felt anything but happy. Rooting in her pocket she pulled out a handkerchief and wiped at her nose, wishing the woman would ease up on the furniture waxing.

Slipping out of her coat, Kitty listened for Bertie coming to greet her, but the only sound was the loud tick of the grandfather clock, the heartbeat of their home. Seeing the Jaguar parked outside had surprised her. Unusual for him to be home so early, but it pleased her because now she could sort out the debacle with Brightlands Lettings and Bertie could find the bank receipt instead of her having to wade through all the documents he kept in the safe. Strange he had not answered her, maybe he was sitting in the garden. Kitty shook her head, dismissing that idea; it was much too cold. Hooking her coat on the coat rack, she sighed with pleasure at being home. Ever since Mr Walker had visited Rosebuds that morning, it had been impossible to settle. His words and those of Mr Foreman had tormented her all day until all she could think of was getting home, talking to Bertie and sorting it out.

As soon as Julie had left, Kitty had closed the shop. Thankfully there were only two orders for delivery the following morning and there was no need to make them up today. As much as Mr Walker had reassured her that Flo Watson had not been contacted regarding the rent arrears, it had concerned her and she needed to be sure, but there had been no possibility of privacy until Julie had gone. The call to Flo had been brief and to her relief her old friend was in good spirits. 'Living like a piggy in poo,' she had chuckled down the phone. Then asked, 'So why are you calling me in the middle of the afternoon? No, don't bother answering. I'll take it Mr Surprise has not failed to come up with something to make your day.'

The hairs on the back of Kitty's neck had risen at Flo's uncanny perception. She should have known her old housekeeper would be suspicious about a call at this time of day. Of course she had laughed it off, insisting she had just fancied saying hello. After a brief chat about nothing in particular Kitty had said goodbye, promising to talk again at the weekend. There had been no mention of rent arrears or letters from Brightlands Lettings. Replacing the receiver, she had been satisfied Flo was none the wiser about the mix up with the agent.

Now, checking her appearance in the mirror above the telephone table, Kitty still bristled at the thought of Mr Walker, with his tombstone teeth and funereal features. All she could think of was proving it was all a gross mistake. Staring at her reflection she noticed how strained she looked. She forced a smile, but it did nothing to change the drawn face glaring back at her. 'Chin up Kitty,' she mumbled, 'you're home now and all will soon be sorted.'

From the corner of her eye she caught sight of Bertie's car keys next to hers on the telephone table reminding her he was home. Why had he not responded when she called out? She checked her watch. It was a little after three-thirty. For the last few weeks she had seen little of him;

most days he arrived home around midnight and then dashed out first thing in the morning. Cynthia had said he had a list of meetings to attend and had no idea when he would return to the office, so why was he here in the middle of the afternoon? Only then did Kitty recall that he had promised to take her out to dinner this evening. Maybe that was why. But then again, he had said that a few times lately and always cried off. She'd had no reason to believe today would be any different.

Unease settled on Kitty's shoulders as she crossed the hall and headed for the kitchen. She stopped in her tracks, some instinct making her turn and push open the door to the drawing room. Immediately she took in the slump of her husband's shoulders as he stood with his back to her, looking out of the window. Before she could open her mouth to speak, he spun round.

'Ah, Kitty, thank goodness you're home!' He came striding across the room towards her.

'I called out to you,' she said, taking a deep breath, all thoughts of Mr Walker and meetings pushed to the back of her mind as she observed Bertie's ruffled hair, the dark shadows under his eyes, his shirt clinging to his chest and damp patches under his arms. Moving to one of the radiators she placed her hand on the top and found it was barely warm. It was January and although the month had started cold today it was quite mild, certainly not hot enough to make anyone perspire unless they'd been out for a run, but Bertie never did that. The image of Mr Walker similarly sweating sprang into her mind.

'Bertie, is everything alright?' she asked, moving to his side and looking anxiously into his taut face. When he did not respond Kitty took hold of his hand and felt the clamminess of his skin. She could see he was far from his usual debonair self. Since she had seen him that morning he appeared to have aged ten years. Meetings, contracts and too much work was taking its toll on her husband.

'Darling you look shattered,' she said squeezing his hand. 'I thought you were spending the day in the office? I tried to call you, but Cynthia said you were out and had no idea when you would return.'

Pulling his hand away, Bertie shrugged his shoulders then dropped down onto one of the soft leather sofas and bowed his head.

'It seems to me you are doing too much, darling. Nothing is worth risking your health,' Kitty said, a feeling of helplessness washing over her. Perching on the arm of the sofa, she placed her hand on his shoulder. 'Bertie, please speak to me.'

Raising his head, a wry smile crossing his face, he looked up at her. 'I'm fine and there is no need for you to worry. It's been one of those days, all part of the business. I arrived in the office first thing to a pile of messages waiting for me to deal with before I had to hot foot it to a supplier. Thankfully our meeting ended earlier than expected and rather than go back to the office and face another mountain of paperwork, I decided to come home,' he said. He reached up and took hold of Kitty's hand, stroking it gently. 'Importantly, I wanted to get back home to see you before I have to leave.'

'Leave! Leave where? Surely not, you look shattered,' she cried. 'Besides, I thought we were going out to dinner.'

'Life does not stop because one looks weary,' he said calmly, getting to his feet. 'Sorry about the dinner, darling, but I only found out this morning and I haven't had a minute to call you. Cynthia never passed on yesterday's messages until I arrived in the office first thing.' He gave a disapproving sniff. 'Honestly, that girl is useless. Had I only the time I would give her the boot and find someone more efficient. You can imagine all hell broke loose when I found out I've to go to a meeting in Southampton tomorrow. What's worse, it's early in the morning, which means I have to drive all the way down there tonight and put up in a hotel.'

Kitty bit her lip, 'Do you *have* to go? Can't you postpone it?'

Afraid not. It's with Didgens, they're a prestigious building company, and it's not just with me, South Coast Architects will be there too,' he moaned, pulling on his ear lobe. 'It's worth a lot to B.C. Builders to be in with them, I can't let it go. I tell you, Kitty, I'll be giving Cynthia the sack on my return.' Bertie turned and strode over to the drinks cabinet.

Annoyance etched on her face, Kitty watched as he stomped over to the bar, every muscle tense as if he had the world riding on his shoulders. The last time she had seen him like this was back in the summer, the day before he was awarded the Town Hall contract and had stayed out all night. That time all his anxiety had been for nothing. Clearly her husband was a worrier, as well as a workaholic. Yet even then she did not recall him being quite this bad. Kitty could feel the tension coming off him in waves.

Becoming increasingly concerned she was sure something else was troubling him... or was it more likely *someone* else? In the few minutes they had been in the room together she had not missed his anxious behaviour or his eyes flickering as he looked everywhere but at her, as if he did not want to make eye contact. She could also tell he was halfway to being drunk, which was not like him so early in the day. Kitty frowned; she could not recall any mention of contacts on the south coast, so where did this meeting suddenly come from? And if it was so prestigious surely he would have known about it before? The more she thought about it the more puzzled she became.

With unnecessary haste, Bertie plucked a cut glass tumbler from the shelf that held their collection of Waterford crystal and placed it down heavily on the bar. He was obviously a bag of nerves. He might think he was hiding his tension from her, but her senses were telling her something did not add up. Why had Cynthia said nothing about Bertie going away when they spoke on the phone earlier? The young woman was a notorious chatterbox, yet this morning had been unusually short on words. At the time, with so much on her mind, Kitty had thought no more about it, but now it struck her as odd. As she grappled for answers to what was going on a disturbing thought leapt into her head. Was Bertie having an affair? It would explain why he refused to make eye contact and looked almost furtive. The chinking of bottles as he rooted through the drinks cabinet brought her out of her reverie and stopped her from straying any further down that murky road of betrayal.

With a bottle of Gordons in his hand, Bertie unscrewed the top and poured the clear liquid into the tumbler, only stopping when it was half-full. Placing the bottle down without its top, he opened a tonic and added a splash to the gin.

'Here,' he said handing her the tumbler, his eyes still not meeting hers. 'I think you need this, you looked frazzled.'

Taking it from him automatically, Kitty watched as he returned the tops to the bottles and wished merely 'frazzled' was all she felt. It wouldn't be so bad as what she was actually feeling: confused and a little afraid. She was increasingly convinced that her husband was hiding something from her and that whatever it was, for now it was staying hidden.

'I'll not join you,' Bertie said. 'I've already had a couple and I need to set off shortly.'

'That's a first,' she said, bemused. When had Bertie ever refused a drink? These days he consumed far too much whisky, often helping himself to several refills. Sniffing the contents of her glass, she added, 'Rather pointless getting squiffy on my own. There's enough for three people in here!'

He made no reply, turning away from her and pacing across the room, one hand rubbing at the stubble on his chin. His behaviour reminded Kitty of a caged animal.

'I take it Cynthia failed to mention Mr Walker too?' she said, unable to prevent a hint of sarcasm entering her voice.

'Who? Walker did you say?' Shaking his head, he stopped his pacing, 'Nope, never heard of him. No doubt another contract meeting I've missed. God, that woman,' he snapped, a fleck of spittle appearing at the corner of his mouth. With the back of his hand he wiped the moisture away and spun on his heels to look in her direction. 'Darling, let's not dwell on Cynthia's shortcomings. She will remain as BCB's receptionist only until I return. Talking of which, I must get my overnight bag together and head for the coast.' He made his way to the door.

Kitty's eyes narrowed. Why was Bertie so impatient to be on his way when his meeting was not until the morning? It wasn't as if Southampton was a million miles away,' she thought, her fear growing. As he reached out for the door knob, she said as calmly as she could, 'Mr Walker has nothing to do with building contracts, Bertie, but he is just as much of a headache, and yes, you have missed a meeting with him.'

'I said it would a meeting,' he called over his shoulder.

Annoyed when he did not turn to face her Kitty ignored his retort and flung back, '*You* might have missed him, but *I* didn't. He came to find me instead.'

This time Bertie did an abrupt about turn, 'What are you talking about?' he snapped, panic gilding his words.

Had she hit a raw nerve or was she imagining that too? 'Bertie, please come back into the room and sit down so I can explain. Surely five minutes won't make any difference to your *tomorrow's meeting*.' She emphasized those two words, wanting him to know she was not taken in by all this Cynthia-not-telling-him nonsense. Maybe her dark suspicions were nearer the truth and Bertie was indeed having an affair. Kitty did not want to believe her husband was hiding anything from her, but what with Mr Walker this morning and now this sudden dash to the coast, she could not suppress the wave of resentment that was welling in her chest, made worse by his reluctance to talk to her.

Bertie hesitated as he hung onto the door knob, 'You don't understand Kitty.'

'You are probably right, but I would appreciate a moment of your time. I need to talk to you. Please Bertie,' she pleaded, needing reassurance and wanting to find out what he knew about Brightlands Lettings.

Sucking in his lips with annoyance Bertie let go of the door knob, stomped back across the room and dropped down on one of the sofas. Crossing his legs he diddled his right foot, an annoying habit he had when stressed. Kitty did not miss his agitation, noting the tic in his temple throbbing like a heartbeat.

'Right, you've got five minutes, so fire away,' he conceded, twiddling his thumbs.

Putting down her untouched drink on the sofa table, Kitty sat next to him. 'This Mr Walker came to find me first thing. He came to the shop demanding money, saying the rent had not been paid on Primrose Cottage and he was there to collect it. I called—' She stopped speaking abruptly as Bertie, his face puce, sprang to his feet as if his backside had been pierced with a sharp needle.

'Kitty, sorry to stop you, but whoever this Mr Walker is he can only be a conman,' he seethed. 'They are everywhere these days, you must be careful. There have been two or three round the office and yard of late.' Bertie glared down at her, 'I cannot emphasise enough that you watch who you speak to. I am not always around and I need to know I can trust you to be careful.' He checked his watch, 'Sorry, but I really do have to go. We can talk about this further on my return.' With that he stormed through the room and disappeared into the hall.

Kitty was stunned into momentary speechlessness at Bertie's outcry; this was not the reaction she had expected. Biting on her bottom lip she stopped herself calling after him that she had spoken to Brightlands Lettings, an inner voice telling her to remain silent. The alarm bells in her head were increasing in volume. What was going on? Bertie's behaviour was far from normal. Maybe she should offer to go with him, that way they could talk and she could find out what was bothering him.

Kitty hurried after him. 'Bertie,' she called, catching up with him half way up the stairs, 'Why don't I pack your bag while you open the safe and find the bank receipt. The one for the transfer you made when you paid Mrs Watson's rent?' Keeping her tone upbeat she added with a smile, 'I'll pack one for me too and keep you company.'

As if her words were arrows of destruction, Bertie's face turned rapidly from puce to white and alarm flashed in his eyes. 'No! No!' Gasping for breath, he added, 'What I really mean is, it would be so boring for you, darling. I will be trapped in a musty old office talking bricks and mortar all day.' He replied too quickly, not given her suggestion a moment's thought. Kitty could see the sheen of sweat springing to his forehead, but she was not about to be thwarted by this lame excuse.

'That would be no problem, Bertie. I could simply go shopping, visit a museum. Then in the evening we could have dinner together. Pretend we were newlyweds again,' she added, placing a hand to his cheek and at the same time raising her eyebrows suggestively.

A strained smile pulled on Bertie's lips, 'Kitty my love, if only life were that simple,' he offered, 'but sadly my darling, as you have seen of late, business often goes on well into the night. There's really no point, you'd be stuck in a hotel room all on your own.' Leaning forward he dropped a dry kiss on her cheek then headed up the stairs.

'But…' she called, the rest of the words sticking in her throat as Bertie thundered towards the landing, the thick pile carpet doing nothing to muffle his retreating steps. Her husband *was* having an affair. Kitty was sure of it now. He did not have time to talk about Mr Walker, Primrose Cottage or anything else, the only time Bertie had was for the woman he was scheduled to meet later.

Gazing after him, Kitty knew she had ignored all the evidence that had been staring her in the face: his heavy perspiring; his furtiveness; his lack of interest in listening to her as if his mind was somewhere else. Always working late, always too tired to make love to her. It all added up. She was a fool. Nor had she missed the dread that pierced his eyes when she had suggested travelling with him to Southampton. There was no doubt in her mind now that Bertie was being unfaithful.

With no idea what to do, feeling as if her legs were about to give way, Kitty returned slowly to the drawing room and picked up the tumbler of gin and tonic. Walking over to the window she allowed her thoughts to travel down the winding road of disquiet, so engrossed in her unhappiness she did not hear Bertie enter the room.

'I'll ring you as soon as I arrive at the hotel,' he called from the doorway, pulling on his dark grey overcoat. His voice startled Kitty. She swung round and her breath caught in her throat. He looked so dapper, freshly shaved, wearing a clean white shirt, his hair slicked back off his face. He was transformed from the nervous wreck of ten minutes ago into the handsome gentleman she loved. Wordlessly she watched as he fastened the buttons on his coat.

'I'll see you soon, Kitty darling, and please... wish me luck,' he said. Then he darted across the room and wrapped his arms around her. 'This time I do need it, Kitty, luck, plenty of it.' He hugged her tight, his voice wobbling with emotion, 'I love you Mrs Costain, don't ever forget that, no matter what happens,' he whispered in her ear. Brushing her cheek with his lips, he let go of her and walked away. Reaching the door, he stopped 'By the way,' he said, looking over his shoulder, 'I've left the safe key on the telephone table for you.'

'Bertie, wait,' she called, her anger evaporating, but it was too late, he had gone. The slamming of the front door resounded through the house.

Standing in front of the window, Kitty watched as Bertie, briefcase in one hand and a small suitcase in the other, sprinted down the steps to his car. She looked on as he dropped the cases into the boot, saw him hurry round to the driver's door, heard the E-type's engine roaring into life. And all the time his disquieting words echoed in her mind, *'No matter what happens.'* What did that mean?

Her heart breaking, tears slipping down her face, Kitty knew she should have expected this. A ten-year age gap made a difference when it was this way round. No doubt he had yearned for a younger woman. Most men did, she knew. Yet whatever your age, betrayal hurt just the same. She felt sick to the pit of her stomach as she watched Bertie swing the gift she had given him out into the road and speed away. Seeing the tail lights flick on as he took the corner too fast, she clutched at her throat. With all that whisky inside him she should never have let him drive. Not that anything she could have said or done would have stopped him.

Turning away from the window, Kitty prayed she was being foolish. Maybe she was wrong and he really *was* off to a business meeting after all. *'Please let me be wrong....'* She wiped the back of her hand across her cheeks. She knew that feeling sorry for herself would not change anything, but a harsh sob tore up her throat and the tears continued to flow. Kitty realised her emotional state was as much down to anger and frustration as despair. It had been a rude shock having a debt collector calling on her, yet Bertie had not stopped to listen to what she had to say, had simply dismissed it. Almost he had criticised her, as if she had somehow allowed herself to be targeted by a conman.

Thinking about Mr Walker had her fretting again. Kitty squared her shoulders, decided the only way to stop it was to find the transfer receipt. That at least was one problem she could deal with. If Bertie was on his way to a love nest somewhere there was nothing she could do about it. The question of the other woman she would deal with later. Retrieving her glass of gin and tonic, she took a gulp and grimaced; it was much too strong. Placing it back on the sofa table she walked into the hall and located the safe key on the telephone table. As she fingered it, the certainty that she would soon have proof of rent payment in her hand stopped her tears. All she had to do was wade through the documents in the safe until she found the slip of paper she needed. *'Oh to be a fly on the wall when I call Brightlands Lettings! That'll put the wind up them and no mistake,'* she thought, a grim smile crossing her face. It lasted barely a second.

A loud knock on the front door startled Kitty, breaking her train of thought. The safe key slipped from her fingers, fell to the floor and slid across the polished parquet. 'What now?' she muttered as the knock sounded again.

With a heavy sigh, Kitty strode to the door, pulled it open and stopped dead in her tracks as she saw who stood on her doorstep.

Chapter Thirty-One

'Mrs Costain? Er, I wondered if there is a possibility I could speak to you?' The young man stepping from one foot to the other on the top step spoke hesitantly. Wrapped in a navy blue duffle coat, a dark blue scarf tied around his neck, he was clearly nervous. When Kitty made no reply, he added, 'My name is Mark Dufton... I'm not sure if you remember me? I came into your shop once... for some pink lilies?' His tone was polite yet laden with anxiety. 'I'm sorry if I'm disturbing you, but I would really appreciate a few moments of your time... if you could spare it?'

Still upset over Bertie's dash to Southampton, Kitty gazed at him blankly. It took several moments before she realised what the young man standing on her doorstep had said. Rubbing her hands together as the cold air nipped at her fingers she stared into his face, noted his pleasant smile as he waited for a response and toyed with the idea of telling him that now was not a good time. Yet something about him made her hesitate. Of course she remembered him coming into Rosebuds. She had been as shocked to see him then as now. How could she forget that face? He might be muffled up in a heavy coat and scarf, but it was the same young man who months earlier had stood on the opposite side of the road staring up at her bedroom window.

Trying to read his expression Kitty wondered what he needed to say to her that had him looking as if he were on his way to the gallows. Mark Dufton, whoever he was, looked young and vulnerable, his eyes pleading. She could see he was nervous and as before, she had the disturbing feeling that she should know him, there was something familiar about his handsome face that made a shiver run down her spine. In an attempt to shake off her unease, she put on her no-nonsense-look, the one she used for recalcitrant children, and in a firm voice said, 'It seems you have the advantage Mr Dufton. You know my name, yet until now I had no idea of yours, and I object to your gawking up at my windows like a prurient schoolboy!'

Colour flushed in Mark Dufton's face and he lowered his gaze to his hands. 'I'm sorry, I can explain. It is not what you may think. I just wanted to talk to you about Mr Costain.'

Alarm bells that had been tinkling away for most of the day now jangled loudly in Kitty's head. Here was someone else wanting to talk to her about Bertie. *'Oh Lord, what now?'* she thought, pulling herself up to her full five-foot-eight inches and glaring at the stranger on her doorstep. 'It is a pity you didn't knock on the door five minutes earlier because you could have spoken to Mr Costain yourself. If it's money you've come to ask for then you're wasting your time,' she said sharply, adding, 'this is a private house. Make an appointment to see him at his office, you'll find the number in the book.' Stepping back she gripped the door for support, her knees feeling suddenly weak. One person demanding money was bad enough, she didn't need another. About to close the door in his face, she registered Mark Dufton's shock.

'Money?' he cried, as if he had been poked with a sharp stick. 'It's nothing to do with money!' Pushing his hands deep into his pockets he looked down at Kitty's feet and took a deep breath before bringing his attention back to her face. 'It is something personal and sensitive and I would appreciate being able to talk to you first. I know Mr Costain is not here, I saw him drive away.' Not giving Kitty an opportunity to speak, Mark rushed on, 'It has taken me months to find the courage to knock on your door. And yes, I did stand on the other side of the street and I apologise if I alarmed you, but I promise you it is not what you might imagine. I was trying to think of how I could say what I needed to say and it's taken me this long to come up with the words. A few moments of your time is all I ask. Please, Mrs Costain,' he pleaded, his breath clouding the frosty air.

Mystified, Kitty wrapped her arms round her chest and wished she had a coat on. It was full dark now and the street lights had come on, bathing Wentworth Place in a soft amber glow. In the glimmer of the porch light she could see the young man was shivering. Wanting to be back in the warmth herself, reluctantly she gave in.

'I must be a fool, but you can have five minutes. Not a moment longer. Any funny business and I'll be calling the police.'

Mark Dufton's eyes flashed with what she took to be relief, though whether it was because she would listen to what he had to say or that he was glad to be out of the cold she wasn't sure. Recalling Bertie's warning, she trusted she had not made a mistake, he didn't *look* like a conman. 'You had better come in, it's freezing out here,' she said, moving aside for him to enter.

'Thank you,' Mark said and stepped over the threshold, his mouth dropping open as he looked around at the opulence of his surroundings.

Taking a step backwards, Kitty's foot landed on the safe key. Almost losing her balance as it slid out from under her, she gasped, swore under her breath and bent to pick it up. Dropping it back on the telephone table she was determined to get rid of Mark Dufton as soon as she could. She would deal with finding the bank receipt the minute he left. Deciding not to invite him further into her home, Kitty turned to face him.

'Well? Your five minutes starts now.' Then, remembering he had stressed the sensitive nature of what he wanted to say, she had second thoughts. Standing in the hall was hardly conducive to a personal conversation. '*Damn and blast*,' she thought, '*I really should have told him to go away.*' It had been a terrible day and having a stranger knocking on her door asking to speak to her about God knew what, was the last straw. She needed a hot cup of tea; the gin she had swallowed tasted sour in her mouth. 'I'll put the kettle on and make us a pot of tea,' she said bluntly and set off towards the kitchen. 'Follow me,' she ordered, over her shoulder.

Mark Dufton, gazing wide-eyed around him, did as he was told.

'Sit yourself down there,' Kitty pointed to one of the kitchen chairs. As Mark settled on the chair she filled the kettle and switched it on, wishing, as she did every day, that Flo Watson would come bustling in. Wanting to delay what she was about to learn, something *personal and sensitive* that concerned Bertie, Kitty busied herself with warming a china teapot. After swishing the warm water round the pot, she emptied it into the sink then reached to the back of the work surface for the tea caddy. Scooping Assam tea into the warm pot she stood and waited for the kettle to boil.

'You have a beautiful house,' Mark said, breaking the silence as he looked around the brightly lit kitchen at all its modern appliances.

Kitty did not miss the way his gaze rested on the silver cutlery as she opened the canteen and picked out two teaspoons. Suddenly she felt very alone. *'Have I made a dreadful mistake letting him in,'* she thought, gripped with sudden anxiety. She hoped not; he didn't look like a burglar. In fact he looked as nervous as she felt. There were plenty of sharp knives in the drawer if needs must, she reassured herself, grimacing at the thought of having to resort to such a desperate act. If it came to it, could she plunge a blade into anyone's chest? Probably not.

Leaving the tea to brew, she placed two cups and saucers on the Formica surface top and fiddled about, filling the matching sugar bowl with cubes and pouring milk from the fridge into a small jug. She was fussing, of that she was aware, but while part of her didn't want to know why this young man wanted to speak to her, the other part was filled with curiosity. Somehow she didn't think he was a conman any more than a thief, so who was he and what did he want? It then occurred to her that maybe this had something to do with Bertie's affair, which, with a sickening lurch, came back to the forefront of her mind. Was Mark here to tell her about it? Was he personally involved in some way? She noticed he was not wearing a wedding ring. His mother then? It was likely he would know if his mum planned to spend two nights in Southampton with Bertie, and he said he had seen her husband drive away. Was that it? Was his mother the 'other woman'? Scrutinizing Mark Dufton, she could think of no other reason why this young man, around twenty five, she judged, had picked today of all days to knock on her door.

The pain of Bertie's betrayal made Kitty feel sick, she didn't want to hear about it; maybe she should ask Mark to leave after all. She placed a hand on her forehead, her head ached; her heart ache was even worse, as if it had been crushed and broken. All of a sudden, the house felt alien to her. Bertie had made such a fuss handing half of it over to her, but whatever papers had been signed, Wentworth Place would always be Bertie's, never hers. And there had been no sign of his ever repaying those huge loans. It had not mattered to her until now. How much of her money had been going on expensive gifts for his mistress, she wondered. In fifty odd years it seemed she had learnt nothing in life except how to be a fool; a rich misguided fool at that.

'I know I have intruded on you,' Mark Dufton's voice filtered into her thoughts and brought her back to the task in hand. Picking up the teapot she poured the tea in to each cup. 'But I more than appreciate your inviting me in,' he said.

Placing the milk jug and sugar bowl on the table in front of him, Kitty returned to the surface top, picked up the filled cups and took them to the table. 'Drink this, it will warm you through and then you can tell me why you are here.' She kept her voice firm for fear of revealing how on edge she was.

'Thank you.' He picked up his cup, his hand trembled and tea splashed into the saucer. Kitty noticed his nervousness, but saying nothing, remained standing at the opposite side of the table.

'You've not been married to Mr Costain very long have you?' he asked, gripping the handle of his cup.

Ignoring the question, Kitty sipped at her tea. What had that to do with him, she wondered, glaring over her tea cup.

Replacing his cup in the saucer, Mark blushed, his pensive expression tinged with embarrassment. 'I don't know where to begin,' he said.

Sinking down into an adjacent chair, Kitty braced herself. 'Well you'd better try,' she said, glancing at her watch.

'This time last year my father died. He had lung cancer. It was a shock. He was a fit man. He liked a drink like most blokes do and he smoked, but who doesn't these days?' he said softly. 'Nothing to excess, except when it came to work, he was a workaholic, though my mother wanted for nothing.' He picked up his tea and took a gulp as if he needed to wet his throat.

Kitty nodded for him to continue.

'In the spring of last year he caught a cold followed by a cough that wouldn't go away. I can't remember him ever being sick.'

Mark was looking at her, but Kitty could see he didn't see her, his eyes had a distant look; whatever story he was revealing to her he was reliving it. What she didn't understand was why was he telling her all this and what it had to do with his mother having an affair with her husband?

'My mother was devastated, she still is,' he said. 'Of course I miss my father, I loved him, but you see Mrs Costain, nothing is what I believed it to be.'

'It never is,' she wanted to say, but decided to keep her thoughts under wraps and let Mark Dufton tell his story.

'When my mother left school she took a secretarial course and with her certificate landed a good office job in the Town Hall, the Planning Department to be precise. She was engaged to my father by then.'

Kitty sipped at her tea and wondered if she was in fact asleep and dreaming because nothing in her day so far seemed real, tempted as she was to pinch herself, she didn't. Instead she listened.

'When my mother married my father she was pregnant, no one knew at the time. When the baby arrived early, my mother told everyone it was premature. That baby was me.'

Mark Dufton was so engrossed in his story that Kitty believed he had forgotten she was there. 'I see,' she said automatically.

She didn't see at all, but felt the need to make some response.

He shook his head, 'Of course you don't,' he said politely. 'I didn't myself until earlier this year when I discovered that the man I thought was my father wasn't.'

'Mark, as moving as your story is, what has all of this to do with me or my husband?'

As the words left her lips, with sudden clarity Kitty understood why this young man, still wearing his coat, sat tense and nervous in her kitchen revealing dark family secrets across her kitchen table. Of course she could be jumping to conclusions, but what she suspected he was about to confirm stared her in the face now she looked at him properly. Kitty blinked; no wonder he seemed so familiar. So that was it! Her husband had long been a philanderer and one of the skeletons in his cupboard had come home to roost. Doubtless this young man was after blackmailing her to keep his secret once he had revealed who he was. She opened her mouth to tell him he was wasting his time, but no words came out.

'I'm getting to that, Mrs Costain, bear with me. In the planning office, Mum had access to a great deal of information, she typed up all the reports and planning applications, you see. She also got to know a few of the councillors and one or two builders. In those days your husband worked for Fairclough's and from time to time he was sent to collect papers from the planning office, which is how he met my mother. She was only eighteen then.' Mark paused, turned his mouth down as if what he was relating was painful for him. 'Mum told me they had a brief secret affair and although she loved Bertie and believed he loved her, she knew her parents would never give their consent or allow the relationship to continue. Back then Mr Costain was just an apprentice bricklayer and my mother was engaged to the man I knew as my father, who was then a junior lawyer.' Pausing again, this time for another sip of tea, he looked around the large fitted kitchen and said, 'Mr Costain has certainly done very well.'

'*Yes, he has, hasn't he,*' Kitty thought, leaving her tea to go cold as she tried to grasp all she was being told. Today seemed to have been one shock after another and she was reeling with it all, no longer sure what she felt about anything. She nodded, said politely, 'Do go on.'

'Well, it was only after my father's death that my mother told me who my real father was. At first I couldn't take it all in. Even now, a year after his death, I still find it incredible.'

'I'm sure you do,' she said. 'Am I to understand that you believe Ber... my husband to be your father?' He nodded and for the first time since she had opened the door to him he smiled, and in his smile she saw Bertie's ghost.

'On the two occasions I mustered enough courage to speak to him,' Mark said, 'he wasn't in his office and the other time he was in a meeting.'

Kitty raised her eyebrow, 'Which is why I saw you back in the summer looking up at the house?'

He had the manners to look sheepish, 'I'm sorry I didn't mean to frighten you. I had only just learned of the address from my mother and I was curious.'

'Like the other week when you came into my shop to buy flowers?'

'Yes,' he said, shamefaced.

'And what does your mother have to say about you trying to find your father?'

As yet she doesn't know. I was going to tell her if I was successful.' His voice sounded lighter, as if talking about his secret had lifted a weight from his shoulders.

'I see.' She didn't see at all. She couldn't begin to grasp that this young man was in fact her stepson. It was too extraordinary for words. Were it not for that faint resemblance to Bertie when he smiled, she would not have accepted he was telling the truth. Unsure what to say, she stood up. 'The tea's gone cold would you like a fresh cup? And do take your coat off or you'll never feel the benefit when you leave. *'Goodness, I'm already talking to him as if I was his mother!'* she thought.

'Another cup would be good, thank you,' Mark nodded in agreement. Standing, he removed his coat and dropped it over the back of the chair before sitting down again. While she brewed a fresh pot of tea he remained silent. The house was so quiet that she could hear the tick-tock of the grandfather clock in the hall.

'What I don't understand Mark, is why you have told *me* all of this,' Kitty said, carrying the teapot to the table.

Mark hesitated as if searching for the right words. 'I would like to meet the man who was responsible for bringing me into the world. I have tried, but he's a very busy man who is seldom at his office. On top of this, my confidence lurches from positive to negative, but when I came into your shop, you seemed so… well… nice, I thought maybe it would make things easier if I talked to you first.' He watched as Kitty poured fresh tea into his cup, 'I'm sorry I have burdened you with this, Mrs Costain, but I suppose I hoped you might help with an introduction.'

His eyes met Kitty's as he spoke and she could see his anticipation, the slight flush of pink in his cheeks. And his eyes were china blue! Before she could respond, he added, 'I can't imagine what it must have been like for my mother keeping such a huge secret to herself all these years.

Nervously he linked his fingers then unlinked them and rubbed at his chin – a gesture that so reminded Kitty of Bertie she almost burst into tears. She felt a sudden shaft of sympathy for this young man. It could not have been easy to talk about this, least of all to her. 'You're not married Mark?' she asked, placing the teapot down on the table mat and staring at his left hand.

As if a light had been switched on, Mark's face lit up, 'Yes, I am actually.' He spoke as if marriage were a badge of honour. 'I have a stepson, Andrew, and my wife and I have a baby due in April.' As if needing to explain further, he added, 'Susan was a widow when we met, her first husband was killed in a road accident two months after their son was born, so Andrew will never know his real father. He will be four at the end of the year and although he loves me as his daddy, it is not the same. That is to say, it won't be when he's old enough to understand.' Mark turned his gaze away from Kitty as if considering his own position. 'Unlike Andrew, I've been given the chance to find my father. My stepson doesn't have that choice; he will never know his real dad...' He looked up at her and shrugged, 'I suppose that is what has spurred me to approach Mr Costain. You see, I do have a choice.'

'I understand,' Kitty said, and this time she really did. She sipped her tea, thinking she could do with something stronger. Pushing the thought of gin and tonic from her mind, she let the unsweetened tea slip down her throat, surprised to be warming to this young man. No matter what was going on in her head, Mark Dufton was determined to share what was going on in his. It was a brave person who had the courage to enter a stranger's house and pour out their heart. Noting a tic pulsing in his left temple, she was again starkly reminded of Bertie. A tic always throbbed in his left temple when he was nervous or anxious. Mark's resemblance to Bertie seemed to be growing stronger by the minute. It could just be a coincidence. Maybe she was imagining it because Bertie was so much on her mind. Yet much as she did not want it to be true – her life was complicated enough – Kitty was convinced Mark was indeed Bertie's son. His story sounded plausible, but what could she do? She was still trying to come to terms with Bertie's infidelity, never mind worrying about the Primrose Cottage rent fiasco. And now this!

Chewing at the inside of her bottom lip, Kitty wondered how Bertie would react to the knowledge that he was about to become a grandfather! She had no idea, but as everything tumbled around in her head, one thing she did know was that the man she had married was an enigma. She sighed with weariness. When she had left for work that morning it had been a normal day, and now, in only a few hours, her life had spiralled into a vortex of confusion and anxiety. Resting her elbows on the table she steepled her fingers and gazed steadily over them at Mark.

'Why did your mother never tell Mr Costain she was expecting his child… that is, I assume she did not?'

'No, she told nobody except her fiancée – the man I thought was my father. He was an exceptional man and he loved my mother very much. He not only forgave her, but he raised me as his own. That is how Mum tells it, and I have no reason to disbelieve her.'

Without warning, Mark jumped to his feet and grabbed up his coat. 'I'm sorry, what must you think of me?' Clearly embarrassed he slipped his arm into his duffle coat as he spoke. 'I am a stranger in your house telling you your husband is my father. It must be a dreadful shock.'

Kitty watched in astonishment as Mark fumbled with the large toggles, trying to push them into the loops. Getting to her feet, she reached out and laid a hand on his arm. 'Not so dreadful as you might think, Mark. It's been a day of shocks; your story is the least of them. But anyway, I will talk to Bertie for you. You must remember that I didn't know him all those years ago. He has mentioned he had girlfriends, though he never told me their names or said anything about them. He did admit there was someone special once, but no further details. You must appreciate we both have our own history. At our age you do,' she smiled, a worldly smile designed to convey she did not have answers, 'but what is past is past. When one meets someone and falls in love, one does not dwell too much on what happened before they met. Having said that, I recognise it is important for you to meet the man you believe is your father.'

Mark nodded and Kitty could see he understood.

'Good,' she said. 'Bertie is away for a few days, some business meetings for more contracts, but if you will leave me a contact number or address I will let you know when he returns. But not before I have an opportunity to speak to him about you. I have no doubt that learning he has a grownup son will come as a shock, so do not expect to hear anything too soon.'

Mark nodded again. 'Of course,' he said, a smile creeping across his face making his china-blue eyes twinkle. 'Thank you for everything,' he added.

'You're very like him, you know,' she said, choking back a sob. Turning away so he would not see her tears she left the kitchen, returning moments later with a notepad and pen. 'Here, write down how I can get in touch with you,' she said, placing the items on the table.

He scribbled down his telephone number and address then placing the pen on the table, handed her the pad of paper. Taking one last glance around the kitchen he wrapped his scarf round his neck and followed Kitty to the front door.

For some time Kitty stood on the doorstep, clutching the notepad to her chest and watching Mark as he set off down the road. A strange feeling wrapped itself around her. It had been weird to see shadows of her husband's looks and mannerisms in such a young man. Was that how Bertie had looked a quarter of a century ago? She had no reason to doubt that Mark Dufton was his son. Shivering in the cold night air Kitty hugged her arms tighter to her and wondered what else there was to know about Bertie Costain. She further wondered how on earth she was she going to tell him about Mark when Bertie eventually returned home.

Kitty watched until Mark turned the corner at the end of Wentworth Place. As he disappeared from view, she closed the door and headed to the drawing room to retrieve her gin and tonic.

Chapter Thirty-Two

Driving on automatic pilot, his head filled with panic and his nerves taut as wire, Bertie realised he could not remember gunning the sports car over the junction. Had the traffic lights been green or red? Damn! The last thing he needed was trouble with the cops. His mind buzzed and his heart raced with all that had happened in the last few hours, yet he reasoned the lights must have been green otherwise he would have heard a cacophony of horns blaring and very likely a loud crash! He had heard nothing and glancing in the rear view mirror, no flashing blue lights were in evidence. A pulse twitched in his left temple as he broke out into a fresh sweat of anxiety at the thought of the men in blue hanging on his tail. Not a police patrol car in sight. In fact the road was empty.

'Focus, Bertie, focus,' he muttered, relief flooding through him. He had been drinking and like most days of late, was way over the limit. He was aware he drank far too much. Alcohol was supposed to help with stress, but it took more and more to calm his nerves, to the point he had often consumed a bottle of whisky in one sitting. He exhaled to sniff his breath. The sour odour of stale alcohol made his nose twitch. He spluttered and swore loudly. 'Christ,' the intensity of the toxic fumes was lethal enough to ignite a dead match. He needed a cigarette. Fumbling in his trouser pocket he pulled out a packet. Lighting up, he had no intentions of opening the windows; long gone was his idealistic intention of not smoking in his flashy new car. Right now he needed the stench of tobacco to mask the odour of stale whisky. Bertie knew he had to drive carefully: the recent Act limiting drivers' alcohol consumption – a limit he must be way over – meant the boys in blue could stop motorists for any little misdemeanour. '*Any excuse to persecute the poor bloody motorist,*' he thought, grimacing. In his view PC Plod should be catching criminals not lurking on street corners. If he was stopped and breathalysed he wouldn't stand a snowflake's chance in hell of talking himself out of it. And if being stopped was not enough to contend with, there was the indignity of being asked to piss in a bottle! The country was going to the dogs, he thought, pulling on his Benson and Hedges as he kept an eye on his speed. It would be sod's law if he got pulled over now, on top of everything else. What a sodding awful day it had been. Winding the window down, he flicked out the spent cigarette and tried not to dwell on the shambles of his life. Should anything else happen to him in the near future he might be tempted to commit *hara-kiri*. Winding the window shut, he snorted; under his present circumstance suicide might not be such a bad idea.

With the bustle of London behind him, Bertie headed out to the M1. The more miles he could put between himself and Brian Smith, along with a frighteningly long list of others, including the creepy debt collector Bill Walker, the better. He checked the rear view mirror again to see if someone might be following him; he was not exactly incognito in the E-type.

As busy streets gave way to open fields all Bertie could think about was what he had done to Kitty. He had lied to everyone in one form or another, but deceiving Kitty had given him pain, real pain. This time tomorrow she would know all about the real Bertie; the cheating lying Bertie, and he wished with every fibre of his being that he could shield her from the pain, but it was all too late. Even now his heart still skipped a beat at the shock of seeing her pull up outside the house in the middle of the afternoon. Under normal circumstances, at that time of the day he would have been alone, the cleaner having long gone, and a couple of hours at least before Kitty arrived back from her shop. He had taken to going home in the afternoon several times over the last few weeks when he needed time to think or to escape the wolves baying for his blood or rather, money he did not have. He had also avoided Howard Silvershoes since the debacle with the Town Hall contract. *'There are only so many lectures a man can take,'* Bertie thought ruefully.

He broke out in a sweat recalling with a heavy heart the sight of Kitty arriving at Wentworth Place soon after three. She was a woman of habit; she never closed her shop before five, but she had this afternoon and he had panicked. His mind turning cartwheels he had watched her slip out of her Mini, dropping her handbag on the roof as she leaned inside to retrieve a large carrier bag. Unobserved he had seen her glance up at the drawing room window and had seen how upset she was. His worst fear was confirmed. He hadn't needed to be Dixon of Dock Green to work out why she had come home early looking so distressed. Someone had got to her and the likely candidate was Bill Walker. The wretched man had been sniffing around B.C. Builders for days, but Bertie had never thought the bastard would stoop so low as to pester Kitty.

The consequences of the last few weeks hit Bertie like a sledgehammer as he contemplated his destruction, recalling the way Kitty had looked at him as he had lied in his teeth. He felt crushed, as if someone had physically attacked him and for a moment he was poleaxed. Not only was he about to lose everything he owned, but very likely the woman he had grown to love, for in the midst of his despair he recognised that he had actually fallen in love with Kitty.

The thought filled Bertie with fear as well as shame. What had he done? In all the years since his early twenties when he had been so badly hurt, he had protected himself against it happening again, vowing never to let a woman get close enough to hurt him. His philosophy had always been to have fun with women but never fall in love with them. There had been a string of beauties hanging on his arm and squirming between the sheets, satisfying his physical needs but never touching his heart. And then he had met Kitty Moore and somehow she had succeeded in piercing his hardened heart. Attractive, in control and above all obscenely wealthy, she had waltzed into his life like a breath of fresh air. At first all he had seen was an opportunity to keep the wolves from clawing at his door, and believing marriage was the only way to secure the favours of a lady like Kitty, he had wined and dined her, made passionate love to her and proposed. He had never meant to hurt her, just enjoy her wealth.

Now, aware that he had somehow broken his vow to himself along the way, he bitterly regretted the pain he was about to inflict on his wife. Until this moment he had not regretted marrying her. Now he did, and the knowledge of what he had done, the extent of his betrayal, brought a searing pain to his heart and a sickness to his gut – feelings he had strived for so long to avoid.

Mentally cataloguing the disasters of the last few months, Bertie knew that if he had lost everything, then Kitty would lose too. Wentworth Place; B.C. Builders; the Jaguar… even the Mini Cooper S would be repossessed in the coming days. Oddly, this thought distressed him further. If a car could choose its owner, Zippy would have selected Kitty. They both turned heads and had presence. Whatever happened over the coming days he *had* to find a way to protect Kitty from being dragged down to the depths to which he had sunk. Everything he did was a lie: his life was a lie, his marriage was a lie. Even he was a lie. In the cold light of day Kitty would see who he really was and he would lose her. And that one loss, Bertie now realised, was greater than all the others put together.

Now, as he saw the sign for the motorway light up in his headlights, he knew he was at the point of no return. He could either continue driving to the North or turn round and go home. It was tempting to return to Kitty and try to explain. Beg for forgiveness, praying she would help him. But what kind of a man would do that to the woman he loved? As the markers flashed by counting down to the slip road, Bertie felt as if he was driving over a cliff.

Chapter Thirty-Three

Pouring hot water into a mug of instant coffee powder, Kitty stirred vigorously. It was her third cup of strong black coffee since she had got up this morning and still it had not lifted her spirits or given her the energy boost she needed. Bertie had promised to call her when he arrived at his hotel last night, but she had heard nothing from him. Southampton was hardly the ends of the Earth. He should have arrived by early evening. He must have been too busy having sex with his bit on the side, she thought, probing the pain as one probes an aching tooth, making it hurt even more.

After Mark Dufton had left she had got mildly drunk waiting for the call. It never came. She could not call Bertie as she had no idea where he was staying. This, added to the events of the previous day, meant she had not slept a wink all night. When she had not been heading to the bathroom she had been down in the kitchen making another pot of tea and revisiting Bertie's reason for dashing to Southampton. A hundred different thoughts had raced through her imagination during the long dark hours and as the hands on the clock ticked the night away, the events of the last few weeks had slowly fallen into place. How could she have been so naïve? All the messages she had left with Cynthia had rarely been returned. Bertie was always elusive and not just with her; even Mr Walker and Mark Dufton had been unable to talk to him. The way Bertie had dismissed her when she had tried to tell him about the fiasco over Mrs Watson's rent, even suggesting Mr Walker was a conman, still rankled. Maybe he was, but somehow Kitty did not think so.

Hugging a mug of hot coffee she rested her elbows on the surface top and peered out of the kitchen window.

Daylight had at last broken through the gloom and in the narrow borders she could just make out the clumps of snowdrops she had planted months earlier. Funny how the world could appear so normal when your own world was fracturing at the seams.

Glancing up at the sky, Kitty saw the clouds were thin and a hint of blue was visible. For company she had switched on the radio to listen to the Light Programme and had heard the weather forecast enough times to recite it backwards: 'A dry day with weak sunshine, temperatures average to slightly above for this time of year,' the presenter had announced at regular intervals. Though of course, now she thought of it, it wasn't the Light Programme anymore. The BBC had fiddled around with all the radio stations and made a mess of it all. God alone knew what she was listening to these days. It irritated her that perfectly good services were being messed around with and in her opinion ruined. Tuning out of the presenter's voice Kitty sighed heavily. She felt weary, cheated and worse, an utter fool. What was she doing here? What had she been thinking twelve months ago? How had she allowed herself to believe that Bertie loved her? Not wanting to attempt to answer such an emotional question, knowing it would only add further to her depressive state of mind, Kitty took another gulp of coffee and eyed the state of the lawn. It needed cutting. The mild spell had encouraged it to grow. Maybe the gardener would think it was not too early to give it a quick trim. Ben Bridges looked after several of the Wentworth Place gardens. He came each week to number six, yet to Kitty's eyes it still resembled a wilderness.

With a jaundiced eye, she turned her gaze to the bird bath Flo used to enjoy watching. It too was looking the worse for wear, covered in algae. But it wasn't the state of the winter garden that bothered her, it was what her husband was up to. It was then Kitty remembered the strange phone calls she'd had of late. The caller never spoke, not even to give a name, just hung up when she answered the phone. Now why would someone bother to call and not speak? Was it the other woman? The more she fretted about recent events the more convinced she was that Bertie was having an affair. The burning question: who was she? Do I know her? Kitty wondered. Was it just a passing fling or was it serious? And if it was just a fling, could she bring herself to forgive him?

She was still tormenting herself on the other woman's likely identity when her train of thought was disrupted by a couple of sparrows flying out of the hedge landing on the bird bath. Almost immediately they took flight again and Kitty, casting her gaze around the garden, spied the neighbour's tomcat slinking through the grass. Dark grey with a broad silver stripe down its back, it was at first sight an attractive cat, but there the attractiveness ended: built like a small dog and with a piercing yowl, the tomcat was a bruiser, both by name and nature. Always on the prowl, if he wasn't killing the wildlife, he was pestering the local feline community. *'Bruiser needs seeing to at the vet,'* she thought, adding to herself, *'And so does Bertie!'* Without humour she laughed out loud.

Keeping an eye on the prowling cat, Kitty watched as he leapt onto the top of the fence and without faltering strutted half a dozen paces before disappearing into the neighbour's garden. Unerringly, Kitty continued tormenting herself. The thought of Bertie making love to another woman made her want to throw up. Could it be Cynthia? Surely not! As if looking through the lens of a camera an image of Bertie's receptionist flashed into Kitty's mind: five feet tall with a ruddy complexion that had likely never felt the caring touch of moisturiser, her hair a mixture of light grey and mouse, long enough to be tied in a band at the nape of her neck. Judging the woman's age was difficult, she could just as easily be thirty-five as forty-five. Cynthia's idea of dressing smartly was wearing a pair of too tight, dark-coloured slacks topped with a clinging home-knitted jumper. She had an earthy laugh and flirted outrageously with all the B.C. builders, who apparently found her irresistible. Quite why, Kitty could not fathom, unless it was that Cynthia was blessed with big boobs. Had she flirted with Bertie too? Had the temptation to take it further been too much for him? Was this the person he was seeing after working hours and during them too? Had he protested a little too much when he said he would be giving her the sack?

So many questions! Frowning, Kitty finished the last few drops of coffee and thought back over her various conversations with Cynthia, but was unable to recall detecting even a hint of collusion when they had spoken on the phone. So if it was not she then who was it? Someone from the club he so loved to frequent?

It bothered her now that Bertie had said he did not go to his club these days, 'Too much going on to waste time drinking with the chaps in there,' he had gushed when she had questioned where he had been on one of his late nights home. So where did her husband go if he did not go to Raffles and who with? Was it the same woman he was going to see on this out-of-the-blue two-day trip to Southampton?

For the first time since she had arrived in Wentworth Place, Kitty longed for her apartment in Wimbledon Village, the simple life and the fun of running her little shop without the complications and stress that Bertie caused her. Gone was the man she had married less than a year ago. These days he was anxious, stressed and deceitful; none of them signs of a successful, happily married businessman. Reluctantly, she had to accept that on all the nights she had gone to bed alone her husband had been out with another woman. Even now he was hiding behind work. How many meetings did a builder need to attend?

Kitty knew she was silently rambling, but only because she felt betrayed and angry. She could no more stop her thoughts than she could stop breathing. Turning away from the window, she placed the empty mug down on the side and pulling the belt tight on her housecoat, tried to hold in the pain. She still had not opened the safe. She had wanted to. She had wanted to prove Walker wrong, but after her evening had been hijacked by a young man claiming he was Bertie's son, she couldn't bring herself to do anything at all, let alone go hunting for a bank receipt. Even if she had dug it out after Mark Dufton had left, what could she have done in the middle of the night? She had convinced herself the proof was in the safe and would still be there waiting for her come morning. Oddly enough, she had not lost any sleep over Mark Dufton's visit. If what he said was true it had all happened long before she and Bertie met. It was of no significance to her other than the fact that she had promised to speak to her husband about it. She would deal with that later if she had to. Maybe she should open the safe now, for if nothing else it would take her mind of Bertie's affair for a few minutes. Holding that thought, she headed towards the hall to retrieve the key.

The clatter of the letterbox followed by the sound of letters thudding onto the mat startled her so much she almost jumped out of her skin. 'It's only the postman, you fool,' she muttered, hanging onto the back of a kitchen chair. Sleep deprivation and a mind in overdrive had done nothing for her equilibrium. Rubbing her temples to ease the tension, Kitty went to pick up the post.

Scooping up the envelopes, mostly brown, bills by the look of them, she recalled Bertie's recent eagerness to meet the postman. No matter what time her husband got home each night, he was always bathed and dressed before the post arrived in the morning. He was even known to leave the house at the same time as the postman pushed his bicycle down Wentworth Place. Only last Thursday, observing Bertie through the bedroom window, Kitty had seen him snatch several letters from the bemused man the moment he had parked his bike. Then, stuffing the post in his jacket pocket, Bertie had leapt into his car and roared away, leaving the postman staring after him in a fug of blue exhaust fumes. Was the new love in his life sending him letters too? It seemed likely.

Kitty singled out the two white envelopes and scanned them. Both were addressed to Bertie. One from the bank the other from Middleton's, the garage her car had come from, its logo emblazoned in the corner. But no handwritten letter addressed to her husband. Dropping the post on the telephone table, she picked up the safe key and twiddled it in her fingers. She was just setting off down the hall when a loud knock sounded at the front door. A feeling of *déja vu* had her turning round. 'Pull yourself together, Kitty,' she hissed, remembering that the newspaper had not yet been delivered. No doubt it was the cheeky paperboy apologising for his tardiness. Slipping the key into her pocket and pulling her face into a smile in readiness to greet him, she hurried back down the hall and pulled open the door.

'Mrs Costain?'

The smile slipped from her face. Kitty looked at a mountain of a man whose high, soft voice belied his stature. He was immaculately dressed, reminding her instantly of Mr Walker. Standing behind him was another gentleman built from the same mould.

'Mrs Costain?' he asked again.

'Yes,' Kitty answered, her gaze darting from one face to the other. They certainly were not paperboys nor were they anything to do with Mr Shepherd's newsagent shop. She sucked in her breath. *'Oh God no! Has Bertie had an accident?'* she thought. Before she could voice her sudden anxiety, the man standing closest to her spoke.

'We would like a word with Mr Costain.' He looked back over his shoulder as if to check the road for the Jaguar.

Kitty's relief that it was nothing to do with an accident was instantly replaced with suspicion. Why was Bertie suddenly the man everyone wanted to talk to? Her second thought was that one of these men might be the husband of the woman her husband had skedaddled away with.

'I'm afraid he's not here,' she replied matter-of-factly, not wanting to give anything away.

'Can we step inside please?' The mountain asked, a slow smile revealing white teeth and deepening a scar on the left side of his thin lips.

'If it is Bertie you want you will be wasting your time, he is not here.'

'That's a shame. Nonetheless, we would appreciate a few moments of your time. It is important,' he pressed. His feet remained firmly on the wide top step, his hands linked in front. The other one stood inches behind. He remained silent, but his eyes never left her. Trying not to feel intimidated by the heavy shadows that darkened the doorstep, the words sounded eerily similar to the ones uttered by Mark Dufton the previous night. Surely these two are not about to reveal they are Bertie's sons too, she thought, almost bursting into hysterical laughter. That would push the realms of reality beyond her limits! Or were these others like Mr Walker, collecting non-payment to the milkman or some such bod? Kitty shuddered and held her arms tightly round her middle. Whoever they were, they looked as if they meant business.

As if picking up of her apprehension, the second man spoke, his voice several octaves deeper than his counterpart's. 'We mean you no harm Mrs Costain. It's just business. If we could step inside then we can explain.'

His smile was so menacing that Kitty felt the hairs on her arms stand up. Rubbing at them over the top of her housecoat, she tried to guess what kind of business included the words, '*We mean you no harm*'? Town halls, car parks and semi-detached houses – the kind of business Bertie was involved in – should hardly have burly men knocking on the door before breakfast. Though, now she thought of it, bedding someone's wife might. Could things get any worse?

Trying not to think about all that had happened over the last twenty-four hours, Kitty's wary eyes took in the measure of the two men looming over her. She could tell them to leave and close the door, but somehow she didn't think that would work. The big man's foot would come out quicker than she could spit in his eye. Resigned to having to listen to what they had to say, she shrugged. 'You've not left me with much choice but to let you have your say.' She stepped to one side and indicated for them to enter. She did not want the neighbours seeing her talking to these shifty looking behemoths on the doorstep.

With the door closed, Kitty stood in front of it and folded her arms across her chest, wondering if she should move closer to the telephone.

'I'm Brian Smith the owner of Raffles,' said the high-voiced gorilla. Glancing to his left, he added, 'And this is Kevin Bryant, my manager.

Kitty nodded as if to acknowledge what Brian Smith had said. 'I find it rather odd that you should be calling at this early hour, Mr Smith, even more so since my husband has not set foot in your club for weeks.'

Smith and Bryant exchanged a look. Kitty did not miss the arching of Bryant's eyebrows or the look of disbelief that sparked between the two men. 'Odd indeed, that,' Smith said in a deadpan voice, 'but not our visit at this early hour. What is *odd* is that a man who resembles your husband and drives an E-type Jaguar, blue, same as your Bertie's, has been frequenting the club every night for weeks. So unless your husband has a double, Mr Bertie Costain almost lives at Raffles.'

Kitty's heart took a dive, but somehow she kept a stiff upper lip. 'Surely there has to be some misunderstanding, because B—'

'I only wish there was,' Brian Smith said, cutting Kitty off in mid-sentence, his dark eyes holding her gaze. 'You see Mrs Costain, our visit is about what your husband has been doing in our club. And it is important we know when he will be back and soon. You see, he has a contract with us and failure to meet the deadline will have serious consequences.'

Placing her hands on her hips and moulding her expression into what she hoped was a look of steely determination, Kitty flung back, 'Are you threatening me? Because if you are, I'm calling the police.'

With his hands outstretched, Brian Smith spoke calmly, 'Nobody is threating you, Mrs Costain, but I am afraid we are here because Mr Costain has been gambling at Raffles and the amount outstanding is considerable. Please can we at least sit down and explain?'

Glad that the front door at her back prevented her from falling over, Kitty stared at him unseeing. '*Gambling… the amount outstanding is considerable*,' repeated over and over in her head. She was alerted by an inner instinct. Its light flooded through her tired brain like a shaft of sunlight giving answers to all the questions that had plagued her waking and sleeping hours. Not an adulterer then; a gambler. She'd had no idea. The odd flutter and a drink at his club, but nothing on the scale this man indicated. These men were serious. This was no hoax; these weren't conmen. The bottom line was that Bertie was in deep trouble, but not through having an affair. For the first time in months his behaviour began to make sense. He hadn't been out till all hours of the night discussing building contracts. Nor had he gone to Southampton to have sex with Cynthia or anyone else. Mr Walker's reason for visiting Rosebuds was very likely genuine. Bertie Costain had been gambling and now, when things had got hot, he had done a runner, leaving her to fend off all those to whom he owed money.

Kitty felt a sense of betrayal so deep that she bent over with the pain of it. She wasn't sure which she would have preferred, Bertie carrying on with someone else, or this. Slowly unbending, she focused on the two men standing in her hallway, each gazing at her with a touch of concern in his eyes. They both looked like spivs: former barrow boys, perhaps. Maybe the debt to Raffles wasn't as bad as she was imagining. A considerable sum to these two could be nothing more than the price of a decent new car. Forcing herself to relax Kitty tried to think positively. It could all be a storm in a teacup and Bertie had panicked. A cup of decent coffee and the flash of her cheque book would sort it out. She had calmed Mr Walker down in the same way. She would deal with these two as well and then later, deal with Bertie in private. By God, would she deal with *him*!

Feeling she had a measure of control on the situation, she stepped round the two stooges. 'I'll make a pot of coffee if you'll follow me through to the kitchen and then you can tell me how much Bertie is in debt to you.' Kitty led the way, aware of a slow burning pit of anger smouldering deep within her. When she got hold of Bertie she would kill him for putting her through all this.

Chapter Thirty-Four

The phone shrilled out as Howard Silvershoes entered his office. He glanced at his watch and saw it was just before nine. Lifting the receiver he announced, 'Silvershoes.'

'Howard, it's Kitty Costain. Sorry to trouble you, but do you have a minute?'

The sound of her voice momentarily knocked him off guard. Kitty was the last person he expected to be calling him at any time of the day, let alone first thing in the morning. Mindful that she did not get involved in Bertie's business, instinct told him something was amiss.

'Yes of course. Good morning Kitty,' he said, attempting to mask his unease. 'What can I do for you?'

Without preamble, Kitty asked in a flat voice, 'Do you know anything about the meeting Bertie is attending in Southampton?'

Howard was taken aback by the question; it seemed odd that Kitty should ask him about Bertie's meeting. He had no idea her husband was out of town, but then, how would he these days? They hadn't met in months and from the wall of silence that followed the messages he had left with Cynthia, it seemed Bertie was not so much keeping his distance as pointedly avoiding him. Rumours were circulating that Bertie Costain was gambling heavily and the debt collectors were after him. Howard had not wanted to believe his old associate would go back on his word, back down the road that had almost ruined him a few months earlier, but he was forced to believe it when one of the debt collectors had come into his office last week looking for Bertie and had explained the situation. Did he really have a meeting in Southampton? So far as he knew, B.C. Builders had no contracts on the south coast. Had Bertie played his last game and taken flight? Howard prayed it was not the case, but it would explain why Kitty was calling.

Trying not to put two and two together and come up with five, Howard responded lightly, 'It's been a busy couple of weeks and I've not spoken with Bertie of late, so I'm afraid I know nothing about his movements. Is everything alright?' He heard a sharp intake of breath from the other end and knew something had to be wrong. Bertie's new wife did not make a habit of calling him. He suspected she did not have a great deal of time for him, though wasn't sure why, unless she had picked up on his reservations when Bertie had upped and married her out of the blue.

'What is it Kitty? Is Bertie in trouble?' the words slipped out of his mouth before he could stop them.

A brief pause followed and Howard suspected she was gathering herself, unsure where to begin. When she spoke, her voice sounded forced, as though she was struggling to remain calm.

'Bertie left yesterday afternoon unexpectedly, something to do with a meeting in Southampton. He was in quite a state of agitation. I offered to go with him, but that did not go down too well. He's never mentioned having business in Southampton before and… well… I drew my own conclusions as to why he suddenly needed to go away. I thought he might be seeing someone…'

As if aware she was gabbling, Kitty's voice trailed away. There was another brief silence, but Howard could hear the line was still open and waited for Kitty to continue.

'However, as it turned out, I was wrong,' she went on. 'In fact I could not have been more off the mark. You see, early this morning two gentlemen claiming to own Raffles, Bertie's club, came to the door wanting to see him… Anyway, I urgently need to talk to him, Howard, but I have no contact number. I've tried Cynthia, but she's clueless and I didn't want to say too much. I thought you might know where he is.'

Howard did not miss the tremor in Kitty's voice and the colour drained from his face as he took in the implications of what she was saying. He didn't need to ask why Brian Smith and Kevin Bryant had knocked on the door of number six, Wentworth Place early in the morning. Their visit meant only one thing and as Kitty elucidated further, every word she uttered confirmed his fears.

'The two men – they said their names were Smith and Bryant – have gone away for now, but that's not all, there is more...' again she faltered.

Holding his breath Howard listened as her words tumbled down the line, anger and betrayal filling her voice as she repeated what they had said. Finally, she took a deep breath then added, 'I'll be frank with you, Howard, I'm finding it impossible to take in. I keep pinching myself in the hope I'm having a nightmare and I'll wake up shortly, but that's not going to happen is it? You know about his gambling, don't you.'

It wasn't a question, but he answered it anyway. 'I'm afraid so Kitty, though I hoped he had stopped after the last time he got himself into trouble.' Howard closed his eyes, shock at what she had said making him grip the handset as if to crush it. Bertie must owe a *vast* sum for Smith to have visited the Costains' home. Knowing that for Kitty the nightmare was real and only just beginning, Howard didn't know what to say to her.

'Last time? What trouble? What do you mean? Could you come to the house?' Kitty asked. 'I'd come to you, but it will be difficult for me and to be honest I don't want to leave just now in case Bertie calls. I'd appreciate you saying yes.'

Hearing the pleading in her voice, Howard's heart constricted. Seconds passed before he answered. He took several small breaths to control the anger bubbling up inside him. *'Damn that idiot man,'* he thought, reaching for a cigarette to ease the tension in his muscles and lighting it one-handed. He wanted to keep his voice steady; had no wish to reveal his alarm to this poor woman.

'It goes without saying,' he said at length, exhaling a twin stream of smoke through his nostrils. 'I'll come as soon as I can.' In truth, Howard had no idea what he could do if the situation was as dire as he feared. He was about to say he would be there in no more than the time it took to drive across town, when Kitty spoke again.

'Thank you. I so need to talk to someone who understands him, because I'm sure I don't.' Her voice hardened, 'Of course he knew exactly what he was doing when he charged out of the house yesterday, leaving me to clear up the mess. He lied to me Howard, led me to believe he had business in Southampton, but it can't be true. Cynthia would have at least known that much. You know, he didn't even call to say he had arrived safely at his destination, wherever that was. Heaven only knows where he has actually gone. I've been worried sick in case he's had an accident. The state he was in when he left it wouldn't surprise me.'

'Calm down, Kitty. No news is good news.' Howard could think of several places Bertie might have gone, but if *he* could, so could Smith and Bryant. Bertie might be a fool, but he was not a complete idiot. He would have gone somewhere nobody would expect. 'Please don't worry. I'll come over straight away. And Kitty, don't answer the door to anyone until I arrive,' he added, unsure who Bertie owed money to and who else would be looking for him.

'Thank you Howard, I appreciate your help. I'm so afraid… to be honest I'm at my wit's end.'

He heard the tears in her voice but was unable to think of any words that would suffice to calm her. What Bertie had done would need more than platitudes. Instead he said simply, 'Try not to worry, Kitty. We will find a way to sort it out. I know that sounds impossible right now, but we will try. See you shortly.'

Hearing her tearful goodbye, he replaced the receiver and smoothed the palm of his hand over the top of his silver hair, ruffling the perfect side parting. '*Try not to worry*,' he had said, because there was nothing else he could think to say which would not betray his anxiety. If things had got this bad, it was likely Bertie had lost everything he owned and the bailiffs would soon be knocking on Kitty's door. He wondered if he should call Marcus, warn him Bertie might have to declare bankruptcy. Decided against it; time enough for that later.

Pushing his chair back, Howard stood then dropped back down. Shock and outrage had now turned to numbness. In a similar way to Kitty he felt a sense of betrayal. He had done everything he could to steer Bertie Costain away from the path of inevitable destruction, and the man had promised faithfully that he would stop gambling. Howard placed his elbows on the desk and rested his chin on his hands. He should have seen this coming, but he hadn't. Foolishly he had thought he knew the man; thought Bertie meant to keep his promise; believed the last close shave had taught him a valuable lesson. How wrong he had been. He had heard of people addicted to gambling, losing their entire life's work to the vagaries of chance and ending up down and out in the gutter along with the druggies and winos, but he had never seriously thought Bertie would be one of them. The man had worked so hard to get where he was, why would he risk throwing all those years of hard graft away on a gaming table? It made no sense at all to Howard.

For years he had looked after the financial aspects of B.C. Builders, advising on loans, book keeping and tax. He had access to Bertie's financial affairs or at least he thought he had. Of late there had been such a strain between them that it appeared Bertie was dealing silently with his own finances and keeping them secret. It saddened Howard to think that they had at one time been friends with a mutual trust. Now there was no friendship and clearly no trust. What Kitty had told him beggared believe and yet he knew it was all likely to be true. Bertie Costain had lost control. The crap had hit the proverbial fan and to avoid the immediate fallout Bertie had made himself scarce. What Howard found hard to believe was that the man could have left Kitty to deal with it. What a bastard! Howard did not know her very well and had been shocked when Bertie announced he was to marry her. It had all happened in a heartbeat. At the time Bertie had appeared happy, which he had never really seemed before he met her, but this had not stopped Howard feeling slightly uncomfortable about it. Kitty was attractive, yes, but she was a good few years older than Bertie and according to Marcus, extremely wealthy. Howard had never wanted to believe Bertie had married Kitty solely for her money. Now he wondered. After all, he hadn't believed Bertie was addicted to gambling and moved into the big stake league, either.

Visualizing Brian Smith and his head honcho standing on the steps at Wentworth Place, Howard's blood ran cold. They would have looked so out of place in that genteel residential area, doubtless wearing dark suits, chests pushed out and legs apart to show off their considerable build. They did not need to openly intimidate, their size did that for them. The fact that they had turned up early in the morning indicated the debt was eye watering and one way or another they intended to collect what was owed to them. They were well known for their special tactics when debts were large and it always started with intimidation. If that didn't yield results, physical violence came next. In Bertie's absence they had instead frightened the life out of his wife, damn them. Howard banged his fist down on his desk in frustration and anger. Unfortunately, this time there was no top notch building contract to rescue Bertie Costain. In fact he could think of nothing short of World War Three being declared in the next hour to take the heat out of this dire situation.

With these thoughts tumbling over each other, Howard did not hear Mr Boy pad across the room. Reaching his master's feet, the old dog sat, lifted his front paw and placed it on Howard's leg.

Feeling the soft warm touch, Howard looked down, a smile curving his lips at the sight of his faithful friend, 'Hello boy,' he said, grateful for the distraction. 'You want to go out again?' he asked, stretching his hand out and stroking the grey thinning fur on the old dog's head. To his sadness, Mr Boy could not settle for long before he asked to go out. Earlier in the week Howard had taken him to the vet, but apart from a box of pills, which Mr Boy refused to take without his favourite treat, it seemed old age was catching up with him and for that there was no treatment. 'We all use the lavatory more as we get older,' the vet had told Howard sagely. He didn't like to think his best friend was old, but the changes of late were undeniably noticeable. Although it was inevitable, for now Howard didn't want to go down the road to when Mr Boy would no longer be with him. It hardly seemed like yesterday when the little rascal had raced around the place at breakneck speed. When he wasn't on full throttle digging holes in the park gardens and giving off enough energy to stoke a steam engine, he would be exercising his teeth shredding rugs and shoes and even chewing pieces of furniture. Mr Boy had continued to act like a mad puppy until he was around five. Howard, who had tired of buying new slippers, had waited impatiently for the dog to calm down. Now he wished the time back. Sadly, Mr Boy's madcap days were long gone. He was content to do as little as possible just so long as his master was nearby.

Howard pulled himself up straight. 'Come on, you can cock your leg in the yard,' he said, more cheerfully than he felt. Wishing his own life was as simple as his dog's he smiled down at the old spaniel. Right now he would swap places with Mr Boy in the blink of an eye. At the sound of his master's voice the dog wagged his stump of a tail and staggered to the door, waiting for Howard to let him out.

Leaving Mr Boy to sniff round the courtyard, Howard shut the door to keep out the cold air and moved to the window to watch him doing his rounds of the various stunted weeds. 'Cock your leg' was, of course, a euphemism. If Mr Boy tried that he'd fall over!

The more Howard thought of Kitty's call the more he realised he could not do this on his own. He would call Marcus after all. The solicitor would at least know the legal implications. He would also be able to comfort and help Kitty, whom he had known for many years. 'My God, how did this all get so out of control?' he asked the empty room and with no answers likely to come, walked over to the phone.

Ten minutes later, Howard replaced the receiver. His call to Marcus had proved timely. Kitty had also spoken on the phone to the solicitor. After a brief conversation, Marcus confirmed he was on his way to Wentworth Place. Thankful for this news, Howard felt slightly better.

A short bark sounded from the yard, a reminder that Mr Boy was outside. Striding across the office Howard pulled the door open. A wagging stump and a yap greeted him. 'Come on in,' he beckoned, adding, 'no doubt you've piddled on all the weeds helping to kill them off.' With slow steps Mr Boy dawdled to his water bowl and gulped a drink, then flopped down on the soft mat under the desk. 'Want a biscuit Mr Boy?' Howard said, rattling the tin where he kept small, bone-shaped dog biscuits. At the sound of the tin, Mr Boy's ears pricked up. His deafness was at times selective!

'Here you are, that'll keep you going till I get back,' Howard said, dropping two treats on the mat. Picking up his car keys from the desk, his heart heavy and his thoughts racing, he strode to the door, saying over his shoulder, 'Good boy, have a sleep, I won't be long.' It was usually a lie, but not today, he hoped.

Chapter Thirty-Five

Twisting the safe key round in her hand, Kitty's heart still raced even though it had been nearly an hour since she had closed the door to the two men from Raffles. She had looked on as they strode back to their black limousine and wondered how she had kept her composure. Having never been one for drama, feeling that excess emotions should be contained, especially in the presence of others, and particularly strangers, Kitty's early morning visitors had almost been her downfall.

The two burly men had tried to cushion the blow on the sum of money Bertie allegedly owed them, but no amount of fancy words would change the debt they claimed her husband had run up. Kitty had struggled with the enormity of what Smith told her and as shock gave way to fear, her head had swum and a feeling of giddiness had her clutching the surface top. She had tried to stay upright on legs that had changed from muscle and bone to jelly. Smith and Bryant had warned her that the debt was considerable before disclosing the amount, but until that moment she had not appreciated their definition of the word. Only the previous day she had in the end sorted out Mr Walker with little fuss and ridiculously she had believed a cup of fresh coffee and her signature on a cheque would once again put everything to rights. But the Raffles men were not Mr Walker and she had been not so much wrong as completely out of her depth.

Seeing she was about to slither to the floor, Brian Smith had leapt to his feet and was at her side in an instant. It was only after the room had stopped spinning that she realised how amazingly agile he was for such a heavy built man. 'Mrs Costain,' he had said, concern making his voice sound gentle, and at the same time had encased her cold hand in his bear-sized paw, his other one sliding round her waist to guide her to a seat. She had slumped down on the nearest chair and he had added, 'Mrs Costain, we did not come here to upset you and I am sorry. It is your husband we need to talk to, but as the circumstances are so dire it is important you understand why we are here.'

She had looked up into his face. Close up she had seen he had soft brown eyes, but no matter how soft his eyes were, it did not take away the reason for the men's visit. 'How could you have allowed it to happen?' she had whispered. 'Why didn't you stop him?' But Smith had simply shrugged his shoulders and replied, 'Your husband is not a child, Mrs Costain. It is not for us to tell him "No" as if he were. Believe you me, we have cautioned him on numerous occasions, haven't we Kevin?' He had looked at his colleague, who nodded in confirmation, 'Yes, lots of times,' he said, all the while looking around him in a way that made Kitty's blood run cold. It was as though he was estimating the value of the house and its contents and doing sums in his head.

As the colour returned to her cheeks and she had felt less light-headed, her unwelcome visitors had left, insisting that she call them the moment Bertie returned. After closing and locking the door she had phoned Marcus and as much as her panicky voice would allow, had explained what had taken place. Throughout her garbled speech he had listened in silence. When she had finished he had insisted he was on his way. Grateful was hardly the word that sprang to mind at his concern. He had suggested she call Howard Silvershoes, who might just know where Bertie had gone. This she had done. Finally, she had phoned Julie and asked her to open up the shop and call her immediately if anyone came asking for her. Kitty had not explained further, there would be time enough for that when she could speak without betraying her fear about all that was happening.

Fortunately, Julie had assumed Kitty was unwell. 'You stay tucked up warm in bed and get yourself better, Mrs C. There's no need to worry about a thing,' she had said. The irony of those words did not escape Kitty, who had burst into tears the moment she put the phone down.

Now, looking down at the key in her hand, she braced herself to open the safe. She wanted to believe the transfer slip for the money paid to Brightlands Lettings would be in there; that Bertie would not have left Flo Watson to be evicted; that the men from Raffles were a figment of her imagination, and right now she wanted to believe the moon was made of cheese!

Oh God, how had this all happened without her having any inkling? Everything was so farfetched and unreal. It occurred to her that her husband was in the wrong job, he should be on the stage for he was a consummate actor. Would anyone believe she had no knowledge of what had been going on under her very nose? Kitty sucked in her breath, gripped the safe key tightly and strode down the hall.

Entering the library she crossed over the large Persian rug in the middle of the floor, her eyes focused on the wall panel that hid the safe. Running her finger along the oak panelling she felt for the tiny switch concealed in the dark wood and locating it, pressed hard. The panel flipped open to reveal a large safe. Kitty's heart beat faster as she pushed the key into the lock, turned it and pulled open the heavy steel door. Wide-eyed, she stared at the mound of papers. She had not looked inside the safe for months and was amazed at how much was in there. Kitty expelled her pent-up breath in a loud groan. How on earth would she find a bank receipt amongst all this lot?

Placing both hands in the deep cavity of the safe, she took hold of a pile of documents and laying them down on the floor, began searching.

A noise outside the room stopped her.

Listening, Kitty stood up. Leaving the papers scattered on the floor and the safe open she hurried to the door. Looking down the hall she spied Mrs Dobbs removing her coat. Damn, she had forgotten to phone the cleaner to tell her not to come in today. Kitty winced at her absent-mindedness then accepted it was understandable given the circumstances. It was too late to suggest Mrs Dobbs should put her coat back on and leave. *'Oh God, I wish Flo was here,'* she thought, the ghost of a smile touching her face at the thought of what her old housekeeper would be saying right now. Even Flo's worst fears had not predicted this!

'Good morning Mrs Dobbs.'

Startled, the cleaner stared down the hall, 'Good morning Mrs Costain. I'll admit you're the last person I'd expect to see at this time of the day,' she chirped, bustling forward, a shopping basket balanced on her left arm. She stopped in front of Kitty, a frown darkening her pretty face, 'My, you do look pale, Mrs Costain,' she said, sucking in her lips, 'are you all right?'.

Kitty felt pale and right now Mrs Dobbs was the last person she needed strutting round the house daubing beeswax on every stick of furniture and making the place reek of lavender. How she wished she had remembered to put the woman off, but she hadn't. With resignation, Kitty accepted that for the moment, what was done was done. At least Mrs Dobbs could make a pot of tea for Marcus and Howard when they arrived. Of course, if Bertie could not find the full amount to pay Raffles, the chances of a cleaner continuing to work here were slim. Just thinking about the sum of money her husband owed made Kitty feel sick.

Finding her voice, she replied. 'No I'm not feeling too good today, Mrs Dobbs, but it is nothing to worry about. Maybe you would just tidy up and wipe down the kitchen and leave the rest for today. I have some people arriving shortly. Perhaps you would make up a tray with a pot of tea for them. After that you can take the rest of the day off.' Seeing Mrs Dobbs' mouth turn down, Kitty quickly added, 'Of course you will be paid as a normal day. It's just that after my visitors have gone I'm going to have a lie down.' Heat crept up her neck at the lie. Taking to her bed was the last thing she would be doing, but her cleaner didn't need to know that.

'Whatever you say Mrs Costain, all I ask is you look after yourself. Of course I'll be more than happy to brew a pot of tea. How many people are you expecting if you don't mind me asking?'

'There will be two. Mr Greengrass and Mr Silvershoes,' Kitty informed her.

'Leave it with me,' Mrs Dobbs called, ambling back down the hall and humming *'All things bright and beautiful'* as she went.

Returning to the library, Kitty removed more papers from the safe and scanning each one placed them to the side. The next document she picked up she recognised as the transfer of fifty percent of the house to her name. As she stared down at what she had put her signature to on that day, which now seemed so long ago, bile rose in her throat. She had thought it was a gift; she now realised it had been nothing more than a precaution. Bertie must have known that since she had no liability for any debts, no court would grant his creditors a charging order to sell the house when she owned half of it. So even then, her husband had been fully aware of what he was risking, and yet it had not stopped him gambling. Kitty took a closer look at the document she had signed, realising she had never read it properly before and as she did so now, all the colour left her face. *'Oh God, Bertie, how could you have done this to me?'* she cried out silently, every organ in her body gripped by fear.

Putting the document to one side she rooted frantically through the rest of the papers, grateful to find nothing more with her name on it. But there was no bank receipt for the payment to Brightlands Lettings either. Somehow, from the moment she had opened the safe, Kitty had known it wouldn't be there. She wanted to scream at the top of her voice, tear the papers to shreds, but more than that she wanted to ask Bertie *why*? Taking several deep breaths, she pulled herself to her feet and with anger grabbed at the pile of papers and shoved them back inside the safe. With the floor now clear, Kitty slammed the door shut and locked it. Gripping the key tightly she pushed the wall panel back in place and leaned against it. She needed to do something, but what?

'Mrs Costain,' Mrs Dobbs peered round the door, 'Mr Greengrass has arrived. I've shown him into the drawing room. By the way, I've lit the fire in there so you'll be as warm as toast. I'll go and make the tea now.'

Kitty spun round at the sound of Mrs Dobbs' voice and to her consternation saw pity in the cleaner's eyes. Did she know? Had she suspected what was going on? Who else knew her husband was a cheat and a gambler? 'Thank you Mrs Dobbs, I'll be through in a moment,' Kitty said, trying not to second guess what the woman was thinking.

Slipping the safe key into the pocket of her housecoat and holding the damning document to her chest, she waited for her heart to stop thumping, needing to compose herself before she spoke with Marcus. Some moments later, passing the telephone table in the hall, she picked up two of the envelopes the postman had delivered earlier and slipped them into her pocket with the safe key.

Chapter Thirty-Six

Entering the drawing room, Kitty hesitated at the sight of Marcus standing with his back to the fire, a pensive look making his features appear sharp. From the corner of her eye she saw a tea tray had been brought in and placed on the low table. She was thankful Mrs Dobbs had brought the refreshments before she spoke to Marcus. She didn't know the cleaner well enough to know how discreet she was, but the less she overheard the less she would have to talk about. Now, looking down at herself, Kitty was conscious that she was still in her housecoat.

'You find me in a sorry state,' she said, flustered, biting on her lower lip. 'I'm sorry, Marcus. Oh listen to me, where are my manners. Thank you for coming at such short notice.' She tried to speak lightly, gave a weak smile, but as if her feet had been glued to the floor, she watched Marcus stride towards her and at the sight of the sympathy etched on his face, felt her resolve disintegrate. Clutching the papers to her chest, she blinked back the tears that stung her eyes. Inwardly she felt as if she were drowning.

'My God, Kitty,' Marcus said, his pain visible in his eyes. Arms outstretched he pulled her to him, wrapping her slight body in his embrace and holding her tight. The warmth of her old friend and adviser was too much and the tears she had held at bay cascaded down her face, the pent up emotions of the last twenty-four hours unleashing a storm of sobs.

'It's alright Kitty,' he soothed, keeping his grip around her, 'let it out.'

She let Marcus hold her, glad there was someone to talk to who knew her well enough to accept her dishevelment and distress. Moments passed before she began to feel calmer. Pulling back she looked up into Marcus' face. 'I'm sorry,' she said, her voice strangled.

Slowly removing his arms from around her, he pushed his hand into his trouser pocket and pulled out a clean, folded handkerchief and shaking it out, handed it over. 'Here, take this.'

'Thank you Marcus, I'm so sorry.'

'Stop apologising, there is no need, what has happened would have the good Lord Himself breaking into tears. Come, let us sit down and try to find out what damage Bertie has done,' he said, guiding her to a chair next to the fireplace. As she sat down, he squeezed her arm affectionately. 'We'll sort it out,' he said, his calm voice reassuring her.

Kitty wiped her nose and watched Marcus step round the large, low table before lowering himself into the firm leather sofa opposite.

'From what I have discovered, the damage is quite far reaching,' she said, screwing his handkerchief into a damp ball.

Marcus crossed his legs and leaned back, his gaze not leaving Kitty. 'What have you discovered since I spoke to you on the phone?'

She dropped the papers she had been clutching onto the table between them and rummaging in her pocket pulled out the two letters. 'I found this document in the safe, and these arrived with the post this morning. Both are addressed to Bertie. I know it is wrong, but in light of everything, I think it would be wise to open them.' With a hand that shook she placed the letters on top of the papers.

Marcus shuffled forward and balancing on the edge of the sofa, pulled out his reading glasses from the breast pocket of his jacket. Slipping on the spectacles, he pulled the document from under the envelopes and peering through half-moon lenses, perused them. Without a word, he placed them back on the low table. Reaching out he took the two envelopes. Slitting open the one from the garage, he extracted the contents and read what was written on the single sheet of foolscap. Remaining silent, he slit open the second envelope, pulled out a letter typed on heavily embossed notepaper and read that too, his face revealing nothing. Holding her breath, Kitty watched his every move.

Whipping his reading glasses off, Marcus waved them in the air like a baton. 'Before I talk about the two letters, I'd like to address this,' he tapped the document she had unwittingly signed.

Kitty nodded and remained silent.

'Have you ever loaned money to Bertie?'

The question should not have come as a surprise, nonetheless she had the feeling that whatever she answered would not be a good response. Not meeting his eyes, she nodded. 'There have been two large loans. Bertie said he needed the funds to pay suppliers while B.C. Builders had a temporary cash flow problem. The first loan was a couple of months after we married and the second was whilst he waited for the Town Hall contracts to be signed. Bertie was agitated that he had not been able to pay me back either loan and insisted on giving me fifty percent of the house. He said it was his way of showing how much he appreciated my help. Those were the papers he had drawn up.'

Embarrassed that she had not sought Marcus' advice, which had been her initial instinct before signing the document, she swallowed hard and continued. 'The day we signed we celebrated at Pierre Duval's…' she hesitated and lifting her head made eye contact with Marcus. 'Pierre witnessed our signatures,' she explained. To her own ears it sounded implausible that a woman of her maturity and experience had been so gullible. Shame oozed out of every pore and she did not miss the look Marcus shot her at her disclosure. Was it pity or anger? Under normal circumstances she would not have signed such a document without his seal of approval, but Bertie had reassured her everything was in order. That night her head had been light from vintage champagne and expensive cognac. It had never occurred to her that Bertie would deceive her. She had convinced herself that to insist on her solicitor checking the documents would have been akin to a slap across her husband's face. It was, after all, a gift. Only now, having read the documents before handing them to Marcus, was she aware of what she had really signed her name to and that it was anything but a gift.

'As you say, Bertie appears to have gifted fifty percent of the house to you, but in fact the papers are false and if tested would not hold up in a court of law. However, they look sufficiently authentic for a loan shark to lend against them. It seems to me,' Marcus reached out and grabbed at the papers, pulling one particular sheet to the front, 'he has used you as co-owner to borrow against your name, thus making you liable for the debt. Here are the loan details,' he waved the sheet of paper in the air. 'I'm afraid Bertie used your earlier loans to him as a lever for you to sign this.' He tapped the other sheets before dropping the one in his hand onto the table.

Marcus confirmed her fear. She had been inveigled into signing her name for a large loan against the house. Renewed panic gripped her. Kitty saw Marcus stare at her and knew he was trying to understand why she had done what she had done. Even if she told him every detail, it would sound ridiculous and a betrayal of his trust. Instead, she told him how the papers had come to light that morning. 'Had I not opened the safe to look for the payment slip for Brightlands Lettings I would not have seen the document.'

'Brightlands Lettings?' Marcus questioned, his eyebrows arching.

'Did I not mention that on the phone? Probably because I was so shocked by my visitors from Raffles that Mr Walker paled by comparison.'

'No, you said nothing about Brightlands,' Marcus shook his head. The look on his face disturbed her.

'Yesterday is when it all started,' she began, and proceeded to tell him what had happened, ending, 'I entrusted most of the money for five years rent to Bertie, but it seems he never paid it to the letting company. He told me he had, even showed me what I thought was a bank receipt for the transfer. I was looking for it in the safe this morning, where he told me he'd put it, hoping beyond hope to find it there. I wanted to clutch onto something that was true about Bertie, but of course there was no proof of payment, instead I found the papers about the loan.' Anger and despair swept over Kitty in waves. 'Just where will it all end?' she murmured and saw an answering anxiety creasing Marcus' face into a heavy frown.

'Not wanting to pile more kindle onto the pyre,' he said, 'you need to know about the two letters. The one from the bank is regarding non-payment of the mortgage.'

'Mortgage? What Mortgage?' she cried out.

'The one for here.'

'But Bertie told me he owned the place outright!' She let out a humourless peel of laughter. It was a bitter sound that rang round the room. 'Good God, will it never stop? He told me he had inherited this beautiful house from some old chap after he had agreed to modernize the place. I take it that was another web of lies?'

A sardonic smile twitched on Marcus' lips. 'Believe it or not he was telling the truth that time. He did inherit the house and he did turn the ruin of the place into something extraordinary and beautiful. All of this happened before he started gambling heavily, believing himself invincible. Fifteen months ago he went to the bank for a mortgage and handed them the deeds. I was involved in the legal matters, hence how I know.'

Shocked, Kitty stared unseeing at Marcus, her thoughts turning inward. She had lived a lie for the last year with someone who was a genius at deception. Her marriage was a lie. The road they had travelled down was of one of deceit and treachery. Bertie had deceived her at every turn. He had never loved her. That too was a lie. All he had loved was her money. *'How right you were, Flo, I should have listened to you.'*

Marcus picked up the letter and handed it over to Kitty, 'As you can see from the tone of the letter, legal proceedings will be implemented for repossession if Bertie does not contact them and pay the arrears by the end of the month. I'm surprised they have not started legal proceedings before now. It would appear he has ignored several previous warnings.

'So that's why he was always so eager to meet the postman,' Kitty thought grimly. Not only was she about to lose a considerable amount of money, the house she had believed she jointly owned was on the point of being repossessed. 'Where does that leave Raffles?' she asked.

'Raffles!' Marcus snorted.

'Yes, they mentioned something about taking the house in payment for the debt Bertie owes them.'

Snickering, Marcus said, 'Did they now, well they have no chance, not with the bank snapping at Bertie's heels. It will take precedence, of course.'

'It's like a bad dream, Marcus.'

'More like the worst nightmare,' he commented. Taking hold of the other letter, he held it out to her, but she could guess what it said before Marcus' next words confirmed it. 'This is from the garage. The new car you are driving is not paid for. Michael Middleton is screaming for payment, hence the letter. I fear your car too is about to be repossessed.'

Kitty felt numb and yet she was still breathing and able to speak. 'Why should I be surprised,' she cried. 'Of course, it was another of his so-called gifts. I wonder how many more of those I've received during this marriage have not been paid for. I was deceived into selling my MG Midget, though I have yet to receive any money for it. I imagine Bertie pocketed that too, though in the scheme of things it is of no consequence.'

Marcus nodded. 'I fear so. By the way, I never did draw up the papers for you to hand fifty percent of your Wimbledon apartment and Rosebuds to Bertie, I was waiting for you to insist,' he said, not taking his gaze of Kitty.

Warring feelings of relief, shame and embarrassment tore her apart. 'Did you know about Bertie?' she asked quietly.

'I confess I suspected, but—'

He broke off at a knock on the door. 'Sorry to interrupt, Mrs Costain,' Mrs Dobbs said, pushing open the door, 'I've got Mr Silvershoes in the hall. Shall I bring him through?'

At the sound of Mrs Dobbs' soft voice, Kitty swivelled round in her chair wondering why she had not heard the door knocker. 'Yes, please show Mr Silvershoes through and then would you bring a fresh pot of tea and another cup and saucer. I'm afraid we've not touched this one. And after you've done that, please take the rest of the day off.'

The cleaner nodded resuming her cheerful countenance. 'Are you sure, Mrs Costain, only I've a list of things I could do?'

'I'm sure.' Kitty automatically returned Mrs Dobbs' smile, 'They'll still be there tomorrow.'

'Well, if you say so, Mrs Costain, thank you very much. I'll be back in the morning mind.' Kitty did not argue, she had enough to deal with right now.

As Mrs Dobbs scuttled away, Howard entered the drawing room. Kitty got to her feet and crossed the room to him, holding out her hand. 'Thank you for joining us, Howard. It's good to see you.'

'I wish we could be meeting under different circumstances,' he said, taking her proffered hand.

Kitty did not miss the drawn look on his face or the anxiety in his voice as he held her fingers tightly between his large cold hands. She was aware there was little he could do to sort out what Bertie had done, but she had asked him to come for several reasons. He was an old friend of Bertie's and he had connections with B.C. Builders, or at least she had been led to believe that was the case. Howard also knew Marcus and it made sense to have them here together. She needed Marcus, both as an old friend and also to help her understand, if possible, what her position was in all of this, and Howard may be able to shed a little more light on the 'real' Bertie.

'Please sit down, Howard,' Kitty indicated the seat next to Marcus. 'Mrs Dobbs will bring us a fresh pot of tea,' she said, adding, 'if only drinking tea would solve all our problems, England would be paradise on Earth!' Wondering where that platitude had come from Kitty thought perhaps she was losing her mind along with everything else. To cover her confusion she asked, 'How is Mr Boy?'

'Getting old, like me,' he said, shaking hands with Marcus before settling on the edge of the sofa.

'As aren't we all,' Marcus murmured with a smile.

Rubbing his hands together, Howard grimaced. 'It's cold out today. I'm still trying to get my head round what Bertie has done. I take it you've still not heard from him?'

'Nothing at all,' Kitty sighed, dropping into the chair opposite the two men.

'Nor have I. In fact I've not spoken to Bertie in a long while,' Howard said. Then getting to his feet he paced across the floor and reaching the window spun round and paced back to the sofa. Resting both palms on the back he leaned forward and addressed Marcus, 'B.C. Builders is not in good shape. I've no idea what the books look like today, they were not brilliant after he lost the Town Hall contract and—'

'What do you mean?' Kitty cried out, cutting across whatever Howard had been going to say. She stopped abruptly as a gentle knock on the door sliced into the tense atmosphere of the room.

Three sets of eyes watched as Mrs Dobbs placed a fresh tea tray down on the low table. Then picking up the one she had brought earlier, the contents untouched, she backed out of the room. 'I'll see you tomorrow then, Mrs

Costain,' she said in a hesitant voice, gazing at the two men.

'Thank you Mrs Dobbs,' Kitty said, knowing there would be no work tomorrow or any other day for the new cleaner. Another matter she needed to deal with. She would have to phone the woman later and explain... but explain what, that there was no money for her wages? Kitty shuddered at the thought. It was all too difficult to think about just now.

As the door closed, she sprang to her feet, 'What do you mean he *lost* the Town Hall contract. He told me he had won it. We celebrated his success. He said it would solve all his recent problems with cash flow....' Her voice trailed away, fresh tears springing to her eyes.

Exchanging looks with Howard, Marcus remained silent.

'Please, will one of you tell me about the Town Hall contract,' Kitty cried, staring from one to the other.

'It was a lucrative contract certainly, and Bertie was indeed the favoured builder; that much was true,' Howard ventured. 'But someone connected with Brian Smith also wanted it and Bertie was forced to step out of the frame in lieu of a huge gambling debt to Raffles. I'm sorry, Kitty. It was me who arranged it. At the time it was the only way to get him out of the hole he had dug for himself. I knew it was either that or lose BSB's altogether. At the time Bertie was sure he had been set up and I was inclined to agree with him, but there was no proof. Now I'm not so sure.'

Not missing a beat, Kitty rounded on him. 'So you knew he was gambling for high stakes and therefore what he was capable of doing, and yet you colluded with him. Did it never occur to you to mention it to me?' As soon as the words slipped out of her mouth she regretted them. She could no more blame Howard than anyone else. Bertie was a grown man who knew what he was doing. Or did he?

Dropping back into the chair, the wind gone from her sails, she studied Howard's face and saw as much misery there as she felt. 'I'm sorry, that was uncalled for. You could no more stop Bertie from doing what he wanted than any one of us.'

'I was of the opinion that it was a valuable lesson. I thought Bertie had realised the enormity of his error and would stop before he lost everything. He swore to me that he would stop gambling. Clearly that has not been the case. I'm sorry Kitty, I really am.' Howard met her gaze and there was no doubting that his apology was sincere.

Not sure if she could take any more, Kitty rested her head against the back of the chair and closed her eyes. Right now all she wanted to do was leave Wentworth Place and pretend she had never heard of Bertie Costain. That was exactly what she would do as soon as she knew her position in all of this. And yet, despite everything, deep within herself she still loved him. That is to say, she still loved the man she had thought he was. It was this that cut her to the quick.

Opening her eyes Kitty sat up and observed the tense posture of Marcus and Howard, both of whom looked like condemned men on their way to the guillotine. It was time to take the bull by the horns; she needed to know the full extent of the damage. Gritting her teeth, she asked in a steely voice, 'Between us do we have any idea how much Bertie has lost? More importantly, I want to know how it all affects me.'

She already knew in part: the pages attached to the back of the document she had so foolishly signed that night at Duval's were for a loan that was considerable. Kitty was fairly sure Pierre had not known, recalling that he had not bothered to read what he was witnessing. She had no idea if Marcus would be able to help, but if anything could be done, he would move heaven and earth to help her, of that she had no doubt. With her throat dry and sore, her head pounding, she leant forward and began pouring the tea.

'Whichever way you look at it, unless there is a miracle, Wentworth Place will be lost and probably B.C. Builders too, assuming there is anything there left to lose,'

Marcus said. The debt to Raffles exceeds the value of the house. And the house is worth at least three times the national average. Wentworth Place is only for the seriously rich. The deeds are with the bank, which is screaming for payment of mortgage arrears or repossession. Then, of course, there is this other loan in your name, Kitty,' Marcus tapped the document on the table between them, 'but I will be looking into the validity of this. I will do everything in my power to keep your apartment and business safe. There is also what is owed to Middleton's and Brightlands Lettings. The question is, is this everything?'

'Christ, isn't that enough!' Howard exclaimed, shaking his head.

'Brightlands is not a problem for the time being, Marcus,' Kitty said. 'I gave Walker a cheque for the arrears, drawn on my personal account. I had intended to stop it when I found the bank receipt, but, well....' Kitty shuddered and poured too much tea into a cup, which overflowed into the saucer. Placing the teapot down, she ignored the mess. Her hand trembled and her heart was beating faster than a drum roll. 'Please help yourself.' She sat back on the edge of her chair unable to comprehend the enormity of Bertie's gambling.

Marcus turned to Howard, 'As you heard, we have identified a number of people to whom Bertie owes money. It looks very much as if he has lost *everything*.'

As he spoke he cast a surreptitious glance at Kitty, but spotting it, she did not miss the implication. Bertie had most certainly lost her. Or had he? Once again she felt the twist of pain in her gut. How could any of this be happening? How did one love a man so deeply one minute and fall out of love the next? One didn't of course. None of this was about love. It was about what she had to do to survive this, and that meant cutting Bertie Costain out of her life much as one cut canker out of an apple tree.

'Are you aware of anyone else who might be chasing for money?' Marcus asked, turning to Howard. 'It seems to me that declaring himself bankrupt is the only course left to Bertie now.'

Howard nodded in agreement. 'I feared as much. With regard to B.C. Builders, I have found out Bertie's been doing his own book keeping of late. I've tried to speak to him, but my calls to the office have been ignored. I'll be honest; I don't really know what the financial situation is. Bertie appears to have borrowed from anyone and everyone. There are a number of suppliers not paid and several contractors screaming for their money. I imagine wages have been paid out of loans. Bertie has been taking out loans to pay other loans, and clearly that can't go on.' Howard pushed his hand through his hair, 'I will speak to his bank manager later today. Hopefully Max Morgan will be forthcoming. I am sure anyone who has had financial dealings with Bertie will be trying to find him, more so as word spreads about his debts and his disappearance.'

Marcus nodded his head in agreement, 'For now there is little we can do until Bertie returns.' Turning his gaze to Kitty he gave her a sympathetic smile and asked gently, 'Are you going to stay here until he comes home?'

Kitty did not need to think about this question, she had no intention of staying a moment longer than was necessary in Wentworth Place. She would go to her apartment in Wimbledon Village, it was not occupied. Of course, she could go to her daughter's, but she squirmed at the thought, it was the last thing she wanted to do. Sandra would, like many others no doubt, gloat in the knowledge she had been right about Bertie. She would not let Kitty forget how she had pleaded with her not to marry him. For now, Kitty felt the need to hide away and lick her wounds. She needed to slip on a coat of armour before she tackled her daughter, not to mention her friends and the world at large. More than anything she wanted to talk to Flo Watson, because if anyone understood what was happening, Flo would.

With her mind made up, she answered Marcus. 'I'm not staying here. I need to distance myself from my husband for the time being. I will call Mrs Watson and drive out to Primrose Cottage. I need to reassure myself the letting agency have not been troubling her. I assume I have enough left in my investment account to pay for the car? I can't be without wheels. Would you deal with that for me, please Marcus?'

'Of course.'

'After that I will return to my apartment.'

Both men nodded. 'I think it a wise thing to do,' Marcus said, 'you never know who might come knocking on your door looking for Bertie and I'd be happier knowing you were safely away from here.'

The tea brought in by Mrs Dobbs sat cold in the cups. 'I can't thank you enough, both of you,' Kitty said. They had come to see her in an instant and both of them looked shocked and strained as if they shared the terrible state Bertie had plunged her into. Confident they would do whatever they could to help, for now all she wanted was to be alone. She smiled at them, but what she really wanted to do was sob and scream, not so much because Bertie had gambled everything away, but because she had been duped. She had been warned by everyone. Stupidity, vanity, call it what you want, she had allowed herself to be taken in by a handsome younger man; one whose silver tongue could turn tin into gold – or make a woman in her mid-fifties feel young and attractive, even sexy. It was a story as old as the hills and as she watched Marcus and Howard getting to their feet, she knew they knew it.

'Will you let me drive you out to Epsom?' Marcus asked.

'Thank you, you are more than kind, but if you don't mind I'd much rather drive myself. I need some time alone and the drive will help.'

Marcus nodded his understanding. 'I will pay Middleton's a visit on my way and secure the car for you.'

'Again, thank you. I am truly grateful… to both of you.'

As Howard and Marcus made their way across the room towards the door, Kitty asked, 'Marcus, in your years as a solicitor did you ever come across a lawyer by the name of Jeff Dufton?'

Marcus stopped and turned to look at Kitty, a puzzled expression on his face. 'As a matter of fact I did. A fine and well respected man. He died last year. Why do you ask?'

'Amongst all the hullaballoo of the last twenty-four hours, I had almost forgotten that I had a visitor yesterday evening, a young gentleman by the name of Mark Dufton. Claims Bertie is his father.

'What? I don't understand!' exclaimed Marcus, fixing Kitty with a puzzled stare. 'Jeff Dufton idolised his family. Mark was his eldest son. I can't believe…' his voice trailed away and he frowned, perplexed.

'The young man could be Bertie's,' Kitty said. 'He certainly bears a striking resemblance and he seemed genuine.' She snorted, 'If it's Bertie's money he's after, he's out of luck. He'll have to stand in the queue!'

Listening closely, Howard had remained silent, but Kitty noticed a flicker of something behind his eyes and wondered how much he really knew about Bertie. They went way back, he may even have known about Bertie's liaison with Mark's mother. Kitty suspected he knew a lot more than he was letting on and instinct told her that if anyone knew about Mark Dufton, Howard would. Right now it was unimportant, there were far more pressing things to deal with and nothing could be done to change Mark Dutton's parentage.

Kitty shrugged her shoulders, 'It seems to me Bertie Costain is an enigma to everyone.'

Chapter Thirty-Seven

Keeping an eye on his speed, Bertie knew that unlike the E-type, his life was spiralling out of control. He had no idea how long he had been cruising up the M1 heading north. Distance was what he needed; he wanted to be as far away as possible from everything and everyone. Beyond that, he hadn't a clue where he was going.

Keeping a comfortable length between the long bonnet of his Jaguar and the driver in front, he kept to the speed limit. Normally he would be showing off his prize car, roaring past in the fast lane, racing down the road like a bullet from a gun, but not today. The last thing he wanted was to draw attention to himself. Settling into a steady seventy miles per hour, the engine purring and the road noise creating a background hum, he allowed his thoughts to wander. How was it possible that something as simple as a flutter and the odd bet could turn into this nightmare of destruction?

Years ago Wentworth Place had been a gamble, as had his parents' home. He had acquired both in the same way and both had been safe bets, it had never occurred to him that he would lose. As the humdrum years had slipped by and his building company had gone through the highs and lows of an industry that swung like a pendulum according to housing demand, he had found a solution to keeping the lifestyle he enjoyed. He had also found the pleasure and thrill of being a member of an exclusive club; one that had a casino. His bets had started low, bets that he could painlessly afford to lose should his luck desert him and from time to time it did, but each time he lost he was gripped by the conviction that one more bet would make things right. The more he won, the greater his euphoria and the higher the stakes, always thirsting for that adrenalin rush that made him feel invincible. Like a god. Bertie couldn't pinpoint the turning point when he realised he was addicted because it seemed to happen overnight. During the last eighteen months, he was painfully aware his company had suffered. He was seldom there. As more and more people came looking for him he had got into the habit of making himself scarce. Eventually he had been forced to borrow money to pay his creditors, always with the intention of paying it back. Always convinced the wheel would spin in his favour. And from time to time so it did, hugely, allowing him to repay some of his debts, yet there was always a need to borrow more. Then he had married Kitty. So desperate was he that soon after their marriage he had risked asking her for a loan. Fortunately, she had believed his explanation about a cash flow glitch. Even the second time it happened she had not questioned it, such was her faith in him. He had meant to pay her back, but as time had gone on and she insisted he should not worry about it, he had taken her at her word. The chances of repaying her now – or anyone else, come to that – were zilch.

Bertie felt his heartbeat quicken and to distract his thoughts he checked his rear view mirror then flicking the right indicator, pulled out to overtake the heavy goods vehicle in front of him, enjoying the sudden surge of power as he put his foot down. Back in the middle lane, he turned up the volume on the car radio, but after a couple of miles the sounds emitted through the speakers jarred on his nerves and he switched it off. The only thing his mind wanted to process was the list of casualties from his gambling. It was a pitifully long list. To feed his addiction he had taken money from any source he could access, legally or illegally, in the hope of stemming the haemorrhaging. He had known he was losing more than he could earn or owned, yet he found it impossible to stop. It didn't take a genius to work out that in the last few days he had reached the end of the line. He was left with nothing; all lost on gambling. And instead of dealing with it, here he was, on the brink of a nervous breakdown, motoring up the M1 when he should be at home finding a solution and not leaving others to mop up the mess. Not leaving Kitty to mop up the mess, he corrected himself. For perhaps the first time in his life, Bertie was filled with self-contempt and loathing.

As the sign for junction ten came in to view, he slowed his speed and indicated to leave the motorway. He needed to stop. He needed to stretch his legs and he needed to take a pee. More importantly, he needed to close his eyes and try to think of a way out of the impossible.

Once off the M1 the traffic thinned to a point where he found himself the only vehicle on the narrow road. Relieved to see a layby, he slowed, pulled over, killed the engine and switched off the headlights. Getting out of the car, he emptied his bladder into the hedge. It was dark. All he could hear was the distant hum of the motorway. Bertie felt very much alone. Returning to the driver's seat, he gripped the top of the steering wheel, rested his head on his hands and groaned, wishing with every fibre of his being that he could render himself invisible. When had it all got out of control? And how did a decent, hard-working bloke end up running away, not only from all he had worked for, but from the woman he loved; the woman he had deceived, cheated and lied to. At the thought of what he had done to her his groan turned into a sob. Tears squeezed out of his eyes and spilled down his cheeks. He stuffed his fists into his mouth but it had no effect, he could not stop sobbing. He had not cried since he was a small boy, but right now, after all the years of needing to prove he was a big man, it seemed he was nothing short of a cry baby, a big sissy, and far more degrading, a thief and a liar. Worse even than that. Sobs racked his body, he was a broken man. The question was, would he ever be able to put right all he had destroyed? Not sitting here, that was for sure. Bertie knew he needed to go back home and face the music. It was either that or take the coward's way out: turn the car, drive south to Beachy Head and jump off. For a moment he was tempted. Almost. But an image of Kitty came into his head and he knew he couldn't do that to her.

Unchecked, his tears dripped onto his tailored trousers, he couldn't seem to stop. All the losses, the shame, the guilt of the past weeks surged into his throat and he wept like a child. Not trusting himself to drive, Bertie sat in his car and cried himself into an exhausted sleep.

The rattling sound of a tractor rumbling down the lane woke him from a fitful slumber. Opening eyes that were puffy and glued with dried tears, Bertie unfolded himself from his scrunched up position and winced, every muscle in his body screaming with pain. God, he was cold! Confused, for a moment he forgot where he was. Peering through the misted windscreen to take in his surroundings, he groaned loudly as everything crashed back into his thoughts. He needed fresh air. Pulling on the door lever, he nudged the door open and stepped stiffly out of his car, his teeth chattering. The air was frigid, the hedge white with frost, as was the car. He exhaled, his breath creating a cloud of steam in front of his face. His lightweight suit, now crumpled and creased, did nothing to keep the morning chill from his bones. Apart from the distant throb of a tractor and a few birds chirping, the place was silent. No vehicles passed him; it seemed the road was little used; more of a lane, in fact. Reluctant as he was to expose any more parts of his body, he needed to relieve himself. He turned to face the hedge, bare of leaves now, and proceeded to create another cloud of steam.

Returning to his car, Bertie slipped back into the driver's seat and felt beneath it for his road atlas, failed to find it. Where the hell was he? He was lost. In every sense of the word! He vaguely remembered coming off the motorway at junction ten, somewhere in Bedfordshire then? All he had to do was go back the way he had come. That shouldn't be difficult. Running his fingers through his ruffled hair, Bertie pulled a crumpled pack of Bensons out of his jacket pocket and lit up. The smoke caught in his throat and made him cough. It tasted foul. *A stupid habit,* he thought. Winding down the window he flicked the unsmoked cigarette into the hedge then turned on the ignition.

First things first: pulling out into the quiet lane, he set off. He needed to find his way home to Kitty. He couldn't begin to imagine what he would say to her, but he'd think of something. He always did.

Chapter Thirty-Eight

Picking up the tea tray, Kitty tried to take in everything that happened, but try as she might, it was all too much. Bertie's activities were akin to a toilet roll. The more you pulled the more it unrolled until it was in free roll, spilling out into a huge pile. She had believed Bertie was having an affair, had gone rushing out of the house to meet a younger woman. It had broken her heart to think he was cheating on her, but now she wished he was. It would have been easier to accept than the real reason for his sudden departure.

Heading toward the kitchen with half-filled cups of cold tea sloshing around in the bone china cups, a sudden noise stopped her in her tracks. Marcus and Howard had left, the cleaner had gone home, she was alone in the house, or was she? Holding her breath she listened again. The sound came from the kitchen. Unsure what to do, she debated calling the police or perhaps she should enter the kitchen and throw the contents of the tray over the intruder. Hearing the noise again, Kitty inched her way to the kitchen door, kicked it open and found herself face to face with a sheepish Mrs Dobbs.

'Good God, Mrs Dobbs what are you doing here?' she squealed, her taut nerves at snapping point.

"I'm sorry if I startled you, Mrs Costain, it wasn't my intention, only I couldn't just go and leave you. I know you told me to, but seeing you so fraught and on the verge of tears as I brought the tea things in, I just had to stay to make sure you were alright.' As she spoke she bustled over to Kitty and took the tray from her hands. 'I'll take care of these and make you a cup of coffee. What do you say to that?'

Speechless, Kitty looked on as her cleaner took charge of the tray, placing it on the drainer before filling the kettle. 'I'm not sure how your coffee thingy works, so I'll make a cup of instant for you,' Mrs Dobbs called over her shoulder, a soft smile deepening the lines around her eyes. 'Sit yourself down before you fall down,' she added, spooning coffee powder into two large cups she had taken from the cupboard.

Moving across the kitchen to where Mrs Dobbs was fussing with the coffee, Kitty tried to focus on keeping her emotions in check, but there were so many thoughts jostling for space in her head it was difficult. 'Thank you Mrs Dobbs, that is very kind of you,' she said, leaning against the top of the work surface. Kitty was afraid that if she sat down she would not be able to get up again and right now she needed her legs to carry her upstairs. There were a few things she had to pack before she left Wentworth Place, and before she could seek the haven of her old home in Wimbledon she had to drive to Primrose Cottage. Of course she must phone Flo first to warn her of her visit. Kitty wished she had the van from Rosebuds, it would be far more useful than the Mini, but Julie would need it. She sighed as she added the need to talk to Julie to her 'things to do' list, which was growing in her cluttered head by the minute, but until the cleaner was out of the way, Kitty wasn't doing anything.

Handing her a mug of coffee, Mrs Dobbs said. 'I've not been here that long, but long enough to get the measure of what's going on and I just want to say that if there is anything I can do, don't be afraid to ask.' She took a sip of the hot coffee before adding, 'I've some idea what you are going through. I wasn't always a cleaner Mrs Costain. I know it's no comfort to you now, but there were telltale signs when you knew what to look for and I wish I'd said something sooner.'

Kitty closed her eyes, appalled that her private business seemed to be common knowledge. Who else knew, she wondered, striving to stop herself from falling apart in front of this woman, who clearly had more idea of what was going on than she ever could. Opening her eyes, she swallowed hard, had Mrs Dobbs suffered the indignity and loss from someone out of control too? Kitty wanted to ask. She wanted to know if the nightmare ever ended, but she couldn't. The shame, the humiliation and the heart-stopping shock was too much. So instead she found words of gratitude, 'Thank you Mrs Dobbs, you have no idea how much I appreciate your concern.' Kitty knew if she said any more it would be her downfall, she would be pouring out her heart. Lifting the cup to her trembling lips she took refuge in a sip of scalding hot coffee.

'For the record, Mrs Costain, I'm no gossip. What happens in this house stays in this house and should you ever feel you want to talk, I'm a good listener. Believe you me it might feel like the end of the world, and for a time it will seem that way, but it's not. I promise you it's not. Time is a healer, it really is, as I have cause to know.'

Kitty watched as Mrs Dobbs' reached over to touch her arm and then, as if thinking better of it, pulled back her hand and wrapped it round her coffee cup instead. Seeing her in a different light, Kitty was curious to know what had happened in the cleaner's life that she could speak with such authority. Clearly something had and it made it doubly difficult to say to her what now had to be said. Clearing her throat, as a preamble to the blow she had to deliver to this perceptive woman, Kitty began, 'Thank you for your kind words and offer of a sympathetic ear, Mrs Dobbs. Please don't think I don't appreciate it. Somehow I believe you have an idea of what I am going through, but I can't say anything right now because everything is in a state of flux. And because of this, I'm afraid for now there is no position for you here. I am sorry, but I will pay you two weeks wages so you have a time to find a new position without being out of pocket.'

Disappointment flitted across Mrs Dobbs' face before it was replaced with a knowing nod. 'I understand. Thank you too for...' she looked down at her coffee cup before finishing her sentence, '...for the extra. It is very much appreciated and if I get something soon, I'll pay you back.' This said, Mrs Dobbs turned to the sink and poured the remains of the coffee down the plug hole.

'Heavens,' Kitty managed a weak smile, 'there is no need for that. I hope you find another position soon. If you will wait a few moments I will write you out a good reference – I have never known the house to be so sparkling clean.'

Returning Kitty's smile, Mrs Dobbs nodded at the compliment. 'Thank you. Now you go and sort yourself out while I finish in here. Forgive me for saying so, but you look like you're about to drop. I've put clean sheets on your bed, which is where you ought to be. Get some rest. Sleep is the best medicine. I don't want to leave until I know you are comfortable.'

Kitty had no strength to argue. She placed her cup down on the surface top and after thanking Mrs Dobbs once again for her kindness, headed for the library. Pulling her writing paper and pen from the desk drawer she wrote a glowing reference and folded it into an envelope together with some cash retrieved from the wad of contingency money she kept in the same drawer. *'I wonder how Bertie missed that,'* she thought caustically. Writing 'Mrs Dobbs' on the envelope she took it to the hall and propped it against the cleaner's handbag on the hall table. She could hear the woman humming and the clatter of dishes being washed.

Thankful that Mrs Dobbs was still ensconced in the kitchen, Kitty headed upstairs, her mind now teeming with the things she must not forget to pack.

Chapter Thirty-Nine

Bertie swung the car into Wentworth Place, his heart skipping a beat at the sight of Kitty's Mini parked outside the house. It was gone ten o'clock. '*What is she doing still at home?*' he cried silently, his panic bringing him out in a fresh rush of perspiration. He had needed time to get himself together before facing her.

Taking his foot off the accelerator, he let the car slow to a crawl as he attempted to work out why Kitty was not at work. He was so sure she would be at Rosebuds as usual. So why in the late morning was she still here? Bertie was filled with dread at the thought of having to face her. His mind raced, had she tried to ring hotels in Southampton and found him not booked in any one of them? He could explain. He could say he'd stayed with a colleague. Yes, that was it. Then the hairs rose on the back of his neck as a frightening thought wended its way into his head. Gasping at the very idea, he dismissed it immediately. No way would Brain Smith turn up at the house, they had an agreement, he would never do that. But what if he had? Suddenly, Bertie could hardly breathe, it was as if a cold hand was squeezing his chest as he imagined the scene.

He had racked his brains all the way back from Bedfordshire, but he had yet to find an answer on how he could pay back what he had lost at Raffles. The house was spoken for by the bank and no way had he assets to cover even half of what he owed. He swallowed hard, for now he needed to concentrate on why Kitty was home and formulate what he would say to her. He had deliberately left the safe key behind in the knowledge that she would delve into the safe expecting to find the receipt for the rent. Of course there wasn't one. What he had thrust under her nose that night was nothing more than a till receipt from the petrol station. He had known she wouldn't look at it. The only paper she would find of interest in the safe would be the one she had signed in front of Pierre Duval. As the memory replayed in his head of what he'd had to do in order to save himself from the dire situation he had found himself in, shame swept over him. On anyone's scale he was the lowest of the low. A worm's belly was not as low as he was right now. He had plummeted to such a depth he wondered if he would ever see daylight again. Borrowing, gambling, borrowing more… it had turned into a vicious circle. There was no doubt in Bertie's mind that desperation brought out evil traits in people and that was what it had done to him. He was vile. Even leaving the safe key so his wife would discover what he had done was selfishness. Kitty finding out how she had been duped would be the preamble to everything else he needed to tell her. At least that was his intention… eventually.

As he drew level with the red Mini his mind continued to spin, knowing he had no time to clean himself up and prepare for what he had to do. During the long drive he had rehearsed every word he needed to say and here he was in Wentworth Place, struggling to catch his breath, floored by the fact that Kitty was home, panic gripping him like a vice. As he tried to calm down, he could not believe it was only yesterday that he had left here, having lied to Kitty about meetings in Southampton so he could run away, leave everything and everyone behind. He felt as if he had lived a hundred years in the last twenty-four hours.

The journey back had been a nightmare. The E-type was everything it said it should be, thirsty being one of them. The petrol gauge was registering close to empty before he found a small garage open. It was situated on the edge of a picture postcard village: 'Last petrol before the motorway' was written on a large piece of cardboard propped against the single pump. As the owner rushed out to serve him, clearly impressed by the car, the man had insisted on knowing as much about the performance and the body work of the E-type as if he were considering buying for one himself. It still baffled Bertie how he had kept his cool and answered all the questions. As it turned out, the delay at the garage had worked in his favour. Next door was a café and by the time he had explained the whys and wherefores of his car, the place had opened. Thankful for the chance to freshen up and something to wet his lips, Bertie had gone inside. The smell of frying bacon assailing his nostrils reminded him he had eaten nothing other than a sandwich since breakfast the day before. Ravenous, he'd ordered a full English and while the food was sizzling in the frying pan, he had gone to the gents for a wash and brush-up. When he returned to the table, feeling somewhat fresher than before, a large plate of bacon, eggs, sausage, tomato and fried bread was placed on the plastic tablecloth in front of him, together with a manky bottle of brown sauce. With a smile, the thin woman with a cigarette dangling from the corner of her mouth appraised him and winked. He barely noticed; he had long been used to the effect he had on women. Thanking her he had tucked in and despite the specks of cigarette ash, food had rarely tasted so good.

Two cups of strong coffee later, he had got directions to the motorway from fag-ash Lil and left the village. As is so often the way with directions, he had taken several wrong turnings and driven for miles before he eventually found the link road to the M1 southbound. By this time it was busy with commuters heading for London, a slow crawl of snarled up traffic in a blue haze of exhaust fumes. As he joined them all he could think of was Kitty and what he had done to her, and these thoughts were still occupying his mind as he arrived in Wentworth Place.

Seeing no space outside his home, Bertie carried on driving a few yards until he spied a slot further down the road. Parking neatly, he switched the engine off. The question as to why Kitty was at home still nagged away at him. Reasoning he was about to find out and there was no sense in worrying about it, he rubbed his hand over his chin, now thick with stubble, pushed open the car door and stepped onto the pavement. Ignoring the briefcase and suitcase in the boot, he slammed the door shut and locked it. Gritting his teeth he made his way to the front door, fighting against the temptation to flee that weighed him down with every step he took.

Pausing at the bottom of the short flight of steps, Bertie took a deep breath, his gaze resting on the large brass knob in the centre of the door. 'It's decision time, Bertie Costain,' he muttered under his breath, 'your last chance to escape and forget Kitty and all the debt that hangs over your head. So what is it to be? Flight or fight? The question was as heavy as each choice. If he was honest, he had no energy for either. Slipping his left hand into his jacket pocket he pulled out a set of keys. Staring down at them, he gripped them between his fingers, raised his head and with a false bravado marched up the steps. He had made his decision.

Chapter Forty

Kitty sighed with relief when she heard Mrs Dobbs call up the stairs, 'Goodbye then Mrs Costain, I'm off now. I'm fussing I know, but if you don't mind, I'll call you later just to make sure you are alright.'

Kitty wondered if Mrs Dobbs thought she intended to harm herself. Nothing was further from her mind. What she would really like to do was harm Bertie! As grateful as she was for the woman's obvious concern, she knew she would cope much better if she was left alone. It wasn't Mrs Dobbs' fault her life had turned upside down, but Kitty wished she had the personality to be rude and tell her, 'Please just go!' She walked out of her bedroom onto the landing and hung over the bannister, watching with frustration as the cleaner shuffled slowly to the hat stand, pulled her coat from the hook and shrugged into it then fumbled with the buttons, getting them wrong and having to start again. Tempted as Kitty was to rush down the stairs, button up the coat and speed Mrs Dobbs out of the door, she remained on the landing saying nothing, an inane smile on her face.

Looking up, Mrs Dobbs saw her there. 'You should be in bed, Mrs Costain,' she admonished. Take care of yourself and thank you for this.' She waved the envelope at Kitty before stuffing it into her shopping bag. Pulling the door open, she paused, turned towards the stairs again. 'I'm sorry, Mrs Costain, I really am.'

Swallowing hard to keep control and unable to speak for fear of revealing how distraught she really was, Kitty raised her hand to acknowledge she had heard, knowing the minute Mrs Dobbs was out of sight she would no longer be able to stem the flood tide.

As the front door closed and clicked shut, Kitty released her anguish in a storm of sobbing, a torrent of hot, angry tears sliding down her face that did nothing to erase the knowledge of what Bertie had done. Letting the tears drip unchecked to the floor, she pushed herself away from the bannister and with a rush of energy she had no idea she possessed, bolted along the corridor to the large store cupboard at the end and flung open the double doors, the force making each door bang in protest against the wall. Spying a small suitcase, she dragged it out and leaving the doors wide open, marched back to the bedroom. The same bedroom she had shared with Bertie for nearly a year. Entering the room, thoughts sprang involuntarily to mind of all the nights she had lain in his arms; the arms of the man who had deceived her from the moment they had met. With all the force she could muster, she pushed these unwelcome memories away. Dropping the case onto the bed, she snapped it open and in a frenzy of activity pulled clothes from the wardrobe and out of the drawers, flinging them carelessly into the case. As the case disappeared under the avalanche, Kitty stared at the pile of her belongings and swore loudly. 'Damn, damn and double bloody damn,' she yelled, and once again wished she had the van. At least she could have packed up boxes and thrown the lot inside. As it was, she was confined to a suitcase that barely held her underwear. Ploughing through the mountain of clothes, she picked out enough to take for the night. At this moment, she couldn't think beyond getting through today. Pushing the lid down she sat on it and managed to engage the catches until they locked. Hurtling into the bathroom, she filled up her wash bag and took a clean towel from the rail. They would have to go in a carrier bag.

Ten minutes later, gripping these few meagre belongings, she steeled herself to take one last look around the bedroom. She'd had it decorated to her own taste, adding new furniture to make the place feel like hers when she had agreed to live here. She had loved the house the moment she saw it, but then, she had loved Bertie too, so what did that say about her and love these days? It was a question others would be happy to answer for her and she could already second guess their responses. Enraged as she felt, Kitty was hurting and again felt the sting of tears at the back of her eyes. 'You must stop this, Kitty,' she whispered, her voice breaking. She wiped the back of hand over her eyes determined not to weep again, but at the sight of her various toiletries on the dresser, most of them presents from Bertie, she felt a lump of despair in her throat. Catching her reflection in the mirror, she winced. No amount of face powder, rouge and lipstick would do anything to cover her shell-shocked appearance. Making up her face was not important; time was of the essence. She had to leave before any more debt-collectors came calling. Shrugging at the futility of it all Kitty walked out of the bedroom.

Needing to keep control of her emotions, she forced herself to focus on driving to Epsom. She would call Flo from a call box as soon as she was out of town. To stop and telephone her now would delay leaving. What about Julie? That could wait. As she headed down the stairs all Kitty could think of was putting as much distance as she could between herself and Wentworth Place in the shortest possible time.

Reaching the hall she dropped her case and the carrier bag by the table. She needed to collect her handbag and the keys to the Mini – assuming it was still parked in the road and the garage had not towed it away. But no, Marcus would never have allowed that to happen. At this thought, she still wondered what had happened to her MG Midget. The memory popped into her head of Julie telling her she had seen a blonde woman driving it. Kitty had wanted to believe it was a mistake, but after the events of the last few hours she knew it wasn't. Her garage had not known what she was talking about when she had phoned them. It was obvious to her now that Bertie had been lying and had either sold her car or given it away against a gambling debt. Who was the blonde he had owed the money to and what for, she wondered, certain now it was how her car had gone missing. No point in thinking about it; the loss of her Midget paled into insignificance beside the enormity of what else Bertie had done.

Gathering up her keys and handbag, Kitty pulled on her coat, not bothering to button it up, tucked her bag under her arm and was bending down to pick up the suitcase when she was startled by a loud click. Swinging round to where the noise had come from, she saw the front door swing open.

Frozen to the spot, her breath held, she watched as Bertie entered the house. He appeared unaware she was there as he kicked the door shut. Juggling his keys in his hand he turned towards the staircase and stopped dead in his tracks as he saw her.

Kitty opened her mouth to speak, but nothing came out. Feeling her legs about to give way, she backed away, grabbed the balustrade and sank down onto the bottom step.

'Kitty!' Bertie cried, the shock of her presence registering on his haggard face.

She heard her name called out in a voice she barely recognised, one that verged on hysteria. Not trusting herself to say anything at all for fear of what might come tumbling out of her mouth, she remained silent, looking up at the shambles of the man she had married. Gone was the dapper gentleman who oozed confidence and allure, in his place stood a crumpled, dishevelled, unshaven stranger; the china blue eyes, which once had sparkled as he charmed his way into her life, stared back at her, red-rimmed, dull and lacklustre. He appeared to have shrunk in height. Shoulders that were usually held back now stooped forward as if the weight of his head was too much for his neck to support. Taking in the pitiful sight, Kitty wondered dully if this was yet another ruse in order to gain her sympathy, for as she now had cause to know, he was a past master at deception. Staring at the wreck of the man in front of her, it dawned on Kitty that she would never trust him again. No matter how he looked or what he said, nothing would make things right. It was too late for that now.

'Kitty, why are you home? I wasn't expecting you to be here,' he said, slicing into her thoughts.

His voice galvanized her to her feet, anger racing through her like a firestorm. 'What?' she snapped, before she could stop herself. 'Why am I home? You of all people should know the answer to that, or did you believe that you not being here would stop people looking for you?' She stepped towards Bertie and at the same moment he stepped back. 'You ask me why am I home, well I'll tell you. Have you any idea who has been knocking on the door? Have you any idea what you have destroyed? Have you? Have you? Have you?' She stabbed her index finger at him three times, wanting to scream and shout and say more, much more, but her heart thumped as if it was about to burst out of her chest making her pant for breath.

Flinching, Bertie stood silent staring at her.

'Well?' she asked glaring at him, trying with all the will power she could muster to ignore the broken man standing before her, but now she had started she could not stop. Her anger was like a tornado that was growing in momentum and strength, she could feel the muscles around her mouth tightening, a warning to stop, but she couldn't.

'Whilst you did a disappearing act, I have had the men from Raffles here, Brian Smith and his partner, hanging on the door before breakfast seeking you out. When they eventually accepted you were not here, they sat me down and told me everything. Everything they know, which in fact isn't everything, because there is more, as you well know.' Kitty paced over to the telephone table and back, 'I've rifled through the safe and found papers I signed for loans I knew nothing about, I take it you left the key for me to find that out?'

Bertie opened his mouth to speak, raising her hand, Kitty silenced him. 'You see, Marcus and Howard have also been here telling me more hair-raising stories. The thing is Bertie, you're so stupid you believed you could do all this without anyone finding out. Well Mr Costain, the balloon has gone up and we are all feeling the fallout. I just want to know why Bertie. Why? WHY?' Kitty was aware she was shouting at the top of her voice, but she couldn't stop. 'How could you do this to me?'

Seeing the tic twitch rapidly in his left temple, Kitty was reminded of Mark Dufton. It was the final straw. She could not take any more. Dropping her gaze she sank down onto the bottom step and covered her face with her hands. Never in her life had she screamed and roared like a fish wife before and it had robbed her of every ounce of energy. It seemed that even the tears that welled in her eyes were to weary to fall. How had it all come to this? she asked herself, knowing there was no answer. All she wanted was to blot out everything including the heartrending sight of the man she had once loved.

Several minutes passed before Kitty felt the warmth of his body sitting next to her. 'I'm sorry Kitty,' Bertie said, his voice faltering, head bowed and his hands dangling between his knees. 'I know it is a totally inadequate word to utter, but you must believe me, I am truly sorry. What I have done is unforgiveable and unforgettable. I never expected it to get so out of control. It all happened so quickly.'

Lowering her hands from her face, Kitty turned and gazed at the slumped posture of her husband sitting inches away from her. 'Why did you do it to me?' she whispered. Appalled, she heard Bertie give out a sob. Kitty sucked in her top lip willing herself to ignore the pitiful sound. God, was he crying? She had never seen a man cry, apart from John the day he had been diagnosed with inoperable cancer.

'I never meant for it all to get out of hand,' Bertie said in a hesitant, tearful voice. 'I was convinced I would be able to put everything right. I just needed a little time.' Raising his head he turned his tearstained face to her, 'I had planned to pay every penny back as soon as my luck changed and you would never have known what had been going on.' He stopped as if needing to consider his next words, 'No matter what I did, the losses kept growing. I'd always been so lucky in the past, but nothing seemed to work for me anymore.' He reached over and placed his hand on hers. 'It was bigger than me. I couldn't stop. I needed help, I know that now, but I was too stupid to see it then. I'm so sorry....'

Kitty looked down and found she hadn't the heart to pull her hand away. Bertie continued, 'I came back today to tell you everything, but seeing you here threw me. I wanted to have time to freshen up before I confessed to you what I'd done. I planned to tell you everything as soon as you got home. It was important to me that I told you everything. I didn't want everyone else to do that.'

Well you left it a bit late,' she muttered, 'they already did.'

He squeezed her hand, 'I'm so sorry. I'm so very sorry. I had never imagined Smith and Bryant would come to the house or that you would need to involve Howard and Marcus. I thought I could come up with a plan by myself, somehow pay off my debts to everyone, including you; you most of all...' his voice faltered and he drew in a sobbing breath.

Kitty listened, alarmed and shaken by Bertie's confession, but as much as she tried to understand what he was telling her, nothing he said took away what he had done to her. He had lied from the minute they first met. 'What is destroying me Bertie, more than anything, is that I loved and trusted you. I feel betrayed. It is clear to me you never loved me. It has all been one big lie.' She saw the pain in his eyes as he listened. It couldn't match the pain she was feeling.

You think I don't love you? You are wrong there Kitty. My problem is I did not realise how much until it was too late. Until I met you there had only been one person I had ever loved. That was a love that was not meant to be and when it ended I thought I'd never love anyone again. I never meant to; who wants to get hurt? But then I met you and despite my fear I couldn't help myself. I kept telling myself that I didn't really love you, that it was just affection and I couldn't be hurt. But I was fooling myself.'

Kitty wondered if the woman he had loved was the one who had given birth to Mark Dufton. She would like to ask, but her composure was crumbling and she needed to get away.

Bertie paused, cleared his throat, said, 'You're right saying I'm stupid. I'm the worst kind of self-deluding fool.' His hoarse voice drifted across the small gap between them and their eyes locked.

'I don't believe you, Bertie. You led me to believe you loved me when in fact all you wanted was my money. Well let me tell you this: there is no money left for you so you can stop the big act. For a moment there you almost had me convinced, but nobody who loved someone could hurt them like you've hurt me.' She stood up, looked down at him then stepping forward picked up her case and the carrier bag.

Bertie sprang to his feet surprising Kitty at his speed, 'Where are you going?'

'As far away from here as possible,' she retorted, the sting having left her voice.

'Please Kitty, no,' Bertie cried, panic flashing in his eyes. Reaching out he took hold of her shoulders and turned her to face him. 'I have made a mess of everything and I have probably lost all that I possess, but you leaving me will destroy me. Please don't go, I don't think I can live without you. Kitty I love you. It is not an act. I will do anything to prove it to you. I'm begging you, pleading, please don't go, Kitty, please believe me,' he begged. 'I love you so much. More than anyone or anything I have ever known.'

'Even more than the roulette wheel?' Kitty couldn't help saying as her eyes met Bertie's. She swallowed down a sob as more tears pooled in his eyes. His words reverberated in her head, she took in the great sadness and strain reflected in his ashen face, the dark hollows round his eyes, yet in that moment all she could see was the Bertie she had fallen in love with. The Bertie who had made her laugh, the Bertie who had made her feel alive, young, full of energy and who had delighted in spoiling her with special dinners, holidays and presents. The same Bertie she had been so proud to be with, hanging onto his arm, poo-pooing the misgivings of her friends, putting them down to envy. Now, with these images filling her mind, Kitty's heart twisted. All she had to do was wrap her arms around him knowing he would wind his around her, hold her tight in his embrace and kiss her as if they were young and carefree. As if nothing had happened. They would fall to the floor and make love as they had done so many times before, falling asleep in each other's arms exhausted. Tears pricked her moist eyes and her arms, as if of their own volition, moved towards him. She saw hope flare in Bertie's eyes. They were so close, their fingertips almost touching. Kitty wanted to do it. She wanted to feel his embrace again, his soft lips on hers. Suddenly, desperately, she ached with wanting him.

But she could not let it happen. She could not trust him and never ever again did she want to feel this much pain. Lowering her arms, she bent down and snatching up her bags, hurried to the front door. Stepping outside, she peered with blurred vision down the ceramic-tiled steps then turned back to Bertie and saw the tears rolling down his face.

'I love you Bertie. I always have,' she said, her voice low, filled with anguish and pain, 'but right now I don't like you very much.' Not waiting for a response, she dashed to her car. She had to keep going, hang onto her resolve or she would never be able to leave him.

Fumbling with the key to unlock the driver's door, Kitty was aware he was following, heading down the steps. She flung her belongings and handbag into the little car and dropped into the driver's seat. The Mini started at the first pull. Within moments she had pulled away from the kerb. Wiping her hand over her face, she checked the rear view mirror. Bertie stood in the middle of the road his arms outstretched beseeching, his mouth wide open as if howling. Kitty stabbed on her brakes and saw him lower his arms. She wanted to jump out of the car and run to him and hold him and tell him they could work it out together. 'Bertie,' she cried, but then she remembered all the lies and deceit. Barely able to see through her tears, she stabbed at the accelerator making the tyres squeal in protest as she headed down Wentworth Place.

Turning the corner, she slowed down. Almost she stopped. What would become of him? Or of her come to that? *'I can't think about that just now,'* she thought. The ending of *'Gone With the Wind'* came into her mind: *'I'll think about that tomorrow… after all, tomorrow is another day.'* It seemed like good advice. Picking up speed, Kitty headed for Epsom. She had no idea if she would make it to Flo Watson's house, but she needed to try.

Chapter Forty-One

Three years later.

Leaning against the back door jamb, Kitty tugged off her Wellington Boots and dropped them to the ground. Still in her stocking feet, the cold seeping through her socks, she lingered on the step to look out across the garden and smiled with satisfaction at what she saw. It had been a labour of love to turn this overgrown plot into a productive and very pretty garden. The greenhouse nearest the cottage was filled with pots of yellow and purple crocus. In front of it were two long rows of daffodils that were close to flowering, their bursting buds nodding in the early morning breeze. In the large border beyond the small lawn, the ornamental cherry tree, which she had planted two years ago, was rewarding her with a cloud of the palest pink blossom and beside it, like a clump of sunshine, the witch hazel was in full flower, as were the primroses at its feet. The winter had been cold and wet, yet everything was coming on nicely. The garden had weathered the worst of the storms and in more ways than one, thought Kitty, she had weathered them too. It had not been easy, but for her this garden had been a life-saver.

The last three years she had put her energy and time into rebuilding her life, and she had succeeded, though would freely admit that it was not perfect, but then, whose life ever was?

A high-pitched squeaking sound like chalk on a blackboard brought Kitty out of her reverie. She rubbed at her mouth as if to ward off the noise putting her teeth on edge and casting her gaze across the garden, spied Alan Broxup. He was bent over the old wheelbarrow, wheeling it along the path from the far greenhouse. Seeing her, he stopped, eased his back and waved. She waved back and smiling, mimed putting her fingers in her ears. Grinning, he nodded then continued on his squeaky way.

Slipping her feet into the soft leather slippers inside the back porch, Kitty headed to the hall to collect the post which, having seen the postman cycle down the lane five minutes earlier, she knew would be on the mat. Bending to retrieve it, her heart skipped a beat as she saw the Middleton logo on the envelope.

'Goodness, get a grip woman,' she berated herself. But no matter how many times she saw it, the logo never failed to bring back that dreadful January day. Hard to believe it was more than three years ago now. Maybe she should have sold Zippy along with everything else, but she'd had enough to do at the time and besides, she had grown to love that little car. It reminded her of Bertie, the *real* Bertie; the one who had stolen her heart at fifty-five. Her breath caught in her throat: no matter how much time had slipped by, thinking about Bertie still managed to create within her a tangle of emotions. If she was honest with herself, she still loved him. It was a problem that refused to go away.

With her thoughts on Bertie, Kitty carried the letter through to the kitchen and only then did she notice the trail of muddy paw prints on the linoleum floor. 'For heaven's sake,' she cried, knowing full well that Poppy, her young springer spaniel, would roll over in abject submission at the sound of her cross voice, paws waving in the air at the sight of her. And as always, Poppy did not disappoint. She wriggled onto her back, mouth open, tongue lolling, looking for all the world as if she were laughing; her feathery tail – left undocked the way nature intended – wagging furiously. It was impossible to stay cross with her. 'What are you doing in here, you rascal?' Kitty scolded, trying to sound stern and failing. She bent to rub the spaniel's belly, murmured, 'Daft dog. You're supposed to be outside with Alan, not muddying my kitchen floor.'

Knowing she was forgiven, Poppy sprang to her feet and almost as if she understood the ache in her mistress's heart, licked Kitty's hand with a soft, warm tongue. Patting the silky head, Kitty pointed to the back door. 'Out,' she said. 'Go find Alan.' Tail still wagging, the spaniel bounded out into the garden and disappeared up the path.

Dropping the offending letter on the work surface, Kitty knew it could be nothing more than a reminder that her Mini Cooper was due a service. Why did she still allow things to affect her in this way? Just thinking about Bertie upset her equilibrium. Why couldn't she just blank her mind and forget him?

What she needed was a cup of strong coffee. Filling the kettle, Kitty plugged it in and switched it on. Waiting for it to boil, she mopped up the worst of the mud. She was acutely aware that Poppy had been part of her healing process. After her life had imploded, when the full extent of Bertie's deception and his debts had been revealed, she would never have believed that having a dog to look after would help ease her pain. At the time she had hardly felt capable of looking after herself, never mind a lively springer spaniel. But to her surprise the puppy had enriched her life in a way she could never have imagined. The tiny creature had needed her; depended on her. And because of that Kitty had been forced to get up and go out, which had led to her once again becoming part of a community. Needless to say, she had not gone looking for a dog. In fact the whole idea had been down to Howard Silvershoes, who had telephoned her out of the blue one afternoon two years or so ago.

'I wondered if it would be convenient to call in and see you at your new home?' he had asked. The sound of his deep voice had taken Kitty by surprise making her catch her breath, her heart racing as her thoughts turned immediately to Bertie. Had Howard news of him and was that news so bad he needed to break it to her in person? She had hesitated and as if he had read her mind, he had added, 'No special reason, it's just that I am in the area and wanted to see how things are with you.'

Of course she had agreed to see him and to her relief they had barely spoken about her husband. Having ascertained that Bertie was well, she had not wanted to venture further into what her ex might be doing. Howard must have realised this for instead he had talked almost exclusively about Mr Boy.

'No matter how much you prepare yourself for losing your pet,' he had said, 'it makes no difference to your feelings when they die. Mr Boy was at my feet when he closed his eyes for the last time. The vet said he had not suffered. It was his heart. It was time for him to go.'

Although Howard's voice was even, Kitty had seen the deep pain in his eyes and had felt the weight of his grief. She knew that words, no matter how sincerely spoken, would never fill the hole that Howard's beloved spaniel had left in his heart. And so she had kept silent and let him talk.

'It's been several months since I lost him and yet the house and the office still feel silent and empty. I confess I am lonely without him. I keep expecting him to come shuffling from his bed to sit at my feet, his head on my knee. He was special, Kitty; not just a special dog, but a special friend too. Of course I can never replace him, but having said that, I so miss having a dog in the house and the closeness they bring that I have decided to get myself a puppy, hence why I am in the area.'

Howard had looked down at his knee as if he was seeing Mr Boy's head resting there. Returning his gaze to Kitty, he had smiled, 'Forgive me; I am going on a bit aren't I? Anyway, I have driven to Epsom to take a look at some springer spaniel puppies and having seen them I have decided to have one. I need to return in three weeks to collect him and I can hardly wait!'

Returning his smile, Kitty had thought he looked peaceful, as if the weight of losing his dog had been lifted by this decision to have another.

'Have you ever thought of having a dog, Kitty?' Howard had asked. 'They are very good company. I can vouch for that. A dog is loyal and makes a devoted friend, one whose love is unconditional and will never let you down.' There had been no malice in his words, but Kitty had understood what he was implying. Loyalty and devotion had been sorely lacking in her life for a long while.

Two days after Howard's visit, clutching the address he had given her, Kitty had gone to see the puppies. In fact there had been only one left: a liver and white bitch. Staring up at her, the pup's appealing brown eyes had seemed to beg her, *'Take me home.'* Of course, Kitty's heart was lost in an instant. Not long afterwards, the furry bundle of mischief was duly ensconced in Primrose Cottage, which had at the time been Kitty's home for almost a year.

Howard had returned on several occasions, bringing with him Poppy's litter brother, which he had named 'Blu'. Watching their antics as they played together had made Kitty laugh out loud for what had seemed the first time in ages. Since then Howard had become a close friend and she looked forward to his visits, as indeed did Poppy.

With these happy thoughts filling her mind, Kitty picked up the envelope from the garage, opened it and pulled out the letter. It was nothing more than a reminder that her car needed its first MOT. It occurred to her that in one sense the last three years had flown by, and yet in another it seemed a lifetime ago that Zippy had been delivered. Her husband had certainly been one for surprises. And in the letter of the law he *was* still her husband. No matter how many times she had decided to end their marriage legally, she had never quite managed to bring herself to start divorce proceedings, despite Marcus insisting she did so before he retired. For some strange reason that Kitty could not fathom, she had been unable to commit her signature to a document that would spell finality to her relationship with Bertie.

'Damn and double-damn,' she muttered to herself. Why did her thoughts *always* return to Bertie? Pondering this, Kitty carried the mop out to the scullery and washed it under the tap in the Belfast sink, watching the muddy water swirl down the plughole. Still thinking about him, something she did increasingly these days it seemed, she wondered how he was. Was he happy? Had he found someone else? Was he keeping to his word about never gambling? Had he and his son become good friends? So many questions, but Kitty found herself hoping that whatever he was doing now, he was content. She did not wish him ill, not any more. For many months she had wanted to hurt him; make him pay for what he had done; suffer the way she had suffered. And she *had* suffered, not just financially but emotionally.

In order to pay the debt Bertie had borrowed against her name, Kitty had sold her Wimbledon apartment. Marcus had tried to get a reduction in the amount owing, but his intervention had only caused more issues and in the end Kitty had been forced to pay up. Fortunately, the sale had coincided with a sharp rise in property prices, which had enabled her to clear the debt completely, though left her with very little capital. The small fortune left to her by her parents had all gone, but for a time she had managed to pay Flo's rent as she had promised, and Flo had been none the wiser.

Then there had been the sale of Rosebuds, for as much as she had loved her florist shop, the joy had gone out of it. Bertie's bankruptcy had been the talk of the neighbourhood and Kitty, on the verge of a nervous breakdown and unable to bear facing her customers – or anyone else, come to that – had decided to sell up. To her absolute delight, Julie, who had recently inherited a tidy sum from an elderly uncle, had asked if she could buy it. Kitty smiled at the memory of her assistant's joy when she had ceremoniously handed over the keys. She had known Julie would make a great success of the business, and so it proved.

After the sale of Rosebuds had gone through, Kitty had determined that once she regained her self-respect, she would not sit around feeling sorry for herself, falling deeper into depression. She had to find something to do that would get her life back on track and bring in a reasonable income. But what? She didn't much fancy going back into the hotel trade, which aside from selling flowers was all she knew.

By coincidence, not long after selling her shop, it turned out that Flo Watson no longer needed Primrose Cottage. Like a bolt from the blue, Kitty conceived an idea. Flowers had always been her chief love, why not grow them to supply florist shops? She would start a new business, a garden nursery, and Primrose Cottage was in exactly the right place. She had cashed in two small investments, which thanks to Marcus had yielded enough together with the proceeds of Rosebuds to buy the vacated cottage, along with a small parcel of adjacent land, which was ideal for her purposes.

Fired with enthusiasm – she could still remember how her anger had fuelled her energy – Kitty had worked until she dropped. She had been out in all weathers, from dawn until well after dusk; never relenting, knowing it was the only way to still her mind from dwelling on what had happened and make sure she fell exhausted into bed each night, asleep almost before her head hit the pillow. Her self-imposed regime had worked and gradually she had begun to heal.

Keeping busy and constantly tired had also helped her to deal with those who had called themselves her friends. Naturally, tongues had wagged: a town crier could not have spread the news of her downfall faster, but too weary to care Kitty had ignored them all and left them to gossip. With her daughter it was different and she cared a great deal. The disparaging comments about her 'come-down' to a 'lowly cottage' and the gloating, 'I told you so' remarks – Sandra had been strongly opposed to her marrying Bertie Costain – had rubbed salt into Kitty's wounds and she had flung out a few choice words of her own. They had not parted on good terms, but happily, their estrangement had not lasted long. Once time had gone on and they had forgiven each other they had become friends again, if anything closer than before.

'*All water under the bridge, now,*' Kitty thought, squeezing out the mop and propping it outside the back door to dry. These days she had the beginnings of a successful business, which she had opened as "Maddison's Garden Nursery", not wanting any association with the name Costain. Flo Watson, who seemed to know everyone in the locality, had found Alan for her to help with all the heavy work, and soon afterwards, Linda, a girl from the village with aspirations to become a garden designer, had come on board to assist with the seeding and potting on. It had been less than three years, but this year Kitty had turned a small profit and knew she was doing quite well. It was true, she reflected, Mrs Dobbs had been right, time *was* a healer and as the pain had slowly subsided she found herself remembering the Bertie she had first met, the Bertie who had swept her off her feet; the man who had made her feel like a million dollars and who, despite everything, she still loved. But the only being she would admit this to was the four-legged one, presently outside snuffling among the rows of daffodils, doubtless having found the scent of some timorous beastie.

Deep in thought, Kitty returned to the kitchen, almost jumping out of her skin when a voice said, 'Ah, there you are! Goodness me, you were miles away.'

'Flo, what are you doing here?' Kitty asked, puckering her brow having not heard her old friend arrive. Unusually, she must have come in the front way.

Reaching over to switch off the kettle, Flo flapped her hands at the billowing steam that was clouding the window with condensation. 'For a start I'm saving your kettle element from burning out – that kettle almost boiled dry,' she tutted. Pulling two mugs from the pine mug tree and placing them on the surface top, she added, 'And having done my rescue bit, I'm making us a cup of coffee, and then I'm going to tell you my news.'

'What news?' Kitty asked, watching as Flo unscrewed the top off a jar of instant and spooned coffee powder into the mugs.

'I'll tell you just as soon as I've made these.'

As Flo bustled around in her kitchen Kitty wondered if her old housekeeper would ever get used to the fact that Primrose Cottage was no longer her home. The changes in Flo over these last three years were almost unbelievable. Since leaving London, she had turned from a grumpy old woman into a contented, happily smiling old age pensioner. That thought made Kitty laugh out loud, for the woman had more energy than a youngster and anyone less like an OAP would be hard to find.

Flo looked up at Kitty, 'So who's tickled your funny bone?'

'Oddly enough, you have.' Kitty replied. 'I was just thinking that we've reversed roles, you living up in the big farmhouse and me down here in the cottage. Who would have thought it?'

Never in her wildest imaginings would Kitty have dreamt that Flo Watson – Flo Fenton now – could be seduced by an elderly, widowed famer. Brian Fenton no longer owned the land the farmhouse had once been part of, but he was comfortably off. Born and bred in the country he was an honest man who was clearly devoted to Flo. Importantly, he made her happy and after all these years without a man in her life, Flo had found the courage to say 'yes' when he proposed. Married life suited her, that much was plain to see.

'I don't know how you can say that,' Flo retorted, picking up her mug, the steam rising from the hot coffee. 'Mind, having said that, I'm not the one marching around in wellies clart up to the eyeballs with mud, but then, I remember you always did cut a dash in them when you were a horse-mad girl.' Flo placed the mug to her lips and looked over the top at Kitty. 'As you say, who would have thought it? There was me thinking about getting a kitten and before I knew it I was getting a husband into the bargain,' she chuckled. 'Not that I'd been looking for one. Not at my age, but there you are. Anyway, had I not eloped with my old farmer you'd never have been able to buy Primrose Cottage and start growing your own flowers, would you. So I've done you a good turn I reckon. And you've got that nursery of yours looking a bit like Rosebuds, only with clean fresh air. So much healthier,' Flo beamed. 'You're supplying your old shop with flowers now, I gather.'

'Yes, Julie's fast becoming one of my best customers.'

Sipping her hot drink, Kitty wished Flo had not said anything about the shop. It would always have connections with Bertie. One mention of Rosebuds and there he was again, back inside her head, and just when Flo's impromptu visit had served to distract her. Kitty frowned. She should forget him and sort out a divorce. It was the only way she could finally draw a line under the worst time of her life. She would ring Marcus' old office for an appointment just as soon as Flo had gone on her way. Divorce; yes, it was the only way. That is what she must do.

Ignoring the silent cry from her heart and the plunging sensation in her gut, Kitty smiled at her old friend. 'So, Mrs Fenton, what is this news you've been bursting to tell me?'

'I'm going to be a great-grandmother!'

Chapter Forty-Two

Folding the sheet of writing paper in half, Bertie slipped it into an envelope, licked the glued edge and pressed the flap down. Having written the address and found a stamp, he sat for a moment with the letter in his hand, staring down at it, praying that Kitty would not only read what he had written, but would reply to his request.

During the last three years not a day had passed when he had not thought about her. If he was having a good day, he would remember her smile and her energy, but most of all her love for him, which used to shine out of her beautiful green eyes. On bad days, the only image that filled his head was that of a shocked, sobbing woman who had seen him for what he was, her eyes filled with pain, her words revealing her disgust and contempt for him. He could not blame her; he felt the same about the man he had become. Even in his sleep Kitty filled his dreams and there were mornings he woke to find his pillow wet with tears. No matter how much he had lost, and he had lost everything, it all paled into insignificance beside his loss of Kitty.

He had tried to blank out that dreadful morning when she left him, but it kept going round in his head until all he wanted to do was drink himself into a stupor. It didn't help. He had gone to her apartment in Wimbledon and begged her to speak to him. All he wanted was the opportunity to explain, but she had turned him away. He had persisted and eventually she had allowed him in and had listened as he bared his soul and told her every detail of what he had done, begged her to forgive him. Her face had been a picture of misery, and knowing it was all down to him had shattered him into tiny pieces. When he ran out of words, at last she spoke.

'Bertie, you have no idea how much I loved you,' she had said, her voice breaking, 'but not only have you used me, you have destroyed me, both emotionally and financially. I have nothing left. You have taken it all. Worse, you have betrayed my trust. I don't know how I am going to get through the coming months, but somehow I will because I have to.'

He had reached across the low table and taking hold of her hand had held it tightly. 'Kitty, my darling, I am here for you. I will always be here for you. I love you more than anything in the world. I want to protect you from the pain I have caused. Please don't leave me. Together we can work out a plan to sort everything out. Together we will come out the other end of this nightmare still as a couple. Please, darling, give me a chance. Let me show you I am a changed man.'

Even now he could still feel his shock at the way she had looked at him, her expression one of sheer horror. She had pulled her hand away, stood up and paced around the elegant room. For several minutes she said nothing and by the time she eventually spoke, he had convinced himself she was thinking about a way forward, how together they would deal with it all. Then, in a voice that was almost a sob, she crushed his hopes completely.

'I have listened to what you wanted to say to me, Bertie. Now please go. And don't come back. There is nothing here for you.' Striding to the front door she had held it open.

On the brink of collapse he had begged her to reconsider, but his words had fallen on deaf ears. Kitty had remained silent, her taut, white face awash with tears as she continued to hold the door open. He did as she ordered and walked out of the apartment. There was nothing else that he could do, but there and then he made the resolution that he would somehow get her back. He would prove to her that he was the Bertie she had first met, the man with whom she had fallen in love; the determined man who thrived on success. He would show her he was not the lying cheat she thought him. Not any more. Not ever again.

Within days of that bleakest time of his life, the bank had repossessed his home. Nothing had prepared Bertie for the moment when all he had worked for was taken from him in a flurry of legal jargon. Owning a property in Wentworth Place had felt like the jewel in his crown and he had lost it. That was the day he was brought to his knees. The only sliver of light in a storm-laden sky was that the bank had sold the house for a very good price. The sale more than covered the arrears and interest that had accrued over the months of missing his mortgage repayments. Under different circumstances he would have laughed at the irony, instead he felt grateful that even in the most dire moments of his life, luck had not totally deserted him. It did not, of course, take into account his debts to Kitty or the fraudulent loans he had raised in her name, which she now had to repay. The balance from Wentworth Place when eventually returned to him had been used to pay off Raffles. A revised amount had been agreed with Brian Smith who, nervous that he might not see a penny should Bertie be forced to declare himself bankrupt, was quick to accept a deal. It was still not an insignificant amount. To his surprise Smith had invited him back to the club.

'We don't hold a grudge, especially to our top members,' he had said. 'All water under the bridge and as long as you sign a contract that states any debt must be paid within forty-eight hours, then we are all back in business.'

Until then Bertie's sense of humour had deserted him, but at that moment he had laughed out loud. He could not believe how stupid Smith was. The man had absolutely no idea! On reflection, Bertie thought, given his track record it was hardly surprising that Smith should so badly underestimate his determination never to gamble again. Even so, beneath his mocking laughter, Bertie felt a wave of cold fury that Smith thought him so gullible. Clearly the unscrupulous man imagined that once the dust had settled, he would get another chance to wring Bertie Costain dry. Well it wasn't going to happen! Somewhat less than politely, Bertie had told him what he could do with his membership. The shocked expression on Smith's face was priceless.

'If that is your attitude Costain, after all the concessions we've given you, then from now on you are banned from Raffles until you offer an apology in writing... or better still, in blood!' Smith had snarled.

Bertie had responded with a slow smile. 'Hell will freeze over before I ever place a bet again, Smith. You'll get no apology from me. I have no wish ever to set foot in your establishment again. Good day to you.'

Marching out of Raffles, Bertie was almost grateful to Smith. The exchange had stiffened his resolve never to play the tables again. More than anything he needed to prove to Kitty he was no longer a gambler.

His other debts took his building company, his precious E-type and all of the valuable possessions from Wentworth Place. By the end of the day he owned little more than the clothes he stood up in, and still he had debts. Bankruptcy was the only course open to him. Determined to repay every last penny if it killed him – especially what he owed to Kitty – Bertie knew he had to find a job. And it was that more than anything that reassured him he had beaten his demon, for at one time he would have shunned paid employment and gone back to the tables, sure that his luck would turn and make him a million. The thought now filled him with horror; recalling the rush of adrenalin when the roulette wheel began to spin made him feel physically ill.

But finding a job had not been easy. All he knew was the building trade and his reputation had gone before him. Nobody wanted to know. Until one day, his luck had turned and in a way he could never have imagined. Now, three years later, clutching his letter to Kitty, Bertie stood up and pulled his jacket from the back of his desk chair.

He walked through to the front office, calling out to the young woman on reception, 'I'm just popping round the corner to the Post Office, anyone wants me I'll be back shortly.' Slipping into his jacket he headed for the door.

'Righty ho, Mr Costain,' she responded as a light lit up on the switchboard. Pulling her headset on, she answered the call with her usual, 'Good morning, Rounce's Builders, how can I help you?' then listening, held up her hand to stay Bertie. He shook his head and pointing at his watch mouthed *five minutes*. 'Oh dear,' she said into the phone, 'I'm sorry, you've just missed him; he's popped out for five minutes.' She grinned across at Bertie, who had paused in the doorway, 'I'll get him to call you as soon as he returns.' Ending the call, she scribbled a note and left it to one side as Bertie, smiling at her, left the building.

Heading down the road, his mind focused on his letter. Having summoned the courage to write it he wanted to make sure Kitty received it as soon as possible, and handing it over to the post mistress would be speedier than slipping it in the pillar box outside the works entrance. He would rather have delivered it personally, but did not think he would receive a welcome reception. It had been almost a year since they had spoken to each other, meeting by accident on the pavement outside Rosebuds – true it was an accident, but he often walked that way in the hope of seeing her Mini parked outside. The encounter had been stilted; they were like strangers, and the pain was as raw as it had been on the day she had left him. And it still was. After that he had flung himself into work to keep his mind from dwelling on what he then had to accept could never be.

Working all hours had brought its own rewards. These days he was the Building Manager for Rounce's, a small company on the outskirts of London. He was kept busy enough, but he missed being his own boss, maybe one day he would think about doing it all again. On the other hand, he would be fifty next birthday and he wasn't sure he still had the stomach for it. It was dog eat dog out there and of late he had lost his appetite for a good fight. Thinking of dog eat dog he was sharply reminded of Brian Gott, the Poison Dwarf. Though these days he tended to think of him as simply, "the Dwarf". Of all the people – the so-called friends – who had cut him dead or not taken the time to acknowledge him at all after his downfall, Gott had been the exception. It was a strange old world.

'Christ Bertie Boy, what have you done to yourself man?' Gott had cried bumping into him as he shambled out of the furnished bedsit off the Mile End Road that served as home. "Home" was a euphemism, he used the place only as somewhere to eat and sleep while he looked for a job, and resented paying rent that he could ill afford on what was little more than a threadbare cupboard.

'Hell's bells Bertie Boy, how the mighty have fallen,' Gott had said. 'You really have dropped to the bottom haven't you? Come on old man let me buy you a decent cup of tea and a sandwich and then you can tell me what you are really doing dossing in a place like this.'

If he'd had the stamina Bertie might have turned and bolted back into his shabby bedsit, but he'd neither the energy nor the inclination and a bite to eat was a welcome thought.

After a second pot of tea and a full English breakfast in a dirty shack of a cafe, Gott had twisted the knife into Bertie's already bleeding guts. He should have expected it.

'Didn't I tell you gambling is a mug's game? Me, I've given it up; couldn't cope with my own tears when I lost.' Gott had laughed loudly at his own humour. 'Pity about you losing that gaff of yours and of course the motor, but what I can't get me head round is you letting that missus of yours bugger off. What were you thinking?'

'If all you've come to do is gloat then sod off, Gott. I'm down but I'm not out yet, you bastard!' he had retorted, spittle and bits of food flying out of his mouth. Raising his eyebrows, the Dwarf had continued as calmly as if Bertie had thanked him kindly for the breakfast.

'You can't blame me can you? In my shoes you'd be doing the same. I'm only having a bit of fun, Bertie Boy. There but for the grace of God and all that. Anyway, before that tic in the side of your face pulses hard enough to burst a blood vessel, I've something to offer you.'

'Bleeding hell, Gott, I've nothing. Watch my lips, NOTHING left, so the answer must be a NO! I don't gamble any more. Got it, Gott!' Realising what he had said, even Bertie had to laugh.

With his hands clasped together, Gott peered over his glasses, 'Okay, Keep your hair on. I've had my fun. I'll get down to business then. The thing is this: my cousin is looking for a decent bloke as yard manager for his building company. You might be a fool and a bloody big one at that, but even I know you know the building trade inside out. And as I once said to you when you were down on your luck, I'm your friend.' Gott had eyed him with open pity, 'The money's pretty ropey, but it is a job and it's legit. You don't need to worry, everyone knows what you've done, but the right word from me will sort it. What do you say?'

He was shocked at Gott's offer and it had taken him several moments before he could get his head around what the little man had said. But the Gott he knew did not do anything for nothing. 'Depends on what you want from me.'

'Nothing, as it happens. I'm helping my cousin out and it just so fits that I can help you too. You'd do it for me in the same circumstances, wouldn't you?'

Bertie was none too sure about that, but again he had been reminded that his luck was still holding. He had agreed to see Gott's cousin and Rounce's had turned out to be a decent firm. Being in paid employment brought Bertie a measure of self-respect and he had worked his socks off, which had soon brought him promotion. Ten months ago he had become Rounce's Building Manager. To his relief he saw little of Gott, but he was grateful to the Dwarf, whose name went on the list with those Bertie intended to repay in some way when he was comfortably back on his feet.

His luck had not always lingered long enough to favour him and Bertie was crushed by guilt when, six months ago, his parents had died within a few weeks of each other. Their deaths had devastated him. He had caused those two people so much shame that he was convinced they had gone to their graves to escape it all. Of course, the doctor said that was not the case. Both were in their seventies and had been heavy smokers for most of their adult lives. They had been lucky to survive this long, the doctor had reassured him. Whatever he said made no difference. Bertie knew he had destroyed them in the end.

They left their terraced house to him. A scribbled note with his parent's Will explained: *As our son bought the house for us, it should be returned to him along with all our possessions, to do with as he sees fit.* Their possessions were few, but the house was another thing. Bertie thought about living there, but it was too full of the spectre of his parents and his guilt, and so he had sold it. Once again he had been shocked at how house prices had rocketed. Like his earnings, a percentage of the money went against his debts. Even though he was bankrupt, at least he had tried his best to pay everyone, if not all he owed, most of it. He had once said he would pay everyone in time and he had, or almost. There was still Kitty.

Having posted his letter to her, Bertie was walking back from the Post Office when he heard the unmistakeable sound of a twin exhaust. Turning, he watched a Jenson Intercepter cruising towards him. It shot past, the deep roar of its powerful engine filing the air. Watching it go, Bertie smirked; he had once believed he would own one of those. Maybe one day he still would. He had never been afraid of hard work as the last three years had proved, and if he continued as he had who knew what he might achieve?

Arriving at the entrance to Rounce's he pulled the heavy glass door open and made for his office, still thinking about that beautiful car.

'Oh good, you're back,' the receptionist called, handing him a fistful of notes as he passed her desk. 'Mark's been on the line and wants you to call him straight away, said it's important.'

'Thank you,' he said, taking the slips of paper, a broad grin filling his face. He had been waiting for this call for days.

Chapter Forty-Three

Mark Dufton replaced the telephone receiver and folding his arms behind his back, thrust out his chest and paced down the narrow hall of his semi-detached house. Reaching the kitchen door, he turned and retraced his steps. The soft tones of his mother's voice drifted through from the kitchen as she chatted to his daughter. Whatever was being said it was clear that his little girl was happily amused, her ringing laughter brought a smile to Mark's face. At three years old, Sarah was an adorable little girl and he loved her beyond words. And today his cup had run over, for not only did he have a daughter, now he also had a son! *'Another son,'* he quickly corrected himself, for more than anything, he did not intend for his stepson, to feel pushed out by the arrival of a new half-brother.

As soon has Mark had arrived home from the hospital he had rushed indoors to tell his mother all about the baby. Lifting Sarah squealing into his arms he had danced a jig around the kitchen table, had barely paused for breath as the joyous words came tumbling out. There was no point in going to bed, despite having been up all night he was much too excited to sleep. Instead he had phoned round his family and close friends to spill out his news.

Hearing another peal of laughter, he strode back to the kitchen and pushed open the door. His mother looked up and smiled at him. She had dropped everything yesterday afternoon to pick Andrew up from school and stayed to look after both the children while Mark took Jane to hospital. He had spent the night pacing the waiting room until, sometime in the early hours, a weary looking midwife had told him he could stop pacing, the babe had arrived and all was well.

Tears had sprung to his eyes at the sight of his wife cradling their tiny son. 'My God he's beautiful,' he had said, staring down at the little red face.

'Here, you hold him,' Jane had said, her eyes shining, though her exhaustion was plain to see as she skilfully placed the swaddled bundle in his arms. 'He's got your nose,' she smiled.

'Poor little chap,' Mark had responded, returning her smile. As he held baby Nicholas against his chest, the tiny mouth opened and emitted a gurgling sound that had Mark weeping tears of joy. He had felt so proud when Sarah had been born, had thought he could never love another child quite as much. He was wrong; that feeling of overwhelming, unconditional love was not one jot diminished and as he held his son for the first time, he knew he loved both his offspring equally. There was nothing to beat the feeling of fatherhood. It brought home to Mark as nothing else did that he had done the right thing in seeking out his birth father after Sarah was born. It had taken him a long while, so afraid of rejection that he had kept putting it off, but when at last he had plucked up the courage he wished he had done it sooner. It was sheer chance, of course, that when they had finally met, Bertie Costain had so badly needed someone to love.

Now, waiting for his father to return his call, Mark recalled their first meeting; the way Bertie had reached out to embrace him. To Mark, it had felt so *right*, as if there was some chemistry between them; some recognition in their blood, and even though Bertie Costain was a stranger, Mark felt there had never been a time when they had not known each other. They had both cried, letting tears slip down their faces unashamedly and then laughing together, slightly embarrassed by their mutual display of unmanly sentimentality.

Mark had not dared to hope it would be quite as easy as this. On that distant, cold afternoon in January, after he had spoken with Kitty Costain, he had walked away believing her husband would at least make contact. As the weeks slipped by and he heard nothing, he had been tempted to return to Wentworth Place, but in the end had convinced himself that his father wanted nothing to do with him. Feeling rejected, Mark had decided to put it all out of his mind and let sleeping dogs lie. That was until the night he had picked up the Evening Standard and seen the name "Bertie Costain" all over the front page. *"... Proprietor of top building company B.C. Builders declared bankrupt. Gambling debts running into six figures spell ruin for this self-made businessman. His wife, who was not available for comment, is believed to be suing for divorce..."*

Mark had read the article several times and although he had never met the man, he was shocked to the core. No wonder Bertie Costain had made no attempt to contact him, he had far more pressing issues to deal with. Recalling the gorgeous house and the attractive lady who had so kindly listened to his story, Mark had wondered how any man could be so foolish as to throw it all away on a game of chance. It explained why she had seemed so stressed, poor woman. Fool or not, Mark told himself, Bertie Costain was still his father, and one day he would find a way to meet the man who had sired him. Leave it a few more years, he thought.

But that was before his daughter was born. With her arrival Mark had experienced such an immense surge of pride in being a father that it decided him to try again to meet his own. This time he had spoken with his mother about what he wanted to do.

'Of course it is up to you, Mark, but it will never change who your father was. Jeff was the one who brought you up as his own and worshipped the ground you walk on. I'm sure if he was able to look down on us now he would understand your need. I suppose it is only natural. All I ask is that you do not get too close until you feel it is right, and be prepared to be hurt. As I told you before, I did love Bertie Costain; ending the relationship was painful for us both, but I had to. Marrying him was out of the question. It was all very different back then. My parents would never have allowed it, they would have disowned me and we'd have been penniless. And then what sort of a life would it have been for you? Had Jeff not married me and accepted my pregnancy, I would have had no choice but to give you up for adoption. I couldn't have faced that. In some ways I feel guilty for not telling Bertie the truth, but if he'd known, he would have put enormous pressure on me. I didn't know which way to turn… I was only seventeen…'

Seeing her tears, Mark had tried to reassure her. 'I know Mum, I know, please don't distress yourself. It was not my intention to bring it all back and I absolutely don't want to hurt you, but now I am a father myself, I feel I must at least meet him, if only to let him know Sarah and I exist. In no way could it change what I felt for Dad… it never could. I miss him so much and I guess I always will, especially now.'

'Yes darling, me too. How he would have loved being little Sarah's grandad,' his mother had said, dabbing at her cheeks. 'Don't mind me Mark, you go ahead and do what you must do.'

And so he had begun to search, but it seemed Bertie Costain had disappeared off the face of the earth. It had taken a full six months after reading about his father's bankruptcy to locate him, and that had been by sheer chance.

When Sarah was a few months old Mark had been promoted to Branch Manager. With the increase in salary he had been able to raise a mortgage to buy a semi-detached in Croydon. The house had needed one or two minor jobs carried out to meet the terms of the mortgage. His call to a reputable local firm of builders had him speaking to their Yard Manager, none other than Bertie Costain. Mark had almost dropped the phone and before he could recover was told he had been put through to the wrong extension and was switched through to the Building Manager. Of course, he had said nothing at the time, but he had gone to the builders' head office when work on his house was nearing completion and asked if Bertie Costain could sign it off and check that it complied with the bank's specification. Rounce's must have thought it a strange request, for it was hardly the Yard Manager's job, but given that Mark Dufton was their bank manager they had been very obliging and Mr Costain was duly sent out to the house on the appointed day.

As it happened, Mark had been alone at the time, Jane having pushed Sarah in the pram to meet Andrew from school. Opening the door to his father, Mark had experienced a severe attack of nerves: perspiration trickled down his back and a feeling of nausea had him catching his breath. What had he been thinking about? Struck dumb, he ushered Bertie into the house and followed him around as, clipboard in hand, his father inspected the work. When he had finished, he marched towards the front door then turned back, eyes narrowed, to stare at Mark.

'Look, Mr Dufton, I can see nothing but first class craftsmanship here, but something tells me this is not the reason you asked me to come to your house,' Bertie had said bluntly. 'I think you'd better tell me, don't you?'

Taken aback, Mark had asked him into the kitchen, indicated a stool by the pine table and set about making them both a cup of tea, keeping his back turned to Bertie as he did so because it was easier than facing him and seeing a look of horror cross his features. Stumbling over his words Mark had begun to explain and then in a rush everything poured out of him, all the things his mother had told him and more besides.

The man who was his father remained silent for such a long time that Mark turned to look over his shoulder and saw that Bertie was silently weeping. 'Am I ever going to get that cup of tea?' he had asked, smiling through his tears.

Speechless with relief, Mark carried two mugs of tea to the table and sat himself down on the opposite stool.

'Sorry,' he managed, 'that must have been a bit of a shock.'

His voice breaking, Bertie shook his head. 'No, the shock came the other day when I saw you at the builders'. You didn't need to tell me who you were, I knew the minute I clapped eyes on you. It was like looking in a mirror thirty or more years ago.' Wiping the back of his hand across his face, he added. 'Thank you for looking for me. You might not believe me when I say this, but I have wondered about you for most of your life. Your mother thought I had no idea, but I knew. She went from being rosy-cheeked and happy to a pale faced and nervous young woman in my company. She ended our relationship so suddenly and with no obvious reason that I could see, for we could have waited until she no longer needed her parents' permission for us to marry. I loved your mother, Mark, and I know she loved me, but it seemed she had no wish to be married to a penniless brickie, which I was then…' he paused and a slow smile spread across his features, 'as indeed I am still, more or less.' Taking a sip of tea, he continued, 'It hurt at the time, but I suppose I didn't blame her for feeling that way. Then, when she married Jeff Dufton so soon afterwards and only seven months later a baby arrived, I knew you had to be mine. I went to see her, you know, but she turned me away, denying the baby was mine so emphatically that she almost convinced me…' Bertie shrugged his shoulders, 'Well, anyway, she had married a good man and she looked happy. And so I walked away. I still loved her and had no wish to upset the apple cart, but believe you me Mark, given the choice I would have married your mother without hesitation. She was the only woman I ever loved until Kitty walked into my life. And now I have lost her too. According to the old saying, I should have been a lot luckier at cards than I was!' He laughed, but it was hollow sound with no humour in it.

Gazing across the table at his father, it seemed to Mark that he looked even more broken than he had in the photograph splashed all over the Evening Standard back along. His heart went out to the man. Whatever he had done, he surely hadn't deserved such a raw deal in life. Not a lucky man, it seemed; how foolish he had been to take up gambling!

A silence had hung between the two of them as if neither knew what to say next. In the end Bertie had been the one to speak first. Getting up from the table, he said, 'I should go, the last thing you want is me filling your kitchen with my self-pity, but thank you for the tea and I'm really glad to have met you.'

Swallowing the lump in his throat, Mark too had stood. 'Before you go, do you think we could get to know each other a little? Not only are you a father, but you have a granddaughter too. Her name is Sarah. Oh, and yes, you also have a step-grandson, Andrew. He never knew his father and it is largely down to him that I started searching for you.'

It was then that Bertie had reached out blindly to hug him and with that tearful father-son embrace, Mark had known they would one day be close.

That had been two and a half years ago, and since then they had indeed become close.

The shrilling of the phone had Mark striding out of the kitchen and down the hall. Grabbing the receiver, knowing instinctively who would be on the other end, Mark sang out, 'Pops, you have a grandson, 7lbs 8ozs. Mother and baby are both fine, and we've named him Nicholas Costain Dufton.'

Chapter Forty-Four

Kitty read the letter for the third time and each time she felt a shiver run down her spine. How odd that Bertie should choose this moment to write to her when, over the last few weeks, he had crept back into her thoughts to the point that he occupied them for much of the time.

She placed the letter down on the kitchen table reflecting that it had been more than a year since they had last spoken to each other. It had been horrid meeting him like that, outside Rosebuds. She had gone there to discuss supplying Julie with cut seasonal flowers and been delighted when her former assistant, who had blossomed in the role of proprietor, had placed a regular order. Coming out of the shop after a cheerful catch-up, with Julie doing most of the talking as ever, Kitty had seen Bertie loitering by her Mini. Her heart had somersaulted then plummeted. Part of her had yearned to rush into his arms; the other part wanted to run a mile. It was awful; they had been like distant acquaintances, each putting on a false smile and exchanging meaningless small talk, stilted and icily polite. Driving back to Epsom, Kitty, who could not have said exactly what they had talked about, had cried for almost the entire journey. Arriving home to an uproarious welcome from Poppy, she had tired herself out working in the garden for the remainder of the day, not coming in until it was almost too dark to see what she was doing.

Why had he written and not telephoned? she now wondered. Was he afraid she would not speak to him or worse, did he believe she would slam the phone down on hearing his voice? Of course she would do neither, not any more. It had taken her a long time to come to terms with what he had done. Distance and time had helped her to heal and the pain had eventually subsided, so much so that she now thought of Bertie without anger. Almost, she could feel sorry for him. The richness of her life had at last overlaid her memories of that terrible time when she thought nothing would ever again be normal. But now it was, just as Mrs Dobbs had said it would be, given time. She had been a wise and kindly woman; Kitty hoped she had found other work to suit her – maybe something more challenging than cleaning someone else's house.

As she gazed again at Bertie's handwriting, she wondered how anyone could make sense of his scrawl, yet she knew he would have tried to make it as legible as he could. She pictured him hunched over a desk – for in their brief exchange outside Rosebuds he had mentioned something about an office job in a builders' yard – as he sought the right words to express what he wanted to say. She imagined his brow furrowed in concentration. Not that he had written much: *"Dear Kitty, I hope you will not mind my writing to you. I have something for you, and I would much prefer to give it to you personally. Of course, I would not presume we could meet at either of our homes, but in a café of your choosing,* he had written. *Please will you give me a call and let me know when and where?"* Adding his daytime telephone number he had ended, *"Fondest regards, Bertie."*

Is that what their relationship had come down to: *"Dear Kitty; Fondest regards"*? It was so formal. How was it possible for a passion such as they had shared to disappear on the wind like a piece of thistledown, as though it had never been? Kitty snorted at herself. For goodness sake! What had she hoped for – a love letter? Stamping on the fantasy that had begun worming its way into her head she read his words again. What did he have for her this time, another one of his special surprises? But despite her suspicion, she felt a warm feeling at the idea of seeing him again. It would be different to their last chance meeting on the pavement; she would be prepared for it this time. And anyway, it would be the perfect opportunity to let him know she had decided to start divorce proceedings. In fact, that could well be why he wanted to see her. As sad as it would be to finalise their union legally, she was suddenly sure it was what Bertie had been waiting for. 'Yes, I will agree to meet him,' she said out loud.

Kitty's train of thought came to an abrupt end as Poppy let out an excited bark. Simultaneously, Brian Fenton's collie, Cassie, appeared round the back door, nudging it wide open and racing into the kitchen to hurl herself at her doggy friend. 'Outside, both of you,' Kitty said sternly, pointing at the open door and laughing as the two dogs chased each other past Flo, almost knocking her off her feet.

'Still talking to yourself?' Flo said. 'I'm sure you're getting worse. First sign of old age, dear,' she added, pushing the door closed.

'Probably,' Kitty retorted picking up the letter and pushing it into her pocket. She would like to have phoned Bertie there and then before she had time to change her mind, but not while Flo was in her cottage.

'Now what brings you to my kitchen when you should be looking after that wonderful husband of yours?' Kitty asked, aware that Flo's sharp eyes had seen her push the letter out of sight.

'Someone written you a love letter?'

Flo's comment was so close to Kitty's earlier thoughts that she blushed. 'None of your business,' she said, but softened her retort with a smile.

'Well,' Flo began, raising her eyebrows but making no comment. 'I needed some fresh air and Cassie needed a walk so I thought I'd kill two birds with one stone. I came to ask if you'd like to come up to the house for tea. I've made scones to have with a tub of clotted cream and some of my homemade strawberry jam. I thought you might like to join us... but if you're too busy...?' she looked pointedly at Kitty's pocket.

Under normal circumstances Kitty would have jumped at the opportunity to enjoy Flo's delicious baking, but right now, her head full of Bertie, she didn't want the distraction. 'Thank you, Flo, but for once I'm going to resist the temptation and say no. You're right, I've a mountain of things to do and I need to get on with them. I've had an invitation to meet up with an old friend, so I want to make sure today's orders are all done and dusted before I go to meet her.' It was not a total lie; the only difference was the gender of her 'old friend.'

'Glad to hear you are getting yourself out again, dear. Work is all well and good, but you need to keep in touch with your friends,' Flo said. 'And make new ones too,' she added, a warm, motherly smile on her homely face.

'You're mothering me again, Flo,' Kitty grinned, knowing her old housekeeper was at her best when playing Mother Hen. *God alone knows what she'd say if she had any idea it's Bertie I'm planning to see*, thought Kitty.

Flo sniffed, 'Right then, I'll get back to my baking,' she said, pulling on the back door handle. Glancing back, her gaze rested once more on Kitty's pocket then rose to her face, 'Look after yourself Kitty, I mean, when you goes to meet your *friend*.' Pulling the door open and calling for Cassie, she stepped out into the mild morning air.

'Bye for now, Flo, and thanks again. Give my regards to Brian,' Kitty said. She had not missed the questioning, slightly anxious look Flo had flung at her. It was uncanny. '*It's like she knows who sent the letter that's burning a hole in my pocket,*' Kitty thought. She frowned; she fully intended to look after herself. That was why she was about to sever for good the final tie with Bertie. That done, perhaps she could at last move on and, as Flo had advised, make new friends – maybe someone special; who knew what was around the corner? But even as the thought came into her mind, her heart cried, '*No!*' How could she ever love another man when deep down she was still in love with Bertie? The old Bertie; the man she had met and married. Did he still exist or had it all been a fantasy?

With these thoughts playing a non-stop game of tag in her head, by the time twenty-four hours had passed, Kitty was a nervous wreck. Who would have thought that meeting up with her soon-to-be ex-husband would have this effect on her after all this time? When she had telephoned him to agree to meet, he had sounded surprised then overwhelmed, gushing with gratitude and eagerness to see her. Kitty had convinced herself that his urgency to talk was to discuss the divorce. After all, they had not cohabited for three years. He was an attractive man; he had most likely met someone else and wanted to be free to remarry. Kitty didn't dwell on that thought; the aching pain it caused made her feel sick.

Bertie had insisted that he had "something" he wanted to give her. Why could he not have told her what it was instead of being so secretive? And why in God's name had she been afraid to ask? Maybe it was an incentive; a sweetener to get her to agree to irretrievable breakdown as the grounds for their divorce. Well if that was the case he would not be disappointed. She had no wish to accuse him of mental cruelty and as far as she knew there had been no adultery – at least, not while they were together.

As the appointed hour drew near, Kitty became increasingly nervous and by the time she was walking into the café on the corner of East Street, she was finding it hard to breathe. She felt Bertie's gaze on her and spotted him sitting at a table opposite the door. At the sight of him her heart lurched and it was with faltering steps that she made her way over to his table.

He got to his feet, a wide smile splashing across his tanned face, his china-blue eyes meeting hers. It was like going back in time, he looked exactly as he had when they first met, perhaps a little thinner, but the effect was just the same. Kitty had to swallow down the lump of emotion that had gathered in her throat, sternly telling herself to control her traitorous tears. *'Pull yourself together, woman,'* she thought, but it was hopeless. He was still so charming, so engagingly handsome; immaculately dressed in a dark suit.

He now had streaks of grey at his temples, but they suited him, made him look debonair, yet with a new maturity.

Absorbing every little detail, her heart racing, Kitty wondered if she had done the right thing in agreeing to meet him. Until entering the café she had convinced herself they would sit down, drink a cup of coffee, listen to what they each had to say and then agree to proceed with the divorce, before leaving to get on with their separate lives. Who had she been kidding? It could never be that easy.

'Hello Kitty.' Bertie's voice was soft and measured as he took hold of her hand. 'Thank you for agreeing to see me, you have no idea what it means to me,' he said, his eyes gazing deeply into hers. Kitty felt him gently squeeze her fingers; it was more like a caress than a formal handshake and she tingled at his touch.

'Hello Bertie, it's been a long time since we met and you look well,' she said, knowing it was a ridiculous thing to say, it had only been a year after all, but her mouth was suddenly dry and her head could not think of the right words.

'Yes, you do too,' he replied. 'A lot of water has gone under the bridge these last three years... for both of us.'

Had he too forgotten their accidental meeting outside Rosebuds? Could it be he felt as nervous as she did? 'Yes, indeed,' she murmured, acutely aware that he was still holding both her hand and her gaze, and even though she knew the cafe was half-full of customers, it seemed to Kitty that she and Bertie were the only two people in the room, so that when a young waitress materialised at her side, Kitty started in surprise.

Taking in the scene the young woman gave a knowing smile and asked, 'Would that be tea or coffee?'

'Coffee for me,' Kitty replied. White, no sugar, thank you.'

'The same for me,' Bertie chimed.

Flustered, Kitty pulled her hand away and fumbled to loosen the buttons of her jacket.

Bertie pulled out a chair next to his, 'Let's sit down. Drinking coffee standing up is not quite the same,' he smiled as he spoke, 'especially when one's knees are wobbling like one of Mrs Watson's jellies.'

'She's Mrs Fenton now,' Kitty murmured, somehow comforted by Bertie's admission of nervousness.

'Good heavens! Really? He must be a brave man to have taken her on,' he grinned. 'Is she still happy being miserable?'

'Yes... I mean no, she's very happy. He's nice, a farmer...' her voice trailed away. Why was she allowing herself to drift into small talk? Strung as taut as a tuned violin, Kitty seated herself on the edge of the Lloyd Loom chair and placing her handbag down by her side, decided to come straight to the point.

'So, you have something to tell me,' she said, looking down at her fingers and twisting her wedding ring round and round. It was a nervous habit. She had meant to take the ring off ages ago, but had somehow never got around to it.

'It's not so much that I have something to *tell* you, but importantly, something to give you,' Bertie said.

She looked up at him then, her eyebrow rising of its own volition. 'Not another of your surprises, I hope,' she said, her lips curving in a weak smile.

He looked a little sheepish, 'Well, it might be a surprise,' he said. Delving into his inside jacket pocket he pulled out a foolscap envelope. 'This is for you,' he said, holding it out to her. 'I'm sorry it has been so long in coming.'

Kitty did not miss the tic that had started throbbing in Bertie's left temple, a sure sign that he was stressed. What was he giving her – divorce papers? She wondered how they had come to be sitting so close to each other, yet were talking in strained tones like two strangers, as if they were both afraid to say the wrong thing. As Bertie's gaze rested on hers, Kitty caught a glimpse of his underlying sadness and knew it mirrored her own. Surely it was not meant to be like this. She stared down at the white envelope and took a deep breath. What awaited her? Did she want to know?

'Take it Kitty, it is for you.'

Picking up the envelope, she turned it over, saw that it was sealed. 'Do I have to open it now?'

'Better that you do,' he said.

'Two coffees,' announced a cheerful voice and the young waitress placed two large mugs of steaming coffee on the table, breaking the strained atmosphere.

'Thank you,' Kitty said automatically. Waiting until they were alone again, she nudged her thumb under the seal, ripped open the envelope and pulled out a single piece of paper. *Not divorce papers then,'* she thought. Turning it over she saw it was a cheque. It was so unexpected that she gasped and biting her top lip, asked weakly, 'What is this?' Staring down at the amount, her eyes widened with shock.

'It's a cheque to you. As you see, I'm paying you back with interest for the two loans you lent to me soon after we were married. I could think of a thousand words to say to you about your kindness and generosity, but I don't think after what we have been through it would be a good idea. Please would you accept a simple thank you for lending me the money? I'm sorry it has taken me so long to repay you, Kitty. By the way, I will also pay you back for the other loan. The one I took out in your name. If it takes the rest of my life, I will make sure everything I took from you is repaid.'

Kitty listened unable to speak, her eyes filling with salty tears as she absorbed the implication of the payment. She had never dreamt he would honour his word to pay her back and with interest too, but here it was; a sum much larger than the original loans. Had she misjudged him? As taken aback as she was, a sudden suspicion flashed into Kitty's mind and her heart plummeted.

'Thank you Bertie, but I simply cannot take this because I don't even want to *think* where this amount of money has come from. I'll be honest, I'd rather not have seen the cheque and continued to live in the belief that you had changed.' Trying not to let her tears of disappointment escape, she laid the cheque down on the table. Nothing had prepared her for this. She had expected Bertie to be begging her for a divorce so he could remarry, instead of which, he was offering her everything he owed her and more. Clearly he'd had a very big win. After all those abject promises, he was gambling again.

'Kitty, no! I *have* changed,' he cried, pointing to the cheque. 'This is not from gambling if that's what you're thinking. I've told you that is all behind me and it really is. I would rather slit my own throat than risk a single pound on a game of chance ever again. Please believe me. I suppose I can't blame you for thinking the worst. I'd pinned my hopes on proving to you that here before you sits the leopard that really *has* changed his spots, the exception to prove the rule.' He gave her a weak smile, but Kitty saw the desolation in his face and her heart turned over. 'Believe you me,' he said, 'I have learnt a bitter and very hard lesson. I have lost everything I owned, but far worse than that, I lost the most precious person in the world to me.'

He dashed a hand across his eyes, but not before Kitty had seen the sparkle of tears. She opened her mouth to speak, but he continued talking, 'My dad and then my mum passed away a few months ago. They left me their house. I believe it was down to me that they died,' he said, his voice breaking. 'Needless to say, they were shattered by my bankruptcy.'

Kitty held on tight to her disappointment. For just a second she had thought he meant her, but of course not; his dad was far more precious to him than she had ever been. She murmured the conventional condolences. She had met Bertie's parents only a couple of times and they had seemed kindly people, both a little shocked at the speed with which their only son had married, but neither had given her the feeling they disapproved of her, despite the age gap. It had seemed their son could do no wrong in their eyes, so his downfall must indeed have been devastating for them.

'The thing is, Kitty,' Bertie was saying, 'I sold the house for a very good price. It is that which enables me to pay back much of what I owe you.' He picked up the cheque and handed it back to her. 'So *please* accept it.'

'I never expected you to pay me back, Bertie. You will recall I always said you were not to worry about it, and I meant it. It was never about the money, it was your deceit that hurt me so badly...' Kitty's voice wobbled, but she soldiered on. 'Since then I have turned the corner and now I own a successful business near Epsom. I am more than comfortable, financially that is. I don't need your money. You keep it and repay everyone else so that you are no longer bankrupt.'

'I'm not, Kitty. Not now. Every creditor but you has been paid. I too have turned a corner. I have a good job and am earning a respectable wage. So please Kitty, take the cheque. I have been many things in the past: a risk-taker, a liar, a fraudster and a cheat, you don't need to remind me. You could not possibly hate me as much as I hate myself, but I vowed I would pay you back and I fully intend to.'

'I have never hated you, Bertie.' Kitty said quietly. She wanted to shout out that she loved him, but it was too late for that now. She took the cheque and as she did so their hands touched. Her voice caught in her throat at the frisson of chemistry between them. 'Thank you. If it means so much to you I will accept it, but only if you will forget about the other debt. It is gone. As you say, water under the bridge. I don't want it and will not accept it. If you must give your money away, give it to your s—'

Abruptly she stopped speaking, pressed her hand to her throat, confused, grabbed her mug and took a gulp of coffee. Supposing he did not know about Mark? She had almost blurted it out. Now was hardly the time to tell him. Not when they were supposed to be discussing divorce.

Bertie let go of the cheque and picked up his own coffee. Taking a mouthful, he placed the mug down then smiled. 'You know, Kitty, I have so much to ask you and so many things to tell you, I could sit here all day and barely scratch the surface. But I know you know about Mark, he told me. Getting to know my son has been almost the best thing that ever happened to me.' He smiled proudly, 'And I am a grandfather now – twice over.' He paused and his grin grew even wider. 'I suppose that makes you a step-grandmother!'

Fingering the cheque, Kitty stared at Bertie in amazement. The transformation in him when he mentioned his new family was extraordinary. Gone was the sadness; the lines in his face, particularly about his eyes, seemed to smooth away; his laugh was one of genuine delight at the expression on her face. For three years she had believed he would quickly revert to his old ways. How wrong she had been. Where did this leave her, because the man sitting next to her was the Bertie she had fallen in love with and as much as she had tried to deny it to herself, there was no denying it now. Even when she hadn't liked him very much, she had never stopped loving him. *'Oh my God,'* she thought, *'why did I agree to see him, why didn't I keep to my resolve to stay away'*?

'Do you think we could have dinner one evening?' Bertie asked cutting into her thoughts. 'We could go to Pierre Duval's again.'

As his words turned her world upside down a peal of surprised laughter escaped Kitty's lips, she could not believe what she had just heard. 'Bertie Costain, you have not changed one iota and Duval's is out of the question. Aside from anything else, it is much too expensive.'

'Not really. Please, do you think you could say yes? There is so much we have to discuss.'

'You mean divorce?' she said bluntly.

The effect on Bertie could not have been greater if she'd slapped him. His face went white and he gasped. 'God, no!' he blurted out, his eyes filling with tears. 'I'm so sorry, Kitty, what I did was unforgiveable, but I always hoped... that is to say, you might justifiably believe that if I had really loved you, I would never have hurt you as I did, but in truth I never ever stopped loving you, even when I was destroying you. It is no excuse, I know that, but I was in the grip of an addiction so strong it blew everything out of my mind except the thrill of playing to win. It made me feel invincible, like a God.' He shrugged, 'I recognise it for what it was now. An empty fantasy; nothing but fool's gold. The shock of losing everything – of losing you – made me see what a fool I really was. As someone told me not so long ago, gambling is a mug's game. I am not a mug, Kitty, and I love you from the bottom of my heart. Tell me there is still hope for me. I asked you this once before, but please, give me another chance. Let me try to make you fall in love with me all over again.'

He had spoken of fantasy, and this had been hers. Was she dreaming, Kitty wondered, was this real? Almost she pinched herself.

'If you'd only stop talking for a minute, Bertie,' she said, smiling through her tears, 'I can tell you there was a time when I could happily have had you locked in the stocks and pelted you with rotten eggs, and worse. But through it all, even in my darkest moments, I loved you. I still do. My problem is that distrust is a hard lesson to unlearn. But I will try. You will have to give me time.'

'As much time as you need, my darling,' he said hoarsely.

'If you think you can just waltz back into my life and take it over, Bertie Costain, you are sadly mistaken. I am settled. I like what I do, I even find I quite like being single. So it is going to take a lot of wooing and seduction on your part! So yes, maybe Duval's is a good idea after all. I do believe we have something to celebrate. And then perhaps we can take things slowly and see where it leads us. But for God's sake, no more of your surprises!'

'Thank you,' he said simply, and reaching for her hand, he brought it to his lips and placed a soft, warm kiss on her palm that made her shudder with longing.

'Despite everything, Bertie, you are still a charmer and an opportunist,' she said, giving up the battle to hold back her tears. She had no idea what would happen in the future, but for now she would enjoy the company of the only man who had ever swept her off her feet, the man she still loved: her husband, Bertie Costain.

The End

To learn more about Pauline, please visit her web site
www.paulinebarclay.co.uk

Magnolia House

When Jane Leonard gave half of her house to her only son, little did she realise that within twelve months, she would be forced to sell the home she had lived in for nearly five decades.

The choice for this action was not hers, but the events that led up to her handing over fifty percent of Magnolia House paled by comparison to what happened after the ink had dried on the documents that named the new owners.

As Magnolia House is put on the market for sale, love and betrayal, hopes and dreams and ultimately family loyalty will affect the lives of all of those who become involved.

Satchfield Hall

When the news reached Henry Bryant-Smythe about his daughter's indiscretion, he not only dealt with it, but stamped on it with such a resounding thud, that the consequences ricocheted through the years and well into the future. Henry Bryant-Smythe cared nothing for the consequences of his actions and even less for the feelings of those involved, with the exception of his own, and these he cosseted.

Celia's Bryant-Smythe's disgrace set in motion events that would affect the lives of many people, taking decades to unravel. Lives would be lost and destroyed and it would take until the death of the one man who had callously started it all, Henry Bryant-Smythe, until it was finally over.

Satchfield Hall is not about gentleness, tranquillity and privilege; it is about, power, love, lives and in the end revenge.

Sometimes It Happens…

Winning the lottery was just the beginning for Doreen Wilkinson, nothing prepared Doreen and her seventeen year old daughter for their holiday at the luxury Villas Bonitas and nothing prepared Villas Bonitas for the Wilkinsons.

Sometimes It Happens…as a cast of characters, all have secrets and as Doreen and her daughter mingle with the rich, they find that deception, love, lies and laughter turns their holiday into one they will never forget.

Storm Clouds Gathering

Storm clouds are gathering, silently and slowly, too far away to worry about. Or so it seems. But ignoring what is brewing will have dire consequences for the people caught up in the maelstrom.

Shirley Burton is too busy cheating on her husband, having a laugh and looking for fun to alleviate the boredom of her childless marriage. Kathleen Mitchell is too wrapped up in running around after her beautiful family to worry about her health. Anne Simpson has two things on her mind: her forthcoming marriage to Paul Betham, who seems to want to control her, and her career, which she does not want to give up.

Can Shirley really expect to deceive her husband and get away with it? Can Kathleen hold it all together, and is Anne able to have the best of everything?

Storm Clouds Gathering is a story of human emotion, passion and heart-rending grief. Set against the backdrop of the mid-sixties, these three families will be tested to the limit as betrayal, loss and love threaten to change their lives forever.

All books available in Kindle and Paperback

Ghosts in Glass Houses

A Marti Mickkleson Mystery

Kay Charles

This book is a work of fiction. Names, characters, places and incidents are either the product of the author's imagination or are used fictionally. Any resemblance to actual persons, living or dead, or to actual events or locales is entirely coincidental.

Copyright © 2017 by Patricia Lillie

All rights reserved.

No part of this book may be reproduced in any form or by any electronic or mechanical means, including information storage and retrieval systems, without written permission from the author, except for the use of brief quotations in a book review.

ISBN-13: 978-1973797951
ISBN-10: 197379795X

Ebook edition published by Kindle Press, 2017.

www.KayCharles.com

For my cousin Jennifer

ONE

When the kid in the movie said, "I see dead people," Marti's first reaction was *Join the club*, followed quickly by *Don't let them drug you—it only makes it worse*.

The movie didn't provide any answers. As far as she knew, none of her ghosts wanted anything important from her, except maybe her great-grandmother. Grandma Bertie constantly badgered Marti to clean up her act. Since Grandma died exactly twenty-four hours before Marti was born, they had different definitions of "clean act." As far as Marti was concerned, keeping up with the laundry and showering once a day qualified. She sometimes failed to meet her own standards, let alone Grandma's.

"Why do you think you feel the need to search for answers in movies?" her shrink, the sixth or eighth so far on her lifetime list of head-doctors, asked.

The woman behind him shook her head. "Tell the pompous brat his aunt Susan says hello, and that trashy slut he married is cheating on him."

Marti wanted to ask where she got her dress but instead relayed the message. Dr. Calm-and-Steady's flinch was better than the dress. Wherever the dress came from, the store was long gone anyway. As was Aunt Susan. It didn't matter. Shopping wasn't in Marti's budget.

"Have you been taking your meds?" the doctor asked.

"Aunt Susan's right. You are a pompous brat. Although I would have said pompous prick."

She never went back, but she upped her self-medication, which was no more help than legal and prescribed drugs but a whole bunch more fun.

Self-medication stopped being fun the morning she woke up on the cold asphalt in the shadow of the Franklinville Public Library's dumpster, wrapped around the town's most infamous homeless man-about-town. At least she was the big spoon. She disengaged herself and did a quick inventory. Her clothes were all accounted for. Her jeans were buttoned and zipped. She hadn't done anything she shouldn't have. Probably.

"You didn't." Ozzie's voice came from behind her, but his body lay motionless on the ground beside her.

Crap. She didn't know whether to believe him. The dead lied as much as the living. More. Their chances of getting caught were lower.

She wasn't surprised to find Grandma Bertie tsk-tsking over her, but the sight of her father, his face wet with tears, shocked her. The Judge never cried. If she had done Ozzie, she hoped he hadn't seen.

"When did you die?" she said.

"Pass. *Pass* sounds much nicer. Less final," her grandmother said.

"Last night," Ozzie said.

"I wasn't talking to you."

"A month ago," her father said.

"No one called me."

"No one knew where to find you." The Judge turned the simple statement into an indictment.

"You did," Marti said.

"That's different. And it took me a while." No more tears. The Honorable Thaddeus A. Mickkleson's voice dripped with the disdain Marti—and legions of Battlesburough County juvenile offenders—knew and feared.

"Are you going to follow me home?"

"Of course." The Judge's powers of condescension remained intact. Death didn't change people.

"I wasn't talking to you," Marti said.

"Me?" Layers of grime and a snarled beard masked Ozzie's expression, but he sounded astonished. And pleased.

"That wasn't an invitation," Marti said.

"'S okay. I hate to be cooped up." Ozzie stepped over his corporeal counterpart without a glance.

"See you around." She left him struggling to lift the lid of the dumpster.

It wouldn't take him long to figure out he didn't need to open it. In his new state, even locked dumpsters were his to explore. Not that their contents were any use to him. Marti hoped he wouldn't be too brokenhearted when he discovered he couldn't maneuver his overloaded and ever-present shopping cart. He might be bound to the shopping cart. Or to the dumpster. Marti didn't understand how that worked, but either one would stink. As long as he wasn't bound to her, she didn't care. Grandma was enough. And The Judge. If she was stuck with her father for the rest of her life, she didn't know what she'd do.

Grandma and The Judge escorted her home.

"We should call somebody about that man," her great-grandmother said.

"We? Since when can you use a phone?"

"Don't you have a car?" her father asked.

"Somewhere."

"I'll tell her where it is when she sobers up," Grandma Bertie said.

Sometimes, the dead had their uses. Mostly, they nagged.

"This place isn't as bad as I thought it would be." Coming from The Judge, that was as close to a compliment as Marti expected.

"At least she keeps it clean," her great-grandmother said.

"Don't get me wrong. It's a dump. But after this morning, I expected worse."

"It's shabby chic. That's—what do they call it—a *thing*, you know." The Judge had nothing on Grandma Bertie in the condescension department.

The one-room, furnished apartment *was* shabby. Two mismatched chairs shoved up to a vinyl-topped folding table passed for a dining area. Duct tape patches adorned a sofa bed that housed a mattress so nasty Marti never bothered to pull it out. Sleeping on the sofa was fine with her. As for chic, Grandma was stretching it, but the place met Marti's needs. Aside from a stray cockroach or two, she and Grandma were the sole occupants, and a place with no haunts was hard to find in the aged buildings within her budget. She had no attachment to the place or possessions to weigh her down. Even the dishes in the tiny kitchen corner came with the rental. When it was time to move on, she would toss her clothes into the back of her car, leave, and never look back.

Her clothes and her quilt. The faded patchwork blanket draped over the back of the sofa was the only decoration in the studio apartment—the only bit of Marti and the only connection to her childhood. It also came in handy when she ended up sleeping in her car. She hoped The Judge didn't recognize it.

He did. "I thought your mother threw that away."

She'd tried more than once, but each time Marti rescued it from the Goodwill donation bag or the trash bag or wherever, until her mother gave up. When Marti left home for good, she took only the quilt and one small suitcase. The quilt always went with her. The one time she tried to leave it behind, she made it as far as her car before she felt compelled to turn around and go back and get it.

Her head hurt, and the scents of Ozzie and parking lot clung to her.

"I need a shower," she said.

The hot water pounded the back of her neck, and the three Advil she swallowed began to take effect, but Marti couldn't relax. It wasn't—yet—a bad day, but it wasn't a good day either.

A bad day would be finding signs Ozzie lied about the closeness of their encounter.

A bad day would be her father following her into the bathroom. The Judge never would have done such a thing in life, but she didn't know what to expect from Dead Dad. About too many things, the dead made their own rules.

On a good day, her great-grandmother would have stayed in the other room and caught up on family gossip with The Judge, but she had no compunction about following Marti into the bathroom or anywhere else.

"You're not even listening to me, are you?" Grandma said.

"Don't you and Daddy Dearest have things to talk about?"

"Pfft. That man always was in love with the sound of his own voice."

"Pot. Kettle."

"Be nice. Besides, we had a long chat while you were snoozing."

"I'll bet you did." If *snoozing* was Grandma's euphemism for *passed out in a parking lot next to a dead bum*, she was gearing up for a lecture. Great-Grandma Bertie was Marti's proof the passive-aggressive gene ran strong in her family, at least on the maternal side. Alive, The Judge didn't have a passive bone in his body. She doubted the loss of those bones changed anything.

"Your father wants to talk to you."

"La, la, la, la. I can't hear you."

"Of course you can. He has a favor—"

"The worms crawl in. The worms crawl out," Marti sang. The worm song made Grandma's skin crawl. Metaphorically, of course. Grandma hadn't had any skin to crawl for thirty-two years, and Marti had used the ditty to irritate her for twenty-seven of those years.

"Marcile!" The use of her formal name meant Grandma was wishing she had the ability to slap her great-granddaughter. Not for the first time, Marti was glad she didn't.

"THE WORMS PLAY PINOCHLE ON YOUR SNOUT." Marti

suspected her own inability to carry a tune irritated the old ghost more than the worms. According to Grandma, she'd been quite the songbird in her day. Marti turned off the shower.

"I was cremated!" The Judge shouted from the other room.

It might take more than Advil to get her through the day.

"What the hell are you wearing?" The Judge said.

He had to be the last soul on earth who didn't recognize Marti's neon-orange-and-green Burger Buster uniform or the smell of bacon grease and garlic pickles that wouldn't come out no matter how many times she washed it. One of her coworkers had a theory the signature scent was woven in with the synthetic fibers of the fabric—orange for the grease and green for the pickles. Eau de fast food. Olfactory advertisement. When a Burger Buster drone in full regalia walked past, mouths watered. Dogs barked. Arteries clogged.

"I have to go to work. And since I'm walking, I need to leave now."

They followed her. Chatted with each other. Marti tried to tune out her father's updates on her mother and sister. Her family was dead to her. No, they weren't. If they were dead, they'd probably be stalking her along with Dead Dad. She shuddered at the thought.

She clocked in with a minute to spare and took her place at the Burger Buster grill, ready to flip burgers.

"This isn't why I paid for you to go to college." Her father didn't mention the part where she never graduated.

She spent her last semester as a patient rather than a student. Too many campus spirits, both the roaming and the drinkable varieties, sent her back for her second stay at the Birches and her first round of shock treatment. On the bright side, tuition for the Birches was higher than for Marydale College, which wasn't cheap. *That* had to have hurt The Judge.

She wanted to tell him *at least it's a job*, but kept her mouth shut. Dead or alive, The Judge didn't need to know the things she'd done or the places she'd slept when unemployed and broke.

"We need to talk," The Judge said.

Marti checked the screen in front of her, tossed four preformed sort-of-beef patties on the grill, and hit the timer. A robot could do her job, which was exactly why she liked it.

"She won't talk to us when she's at work," her grandmother said. "That's how she lost the last job."

She stood in the parking lot and searched for her beat-up Taurus.

"Scooter's," Grandma said.

Oh yeah. Scooter's Bar and Grille. The grill part shut down long before Marti moved to town, most likely at the insistence of the health department. She couldn't imagine anyone wanted to eat there, but she did like to drink there. The bartenders all knew her and could be trusted to take away her car key when needed. She didn't mind being seen as a falling-down drunk—on occasion—but driving drunk was another matter. She wouldn't be responsible for adding to the revenant population.

Scooter's sat just outside of town. She had no clue how she made it from there to the library parking lot. When the bartenders took her keys, they arranged a ride home for her, and the ride always dropped her off in front of her apartment. Maybe they did, and she'd decided it was time for a new book or two. She did like to read. She could ask Grandma. Or not. She decided it wasn't important.

The Judge cleared his throat. "Marti—"

"Time for a walk." She cut The Judge off. He was about to tell her something she didn't want to hear. He'd used the same tone every time he shipped her off to a new doctor or hospital.

"Marcile—" The Judge spoke her name slowly, as if he were talking to a problem child. His problem child. Marti ignored him and set off for Scooter's.

"No talking while walking," Grandma said. "People will think she's talking to herself. Might think she's disturbed and medicate her. Lock her up somewhere. Shock treatment isn't a whole lot of fun, you know."

Go Grandma! Marti couldn't resist a glance at her father. He was either suffering from a bit of afterlife indigestion or feeling sheepish. Score one for Great-Grandma Bertie.

"Don't be ridiculous," The Judge said. "People will think she's talking on her phone."

"What?" Grandma said.

Crap. Leave it to The Judge. She and Grandma spent the last ten years in backwater towns. Pretty much the only people walking around and chatting on unseen cell phones were teenagers. Since Grandma was convinced insanity was an inherent part of adolescence, Marti had no problem enforcing the no-talking-while-walking rule. She developed a fondness for long walks. Sometimes it was the only way to shut up her great-grandmother's ghost, and The Judge was about to blow it.

"Her cell phone, you stupid old woman," The Judge said.

Maybe not. Insulting Grandma was asking for trouble.

"No talking while walking." Grandma's command voice was the stuff ghost stories were made of. It sent a shiver up Marti's spine, and she knew Grandma learned it from movies.

It didn't stop The Judge. "Marcile—*Ouch!*"

Marti didn't see what Grandma did—her companions had fallen behind her—but whatever it was, it worked. The Judge shut up.

They walked in silence until the sidewalk ran out. Marti kept her head down and crunched through the dry brown leaves along the roadside. She trusted the afternoon sunshine to light up her Burger Buster uniform's combination of hunter-don't-shoot-me orange and road-crew-don't-hit-me green, and alert any passing drivers to her presence.

"Watch where you're walking," The Judge said.

She pretended not to hear him over the traffic, the honking horns, and the occasional idiot who rolled down his window and warbled "Buuuuur-ger Bust-eeeeer!" at her. The theme song was more memorable than the food.

She heard The Judge just fine. She had no choice. If Marti heard the dead with her ears, she would have long ago solved her problem. Their voices echoed inside her head. It would take more than a good set of earplugs or a quick jab with a Q-tip to shut them out.

SCOOTER'S PARKING LOT was empty except for two pickups, Marti's Taurus, a few dried leaves, and George. Back when he realized Marti could see him, George told her he didn't mind being dead but wanted to shoot one last game of pool. Since that was impossible, he loitered at the bar's front door and greeted customers with a doleful, "Have a good time. Drink one for me. I'll just wait out here." No one other than Marti heard him. She classified him as an Eeyore ghost.

"We need to talk now." The Judge's orders didn't carry the same oomph they did when he was alive.

She had a decision to make. Retrieve the spare key from its magnetic holder stashed in the wheel well? Or go inside and retrieve the key she left behind the night before? The first was a pain in the butt. She deliberately made the key hard to get to. She didn't want to risk using it as a backup system when her judgment—not to mention her coordination and driving ability—was impaired.

The latter carried its own risks. It wouldn't be the first time she claimed her key only to have it repossessed. The latter was definitely the more attractive option.

"I owe you an apology," The Judge said.

"You owe me more than one." One drink. She could go in, have *one drink*, get her key, and leave.

"We took you to doctors."

"You gave me drugs." If any of the muckety-mucks from Burger Buster caught her drinking in uniform, she'd lose her job.

"You were better when you took them."

"I was better when you thought I took them. When I took them, I couldn't shut out the dead. You all talked at once, so I stopped." What were the chances of Burger Buster bosses drinking at a redneck bar in midafternoon? She didn't recognize either of the trucks, but that didn't mean anything.

"We did what we thought was best."

"Best for you. Not me." A fellow employee might spot her. Some of them would rat her out in a heartbeat. She could send Grandma in on a recon mission, except Grandma refused to set foot in Scooter's. She hung out with George while Marti went inside—the main reason it was her favorite drinking establishment.

"I need to tell your mother," The Judge said.

"Tell her what? That her crazy daughter's not totally loony tunes after all? ''Cause ghosts is real and I are one.'? What makes you think she'd believe you? Or see you? You're *dead*." One drink. Maybe two. She could hide in a dark corner. Scooter's had lots of dark corners.

"Marcile Tobias Mickkleson. Look at me." The Judge went from apologetic to apoplectic in under sixty and along the way reduced Marti to the quivering lump of her twelve-year-old self. She couldn't help it. She obeyed.

"I was murdered."

She laughed. Not at her father. He was dead serious. Grandma was long dead but not serious. In an eye-rolling contest with an army of live sixteen-year-olds, Alberta Marcile Ferguson would beat them all.

"I'm going to get my car key," Marti said.

TWO

"Jack Daniel's. And whatever's on tap." One drink. That was all. One drink, then she'd get her car key from Carl the Bartender and go outside and go home. She'd finish her conversation with The Judge. Or not. He stayed outside with Grandma and George. Maybe the two of them managed to get rid of him while she was inside. Better have two drinks. Give them time to work.

"Hey, Marti. Didn't expect to see you again so soon." Just Call Me Joe perched atop the cash register, his malevolent grin at odds with his friendly greeting. Marti classified him as a cantankerous old coot, even if he was dead.

Instead of putting a coaster in front of her and pouring her drink, Carl rummaged in a drawer beneath the bar, pulled out her key on its bright pink clip, and tossed it in front of her.

"Sorry. Boss says you're eighty-sixed." He delivered the bad news in a soothing Johnny Cash drawl. Marti knew the rich bass tones were real, but when he came into Burger Buster, the drawl was missing. She assumed he put it on and played it up for the Scooter's clientele. Adorable as it was, it didn't soften the news of her banishment.

Her key, with its paper tag that said *Marti M* along with the date and time of confiscation, wasn't adorable either. Carl recycled tags. Hers bore six dates, and according to the most recent, she lost her driving privileges shortly after midnight, well before last call.

Just Call Me Joe hopped off his roost. The night Marti, after a few too many rum and cokes, confessed she could see and hear him, he wasn't pleased. He refused to tell her his name, and she didn't care enough to press the matter. When he said, "Just call me Joe," she went with it.

At the moment, he looked mighty pleased with himself. Marti had a suspicion whatever caused her exile, it had nothing to do with the six strikes listed on her key tag.

"For how long?" The last time she was banned for life from Scooter's, it lasted two weeks. A long two weeks. Not because she missed the drinking. That, she could do anywhere.

Grandma wouldn't tell her why she refused to enter Scooter's. Maybe she and Just Call Me Joe had a history. Whatever. The dark bar, with its hidden corners and jukebox full of old-time country hits—no boy bands or twerking tarts allowed, only Patsy and Hank and crew—was her haven. It wasn't the alcohol, although recently she'd been indulging in more than she knew was good for her. Some nights she sipped a Sprite in a corner. Just Call Me Joe rarely joined her in a booth, and he was the only spirit—of the ethereal sort—in the place.

"I dunno. Could be for real this time," Carl said.

Just Call Me Joe did a little two step. His grin widened. Crooked teeth twinkled, but neither his smile nor his eyes lit up his leathery face. Whatever he did while alive, he'd spent a lot of time in the sun.

Jimmy, Scooter's owner, despised her but liked money. Regular customers meant regular cash, and Marti was a regular. For reasons he never bothered to share, Just Call Me Joe hated Jimmy worse than Jimmy hated her. Whatever she'd done, there was a good chance Just Call Me Joe either instigated it or, at the least, egged her on.

"You! Crazy girl! Out! Now!" Jimmy burst through the swinging door between the bar and the unused kitchen. Whatever she'd done, it really irritated him.

"The worms crawl in, the worms crawl out," Just Call Me Joe

sang and jumped onto the bar. "Hey, Marti? Wanna sing another duet?" Cantankerous was an understatement. He was an evil jerk.

He capered in front of her and grabbed his crotch.

Marti shuddered. It was just as well Carl and Jimmy couldn't see or hear him. No one needed to see the scrawny old ghost shake his booty in Carl's face.

"Come on up here and join me, Sweet Cheeks." He planted his scuffed brown shitkicker on top of her car key. She steeled herself for the shock, reached through his foot, and grabbed the key. Even though she knew what was coming, the icy burn made her flinch. She let out a yelp.

Just Call Me Joe cackled.

"You prick," she said.

"Out, crazy girl!" Jimmy shouted.

"I didn't mean you," she said.

Jimmy didn't buy it. "Out! Out! Out!" His face turned purple, and the veins on his neck bulged and throbbed.

"You really need to leave. You *really* pissed him off this time," Carl said.

Marti didn't have a clue what she'd done and wasn't sure she wanted to know, but she did want a drink.

"My dad died." She pulled a sad face. Jimmy had kids and, she assumed, a father. He looked, and sometimes smelled, like he'd crawled out from under a swamp log, but the odds were in favor of traditional parentage. Maybe she'd get a sympathy beer. She'd settle for cheap. Milwaukee's Best, in a can.

"I don't care. Out! Before I call the police!" Jimmy picked up the bar phone.

He probably kept the cops on speed dial. *At least he didn't call them last night.* Knowing whatever went on wasn't cop-level bad was a comfort. A small comfort, since blood needed to be spilled before Jimmy willingly brought on-duty police into his bar, but a comfort all the same.

"The worms play pinochle on your snout," Just Call Me Joe

crooned, Dean Martin with a country-twang. "Come on. Sing! Dance! Last night was a hoot!"

Marti had no doubt it was. She could stop at the Iroquois Lounge on the way home. The Iroquois was better lit than Scooter's, they played Muzak instead of letting the customers control a jukebox, and Grandma *always* followed her inside, but they never banned her.

"Never laugh as the hearse goes by, for you may be the next to die." Just Call Me Joe switched from Dino to Hank Williams, and his yodel followed her out the door.

He really sang well. For a dead guy.

Grandma and The Judge waited in her car. Grandma must have called shot-gun. The Judge huddled in the back seat, arms crossed, mouth downturned, and generally pissed off. Marti unlocked the door and got in. Neither greeted her.

"Hey, guys. Have a nice chat while I was gone? Are we ready to party? Or should we aim for a nice quiet family night at home?"

Grandma gave her the evil eye.

"Somebody murdered me," The Judge said.

"Gosh. Who could have *possibly* wanted to do that?" The Judge never picked up on Marti's sarcasm when he was alive. She wondered if he'd gained the ability in death.

"There are rumors it was your mother." He hadn't.

"You certainly gave her enough reason."

"What do you mean?"

"Well, let's see. You're cheap." Marti held up one finger. "You're controlling." A second finger. "And then there's that little thing with Mrs. McDonagh." She wagged her whole hand. The Judge and Sheila McDonagh were worth five fingers on their own.

"Who told you about her? Alberta? Was it you?"

Grandma snorted. "As if anyone needed to tell her. The whole town knew."

No one told her. In her junior year of high school—for the

first time since third grade when she'd ceased being the rich girl everyone wanted for their friend and became the crazy outcast kid—Marti had friends. Bicklesburg's group of small-town Goth wannabes thought her loony bin stays were romantic. Oliver, his girlfriend Ashley-but-please-call-me-Raven, and Marti's sort-of boyfriend, Dmitri, pretended to believe her when she talked about seeing the dead. It gave her spooky-Goth cred, and it was a relief to be around people with whom she didn't need to pretend.

Her junior year she was still the weird girl, but that was a *good* thing and she wasn't alone.

The four of them went on a Friday night double date. A concert or a movie or simply driving around town. She couldn't remember where they'd been, but she knew she'd had fun. She'd laughed. She was happy. They might have been—probably were—a little high. Oliver parked on the street in front of Dmitri's house. Dmitri got out but, instead of heading to the house, he jumped on the hood of Oliver's Camaro and belted out a Misfits song.

Oliver honked the horn. Marti and Raven screamed and applauded. Lights appeared in windows up and down the street. They didn't care. Loud, rowdy, having a good time, they were unwilling to let the night end—until they saw The Judge standing in Mrs. McDonagh's front window.

"Yo! Judge! Welcome to the neighborhood!" Dmitri shouted. "Make yourself right at home—at least until Ralphy gets back!"

In the backseat, Marti ducked. She didn't think her father saw her.

Ralph McDonagh was a truck driver. He was gone a lot.

Marti's mother's career was being The Judge's wife. She sat home alone a lot.

Marti spent the weekend avoiding her father.

On Monday, the school conducted a locker search. Dmitri and Oliver were busted for weed. They claimed it wasn't theirs, and Marti knew Dmitri was telling the truth. He never brought his to school. Oliver she wasn't sure about, but it didn't make any difference. Both boys came up before Judge Zero-Tolerance Mickkleson, who shipped them off to a youthful offender facility on the other side of the state. She never saw Dmitri again. Although their relationship was based mostly on the fact his parents hated her as much as hers hated him, she missed him. Raven washed the purple out of her hair, bought a new wardrobe full of preppy labels, went back to being Ashley, and never spoke to Marti again. Marti spent her first summer at the Birches, her parents' latest expensive Bin of Choice for Recalcitrant Daughters.

Her senior year, she was friendless but not alone. Never alone. She always had Grandma. And according to the buzz in Bicklesburg, The Judge still had Mrs. McDonagh. Probably not as often as the gossip mill reported. Mr. McDonagh was home *sometimes*.

"Don't exaggerate," The Judge said. "We were discreet."

"Ha," Grandma said.

"Discreet? Remind me to get you a dictionary," Marti said.

A dark SUV, followed by a humongous pickup, pulled into Scooter's parking lot. Shift-change time at the local factories, and it was Friday. Payday. The bar would soon be packed, and it wouldn't do to be spotted sitting alone in her car talking to herself. Or sitting listening to Grandma and The Judge argue. If Jimmy spotted her taking up a parking place without spending money, he'd never revoke her sentence.

"You both need to shut up." She turned the key. The Taurus shuddered and roared to life. She needed to get the muffler fixed. She waited for The Judge to point out the obvious. Grandma saved her nagging for more important issues than car repair, although she would no doubt have something to say if the muffler actually fell off the car. Neither of her passengers spoke. Their silence lasted until she was on the road.

"I left you money," The Judge said.

Marti hadn't thought about an inheritance. After a decade of cutting her family out of her life, she figured she was cut from theirs, and that included The Judge's will. "How much?"

"Enough."

"How much?" She didn't know how large a sum it would take to get her to return to Bicklesburg and her family, but it would need to be a lot.

"Go home. Find out. And while you're there, figure out who killed me. You're smart enough."

"How much money?"

"Do it for your mother. She's not well."

"You know you're a cliché, right?"

"What do you mean?"

"Dead guy. Ghost with a problem. Help me, Obi-Wan-psycho-daughter! You're my only hope!" Her father had been a cliché—rich old white guy on a power trip—when he was alive, but she decided not to bring it up.

"Isn't that how it works?" The Judge not only was a cliché, he believed in clichés.

"As long as he believes that old chestnut, he'll never move on," Grandma said.

"Someone murdered me," The Judge said, "and I want to know who, even if you don't."

"You killed yourself," Grandma said.

"I certainly did not!"

"All those years of drinking and eating like a pig finally caught up to you." Grandma wasn't cutting The Judge any slack.

"I hate to interrupt this conversation, but do you guys smell something?" A whiff of smoke. Marti couldn't tell where it came from. She hoped it wasn't the Taurus's engine. The car was a heap, but it was all she had.

"Just you and that gawd-awful uniform," The Judge said.

"Liar," Grandma said. "We're dead. We have no sense of smell."

Sirens. Red lights in the rearview mirror. Marti pulled to the side of the road and stopped.

Two fire trucks and a police car roared past. The Taurus was good.

A few blocks ahead, the fire trucks turned at—*Crap.* Maybe it was the CVS or the pizza place or any of the other small businesses that lined the side street. Just because they turned on Stanley Street didn't mean it was the Burger Buster.

She slowed to a crawl as she passed Stanley. The police had the street blocked off.

"Can you guys see anything?"

"Stop referring to your father and me as *you guys*. And, no."

"There's a fire. It'll probably improve the landscape around here," The Judge said.

Marti turned into a tiny strip mall and parked in front of the Iroquois.

"Do you think that's a good idea?" Grandma said.

"I'm not going in." She wasn't. At least not yet. On foot, she cut behind the mall and through the library parking lot. Ozzie didn't acknowledge her. She hoped somebody had found him and removed his remains, but the dumpster blocked her view of her early-morning resting place. Ozzie's almost-final resting place. She headed down the alley between Whiffler's Insurance Agency and Color Me Crazy Stylists. A crowd jammed the sidewalk in front of the salon. She weaseled her way through the onlookers until she made it to the police tape.

It wasn't the drugstore or the pizza place. The day officially became not simply a bad day, but a close the lid on the toilet and flush day.

"So, what happened?" a guy in a suit asked.

"How would—Oh." Her uniform. "I don't know. I got off an hour ago. Just haven't been home to change. Did everyone get out?"

"Looks like it." Suit Guy pointed to a knot of people huddled in the CVS parking lot. Marti didn't know how she'd missed the blaze of green and orange polyester. One of her coworkers jumped up and down and shouted.

"Look. It's your little friend," Grandma said.

"Sh—" Marti caught herself before she told her grandmother to shut up. Suit Guy wouldn't understand.

Darrell Something-or-other headed across the street toward her. She couldn't remember his last name. She thought of him as Weasel Boy. They didn't often work the same shift, but when they did, Weasel Boy attached himself to her like Velcro.

Grandma maintained he had a crush on her. Marti didn't want to go there.

"Pretty cool, huh?" Weasel Boy ducked under the police tape and inserted himself between Marti and Suit Guy. She edged away from him and stepped on someone's foot.

"Hey!"

"Sorry," Marti said. Suit Guy snickered.

"We should have marshmallows." Weasel Boy was enjoying himself.

"What happened?"

"I dunno. I was mopping the storeroom and the alarm went off and here we are. Looks like we're gonna get a long vacation."

He was right. With the amount of water the firemen were pouring through the roof, this was not a little grease fire. Even if the Burger Buster survived, cleanup would take weeks. Weeks without a paycheck.

"Fine for you," Marti said. Weasel Boy was in his early twenties but lived with his mother. He didn't need to worry about rent or groceries. "I need a paycheck."

"You can come eat dinner at my house whenever you want. Mother's a really good cook, and she's always telling me I should invite friends over."

"I'll start looking for another job."

"Good luck with that in Franklinville."

Suit Guy snickered again.

Even crap jobs were few and far between in the depressed town. Marti and Weasel Boy were lucky to be Burger Buster drones. Half of their coworkers had graduate degrees. Marti had no savings. Anything left after necessities—and it wasn't much—she deposited at the National Bank of Scooter's. All deposit. No return.

"It's a trust fund," The Judge said. "Your sister's in charge, but there's an upfront sum just waiting for you."

"How much?" Marti said.

"What?" Weasel Boy leaned in close to her.

Marti sprang back and landed on a foot again. Same guy's. She recognized his voice when he swore at her. Weasel Boy grabbed her before she toppled over.

"I can't take this." Marti freed herself from Weasel Boy's grasp and pushed her way back through the crowd.

"Don't forget! Free dinner!" Weasel Boy's shout followed her.

"He likes you a lot," Grandma said.

In the strip mall parking lot, Marti stared longingly at the entrance to the Iroquois.

"What do I have to do to get this money?" she said.

"Go home. Prove to your sister you're responsible," The Judge answered.

"I'll die a pauper before I manage that."

"You get the first check just for going home."

"How much is it?"

"Enough for six months. Stay in Bicklesburg. Prove you can take care of yourself, and the trust fund floweth. It'll be a tightly controlled flow, but it will flow."

"And if I take the money and run?"

"The account gets held to cover any future hospitalization bills or worst case scenario, bail. Or your long-term care if necessary."

No savings. Nada. All she had was the cash in her wallet, and after last night, she didn't know how much that was.

She opened the door of the Taurus and got in. Grandma and The Judge didn't follow.

"Six months? That's all?"

"Plenty of time for you to find out who killed me."

Grandma snorted and, once again, demonstrated her prize-winning eye roll.

Marti slammed the car door and rested her head on the steering wheel. Six months wasn't long. She'd learned a lot of survival skills after she left home. She'd gone at least eight months at a time before people started giving her sidewise looks and whispering behind her back. If the trust-fund payments were large enough, she and Grandma could find a house in the middle of nowhere. Way out in boo foo land. A place where she could go for days without seeing another living soul. A place not overrun with dead souls. A place with no Burger Buster. As a long-term stress-reduction plan, it was solid.

And The Judge mentioned something about her mother not being well. Her relationship with her mother was complicated, to say the least, but if Mom's health was bad enough for The Judge to notice, it worried her.

She rolled down the window.

"I figure out who murdered you and you go away?"

"Yes."

"No one murdered him. He could go now if he wanted," Grandma said. "Problem is, he doesn't want."

"I prove no one murdered you and you go away?"

The Judge didn't answer.

"Well? That one's a deal breaker."

"Okay, but—"

"Are you two going to get in the car or run along beside me?"

THREE

AFTER A FEW HOURS' SLEEP—SHE NEEDED TO GATHER HER strength before she returned to what was left of the rock-hard bosom of her family—Marti spent all of fifteen minutes throwing her belongings into plastic bags. Two large black trash bags held it all. If not for the quilt, she could have made do with one. She briefly considered leaving it.

"Don't even think about it," Grandma said.

"It's not worth hauling around," The Judge said.

Her father's comment was the clincher. She packed it.

The rent was paid until the end of the month. That gave her three weeks if she decided to come back. If she stayed in Bicklesburg or moved on to parts unknown, someone from the management company would come banging on the door on the third day of unpaid rent. They'd find the place empty. Her rent covered all utilities but the phone, and she'd take care of that later. If she came back before the end of the month, she might want it. If not, she'd cancel it from wherever she was. Not returning meant she'd lose her security deposit, but if things worked out in Bicklesburg, she wouldn't need it.

Her Burger Buster uniforms gave her pause. Technically, they belonged to the company. She should return them, but with the Franklinville Burger Buster closed, she had no idea where to take them.

"Hey, Dad, did Bicklesburg get a Burger Buster yet?"

The Judge scowled in answer. Marti assumed that meant no. She wanted to needle him with an *Over your dead body, right?*

but resisted. The drive ahead was long enough, and he already looked like he was in a foul mood.

"Darrell would turn them in for you," Grandma said.

Weasel Boy. Marti mimed sticking her finger down her throat and gagged. She folded the two sets of tunics and pants and stacked them neatly on the sofa, the only sign she'd ever occupied the place. The scent of pickles and grease followed her out the door.

Before she hit the road, she ran by the library one last time and dropped her books in the deposit box. If she ever returned to Franklinville, she wanted her library card in good standing. No matter where she'd lived or what she'd done, she was always a good library patron. She considered it a point of pride, her single concession to responsible adulthood. She swung around back and checked for Ozzie. His body and shopping cart were gone, but he wasn't. He shimmered in her headlights, slumped on the ground next to the dumpster. She hoped he just hadn't yet figured out how to wander. It would suck to be tied to a garbage bin for eternity. She waved, but he didn't wave back.

"Are we ever going to get going?" The Judge asked.

"I feel like I ought to go give him a pep talk or something." As accustomed as she was to—and as much as she disliked—being surrounded by roving spirits, she felt a responsibility to Ozzie. Almost a maternal instinct. His demise was the first time she'd been present when a soul passed from the living sphere to the dead, even if she didn't remember the event. "He looks so dejected."

"He'll be fine," Grandma said. Marti didn't ask how she knew. Grandma had a few connections in the afterlife, or at least a better understanding of how things worked, than Marti did but was reticent on the details.

In the wee hours of the morning, with the dim lights of the sleeping town in her rearview mirror, Marti realized her closest connection in Franklinville was a dead, homeless bum. If she still talked to shrinks, it would be a subject worth exploring. She was glad she didn't.

The drive to Bicklesburg was less than two hundred miles. The pouty-child voice in her head whispered her mother and sister could have found *her* after The Judge's death, if they'd wanted to. The slightly saner, grown-up voice pointed out she'd moved so many times in the past ten years she'd lost count, and she was *really* good at hiding from them. It was her special talent. That and the ghost thing.

She made it to the center of Bicklesburg as the sun came up. The village square was deserted. Almost. Mrs. Heedly, her third-grade teacher, sat in the gazebo's hanging swing. Marti spent a large part of third grade sitting in the hallway outside the classroom door. Mrs. Heedly had no patience for Marti's "troublemaking" and delighted in separating her, desk and all, from the rest of the class. Marti was vindicated seven years later when she said hello to her former tormentor—at the woman's funeral.

Marti slowed the Taurus to a crawl and drove around the square. She hadn't seen a sign, but the speed limit used to be ridiculously low, like ten or fifteen miles an hour, and she doubted it had changed. Even in the wee hours of the morning, there was a good chance the village speed trap was operating. Rowdy teens and outsiders, scofflaws all, sometimes hit twenty-five and kept the village coffers full.

Bicklesburg was the county seat—the Emerald City to Battlesburough County's Oz—and took its importance seriously. The village square was more oval than square. Its central park—"the Green" in Bickles-speak—was surrounded by carefully conserved Greek Revival buildings, each bearing a historical landmark plaque. Nobody tore down history and replaced it with a parking lot or chain store there. The Bicklesburg powers-that-be were convinced if they kept up the appearance of a more genteel time—or what they thought of as a more genteel time—

the village would stay a *nice* place to live. Somewhere along the line, the Bicklesburg hive mind chose one good year and stuck with it. The downtown facade hadn't changed since 1959 when the town fathers apparently decided to remain in 1859. Ward and June Cleaver, Wally, and the Beaver would be right at home in Bicklesburg.

Eddie Haskell wasn't welcome. The square-peg-in-a-round-hole Marti Mickklesons of the world weren't either.

When she drove past the county courthouse, its front lawn crowded with souls ranging from civil war veterans to recently deceased petty thieves, she expected commentary from The Judge. More than a few of the not-so-dearly departed from the last four decades must have appeared before him at some point.

Not a peep came from the back seat. She checked her rearview mirror. He was still there. *Darn.*

Grandma and The Judge hadn't spoken to each other or her for miles. They'd bickered for the first two-thirds of the drive. Now that they were both dead, Marti discovered how much they disliked each other in life.

Grandma warned Marti's mother not to marry Thaddeus Mickkleson. He was a scoundrel and a cheat from a long line of scoundrels and cheats and would break her only granddaughter's heart. The Judge considered Grandma Bertie an interfering old biddy and blamed any problems in his marriage—which, according to Grandma, meant any time he didn't get his own way—on her.

At the time of her death and Marti's birth, Grandma was banned from his house. Fat lot of good that did in the long run. It did explain why Marti's childhood talk of Grandma Bertie, out of all her so-called imaginary friends, caused The Judge to turn funny colors and the veins in the side of his neck to throb.

Marti'd never heard a peep about their feud. In the Mickkleson family, the living didn't air their dirty laundry in front of each other, let alone the public.

For the first hour of the drive, their squabbling entertained her. In the second hour, she would have killed them if it wasn't redundant. By the last hour, they quit speaking to each other, much to Marti's relief. She didn't know how much longer they could keep it up and wondered who would speak first. Her money was on The Judge.

It was too early to show up at her mother's house. *Her mother's house.* No longer *The Judge's house.* Would that change anything? She wasn't yet ready to find out. A little drive around her old stomping grounds was in order.

Three-quarters of the way around the square, she hung a right off Bickle Circle and left the time warp. A CVS stood next to a Domino's Pizza. A tiny strip mall held a laundromat, a thrift shop and—

"Oh my gawd, is that a *pawn shop*?" The Golden Pawn nestled shoulder to shoulder with the Quik Cash Loan Store. The Bicklesburg where Marti grew up enforced architectural guideline ordinances, sign ordinances, lighting ordinances, noise ordinances, and pretty-much-anything-else-one-could-think-of ordinances. The only ordinance the commercial block didn't violate was the tall grass ordinance. The squat, utilitarian buildings sat in a sea of black asphalt. She wondered if there was a parking lot size ordinance. If there was, it was in shambles too.

"Newcomers got elected to the village council and took over the zoning committee." The Judge didn't bother to hide his disgust.

Newcomers. The one thing worse in The Judge's eyes than delinquent teens.

Grandma maintained her stony silence.

"Well, I won that bet," Marti said.

"Don't tell me you've taken up gambling too." Gamblers were a hair's breadth above juvenile miscreants on The Judge's scale.

Grandma snorted. "So sayeth the pillar of moral rectitude."

Just past the Dollar General—the village was going to hell in a handbasket—was a fast food joint. Not Burger Buster, thank goodness. She hit the So-nutt-ee Donut drive-through.

She didn't recognize the pimply teen who took her money in exchange for an extra-large black coffee and two chocolate-iced, custard-filled donuts, but she knew his face. The sleepy young man was unquestionably a Pernelli. The same faces showed up in Bicklesburg generation after generation, the result of either strong genes or inbreeding. Dawn Pernelli, Marti's high school tormentor-in chief, had a passel of brothers—six or seven. Marti couldn't recall exactly how many, but there were a lot. The youngest started school the year after she and Dawn graduated. Pimples might be Dawn's baby brother, one of the others, or a cousin. Oliver was Dawn's cousin and bore the Pernelli stamp, although he didn't bear the name.

Most of the students at Bicklesburg High ignored her, intimidated by The Judge. Even the staff kowtowed to her father, who was rumored to control the school board from behind the scenes, although most were unable to mask their dislike of her. Dawn was different. In her presence, Marti wasn't the invisible weird girl with the all-powerful daddy. She was a target.

When they were freshmen, Marti walked into the school bathroom and found Dawn changing names on ballots for the homecoming court. Dawn ended up the freshman attendant. Marti never told anyone what she saw. Who would she tell and why would anyone believe her if she did? Still, word somehow got out. Dawn probably couldn't keep her own mouth shut. If the administration heard, they didn't do anything, but there was a lot of sniggering among the students. Through it all, Dawn held her head and tiara high.

Then she came after Marti.

Dawn had an extra portion of mean but wasn't overly blessed with brains, so she stuck to the classics. Hallway taunts. Bathroom graffiti. Tripping Marti in the cafeteria. Papering the outside of Marti's locker with borderline obscene pictures when she wasn't having her minions attempt to stuff Marti into it. Marti was too tall for that trick. They never managed to shut the door. Dawn stopped short of posting her Marti Humiliation Achievement List on the Internet, and after Oliver and Dmitri disappeared from Bicklesburg, she got sneakier in her torture or at least more careful about getting caught. She let her followers do the dirty work.

No one ever tried to stop her. Dawn Pernelli was everybody's designated missile, aimed at misfit Marti, doing the things they all—students and teachers—wished they could get away with. The one time Marti complained, both her mother and the school guidance counselor lectured her on trying harder to fit in. Grandma Bertie was her only advocate. Too bad Marti was the only one who heard her.

Pimples didn't appear to recognize her. That was a good thing. The Bicklesburg grapevine was a marvel of efficiency when she lived there, and she didn't count on that having changed. Her nomadic lifestyle taught her two important things. All small towns were Peyton Place, and you never truly got out of high school. Pimples might not be Dawn's baby brother, but he was some sort of a relative. She didn't need him alerting Dawn to her presence.

"Hey lady. You gonna take this or what?" Pimples held out her order.

She thanked him and took the brown bag. She made a point of being polite to fast-food workers. Solidarity and all that. He grunted in return. Definitely had all the verbal skills of a Pernelli. She pulled around to the back of the building and parked in the far corner next to the dumpster.

"What is it with you and dumpsters?" The Judge asked.

"Shush," Grandma said.

Marti decided to let Grandma handle The Judge. With any luck, they'd stop talking to each other again, and she could drink her coffee and eat her donuts in peace while she waited until a more reasonable hour to knock on Mom's door.

And geared up her courage. She didn't expect a prodigal daughter greeting—she certainly wasn't repentant enough to rate a feast—but she didn't know what to expect or what she would say. *Hi, Mom. I'm home!* seemed inadequate. Maybe the shock would render her mother speechless. The shock. What did The Judge mean by "not well"?

"You said Mom wasn't well. What's wrong?"

"It's complicated," The Judge said. "You'll see."

Marti debated pushing for details. If he didn't want to tell her, it would be an exercise in futility. Between heredity and environment, she came by her own stubbornness honestly. From both sides of the family.

"Me showing up at her door. It's not going to—you know—make her keel over or anything?"

"Maybe you should call first."

"I don't have a cell phone."

"You're kidding. Even I have one. Had one." Alive, The Judge hated technology but loved expensive toys.

"Nope." Marti loved technology but couldn't afford expensive toys.

"You could go inside and—"

"No." Marti wasn't getting out of the car until she got to her mother's house. Pimples Pernelli was all the Bicklesburg she could take before seeing her mother. If anyone recognized her, she might pack it in and leave. The idea was already tempting enough. "Who thinks Mom murdered you?" *Why* wasn't in question.

"It's just gossip, but she doesn't need it. And I don't like it," The Judge said.

"You should be used to gossip."

A shiny black Cadillac Escalade pulled in, parked across three spaces, and disgorged its occupants.

Sheila McDonagh had not aged well. Her hair was still an unlikely shade of blonde and still shellacked into a canary-yellow helmet, but there was three times the Mrs. McDonagh Marti remembered and all crammed into what appeared to be the same size—and style—jeans she wore over a decade ago. The red puffer jacket wasn't doing her any favors either, nor was the glow-in-the-dark orange fake tan.

Back in the day, Marti knew she should hate the woman with whom her father betrayed her mother. She'd read enough angsty teen novels to get that. Somehow she never summoned up the energy. Mrs. McDonagh worked as the receptionist at the front desk at the courthouse. She was all sweetness and sunshine the few times they'd interacted before Marti found out about her and The Judge.

After Marti found out, she avoided the courthouse. Back then Sheila McDonagh didn't look much like a floozy—at least not Marti's Hollywood inspired idea of one—other than her big yellow hair. Since Marti's own driver's license had a color wheel in place of hair color, she wouldn't judge the woman on a dye job. The current edition of Sheila teetered along on her high-heeled boots behind her husband, her mouth going a mile a minute, the central casting picture of overblown and aging floozy.

Ralph McDonagh *had* aged well. Despite the early-morning chill, he didn't wear a jacket. No beer belly on him. His plaid shirt was tucked into worn Levi's ending above the heels of pointy-toed cowboy boots that made him look all the more lean and rangy. Marti was sure the exaggerated silver pompadour existed solely to show off just how much hair he had left. His face had a few creases, but a lean, mean, aging Harrison Ford in a wig could play him in a movie. What had Sheila ever seen in her father?

"He's got more hair than you. Taller too." Marti turned to look at The Judge. He hunkered down in the back seat. "Relax. It's not like he can see you."

Her father sat up straight and attempted to reassemble what was left of his dignity. Stripped of his judicial robes and any real power over her, he wasn't much. An average little man in an expensive suit. A short, tubby old man with a comb-over. A dead man. The thought should have roused more sympathy in her than it did.

Maybe she couldn't yet mourn what wasn't gone.

"Looks like Ralph did pretty well for himself. That's a nice car." The shiny Escalade bore thirty-day tags. Marti couldn't read the dates, but it was less than a month old.

"I really wouldn't know," The Judge said.

"Not privy to Sheila's finances?"

"We came to a parting of the ways."

"Mom found out?"

No answer from The Judge.

"Ralph found out?"

"This is none of your business."

"If he did, he's a prime suspect for killing you." *Along with at least two hundred and ninety seven others.*

"He was not murdered," Grandma said.

"It speaks, but it makes no sense," The Judge said.

"He should have been murdered long ago. Drowned at birth. But he wasn't." Grandma said.

"Then you wouldn't have me," Marti said.

"Ha!" The Judge said.

"At least you take after your mother's side," Grandma said.

"So it's your fault she has this . . . thing? I knew it had nothing to do with *my* side of the family."

"Nothing comes from your people except a few of her bad habits."

"Enough." Marti told herself her great-grandmother was just trying to annoy The Judge. She was *nothing* like her father. She turned the key and the Taurus roared. She really needed to take care of that muffler. In Bicklesburg she'd end up with a ticket in no time, unless the noise ordinance was as outdated as the zoning ordinances. "So, has the newcomer strip-mall crowd taken over the police department too?"

"Oh no," The Judge said. "Big Fysh is the chief now."

Great. Billy "Big" Fysh Jr. was Dawn's high school boyfriend and former cocaptain of the football team. He'd played one of those positions mainly consisting of mowing down opposing players. His resemblance to the Hulk resulted in *Fysh Smash* banners festooning the school on game days.

"He rose through the ranks quickly," Marti said.

"Had the position since his dad retired."

"Gotta love Bicklesburg and small ponds." Except she didn't. In her experience, the smaller the pond, the more the likelihood of the minnows being swallowed alive.

With Big Fysh in charge of the Bicklesburg police force, the first thing she needed to do when she got her hands on some cash was take care of the muffler. Big was Dawn's number-one Marti-torturing minion, and Marti had no reason to believe he'd changed.

FOUR

Six large houses, mansions by modern standards, lined the corridor of Albion Court, known to longtime locals as "the Avenue." The imposing brick houses, all built by the town's founding fathers and set well back from the street, had a certain sameness to them—an early nineteenth-century housing development for the wealthy. Hedge-lined walks led to front steps and porches flanked by white columns. Behind heavy wood doors and tastefully curtained windows dwelled the current generation of Bicklesburg aristocracy.

The Avenue wasn't Philadelphia's Main Line or Long Island's North Shore. The residents weren't Boston Brahmins or New York Knickerbockers. Which was a problem. The second-class status of the small-town nobility made its members take their positions and themselves all the more seriously.

The street ended in a large circle in front of the seventh house, the largest and scariest of them all.

Bickle House, home of the Mickklesons, or what was left of them.

The Bickle family name had daughtered out, and the remnants of the line died off or deserted Bicklesburg ages ago, but their castle still stood, a stern emperor presiding over the minor royalty lining the path to the throne. Bickle House was the top rung of the local social ladder. The Mickklesons didn't create the rung, but they stood on it now, and that was all that mattered.

Her sister was born in Bickle House. Marti wasn't. She was a baby when The Judge, second generation of Mickklesons to own the crown jewel of Bicklesburg real estate, inherited the manse. It was the only home she remembered. Although *home* was stretching it. *Housing* was more apt. *Prison* was even better.

How The Judge's father acquired the property remained a mystery. Rumor had it he won it in a poker game. Thanks to The Judge's refusal to talk about it and the air of secrecy and shame he took on whenever Marti brought up the subject, she spent most of her youth imagining far more nefarious scenarios. Her favorite involved pirates.

She supposed her mother owned it now. Eventually, it would go to her little sister. On The Judge's list of lifetime disappointments, his lack of sons came in second only to everything about his eldest daughter, but Mom shut the baby machine down after two girls. She'd risked her girlish figure twice and considered that fulfillment of her duty.

All the Avenue's houses were outrageously expensive to maintain and far too large for single families, especially without the large live-in staffs of past eras. When Marti left home, two sat empty. When she was in high school, a young entrepreneur tried to get the street rezoned for multifamily dwellings, intending to turn the empty monstrosities into upscale apartments. The Judge and the other remaining Avenue occupants fought the change and won. They preferred empty houses over undesirable neighbors, and they had more pull with the village council than some upstart real estate wannabe.

Marti's sister later married the uppity would-be mogul. Marti missed the wedding, but she kept up with Bicklesburg news online. The *Bicklesburg Gazette* published a print edition once a week but, in a rare Bicklesburg nod to the modern world, had a great website. After her last laptop died, Marti was limited to using the computers at the library. She hadn't managed to read the hometown news for over a month. If she had, Dad's re-entry into her life wouldn't have been such a surprise.

She didn't imagine her parents were overjoyed with an upstart son-in-law from the wrong side of town and a good ten years older than his bride, but they always believed throwing money at a bad situation made it better. The wedding was the social event of the year. The *Gazette*'s website published the equivalent of a double-page spread full of photos, and in each, her sister glowed. They either hired an excellent photographer or the bride truly was happy. The groom looked smug.

Since the *Bicklesburg Gazette* was big on social news, she knew the wedding was quickly followed by two babies. Too quickly with the first. Her sister wasn't so perfect after all. The first child was a boy, and they named him after The Judge. Marti was willing to bet everything she owned—little though it was—the continuation of the long line of Thaddeus Aaron Mickklesons, even if the latest was Thaddeus Aaron Mickkleson Rudawski, made everything shiny and transformed the social-climbing husband into a saint.

She pointed the Taurus at the brick behemoth and crept toward the circle at the end of the street, a peasant approaching her king. As long as she didn't give the car too much gas, the muffler didn't roar. She parked beneath a giant maple tree that had yet to shed its blazing red leaves. Once it did, they would be disposed of daily—twice a day if needed—by the yard service employed by the Avenue's Residents' Council. No crunchy brown leaves allowed to mar the beauty of the Avenue. No opportunities for jumping into piles of fall leaves for the Avenue's children, if there were still any resident children.

"You can't leave this heap here," The Judge said. "Go back around and park by the garage."

The Avenue's driveways and garages were hidden behind the main houses and only accessible from parallel alleyways that ran behind the houses. The private lanes provided an extra layer of insulation between the royalty and the peons of Bicklesburg. The garages—former stables and carriage houses—were each big enough to house a family of ten plus multiple pets. To park by the garage, she'd need to leave the Avenue, go back to Strafing

Street, and turn into an alley. Either one. They met and joined behind Bickle House. *All roads lead home.*

"Leave her alone," Grandma said.

"I'm good here," Marti said.

She wasn't good. She wasn't ready to return to her parents' house. She needed to get out of the car. Go up the front walk, climb the front steps, pass between the unwelcoming white columns, cross the porch, and ring the bell. *Easy-peasy. Not so much.*

If she sat there much longer, someone would call the police, or worse, the Avenue's private security watchdogs would show up. Her ancient Taurus did not fit the landscape. On the plus side, if she ended up at the police station, she might feel more at home than she did on the Avenue. Big must have outgrown "Fysh Smash." The private Albion Court Security thugs, chosen by her father to safeguard the Avenue and its residents, weren't bound by the same constraints as the police. Maybe things had changed. Maybe the ACS had morphed into a fluffy, friendly welcoming committee. Maybe she should sit there long enough to find out. Maybe pigs flew, chocolate contained zero calories, and she would learn to love okra.

"What are you waiting for?" The Judge was out of the car. His ineffectual attempt to bang on the driver's side window made Grandma Bertie laugh. Marti flinched and winced as his fist caught and passed through her ear.

"Oh my gawd. I'm sorry!" The Judge was horrified. He obviously thought he'd hit her, and physical violence was never part of his repertoire. In fact, he abhorred it.

Marti saw no reason to enlighten him. If his fist had gone through her head, the effect would have been worse than a blow. Besides, his discomfort cheered her.

"So, let's do this, shall we?" she said. She'd come this far. She might as well see it through. Not to mention, the needle on the Taurus's gas gauge was in the red zone, and she wasn't sure she could afford the gas to get back to Franklinville or the muffler wouldn't fall off before she made it out of town.

Her overly bright words were met with a sad smile from Grandma and an impatient grunt from The Judge.

One. *Inhale.* Two. *Exhale.* The waist-high shrubs along the front walk grew and closed in on her. Or maybe she'd shrunk and was six years old again, the thorns of the bushes reaching to grab her. *One foot in front of the other. Breathe.* With each step, Marti fought to calm the pounding in her head and silence the ringing in her ears. *This is ridiculous. I am an adult. I can do this.*

She didn't feel like an adult. "Grandma?" Marti's voice trailed off. She sounded as pathetic as she felt.

"You'll be fine. I'm here."

Marti knew Grandma Bertie couldn't *do* anything except be there, but her great-grandmother's words reassured her as they'd done when Marti was a frightened six-year-old.

"I don't understand the issue here. Get up there and ring the bell." The Judge never understood Marti or her fears. There was no reason for him to start now.

Four stairs and she would be on the front porch. The spacious porch made a perfect place for children to play, were they permitted to. The young Marti and her sister were restricted to the backyard. Children frolicking in front of the grand house was deemed unseemly. The magnificent porch was only used during her parents' annual summer party, when it was decorated with fairy lights and filled with linen-covered tables and Bicklesburg's most influential citizens—all two dozen of them, twelve there on sufferance—dressed to the hilt. Every summer, someone drank too much and tumbled over the rail into the flower bed. Usually her father. Good thing it was a short fall.

Marti grabbed the wrought-iron handrail, steadied herself, and ascended the brick stairs.

Six steps across the polished wood floor—*breathe*—and she stood before the entrance to her childhood home.

All the years she was gone, she kept a door key on her ring. Even if the lock hadn't been changed, it didn't feel right to open the door and walk in. For all she knew, her mother wouldn't recognize her. She might call the cops. Or the ACS thugs. Or shoot her. The Judge made a big deal out of making sure all his girls—Mom, RachelAnne, and Marti the Unstable—knew how to handle a firearm.

It even felt wrong to knock on the heavy mahogany front door. She didn't have to do this. She could leave. Turn and run. Drive away. Somewhere. Anywhere. Farther away than Franklinville. Start over for the umpteenth time. No one need know about her brief return to Bicklesburg.

Unless the Taurus ran out of gas inside the town limits.

Or the muffler fell off.

Or the cops stopped her for driving a noisy, ugly vehicle in their candy-box town.

"If I got arrested, and Big threw away the key for six months, would I get paid?"

"Stop procrastinating. Ring the bell." The Judge's imperial command didn't encourage her.

She stuck her hands in her pockets. "Why am I doing this again?"

"Justice," The Judge said.

"To get rid of him," Grandma said.

"Nifty cashy-money," Marti said. She steeled herself, removed her hands from her pockets, and lifted the heavy brass, faux door knocker. She knew the lion's head was a doorbell in disguise and, unless the melody had been changed, the familiar tones of Big Ben rang throughout the house. Big Ben, the *all clear* signal in Franklinville's emergency alert system test, might be a good omen. She doubted it.

She waited.

"Ring it again," The Judge said.

"Leave her alone," Grandma said.

"You two need to shut up. This is hard enough. Be quiet and let me do it on my own."

She reached for the knocker. The heavy door swung open. Marti found herself not face to face with her mother, but with her hand in the air, fingers curled and ready to claw out the eyes of her sister, the ever-perfect RachelAnne.

RachelAnne—*one word please and a capital* A *and don't forget the* e *at the end*—hadn't changed much in the last decade. If anything, she'd become more RachelAnne. Every hair of her tasteful hairstyle was perfectly in place. Not puffed and shellacked like Mrs. McDonagh's. RachelAnne's hair lay artfully tousled, as if Mother Nature herself arranged it and there was no other way for it to be. She'd probably spent a good hour on it. The blonde was no more natural than Mrs. McDonagh's, but it must have cost a pretty penny to make it appear colored by genetics and highlighted by the sun rather than by chemicals and a talented stylist. Makeup—not too much, exactly enough to show she cared to make the effort—perfect. Two children—not present but no doubt also perfect—hadn't affected her perfect figure, which was clothed in the perfect outfit for the perfect homecoming queen turned perfect small-town aristocracy heiress apparent.

Marti's jeans and sweatshirt were clean, and she'd brushed her teeth and hair before throwing her plastic bags in the car and taking off. If she had a look, it was "Needs More Coffee."

"So. You heard," RachelAnne said.

"Hi Marti! Welcome home! How the heck are you?" Marti couldn't keep the sarcasm out of her voice. RachelAnne had that effect on her. It wasn't like she expected hugs and kisses. The Mickklesons weren't much on physical displays, but some sort of greeting would be nice.

"Don't. Just—don't. It's been a rough enough morning already," RachelAnne said.

Instead of asking why, Marti kept her mouth shut. RachelAnne looked pained. Marti didn't want to give her the opportunity to move into martyr territory, especially not if her presence was the cause. The sisters stared at each other in silence until Marti couldn't take it.

"So, how's Mom?"

"You'd better come in." RachelAnne's tone skirted the borders of martyrdom.

Her sister stepped back, and Marti stepped into her parents' house for the first time in a decade. Nausea hit her. She swayed and grabbed the doorframe.

"Are you okay?"

"This isn't easy for me either." The wobble in Marti's voice irritated her. She knew better than to show weakness in front of the enemy. Worse than the enemy, her baby sister.

"Mom's in the kitchen." RachelAnne's voice softened. "You know, I think she'll be happy to see you."

Mom was tucked into the corner breakfast nook, cup and saucer, teapot, toast, and jam jar in front of her.

The stench of Mom's special tea hung in the air like fog.

Mom never drank coffee. She drank tea made with her own mixture of tea leaves and herbs brewed in an elegant pot from her considerable collection of antique china cups, saucers, and teapots.

The fetid odor of the tea didn't appear to bother Mom or RachelAnne. Marti's eyes watered. She took shallow breaths. The familiar dirty-socks-and-cat-pee scent of Valerian—Mom's tea always smelled so bad no one else touched it—was joined by dead skunk. Mom had a new recipe, and it reeked worse than the old one. Marti hoped it tasted better than it smelled. She didn't intend to find out.

She recognized the blue and gold lusterware teapot and cup, with their iridescent glaze and hand-painted cherry blossoms, as a set handed down from Grandma Bertie. On the table next to the pot lay the heart-shaped silver tea infuser Marti gave her mother for Christmas—how many years ago? She couldn't have been older than ten.

"Hi, Mom." Marti left out the *Honey, I'm home*. She needed to rein in her smart-aleck tendencies, at least until she found out what hoops her sister would make her jump through to get her inheritance.

"Oh, Marti. Your father's not here." Mom idly picked up her spoon, gave her tea a slow stir, and stared into her cup.

Aside from the fact that The Judge was standing right beside Marti, it was not the greeting she expected.

"Play along." RachelAnne's stage whisper was as good as a shout. Mom didn't notice, or if she did, she ignored her younger daughter.

"Oh dear. Just like Aunt Alice Bradley," Grandma Bertie said.

"I told you she wasn't well," The Judge said.

Margaret Mickkleson was, like her younger daughter, perfectly coiffed and neatly dressed, but something was off kilter. She wasn't her imperious self, not the one Marti remembered. Although totally submissive to The Judge—at least to his face—Marti's mother ruled her daughters with an iron fist in a velvet glove.

Marti played a round of "What's Wrong With This Picture."

Mom slumped, her shoulders the tiniest bit rounded. She leaned on her elbows. Not much for anyone else, but for the woman who equated ramrod-straight posture with good breeding, she might as well be slouched with her legs splayed in front of her.

The iron was missing. The glove was empty.

One buttered triangle of wheat toast lay untouched on her plate. The other, spread with jam, was shredded. Dark purple smeared Mom's fingers. *Jam?* Marti's fondness for blackberry jam always provoked a lift of her mother's perfectly arched eyebrows and a "Do you really think you need the extra calories, dear?" Mom never touched the stuff.

Those perfectly arched eyebrows hadn't seen tweezers in too long. They looked like caterpillars, or like Marti's brows. Below the unkempt brows, the tiny crow's feet around her mother's eyes could be the result of time, but the unfocussed gaze couldn't be blamed on age. Grandma Bertie's ghost eyes held more spark than Mom's.

"I wonder what's keeping The Judge? It's not like him to be late." Mom contemplated her sticky hand then licked her fingers.

The Queen Consort was gone. The woman at the table appeared . . . human.

Marti's eyes burned. Her knees wobbled. Her father's death barely fazed her. From her point of view, he was still around, and he was still himself. Her mother—Marti didn't know who this old woman was. She did some quick calculations. Her mother was sixty-two. Not old at all. Whatever was wrong, it was more than the effects of time and grief.

Marti sat down across from her mother, picked up the uneaten slice of toast, and bit into it. Cold.

"I came as soon as I heard," she said. "I'm sorry I wasn't here sooner."

"Don't talk with your mouth full." The words were Mom's, but the tone was listless, an auto-response. "Would you like some tea? Your father likes sweet tea. Sweeties of all sorts, really. Sometimes I sweeten things a little extra for him."

"Mom!" RachelAnne loaded the single word with multiple commands, including "Don't say that" and "Hush" and a half dozen more Marti didn't want to think about. Her sister sounded more like Mom than her mother did.

"No thanks." Marti didn't see any reason in her mother's words for her sister's censure. The Judge did like sweet tea. Had liked sweet tea. Sweet, tart, tangy—it no longer made any difference, since The Judge was beyond drinking anything.

"Then you'd better go get ready for church. You certainly can't go with us dressed like *that*."

Her mother's disapproval was the first thing that made Marti feel she was truly home. Her throat tightened, and she blinked away tears. She would not cry.

"I think I'm going to skip church today." She'd skipped it every Sunday since she was twelve. After scandalizing her Sunday school class with the story of the Reverend Bartleby Stoker's unseemly death in the bed of the wife of a church deacon, talking her parents into letting her stay home was a piece of cake. Insisting she heard the story from the reverend himself was the icing on the cake. It was also a lie. She heard the story from the cuckolded and long-dead deacon.

Marti put down the toast and patted her mother's hand. An unfamiliar welling of sympathy disconcerted her. She'd battled her mother for years. Mom was the enemy, responsible for the misery of her teenage years, but the woman across the table wasn't the same woman whose standards Marti consistently failed to meet.

"I don't think that's a good idea, dear. Your father won't be pleased." Mom picked up the jar of blackberry jam and contemplated the contents. "Oh, what the hell. I'm hungry." She scooped a finger full and and stuck it in her mouth.

Marti stayed stock-still and tried to keep her shock off her face, but didn't know if she succeeded. Inside, she felt like a cartoon character—her eyes bugged and her jaw dropped to the table. Mom's use of the *h-e*-double-hockey-sticks word, her admission she was hungry, the blackberry jam—on her finger no less—any of those things alone would have surprised Marti. The combination left her dumbfounded.

The Judge harrumphed.

Grandma tsk-tsked.

"Here, Mom. Use a spoon." RachelAnne handed her mother a small, silver spoon.

The pickle spoon from the formal silver, reserved for special occasions. Occasions so special Marti only remembered it being hauled out once, and for a function so highfalutin she wasn't allowed to attend. The misuse of family heirlooms, a major misdeed in Mom's lexicon of sins, would surely bring her mother back to earth.

Her mother took the spoon, ladled more jam into her mouth, and giggled.

The high-pitched giggle did it. Margaret Alberta Dibble Mickkleson *never* giggled.

"Who are you and what have you done with my mother?" Marti said.

FiVE

"Marti." RachelAnne's urgent whisper was as subtle as a herd of stampeding purple elephants. She shifted her weight from foot to foot and glanced at the kitchen door, her body language more obvious than her tone. Her eyebrows—no need for tweezers there—raised and her lips pinched, she channeled Old Mom, the definition of impatient disapproval. She glanced at the door, then at Marti and back to the door. Irritation rolled off her like steam.

"Okay, Mom." Marti directed her answer at her sister. RachelAnne's neck flushed scarlet, and the color crept to her cheeks. Baby Sister might be Mom's heiress-in-waiting, but she still had a few things to learn. Mom *never* blushed.

"I'll see if I can find Marti something to wear to church." Her sister's words were for Mom, but Marti knew the frosty tone was for her.

She was in for a grand time.

"That's nice dear. I don't think her old clothes will fit her anymore." Mom spoke through a mouthful of jam. The blackberries stained her lips a lovely Goth purple. The first time Marti showed up at the dinner table with her hair dyed jet-black and wearing blackberry-colored lipstick, her mother cried. The idea of being mother to Morticia Addams was too much for her. Marti suspected hormones were involved. Mom seldom let emotions get the better of her, but even Margaret the Great was no match for PMS.

"You're looking a little chunky, Marcile. You should get more exercise," Mom said. "Or maybe it's your outfit. What *are* you wearing?"

"Top-o-the line Salvation Army thrift shop," Marti said. She wasn't being snotty. It was the truth.

"*Marti.*" Again with the drama-queen whisper. Whatever RachelAnne wanted, it couldn't be anywhere near as weird as watching her mother turn into a jam-swilling Goth princess.

She followed her sister out of the kitchen.

"Martiiiiiii!" A pint-size apparition in late-nineteenth-century dress materialized at the far end of the long central hallway and barreled at her. Amity Bickle was Marti's oldest friend, in all senses of the term. For most of her childhood, Amity was her only friend other than Grandma Bertie. When they were both children, Amity was more in need of a friend than Marti. Amity had been eight years old for a whole lot of years.

The late, but still lovely, child flew down the hall, her arms outstretched.

Marti braced herself for what she knew was coming. Amity never remembered her limitations or her effect on others. The little ghost hit with the force of a thousand icy knives. Marti shuddered and clenched her teeth to keep from screaming or, at the very least, moaning. Putting her hand though Just Call Me Joe's foot was one thing, but a full-body spirit pass-through was agonizing. If it hadn't been quick, she might have passed out.

"Sorry about that, Miss Marcile." Edwards trailed Amity. "Welcome home." The original Bicklesburg Bickles' butler gave her a slight but elegant bow. "Groovy to have you back." During the eras he'd roamed the house unseen, he developed a fondness for slang. His conversation was often at odds with his formal demeanor but always delivered in the most dignified of tones. It was one of the many things Marti loved about him. "Hoity-toity House hasn't been the same without you." His complete lack of respect for the upstart Mickklesons was another. "Miss

Amity has missed you." His devotion to the tiny girl ghost was the thing she loved best.

She classified both Amity and Edwards as Caspers, the kind of friendly spirits she didn't mind having around. It was nothing short of a miracle a place as old as Bickle House only held two ghosts, and two so amiable their presence in no way prepared her for the Just Call Me Joes of the world.

"Are you okay?" RachelAnne stood stiffly by the door of The Judge's study. Everything from her posture to her expression radiated disapproval—even more than her voice, which was saying something.

Marti wanted to return Edwards's greeting. Unlike her living family, he and Amity were happy to see her. RachelAnne narrowed her eyes and frowned, as if she expected Marti to start drooling and gibbering at any moment.

Talking to her invisible friends was a bad idea.

"Just . . . remembering," she said. Her sister accepted the lame explanation. At least that was how Marti chose to interpret RachelAnne's slight nod.

Edwards took stock of the situation and took appropriate action. "Come, Miss Amity. Miss Marcile needs to spend time with her sister. I'm sure she will find time to play later. Amscray." He collected his charge and hustled her away.

"See you later, alligator," Amity called over her shoulder. More than a century of Edwards's company had enlivened her vocabulary.

"Why is Mom going to church on Saturday?" Marti hurried to catch up to her sister.

The Mickklesons attended the First United Methodist Church, but Marti saw their presence, lined up in the front pew every Sunday, as a matter of show not devotion. Did the Methodist church even hold Saturday services?

"She's not. She thinks it's Sunday." RachelAnne pulled a key from her pocket and unlocked the door.

"You girls aren't allowed in my study!" Any remains of the pathetic little man hunched in her backseat in the donut store parking lot vanished. The Judge was back and on his home turf. His roar filled the hallway and shook the paintings on the walls.

Metaphorically, of course. RachelAnne didn't have a clue her father was present and in high dudgeon.

Marti bit her tongue to prevent herself from asking The Judge who was going to stop them.

Metaphorically, of course. On the outside she was all smiles. No one was going to stop them.

"We'll just stay out here and let you two get reacquainted," Grandma said. "We can go talk to Edwards. Unlike some, *he's* a gentleman."

Grandma and Edwards got along well, to the point Marti once accused Grandma of spectral hanky-panky. Grandma snorted and informed Marti they were bonding over the trials and tribulations of caring for mouthy little girls.

"Speak for yourself." The Judge preceded Marti and her sister into what was once his hallowed ground, the room reserved for the King of the Castle, those select few he invited in, and daughters—mostly one—in need of a stern talking to.

With her patent eye roll and shrug, Grandma joined them.

DESPITE THE MANY times Marti stood before the massive oak desk and listened to The Judge catalog her shortcomings, she loved his study. In front of her angry father, she'd stood at attention, a prisoner in the dock. She never looked at him. She memorized the pattern of colors on the book-lined walls and irritated him by spinning the giant globe—not the antique it appeared to be, but a hidden stash of booze. Not the good stuff. The Judge kept the good stuff under lock and key.

A large, ornately framed photo of greeting-card-caliber sweetness hung over the fireplace. Two towheaded little girls, their backs to the photographer, wandered hand in hand through a field of tall grass and wildflowers. Saccharine enough to induce sugar shock in the most cynical of souls, it was out of place in the somber study. The little girls were Marti and RachelAnne. The photograph won grand prize at the county fair the year The Judge took it. Its presence in his study was a trophy, not a sign of paternal affection.

Family legend had it that seconds after the photo was snapped, Marti dropped her baby sister's hand, clotheslined the unsuspecting toddler, then solicitously helped her up. Marti had no recollection of the incident, but Grandma Bertie assured her it was true.

"However," Grandma told her, "they always leave out the part where you took three more steps and clotheslined the poor little thing *again*. The second time, she came up fighting. The two of you went after each other like wildcats and had to be pulled apart. An hour later you were playing together like best friends."

Their entire sisterly relationship captured in one trite photograph.

The Judge ensconced himself in the red-leather desk chair but leapt out before RachelAnne settled herself into his lap. Through his lap. RachelAnne shivered. The Judge hadn't made it out quite in time.

Taking the throne and leaving Marti standing on the other side of the vast desk was a power play, but RachelAnne had a long way to go to reach the intimidation level of their father. Marti dragged one of the smaller wingback chairs closer, plopped her butt in it, and propped her feet up on the desk. Her sister's gasp matched The Judge's.

"Why are you here?" RachelAnne didn't bother to directly address Marti's show of disrespect. Her tone said it all.

Marti's rude feet-on-the-desk slump had the intended effect on The Judge, who would have tried—unsuccessfully, of course—to yank her from the chair if Grandma didn't stop him. RachelAnne, after her initial reaction, wasn't the least bit impressed.

Her head shake and frown said as far as she was concerned, Marti was simply living up to expectations. Low expectations.

Worse, Marti's position was bad for conversation and made her back hurt. Better to look her sister in the eye rather than peer at her through parted knees. She put her feet on the floor, sat up straight, and leaned forward.

"Our father died. Can't I come see our mother?" She wasn't supposed to know about the trust fund. RachelAnne would have to bring it up sooner or later.

"How did you hear about Dad?" RachelAnne's rear planted in The Judge's chair gave her the uncanny ability to make his courtroom voice come out of her mouth.

"What, did you become a lawyer behind my back? Or a cop?" Belligerence was the wrong approach, but it was one of Marti's strengths. She needed all the strength she could muster.

"I'm curious. We haven't heard a word from you in, what? Eight years?"

"Ten." Was her sister trying to trip her up, or did she really not remember how long Marti was gone? "And I read about Dad's death in the *Gazette*. Online."

"You did not," The Judge said.

"Passing. His passing," Grandma said. "And what's she supposed to do? Tell her the truth?"

At times lying was not only expedient, it was necessary. "Oh, Dad showed up and told me" was the truth but wouldn't go far in convincing RachelAnne she was stable and sane. Not to mention, grown-up RachelAnne might not be Judge caliber, but she was way more intimidating than the baby sister Marti clotheslined with regularity.

"And you couldn't be bothered to show up for the funeral?" RachelAnne leaned forward, elbows on the desk, hands clasped in front of her.

"I didn't see it until yesterday." *Keep the story simple, don't get caught.* RachelAnne was in charge of the trust fund dollars.

Explaining The Judge's post-death visit would get things off to a bad start. Getting tripped up in her own lies—she preferred to think of them as fibs or half-truths—wouldn't help either.

"Tell her I was murdered," The Judge said.

"Oh, that's a *fine* idea when they're getting along so well," Grandma said.

Marti wondered at Grandma's idea of *so well*. Maybe not tearing out each other's hair counted.

"Why should I believe you? You just show up after all this time and waltz in the door..."

Part of Marti's brain told her *Do not engage. Do not rise to the bait*. She ignored that part. "It wasn't a waltz. It was a two-step."

Not a rise out of her sister. She knew she could do better. "So, how's Peter? The kids? And speaking of the progeny, how did Mummy and Daddy feel about grandchildren named Rudawski?"

"Marthi..."

There it was. Little sister's one socially unacceptable flaw.

Marti's wide grin was reflex. Triumph. She wasn't mocking her baby sister. Okay, maybe a little.

RachelAnne's baby lisp hung around long after it was considered cute, long enough for her concerned parents to take her to a speech therapist. Since Baby Sister couldn't say Marcile, or Marci, everyone started calling big sister Marti, which RachelAnne could and did say. No one consulted Marti on the name change. RachelAnne eventually conquered the lisp, except when stressed, but Marcile remained Marti.

RachelAnne clamped her mouth shut. Marti imagined her silently counting to ten.

"Marthile." Counting hadn't worked.

Marti snickered. Whoever said "you can't go home again" was wrong. You could, and you could pick right up where you left off. Which might not be a good thing, but at that moment it was fun.

RachelAnne flushed. Marti braced herself for the screeching

to begin. Instead, her sister smiled—a cat who swallowed the canary smile.

"As a matter of fact, I *am* a lawyer and, after I pass the bar exam, I'll be an attorney." Two sibilants. Zero lisp. Baby Sister had regained her composure.

"You're a *what*?" Marti was floored. If asked, she would say her sister's goals in life were dress well, marry well, have stunning children, and stay thin. Law school wasn't a blip on the radar.

RachelAnne, always the good daughter to Marti's bad daughter, was destined to follow Mom's footsteps, not The Judge's, although neither of their parents were an easy act to follow.

Mom's "oh no dear, I don't work" was an outright lie. Between the committees she chaired, the charities and fundraisers she oversaw, and keeping up appearances as the Honorable Judge Mickkleson's wife, she had more on her plate than any Fortune 500 executive. She was the de facto first lady of Bicklesburg. Mayors wives—and since the election of the village's first woman mayor, mayors—came and went, but Margaret Mickkleson ruled for life. She handled it all better than any high-powered CEO and with more style.

Maybe RachelAnne decided the Dad route was easier. Or maybe she was taking both paths at once. She was, after all, raised to be Superwoman in tasteful attire.

"I went back to school after Little Thad was born. You know, maybe we should stop calling him 'Little' now that Papa Thad is gone."

Papa Thad, aka The Judge, cleared his throat. Marti wasn't about to tell her sister Papa Thad was far from gone.

"And became a *lawyer*?" Maybe she couldn't go home again. The only member of her family who was anything like she left them was The Judge—other than his whole being dead thing.

"I graduated from law school before Daddy passed. I still need to take—and pass—the bar exam."

Never underestimate Superwoman. "The Judge must have

been proud. Are you going to hang out a shingle? Or are you aiming for his place on the bench?" The admiration in Marti's voice wasn't an act. Baby Sister not only surprised her, she impressed her.

RachelAnne's smug grin widened. "Actually, I've been working in the public defender's office. Lawrence Brumble is retiring in a few months. He agreed to stay until I was legally legal."

"It would have never happened while I was alive," The Judge bellowed.

"And you're not, so it gets to happen over your dead body," Grandma said.

"Wow," Marti said.

RachelAnne beamed.

The passive-aggressive gene didn't skip her sister. Not only did she have it, she knew how to use it. The Judge might have been proud of his younger daughter—or at least been able to fake it—if she'd chosen corporate law. Tax law. Joined the district attorney's office or gone into family law. Marti knew, by The Judge's standards, RachelAnne was on the one route worse than personal injury or bankruptcy law, which made her accomplishments all the more awesome.

"Unless Larry decides to stay. Since Daddy's been gone, he's had one client get parole and one found innocent," RachelAnne said. "Success is a whole new world for him."

Lawrence "Bumbles" Brumble's photo was rumored to appear in the dictionary next to the words *incompetent* and *nincompoop*, and those rumors were started by people who actually liked him. Although The Judge had no patience for fools and sycophants— and Bumbles was both—it wasn't incompetence that made him loathe the public defender. It was the public defender thing. The Judge believed anyone who couldn't afford a decent attorney was obviously guilty of something and didn't belong in his county. An appearance before Zero-Tolerance Mickkleson with Bumbles McBumbler as defense was a near guarantee of deportation from

Battlesburough County—as Oliver and Dmitri, wherever they were, could attest.

Marti found it entirely possible the thought of his baby girl—the good daughter—becoming a public defender killed The Judge. One thing for sure, RachelAnne earned any position she held in that office. The Judge was a big believer in small-town nepotism, but only when it fit his own purposes.

"The Judge must have loved that," Marti said.

"He wasn't too pleased," RachelAnne said.

"I'm surprised he *permitted* it." Marti was also surprised The Judge hadn't responded to Grandma's "over your dead body" comment. The last she knew they were hovering behind her. A quiet Judge could not be a good thing.

"He made some noise, but Battlesburough County's acquired some new blood. His strings didn't pull as easily as they used to, but he was still trying to yank them when he passed." RachelAnne's grin faded.

Passed. Grandma should be pleased with RachelAnne's choice of words. The Judge, not so much with their meaning. Marti waited for him to make noise. Not a peep. No "I didn't pass. I was murdered."

"What happened? I just know he died, no details." Marti stood, sauntered to the fireplace, and examined the photograph over the mantle. She and RachelAnne were adorable toddlers, at least from the back.

"He had a stroke. You know how he was. He ate and drank whatever he wanted. No one could tell him anything, not even after he was diagnosed with diabetes."

The Judge maintained radio silence.

Marti turned to face her sister and snuck a glance at the room. Grandma stood behind The Judge. He'd been a short man and made a short ghost. Grandma Bertie'd been a tall woman. She had one arm around his neck in a hold worthy of any professional wrestler and one hand clamped over his mouth. His bulging eyes had to be from rage since he was beyond suffocation.

"Diabetes?" Marti struggled to concentrate on the conversation and keep her amusement at the scene out of her voice. Mom said The Judge liked sweet things, but Marti remembered him as a bourbon man. Three fingers, straight. Marti didn't remember him liking anything sweet, other than tea and RachelAnne.

From the time she was a toddler, Baby Sister went full-force sugar bomb around her darling daddy. Her doll-baby act made Marti look ornerier by comparison. It also made Marti ornerier in reality.

"About five years ago, and true to form, it coincided with his sudden development of a sweet tooth."

The Judge managed to shake Grandma's hand off. "I was perfectly healthy," he said. "Someone poisoned me."

Marti wondered if her father was more than a little crazy himself. With all the youthful offenders he sent away over the years, a little paranoia wasn't out of line, but denying a life-threatening diagnosis was nuts even for a guy with an ego the size of Alaska.

In a lightning-fast move, Grandma changed her hold on The Judge—the years she spent watching WWE with Marti weren't wasted—and dragged him backward through the wall and out of the den. Marti faked a fit of coughing to cover her laughter.

She strolled around the desk and gave the globe a spin before returning to her chair. She sat primly and stared at her hands folded in her lap. The image of her great-grandmother dragging the most powerful man in not only Battlesburough County but in Marti's life away was too much. She shook with repressed giggles and hoped her sister didn't notice.

"Would you like a drink?" RachelAnne asked. "I have the key to the liquor cabinet."

At this hour of the morning? RachelAnne had changed. Unless—Marti looked at her sister. The Mom-like stare told her what she needed to know. Bonding time was fading fast.

"It's a little early don't you think?" The drink offer wasn't an invitation. It was a trap. RachelAnne had picked up a few clothesline tricks of her own. She would make a terrific lawyer. Marti needed to stay on her toes. "And what's wrong with Mom?"

RachelAnne's face fell. "That's—"

Attention. Back door open. Back door open.

The mechanical voice was clear and calm. Open doors left the unseen robot woman unruffled. Not so RachelAnne.

"Crap!" RachelAnne jumped up.

The back door was off the kitchen. RachelAnne took off, Marti at her heels.

The kitchen was empty. Almost empty. Grandma and The Judge were the sole occupants.

"She went that way." Grandma pointed to the open door. The only sign of Mom was a pair of spiky pumps lying in the middle of the floor. Satin with tiny rhinestone bows on the heels, they weren't typical Sunday go-to-church shoes. Outrageous shoes were Margaret Mickkleson's trademark, the single visible sign of rebellion in her otherwise conservative respectability.

The Judge sat on the floor, trying and failing to pick up one of the gaudy purple shoes. "Do something," he wailed. "She's not well!"

Six

RachelAnne shot out the back door and shouted for Mom.

Her sister didn't know there were two witnesses to their mother's departure—or disappearance. Marti didn't want to think about the implications of the latter.

"What happened?" she said.

Grandma threw up her hands. "You got me. She just stood up, kicked off her shoes, and marched out the door."

"She didn't say anything?" *Why would she?* Mom didn't know she had company in the kitchen.

"She was singing. More like humming. The song she sang with you girls when you were little." Grandma hummed a few bars.

"Going to the Zoo." One of Marti's favorite childhood songs, but she failed to see how it was any help in the current situation. The closest zoo was fifty miles away. If Mom planned to walk there, it was no wonder she left her high heels behind.

"Marti! What are you doing? Get out here. Help me look for Mom!" RachelAnne screeched.

"Listen to your sister!" The Judge was up and out the door.

She made it to the backyard in time to see a man in uniform round the corner of the house. Tall, dark curly hair, vaguely familiar. *No. Can't be.*

He stopped. "Marti?"

It was. The years were kind to Dmitri Doyle. He'd filled out, and in all the right places. The crisp uniform—he couldn't be a cop, he had a record—must have been tailored. Grown up Dmitri didn't have an off-the-rack body, and the dark-gray shirt and black pants fit him like a glove. His face glowed with healthy tan, not Goth pallor. Or prison pallor. He was taller than she remembered. At least on the outside, this new Dmitri was a huge improvement on the scrawny teenager she'd last seen being hauled away by the police.

"*Mommy's taking us to the . . .*" Not Mom's voice. Smooth. Professional. Recorded. Male.

RachelAnne rushed out the side door of the garage, cell phone to her ear. "What?" she snapped.

"Yep. It's me," Marti said. Dmitri's uniform wasn't police. The blue, oval patch on the front pocket read "ACS." He was an Albion Court Security gorilla.

He sure didn't look like a gorilla. She wondered how long he'd been on the job. It was hard to imagine The Judge hiring one of the delinquents he sent to prison to guard his castle. Foxes didn't get to guard the hen house, no matter how good looking they were.

"It's not babysitting," RachelAnne said into her phone. "They're your kids, and when they're your own kids, it's not babysitting. It's parenting."

Marti guessed RachelAnne was talking to Peter. She'd never met her brother-in-law, but if he didn't get the point of her sister's if-you-don't-listen-to-me-and-listen-now-your-world-will-end-and-end-in-pain tone, he was a few beans short of a full burrito.

"That your car out front?" Dmitri looked her up and down.

"Yep." For the second time that day, she was acutely aware of her ratty sweatshirt and ill-fitting jeans and regretted her wardrobe choice. Regretted her entire wardrobe, in fact.

"Alarm went off in the guardhouse. Everything okay here?" He didn't sound much like the teenage wild man she remembered. He sounded like a responsible adult. Not to mention a bit intimidating.

"Mom's missing. Wandered out the back door." If New Dmitri was terse, she could be too. Especially with those blue eyes staring at her.

"Attention. Back door open. Back door open." Lady Electro-Voice backed Marti up.

"You'll just have to deal with it. I will be there when I get there. Which, at this point, may be tomorrow." RachelAnne wasn't terse. She was furious. She stabbed a finger at her phone and stuck it back in her pocket. "I checked the garage. Her car's there. She's not. I'll go that way. Dmitri, go that way. Marti, that way. Call me if you find her."

"Ummm . . ." RachelAnne was still in she-who-must-be-obeyed mode, and, contrary to popular opinion, Marti's burrito was stocked full of beans.

"What are you waiting for? *Go!*"

"I don't have a phone, but I like your ringtone."

The two of them stared at her like she'd said she was a virgin. Dmitri knew better.

"What? I just never got a cell phone. Never really needed one." It was true. The only reason she had a landline back in Franklinville was so the Burger Buster could call her in for extra shifts. She had nobody to call and no one she wanted to call her.

"You and Dmitri stick together. You'd probably end up lost on your own anyway."

"Attention. Back door open. Back door open." Electro-Woman sounded panicked. Or Marti was projecting. Her sister in command mode, her possibly senile mother going walkabout, her old boyfriend showing up and, well, *looking* at her—her stomach did a flip-flop and her ears buzzed. *Welcome home to me,* she thought.

"Somebody shut that door! Let's go. *Mom!*" RachelAnne's shout was enough to wake the dead, let alone any neighbors still asleep.

If Mom heard, she didn't answer.

MARTI AND DMITRI zigzagged through backyards and front yards, randomly shouting, "Mom!" "Mrs. Mickkleson!" and "Margaret!" None got an answer. Before crossing streets, they shouted and looked up and down the sidewalk. They didn't see a living soul. It was still early, but it was Saturday. Someone should be up and about. If they weren't already, you'd think they'd wake up and stick their heads out to see what the hullabaloo was about. Maybe all of Bicklesburg had been kidnapped and replaced by pod people. From what she remembered, it would be hard to tell the difference.

The Judge and Grandma tagged along. They greeted and were greeted by a dozen loitering spirits. Some Marti recognized. Some she didn't. She ignored them all. The ones she didn't know weren't aware she saw them. They wouldn't find out unless she let on, which she wasn't about to do. As for the ones she did know, as much as she wanted to ask if they'd seen her mother, speaking to them in front of Dmitri was out of the question. She left the spiritual interrogation to her ghostly companions.

The ones Grandma asked didn't have an answer. The ones The Judge spoke to ignored him. The Honorable Thaddeus A. Mickkleson didn't inspire the same awe in the afterlife he had commanded in life.

They crossed streets and countless yards before they spotted a real live person. The slim woman looked up from raking leaves and purred, "Hi, Dmitri."

Dawn Pernelli's appreciation for the grown-up Dmitri oozed like syrup. She'd changed in at least one way since high school. Teen Dawn had about as much respect for Teen Dmitri as she had for Teen Marti. Adult Dawn pulled off her gloves, put one hand on her cocked hip, struck a cheerleader pose, and beamed at Adult Dmitri. Attitude wasn't the only change. The universe had balanced out the kindness of the years it spent on Dmitri with what it took from Dawn. The phrase "rode hard and put away wet" sprang to mind.

"Have you seen Mrs. Mickkleson?" Dmitri said.

"She wandered through here a few minutes ago. Didn't bother to speak to me."

"You didn't think to call someone? Haven't you heard she's been . . . unwell?" He glanced at Marti.

"Eh. I've never understood anything the Mickklesons did. As far as I'm concerned, they've always been a bunch of loony tunes. All of 'em." She tore herself away from Dmitri's baby blues. "Hey, Marti. When did you get home?"

From someone else, Marti might have credited the forced surprise to bad acting. From Dawn, it was no doubt intentional. Subtlety was never one of her strong points. Appearance to the contrary, the former high school queen bee hadn't changed all that much.

"Hey, Dawn. Nice tan," Marti said. Rather than paint her old nemesis with Dmitri's healthy glow, the sun had shriveled her like a prune. Marti might be dressed like a thrift-store reject, but Dawn had the leather skin and crow's feet of someone three times her age. Or of Just Call Me Joe. She'd kept her cheerleader shape. Marti supposed having her morph into a potato was too much to ask.

"Be nice," Grandma said.

"Stop dawdling. We need to find your mother," The Judge said.

Dmitri looked from one woman to the other. The corners of his mouth twitched, but he stuck with playing the strong and silent type. Marti wondered if he was waiting for a cat fight. He wasn't going to get one. She was well out of high school, even if Dawn wasn't.

"Which way did my mother go?"

"So, Dmitri, any big plans this weekend? Because —"

"Dawn. Answer Marti. Which way did Mrs. Mickkleson go?"

Dawn pointed a limp finger toward the front of the house. "Like I said, she just wandered through. Actually, *wandered* is the wrong word. She looked like she knew where she was going. I don't think she even noticed me. About tonight, there's a—"

"Dawn. One word. Sunscreen." Marti took off. Dmitri could follow or stay and make a date and bask in Pernelli adoration. She didn't care.

"Dmitri! Call me!" Dawn's wheedle was more of a whine, but Dmitri was at Marti's side. Of course he was. He was paid to provide security to the Avenue's residents, including—probably most of all—The Judge's missing widow.

"So. Dawn's single?" Marti said.

"Nope," Dmitri said.

"Still classy then."

Dmitri snorted, or maybe it was an embarrassed laugh. Marti hoped he didn't have a lot be embarrassed about where Dawn Pernelli was concerned. She hadn't made up her mind about New Dmitri, but she was leaning toward liking him. A Dawn-Dmitri duo would put that to rest in a hurry.

They crossed the street in front of Dawn's house. They cut through back and front yards. They crossed another street. No sign of Mom.

"How far could she have gone?"

"Depends on how determined she was," Dmitri said. "And if she's been moving in a straight line while we wander back and forth . . ."

"That's not encouraging." If insistence on getting her own way qualified as determination, her mother could walk all the way to Franklinville before they found her.

Marti wouldn't make it that far. The past few days—starting with her mysterious Scooter's bender—were catching up with her fast. Her head hurt. Her feet hurt. Finding Mom was only half the trek. Once they found her, they had to walk home again.

"Stop for a sec," she said.

"You see something?"

"I just need to get my . . . bearings." She caught herself before she said "breath." Dmitri hadn't broken a sweat. No point letting him know what a wimp she was.

Bearings wasn't a total lie. She had no idea where they were. The yards were small and could benefit from the attention of Dawn and her rake. The houses were tiny, and a few cried out for new paint jobs. The cars in the driveways were in better shape than her Taurus—no surprise there—but none were new, nor were they luxury models. She'd left the Avenue behind in more than distance.

She wondered where her sister was and hoped RachelAnne was having better luck. With luck, the Fates would smile on them and Mom would turn up before Marti sat down in the middle of some stranger's yard and told Dmitri to go on without her, she'd be fine.

"*Mom! Paging Margaret Dibble Micklleson!*" Marti was past caring if she woke the entire planet.

"Here, dear."

Mom. Marti and her entourage trotted around the house. Grandma and The Judge got there first. Gravity didn't slow them down.

Mom sat on the porch swing, one leg curled beneath her. With her other foot, she gently rocked the swing. The foot was bare, her stocking shredded. She cradled something in her lap.

"Oh, Marcile," she said. "Your father will not be happy at you keeping company with that boy again." She appeared oblivious to Sheila McDonagh, seated next to her on the swing.

Marti'd never seen The Judge's wife and his girlfriend in the same room, let alone in such close proximity to each other.

Not while they were both alive.

Dmitri pulled out his phone and hit a button. "We found her," he said.

"Going to the zoo, zoo, zoo." Mom rocked and sang to the thing in her lap.

Sheila wasn't oblivious to Mom's presence. Even dead, she wasn't happy at sharing a swing with the woman she'd shared The Judge with.

"Go away and leave me alone, you harpy." Dead Sheila was unpleasant, to say the least.

Mom cooed and cuddled the thing in her lap. Marti strained to get a look at it, but between the angle and Mom's protective cradling, she couldn't.

"Where are we?" Marti asked.

"The McDonaghs," Dmitri said. "Don't recognize it? Neighborhood hasn't changed much."

"Oh. I . . ." Marti turned. Across the street, a For Sale sign graced the lawn of Dmitri's teenage home. The curtain-less windows were dark. Other than its general air of abandonment, the Doyle house hadn't changed.

The McDonagh house had changed. The last time she saw it, a few cement steps lead to the front door. The big front window now looked out on a spacious porch. The newness of the unpainted wood meant the porch was a recent addition. Very recent.

Marti had a flashback of her father framed by the window, accompanied by a twinge of guilt. She should have recognized the place where Dmitri's life changed. To be fair, the house wasn't the problem. Her father's presence there all those years ago was the problem. And it was dark that night. And she was a little buzzed. And it was so long ago, it was another lifetime. And—

"Get off my porch, you witch." Sheila put a halt to Marti's self-justification party.

"Mom? I think we should head home now," Marti said.

"Oh no, dear. I'll just sit here and wait for your father."

"I'm gonna call the cops." Sheila leapt off the seat, grabbed one of the chains the swing hung by, and shook it. Or tried to. Nothing happened. She stared at her hand and waggled her fingers, dazed.

"Oh dear," Grandma said. "She has a lot to learn."

Marti hoped she didn't decide to spend eternity—or even the next few days—hanging out with The Judge. Maybe she'd stick with Ralph. Where was he, anyway? For that matter, where was Sheila? The earthly Sheila.

The garage door was open. An older Toyota took up one side

of the interior. The spot next to the compact car was empty. If the Escalade wasn't there, maybe Sheila wasn't either, not in the flesh. Getting Mom out of there was an excellent plan.

A white car rolled up the street and turned into the drive, cherry light flashing but no siren. The cavalry—and Mom's ride home—had arrived. Marti hoped she could hitch a ride too. It wouldn't be the first time she rode in the back of a vehicle emblazoned with the words "Police. Village of Bicklesburg."

RachelAnne jumped from the front passenger side and ran to the foot of the porch. "Mom! Are you okay? What are you doing here?"

"I'm looking for The Judge. I don't think he's here, but he'll turn up sooner or later." Margaret Mickkleson was serene, a Madonna and—whatever was in her lap.

"Why would Daddy be here?" RachelAnne evidently accepted her mother's search for her dead father but not the location.

Marti felt like the sanest member of the Mickkleson clan. "Seriously? You didn't know?" she said.

Her sister was a docile teen, but Marti never considered her naive. True, Marti found out about The Judge and his girlfriend by accident, but RachelAnne had been far better socialized and in touch with the goings-on around town. Her sister must have heard the gossip at some point.

"Bless your heart, dear. Sheila McDonagh is your father's bimbo."

"Mom!" Apparently the scuttlebutt never made it to RachelAnne.

Sheila slapped Mom. Her hand passed through Mom's cheek and came out the other side of her face.

Mom shuddered. "Like animals," she said. "They were at it all the time and thought I didn't know. It makes me cold just thinking about it."

"Big! Arrest her. She's trespassing." Sheila tried and failed to shake the porch swing.

"I don't think she knows she's dead." Marti'd forgotten about The Judge, but Sheila heard him. Her eyes widened. She flickered.

"It's okay, Sheel. It's not as bad as you think," he said.

"Wow." Marti'd never seen a ghost faint and didn't know it was possible.

"Conditioned reflex," Grandma said.

"Should we see if she's okay?" The Judge's concern would have been more touching if it were for his wife, not his girlfriend.

"She's dead, you dolt," Grandma said.

"Not her. Margaret." Both Marti and Grandma had misjudged The Judge. Marti chalked it up to karma. The Judge had a lot to answer for in that department.

"It's okay, little man," Mom crooned to the thing in her lap. "We'll get you fixed up in no time."

"Mom, what is that?" Marti hoped whatever it was, it had nothing to do with Sheila McDonagh's death.

"Sheila always liked stumpy little things, which explains her fondness for your father." Mom ran her hand through her hair and left a dark streak in the blonde. The thing in her lap rolled off and hit the floor with a thud, narrowly missing her bare foot.

"Mom, are you hurt?" RachelAnne dashed for the porch, Dmitri right behind her. Marti stayed put.

"No, dear. The poor little thing missed me. I hope he isn't broken. I think he's an antique. Also like your father."

"Why is she so angry at me?" The Judge said, perplexed.

Marti glared at her father. No one could be that stupid. Her father wasn't, but he was that self-centered.

The large—and live—man in uniform at The Judge's side thought the glare was for him. "Hey. Marti Cray-Cray," Big Fysh said.

He turned beet red as soon as the words were out.

Terrific. The chief of police addressed her by her high school nickname. She wanted to use a few of his—the ones used behind his back, not to his face. Instead, she joined her sister on the porch.

"Big. Call the ambulance." RachelAnne's concern wasn't for her mother's toes or for the garden gnome lying next to them. The little guy *was* an antique, cast from concrete, not molded from cheap plastic. Layers of colorful paint and repaint jobs cracked and peeled. He looked beaten and bruised.

The dark stain covering half his face wasn't from his wounds. It matched the streak in Mom's hair.

"Mrs. Mickkleson? Are you sure you're okay?" Dmitri gently lifted and examined her hand. "I don't think it's her blood."

"I'm fine, honey. But I'm afraid poor little Mr. Stumpy might be hurt." She nudged the gnome with her foot, and he rolled across the porch.

"Mrs. Mickkleson? Do you know where Sheila McDonagh is?" Big joined the crowd on the porch but didn't make it as far as the swing. He stopped by the large window and peered inside.

"Oh, she's probably off with my husband somewhere. Check the cheap motels."

Mom was close. In one sense, Sheila was with the departed Judge, but he hovered over his widow looking concerned, and his girlfriend was nowhere to be seen. Ghost Sheila had disappeared or dissipated or evaporated or whatever it was spirits did.

Marti joined Big at the window.

Something all too solid and Sheila-sized splayed across the coffee table. Marti willed it to be a pile of blankets or laundry in need of folding. Blankets and laundry the color of Sheila's red jacket and yellow hair.

A So-nutt-ee Donut cup lay on the floor in front of the largest TV Marti'd ever seen. The cup's dark contents splattered and stained the white carpet. At least, Marti hoped the stain came from the coffee cup.

Her first thought was *as last meals go, donuts are better than Burger Buster*, and she hated herself for it.

Sheila McDonagh was dead. Marti knew as soon as she saw her on the swing next to Mom. She had the special shimmer, a dead giveaway of the dead, but her body was supposed to be—Marti didn't know where. Off in a ditch in a wrecked Escalade or on the floor of the donut place. Somewhere else. Anywhere else.

It could be an accident. A heart attack. A natural death. Just because her big, yellow hair appeared to be crushed and stained to match the bloody smear on Mom's dress didn't mean it was true.

"I think Mr. Stumpy there is beyond help. I'm cold and I want to go home now," Mom said.

The little garden gnome's vacant eyes stared at the ceiling.

"Not yet, Mrs. Mickkleson." Big took out his phone. "Not yet."

SEVEN

"Mrs. McDonagh!" Big pounded the front door. "Are you okay?" He jiggled the door knob.

"I'll check the back," Dmitri said.

Marti stared through the window. "Maybe she was making a scarecrow."

Big's expression implied she'd reconfirmed her status as Marti Cray-Cray. It didn't imply he was surprised.

The lump in the front room didn't budge. Sheila's death might be an accident. She'd tripped. Fallen. Hit her head. The gnome—and Mom—had nothing to do with it.

Dmitri returned. "Back's locked too."

"We'll have to break in," Big said.

Fysh Smash. To give the chief a little credit, he *was* in a hurry to get inside and confirm what she already knew—what she suspected Big knew too.

Sheila McDonagh was beyond any help the police chief or anyone else could provide, and it wasn't an accident.

"Wait." Dmitri bent and rummaged in the shrubs at the foot of the stairs.

"I want to go home now," Mom said.

"Shhhh." RachelAnne, pale and wide-eyed, sat by Mom's side in the space vacated by the departed Sheila. She hadn't looked through the window and couldn't have seen Ghost Sheila, but she obviously knew something was up. Something bad.

Dmitri came up with a faded-green plastic frog.

"I don't like frogs," Mom said. "Nasty little things."

He flipped the tacky ornament and did something to its nether region. It belched and its white belly popped open.

"Is it a toad? Toads are worse than frogs. RachelAnne, take me home this instant." Mom managed to combine imperious and whiny in a single tone.

Dimitri pulled a key from the frog's innards and tossed it to Big, who snatched it from the air.

"Your father was a toad. I kissed him. Sheila kissed him. Lord knows who else kissed him, but he never turned into a prince."

"*Mom!*" RachelAnne needed to get a grip. She was pale enough to be mistaken for a ghost.

"At least he thought he was a king," Mom said.

"How did you know the key was there?" Big ignored both Mom and RachelAnne and addressed Dmitri.

"Stupid frog is in a thousand mail-order junk catalogs and now it's on even more online junk-shopping websites. Sticking one by your door is like advertising 'Hey! Here's a key! Come on in!'" Dmitri said.

"Guess we need to do just that." The police chief unlocked and opened the front door. "Mrs. McDonagh?"

"Stay here," Dmitri told Marti.

"Sheila?" Big entered the McDonagh house with Dmitri right behind him.

And Marti right behind them.

The lump in the living room wasn't blankets or laundry or a half-finished scarecrow. Sheila's moussed and sprayed hair helmet hadn't protected her.

Her skull was caved in.

"I don't suppose she tripped and fell?" Marti said, still grasping at straws.

"What's she doing in here? Get her out!" Big glared.

"I saw her this morning. Alive," Marti said.

"When? Where?" Big said.

"Early. At the Do Not—the Sough Not—the Too Nutty—there."

She pointed at the paper coffee cup on the floor. Her tongue was thick and didn't work. She couldn't think. The dark spill of coffee shimmered against the white carpet. A ghostly shimmer. *Did coffee leave ghosts?* The floor tilted and rippled.

"Marti? Are you okay?" Dimitri said.

"I think I'm going to be sick." She'd dealt with the dead her entire life, but *her* dead were basically alive. At least to her. For the second time in as many days, she was in the presence of a dead body. A really, really dead body. A recently dead body.

Sheila dead was worse than Ozzie dead.

Maybe because Marti was completely sober and awake.

Maybe because she'd just seen Sheila, alive and kicking.

Maybe it was the blood.

Probably the blood.

Definitely the blood.

"I know I'm going to be sick," she said.

"Not in here," Big roared.

Dmitri hauled her outside, and just in time. She finished vomiting over the porch rail as the rest of the cavalry arrived, with lights *and* sirens. Bicklesburg had more cop cars than she remembered.

"We need to get you home, and I'll make you a nice hot cup of tea. My special recipe," Mom said. "It'll make you feel better."

Marti threw up again.

By the time she, her sister, and her mother were allowed to leave, Marti couldn't have crawled from the McDonaghs' to Bickle House, let alone walk. She wasn't sure she could find her way home if left to her own devices. Instead, she rode home in the back seat of a police car. Their baby-faced chauffeur handed her a pink plastic bag when she got in.

"Just in case," he said.

He needn't have worried. Her stomach still pitched and roiled, but there wasn't anything left to come up.

Mom sat next to her, poised and calm. How she remained untouched by the morning's events was beyond Marti.

Maybe she *should* try some of Mom's tea.

Up front, RachelAnne chatted with the baby-faced cop. Grandma and The Judge were nowhere to be seen, but Marti knew they were close. At least Grandma was. She didn't know how it worked with The Judge, but Grandma had a limited range. If Marti managed to get much more than the length of a football field away from her, an invisible bungee cord snapped her back to Marti's side.

Marti had a vague idea civilians—and RachelAnne was a civilian despite her position in the public defender's office—riding in the front seat violated some regulation or another, but it came from books and movies. It didn't matter. Bicklesburg was its own law, as far removed from reality as any sitcom or reality show.

Baby Face chuckled. He was either sucking up to RachelAnne or flirting with her. There'd been no sucking up or flirting when he interviewed her.

In truth, she got off easy with the questions. Sometime over the past decade, Dmitri had acquired a sterling reputation. He and Big acted like best buddies. Easy with each other. Comfortable. Like old friends. Maybe even bromance. She got the impression Dmitri was above reproach or suspicion. Since she'd been in his company from the time she left the house and before that with RachelAnne, she had a solid alibi. For most of the morning.

Baby Face—he told her his name, but it went in one ear and out the other—was extremely interested in what time she saw Sheila and Ralph at the donut place. She couldn't remember the exact time.

"Early. Seven-ish, maybe before," she said and assured him the McDonaghs were both very much alive when they walked through the So-nutt-ee door and didn't walk back out of it before she left.

"My donut bag is still in my car. The receipt will have the time on it." She did know how fast food joints worked.

"You say you were in the parking lot eating your donut when Sheila and Ralph arrived. Can anyone confirm that?"

Sure. My dead great-grandmother and dead father were there nagging me and fighting with each other. "No one I know of. Why does it matter?"

"Just covering all the bases, ma'am."

The baby-faced cop called her *ma'am*. If Marti wasn't already feeling old, exhausted, and used-up, *ma'am* would have done it. He had to be a Bicklesburg newcomer. She couldn't place his face in any of the families she remembered. His manner was obsequious, but otherwise straightforward. Translation—he knew she was a member of the powerful Mickkleson clan, but not that she was the wayward offspring. He'd find out soon enough. His cohorts smirked while he took her statement. Maybe he was brand new and dealing with Marti Cray-Cray was some form of initiation.

As befitting her mother's status, Big had dealt with Mom while RachelAnne and The Judge hovered. Once Baby Cop turned her loose, Marti stood to the side and eavesdropped. Dmitri and Grandma glued themselves to her. Grandma, she understood. Dmitri, not so much.

Mom went from talking nonsense, "Mr. Stumpy has a secret," to haughty, "Young man. Take me home. I can have your badge, you know," to cranky and confused, "Where am I? Where are my shoes? I'm cold. I want to go home." Big kept a straight face and treated Mom with kindness and respect, even when she insulted him. "Aren't you Billy Fysh's son? The dim one? Your brother, now *there's* a young man with a future."

In between the many faces of Mom, Marti gleaned she'd tripped on the gnome, picked him up, and taken him to the swing to comfort him. Whether the McDonagh house was her destination all along or she'd stopped to help a gnome in need, Mom was concerned about the little fellow. "Mr. Stumpy's an antique, you know. He's been mistreated. It makes him sad."

Mom wasn't the only one interested in Mr. Stumpy. A couple of cops took pictures, carefully bagged him and tagged him, hustled him into a car, and sped away. The gnome made it out before Sheila. Maybe they thought he could be saved. More likely, they thought he was responsible for the damage to Sheila's hairdo, not to mention to her skull.

When Mom stuck out her lower lip and refused to answer any more questions, Big gave up and recruited Baby Cop to drive them home, with instructions to take Mom's dress as evidence. Marti's crime scene investigation skills all came from Hollywood, but she didn't see what Mom's lavender silk Anne Taylor sheath would tell them. The dark stain was in her lap and, as far as Marti could tell, came from Mr. Stumpy. If Mom used the little concrete man on Sheila, there should be more blood. There always was in the movies.

Baby Cop hit a pothole. The car lurched and Marti's stomach heaved. Good thing she hadn't eaten a third donut.

"Marcile? What are you doing here?" Mom asked.

"Good question," Marti answered.

"I'm glad you're home." Mom took her hand and squeezed.

The connection was more disconcerting than Sheila's dead body. The two of them hadn't held hands since Marti was five, and then only to cross the street.

BABY COP TURNED onto the Avenue, and Marti clutched her pink barf bag. It wasn't the young officer's driving. After the pothole, he slowed. She could walk faster than he drove. The sight of Bickle House left her breathless, and not in a good way. In a suffocating, why-did-she-think-she-could-ever-come-back way.

Her Taurus was no longer alone on the street. A bright red Hummer with dealer plates towered over her aged sedan like a gigantosaurus moving in for the kill. Marti didn't think anybody still drove those things. Officer Baby Face pulled in behind the monster.

"Wonder if that thing qualifies for collector plates yet?" Marti said.

"Crap," RachelAnne said.

The end of the Avenue was a hive of activity. A small boy, five or six years old, and a toddler ran laps in Bickle House's front yard. The boy chased the little girl, caught up with her, then paused long enough for her to squeal and get away.

"I'll get you," he shouted and resumed the chase.

"My grandbeauties!" Mom pulled her hand from Marti's and attacked the door. It didn't open. "Young man! Unlock this door immediately."

"Please be patient, ma'am." Officer Baby Face got out and scanned the yard. All he needed was a black suit, Ray-Bans, and another ten years on him to look like Secret Service.

The boy dropped his pursuit and stared at the police car. His sister quit squealing and joined him, her thumb in her mouth.

The children apparently posed no threat. Baby Cop opened Mom's door. She jumped out and spread her arms wide.

"My pretties!" she said.

Marti had a flash of Margaret Hamilton, the Wicked Witch of the West, and Flying Monkeys. The kids—Marti assumed they were her niece and nephew—were either too young to get the probably unintended reference or didn't care.

"Nana!" The kids hurtled at their grandmother.

RachelAnne and Baby Cop intercepted the dual kid missiles. RachelAnne deftly scooped up her daughter. Baby Face took a full-on hit from the boy. He teetered for a second, but regained his balance and tried to look stern. He didn't have the face for it.

"Nana, what's that all over your dress?" the boy asked.

Mom looked down. "Oh. There was a sad little man . . ." She sounded confused, but before she finished her thought, another little man—one not made of concrete—popped from behind the Hummer.

"Kids! Back off and leave your grandmother alone. Hello, Rodney." He nodded at Baby Cop, who certainly didn't look like a Rodney. More like a Brandon or a Kyle or a Justin. "Glad you're here. I don't know who this heap belongs to. I was about to call a tow truck myself, since I can't seem to raise anyone in the ACS office. If Doyle wants to keep his job, he'd better get on the ball. Never understood why Pop Mickkleson hired him in the first place."

Marti was willing to bet her entire inheritance—the one she wasn't supposed to know about—she'd found the cause of The Judge's death. If his son-in-law called him "Pop Mickkleson" to his face, it was a wonder he didn't have a stroke years ago.

"Um, that's mine," she said, also willing to bet the heap in question wasn't the Hummer.

"My dad says it's an eyesore." The boy had to be the latest addition to the Thaddeus line. The little girl, whose name Marti didn't know, kept her thumb in her mouth and stared.

"Marti, this is my husband, Peter Rudawski. Peter, my sister Marcile. We call her Marti."

"Do you think she knows?" Grandma Bertie said.

"He's beneath her," The Judge said.

Peter Rudawski stood before her, hand outstretched. He was all but a carbon copy of a younger Judge. Same height, same build. Different hair. When Walt's on the Green closed and took its red-and-white striped pole with it, The Judge insisted the salon stylists who replaced the barber stick to the same basic cut he'd worn for years. Short on the sides. Short on the top. Tapered in the back. No wussy hair product or fussing with a blow dryer for The Judge, and he would have died before letting anyone add the artful highlights his son-in-law sported. By the time he did die, he didn't have enough hair left to bother with.

"Good to finally meet you." Marti took his proffered hand and shook. Peter's sweaty and limp grip, nothing like The Judge's, wasn't the only thing mushy. On closer inspection, his facial features, although in the same ballpark as The Judge's, were doughy, blurred. Any air of kindness the softness might provide was counteracted by his eyes, which were as cold and hard as her father's at his angriest. She was being judged and found lacking. Liking him wouldn't be easy, but she'd give it a try.

For RachelAnne's sake.

For her own sake, since she needed to get along with RachelAnne in order to finance her own future.

"You too," he said. "I've heard a lot about you."

"You can believe it all." Maybe at least some of what he'd heard was good. She doubted it.

"Oh, I do." His oily voice left Marti feeling like she'd done a double shift over the Burger Buster grill. What did RachelAnne see in him? If it was the obvious, Marti wasn't the only sister with daddy issues.

"And our children, Thaddeus and Margaret," RachelAnne said.

"Nice names," Marti said. *Margaret.* Of course. The Mickkleson surname might daughter out with the current generation, but thanks to Baby Sister, the last of the monarchs would be remembered. Poor kids.

"What happened to Eric and Ariel?" Grandma said.

When they were kids—even when they were teens—RachelAnne vowed she'd name her future children after the Disney prince and princess. Naming them after the king and queen of Bicklesburg lacked the same sense of romance. RachelAnne's idea or Peter's?

"Call me T3." The boy stuck out his hand.

"T3?" Marti said. The kid had a more impressive handshake than his father.

"My superhero name."

"Got it."

"Call my sister Maggie. She doesn't have a superhero name yet. We don't know what her superpower is."

"What's yours?"

"I'd tell you, but then I'd have to kill you."

"Thad!" Peter apparently didn't subscribe to the T3 ruling.

The boy shrugged off his father's reprimand and turned his

attention to Baby Face Rodney. "Do you have a gun? Is my nana under arrest? What'd she do?"

Marti decided she liked her nephew.

"Thad!" RachelAnne echoed her husband, and T3 backed off.

Maggie hid behind her mother and peeked around RachelAnne's legs. "Who's that yady?" she said and pointed.

"Lllllllady," RachelAnne said, "and she's your aunt Marti."

RachelAnne couldn't see her daughter, but Marti could. She had no clue what Maggie's superhero name was, but she was afraid she knew what her super power was. The little girl didn't point at Marti when she asked her question. She pointed to Marti's left.

The yady in question was Grandma Bertie.

BABY FACE RODNEY escorted Mom and RachelAnne into the house. The Judge trailed along. Marti needed an aspirin, but she stayed outside with Peter and the kids—and Grandma Bertie, whom Maggie didn't take her eyes off of.

"So. Why are you here?" her brother-in-law said. Any pretense of manners and welcome left with his wife and mother-in-law.

"My father died. I came to see my mother and sister." She was sticking to her story come hell or high water.

"Staying long?" Like his wife, her brother-in-law managed to load a whole lot of accusation into a few simple words. Maybe it was their special talent and drew them together, a match made in heaven.

She wondered if T3 had superhero names for his parents.

"My, my. He even sounds like your father, doesn't he?" Grandma Bertie's disapproval and dislike of The Judge extended to RachelAnne's husband.

"I don't know," Marti answered Peter. She agreed 100 percent with her great-grandmother.

"Well, you can't leave that wreck sitting in the street," Peter said.

"I don't plan on it." Marti pulled her keys from her back pocket.

They still bore their Scooter's confiscation tag. She ripped it off and shoved it back in her pocket.

"What's that?" T3 asked.

"I'd tell you, but then I'd have to kill you," Marti said and was rewarded with a heart-melting smile. It was hard to believe her brother-in-law had any part in the making of the kid.

To Peter she said, "I'll move it around back. Right away, since it bothers you so much." Not to mention, it gave her a good excuse to get away from him.

The Taurus didn't cooperate. Marti turned the key. It coughed and died. She tried again. Same result.

"Come on baby, don't do this to me now. Not in front of Dad, the Sequel," she begged.

The car ignored her. After her fourteenth failed attempt—she didn't count, but T3 did and loud enough to be heard back in Franklinville—she admitted defeat and got out.

"I don't suppose you have Triple-A?" Peter said.

Peter's smirk begged for the pie-in-the-face treatment, but she didn't have a pie handy. She couldn't say the words that popped to mind in front of the children, so she settled for shaking her head. "I don't suppose you want to help me push it down the Avenue, 'round to the alley, and up the alley to the back of the house? No? Then I guess it'll have to sit here for a while."

"Oh! Oh! I'll help push!" T3 jumped up and down.

Maggie took her thumb from her mouth. "Me too."

Peter scowled at his offspring and took out his phone. "I'll call a tow. I own a car lot."

Marti remembered Rudawski Motors, Bicklesburg's only used car lot. Before his exile, Dmitri was saving for a car of his own. Together, they wandered the lot and imagined themselves driving off into the sunset in a "fully guaranteed, gently used, previously owned auto-moh-beeeeel." She remembered the owner as a good-natured old guy with a slight accent. He must have been Peter's father. Or grandfather.

"If my mechanics can stop laughing long enough, they might be able to find out what's wrong," he continued. "If not, we'll tow it to the junkyard. They'll give you a few dollars for scrap value."

Marti wondered if the "if not" referred to the laughter of the mechanics or the repairability of the Taurus.

RachelAnne, Mom, and Baby Face Rodney returned.

"What's wrong?" Mom wore tailored slacks and a crisp blouse. Her feet were shod in comfy looking flats. Glitter-encrusted red flats.

"Aunt Marti's car's dead." T3 got down on his hands and knees and peered under the Taurus. "Looks good down here," he said.

Maggie jumped on his back and shouted, "Giddyap!"

"Hang on." T3 scuttled away.

"There's a shock," RachelAnne said, ignoring her kids.

Mom simply looked at the Taurus and raised her eyebrows. When it came to expressing disdain, disapproval, dislike, or dis-about-anything, Margaret Mickkleson did not need words.

Baby Face held a sealed bag. Mom's lavender silk dress was stuffed inside, the dark stain of Sheila's—or Mr. Stumpy's—blood visible through the clear plastic.

"I'll get this to the station. Someone will be in touch," he said and left. No one said goodbye.

RachelAnne corralled her kids. "I don't suppose they've had lunch?"

"You'll have to take care of that. I have a meeting." Peter stuck a pair of mirrored aviator sunglasses on his face and ran his hand through his hair.

Marti was beginning to think of him as "The Judge, Extra-Special Sleazebag Edition."

"Peter, this is no place for the kids right now." RachelAnne let go of her children.

Maggie dashed away and squealed. "T3! Chase me!"

Super Brother complied.

Peter shrugged. "They look happy enough to me. I have things to do. I don't have time to babysit this afternoon. I'll come by when I'm done. See what's up."

RachelAnne got the mad mom look. Pinched lips. Narrowed eyes.

"She's gonna blow," Grandma said.

If Peter knew what was good for him, Marti thought, he'd back down and back away.

He didn't. "Look. They'll be good for your mother." He cocked his head toward the front yard, where Mom chased T3 who chased Maggie. All three were laughing.

Of the multiple versions of her mother she'd seen so far, Happy Fun Grandmother-Mom was the most unfamiliar. And the one she liked best.

RachelAnne closed her eyes and gave a barely perceptible shake of her head.

Peter took it for agreement. "As soon as I get your sister's car sorted out, I'm outta here." He held up his phone. "And if I don't call the tow truck, that won't happen." He stuck his phone to his ear.

RachelAnne sighed, rounded up Mom and the kids, and herded them toward the house.

"Is the yady coming with us?" Maggie said.

"Lllllady." RachelAnne corrected her daughter. "Marti?"

"I'll be in after I take care of the car."

"Ten minutes," Peter said. "Moved you to the top of the list. Being the boss has its perks. Kids, behave for your mother." His phone chirped. He waved at his family and stuck it to his ear again.

Marti remembered why she hated the stupid things.

"Almost on my way . . . be there soon . . . I'm trying. Really . . . fifteen minutes. Twenty at the most." He stuck the phone back in his pocket. "Where the hell is that truck?"

He was anxious to meet someone. A thousand snotty remarks went through Marti's head, but she decided discretion was the better part of valor—and the safest route. She quietly unloaded her two black garbage bags from the car.

"Nice luggage," Peter said.

"I like it. Easy to store when not in use. Easy to replace when lost. Best of all, the color goes with everything."

Whatever did RachelAnne see in him? The parental-annoyance factor of marrying into the wrong small-town social class was hardly enough to make up for his sterling personality. It was also more Marti's style than her sister's. Maybe he was nicer when the two of them were alone. She hoped so.

She felt a pang of—something, she wasn't sure what—when the tow truck driver loaded the Taurus onto his flatbed. She didn't love the car, nor did she hate it. It was transportation, nothing more, nothing less, but it was hers. It didn't fit in on the Avenue any more than she did. She and her car were two of a kind. Beat up, but still kicking. Until now. She hoped the Taurus's demise—and she had the feeling whatever was wrong was fatal—wasn't an omen, a sign they'd haul her away next.

The Rudawski Motors Towing truck disappeared around the corner.

"Bye-bye, little car," she said.

"You *are* strange," Peter said.

"Oh crap." Marti kicked the black bag by her feet.

"Forget something?" Peter and Grandma said in unison.

"Nothing important," Marti said. The So-nutt-ee Donut receipt was still in the front seat, stapled to the empty donut bag. Oh well. She could get it later. If not, Pimples Pernelli or some other donut drone must have seen the McDonaghs. Big could interrogate Pimples.

That, she'd pay money to watch—once she had some.

EiGHT

"Looks like they ate and ran," Grandma said.

Dirty plates and empty glasses, along with Mom's teapot and empty cup, littered the table in the breakfast nook. It had been pressed into service as a lunch nook, which made sense. The island counter in the center of the large kitchen was for lunch, snacks, and all lesser meals, but the kids were too short for the stools. The family dining room was only used for evening dinners and the formal dining room for entertaining. Old Mom believed in rules and ritual. New Mom either adjusted or didn't notice.

Marti longed to stay in the deserted kitchen and enjoy the quiet, but it would only delay the inevitable. She was back in the bosom of her family. Time to get used to it.

"RachelAnne? Mom?" Marti waited for her bellow to provoke Mom's usual "don't screech like a banshee" reprimand, which itself sounded a lot like a banshee screech.

No reaction from New Mom. The changes in her living parent were creepier than her father's demise and reappearance.

"In here!" RachelAnne failed to specify the "here," but Marti had a good idea where she'd find her sister and posse.

She followed her sister's voice down the hall to the family parlor. She never understood why her mother insisted on the archaic *parlor* rather than *room*, but hers was not to reason why.

Other than the girls' bedrooms, the family parlor was Bickle House's one room not stuffed with museum-quality antiques left by the original Bickles, mixed with a few Mickkleson pieces and even fewer pieces from Mom's family. Most of Bickle House remained frozen in its elegant past, but Mom decorated and redecorated the family room every three years. She called it their "casual space." Unfortunately, Mom's idea of casual came from *Architectural Digest*. The family parlor was only slightly less intimidating than the rest of the house.

Marti stopped a few steps short of the door. Returning to the scene of her parents' version of family togetherness stirred up a stress-pool of memories.

Every evening after dinner, for exactly one hour, the four of them gathered in the family parlor for "sharing time." Translation: Mom and The Judge sat regally in their parental thrones and interrogated their daughters, seated like penitents on the couch across from their monarchs.

When they were little, both sisters enjoyed recounting the highlights of their day—a goal scored in soccer, a funny comment from a friend, finding a rock that looked like a polished heart.

Mom overrode the girls' stories with admonishments on their posture. *Sit up straight. Knees together. If you must cross something, make it your ankles, not your legs. Stop playing with your hair. Hands folded in your laps. Honestly, people will think you were raised by wolves.*

The Judge mostly grunted.

The conversations grew more and more awkward as the sisters grew older. By the time they were teenagers, her father's unvarying dismissal, "Well, off with you now," was everyone's favorite part of the evening. The nightly ritual remained a requirement for living in Bickle House until the day Marti left.

She last saw both her parents alive in this room. RachelAnne was off at Vassar making her parents proud. Marti'd returned from her last stay at the Birches and spent a month hiding in her room. Every night, The Judge asked about her plans for the future. Her mother asked when she was going to do something about her hair. That last night, Marti sat up straight, crossed her ankles, folded her hands in her lap, and lied through her teeth to both of them. Her bag was already packed and stashed in her closet.

She took a deep breath, squared her shoulders, and stepped into her past.

Not her past. Somebody else's past. Bizarro-opposite land.

The family parlor had been redecorated, probably more than once, since she left. The refurbishing of the parlor was nothing compared to the refurbishing of the family.

Proper posture was obviously no longer important. Mom sprawled on a comfy-looking couch, her feet propped on the coffee table. Maggie curled up next to her, half on and half off her lap. T3 perched on the coffee table, his hands behind his back, and watched his mother shift toys and magazines. RachelAnne knelt, ran her hand under an overstuffed chair, and stood up looking exasperated.

"Hey," Marti said.

"Has anybody seen the remote?" RachelAnne nodded at her sister and kicked aside a pillow.

A pillow. On the floor. The room was a mess. Mom didn't do housework—heaven forbid—but what happened to the staff?

"Peter said he had an important meeting and he'll check in with you later." Her brother-in-law left as soon as the tow truck left. He didn't bother to go in and say goodbye to his wife and children. Instead, he drafted Marti as his messenger.

"Probably a golf date," RachelAnne said. "Thad, check the toy box. Stupid thing has to be here someplace."

"Who wants to watch ponies?" Mom said.

"I do! I do!" Maggie shouted.

T3 groaned, but it was a halfhearted protest. He pulled the remote from behind his back and handed it to his mother.

"Did you have that the whole time I was looking for it?" his mother asked. He answered with an ear-to-ear grin.

RachelAnne really did make cute kids. It was hard to believe Peter had any input.

"That's new," Marti said. Across from the couch, on the wall once covered by expensively framed examples of The Judge's amateur photography, hung a huge flat-screen television. Not as gigantic as the one at the McDonaghs' but close. In Marti's day, television was relegated to the bedrooms, the sets deemed too ugly and the act of watching them too crass for the grander areas of the house.

"Grandparent syndrome. Check out this room." RachelAnne circled one hand in the air and handled the remote with the other. The TV sprang to life. Sometime in the last ten years, the family parlor had too. It looked like Mom dumped *Architectural Digest* in favor of *Homey Living for Normal Folk (of the Wealthy Variety)* or *Appearances? Who Cares?*

Beneath the clutter the furnishings still reeked of money, but the new style was inviting, not daunting. Every seat looked like a good place to curl up and relax. Instead of being arranged for what her mother called "the facilitation of civilized conversation," the couches and chairs all pointed at the TV. Pillows and soft-looking throws abounded. Grandparent syndrome or not, Marti couldn't imagine her mother wielding knitting needles and wondered if she ordered the afghans from a catalog or had them custom made. Probably the latter, since their colors coordinated perfectly with the whimsical fairy-tale scene painted on the toy box in the corner.

"It started with the toy box. When Thad was born, Mom found it at an art fair and filled it with appropriately educational toys," RachelAnne said.

Marti looked at the plastic superheroes and neon critters scattered on the floor.

"Yeah. Mom's definition of *appropriate* changed to 'but they love it' as the kids grew, but the toy box was the centerpiece of her next room rehab. I think she likes it more than the kids do,"

RachelAnne said. "They bought the television to watch movies with the kids, which led to getting cable, which led to, well, that." RachelAnne pointed at Maggie and T3 snuggled with their grandmother on the overstuffed sofa.

"Did we ever do that?" Marti asked. "The snuggling. Not the television watching."

"We must have, but I don't remember," RachelAnne answered.

Neon-colored talking ponies cavorted on the television screen. The couch crew giggled. One of the ponies—or maybe it was a unicorn—matched the one on Maggie's T-shirt. An identical plastic pony lay on the floor next to Marti's foot.

Even The Judge was entranced by the cartoon. He couldn't cuddle with his widow and grandchildren, but he giggled along with them from the back of the sofa.

The sight and sound of a giggling Judge was something Marti could have done without.

"Practically perfect prancing ponies!" Mom sang along with the rainbow herd.

T3 and Maggie whinnied in return.

"Bizarro-opposite world," Marti said.

"Indeed," RachelAnne said.

The Judge reached out and touched Mom's shoulder. She shivered. Maggie flinched and pulled away from her grandmother.

"Did you see that?" Grandma Bertie asked.

Marti bit her lower lip. The last thing she needed or wanted was to get sucked in by the newest generation of Mickklesons, even if they were named Rudawski.

Grandma and Marti weren't the only ones who noticed Maggie's recoil—or to understand the implication. The Judge leapt off the sofa back and landed in front of Marti and her great-grandmother. He'd gotten pretty spry in his afterlife.

"This is somehow your fault," he said.

"Unbelievable," Marti said.

"Like your family tree is flawless," Grandma said. "I've met your grandfather. He's a scoundrel even in the afterlife. The apple doesn't fall far from the tree, as they say."

"Believe it," RachelAnne said. "Come on. They'll all be fine as long as the ponies are on. Anyone who doesn't believe in using TV as a babysitter never had kids. Of any age."

"Get out of my house," The Judge roared.

"If I leave, Marti leaves," Grandma said.

Marti wished she could. She couldn't—yet—get out of the house, but she could follow her sister to the kitchen.

Much to Marti's relief, The Judge stayed and went back to pony watching.

Grandma Bertie didn't. "That man. He's got secrets, you know. Whatever's wrong with your mother, I blame him. Living with him would be enough to drive anyone around the bend."

Pot, kettle, Marti thought. Grandma chattered away, complaining about The Judge, like Sheila following her husband in the So-nutt-ee parking lot. If Ralph McDonagh bashed in his wife's skull and took off, Marti understood the motive.

Grandma didn't shut up until they got to the kitchen, where Edwards greeted them with a slight bow and Amity with a squeal. Grandma reciprocated with an awkward curtsy, and Amity laughed.

"How's Mrs. Partridge?" Marti asked.

"Retired. Living in Florida," RachelAnne said.

Which explained the state of the family parlor. The former housekeeper would approve of the new decor, but dirt and disarray were not permitted on her watch. Dust bunnies vaporized themselves in her presence.

"Good for her!" Grandma Bertie said.

"It was her dream," Edwards said.

In the old days, the kitchen was Marti's favorite place. She read about "home" in books and saw it in sappy sweet movies, but Mrs. Partridge's base of operations was the single place she felt it.

Mrs. Partridge was the one who picked the girls up from school, ran them to all the various activities they were enrolled in whether they liked it or not, bandaged scraped knees, and hugged away hurt feelings. She slipped them forbidden treats in the kitchen. The kitchen was Mrs. Partridge's domain, the one place Mom never interfered. Sometimes Marti suspected her mother knew about the cookies and that maybe, just maybe, Mrs. Partridge fed her secret cookies too.

The housekeeper never knew it, but Grandma Bertie adored her. Marti tried to tell her once, but Mrs. Partridge hushed her and gently pointed out that she'd have a much easier time of it if she "quit with the crazy talk." Nobody was perfect, not even Mrs. Partridge, but she came close.

"Marti, come play with me," Amity said.

"Shut your trap," Edwards said, his gentle tone at odds with his words. He managed the language but not the finer points of slang—and had more in common with Mrs. Partridge than he knew.

"Martiiiiiiiiiii. Play with me." Amity ignored Edwards.

"Sorry, miss. She's been lonely since you skedaddled."

"*She* sent a card when Dad died," RachelAnne continued.

"Humph," Grandma said. "That was manners, not sympathy. She had no use for your father either."

"I didn't know." Marti gripped the kitchen table and took a deep breath. She wanted to tell all of them to shut their traps, and in a decidedly different tone than Edwards's. Grandma she was used to, and Grandma knew the rules. She didn't expect answers and knew when to back off and shut up. Edwards seemed to have forgotten the rules. Amity always ignored them. RachelAnne might not have meant her words as an accusation, but they felt like one. Marti's head was ready to explode. With Mrs. Partridge gone, she wondered who would get stuck cleaning up the mess.

Lucky for her, Grandma knew her well enough to see her distress. "Come, Amity. I'll play with you. Marti's busy right now."

"But you can't make the dollies move!" Amity stamped her foot.

"Are you okay?" RachelAnne said.

"We'll find something else to play." Grandma and the butler hustled the little girl away, and Marti was left alone with her sister.

"Just . . . tired. The morning's been a little—"

"I don't want to talk about this morning. Not now." RachelAnne opened a cupboard door.

"Works for me," Marti said. Denial was a Mickkleson specialty. She gathered the lunch dishes. Her stomach heaved at the stench from the teapot. Good thing she'd left her coffee and donuts in the McDonaghs' front yard.

"Would you like some tea?" RachelAnne asked.

"You've got to be kidding me." Marti held her breath and poured the dregs of Mom's leftover tea down the drain.

"Not *that* stuff." RachelAnne waved a yellow box. Lemon Lift. Decaffeinated.

Marti preferred coffee and never understood the point of decaffeinated anything, but said "Sure." With the state her tummy was in, tea might be a better idea.

"Even Mrs. Ward won't touch Mom's potion, and she worships the ground Mom walks on."

"Mrs. Ward?"

"The new Mrs. Partridge. In title, anyway. Myrna."

"*Myrna?*"

"She insists we call her Mrs. Ward now, as 'befitting her new station.'" RachelAnne sniffed and stuck her nose in the air. "La-di-da."

Mom and Mrs. Partridge had, if not a friendship, a mutual respect. The older woman made sure the house ran smoothly and handled the parenting trivialities. Mom took the public glory and made sure the girls grew into the right sort of people—in Marti's case, a losing battle. Neither crossed into the other's territory.

Myrna was another matter. Mom's attitude toward the part-time help—the young Myrna LaRue came in to help Mrs. Partridge three days a week and for special occasions—was straight out of a BBC period piece. The younger woman was the lowliest of scullery maids, and Mom was the grandest duchess with a moral imperative to instruct and improve the unwashed working class.

Mom instructed the same way she mothered. Everything Myrna did fell short of the expected perfection. Mom tormented and criticized every chance she got, all under the guise of "helping the poor girl better herself."

Marti would have sympathized, but Myrna took her revenge on the girls. It was impossible to like someone who called her names and pinched her and whispered, "Tell on me. Try it. Who's going to believe you, crazy girl?"

Myrna bullied. Marti kept her mouth shut. RachelAnne complained.

Mom put on her martyr hat and said, "We must be patient with her. She needs the job."

The Judge never acknowledged the existence of Mrs. Partridge or Myrna or any other help who passed through his employ. If she and RachelAnne had ratted Myrna out to him, he would have said, "Talk to your mother."

Looking back, Marti wondered why they didn't tell Mrs. Partridge, who *might* have believed them. The best explanation she came up with was they were kids, and kids are weird.

"Myrna LaRue?" Marti said. The former maid hardly seemed like a fair replacement for Mrs. Partridge. At least she wouldn't pinch the adult Marti. Probably.

"I know," RachelAnne said. "But I have to admit, since Mom took a turn for the worse, she's been a great help. Dropped her other clients—customers—whatever housekeepers call the people they work for—and came to work for Mom full-time, or at least five days a week. She'd been coming to do the house three days a week."

Mrs. Partridge had lived in and pretty much been available twenty-four seven, with a few evenings off.

"Mom and The Judge survived with three-day help? What did they eat?"

"Mom took up cooking. She isn't good at it, but she likes it."

Marti hoped Mom's meals smelled better than her tea. Maybe she had poisoned The Judge.

RachelAnne set two steaming mugs on the table. "Of course, one of those people she dropped was my boss and he's none too happy, so I get to hear about it. Ev-e-ry day," she said. "There must be cookies stashed around here somewhere." She pulled a half bag of Oreos from a ceramic canister marked *Flour*. "Bingo. I don't need a plate if you don't."

"Plate? What is this 'plate' you speak of?" At the sight of the cookies, Marti's stomach growled. Which was better than heaving. Donuts. Oreos. She was having a high nutritional-risk day, but Oreos were good for the soul, if not the body. "I can't believe you found Oreos. Does Myrna—excuse me, *Mrs. Ward* have secret vices?"

"They're Mom's. She slips them to the kids when they visit and thinks I don't know. Like I don't recognize Oreo breath."

"Wow." Television, cooking, and now Oreos.

Oreos, along with all mass-produced cookies, cakes, chips, cheese puffs, soda pop, and other delicious forms of poisonous junk food, were on Mom's list of forbidden foods. She not only feared having pimply, tubby daughters, she wanted them to develop a "refined palate."

Mrs. Partridge's home-baked cookies were heavenly, but Oreos were something else. Of all the forbidden treats, Oreos were the one that ensnared Marti. She'd passed her addiction on to her baby sister. The two of them hid in the back alleys—meaning backyards and parking lots—of Bicklesburg, stuffed their faces, and chased their Oreo highs. They lived in fear of returning home with telltale black teeth. After cookie benders, they checked each other for crumbs and Oreo breath.

"Did this start before or after she got—well, you know?"

"Before. Around the time TV became an acceptable vice."

"Is this the same woman who raised us?"

"Oh, you won't believe the things my kids get away with," RachelAnne said. "Even when Dad was alive. Have I mentioned grandparent syndrome?"

"More than once," Marti said.

"It's a real thing and incurable. It's ugly. Unless, of course, you're the grandchildren. There's probably some milk if you want to dunk."

"No need."

"I didn't think so," RachelAnne said.

Oreo addiction was one of their few sisterly bonding experiences, and dunking the little round gems in milk wasn't part of the equation. It had been tough enough to score cookies without Mom finding out. Milk was out of the question.

RachelAnne set the bag of cookies in the center of the table.

"Oh my. Double Stuf," Marti said.

Each sister took a cookie and twisted. They pulled apart the dark wafers and solemnly licked the white filling.

Six cookies—each—later, RachelAnne said, "You have white stuff on your chin."

"You too."

Their laughter was loud, long, and totally out of proportion for the situation.

"It wasn't that funny." RachelAnne wiped her eyes.

"Apparently, we needed it. Or something." Marti wiped the Oreo filling from her chin. "You really didn't know about The Judge and Sheila?"

"Every day it becomes more and more obvious to me that I grew up in a bubble," RachelAnne said.

If Peter was any indication, she still lived in one. Marti wasn't ready to open that can of worms. "Tell me about Mom." She didn't want to deal with the Mom can of worms either, but it was necessary.

RachelAnne took an Oreo and examined it. "I'm not really sure. We have another doctor's appointment next week. Maybe we'll get answers then."

"Another? How long has she been . . . not herself? Other than the grandparent thing?"

"I'm not sure about that either." RachelAnne pulled apart the cookie and contemplated the filling. "Mrs. Ward says months. I was so busy with school and work and the kids, I never noticed." She put down the cookie, crème filling intact. "When Dad died, she . . . I don't know, had some sort of breakdown or something." She poked the white icing hard enough to break the wafer into pieces.

Oreo destruction meant serious stress. Time for a temporary change of subject. "What happened to The Judge?"

RachelAnne lined up the pieces of broken cookie. Marti took another cookie, began the sacred Oreo ritual, and waited for her sister to answer.

"He'd been out with the Tams." RachelAnne straightened the row of cookie pieces. Five little crumbly soldiers marched in perfect formation.

Marti slowly licked the crème from her cookie. The Tams was a secretive club made up of the county's wealthiest and most influential citizens. The membership roster was an open secret. All male. All powerful. Everybody knew the Tams existed, but nobody other than the initiates knew what went on in their closed-door meetings. No one even knew what the name meant. Publicly, they were a do-good organization, sort of like the Rotary. Select members got their pictures—handing giant checks to charitable organizations—in the newspaper.

Local conspiracy theorists cast them as a mini Illuminati in control of the local government, the local economy, and the local weather. Other than the weather, there was a good chance their control was more practice than theory.

Judging by the condition her father was in when he returned

from their monthly meetings, the gatherings were devoted to drinking, eating, drinking, backroom wheeling and dealing, and drinking. And possibly strippers.

If The Judge was murdered by one of his fellow old-guy fraternity brothers, Marti had zero chance of finding out who it was. If overindulgence in shenanigans while in their company contributed to his natural demise, she had even less of a chance of proving it. Neither the Tams nor anyone connected to them would talk.

She wondered if Sheila was involved with any of the Tams. Any still alive.

"Dmitri drove him to and from the meeting," RachelAnne said.

The Judge always pulled a driver from the ACS force when he knew he'd end up too far gone to drive.

"He said Dad was in his usual state when he brought him home. Mom waited up for him. She fixed him a whiskey sour—like he needed another drink—and went to bed. Myrna got here in the morning—Mom was still asleep—and found him. Stroke. He ate what he wanted and drank what he wanted and counted on medication to control his diabetes. He was probably worse after the diagnosis. You know how he was. No one could tell him anything. It finally caught up to him and killed him."

It was RachelAnne's longest speech since Marti's arrival, and her most expressionless. She might as well be describing beige.

"And Mom? You said she had a breakdown," Marti said.

"At first she insisted he wasn't dead. Then she became convinced she killed him with the whiskey sour. Something about making it extra sweet. That caused a lot of gossip. There was a case of a woman poisoning her husband with antifreeze over in Cooperstown last year. I think the locals were jealous. Wanted a good poisoning of their own." RachelAnne slumped in her seat, took another Oreo, and stuffed it into her mouth in one piece.

Marti stayed quiet and watched her sister chew.

RachelAnne swallowed and continued. "Mom made it through

the funeral, then completely fell apart. She has days when she seems to be her old self—almost, but not quite. She talks about Daddy like he's still alive. A few days after the funeral, I came by and found her on the phone hiring caterers for a DAR meeting. She said she was hosting twenty guests for high tea. She and Biddy Cromwell are the only local members left. They haven't met anywhere other than restaurants for years. That night, she put the tea kettle on the stove, went out to the backyard, lay down, and fell asleep on the lawn. Almost burned the house down. Would have, if Dmitri hadn't found her."

When Marti got ahold of The Judge, she would—well, she didn't know what she'd do. Killing him was superfluous. His "your mother's not well" was wholly inadequate.

"I haven't left her alone in the house since. Myrna—Mrs. Ward. Don't tell her I keep calling her Myrna—comes in Monday through Friday. I've hired a nursing service for the nights. I tried day nurses on the weekends, but it didn't work out. They upset Mom and made her worse. I spend my Saturdays and Sundays here until the night nurse arrives. Weekdays, I come over after work and stay with her between the time Myrna leaves and the nurse gets here. Peter's lost patience with the situation. He says we either need to move in to Bickle House—all of us—or put her somewhere. I think he wants both. I don't know what to do."

"What does her doctor say?" Marti didn't have any practice supplying reassuring words. Showing an interest was better than nothing.

RachelAnne shrugged, more a gesture of defeat than anything else. "They did an MRI. She doesn't have a tumor. Other than that, at this point, it's all guesswork. Alzheimer's? Something else? If there's any family history, no one talked about it. Nothing except for—"

"Me."

"Aunt Alice Bradley," Grandma said. "You are perfectly sane and you know it." Grandma'd snuck back in while Marti was listening to RachelAnne. At least Edwards and Amity weren't with her.

RachelAnne squirmed. "I'm sorry but—"

"Don't worry about it."

RachelAnne laughed. "At the moment, you're the sanest relative I've got. Not sure how I feel about that."

"I can stay as long as you need me," Marti said, and not just because Mom's—and RachelAnne's—needs fit in with her own goals.

"Don't you have a job to get back to?"

"That's sort of up in the air right now."

"Did you get fired? Is that why you came back?" RachelAnne perked up.

"I'm on unpaid leave while they remodel." It was a truth. Not the whole truth, but a truth.

"So you're here because you need money."

RachelAnne was half-right, but Marti decided to neither confirm nor deny. "I'm broke, but I left the nest ten years ago. Trust me, if I'd run home every time I ran out of money, you'd have seen me a long time ago. And seen a lot of me. I came home because I heard about The Judge. He was my father too, you know."

"I didn't mean . . ." RachelAnne pulled herself together. "Do you remember Benjamin Bowman?"

"The Judge's golf buddy." That wasn't all he was. Marti picked up an Oreo and inspected it—she hoped nonchalantly. *Here it comes*, she thought.

"And his lawyer. We need to see him."

Bingo. "Why?" Marti hoped she wasn't overacting the I-know-nothing thing.

"You're not broke. Not rich, but not broke. The Judge . . . it's complicated. I'll call Mr. Bowman today and make an appointment."

"On a Saturday?"

"We're Micklesons. I have his home number."

"Good point," Marti said.

"I never should have left Mom alone this morning."

"Stop beating yourself up. If anything, it was my fault for surprising you. Have another Oreo." Marti shoved the package across the table at her sister. If Mom couldn't be left alone for ten minutes in her own house, things were bad.

Maggie wandered in and pulled her thumb out of her mouth. "Nana's seeping," she said.

"Slllllllleeping, honey. Slllllllleeping." RachelAnne lifted her daughter onto her lap, and the little girl snuggled in. "At least, I hope she's not seeping."

"Nana?"

"She adores the kids. She's the poster woman for grandparent syndrome but still doesn't like thinking of herself as a grandmother."

"Amity wants to pay," Maggie mumbled.

"Pllllay. Did you bring her with you?" RachelAnne said. "Amity's her favorite doll. Didn't you have a doll named Amity?"

"Something like that," Marti said.

"I don't know where either of you got that name."

Marti did.

"I think she's mad," Maggie mumbled.

"What's Thad doing? Is he sleeping?"

"T3 changed the TV." Maggie's eyes fluttered. She'd be seeping herself in a second.

"I probably should go see what he's watching," RachelAnne said but didn't move.

Maggie's thumb went to her mouth, and she nodded off, content against her mother's chest.

"I'll go," Marti said.

NiNE

MOM WAS INDEED SLEEPING, HER HEAD THROWN BACK AND HER mouth wide open. She snored. Loud chainsaw snores. If she could see herself, let alone hear herself, she'd be humiliated. At least she wasn't seeping. Not as far as Marti could tell, and she wasn't going to check.

T3'd not only changed the channel, he'd upped the volume to blare. Instead of colorful ponies, superheroes battled supervillains across the large screen. Explosions boomed. Heroes zoomed. Villains were doomed. Whether it was new characters or new costumes on old characters, Marti didn't recognize the show. The Judge and T3 were mesmerized. Neither acknowledged her.

A shrill ring cut above the roar of the TV, and everyone—including The Judge—jumped. Everyone except Mom. She was out for the count.

"What's that?" Marti said.

"The phone," The Judge and T3 said and went back to the show.

By the third ring, after she stepped on and destroyed one plastic pony and two unidentifiable action figures, she found the handset under a pile of magazines. She let the phone ring again, trying to decide if she should answer it. It might be the police. More likely, it was some gossipy old biddy after an insider account of the morning's events. Anyone close enough to her parents to have their unlisted number was sure to be someone she didn't want to talk to.

"Marti! Can you get that?" RachelAnne called.

"Got it!"

The Judge and T3 cheered. Not for her. Animated explosions filled the TV screen.

Mom snored on.

"Mickkleson residence." She did her best to emulate the smooth electronic tones of the "back door open" lady. If the caller heard the television, they'd think they'd called a construction site. Or a war zone.

"I know what you did. Don't think you'll get away with it." The voice on the other end of the line was deep and rough and inhuman.

"Who is this?" She couldn't tell whether the caller was a man or a woman.

"You killed them both. Don't think you'll get away with it just because you're a Mickkleson, you b—" The caller spewed a stream of invective vile enough to shock her, and she'd pretty much heard everything. Just not strung together and directed at her. At least not with such intensity.

"Listen up, you crazy—" The distorted alien voice railed on.

How many people knew she was home? Her family, Dmitri, the cops, Dawn Pernelli—Dawn. No doubt the whole county knew.

"Marti? When did you get here? Whom are you calling?" Mom was awake.

The caller laughed, a high-pitched giggle that sounded almost human. Almost, but not quite. "Two dead . . . vengeance is coming, you filthy wh—"

"No one." She cut the connection. "I'm not calling anyone." The call wasn't aimed at her. It was aimed at her mother. She'd only been in Bicklesburg for Sheila's death. Mom was there for both The Judge and Sheila.

Unless the caller knew about Ozzie, which was impossible.

"I'm cold. Where's Myrna? I need my tea." Mom pulled a brightly colored afghan from the back of the couch, wrapped herself in it, and fell back asleep.

"Got 'em!" T3 said.

The Judge put his hand up for a high five and nonchalantly ran it over his head when when none came.

RachelAnne appeared, carrying her half-awake daughter.

"Aunt Marti yooks scared," Maggie said.

"Who was it?" RachelAnne didn't bother to correct the little girl's speech. "You look like you've seen a ghost." She blushed. "I'm sorry. You know what I mean."

"Wrong number," Marti said. The phone call left her feeling violated. Dirty. For both her mother and herself. And everyone else in a two-mile radius.

RachelAnne called Benjamin Bowman, and he agreed to see them the next day. On a Sunday afternoon. The Judge was dead. Long live the power of the Mickkleson name.

Or else there was a whole lot more money at stake than Marti thought there was. Enough to disappear again. For good this time. For enough money, she might be willing to put up with The Judge hanging around. Maybe not. She wanted to press her sister for details. RachelAnne *had* mentioned money in a roundabout way. She didn't want to look greedy. She was, but she didn't need to telegraph it.

Marti had a million questions for her sister and no chance to ask them.

Questions about The Judge's death. The little her sister told her backed Grandma Bertie's he-ate-and-drank-himself to death theory. The Judge Marti remembered wouldn't pay any attention to doctors. He was untouchable. Immortal. Immune to the laws of nature, if devoted to the laws of man. Death by Enormous Ego. How she could prove Natural Causes of His Own Making to the owner of that ego was beyond her.

And Mom. There had to be more to Mom's condition than RachelAnne was saying. The MRI and no tumor was good news, but weren't there more tests? Did the doctor have any idea what was wrong? Marti spent the day watching her mother, searching for the Mom she remembered.

Margaret Alberta Dibble Mickkleson, Queen of Everything, appeared now and then—"Marcile. What in the world are you wearing? Are you planning on indulging in manual labor? If so, you are severely underdressed"—only to be replaced by a quivering and confused woman much older than her years—"Where's my tea? Who took my tea? Where's Myrna? It's Wednesday. She's late."

Once in a while, another Mom put in an appearance. The Mom from behind door number three possessed all of Mom's attitude, but none of her acuity. "Marcile. When did you get here? What are you wearing? Did you forget your medication? You'd better change into more appropriate attire before your father sees you."

All three Moms had a few things in common. First, they all downed pot after pot of disgusting tea. Second, Sheila McDonagh's death had no effect on them whatsoever, if they remembered the morning's events at all. And last, they all adored T3 and Maggie.

To anyone who didn't know her, Mom would look like any other grandmother doting on her grandchildren. To Marti, the easy, playful, and most of all nonjudgmental relationship her mother had with RachelAnne's children was downright surreal. They cuddled. They sang. Not only the zoo song, which was the only song Marti remembered her mother singing to her. Somewhere along the line, Mom developed an entire repertoire of kid songs. She might not know what day it was or remember her husband was now her late husband, but she remembered the lyrics to two dozen silly songs, including the one that got a six-year-old Marti into a bucket of trouble.

At one postdinner family-bonding session, she announced she'd learned a new song. Her parents asked to hear it. Their pained expression when she sang "There were three jolly fishermen, fisher-fisher-men-men-men" was probably due to her inability to carry a tune. She made it all the way to "Amster-Amster-dam-dam-*dam*" before they stopped her.

"Young ladies do not use *language*," her mother said.

In retrospect, the scandalous song wasn't the reason for her banishment from polite company. The parental disapproval level hit code red when she informed them Grandma Bertie taught her the song. She was sent to her room and ordered to be grateful they didn't have Mrs. Partridge wash her mouth out with soap.

New Mom sat on the couch with her grandchildren, in the new version of the same room, and led them in a sing-along. Both she and The Judge belted out the offensive chorus at the top of their lungs. The kids matched them word-for-word and decibel-for-decibel. They followed it up with the zoo song. They followed every song with the zoo song.

RachelAnne sat in the corner and flipped through a magazine, oblivious to the total weirdness of the situation.

"Look at all the monkeys swinging in the trees," Mom and Maggie sang.

T3 capered and scratched his armpits and made chimp noises. "Can we go to the zoo tomorrow?" he asked.

"No, dear, maybe another time." RachelAnne didn't look up from her magazine.

"Next week?" T3 said.

"Maybe." RachelAnne turned a page.

"Yay! Mommy's taking us to the zoo next week," he sang.

"That's a fine idea," The Judge said.

"You should go too," Grandma Bertie said.

As far as Marti was concerned, she was already at—or in—a zoo.

"Did I say that?" RachelAnne pulled her nose out of the magazine and looked at Marti.

"If you did, I missed it," Marti said. "Maybe he'll forget in a week."

"You obviously don't have children," RachelAnne said. She

went back to flipping pages, not overly concerned about keeping a promise she didn't make or overly interested in the magazine's contents.

Marti not only didn't have children, she'd never spent any time with kids. Never wanted to. However, even to her unpracticed eye, her niece and nephew were something special.

T3 was five—five and three-quarters to be specific, and he was specific—going on fourteen. Marti fell in love with him at "if I tell you, I'll have to kill you," and the more she listened to him talk, the deeper she sank. He spoke like a mini-adult with the whimsy of a child. They'd exchanged few words, brief conversations before he zoomed off to something more interesting, but she enjoyed talking to him more than any other member of her family, living or dead. He was too realistic to truly believe the superhero thing, but he pretended with every fiber of his being. Marti was ready to find herself a cape and run off to defend the universe with him. She drew the line at spandex, but since T3 wore a T-shirt, jeans, and sneakers, she thought he'd let her off the hook.

She was equally taken with his little sister. Maggie was a solemn little thing. Other than her problem pronouncing words with *l*'s, she was nearly as verbally skilled as her big brother. By the time she reached his age—another two and one-quarter years, according to T3—she'd run conversational loops around him. Not that Marti actually had a direct conversation with her niece. The little girl kept her distance and mostly stared at her. When she spoke to Marti, it was through her brother or mother, and all too often, she mentioned "the yady." RachelAnne assumed her daughter meant Marti and corrected her with, "She's your aunt Marti, sweetheart." At least she skipped the dreaded *l* and didn't try to force Maggie to say "Aunt Marcile." Maybe she sympathized with her daughter's speech struggles.

Marti sympathized with a struggle she didn't think the little girl or her mother were yet aware of. Her first impression was on the money. The "yady" in question was Grandma Bertie, and

Maggie's frequent mentions of Papa Thad weren't because she missed her grandfather. Marti found it hard to believe RachelAnne didn't suspect something when Maggie named her doll Amity. Her sister was either taking denial to a new level or completely blocking out a large part of their childhood.

If she stayed, she needed to make friends with her niece. Maggie would need a friend who understood. As it was, she let the little girl keep her distance. *For her own good*, she told herself. It wouldn't be fair to get close then jump ship. Not fair to Maggie.

It didn't make any difference to her. She'd survived the past decade family-free and liked it that way. It wasn't like she needed a friend or anything. A living friend. She had Grandma. What kind of friend would a three-year-old make anyway? Three and a half years old.

"I think I yike the yady," Maggie said.

"I like you too, sweetheart." Grandma beamed. Maggie stuck her thumb in her mouth.

"Llllady." RachelAnne closed her magazine. She apparently kept an eye—and an ear—on the goings-on of her kids even with her nose buried in the magazine.

"There was an old lady who swallowed a horse," T3 sang.

"She died of course!" Mom shouted. "Has anyone seen Mr. Stumpy?"

"That's it. Where's the remote? It's time for ponies," RachelAnne said.

The remote lay next to the phone on an end table, just out of RachelAnne's reach.

"It's here." Marti reached for it, and the phone shrieked. She grabbed it instead.

"I know what you did, you b—"

She cut the connection and tossed the receiver under the table.

"Who was that?" T3 said.

"Was it your father? Did he say when he's coming home?" Mom said.

"Wrong number," Marti said.

"Really." RachelAnne did the skeptical eyebrow lift thing. She looked far too much like Mom.

"Aunt Marti yooks yike she saw a ghost," Maggie said.

"Absolutely. Who wants to play outside?" Marti needed to get out of the room, out of the house. Out of Bicklesburg, but that wasn't going to happen. Not yet.

"I do! I do!" T3 was raring to go, but his sister shrank into the corner. "Come on, Mags, bet you can't beat me there."

He knew his little sister. Her face went from shy to determined, and she was off the couch and out the door in an instant. He hung back for a split second, then raced after her shouting, "I'll catch you!"

Marti really liked him, despite the fact—or maybe because of the fact—he was a much better big brother than she'd ever been a big sister.

"I think I'll just stay here and take a nap." Mom shut her eyes.

"I'll stay with her," The Judge said.

RachelAnne looked from Marti to their mother. "I'll stay with Mom." She didn't sound entirely convinced leaving her children alone with their long-lost, possibly certifiable, and definitely irresponsible aunt was better than leaving Mom unattended.

The Judge didn't count, since RachelAnne didn't know he was there.

"I like your kids," Marti said, "and I'm no more crazy than you are."

"That's not exactly reassuring," RachelAnne said, but she said it with a smile.

"Wait'll they find out how good I am at hide-and-go-seek."

"You've certainly had a lot of practice at hiding."

"When it comes to hiding, I am killer," Marti said.

RachelAnne's smile vanished. Marti left without apologizing for her poor choice of words—and before RachelAnne had a chance to reconsider her decision to let the kids out with their crazy aunt.

Marti and the kids ran races and played chase the Maggie, never managing to catch her.

"Maybe when she gets bigger," T3 whispered.

They threw their all into heroes and villains. Marti was the bad guy, intent on world domination, but T3 and his sidekick tackled her and saved the day.

They never got to hide-and-go-seek.

Amity threw a minor temper tantrum at Marti playing with T3 and Maggie instead of her. When Marti ignored her, the tantrum went nuclear. The spoiled ghost threw herself on the ground and rolled. Before she could move, Marti found herself standing in a puddle of ghost, shivering and shaking while tiny icicles darted from her feet to her shoulders.

"That's mean!" Maggie said. Amity leapt and dove at the living girl.

Edwards arrived just in time to snare the bratty ghost girl and drag her off, kicking and screaming.

RachelAnne and Mom arrived at the same time.

"Are you okay?" RachelAnne said.

Marti's teeth chattered. Quick pass-throughs were bad enough. Amity planted herself and stayed. She was frozen to the core.

"Aunt Marti stepped on a ghost," Maggie said.

"A super ghost! Take her down!" T3 lunged at Marti.

"Are you sure you're not sick?" RachelAnne grabbed her son.

"I th-think it's t-t-time to g-go inside," Marti said.

When Peter returned from his important meeting, Marti was wrapped in one of the knitted blankets, Maggie on her lap, next to Mom on the family room couch. Amity's tantrum turned her into a temporary Marti-sicle, but it broke the ice with her niece. The toddler either cottoned on to their shared secret or felt sorry for her aunt. Marti didn't care which. She was grateful for the extra warmth.

"Everybody ready to go home?" Peter said.

"Can we watch the rest of the movie?" T3 said.

Maggie and Mom didn't say anything. Neither did Marti. He certainly wasn't talking to her unless he was suggesting she leave. The look he gave her when he arrived said it was a distinct possibility.

"We need to talk," RachelAnne said. "Alone." She and her husband disappeared.

"You want me to go eavesdrop?" Grandma said.

Maggie stared wide-eyed at the two of them. Marti shook her head. The acting-like-a-responsible-adult thing was harder than usual with her niece watching.

RachelAnne and Peter weren't gone long.

"Kids, Daddy's taking you home, and I'm having a sleepover with Aunt Marti," RachelAnne announced.

T3 groaned.

"Won't that be fun," Marti said. RachelAnne—or Peter—didn't want to return the next day to find Marti and the family silver gone.

"I want to seep over with Aunt Marti," Maggie said.

Peter scowled. "You've obviously made a conquest."

"Sllllllleep," RachelAnne said. "And you're both going home with Daddy. How about if we order pizza first?"

"Pizza!" both kids shouted.

Mom turned her nose up at the pizza. While RachelAnne served pizza with the works for everyone else, Marti prepared toast and stinky tea for her mother. Everyone was happy except Peter. His mood matched the tea funk.

After dinner, RachelAnne's crew departed in a flurry of hugs and kisses. The flurry was for—and from—the kids. Peter exchanged stiff hugs and pecks on the cheek with both his wife and mother-in-law.

Marti got, "I'll let you know as soon as I hear anything about your car." Which was okay. That was all she wanted from him.

"The night nurse will be here soon." RachelAnne shut and locked the front door, silencing Electro-Woman and her "Front door open. Front door, open."

"She really needs to expand her vocabulary," Marti said.

"Huh?" RachelAnne looked confused.

"The alarm lady."

"Oh. Was that a joke?"

"Apparently not a good one."

"I never know with you."

"And you a lawyer. Don't they train you to read people or something? Here I was, getting all excited at having my own highly skilled private defense lawyer in the family. Who knows when it might come in handy." Marti yawned.

"I hope that's a joke," RachelAnne said.

"You never know."

"If you're going to get into trouble, at least wait until I pass the bar."

"I'll do my best." As witty banter went, it wasn't much, but as exhausted as Marti was, it was all she had. RachelAnne didn't appear to be in any better shape.

"Back door open. Back door open."

"Crap," RachelAnne said. Marti said something a bit stronger, but the meaning was the same. Both ran for the kitchen.

Grandma and The Judge beat them there.

Mom stood at the open back door. Rather than going out, she ushered in a young woman dressed in jeans and T-shirt. A tight T-shirt. She carried an overnight bag adorned with a badly drawn logo of two clasped hands.

"Oh, thank goodness." It was hard to tell if RachelAnne was near tears or relieved. Considering what happened the last time Electro-Woman—she really needed a name—got all excited about the back door, Marti didn't blame her.

"You're early." RachelAnne shut and locked the door. "Marti, this is Winter Adams, from Helping Hands Home Care. She's here three nights a week. Georgia Harrison comes in the other four," RachelAnne said.

"But Mrs. Mickkleson likes me better, don't you sweetie?"

Mom stuck out her tongue.

Adams my foot, Marti thought. The girl—young woman—was a Pernelli if she'd ever seen one, and she'd seen more than one.

"Winter, my sister Marti. She's here for the night. Longer if we're lucky."

"So happy to meet you. I've heard all about you from my aunt." Winter held out her hand, and Marti shook it.

"Your aunt?"

"My aunt Dawn. You went to school together or something." Winter giggled.

A high-pitched giggle. Like the one on the phone. Marti narrowed her eyes. The nurse looked a lot like her aunt. The young version, before the sun damage and wrinkles set in. Other than her resemblance to Dawn, she seemed harmless, but she was a Pernelli. As far as Marti was concerned, they were all as harmless as rattlesnakes. "I went to school with a lot of Pernellis," she said.

The nurse giggled again. "We're like *marabunta* army ants. If you see one of us, there's a horde around somewhere."

Marti wasn't reassured. Army ants killed and devoured everything and anything in their path. Maybe *marabunta* were some special species, all fluffy and friendly. She doubted it. Not if there were Pernellis involved.

"I'm staying tonight to welcome my sister home," RachelAnne said, "but you can go about business as usual. Mom had a rough day. Routine will be good for her."

"I heard," Winter said. "About the day, I mean."

I'll bet you did, Marti thought.

"Mrs. Mickkleson. Let's get you upstairs." Winter bounced away and took charge of Mom.

"I want tea," Mom said.

"One cup. That's all." Winter headed for the china cabinet, right at home in the Mickkleson house. "And which pot would we like tonight? How about these darling roses?"

"I want the Staffordshire," Mom said.

Winter put the roses back on the shelf and pulled out a pot with a spout shaped like a duck.

"I usually leave now, so we're off duty," RachelAnne said.

"Thank goodness," Marti said. Winter irritated her.

The sisters spent the evening in front of the TV, watching inane sitcoms. Marti had no idea what they were about and didn't care. RachelAnne claimed to watch them regularly and enjoy them but didn't act the least bit entertained. She acted worn out and worried.

Marti snuck peeks at the clock and wondered how soon she could announce she was off to bed without looking antisocial.

Her sister didn't care about antisocial. Shortly after nine, RachelAnne said she was calling it a day. "It's been a long one and I can't keep my eyes open."

"I love you," Marti said and meant it.

SHE RETRIEVED HER garbage bags from the kitchen, grateful no one stuck them out with the trash, and headed upstairs.

At first glance, her childhood room was as she'd left it. Cleaner, but that was no surprise.

On closer examination, the changes were subtle. Posters leftover from her teenage years still adorned the walls, but the Misfits and her cheap print of Edvard Munch's *The Scream* hung in neat frames, no longer tacked to the wall with blue putty. Her collection of dancing skeletons cavorted on the desk, rather than hiding in the nooks and crannies of her bookshelf where the books were now arranged by spine height and color. The plain black bedspread was new, but went with the rest of the room. She hadn't changed the decor after her Goth phase. Someone had preserved and upgraded her adolescence. It was the Museum of Marti, and it creeped her out.

The dresser drawers were empty. She unloaded her bag of sweatshirts, jeans, pajamas, and undies. Other than her hairbrush and toothbrush, that was the sum of her belongings.

Almost.

"Get it out," Grandma said.

"Give me a chance." Marti pulled the new spread off the bed and replaced it with her quilt.

"That's better," Grandma said.

Better wasn't the word Marti would choose. The faded quilt meant home to her, *her* home, not Bickle House. On her old bed, in her old room, it looked right. Natural. Like it belonged there, and she didn't. She snatched it off the bed and balled it up.

"So. What's your plan?" The Judge said.

"What do you mean?" Marti opened the closet. The clothes she left behind still hung inside, neatly organized by blouses, skirts, and dresses. She threw the quilt in and kicked it to the back, stubbing her toe on a pair of purple Doc Martens in the process. "Ouch!"

"What's wrong?" Grandma said.

"My past just bit me," Marti said. She'd always liked those boots too.

"That's what you get," Grandma said. "Poor quilt."

"Stick to the subject," The Judge said. "Whoever did—that thing—to poor Sheila was likely the same person who murdered me."

"He wasn't murdered," Grandma said.

"He just went to sleep and never woke up." Amity and her keeper appeared in the closet. "Marti, why is your blanket on the floor?"

Marti shut the door. Not that it kept them in.

"Can we play now? Pleeeeease?" All smiles and bouncing curls, Amity evidently forgave Marti her transgression.

"Maybe when I warm up." Marti wasn't ready to forgive the spoiled brat. The memory of standing ankle-deep in ghost made her shiver.

Amity pouted. She knew exactly what she'd done, but Marti knew better than to expect an apology.

"Come along now, Miss Marcile needs to sleep." Edwards took his charge's hand and looked pointedly at The Judge.

Her father settled himself on her dresser. "Who is—was—this man and why is he in my house?"

"He's been here longer than you have," Marti said.

"And he's nicer, too," Amity said.

"You've got that right," Grandma said.

"Everybody out!" The Judge bellowed.

"Good idea. It's my room. You leave." Ghost Judge didn't intimidate her. She considered it an improvement in their relationship.

He didn't. "Do not talk back to me, young lady!"

"You are a mean, mean man and you should go away," Amity said.

The Judge sputtered.

Edwards corralled his charge. "Nighty night, sleep tight, Miss Marcile. Don't let the bed bugs bite." He and Amity disappeared.

Business as usual in Marti Mickkleson Land.

"Normal is what you're used to," she said.

"What?" The Judge was sullen.

"Oh lord. Now I *am* talking to myself. Edwards is right. I need sleep."

"First, tell me what your plans are," The Judge said.

"To take two aspirin—if I can find any—and get a good night's sleep. I'll call you in the morning."

"This is serious. Did you *see* poor Sheila?"

Marti didn't bother to answer. He knew she had. She still saw poor Sheila and her crushed skull every time she closed her eyes.

"Thaddeus, leave the girl alone," Grandma said.

"She needs a plan."

Marti's patience, which she had little of to start with, was wearing thin. "Look. I'll bet anything it was Ralph. He probably got tired of her incessant chattering. Or the smell of hairspray. Or he found out about you and had a delayed reaction. Whatever. He broke. I'm sorry your bit on the side is dead. Nobody deserves that. But since Mom's here and bimbo's there, why don't you go off and find Sheila Hair Helmet? You two can have a few uninterrupted years together before Mom joins you."

She hoped the last part was true.

"Good for you." Grandma beamed.

"I'm not going anywhere until we have a plan," The Judge said.

"*We?* I'm going to bed now. Stay or leave. Just shut up." She started to pull her sweatshirt over her head. She'd barely lifted the hem before The Judge fled.

"I'm so proud of you. Don't let him bully you," Grandma said.

"If you're staying, be quiet. I need sleep."

"Do you want me to sing you a lullaby? Like I used to?"

"NO!"

"Marti? Are you okay?" RachelAnne tapped at the door.

Marti threw a pillow at her great-grandmother.

Grandma had the grace to look sheepish.

"Bad dream," Marti said.

"Can I come in?"

Marti cracked the door and slumped against the doorframe. She didn't need to act. She was drained. She did need to fib, just a little. "I sat down, closed my eyes for a second, and fell asleep. Bad dream."

"You're not. . ." RachelAnne stared at Marti's feet. "Well . . . hearing voices again, are you?"

"Only yours."

"Do you want to talk?" RachelAnne didn't look her in the eye. The offer didn't hold much sincerity. No surprise. They'd both been through the same wringer.

Mostly the same. Her sister no longer had to deal with The Judge. "I just want to go to bed."

RachelAnne didn't press the matter. "Okay. See you in the morning."

Marti closed the door and glared at her grandmother.

Grandma made the universal sign for *my lips are zipped*, and

Marti crawled into bed, still dressed.

She slept—she thought—but not long or well. The Judge and Grandma Bertie's arguing might have been real. Amity's pleas for someone to play with and Edwards's consoling replies might have been real. The laughter of the concrete garden gnome with the bloody head definitely wasn't.

When the sun peeked around the curtains, she was wide awake but not rested and ready to face the day.

"Get up. You've got things to do. Places to go," The Judge said.

She definitely wasn't ready to deal with The Judge, but she did have a question for him. One that nagged her all night.

"Dad? Why are you so worried about who killed your bimbo?"

He disappeared.

TEN

"Your father left you a sizable bequest in the form of a trust fund. He also set some unusual and explicit conditions on your inheritance." Benjamin Bowman straightened the small stack of papers in front of him and squared them with the edge of his desk. He was the late Judge's lawyer and the closest thing her father had to a best friend.

"Of course he did." Marti knew the conditions—unless The Judge left something out, which she wouldn't put past him. He'd made himself scarce after her still unanswered Sheila-question, until he insisted on accompanying them to the lawyer's office. In the car, he was quiet. Too quiet. He didn't even react to Grandma Bertie's barbs.

"Shut up and listen," RachelAnne said.

Their tentative sisterly bond came and went so fast it made Marti dizzy. They were pleasant to each other over coffee and breakfast. RachelAnne's attitude changed when Peter and the kids came to sit with Mom while the two of them were gone. As soon as they arrived, she and her husband slipped off into another room. Marti couldn't make out most of their words, but she heard her own name, and their raised voices gave her the general gist of the conversation. Her sister barely spoke to her afterward, and when she did, she snapped. Marti tried not to take it personally. It wasn't easy.

Bowman picked up the top paper and read aloud. The language was legalese, but Marti understood.

The first stipulation decreed she return to Bicklesburg and the bosom of her family on her own. It didn't matter why she came back, but she was not to be enticed by the promise of money. Rejoining her family had to be her decision.

She shot The Judge a look at that one.

"Made sense at the time," he said.

Grandma rolled her eyes.

"As you're here, I believe we can consider the first condition met," Bowman said.

"Go, me," Marti said. Neither her sister nor the lawyer knew the dearly departed had blown his own demand. Marti wouldn't tell, and Grandma Bertie and The Judge couldn't, so it was all good.

Bowman read a pompous passage explaining how The Judge, as her father, had her best interests at heart. With her "disability," he didn't expect her to be able to fully care for herself, so the conditions he set were for her own protection.

Blah, blah, blah.

Her father never considered she might have a full and successful life of her own. She didn't, but it still rankled to know he assumed she'd end up worse than what she was—a fast-food employee who lived in a one-room dive and once in a while drank a little too much and *needed* money.

What really irritated her was she couldn't argue with him. Well, technically she *could*, as long as they were out of earshot of Rachel-Anne and Bowman and the rest of the living population. But any leg she had to stand on was more ephemeral than either of his.

If she wanted the money, any semblance of freedom pretty much ended once she returned, but the payout was excellent. A little mental arithmetic—minimum wage times forty hours a week times fifty-two weeks a year—at her current Burger Buster standard of living, she could live for six years and then some on the first payment alone. The one she got for simply showing up. The one The Judge called enough to live on for six months.

During that six months—to be spent in Bicklesburg at a residence of her own choosing, but he hoped she would stay with her mother—she was to prove to her baby sister she was trustworthy. Sober. Responsible. Able to take care of herself and manage her finances.

She had to prove herself not crazy. Bowman didn't use the despicable word, but it was the essence of her father's message.

Should she manage to meet the standards as outlined, she would receive a monthly allowance from the trust and, unless she ended up in prison or institutionalized, be allowed to live her life with minimal interference from RachelAnne or anyone else.

He trusted RachelAnne to be a better judge of her sister's character and state of mind than she'd been in certain other areas of her own life. Marti wondered if Baby Sister's misstep was her choice in husbands or careers. Not even the perfect daughter escaped The Judge's disapproval.

As for the size of the trust fund, Marti knew her family was well off—who in Bicklesburg didn't—but she had no idea they were *that* well off. The monthly allowance was equal to half the first payout. Bye-bye Burger Buster budget. She and Grandma could live out their days wherever they wanted. She could. Grandma'd already done her living.

If she lasted six months in Bicklesburg and made her sister happy—a big if.

RachelAnne's back was ramrod straight. She stared straight ahead. Marti couldn't tell if she was watching Bowman or examining her own reflection in the large, gilt-framed mirror on the wall behind him. Her sister pinched her lips. Her nostrils flared. Even in the reflection, she didn't look at Marti. Marti felt the hot waves of something—anger? hatred?—rolling off her sister and wondered whether it was the responsibility or the money or the insult from Daddy Dearest that infuriated her. It couldn't be the first time she'd heard the terms of The Judge's bequest.

Bowman looked from sister to sister. "Any questions so far?" Marti shook her head. RachelAnne didn't respond. He went back to reading.

Should Marti fail to prove herself worthy of The Judge's largesse, she would receive a greatly reduced monthly allowance—little more than her monthly take-home from Burger Buster—but only if she remained in Bicklesburg and lived with her mother or, in the event of her mother's death, in housing approved of by RachelAnne.

At least he didn't decree the sisters live together.

In the event Marti failed to prove she was a responsible adult, RachelAnne was required to provide documentation of her shortcomings. Simply pissing her sister off wouldn't be a problem. Which was good. Baby Sister was looking more and more pissed off with every word Bowman read.

The trust would pay for emergencies, including medical bills, bail, legal representation, or, in the sad event her *disability*—she wanted to scream and throw things every time Bowman used the word—got the better of her, her long-term care at the Birches or a similar facility.

When she died, the trust would pay her funeral expenses and the remaining capital would go to charity. She didn't recognize the name of the organization. It sounded like a support group for the parents of wayward children.

Thomas Wolfe was wrong. She could go home again if she was willing to return to the person she was, or thought she was, when she left. Or the person everyone else thought she was. By the time Bowman finished reading, Marti was again a helpless and dejected teenager living under The Judge's thumb, wondering if she did suffer from a mental illness.

The transformation wasn't only in her head. The mirror reflected a portrait of two deeply unhappy women. While RachelAnne looked like a miserable and angry adult, Marti was a sullen adolescent. Without realizing it, she'd slid down in her chair. Her legs stuck straight out in front of her, crossed at the ankles. She gripped the arms of her chair so hard pain spread from her hands to her shoulders. She hoped The Judge was pleased with himself.

She sat up straight, put on her responsible adult face, and checked the mirror. Her version of a responsible adult face made her appear demented, but it went well with her Porky Pig sweatshirt. She wondered if RachelAnne would crack a smile if she stuck out her tongue and let loose with a "Th-Th-Th-Th-Th-That's all, folks."

Probably not, and she'd seen no sign Bowman possessed a sense of humor.

The lawyer cleared his throat. "Do you have a bank account? I can arrange an electronic transfer of the immediate settlement."

She assumed the bank account was a rhetorical question. Her savings account in Franklinville held enough to keep it open and allow her to cash her Burger Buster checks. The habits she developed when she first ran away stuck with her long after she assumed—hoped—her family quit searching for her. If they searched for her.

She paid cash for everything. When she couldn't, she went to the post office and bought a money order. Her paper trail was as narrow as she could make it, and her digital vapor—financially at least—was as close to nonexistent as she could make it. She didn't even have an ATM card.

If she stayed in Bicklesburg, putting the money in the Franklinville Community Credit Union wouldn't do her a whole lot of good.

On the other hand, she only needed to stay there if she wanted the whole pie. Once she got the first slice, there was nothing to stop her from returning to Franklinville, emptying the account, and moving on.

Nothing other than the Taurus needing repairs.

And being stuck for who knew how long with The Judge if she didn't fulfill her end of the bargain.

And Mom. To her surprise, no matter how angry she was at her not-so-departed father, she found she didn't want to abandon her mother.

"Of course I have a bank account," she said. "A bare-bones savings account at the Franklinville Community Credit Union. No bells and whistles. Not sure it's set up for electronic transfers."

"You really do live in the stone age, don't you?" RachelAnne said.

Marti shrugged. "You can probably make a deposit, but I have to go make withdrawals in person."

"What about your F-n-R account?" RachelAnne said.

"F-n-R account" was what she and her sister called their childhood savings accounts. The Judge had ruled half of their weekly allowances and 80 percent of any birthday, Christmas, or whatever monetary gifts went straight to the bank. He maintained it taught them fiscal responsibility—the original meaning of "F" and "R." In reality, both sisters learned embezzlement skills early, and when they were teens, they found a new meaning for the "F." Her parents' names were on the account along with hers, so she hadn't closed it, but ten years ago, her last stop in Bicklesburg was the bank. She all but drained the account and hit the road before they knew she and the money were gone. Despite everything she'd skimmed off the top over the years, Marti's F-n-R account provided seed money for her new life.

"You're right. If The Judge didn't close it, the ten bucks I left in it might be twenty by now."

"It's still there," The Judge said.

"Account number?" Bowman asked.

Marti waited for The Judge to supply the number, so she could parrot it to the lawyer. When he didn't, she said, "I have no idea. How about I go to the bank tomorrow? Check on that account, open a new one—or something."

Everyone agreed it was a fine idea. Bowman, gravely. RachelAnne, sullenly. Grandma, enthusiastically. The Judge, silently. At least Marti assumed his stiff nod was agreement.

Bowman handed her a bundle of papers. "Please read this over. If you agree to your father's terms, initial each page, and sign the last."

She skimmed the pages. No surprises. She initialed, signed, and handed the papers back to the lawyer.

"I believe that's about it for today." Bowman stood and walked around the desk, hand extended. "Marcile, it's wonderful to have you back. I'm just sorry your father is not here to enjoy it."

Her father was there, and from his expression, he wasn't enjoying it any more than she was.

RachelAnne unlocked her Subaru wagon, tasteful transportation for a busy mother of two, soon-to-be lawyer, and small town princess. Unlike Peter's Hummer, it had real plates, so it was RachelAnne's rather than a Rudawski Motors loaner. She hadn't spoken since saying goodbye to the lawyer. Her angry pout was gone, but she didn't look happy. The last time Marti saw happy on her sister's face was online in the wedding photos.

"So, no BMW?" Marti said, testing the waters.

"Some of us are on a budget."

The waters were dark and muddy.

"Looks like you're now the boss of me. At least for six months," Marti said.

"Only if you stay. And it's more like the judge and jury."

"Well then, your law-school education won't go to waste defending obviously guilty lawbreakers," Marti said brightly. "See, The Judge *did* appreciate you."

RachelAnne didn't laugh. To be fair, the joke was lame.

"Did he put someone else in charge of your trust fund?" Surely The Judge trusted RachelAnne to handle her own affairs as well as her flaky sister's.

"He didn't leave me anything. Other than your trust fund, bequests for Thad and Maggie they'll get when they turn twenty-one, and a few minor gifts to charity, it all went to Mom. Most of it was already in her name anyway."

Marti was stunned. "Rach—"

"Guess he figured *I* could take care of myself. And you."

"Look. I didn't ask for any of this. You're the one who wants me to stay."

"See what you did? They're fighting," Grandma said from the back seat. The Judge didn't answer.

Neither did RachelAnne.

Her sister's silence sucked the air from the car.

The tension grew until Marti couldn't take it anymore.

"The Judge is a dick," she said, and immediately regretted it. Not calling her father a name. Too late, she realized she said *is* instead of *was*.

Grandma snorted. The Judge let out an indecipherable gurgle. Marti hoped he was choking on his own ego.

RachelAnne stared at her. Marti waited for her sister to jump on her use of the present tense. Instead, she burst out laughing.

The air in the Subaru returned to breathable.

"He really was, wasn't he?" RachelAnne said.

Whew. Her sister didn't notice her little grammatical oopsy. Unless she was filing it away and compiling a list for later use. The roles The Judge forced on the two of them didn't help Marti's trust issues.

"It doesn't really bother me," RachelAnne said. "Not a lot, anyway. Peter's pretty pissed."

"Say that three times fast," Marti said. If her sister denied any disappointment at being shafted in The Judge's will, Marti would have worried. No one was that saintly. Peter was probably throwing snit fits.

"Oh, I have." RachelAnne started the car. "Peter's pushing hard for us to move into Bickle House with Mom. More so since you got here."

Of course he was. "Maybe he's just worried about Mom. After . . . you know . . . yesterday." Marti was loath to mention Sheila's murder. Denial was a vacation home for her family.

"Peter doesn't worry about anybody but himself."

Marti waited for RachelAnne to elaborate and hoped she wouldn't.

RachelAnne didn't say anything more. If she was waiting for Marti to ask, she'd have a long wait. Getting sucked into RachelAnne's marital problems was not on her to-do list.

"If it helps, Mom will probably leave you everything to make up for Dad only leaving you me," she said.

"Don't say things like that." RachelAnne pulled out and aimed the Subaru away from glorious downtown Bicklesburg.

"Um, isn't this the wrong way?" Marti said. They'd passed through town on their way to Bowman's office.

"Errands. As long as Peter's mom-sitting, we'll take advantage of it. He can pretend he's king of the castle for another hour."

The hints of strain in the Mickkleson-Rudawski marriage didn't come as a surprise. She'd spent little time in the company of her brother-in-law, but her dislike went deep, deeper than his resemblance to The Judge. She didn't trust the dirt bag any farther than she could throw him. Not even that far. He wasn't big.

If RachelAnne was willing to spill her problems to Marti, she had to be desperate for someone to talk to.

"How fun for him," Marti mumbled. She was not only the Bad Sister, she was *a* bad sister, and she was okay with it.

"I don't want to go back to that house," RachelAnne said.

"Now *that* I completely understand," Marti said.

They rode in silence, but this time it was a comfortable silence. Companionable. Marti concentrated on the six months ahead and the plates she had to juggle. On long months of getting along with RachelAnne. On her parents, the dead one in better shape than the live one. On Maggie's ability to see Grandma Bertie. She wasn't juggling plates. She was juggling knives. Or cats. She tried to remember how much she understood about her own situation at Maggie's age, but it was a long time ago and the car was warm and the ride was smooth and the little bit of sleep she'd managed the night before wore off. She dozed.

"No. I ABSOLUTELY forbid it!" The Judge's bark woke her.

They were in a parking lot. A big parking lot.

"Seriously?" Marti said. Walmart and RachelAnne did not compute. Walmart and Bicklesburg—even the outskirts of town—did not compute. The invasion of Wally World was worse than the pawn shop.

"If you're going to stay, we need to get you a phone. This is the closest place. Also, I need to get cat food. Don't tell Mom." RachelAnne checked her makeup in the rearview mirror.

"That you have a cat?" When they were children, the only pets allowed were goldfish. No messy, smelly, shedding animals in the house, and a simple flush down the toilet following their inevitable deaths.

"She'd be humiliated," RachelAnne said.

"The cat? Cats don't care enough to be humiliated."

"Mom."

"At the cat? No pedigree?" Marti couldn't resist. She knew the cat wasn't what RachelAnne meant. While others had political or economic objections to the omnipresent superstore, her parents' Walmart disapproval wasn't so noble.

"Don't be a brat."

"Why do I need a phone? They're annoying. You can't have a face-to-face conversation without them ringing and—"

Right on cue, RachelAnne's purse sang the zoo song. She pulled out her phone, stabbed the screen, and tossed it back in her purse. "We need to hurry. Peter's getting impatient."

"You didn't answer it."

"I don't need to. You need a phone so you can keep in touch. What if something happens with Mom? And so I can get in touch with you."

Keep track of me, Marti thought.

"Time to join the real world," RachelAnne said.

The last place Marti wanted to be was the real world, Rachel-Anne edition. "What if I don't answer it? How do you know that call wasn't about Mom?"

"Sometimes I hate you." RachelAnne opened her purse. The phone chimed, and she grabbed it. "Oh. Look. Voice mail." She put it on speaker phone.

"Since you're not answering, I'm going to assume you're still with Bowman. If you're listening to this, I'm going to assume you're finished. Get yourself back here. I don't know who's worse, your mother or your kids, but I've got better things to do than babysit. So no stops. No shopping. And don't go buying anything for your dip-stick sister. She should be buying stuff for you."

"Well then," Marti said.

The sisters looked at each other.

"Peter's pretty pissed," they said in unison.

Neither laughed.

"I could apologize for my husband, but—"

"Mom never apologized for The Judge," Marti said. Baby Sister married a man worse than a daddy clone. No matter what The Judge did behind Mom's back, to her face he treated her with respect. Speaking of The Judge, he was awfully quiet. She pretended to check out the parking lot and snuck a peek at the backseat.

Grandma held him in a chokehold, one hand clamped over his mouth. "We'll just stay here. You girls go do what you need to do," she said.

"It's a big store," Marti said.

"It's a supercenter," RachelAnne said. "Which is why they have everything, including a phone store."

Grandma sized up the parking lot. RachelAnne had managed to snag a parking space within minimal walking distance to the door.

"Maybe I should have worn my hiking boots," Marti said. Not that she owned a pair, unless her old Doc Martens counted.

"Don't be such a wimp," RachelAnne said. "The phone center is at the front of the store, right inside the door. Next to the Pizza Pizza. We can grab dinner to take home."

"If you don't go wandering too far into the store," Grandma said, "Cranky Pants and I should be fine outside."

If she did wander too far inside the store, it would be bungee-Grandma time. Unfortunately, The Judge would probably come along for the ride.

"Go in and grab your cat food and I'll wait out here," Marti said.

"What is your problem? Is it Walmart? Deal with it. If it's the phone, it's time to put on your big girl panties and join the modern world."

"I don't have any money," Marti said. "Not yet. The phone can wait." She'd already run into too many people from her high school days. Who knew how many more lurked inside the superstore? From the looks of the parking lot, three-quarters of the population of Battlesburough County was inside.

"Eh. They'll put most of it on your first bill. You'll have money by then. Use a card today."

"I don't have one." Her under-the-radar existence didn't result in bad credit. It gave her no credit record. She liked it that way. Businesses didn't. Marti knew enough about cell companies to know they'd want a deposit. She shouldn't care, but she didn't want to go through the credit denial thing in front of her sister. "Besides, I don't want to sign any long-term contracts. Commitment's not my bestest thing."

"So we'll buy you a phone, and you can go month-to-month. I'll use one of my cards. What Peter doesn't know won't hurt him."

Definitely trouble in paradise. "You're not going to take no for an answer, are you?"

"Nope," RachelAnne said.

"Just go and get it over with," Grandma said.

"I'll pay you back," Marti said.

"You bet you will," RachelAnne said.

Marti meant payback for dragging her into the store and forcing her to get a phone, not the money.

The phone center was, like her sister promised, right inside the door. Other than one bored-looking saleswoman, it was deserted. Marti headed for the most basic phones she saw, under a banner that shouted *NO CONTRACT NEEDED* in two-foot-high black letters. The sooner they got this done with, the better.

"Those are crap." RachelAnne dragged her to the smartphone display. "Look at these."

The latest iPhones. Marti read the display tag. "Oh my gawd." The cheapest version cost half of what she made in a month. Used to make.

"You can afford it," RachelAnne said.

"I thought I was supposed to be proving I can manage my money."

"That doesn't mean not spending it. You need a phone. Since you'll be Mom's major caretaker, at least for a while, I insist on it."

"Major caretaker? What about Myrna Ward?"

"You're family. She's an employee."

Marti gave up. "I need *a* phone," she said. "I don't need *this* phone."

"Marti. Live a little." Something in RachelAnne's voice made Marti want to cry. Pity? Compassion? Whatever it was, she didn't like the lump it brought to her throat.

"You can afford it. You can also afford some new clothes, but not today. And not here," RachelAnne said.

Disapproval Marti recognized. The lump dissolved. She examined the phone. It sure was pretty.

"Hi. I'm Pris. How can I help you today?" The saleswoman—sales-child, she couldn't have been more than nineteen—looked Marti up and down and turned her attention to RachelAnne.

The two of them put their heads together. Before she knew it, Marti was the owner of not the basic, but the middle-of-the-line iPhone, a month-to-month plan with more minutes than she'd ever use, lots of data she did plan on using, and a phone case. Marti intervened once. No way was she carrying the pink-and-green case RachelAnne chose. RachelAnne rolled her eyes—and looked a lot like Grandma Bertie doing so—at Marti's plain navy-blue selection, but Pris cheerfully assured them the simple case had "excellent protective qualities, and that's *always* a plus." The sidewise glance she gave Marti while addressing RachelAnne said more than her words.

It also cost half as much as the designer label case RachelAnne liked so much. When Marti turned the atrocity down, her sister bought it for herself.

Despite the small economy, Marti blanched when Perky Pris announced the total and her sister handed over her credit card. She'd lived on less per month. "Rachel—"

"Don't thank me. Just remember who you're writing your first check to."

Pris rattled off Marti's new number. RachelAnne entered it into her own phone and frowned when the zoo song played again. This time, she answered it. Her side of the conversation consisted of "We're on our way," "Soon," and "The longer I talk to you, the later we'll be." She ended the call. No "Goodbye." No "See you soon." No "Love ya."

"*Looooove* the ringtone," Perky Pris warbled. RachelAnne was her new best friend, her idol.

"My children chose it. Their grandmother sings it to them." Princess RachelAnne tossed a snippet to her peon fan club.

Or a cookie to a puppy. "Ohhh. Maybe I'll put it on mine. My niece would *adore* it." The puppy wagged its tail.

Perky Miss Perky Pants had served her purpose. RachelAnne ignored her and informed Marti she was going to go get cat food while Pris finished the phone setup. "Meet me this side of the check out," she commanded and left.

"That's me, not you," Marti said to the beaming saleswoman.

"Let's get this taken care of," Pris said.

Once RachelAnne and her credit card disappeared, Perky Pris morphed into a model of efficiency.

"Any problems, don't hesitate to call. Thank you and have a nice day." The model of efficiency spoke like a robot.

Marti headed out of the phone center to wait for her sister.

"I'm telling you, Queen Margaret did it and they'll cover it up."

Marti would have recognized Dawn's nasal voice even if she hadn't heard it the day before. Teenage nightmares stuck around forever, at least hers did. Sure enough, Dawn, dressed in a royal-blue shirt and khaki pants, manned a register. The customer in front of her waggled a handful of coupons. Dawn paid no attention.

"Nah. It was Ralph." The cashier at the next register was as loud as Dawn, but less nasal. And less annoying, but who wasn't? "He finally snapped. It was one thing when he was on the road all the time, but after he retired he had to put up with Sheila full time. It had to be painful."

"I'm telling you, it was Mrs. My Poop Don't Stink. All those freaking Mickklesons are crazy," Dawn said. "Did you hear Marti Cray-Cray's back? She looks like some homeless bum. Maybe she helped her mother get rid of Sheila."

"Hey! Pernelli!" Dawn's customer leaned across the counter and stuck a wad of paper in the cashier's face. "I have coupons, and you're wrong."

The woman looked vaguely familiar. Marti couldn't place her, but she liked her.

Dawn grabbed the handful of coupons—so much for service with a smile. "What makes you think I'm wrong?"

In Pernelli World, the customer wasn't always right.

"First, Mrs. Mickkleson wouldn't hurt a fly."

"Yeah, yeah. How much does she pay you? Never thought I'd see the day when Myrna LaRue joined the Mighty Mighty Mickkleson Fan Club."

"It's Ward. Myrna *Ward*."

No wonder the woman was familiar. Marti tried to see the nasty young woman she remembered, but all she saw was someone who could be Myrna the Maid's mother. It was twenty years, give or take, since she left the Mickkleson's employ, and they weren't kind years. The once-voluptuous young maid now bore a startling resemblance to an insect. A well-dressed praying mantis, although preying mantis would be more apt. Marti wondered if Myrna was wearing hand-me-downs from Mom.

"Yeah, yeah," Dawn said. "Too bad no one around here ever met *Mr. Ward.*"

Pinch her. Go ahead. Pinch her, Marti thought.

"Second, it *was* Ralph," Myrna Ward said. "I saw him heading out of town in that new car of his yesterday, going like a bat out of hell. He almost ran me off the road. Guess we know why now. I went to the police station this morning and told them *all* about it." Her gravelly voice carried and halted the chatter around her.

That voice. Myrna could be the anonymous caller, but she was defending Mom to Dawn. It might be a smokescreen.

"Queen Margaret pay you enough to lie for her?" Dawn was a more likely suspect for the obscene calls. Marti knew from experience she had the vocabulary.

The line at Dawn's register grew, and the natives grew restless.

"Chief Fysh seemed to believe me. Larry Brumble is devastated. He and Ralph are second cousins you know," Myrna said.

"Hey! Ladies! Save it for the beauty parlor! I got things to do." An old guy in a track suit, three back in line, shook his fist in the air.

"Hold your horses, Uncle Herb," Dawn said. "Your total is seventy-eight dollars and ninety-seven cents," she informed Myrna.

"You must have missed a coupon," Myrna said. "Go back and check."

"Everything all right here?" A bottle redhead joined them. Marti recognized the color. She'd used it herself. It wasn't intended to mimic anything natural. Dawn's face flushed brighter than the woman's hair. Marti guessed the newcomer was her boss.

"Just fine." Myrna's terse answer brimmed with the perfect combination of condescending grace and displeasure to let the manager know that no, things were *not* all right, thank you very much. She regally swiped her card. Her body language matched

Mom's at her haughtiest to a tee. The woman was a whiskey-voiced, bargain-basement Margaret Mickkleson knockoff.

Dawn handed Myrna her receipt and mumbled. Marti couldn't hear her. Since the manager had stepped away, it could have been either "Have a nice day" or "Drop dead, you cow."

Myrna LaRue Ward took her bags and left the register. She made it a few steps before the redhead stopped her.

"I heard you say you saw Ralph McDonagh yesterday morning. I did too!" The redhead leaned in, up for a good round of dirt dishing. Marti moved closer, up for a good round of eavesdropping.

Myrna was having none of it. "Really? Did you report it to the police?"

"I, um, no. I didn't want to get involved." The redhead deflated.

"Well, you should, you know. It *is* your civic duty." Myrna sailed off.

"You ready?" RachelAnne nudged Marti with a cart full of bright-blue plastic bags.

"That's an awful lot of cat food. What do you have? A lion? I think I just saw Myrna. Did you catch any of the little exchange between her and Dawn Pernelli?"

"I grabbed a few extra things since I was here. Don't tell Mom. And goodness no. If at all possible, I go to the checkout as far away from Dawn as I can get."

"Good plan." Baby Sister could have warned her.

"She still hasn't forgiven Dad for sending Oliver away. Dmitri's put it all behind him, so I don't see why Oliver and Dawn and that whole bunch can't. After all, it *was* about drugs."

In their school days, Dawn's family connection to Oliver was a source of humiliation. Once he started hanging out with Marti, she told people he was adopted. When he got in trouble, the Pernellis circled the wagons. They could trash-talk their own all they wanted, but outsiders—especially Mickklesons—were a diffcrent matter.

"She still insists he was framed," RachelAnne continued.

"There's a fifty-fifty chance he was," Marti said. "Dmitri too. Maybe even sixty-forty."

"I forgot you hung out with them," RachelAnne said.

That's what got them in trouble, Marti thought, *that and The Judge and Sheila McDonagh.* "For a while," she said.

"Well, Daddy wouldn't have sent them away if they didn't deserve it. Dmitri's turned himself around. Oliver is a disgrace. Still in and out of jail, practically homeless."

"I'm a little worried about your future in the public defender's office," Marti said. Every time she started to like her little sister, RachelAnne went and proved she was a Mickkleson, a judgmental snob through and through. "How can someone be practically homeless?"

"Oh, his mother takes him in sometimes. Other times, he sleeps in parking lots—or the gazebo in the Green. Can you imagine what that looks like to visitors? In the winter, I think Big arrests him just to give him a warm place to sleep."

Oliver sounded a lot like Ozzie. What was it about men with the initial O? As long as she didn't wake up in a parking lot curled around Oliver's dead body, Marti wasn't going to think too hard on it. She had enough to deal with.

Mommy's taking us to the zoooooo tomorrow—

"Your purse is singing again," Marti said.

"I guess we can't put it off any longer." RachelAnne didn't bother to answer the call. "Time to head home."

ELEVEN

"Why does she always sleep so late?" The Judge said.

"Leave her alone," Grandma said.

"I want to play," Amity said. "When will she wake up?"

"Shush," Edwards said.

"Grand idea. Everybody shush," Grandma said.

Marti surrendered and opened her eyes. "I'm awake," she said.

"You can't lie in bed all day," The Judge said.

"That makes you a lazybones," Amity said.

Marti grabbed her phone from the bedside. Six thirty. Hardly "all day."

"Getupgetupgetup," Amity said.

"I'm sorry, Miss," Edwards said.

"Don't worry about it." Even if they all evaporated, Marti knew she wouldn't fall back to sleep. She hauled herself out of bed, pulled on a sweatshirt, and went downstairs in search of coffee.

Myrna LaRue Ward, a white, frilly apron over her navy jacket and slacks, puttered in the kitchen.

"Hi Myr—Mrs. Ward." Marti didn't do perky or friendly until after her third cup of coffee, but if the former maid preferred "Mrs. Ward," she could manage it. No point getting off on the wrong foot, but if Myrna tried to pinch her, she was pinching back.

"Hello, Marti. My condolences on your father's passing."

"Thank you." During Myrna's first turn in Bickle House, Mom insisted she address the girls as "Miss Marcile" and "Miss RachelAnne." The whole upstairs-downstairs thing humiliated the girls. Myrna, it pissed off. "Is my sister up?" Peter was less than thrilled—understatement—at RachelAnne's decision to spend another night at Bickle House. She promised to be home early, in time to see him off to work, pack T3 off to school, and take Maggie to daycare on her way to work.

"Gone before I arrived. She left a note telling me you were here, and I am to go about my duties as usual."

"I'll do my best to stay out of your way." Marti lifted the tea kettle on the stove. It felt full, so she turned the burner underneath to high and took the French press from the cupboard.

Her first morning home, she was disappointed by the lack of an automatic coffee maker in the otherwise high-tech, top-of-the-line kitchen. *Disappointed* was the wrong word. *Panicked* was the word. Since her father was the one who drank coffee, Marti'd hoped her parents had invested in one of those fancy single cup brewers. The kind that would supply her with an endless stream of fresh cups of steaming heaven in a cup on demand.

The Judge no longer needed the caffeine, but she did. When RachelAnne answered her pathetic *coffffeeeeee* by pulling the press and a bag of Lavazza espresso from the cupboard, Marti said, "You're my favorite sister."

The coffee press made it to the counter, but she dropped the bag of ground coffee. It bounced, but stayed sealed. No mess to clean up.

"I can do that for you," Myrna said.

Marti waved her off. "I'm good."

"You're just like your father," Myrna said.

Marti frowned. Her second night in her childhood bed hadn't gone much better than her first. Lack of sleep left her feeling dead, but not as dead as The Judge. As far as she was concerned, that was as close to having anything in common with her father as she wanted to come.

"Not exactly eloquent until you get a cup of coffee inside you," Myrna explained.

"More like three," Marti said.

Myrna folded a linen napkin and placed it on a bed tray.

"How is my mother this morning?"

"We'll see," Myrna said. "I'll take her breakfast up in a few minutes."

On Sunday, Mom made her own toast and stinky tea.

"Why does she need breakfast in bed? What's wrong?"

"I do this every morning." Myrna chose a teapot and cup and saucer from the glass-fronted cabinet. "When I'm here, that is."

Marti wondered whether the morning pampering was instigated by her mother or the housekeeper. The kettle whistled, and she filled the coffee press with boiling water.

Mrs. Partridge's former underling couldn't be much more than ten years older than Marti. She wasn't much more than an awkward teenager during her first stint in Mickkleson Land. Back then, she wore the classic maid's outfit—black dress and white apron, sensible shoes, and dark hose. Mom abhorred bare-legged women in skirts. In front of Marti's parents, Myrna had worn a subservient attitude to match the uniform.

The adult Myrna LaRue Ward refilled the kettle and set it on the stove. From far away, in dim light, if she squinted, Marti might mistake her for Mom. On closer inspection, she missed the mark. Both women were tall, but where Mom was gracefully slim, Myrna was scrawny. She wasn't wearing Mom's hand-me-downs. Maybe she saved those for Sundays or trips to Walmart. Her trousers and blazer were off the rack and off a chain-store rack, at that. Marti placed them higher than Kmart, possibly JCPenny level, but they weren't the product of anywhere her mother deigned to shop. She wondered if Myrna knew Mom wouldn't view the housekeeper's subpar new clothing with any greater regard than Marti's thrift-shop sweatshirts and jeans. At least Old Mom wouldn't. Who knew about New Mom?

The difference went deeper than window dressing. Although Myrna managed to give the impression of holding her head high and her nose in the air while loading the dishwasher, it came off stiff. "Putting on airs," Grandma Bertie called it.

Mom would maintain her elegance while plunging a clogged toilet. Not that she would ever lower herself to such a menial task, but if she did, toilet plunging would become the next big thing among the Bicklesburg ladies-who-lunch crowd. Mom called it breeding. Marti called it training. Training that never took for her. Mom's attempts to improve the young Myrna must have eventually sunk in, but like the housekeeper's clothes, didn't fit quite right.

Myrna filled the silver tea infuser with Mom's special blend. Even dry, the mix was pungent.

"Ugh. What does Mom put in that stuff? It's worse than I remember."

"Chamomile." Myrna added hot water to the teapot.

Instant toxic fumes. "That stink is *not* chamomile. It's not even valerian. *That* smells like dirty socks and cat pee, and whatever is in that so-called tea makes valerian smell like roses," Marti said.

"I'm sure I don't know." Other than the gravelly voice, Myrna delivered the line in pitch-perfect imitation of Mom. She opened a white paper bag, took out a croissant, and arranged it on the tray next to the tea and blackberry jam.

"Ohhh—that looks yummy," Marti said. Maybe the new Bicklesburg wasn't all drive-through donuts and Walmart.

"I brought one, for your mother." The housekeeper lifted the bed tray. "Will you be staying for lunch?"

"I have errands to run." One errand. The bank. "I should be back for lunch."

"I'll let your mother know." Myrna swept out of the kitchen, a lady-in-waiting bearing gifts for her queen.

Marti might be a daughter of the house, but it was obvious Myrna felt she held a loftier status. She was probably right.

WITH THE FATE of her Taurus still up in the air, RachelAnne had suggested Marti use one of their parents' cars. Since neither Mom nor The Judge was in any shape to use the vehicles themselves, she accepted. Much to The Judge's displeasure, she chose her mother's sports car over his Lexus LX.

"I don't know what she sees in this thing," he said.

"I do." The car was beauteous. Blue so deep it was almost black, red leather seats—even the shape of the little coupe was perfect. Whoever designed the Audi TT designed cars like Apple designed electronics. The TT was a luxury show car, but Marti liked it. The Judge's SUV was ostentatious and intimidating. Like him. Besides, she'd never driven anything that large in her life.

She settled into the TT's driver seat, Grandma and The Judge in the back, and decided she might be in love.

"This back seat is ridiculous," The Judge said.

"You can stay home," Marti said.

"I like it," Grandma said.

"You can drive stick, right?" The Judge squirmed.

"Puh-leeze." The Taurus had a standard transmission.

"I wish I could fasten my seat belt," The Judge said.

"A little redundant, don't you think?" Marti stalled the TT twice before she got used to the stick. First gear wasn't in the same place it was on the Taurus, and unlike the Taurus, the TT's transmission wasn't so worn it didn't know the difference between first and second.

By the time she hit the road into town, she had a feel for the car, and it was good. Too good. She checked the speedometer and slowed down. Getting a speeding ticket wasn't in her plans. She had enough of cops on Saturday to last a lifetime. On the other hand, she suspected she was driving the single midnight-blue TT—the only TT—in town. She wouldn't be surprised if Margaret Mickkleson was ticket-proof.

Which might condemn the Queen of Bicklesburg, in the eyes of the good citizens if not the law, for murder.

The anonymous caller sounded convinced. However, as vile as

the call was, Marti decided not to take it seriously. She blamed small-town jealousy, put it out of her mind, and hit the gas pedal.

The Bicklesburg First Seventh Federal Bank sat on the square in the same building it occupied for two hundred years. Over the decades, its name changed and grew with consolidations and mergers, but compared to Wells Fargo or Bank One, it was small. Marti was willing to bet the entire ten dollars she left in her F n R account all but the newest residents still called it Bicklesburg Banking Company or simply the Bicklesburg. She might even bet the ten years' worth of interest on those ten big ones.

She slowed the TT and prowled the square in search of a parking spot.

"Doesn't anybody work in this town?" The Green wasn't crowded, but people stood in knots, talking and gesturing wildly. Live people. Only a few turned and stared when she crept past, but she felt like every pair of eyes in Bicklesburg was on her. The TT begged her to floor the gas pedal and take off. It didn't like going slow. That was probably her imagination.

You killed them both. She wasn't doing a bang-up job of putting the blasted phone call out of her mind.

She stopped and waited while a hybrid backed from a space directly in front of the bank. Good Parking Fu was on her side. Minimal exposure to the park crowd. In Bicklesburg, wherever two or more were gathered, gossip blossomed.

Which might not be a bad thing. Maybe the caller was in the park.

Most Bicklesburgians weren't as obvious as Dawn Pernelli. If they were talking about her family—and they couldn't discuss Sheila's murder without bringing up the Mickklesons—they were likely to clam up if she wandered over, but she had a secret weapon. Even if the caller wasn't in the park, it wouldn't hurt to know what the rest of the town was saying behind her—not to mention Mom's and RachelAnne's—back.

"Grandma? I have a job for you."

Grandma Bertie headed across the street to the park. She'd gladly accepted her mission to eavesdrop on any conversation she could get close to. Marti went into the bank to take care of business. With Grandma's limited away-from-Marti range, she could only cover the near side of the Green, but that wasn't a problem. She and Mrs. Heedly were old friends, and Marti's old teacher had the run of the park. Marti was sure Mrs. Heedly listened in on all the gossip and was aching for someone to share it with.

The Judge went inside with Marti. The grand old bank was a museum, an ode to a slower, more graceful era. A paean to wealth. The black-and-white marble floor glowed. Well-dressed tellers, fewer than in the old days but still present, sat stationed behind a long oak counter, separated from their customers by bars. Ornate columns supported the vaulted ceiling. The central chandelier gave the one from *Phantom of the Opera* a run for its money. Its baby sisters and brothers lit the far corners of the expansive room, shining soft light on scattered desks. Computer monitors at the teller stations and desks were the sole sign of the modern world.

Not quite the sole sign. She didn't remember the uniformed security guard, gun on his hip. She didn't recognize him, and from the way he sized her up, he either didn't know or didn't recognize her. She was stranger danger, and loitering in the middle of the hushed Victorian splendor looking like a lost street person didn't help.

"Don't just stand there. Go talk to the manager," The Judge said.

She would, if she knew who and where the bank manager was. She wondered if the guard could help her. He looked more than willing to shoot her.

A sensibly dressed woman hurried toward her. Short, brunette, wearing a well-cut gray tweed suit and conservative heels, she was either more security or a bank employee.

"Marti?" she said, her squeal at odds with her businesslike stride.

"Raven?" It couldn't be. "I mean, Ashley?" It had to be. Raven-Ashley Carlyle was the only person she'd ever come across who actually sounded like a cartoon character.

Ashley laughed. "That was a *long* time ago. Your sister called and said you would be in today. Follow me."

"I forgot you two knew each other," The Judge said.

He was flustered, which in turn made Marti suspicious. No one ever said Sheila was his sole conquest, and with The Judge's track record—no. If he had tried anything with her old classmate, Ashley was the sensible type, even when she was Raven of the purple hair and Betty Boop voice. And quiet—she was Sheila's opposite in every way. But then, what else would The Judge have to be nervous over?

Marti followed her old acquaintance—*friend* was too strong a word—to a large office in the back. Other than the keyboard and monitor on the desk, the office was as old-fashioned as the front of the bank. The name plate sitting on the desk was carved wood, not tacky metal and plastic. *Ashley Fysh, Bank Manager*.

"You married Big?" Marti couldn't wrap her head around the match.

"Goodness, no. His brother, and he goes by Jim now, not Little. Would you like coffee? Tea?"

Marti credited the warmth in Ashley's voice to her job. Bicklesburg Bank plus Mickkleson money equaled instant friendship. "I'm beginning to think I'm the only person to ever leave Bicklesburg," she said.

"Almost. But now you're back. We're a lot like the Hotel California here."

"I can check out any time I like—"

"But you can never leave." Ashley finished the lyric.

"Well, now I'm depressed," Marti said, "and I still hate the Eagles." Ashley was either happy to see her or a darned good actress.

"Me too. The Eagles, that is. Not the depressed. Let's see if we can cheer you up." Ashley tapped her keyboard and examined the screen. "RachelAnne told me why you were coming in, and you do indeed still have an account with us. Even though I know you, I'll need official verification. Do you remember the account number after all these years?"

"879 625278," The Judge said.

"879 625278," Marti repeated, hiding her irritation with her father.

"Wow. I'm surprised and impressed. Most people—including those who've been in regularly for the last decade—can't rattle off their account number."

"I'm a little surprised myself." The ease with which The Judge rattled off the number was especially surprising considering his clueless act in Bowman's office.

"Here's an easy one. Social Security number?"

That Marti supplied without any prompting and when asked for ID, she produced her driver's license. She skimmed the papers Ashley slid across the desk—blah, blah, blah, signature—and signed them with a flourish. Ashley pushed a few more keys. A hidden printer whirred. She reached under the desk and came up with a thin sheet of yellow paper.

The Judge paced. He was getting more exercise dead than he ever got alive.

She ignored him and read the receipt Ashley handed her.

Holy cow. "There must be some mistake here. I mean, I know interest rates go up and down, but I cleaned out this account when I left. All except for ten bucks." Marti handed the paper back to Ashley, who checked it against her computer screen.

"No, that's the balance."

"Did Mr. Bowman already arrange for a deposit?" Didn't seem likely with all the formalities she just went through, not to mention the balance was close to fifteen times the amount of the expected deposit.

"No," Ashley said. "The last deposit was, let's see, seven weeks ago."

"I don't suppose you can tell me who made it?"

"No, just the amount. It looks like there's been regular monthly deposits, ever since—well, as far back as I have access to. Not long after you left town."

"Don't look at me," The Judge said. "It must be your Mother." If it was possible for ghosts to sweat, his upper lip and forehead would be beaded with moisture.

"I—wow." Marti didn't know what to say—or think. The money in her account—wherever it came from—might be a drop in the bucket in Mickkleson terms, but was a small fortune to her. Make that a medium fortune. Bordering on medium-large.

She could leave Bicklesburg again and never come back. She didn't need The Judge's trust fund.

Except she'd be stuck with him. If she didn't fulfill her end of their bargain, her father would never leave her alone.

And her Mother. Despite the vile phone call, she couldn't seriously be a suspect in Sheila's death, but *something* serious was wrong with her.

Marti checked the bank balance again. Okay, a large fortune.

RachelAnne was perfectly capable of taking care of Mom without her help and would be much happier without her black sheep of a sister in her life.

"Are you okay?" Ashley said.

"I'm stunned," Marti said.

The Judge said nothing. If he stayed this quiet all the time, she might get used to having him around.

Marti tried to think of one good reason not to withdraw everything then and there, hop in the TT, and drive. The only thing she came up with was RachelAnne would report the car stolen and have her arrested.

She had enough money to buy her own TT. Or whatever she wanted.

She didn't have to decide now.

"Any more questions—ones I can answer? Can I help you with anything else?"

Marti checked the yellow paper again. She did have another question. "My father's name used to be on this account. I don't see it here."

Not exactly phrased as a question, but Ashley got the gist. She checked her screen. "Nope. It's just you and your mother. He must have taken himself off at some point."

"You were an adult. It seemed like a good idea," The Judge said.

Marti didn't believe him. He'd never treated her like an adult when he was alive. Not so much now that he was dead either, but he had to be alive when he removed himself from her savings account. And her mother's name was still there. She couldn't take it up with him in front of Ashley.

"Someone must be paying taxes on the interest," Marti said. Ghosts were a piece of cake. The IRS scared her.

"The Form 1099-INT is issued to Margaret Mickkleson," Ashley said.

As long as Mom or her accountants did whatever they were supposed to do, that was one less thing for her to worry about.

"I guess I need to set up a checking account and move some of this money into it. And get an ATM card. And I need the information for an EFT and ... wow." Marti looked at the printout and shook her head.

GRANDMA BERTIE FLUTTERED impatiently around the TT. "What took you so long?"

Marti strode to the car and ignored Grandma, The Judge, and all the nosey parkers watching from the Green. Unfortunately, she hit the wrong button on the electronic key fob. The horn blared and the little car lit up like a Christmas tree. A classy Christmas tree, but still an attention magnet. By the time she found the correct button and shut it up, everyone in the park was staring.

They probably needed fresh grist for the mill. She'd call it her public service for the day.

Inside the car, she put her new phone to her ear.

"Who are you calling?" The Judge said.

"No one. I have an audience. No use talking to myself and giving them the Crazy Marti show. Why is there so much money in my account?"

"I have no idea. It must have been your mother. Maybe she was worried about you."

"How were you so quick with the account number?"

Marti watched him in the rearview mirror. The Judge clamped his mouth shut and crossed his arms. "You look like a two-year-old in a snit," she said, which didn't help. He turned and watched the people in the park. Most of them no longer appeared to be paying attention to her.

She couldn't force him to talk. She shifted her attention to her grandmother who, for a change, sat in the front seat next to Marti. "Did you get anything out of Mrs. Heedly?"

"Did I ever." Grandma wasn't sitting. She hovered a few inches above the red leather.

"Well?"

"I'm not sure you want to hear." Grandma obviously wanted to tell.

"She doesn't." The Judge was willing to talk, just not about what she wanted to talk about. "The woman never made sense when she was alive. I have no doubt she's still a nasty old crone."

"Too bad you didn't believe that when she made me spend third grade sitting in the hallway. Grandma, spill."

"Lots of theories about Sheila. No one's really talking about your father. That's why he's so cranky."

"It is not," The Judge said.

"Dad, shut up."

"Well," Grandma said, "a couple of folks claim to have an inside track on the investigation, and they say Ralph's officially the number-one suspect."

"Makes sense," Marti said. "Don't they always suspect the

spouse first?" If Grandma wasn't so adamant The Judge wasn't murdered, Ralph would be her number-one suspect for knocking him off too.

"They're the boring ones, not to mention the minority. Want to hear the other theories?"

"No," The Judge said.

"Yes," Marti said.

"Theory One. Your mother did it and there's a cover-up because Mickklesons can get away with anything." Grandma rose another inch off the seat. Any higher and she'd stick her head through the roof.

"Of course."

"Told you she was a nasty old bat," The Judge said.

"Dad—"

"Theory Two. Ralph and your mother did it together. They've been carrying on for years and she'll soon be joining him in some tropical paradise with no extradition treaty. Because Mickklesons can get away with anything."

"Interesting. Anything to back it up? The Ralph and Mom thing, not the tropical paradise." Marti didn't believe there was, but the idea had to irritate The Judge. No point in letting the opportunity pass.

"No, but the Theory Two team seems to think your mother is much smarter than your father ever was, and you can't argue with that. They're not surprised she kept the affair hidden for, well, anything from years to decades. There's some disagreement on the time frame."

"Sounds legit."

"Janice Heedly got the impression there's a lot of admiration for Margaret among the Theory Two crowd. She wasn't sure whether it was for pulling off a murder or for being involved with Ralph McDonagh. The older women think he's a hottie. They have a point."

"True. Nice head of hair."

"Don't be ridiculous. Your mother would never be unfaithful to me. Especially not with a truck driver." The Judge sucked in his spectral belly and ran his hand through the remains of his comb-over. The old saw about good for the goose, good for the gander held no water with him.

Marti couldn't imagine her mother embroiled in an affair, but only because it was messy. All that sneaking around. But who knew? The Judge wouldn't. Not unless her mother wanted him to. "Anything else?"

"Theory Three. Ralph did it on his own. There's a long list of *whys*, but the Theory Three folks figure he's holed up somewhere with a girlfriend from his time on the road. They all expect he'll be caught soon."

Marti liked Theory Three. It left her family out of it. "That's it?"

"Well, there's Theories Four, Five, Six, Seven, Eight, and Nine. Your mother did it, and she killed your father too, because insanity runs in your family. Oh. There's a cover-up because Mickklesons can get away with anything. Then there's Theory Ten."

"Which is?"

"You did it. You came back to town to take revenge for your mother, or on your mother, or because Sheila knew some terrible secret about you, or a hundred other cockamamy reasons. I believe one version involves buried treasure. They're all a little convoluted. Even Janice Heedly doesn't believe them, and she's not your biggest fan. Not a fan at all, for that matter. She blames cable television."

"For me?"

"No. For the crazy theories. Anyway, there'll be a cover-up because—"

"Mickklesons can get away with anything!" Marti and her grandmother said at the same time.

"Even the crazy ones," Grandma said.

"*Especially* the crazy ones," Marti said.

"I don't know what you two find so amusing," The Judge said.

"Marcile, your mother is in trouble here."

"Dad. There's no way she did it. Mom's got some problems." *Understatement.* "But murder isn't one of them. They'll find Ralph. They'll arrest Ralph. End of story. Nothing to do with Mom. Or you. Or me."

"That won't stop the gossip. The Mickkleson name must remain untarnished."

"This is Bicklesburg. *Nothing* stops the gossip. As for the Mickkleson name—"

"I think they found Ralph. Or at least his car." Grandma pointed across the square. "Over there."

A Rudawski Motors flatbed truck slowly rounded the Green. The black Escalade on the back no longer looked shiny and new. The tires were flat. The paint job was muddy and dull. It didn't look much like the Escalade in the So-nutt-ee Donut parking lot, but it was definitely the same car.

It wasn't empty. Ralph McDonagh wouldn't be telling anyone what happened to his wife.

Well, there was one person he could tell.

"Crap," Marti said.

"What?" The Judge said. "They found Ralph's car. Doesn't mean he didn't do it."

"Maybe the girlfriend theory is right," Grandma said. "He killed Sheila and dumped the car. The girlfriend was waiting for him with a getaway car."

"Don't you guys see him?"

"See who?" Grandma said.

"Ralph. In the driver's seat." The tow truck passed them and turned off the square. The Escalade was empty.

"Are you seeing things? You haven't been drinking, have you? Why would he be in his car on the back of a tow truck? In the back of a police car, maybe. You're not making sense." The Judge hadn't caught on to the implications of Marti seeing Ralph.

"He disappeared," Marti said.

"I'm sure it was a trick of the light," Grandma said. "If even the ghost of that good-looking man passed by, I'm sure I would notice."

"Oh." The Judge got it. "Well. *I* didn't see anyone."

"I did," Marti said. *Unless I really am losing it.* "Ralph McDonagh is dead."

TWELVE

"I do hope you're not turning into one of those youngsters with their noses constantly stuck in their phones," Grandma said.

"Shush," Marti said.

"That one! That one! Put that hat on her." Amity pointed to a scarlet bowler adorned with yellow daisies. Marti tapped the screen of her phone, and the hat moved to the head of a blue-eyed, blonde, ringlet-bedecked doll. The virtual girl bore a startling resemblance to Amity. The hat wasn't a great match for the green gingham dress and purple pantaloons they'd already put on her. Amity giggled and pointed to a pair of black Buddy Holly glasses. "Those," she said.

Marti and her ghost crew were assembled in the family parlor. Grandma, The Judge, Amity—the only one not present was Edwards. As much as he adored his little charge, he needed a break. He claimed he hadn't had one since Marti left home. Wherever he was hiding, Marti hoped he was enjoying the quiet. Amity wore her out in ten minutes. Edwards was stuck with her for eternity.

The first thing she'd done when she got home was take out her iPhone and check the local news sites for anything about the discovery of the McDonaghs' Escalade. If any place had the story, it wasn't deemed important enough to be considered breaking news. She learned nothing. The second thing she did was open an App Store account and download the Bicklesburg Bank's mobile app. Their brick-and-mortar presence might be as old school as old school could get, but their customer service was thoroughly modern and up to date.

The third, fourth, and fifth things she did was check her bank balance. It was just as large as it was when Ashley first showed it to her. Maybe it wasn't all that large. Maybe, after a decade of living hand to mouth, her frame of reference was skewed. She checked it again. Still unchanged and still large. Warren Buffett might not be impressed, but she wasn't Warren Buffett. Jimmy Buffett, maybe. She did like margaritas.

And her bank account held a whole bunch of margaritas. She half expected to see it earning interest by the minute. She would have more when Bowman transferred the no-strings portion of her inheritance. Her upbringing proved money couldn't buy happiness, but she was willing to give it a shot with or without the salt and lime.

She had no reason to hang around Bicklesburg. Other than her mother's health and possible status as a murder suspect. But RachelAnne had things under control. Mostly.

Then there was Maggie.

"Why are you just sitting there?" The Judge said. "There are murders to be solved. Starting with mine."

"You weren't murdered," Grandma said. "But keep it up and you might end up exorcised."

"We can do that?" Marti said.

"No, but I know a guy," Grandma said darkly.

"You don't scare me," The Judge said.

"Seen Sheila lately?" Marti said.

If it turned out Mom did knock off the old coot, Marti might give her a medal instead of turning her in. She checked her bank balance again. She could afford a nice medal.

Amity nagged her to play—big surprise—and Marti felt guilty at putting her off yet again. The phone fascinated the ghost girl, so she stopped admiring her bank balance and found a paper doll dress up App. Since Amity couldn't do anything except stick her finger through the screen, she gave orders and Marti used her earthly fingers to carry them out.

Playing virtual paper dolls with Amity and playing should-I-stay-or-should-I-go with herself was better than thinking about Ralph McDonagh's ghost and his now-you-see-me-now-you-don't act. Grandma and The Judge insisted they didn't see him and remained unconvinced of his presence in the Escalade. The Judge was dismissive. Grandma Bertie was worried. Not about Ralph, but that Marti was heading around that bend everyone else thought she rounded years ago.

"Let's do another!" Amity said.

Marti swiped the screen and chose a monkey as their next fashion victim. Amity squealed and hugged her.

She dropped the phone. "D-d-do th-that-t-t ag-g-gain, and-d-d we're d-d-d-done," she said.

Amity pointed at a green Victorian-style crinoline. "Put that on him. It looks like mine."

Marti tapped the dress, and the phone shrieked.

"That's a pretty song," Amity said.

It wasn't pretty and it wasn't a song. It was RachelAnne calling.

Marti barely got out her *hello* before her sister interrupted.

"Marti. Where's Mom?"

"In the kitchen with Myrna. Do you want me to get her?" If RachelAnne wanted to talk to Mom, why call her?

"No! Do they have the TV on? Or the radio?"

"I don't know. Why?"

"I don't have time to explain. Keep Mom away from the television and radio for the rest of the day. And the computer. Anywhere she might hear the news."

"What news?"

"*Any* news. Just do it. And don't answer the landline. Or the door. Call the security office. If Dmitri's on duty, tell him to call in extra help and station them at the house. If Dmitri's not on duty, tell whoever is the same thing and to get Dmitri in. If the press invades the Avenue, don't talk to them."

"Is this about Sheila? Did they find Ralph?"

"No. Apparently Sheila McDonagh wasn't Dad's only secret."

"If you're going to give me orders, you'd better tell me what's going on." Marti never responded well to being bossed around.

"*Just do it.* I'll explain later. It's a madhouse here. I need to go."

"RachelAnne. What is—" She was talking to dead air. Her sister'd hung up on her. *Okay then.* For someone who was practically raised by Ms. Manners—and paid attention to the lessons—Baby Sister had a serious rude going on.

"So, Dad. Anything special you'd like to share with the rest of us?"

"You know all you need to know," The Judge said.

He really was a pompous bore.

"You can tell us about the time Margaret found you passed out in the rose bed and decided to leave you there," Grandma said. "If I remember correctly, the story involves an anthill and a rash."

"Bite me," The Judge said.

"I'll leave that to the ants," Grandma said.

"Sheila taught me to say *bite me*," The Judge said. "It's a polite way of telling you to go—"

"Everybody *shut up*," Marti said.

"Can we play doll babies now? Grandma can play too, but I don't think *he* can." Amity didn't like The Judge dead any better than she'd liked him alive.

"We'll play dolls later," Marti said. "Right now I need you to play Look Out. Do you remember how?"

"Of course." Amity was less than enthusiastic. As a teen, Marti convinced her Look Out was a game. She seldom needed a sentry, but it was a good way to get a break from what amounted to an annoying and adoring little sister who never grew older. Look Out wasn't much fun for the young ghost. Marti suspected she knew she was being used. "But *he's* already here." She stuck out her tongue at The Judge.

"Not him. I want you to stay outside the door and watch for my mother."

"She's in the pantry with Mrs. Ward. They are mixing her medicine." Amity always called Mom's tea "medicine." Marti didn't know why and didn't think Amity knew. Grandma Bertie assured her ghosts had no sense of smell, so it wasn't the stench.

"She's the dragon, and I'm the princess in the cave," Marti said. "Tell me if she sneaks up while I'm burying my treasure." Didn't make a whole lot of sense, but Amity fell for it. She wasn't happy about it. She stuck out her lower lip and floated toward the door.

"We'll play doll babies next," Marti said.

Amity flounced through the wall with all the haughtiness a four-foot-tall ghost could muster. She must have been impressive alive. As long as she stayed in the hallway and didn't flounce herself up to the attic or someplace, Marti didn't care. She needed to keep Mom away while she tried to find out what had RachelAnne in a tizzy.

"Okay. What's going on?" The Judge asked.

"Not a clue, but it sounds like you're involved." Marti found the remote and turned on the television. A game show appeared. *Family Feud*. A little too on the nose for her. She pressed the up arrow. Another game show, one she didn't recognize. "What's the news channel?"

"Which one?" The Judge said. He didn't appear worried.

"Any one. Something regional. Or local." Although she hadn't owned a TV for ages, she knew enough about cable to know news channels bred and multiplied. Sooner or later, every tiny burg in the world would have its own cable news network.

"One-six-nine-five," The Judge said.

Marti punched the numbers on the remote. The giant screen filled with head shots of three well-dressed men. The third was The Judge's official portrait. The headline above the photos in big, bold, red letters, said KIDS FOR CASH REDUX.

"Oh crap," The Judge said.

"Hush," Grandma said. "I want to hear this."

So did Marti. She upped the volume.

"... in a scheme similar to the 2008 Luzerne County, Pennsylvania scandal, which resulted in the conviction and sentencing of two judges on racketeering charges resulting from acceptance of illegal payments from a for-profit juvenile detention corporation. Also implicated, although it's currently unclear how, is the late Judge Thaddeus A. Mickkleson of Battlesburough County. We will be reporting more details as they become available. The state attorney general's office has scheduled a news conference for three o'clock, which we will be covering live." The scene went back to the newscaster, and he moved on to another story. Something about puppies. Marti clicked off the television. "Dad..."

The Judge was gone.

"Where'd he go?"

"Away," Grandma said. "Apparently, he was embarrassed about something."

"Like, away to the kitchen or the basement or...?"

"How am I supposed to know?" Grandma said.

Daddy Perfect, Judge Stickler-for-Law-and-Order, Protector of Peace and Justice and the Battlesburough County Way, had a lot to be embarrassed about.

"Can you get him back?"

"Maybe. Do we really want him back?"

"Good question." The Judge was beyond the reach of investigators, but Marti had a few questions for him. More than a few. She wasn't sure she wanted the answers—or if getting them was worth hauling him back from wherever the dead went when they weren't bothering her. "Go find him," she said.

The house phone rang, and she grabbed it before remembering her sister's orders.

"Mickkles— Peter Plunkett's Pizza Palace," she said.

"This is MaryEllen Pernelli from the *Bicklesburg Gazette*—

"No habla inglés." Marti cut the connection. Her bad accent wouldn't fool anybody.

The best idea was to unplug the landlines. Marti had no clue where the base for the family parlor's cordless phone was or how many phones were in the house. She put the handset on mute and tossed it under the couch. Considering the general state of the room, that counted as hiding it in plain sight.

Amity still stood sentry in the hallway. "The dragon lady is in the kitchen," she said, "and I don't want to play this game. It's boring."

"Me either," Marti said. "Why don't you go find Edwards?"

Amity vanished.

Even if Amity hadn't told her where to find Mom and Myrna, the telltale stench of Mom's tea would have led her to the kitchen. She'd been home—what? Not quite three whole days, and her mother had spent more time in the kitchen than she did in all of Marti's growing-up years put together. Her tea consumption had definitely risen.

Mom sat on a stool at the island counter, sipping from a china cup. Delftware. The teapot sported a different pattern from the cup but in the same telltale blue. Marti wondered if the beauty of her mother's cup and teapot collection was intended to balance the repulsiveness of what she filled them with. What did she put in the vile stuff? Skunk cabbage?

Mrs. Ward leaned on the other side of the counter and chatted on her cell phone. Mom picked something up and pointed it at the small flat-screen television built into the wall.

Marti moved fast, but the housekeeper moved faster. The remote was out of Mom's hand and into Myrna's apron pocket before Marti was halfway across the room. Mom looked from her empty hand to Myrna and pouted.

"Now, sweetie, you know there's nothing on right now. Nothing you like, anyways."

Sweetie? Again? What was it with people calling her mother *sweetie*? Especially the help. Especially Myrna.

"I'll call you back." The housekeeper's phone joined the remote in her apron pocket. "That was Lawrence Brumble. He thought maybe since you're home now, he could have me back one day a week. How long are you staying?"

"I want to watch the ponies." Mom's lower lip trembled.

"I don't know," Marti said. Why was Brumble worrying about housekeeping? RachelAnne said the office was a madhouse, and from what little Marti saw on the news report, she believed it. Either the public defender was as big of an idiot as The Judge claimed or Myrna was speaking in code to let Marti know she knew what was going on. "RachelAnne called," she said.

Myrna nodded. Code it was, which explained the remote snatch and stash.

"Marti? Why aren't you in school?" Mom said.

The landline rang. Myrna grabbed the phone and hit the mute button. "We'll just let the machine get it."

"It might be your father," Mom said.

"Oh, I doubt that," Marti said, "but I'd really like to talk to him myself."

Big Ben rang out. He wasn't telling them the time. Someone was at the front door.

"RachelAnne said not to answer the door," Marti said. Code, shmode. Mom wasn't in touch with reality.

"I'm hungry." Mom reached for the flour-Oreo canister.

"No need," Myrna said. She pulled the remote from her pocket and pointed it at the TV.

The Judge had taken home security seriously. The kitchen television got more than cable. The screen split into four quarters, each showing a different angle of the house and front yard. A woman with a microphone stood in front of the door. A cameraman lurked behind her. Two vans, one bearing the call letters of a local television station and the other the logo of a cable news network, were parked out front.

"Where's security?" Mom said. "There is no soliciting on the Avenue. And somebody stole my Oreos."

The reporter reached for the phony door knocker. Big Ben bonged. Someone pounded on the back door. They were under siege from all sides.

Myrna switched the channel. Four views of the back of the house appeared.

"Aaaaaaand there's security," Marti said. Dmitri had a lock grip on the arm of a skinny guy. The captive's head was down, his face hidden. He was dressed more like Marti than like a reporter.

Dmitri looked straight into the camera. "Get Marti."

"Guess I'll answer that one," she said.

"I'm hungry. I want a cookie," Mom said.

"Come on, sweetie, we can watch the ponies on the big TV," Myrna said.

"Good plan," Marti said. The family parlor was in the center of the ground level and window free.

Grandma appeared behind Myrna. "Your father is in the attic. He says he doesn't wish to discuss the situation."

"I want more tea," Mom said.

"Oh, I think you've had enough for now," Myrna said.

Dmitri banged on the door again. "Mrs. Ward? Marti?" His prisoner lifted his head, and Marti got a good look at him.

Weasel Boy.

"It's your little friend!" Grandma said.

She flung open the back door. "What in the—"

"Back door open. Back door open."

"There's someone back here!" A news crew raced around the corner of the house.

Dmitri hauled Weasel Boy inside. Marti slammed and locked the door.

The news crew pounded on the door. "Mrs. Mickkleson? Mrs. Mickkleson? Do you have a statement on the accusations against your late husband?" More pounding. What was with these people?

"*No habla inglés.* Mrs. Mickkleson, um, *no es agua*," Marti hollered.

"You just said your mother isn't water," Dmitri said.

"Well, she's not," Marti said. "At least she wasn't five minutes ago."

"That's the worst accent I've heard since high school," Weasel Boy said.

"That's where I learned it," Marti said. High school Spanish class was further away for her than it was for him. "Weas—Darrell. What are you doing here?" He clutched a bedraggled bunch of flowers to his chest. The kind sold at gas stations. It was probably in rough shape before he mangled it.

"So you *do* know him." The corners of Dmitri's mouth twitched. "He says he's your boyfriend."

"Here." Weasel Boy offered her the bouquet. A broken carnation waggled and dropped its badly dyed bloom. Marti half expected the flower to explode when it hit the floor. She'd never seen a Burger Buster orange carnation.

She didn't take the flowers.

"Told you he had a crush on you," Grandma said.

"He is *not* my boyfriend," she said. Dmitri's twitch turned into a full grin. A cute grin. She still wanted to smack him.

"Mother wants you to have dinner with us," Weasel Boy said.

"Back in Franklinville?"

"Oh no. She's here."

"*Here?* Why is she here? Why are *you* here?"

"Because he has a crush on you," Grandma said.

"I don't drive. Mother brought me."

"*Why?* How did you find me?"

Weasel Boy pulled a tightly folded square of paper from his pocket and handed it to her.

She opened it and found a computer printout of a news photo. Saturday's scene at the McDonagh house. She stood in the background. Mom was right. She did need to do something about her hair.

"Why would you even see this?" Marti saw no reason for Sheila's murder to be news in Franklinville, almost two hundred miles away.

Weasel Boy shrugged. "I like to read about murders."

Big Ben played again. And again. And again. The hammering on the back door continued. Dmitri smirked. The smirk was the last straw.

"Look. Norman Bates, I don't know why you're here or how you found me, but you are *not my boyfriend*. Go back to Mommy. And you—" She turned on Dmitri. "You are supposed to be security. Act like it. Get rid of these reporters or ghouls or whatever they are. And get Norman here out of my house and out of my sight."

Both the doorbell and the pounding ceased, and silence greeted the end of her tirade.

"I had Big send over a couple of cars. Look." No smirk. All business, Dmitri pointed at the TV where security images of the back door still played. Baby Face Rodney and another of Bicklesburg's finest hustled the camera crew away. "We can't keep the press off the street, but we can contain them. They won't be at your door, but stay away from the windows. Don't answer the phone. If you absolutely must leave the house, call me. Someone will escort you. Don't give them anything to get excited about."

"Why are they here?" Marti said. "It sounded like there were two live judges for them to harass."

"Slow day, I guess," Dmitri said.

"If you need a character witness, I'm willing," Weasel Boy said.

"Get him out of here," Marti said.

"Come on Norman. I bet Mother's worried about you." Dmitri grabbed Weasel Boy's arm.

"Wait!" Weasel Boy held out the flowers. When Marti didn't take them, he threw them at her. She jumped back, and they landed at her feet. "Mother thought you'd like them," he said. "I'll find you something better next time."

"Get him out of here and keep him away from the vultures out front."

"Don't worry, Marti. I won't tell your secrets." Weasel Boy looked at her with puppy-dog eyes.

"Should have believed me," Grandma said. "He luuuurves you."

"OUT!"

She swore Dmitri chuckled on his way out the door.

MARTI FED WEASEL Boy's flowers to the garbage disposal. Much more satisfying than tossing them into the trash and far cheaper than therapy.

First a lime green blossom, then a hot pink—her hair, for a brief time, was that exact hue. She hoped she'd worn it better than the hothouse bloom did. The one white rose, from the center of the bouquet, she saved for last. It wasn't bad, but it was as doomed as its brothers and sisters. She got a rhythm going and enjoyed the sound of the running water and the grinding of the disposal. Down to two carnations, she chose the blue—sort of robin's egg on meth—and sent it to its death.

It shrieked.

The phone on the wall next to the sink screamed a second time, and she grabbed it without thinking. *"What?"*

"I know what you did."

"Who is this?" Marti was about to slam the receiver back on the base but stopped.

". . . away with it. You killed them both. Don't think you'll get away with it just because you're a Mickkleson . . ."

The same raspy, genderless voice spewed the same vile words in the same tones, same cadence, same everything as the first call.

"La, la, la, la. I'm not listening."

The caller didn't pause. Marti missed a few colorful phrases when she hung up the last time, but she didn't need to hear any more. She hung up, not bothering to slam the receiver. There was no one on the other end to hear her if she did. The Mickklesons' obscene caller was a robocaller.

If she discounted Grandma's insistence The Judge's death was due to natural causes, Marti counted one murder and two possibles. If she assumed the caller's target was her mother, not herself, who was Mom supposed to have done in? The Judge and Sheila? That made a certain amount of sense, but why wait till now? They'd carried on for years. According to The Judge, they came to "a parting of the ways." How long ago? If C-3PO was making accusations about Ralph and Sheila, it made no sense. Did anyone besides her know Ralph was dead? She wasn't 100 percent sure he was dead. Maybe she did imagine his presence in the Escalade.

It was all ridiculous anyway. There was no way Margaret Mickkleson killed any of them. Except maybe The Judge, which was perfectly understandable, not to mention justifiable.

THiRTEEN

In the family parlor, Mom snored on the couch, head thrown back, mouth open, feet on the coffee table. Ponies pranced on the TV screen. Myrna sat in an overstuffed armchair and crocheted, shoulders squared, feet firmly planted on the floor. Sitting didn't diminish her resemblance to a stick insect. Her florescent yarn matched the ponies' manes and tails. The orange and green matched the Burger Buster colors. As long as the yarn wasn't scented, Marti was good with it.

"How's she doing?" Marti said. "When she's awake."

"Fine. She always has a bad spell around midday. Then it's nap time. When she wakes up, she'll be a little disoriented, then she'll be herself most of the afternoon. Almost herself. As close as she gets nowadays." Myrna's shoulders slumped. She sighed, looked at Mom, and shook her head.

Marti moved a couple of pillows off the couch and picked up the newspaper. Sheila's murder filled the front page with Weasel Boy's photo smack dab in the center. She wondered if The Judge's misdeeds were enough to bounce his dead mistress to the back pages in the next edition.

"I've hardly had time to keep up with the housework since your mother took her turn for the worse. Your sister promised me help, but it hasn't happened yet." Martyrdom and sadness fought for supremacy in Myrna's voice. Martyrdom had the edge.

"She's probably been a tad busy." Marti was getting used to the clutter, but clutter was the least of the room's problems. Dust bunnies frolicked in the corners. Sticky little handprints—

Maggie's, by the size of them—marred the gloss of the end tables. Help or no help, Mrs. Partridge would never have stood for it. Nor would she have sat and crocheted in the middle of the mess. Marti remembered the family parlor smelling of furniture wax and antiseptic. All she got now was the stale aroma of Mom's obnoxious tea.

Whether it was The Judge's absence or her mother's illness, Bickle House was going to seed. Marti was no great shakes as a housekeeper, but it bothered her enough she considered cleaning the room herself. She needed something to do other than sit and think about murder and scandal, but Myrna was likely to see it as an insult. No point in insulting Myrna. She settled on the couch next to her mother.

"What are your plans? How long are you staying?" Myrna shook out the half-finished blanket.

"I honestly don't know." Marti hoped Myrna didn't play poker. Her attempt at disinterest had the opposite effect. Marti assumed she was after inside information, a tidbit to deal her a full house in the Bicklesburg gossip game. At that game, Marti was sure the housekeeper was an expert.

"So, you still crazy?" Myrna asked the loaded question in a tone more offhand than the last.

"As a loon," Marti said.

"Just so we have that clear." Myrna spread her project over her lap. Marti couldn't imagine a decor in the world it would match.

The snoring stopped. "Mrs. Ward makes my tea now," Mom said.

Interesting that Mom called Myrna *Mrs. Ward*, and Myrna called Mom *sweetie*. Quite a switch from the days Mom said *Myrna* and said it as if it left a bad taste in her mouth, and Myrna called Mom *YesMa'am*, all one word.

"That's nice," Marti said.

"I never did like Sheila McDonagh," Mom said.

"Shhhh, don't say things like that," Myrna said.

"Is tomorrow Wednesday?" Mom said.

"It's Tuesday. Why?" Marti said.

"You need a haircut. And a manicure. I'll take you to the salon with me on Wednesday. They'll fit you in. For me." Old Mom's Wednesday hair and nails appointment was sacrosanct. When Marti's fifth-grade holiday concert was scheduled at the same time as her regular root touch up, Mom chose her stylist over singing ten-year olds.

From the looks of her roots and fingernails, New Mom hadn't been to the salon for some time.

"Maybe." Marti didn't know what else to say.

Myrna concentrated on her yarn and stayed out of the conversation.

"And what are you wearing? You look like something the cat dragged in, and we don't have a cat." Mom stood. "I believe I'll go for a walk. Marti, go change your clothes and come with me. You appear to need the exercise."

Myrna dropped her work and leapt up. "Now, Mrs. Mickkleson, I don't think you want to go out today."

Apparently when Mom was more with it, *sweetie* was out and formal address was in.

"Mom, all I have is sweatshirts and jeans." The return of Old Mom made feeding her to the vultures waiting outside tempting, but she'd promised RachelAnne otherwise. Keeping Mom focused on her multitude of shortcomings was as good a distraction as any.

"Then you need to go shopping. But first borrow some clothes from your sister. Any respectable establishment will think you're a shoplifter. Or a member of the janitorial staff."

She hadn't exactly *promised*.

"And why don't I want to go out? Is it raining?" Mom said.

"Yes," Marti said.

"No," Myrna said.

Mom narrowed her eyes and looked from her housekeeper to

her daughter. "What's going on?" The laser stare awakened the twelve-year-old in Marti.

The twelve-year-old who wasn't known for her honesty, but for telling stories so preposterous no one mistook them for the truth. Marti opened her mouth, prepared to lie her butt off. If she tried hard enough, she might be able to work in aliens. Green ones. With purple spots.

Myrna didn't give her a chance.

"Now, Mrs. Mickkleson. We have plans for the afternoon. We need to get started sorting Judge Mickkleson's things. The people from the Clothing Bank are coming next week."

The Clothing Bank was one of Mom's pet causes. She'd sat on the board for as long as Marti could remember. The clothing they collected was sent to homeless shelters. The Judge's tailor-made suits would be a hit.

"I'll help," Marti said.

"Don't be ridiculous. Your father would not want you pawing through his possessions," Mom said.

"I found your father." Grandma's announcement startled her. Her dearly departed great-grandmother enjoyed popping in and out of the rooms of Bickle House far too much. Not a lot of opportunity for popping in the one room apartments they'd spent the last decade in.

"What's wrong? You twitched. You're not doing drugs, are you?" Mom said.

"No, Mom. I'm fine. Maybe I'll just sit here and watch the ponies."

"See if you can find something appropriate to wear for dinner. *Something* in your closet must fit. If not, Mrs. Ward can find you one of my dresses. Of course, those probably won't fit either. Maybe you should skip dinner."

Marti tried to remember if she'd actually *agreed* to keep Mom away from the vultures. RachelAnne hung up awfully fast.

"Your father will be livid if you show up at the table dressed like an overage street urchin." Mom swept out of the room, her lady-in-waiting trailing.

THE GROWN-UP MARTI in her head told her full-strength, extra-power Old Mom had no power over her. Old Mom's harping meant nothing. The young Marti in her heart didn't listen.

"Calm down," Grandma said. "She's not herself. You heard what she said about your father."

"Oh, some of that was herself." Too much of it was the woman Marti couldn't get away from fast enough. A woman fully capable of dealing with gossip. Capable of dealing with the reporters outside. Capable of crushing the spirit of daughters who saw spirits with one withering glance.

Capable of murdering Sheila McDonagh. Except Old Mom would find a neater way of dispatching her rival. She would never ruin a good—and flattering—silk dress.

New Mom licked blackberry jam from her fingers. New Mom might not care about blood on lavender silk dresses. New Mom could be faking it, but getting rid of Sheila now, after The Judge was gone, made no sense. Why risk it?

Mom was in her early sixties. It could be Alzheimer's.

"Grandma? When we first got here, you mentioned some great aunt or somebody? Said Mom was just like her?"

"Aunt Alice Bradley." Grandma tsked. "Such a shame, that one."

"Tell me about her."

"My father's baby sister. Much younger than Papa. Influenza took my grandparents, both on the same day, poor souls. Papa was her guardian, and I grew up with her."

Whenever her great-grandmother told stories of her youth, Marti was astounded at how long ago she was born. She was ninety-two when she died in a freak boating accident—why someone that age went canoeing without a life jacket was beyond Marti's comprehension. Add in Marti's thirty-two years and Alberta Marcile Ferguson had witnessed well over a century's worth of life.

"She was a famous beauty," Grandma said. "Your mother looks a lot like her, from what I remember. When I was a child, she was my favorite aunt, always laughing and full of fun and more like an older sister than an aunt.

"That doesn't sound like my mother."

"I only said she looked like her. Aunt Alice had suitors by the dozen. They brought her gifts and wrote bad poetry for her. She was my idol. Never married, though. The love of her life died in the Great War, and she took it hard. By the time I was a schoolgirl, she couldn't tell her hat from a shoehorn. In those days, quite shameful. Reflected badly on the whole family. The last time I saw her, I was fifteen or sixteen years old. She was angry, shouting vile things at Papa."

"What happened to her?"

"Papa bought her a small house and hired a companion to take care of her. My sister and I took to calling her Bertha, you know, after the wife in the attic in *Jane Eyre*. Teenagers are so cruel. When the cottage burned and both Aunt Alice and her nurse—what was her name, Lotte? Lotilla? Something with an *L*, doesn't matter—died, Millie and I thought it was somehow our fault. Because of the Bertha thing. I put her out of my mind. Hadn't thought about her for years, until I saw your mother."

"Was this here in Bicklesburg?"

"Oh goodness, no. Back in Massachusetts. I moved to Bicklesburg after your great-grandfather died. Your mother was all the family I had left. Having married beneath her, I feared she'd need me."

Unlike the general Bicklesburg populace, The Judge married an outsider. He and Mom met in college. Her parents were gone, and she had money. He had parents, even more money, and no suitable Battlesburough County-bred bride candidates. Whether their marriage was love or a merger based on social status and family fortunes, Marti had never figured out.

"Does Mom know about Alice?"

"I don't see how. I never talked about her. One didn't, you know."

"What you're saying is insanity doesn't just run in our family, it races, sprints, darts, scampers, and scurries."

"You are quite sane, dear. And your father's side has far worse secrets, I'm sure."

"He kept a doozy or two himself." Marti struggled to wrap her mind around it all. Old Mom. New Mom. The appalling possibility her mother *was* a murderer. If she'd done away with Sheila, maybe she had done away with her husband, despite Grandma's insistence The Judge died of natural causes. Great-Grandma Bertie might be protecting her granddaughter, a *mea culpa* for her treatment of Aunt Alice more than a century ago.

If Marti followed that train of thought much further, she'd have Mom off on a tropical island with Ralph, like the busybodies in the park. But Ralph was dead. Unless she'd imagined—hallucinated—him in the Escalade. One more thing she didn't want to think about. Time to dial up Denials-R-Us and change the subject.

"You said you found The Judge," she said.

"Oh! I did. He's in the house. He doesn't want to talk to you. With good reason, I'd say. But he did say to tell you he is holding you to your agreement. Sooner or later, this nonsense will blow over, and if you don't find out who his imaginary killer is, he'll stick with you the rest of your life. 'Nonsense' was his word. I added 'imaginary.'"

"No comment on what's going on? Did he bother to try to explain or defend himself?" She remembered the Pennsylvania Kids for Cash scandal. If The Judge was remotely involved in anything similar, there was no defense.

"Have you *met* your father?" Grandma said. "Has he ever explained anything? Don't worry. I told Edwards and Amity to keep an eye on him. Edwards promised to stick to him 'like a fly on pig . . .' You get the picture."

Not only did Marti get the picture, she found the simile apt.

Edwards did whatever Grandma asked. Amity hated The Judge. With any luck, she'd go exceptionally pouty and turn on her whine machine. The Judge ought to enjoy that.

Dmitri called. The crowd of press had thinned. "There's only one local crew left out there, but don't think it's over. Consider it the eye of the hurricane. They'll be back in full force. They're in town. County officials are making a public statement. Once that's done, they'll be back. This town hasn't seen this much action since the Civil War."

Bicklesburg had been far from the fighting, but had been a political hotbed, full of abolitionist firebrands. The Bickles and Mickklesons—to their credit—were at the center of that storm too. The Mickklesons were in the middle of everything.

Crap. "You don't think they know about Saturday and Mom and . . ." Marti wanted to say *me* but didn't want to come off as self-centered, even if she was.

Dmitri laughed. "Why do you think the press is camping on your front lawn? One dead judge isn't big news, not when they've got two live ones to hound."

Marti wondered how The Judge would feel at being upstaged. Under the circumstances, he should welcome it, but with him, you never knew. Then again, he was in hiding.

"But when that dead judge's wife is small-town aristocracy and possibly a suspect in the death of that same dead judge's rumored mistress, and one of his daughters works in the justice system and the other is rumored to be . . . colorful, now, that's news. In this part of the country, you guys are better than the Kardashians," Dmitri continued.

"You don't have to sound so gleeful," Marti said.

"I'm not. I was imagining you in one of those slinky celebrity red-carpet dresses."

Marti hung up on him. Anything that came out of her mouth would end up embarrassing her anyway.

GHOSTS IN GLASS HOUSES 171

Since Myrna was keeping Mom occupied upstairs, Marti turned on the TV. She'd missed the big news conference, but what she found was—well, better was the wrong word, but more pertinent to what she wanted to know. The legend across the bottom of the screen read,

>Battlesburough County Courthouse
>Lawrence Brumble
>Battlesburough County Public Defender's Office

An uncomfortable-looking little man in an ill-fitting suit sweated at the podium. RachelAnne's boss. Marti checked the lineup behind him. Her sister wasn't there.

Bumbles Brumble reminded her of someone. She couldn't put her finger on whom, but with all the tangled family trees in Bicklesburg, she wasn't surprised. It was possible she recalled the balding, twitchy attorney from her own past. She'd never needed him. She'd never gotten into any needing-a-lawyer level trouble, and if she had, it wouldn't have made it as far as court. On the off chance it did, her parents would have retained the best representation money could buy. No public defender for her.

". . . completely unfounded," Bumbles said into the microphone. He stuck a finger inside his shirt collar and pulled it away from his neck. His face was an unhealthy gray, and the high-definition television treated Marti to every bead of sweat on his shiny forehead.

The hands of the assembled reporters shot up. Bumbles pointed at one.

"Mr. Brumble. Unlike the situation in Luzerne County, the incarcerated juveniles in Battlesburough County had legal representation, the vast majority of them through your office. Your office—you in particular—has an outstandingly high conviction rate. However, you are the public defender, not the prosecutor. How do you explain this?"

"No comment." Brumble blinked, took out a white handkerchief, and mopped his forehead. "Next. Last question." He had an odd voice. Not squeaky, but high and soft. Maybe nerves turned him into a soprano. Marti couldn't remember if she ever heard him speak.

The sea of hands waved again. Brumble pointed at a middle-aged woman in an orange suit.

"MaryEllen Pernelli, *Bicklesburg Gazette*," the selected reporter said.

She didn't look like a Pernelli. She must have married into the clan.

Bumbles visibly relaxed, like he thought the hometown team was on his side.

"RachelAnne *Mickkleson* Rudawski is an employee of your office. Does she have any comment on the charges against her father? Do you foresee any conflict of interest if the public defender's office becomes part of the current investigation? For any reason?"

"First, no charges have been or can be filed against the *late* Judge Mickkleson. At this time, his *alleged* involvement in the situation is a matter of rumor and speculation."

Bumbles wiped his forehead again and continued. "Second, Ms. *Rudawski* has voluntarily taken indefinite leave while the *allegations* against her late father are being investigated. She states she has no knowledge of her *late* father's activities, and she will be spending time with her recently *bereaved* mother." Bumbles answered MaryEllen Pernelli's question effortlessly. Either the statement was rehearsed or he was so thrilled to have the attention off him and back on The Judge—and RachelAnne—he magically transformed into a skilled public speaker.

"Thank you," he said, mopped his forehead one last time, and stumbled off the stage.

Marti was positive she'd seen him recently. She remembered a younger Larry Brumble, without the potbelly big enough to strain the buttons on his suit and to enter a room fifteen seconds before his backside. Something about him now—no use.

He probably reminded her of some Burger Buster customer in Franklinville.

Her cell phone rang, reminding her why she hated the blasted things. Only two people had her number, and it still went off constantly. The latest caller was her sister.

"How's Mom doing?" RachelAnne asked.

"A little while ago she was full-strength Queen Margaret. She and Myrna are sorting and packing The Judge's clothes or something."

"I'll be there in an hour or two. We need to tell her what's happening. Together. Both of us."

"Okay. If you hurry, you might beat the return of the bloodsuckers. They all took off to feed at that news conference."

"Did you see it?"

"Only the end. Your boss. RachelAnne, I'm sorry." Marti had no idea what the long-term effects would be, but Baby Sister must have felt as if The Judge reached out from the grave to screw up her life, or at least her career. Marti sympathized in ways her sister would never understand.

"I have to go see Peter before I come over. He's been calling and texting all day, and I've been ignoring him. He's probably livid."

"Good luck with that."

By the time RachelAnne called and said she'd be there in five minutes, the vultures were back.

"Call Dmitri and warn him you're on your way. If the idiots staked out the alley, you'll never get through," Marti said. "Unless you run them down. There's a thought."

"Like we don't have enough problems." RachelAnne hung up. *Goodbye* wasn't in her vocabulary.

Mom and Myrna either finished or gave up on their sorting for the day. Marti joined them in the kitchen to wait for her sister. Mom sipped her ever-present tea. Her teapot and cup were adorned with tiny bluebirds. Marti was growing used to the smell. She only gagged once.

It took her sister a little longer than five minutes to make it to Bickle House, and Marti checked the security monitor before answering the back door. The last thing she wanted was to open the door to a reporter, or worse, Weasel Boy.

"Those people are—"

"Vultures?" Marti completed her sister's sentence.

"I was ready to plow right through them, but I didn't want to dent my car. Also, Dmitri and Rodney made them move. Are you wearing the same clothes you wore yesterday?" RachelAnne wrinkled her nose.

"No." Marti's sweatshirt was clean and sported an entirely different design than yesterday's Porky Pig. The one she wore was someone's souvenir of a trip to Carlsbad Caverns. She didn't know whose since she bought all her sweatshirts at Goodwill or Salvation Army. She wore the same jeans, but they'd been clean the day before. They had at least one more day of wear, if not two, left in them.

"I don't understand. You used to have style." RachelAnne shook her head.

"Still do. One that fits my life."

"We really need to take you shopping."

"Are we procrastinating? Just a little?" Marti didn't blame her sister. The talk with Mom would not be fun.

"Shush."

"If you two don't mind, I need to leave. It's well past my usual time." Myrna had her coat on and buttoned. She clutched her purse and waved her car keys.

"You could have left. I was here," Marti said.

"I always wait for RachelAnne."

"Things are a little crazy today. I'm sorry," RachelAnne said.

"They weren't exactly peaches and cream here," Myrna the Martyr said. "I need to get home. I have a plumber coming at six thirty. I do have a life of my own, you know."

"You have plenty of time," Marti said. "It's not even six yet." It would be in a few minutes, but the housekeeper annoyed her. You could get anywhere in Bicklesburg in under fifteen minutes including hitting all the red lights. All three of them.

"I live in Harrison Heights."

"Gosh. I hope you don't run into traffic," Marti said. *Heights* was an exaggeration. "Four Corners" better described the neighboring village, which made Bicklesburg look like bright lights, big city time. A twenty-minute trip, if Myrna drove slow.

"I'll call Dmitri and let him know you're coming through," RachelAnne said.

"Thank you," Myrna said.

Marti held the door open and considered letting it hit the housekeeper on her way out, but thought better of it. RachelAnne got to go home. Marti had to spend the next day and who knew how many days after with her. "Nice car," she said.

Myrna's shiny metallic-blue Camaro, a vintage muscle car, not the wimpy modern version, had either sat in a garage for decades or been flawlessly restored. Its vanity plates read "CLN-QU3N."

"My late husband's," Myrna said.

"I don't get the plates."

"Clean Queen." Myrna sailed out the door.

FOURTEEN

"Front door open. Front door open."

"Oh, hush," Marti told the disembodied watchwoman. She shut the door behind her and silenced the silvery-voiced alarm system.

Mom was in bed and, when Marti peeked in on her, sound asleep. Snowball or Winter or whatever her name was watched Mom, and Edwards watched the nurse. He promised to alert Marti if Mom woke or the snowflake woke her and tried to pump her for gossip. Mom's sitter was, after all, a Pernelli.

There was no one to stop her from sitting on the front porch. No one to tell her it was inappropriate. No one to say, "We are not a bunch of hillbillies." Of course, the shape Mom was in, she might not care if Marti broke the rules. She might join her, given the opportunity.

Lack of chairs was a drawback, so with a porch bigger than her last apartment, Marti settled herself on the front steps. *All I need is a corncob pipe and a jug of moonshine.* She would settle for a beer, but as far as alcohol went, the refrigerator was bare. She refrained from raiding The Judge's stash in case Baby Sister took inventory.

Since the meeting with Bowman, RachelAnne fluctuated between "Let's be sisters" and "I've got my eyes on you" so fast Marti didn't bother trying to keep up. RachelAnne had gone home for the night, but Marti didn't see it as a sign of trust. Her sister had a family to tend to, and Maggie's "I miss you, Mommy" phone call, which RachelAnne put on speakerphone, was heartbreaking even if Peter put the little girl up to it.

Grandma Bertie settled on the porch rail. "You seem to be holding up well, *seem* being the operative word," she said

GHOSTS IN GLASS HOUSES 177

"I'm in no mood for a heart-to-heart. Or advice," Marti said.

"That's fine. Let's just enjoy the evening," Grandma said, "but I do think you're doing well, all things considered."

The Avenue glowed under the streetlights. The reporters were gone. They would be back. The possibly senile widow of a philandering and crooked judge, a small-town society matron who might be involved in the murder of her late husband's mistress, had to be ratings gold. Unless a story involving someone younger and prettier came along to distract them. One could only hope. Still, Marti had a feeling the Mickklesons were destined to star in a ripped-from-the-headlines television show. There was a time when she would have enjoyed seeing her family humiliated, but Mom and RachelAnne deserved better. None of this mess was their making.

The Judge deserved it, and no matter how the situation played out or what he'd done, he'd get off scot-free.

Light flickered in the windows of three of the large houses. The other three were either empty or the occupants turned in early. The last Marti knew, Beadle House still held Beadles, a couple who were ancient when she was a child. If they were still alive and kicking and living on the Avenue, it was possible they hit the sack earlier than her mother.

She considered opting for an early bedtime herself. Her head pounded. Her joints ached. Her mind and nerves were wide awake and dancing the two-step. In four days, she'd dealt with two freshly minted ghosts, not to mention their abandoned bodies, starting with poor Ozzie. Three, if she counted her father. Four, if what she'd seen inside the Escalade wasn't her imagination.

The worst of it wasn't all the death. The worst was the turmoil of the living—and her family sucking her back in. After years of cutting herself off and forcing herself to view them as strangers, she was in danger of caring. Past the danger. Hard as it was to admit, she cared.

She couldn't rid herself of the nagging idea her mother might be a murderer. The logistics of Shella's death, as far as Marti could tell, cleared her mother. Mom had a good head start on the search party, but there couldn't have been enough time for her to dispatch Sheila before she and Dmitri arrived. Dead Sheila was as surprised as anyone to find Margaret Mickkleson on her porch swing. Wouldn't Sheila have known if Mom had wielded Mr. Stumpy?

Not if she surprised her from behind, the evil voice in Marti's head answered. Mom certainly couldn't have taken off with the Escalade. What about Ralph? If he was alive, it *might* clear Mom. If he wasn't, there was no way Mom had anything to do with his death. Both Myrna and the redheaded Walmart manager saw him in the Escalade. If he was alive, he must have killed his wife. If he wasn't, well, that cleared Mom too. She hadn't left the house since her Saturday morning walkabout.

Unless she got someone else to do it. Evil Voice needed to shut up and go away.

As for The Judge's death, Mom did indeed have ample opportunity and motive. The only question was, if she was willing to kill him, why did she wait so long?

Marti didn't want to believe any of it. Evil Voice was simply a reaction to Mom going all Emily Gilmore on her and resurrecting her adolescent anti-parent fantasies.

No denying it, she cared. She didn't want her mother to be a murderer.

Something moved by Beadle House. She sat up straight. Someone emerged from the shadows. She steeled herself and prepared to run. If it was a leftover reporter, the ACS night shift would take care of them, she hoped sooner rather than later. In the meantime, she wasn't going to answer questions. She'd be inside behind the locked door before they made it up the street.

Whoever it was wasn't in any hurry.

"It's your young man," Grandma said.

"Crap." Marti stood. Forget the ACS. She'd call the cops. Weasel Boy creeped her out.

It wasn't Weasel Boy. It was Dmitri. In street clothes. "He's not my young man." Marti sat down.

"I like him."

"You didn't back in the day." Marti spoke softly though Dmitri wasn't yet close enough to hear. She hoped.

"That was different. You were far too young to be doing the things you were doing."

Marti's cheeks burned. Some things she never got used to her great-grandmother knowing.

She was saved from answering. Once Dmitri hit the sidewalk, he went from amble to stride. In no time, his long legs brought him close enough to hear her talking. She didn't think New Dmitri would find Crazy Girl as fascinating as Teen Dmitri did. He'd entered respectable adulthood, a state that eluded her.

"Hey. Can you stand some company?" He carried a brown paper bag.

"Have a seat." Dmitri looked better in jeans and a sweatshirt than she did—and even better than Dmitri in uniform. No wonder Dawn Pernelli went all drooly at the sight of him.

"He did grow up nicely," Grandma said.

Shut up. The thought was for her great-grandmother. Dmitri got a lame smile.

Unfortunately, just because Grandma was a ghost didn't make her telepathic. "And he's a big step up from Weasel Boy," she said.

"How's your mom?" Dmitri lowered himself onto the step next to Marti and set the bag at his feet with the unmistakable clink of glass hitting glass.

"Tired. Sleeping off the day."

"Does she understand what's happening?"

"RachelAnne and I tried to explain. I'm not sure how much she got. What's in the bag?"

"Thought maybe you could use this." He pulled out two bottles of Corona and a church key. "Don't have any lime."

"Thanks." Marti watched him open both beers and took the

one he handed her. He folded the empty bag and stuck it in his back pocket. He'd only brought the two, one for her and one for him, so this—probably—wasn't a trap set by RachelAnne, arbitrator of Marti maturity and holder of the purse strings. *I really need to get over this paranoia.*

Two bottles, which raised another question. "How did you know I was out here?"

"Cameras. Your father put them everywhere. He was a very security-conscious man."

Or more paranoid than I am.

"It appears he had reason to be," Marti said. In the awkward silence that followed, it hit her. How long had The Judge been on the take?

Were her trust fund and the mysterious deposits to her savings account funded by selling Dmitri and others like him?

She added it to her list of questions for The Judge—if he ever showed his face again. Right then, she had a few questions for Dmitri. He couldn't work twenty-four hours a day. He was out of uniform. He had beer. She took a swallow. Cold beer too. She could attempt to get tricky and try to charm answers out of him, but she was too worn out for games, and charm wasn't her forte.

"Do the cameras run all the time? Are we being recorded right now? And why were you watching me? You don't look like you're on duty." Good thing she didn't take the charm route. She was barely making sense on the direct route.

"The cameras do run all the time. They start recording when the house alarm tells them to. If the door is closed in a reasonable amount of time, they stop recording."

"Harriet."

"Who?"

"The 'back door open' lady. I've decided to name her Harriet."

"Okay then." Dmitri examined the label on his beer bottle. He'd hardly made a dent in the contents. Marti's was half-empty.

"Maybe you should slow down," Grandma said. "Don't want to embarrass yourself."

Marti took a swallow and set the bottle on the step beside her. As much as she hated to admit it, Grandma had a point. Whether it was the beer or the cool night air, she was relaxed. More than relaxed. Drowsiness crept over her. If she wasn't careful, she'd curl up right there and fall asleep next to Dmitri, and what would Harriet have to say about that? *Wait.* "Harriet!" She shook herself out of her stupor.

"What?" Dmitri turned those lovely eyes on her.

"Harriet. I first met her when she was going on and on about the back door. Saturday. When Mom wandered off. When Sheila . . . if there is video . . ."

"That's what I came to tell you. Big says your mom is off the hook. Sheila was dead before your mother left the house." He paused. "You're probably in the clear too, but Big says to tell you to find that receipt. The employees at the donut place say Sheila and Ralph were there, but no one remembers you."

Despite the gossip in the Green, Marti never thought anyone seriously considered her a suspect. That might explain Dmitri's off-duty presence on the Avenue. He was keeping an eye on his old girlfriend, murderous Marti Cray-Cray, in case she'd returned to knock off The Judge's wimmen-folk one by one. She edged away, putting a little more space between the two of them.

It didn't explain why Chief Big Fysh used a private security guard as his messenger boy, unless he was so fed up with Mickklesons he didn't want to subject his own minions to them. Sounded legit to her. "I should call RachelAnne. Tell her Mom's in the clear."

"I already did."

"Of course you did." Her flare of jealousy was unreasonable, but old habits were hard to break, especially where her sister was concerned. "I'm not really a suspect, am I?"

He shrugged. "You'll have to ask Big about that."

"So. You and Big. You're buddies now?"

"We get along. He's not such a bad guy."

"He called me *Marti Cray-Cray*."

"Old habit. You took him by surprise."

She and Fysh, after all these years, had something in common. Conditioned reflex. *Fysh smash*. The difference was she managed not to let her reflex pop out her mouth. She didn't like the high school hero turned police chief and didn't see that changing anytime soon. If Dmitri kept defending him, he'd end up on her louse list too. "Tell me he's not married to your number-one fan, Dawn."

"Ha. No. He found a new girlfriend when he went off to college. Married that one. Didn't work out. Dawn tried her darnedest to get him back, but he'd moved on. Don't think she ever quite recovered."

"So, who did she marry?" Marti didn't particularly care, but small talk about the past was better than discussing either Sheila or The Judge.

"Bob Gunderson."

"Don't think I know him." Finally, one of those newcomers she kept hearing about. But then, there was a fifty-fifty chance he was related to someone she did know.

"Moved to town while you were gone. While we both were gone. Drives a tow truck for your brother-in-law." Dmitri swirled the contents of his bottle. He'd caught up to her level of beer drainage.

"Wonder if he's the one who hauled away my car." Or hauled the McDonaghs' Escalade into town. She picked up her Corona. "This is lovely. Thank you. I hardly miss the lime." She took a slug. "Has anyone heard anything from or about Ralph McDonagh?" she said in her best don't-really-care, just-making-conversation voice. To her ears, she sounded as exhausted as she felt, but maybe it passed for casual.

"Why?" Dmitri matched her casual and raised it to nonchalant.

"I thought I saw them hauling in his SUV this morning. When I was leaving the bank. I'd forgotten until you brought up tow trucks." How many little white lies did it take to equal one big whopper? If she kept going, she'd find out.

"I'd say you had other things on your mind." He drained the last of his beer. "Like your little boy toy. Did you get those flowers into some water?"

"Do not start." Marti countered the laughter in his voice with what she hoped was an if-you-keep-it-up-you're-going-to-get-this-beer-bottle-up-alongside-the-head tone.

"You want to tell me about him?"

"Not without another beer." *Not even then.*

"Change of subject then. How's your mom holding up?"

"Good question. When RachelAnne and I tried to explain what's going on, all she had to say was, 'Your father. Such a rascal.'" Grogginess was taking over again, starting at her feet, which felt like rocks, and creeping up her legs. Falling asleep right there next to Dmitri wasn't a bad idea. It would lead to waking up next to Dmitri. Which would be better than waking up next to Ozzie. At least Dmitri smelled better. Much, much better.

She pulled herself together. *Do not start thinking along those lines.* "How did you end up working for The Judge? For ACS. Same thing."

"Came back when my mom died. Couldn't find a job. Your father was expanding security here—I think he really wanted to build a gate around the Avenue but couldn't get the zoning permit—and offered me a job. Maybe he felt guilty."

"Hardly sounds like him."

"Whatever. It's a decent job, and I do a good job." Dmitri pulled the bag from his pocket, stuck the empty bottles in it, and stood. "I should go."

She'd crossed an invisible line. "I didn't mean . . ." She didn't know what she didn't mean. Dmitri loomed in front of her and waited for her to finish. "Sit down. Stay. Even before today, I felt like I owed you an apology. I never expected to have a chance to deliver it. What happened when we were kids, what The Judge did, I'm sorry."

"It wasn't your fault."

"It was. Your big bad crime was keeping company with his unstable daughter. That and discovering his secret. Well, one of his secrets. Who knows how many more he has—had. And . . ." A new idea hit her, one she didn't like.

"And what?" he said.

"Maybe sending you away paid for sending me away." If Judge "Zero Tolerance" Mickkleson was really Judge "Show Me the Money" Mickkleson, it was possible her stays in expensive loony bins, as undeserved as they were, drove her father to violate the law he claimed to revere. The family fortune looked bottomless to her, but was it? Had it always been that way?

Dmitri sat back down. "I don't think his sending me away is connected with the current mess."

"How can you know?"

"For one thing, I went to the old place in Johnsonville. The state-run detention center. Definitely no money or profit involved there. The charges are somehow connected to the new place in Franklinville."

"Wait. There's a prison in Franklinville?" How had she missed that?

"The Wayfair School."

"That's a prison?" She'd heard of the place but assumed it was a private school.

"It's a youth detention facility built and run by an independent contractor. There's big bucks in bad kids." Dmitri must have seen more of the news than she had. Or had a better source of information. "The stuff in my locker wasn't mine, you know."

"I never thought it was." Despite his Goth-rebel shtick, young Dmitri was focused on getting into college. Other than a closet full of black clothes, outstanding taste in music, and his interest in her, his bad-boy act was reserved for off-school hours. He was smart. If it hadn't been for The Judge, he would have made it to college and gone on a free ride. "Hanging out with me really screwed up your life, didn't it?"

GHOSTS IN GLASS HOUSES 185

"Well, I played a part in it. The stuff my mom found in my room? That *was* mine."

"It was a first offense, and my father made you disappear."

"My life isn't all that screwed up," Dmitri said.

"I didn't mean—never mind. My foot is permanently installed in my mouth. What did you do before you came back to Peyton Place?"

"I'll make you a deal. Don't ask about my last ten years, and I won't ask about yours."

"Deal," Marti said and couldn't come up with another topic of conversation.

Sirens rescued them from the awkward silence.

"Great. More excitement," she said. "Are Big Fysh and his minnows up to this much crime?"

"Those are fire trucks," Dmitri said.

"You can tell the difference?"

"They're totally different." A slightly different wail joined the chorus. "Now, *that's* a police car." He grinned. "See, I am good at my job. I do need to go. It's been a long day, and tomorrow has a better-than-average chance of being just as . . . interesting."

"Do you think the reporters will be back?"

"Unless something sexier distracts them, the chances are good."

"They don't—do they—" She was about to risk pissing him off again, but had to ask. "Do they know you're one of the kids The Judge sent away?"

"My juvenile record is sealed."

"But Bicklesburg mouths aren't."

"That could be a problem. See you tomorrow." He stopped halfway down the walk and turned. "Hey, Marti? Be careful."

It wasn't until he was gone she realized he'd sidestepped her question about Ralph McDonagh.

Had she seen Ralph in the Escalade or imagined him? Why she'd start imagining ghosts when there were enough real ones in her life was beyond her, but why didn't Grandma and The Judge see him?

If Ralph was still in the Escalade, she wanted to talk to him. It wasn't like anybody else could.

She checked her phone. Ten o'clock. Not so late her going out would arouse suspicion, even in a town where they rolled up the sidewalks at sundown. Someone in the security office no doubt watched her conversation with Dmitri. They would see her leave. Why would they care? She wasn't a prisoner in her mother's house, but if the press returned the next day, she might be.

The drowsy disappeared. She was wide awake and not looking forward to another night of tossing and turning.

She had the keys to the TT with her. She wasn't sure exactly how the security system worked, and she didn't want to risk Harriet locking her out. Before she came out, she grabbed her mother's key ring. It held both house and car keys.

If nothing else, a nighttime cruise in the sweet little sports car would be fun. She could use some fun.

"Come on, Grandma," she said. "We're going for a ride."

FiFTEEN

The police station was on the outskirts of beautiful downtown Bicklesburg, on the opposite side from Walmart and the strip malls. With the police station, the jail, four churches, and a cemetery, developers must not have considered the east side commercially attractive.

The station was before the cemetery, across from the Episcopal church, a smallish—compared to its neighbors—white clapboard building. The new Municipal Services Center was built around the original village police station when Marti was in junior high. Municipal Services sounded like it should include the sewer and sanitation departments, but the expansion of the old building only housed the police and fire departments. The architect designed the new facade to match the Bicklesburg style, but it needed another hundred years to truly blend in. The burnt-orange brick hadn't yet deepened to red. The columns on either side of the main entrance were still a bit too white.

Behind the building's elegant face, the added sections were ugly utilitarian boxes. The old part was equally grim. Marti considered the contrast the perfect definition of the Bicklesburg lifestyle.

Unless things had changed, a fenced-in lot out back held vehicles confiscated from vicious parking violators and other nefarious criminals. She hoped to find the McDonagh Escalade incarcerated there.

The row of churches was dark and quiet, but the garages at the fire station stood open. The brightly lit bays were empty. A lone patrol car sat in front of the police half of the building.

She passed the Municipal Center and turned at Oakdale Memorial Gardens. She passed under the wrought-iron arch and drove past modern headstones and granite angels and the Mickkleson mausoleum, where her father's ashes were interred. Too bad he didn't stay with them.

Next to the Mickkleson vault lay Grandma Bertie's earthly remains. The Judge refused her admittance to the family vault on the grounds she wasn't a Mickkleson, no matter that she was the last of Mom's family. Mom sprang for a large monument to mark her grandmother's grave. The angel perched on the headstone looked demented. The sculptor had been a friend of Grandma Bertie's.

"Do you want to stop?" Marti asked.

"Nothing here for me," Grandma said.

She kept going. Cemetery residents, the ones not confined to their graves, roamed in the dark. None greeted her.

At the end of the gravel road, in the shadow of one of the last remaining oak trees, she parked the TT and got out to walk. The original cemetery, resting place of Bicklesburg's founders, bordered the impound lot.

The old burial ground was dark but, for her, never quiet.

Mrs. Heedly and a few helpful mothers—Marti's not among them—had shepherded Marti's third grade class there for a lesson in local history. The children, equipped with soft crayons and sheets of paper bigger than they were, were to take rubbings of the weathered gravestones.

The resident spirits brushed against her classmates. The children shivered and giggled. Mrs. Heedly and the Mom brigade made jokes about geese walking on their graves. It was all great fun for everyone except Marti.

The unfamiliar crowd of ghosts terrified her. She'd never seen so many at once.

"Just ignore them. You'll be fine," Grandma told her.

Answering her great-grandmother was a mistake. Her

classmates ignored her, but the haunts realized she could see and hear the dead.

They crowded around her. A few reached out and touched her arms or her legs or her head. Cold and claustrophobia set in, followed by hysteria. The more Grandma Bertie tried to reassure her, the more distressed she grew. Eventually, she became physically ill. The farmer whose headstone she splattered with vomit was not pleased.

The ire of Sven Svenson—Loving Husband of Esther, b. 1796, d. 1864, Mauled to Death by His Prize Pig—was nothing compared to her classmates'. They were pissed at having their field trip cut short. Their mothers whispered and shook their heads.

Marti was sure the adults, not the kids, spread the story all over town. Dawn Pernelli's mother was the town crier.

The field trip solidified her position as a social pariah, the weird girl.

She'd returned to the cemetery only once. Late one night, long past curfew, she, Raven-Ashley, Oliver, and Dmitri brought a blanket and a case of cheap beer to the graveyard. Marti entertained her friends with descriptions and stories, mostly made up, of their ghostly hosts and drank too much too fast. Grandma not only disapproved of the party, she was angry enough to let Sven Svenson give Marti a bad case of ghost freeze. Her friends blamed her shivering and crying on an inability to hold her beer and got her out of there before she baptized another grave.

Grandma Bertie said it served her right.

She loathed the place. The malevolence of the ghosts wasn't her imagination. According to Grandma, those stuck within the confines of Oakdale's wrought-iron fences, cut off from their homes and loved ones but unable to move on, grew bitter and confused over the years. In the original section the years topped two centuries for some, which made for a lot of bitterness.

There were few Caspers in the crowd that watched her make her way among the crumbling headstones. Individually, they couldn't do anything more than give her a bad chill. If they joined forces, the deep freeze would be excruciating, if not worse. As far as she knew, they'd never ganged up on a living soul. People joked about the chills and thrills of the cemetery, but no one ever froze to death there on a summer—or fall—night.

Marti fervently hoped she wouldn't be the first.

"Just keep walking," Grandma said. "Don't run. They're like bears. Running will only excite them."

The bear analogy didn't reassure her.

The dead closed in on her. She swore she heard Grandma growl. They backed off. The Oakdale crowd respected—or feared—Grandma Bertie. Marti didn't understand it, but she appreciated it.

Outside the crumbling Bickle crypt, a woman dressed in a black-ribboned bonnet and a dull black, bell-shaped dress paced and wrung her hands.

"Almira." Grandma barely raised her voice, but Almira Bickle appeared at their side in an instant.

"My Amity?" Amity Bickle's mother's portrait still hung in Bickle House. The Mickklesons took possession of Bickle history as well as status along with the house.

"She's fine," Grandma said. "Edwards takes excellent care of her."

"Does she miss me terribly? Can you not bring her to me?" Almira's chin trembled. She dabbed her eyes with a lace-trimmed hankie.

Each morning, Amity stopped before the painting, dropped a curtsy, wiped away a fake tear, and said, "Sleep tight, dearest Mama, and don't let the bedbugs bite," while Edwards looked on with approval. Other than that, she never appeared to give a thought to her mother.

Almira, however, mourned her daughter long after her own death. According to Edwards, grief for the lost little girl sent her mother to her grave. The Victorian fainting couch in Mom's room once belonged to Almira. She'd spent the twenty years between losing her daughter and her own demise reclining on it.

"Now, you know better," Grandma said.

Almira sighed, a good trick for a corseted ghost. "You've grown," she said to Marti. "Not into a lady, but grown."

"It happens," Marti said and regretted it. Amity hadn't grown. Sending Almira into a fit of the vapors wasn't in her own best interest. Many of the lingering spirits lived during the Bickle era. Almira ruled the cemetery like Mom ruled—or once ruled—Bicklesburg. Having Almira Bickle by her side while she crept through the graveyard added a layer of protection beyond anything her great-grandmother provided. If she distressed their former doyenne, Grandma Bertie might not be able to hold them back.

"Why are you dressed so slovenly? Are you a farmer? A convict?" No vapors. There was more steel in the dead woman than Marti expected. She eyed Marti's sweatshirt and jeans.

Even the dead had something to say about her wardrobe.

"I'm between jobs," Marti said. They reached the edge of the graveyard. She put the hood of her sweatshirt up and pulled it tight around her face. Not much of a disguise, but with the number of surveillance cameras on the Avenue, there was no reason to think the well-lit impound lot wasn't similarly equipped.

Since her last visit, the high chain-link fence had grown by a few feet and acquired a crown of coiled barbed wire. Good thing she didn't intend on scaling it.

The lot was near-empty. A red Chevy with a crumbled fender, a blue Taurus much newer and in better shape than hers, a silver Honda CRV—no hulking black Cadillac Escalade.

"I don't see it," Marti said.

"Listen up." Grandma addressed the assembled dead. She described the McDonagh SUV and asked if anyone had seen it.

Marti hoped at least one of them paid attention to the comings and goings next door. It wasn't like they had anything else to keep them entertained.

"The monster is inside." The booming voice came from a tiny, hunchbacked wraith. Marti couldn't see his face. She assumed it was a he because he wore pants, and those in the oldest part of Oakdale Gardens were buried in a time when women didn't. At least not in Bicklesburg.

"Inside where?" she asked.

"Death rolls with all of us," he intoned.

"Billson was a little . . . eccentric . . . when he was alive," Almira said. "It has worsened through the years." She let loose with another dramatic sigh. "I believe what you are looking for is inside that hideous building."

Engrossed in ghosts and cars, Marti hadn't looked at the station itself. A squat garage, added recently from the color of the brick, stood annexed to the main building. No windows. Unlike the fire truck bays, the overhead door was closed and, Marti guessed, locked tight. A town the size of Bicklesburg was unlikely to have its own crackerjack team of forensic investigators. The Escalade was likely inside awaiting someone from the state police.

"Grandma?"

Grandma Bertie scrutinized the distance to the building. "You're going to need to be a bit closer."

Marti and cortege crept along the fence. She stuck to the shadows and hoped she was hidden from any cameras.

"Skulking is unbecoming," Almira said.

"I think we're close enough," Marti said. To her relief, Grandma agreed.

"You'll be all right here?" Grandma said.

"I'll protect her as if she is my own," Almira said.

"The wrath of monsters shall be averted," Billson said.

"Make it fast," Marti said.

Alberta Marcile Ferguson, unstoppable by fences or locked doors or brick walls, went in search of Ralph McDonagh.

"One dead fish. No Ralph," Grandma reported.

"Did you check the entire garage? Maybe he didn't stay inside the car."

"The devil roams the earth like a lion," Billson said.

"Of course." Grandma gave her a withering look. "I think that car is bigger than our last apartment, but it sure has a cramped front seat. I don't know how that long drink of water ever fit in it."

"The seat moves." Marti met Grandma's wither with a "duh" look. "Just like the Taurus used to." The Taurus driver's seat was stuck in one position for so long, Grandma probably forgot, but Marti wasn't about to cut her any slack. "Forward, backward, up, down, with what that thing cost, it ought to come out and fly around the room on command."

"My. You are a disrespectful young woman," Almira said.

"You see what I have to put up with?" Grandma said.

"You're *sure* Ralph isn't there? You weren't gone long." The seat bothered Marti. In the So-nutt-ee Donut parking lot, Ralph towered over his wife, and Sheila wore heels. Maybe someone, either out-of-town expert or local expert-wannabe, already examined the SUV and moved the seat.

"Are *you* sure you didn't imagine him? You've been under a lot of stress lately." Grandma poured on the put-upon act. Almira was a sympathetic audience.

"Let's go." Marti turned to find a sea of ghosts. From the look of it, every haunt in Oakdale Memorial Gardens joined the retinue while she wasn't paying attention.

"We don't get much excitement here," Almira said.

"The sea claims us all," Billson declared.

"Grandma? I can't." Marti's voice quivered. She'd stand there all night, let Big find her in the morning, let RachelAnne send her back to the Birches—no way was she walking into the shimmering, icy wall of the dead.

Alberta Marcile Ferguson lifted her hand. Almira Bickle nodded her consent. The sea parted.

Grandma and Almira flanked her. Billson fell in behind her. They didn't look like bodyguards, but they were better than the Secret Service. Marti kept her eyes on the ground in front of her and walked—but didn't run—to the TT unmolested.

"Kiss my little girl for me," Almira said.

"I will," Marti said. She had no intention of kissing the ghost girl herself, but she would pass the request to Edwards.

"The sinners shall be taken," Billson said.

"Time to go," Grandma said.

"I DID SEE him." Marti turned the key and the TT purred. "I'm not crazy." She realized she wanted Ralph McDonagh to be dead to prove her right and felt like scum. "You didn't see anything in the Escalade? Tonight, I mean."

"Just that dead fish," Grandma said.

"Maybe he's wherever they found the car. One of the ponds outside of town. We can look for him." Even if Ralph was dead, there was no guarantee he was hanging around anywhere, but she had to check.

"How many ponds are there?"

"A lot." Between reporters and The Judge's cameras, Marti didn't know how she'd get out of the house to visit them all. "It'll take a while."

"Why don't we go to the station and ask?" Grandma said.

"Yeah. Like Big will tell me. *Sure, Marti Cray-Cray. Let me fill you in on my investigation.*"

"Don't get shirty with me, little girl. Billy Fysh may be the *current* chief of police, but he's hardly the only one."

"One-Eye Stash."

"Don't call him that."

Eustace Cunningham, aka One-Eye Stash was once The Law, capitalization required, in Bicklesburg. After losing an eye as a wild young newlywed, either in a barroom brawl or to a wife with no patience for his extracurricular shenanigans depending on which story you believed, he grew a prodigious black handlebar mustache and reformed. If the legends were true, her zero-tolerance father was a bleeding-heart charity worker compared to Stash. In his day, wrongdoers seldom made it to court. He believed in swift justice, right up until the day he disappeared.

The mystery of his disappearance was never solved, but a century later, he still considered himself a member of Bicklesburg's finest.

Death didn't kill his eye for the ladies. He wasn't fond of Marti, but like most old dead guys, he thought Grandma Bertie was just swell.

"Grandma, I love you." Great-Grandma Bertie was the best networker from beyond the grave ever.

"I know, dear."

THE AUTOMATIC GARAGE door went up. The TT's headlights illuminated both the interior and the man looming in the middle of her parking place.

Marti hit the gas pedal and gunned the car. If the TT didn't have excellent brakes, she would have barreled through the back wall.

She figured The Judge's leap to the side was conditioned reflex. It wasn't like she could hurt him.

"Was that really necessary?" Her father appeared in the backseat.

"No, but it was fun." She got out and locked the car. As expected, he followed.

"Sure was," Grandma said.

"Where were you?" he demanded.

"More to the point, where have *you* been?"

"That is my business, not yours."

"Speaking of your business, you want to fill me in on it? For a dead guy, you're getting pretty famous. And not in a good way."

"Also none of your concern. Are you any closer to discovering who murdered me?"

"For the umpteenth time, no one murdered you," Grandma said.

"I hear they're still looking for Ralph. He couldn't have been your biggest fan," Marti said.

"Ralph McDonagh did not kill me. He had no reason to."

"Um, Sheila? His wife? Your girlfriend? He was good with all that?"

"I told you. Sheila and I were finished years ago."

Interesting. He didn't claim Ralph didn't know about the affair, only that it was over. "When did he find out about the two of you?" Marti asked.

The Judge glowered.

"Recently?" she continued. "He found out what you'd been doing all those years he was on the road and lost it? Or maybe he knew all along. Simmering rage, building over the years, finally coming to a boil, and he couldn't stand the thought of you and his wife and—"

"Stop. I was worth more to him alive than dead."

"What?"

"Sheila and I broke it off when he found out. She wasn't aging well anyway. I paid him to keep quiet. Not a lot, but regularly and in cash."

"Ralph McDonagh was *blackmailing* you?"

"I don't like to think of it that way. He was a write-off. A nothing. I didn't want your mother to find out."

"Well, he put one over on you, didn't he? Mom knew all along. And what did the lovely Sheila have to say about this?"

"She didn't know."

"What makes you think so?"

"She was smarter than he is. He's an idiot. He could have asked for a lot more money. She would have."

"I don't think he *is*. I think he *was*. I think he's dead too."

The Judge snorted.

"I saw him. In the Escalade."

He turned to Grandma Bertie. "She's still stuck on that? I didn't see him. You didn't see him."

Grandma shrugged. "If Marti says she saw him, she did."

Whether Grandma believed her or wanted to argue with The Judge, he fell for it.

"This is not good," The Judge said. "If he is dead, you have to find out who killed him."

"Why do you care? I'm pretty sure he can't blackmail you anymore."

"He said he had an insurance policy, right out of a bad movie. The man has no imagination. He wrote a letter. I don't know where he left it or what it says, but he said if anything happened to him, I'd be sorry."

"Dad. You're d-e-a-d. What can he do to you?"

"My reputation."

"Have you been paying attention? I don't think you've got much of a reputation left. At least not one worth protecting."

"Pfft. That's nothing."

"Seriously? You're national news—and not of the good sort."

"Shhhh. Keep your voice down," Grandma said.

"I did nothing wrong. Anything I may *allegedly* have done, I did for the good of the county." The Judge lowered his voice.

"Great. Now he listens to me," Grandma said. "You're not the one I was talking to."

"Taking money in exchange for locking up kids? Kids like Dmitri?" Marti didn't care who heard her.

"It certainly straightened him out. And I took nothing for myself. I did it for the greater good."

"What? You did it for the puppies and kittens? For starving orphans in third-world countries?"

"Ms. Mickkleson? Are you all right? Who are you yell—talking to?" A young man in an ACS uniform stood in front of the open garage door.

"No one. I'm the crazy daughter. Didn't anyone tell you?" She strode past him and let herself into the house.

"Back door open. Back door open," Harriet said.

"Oh, shut up." Marti slammed the door. The sound echoed in the night, loud enough to wake the dead. If they weren't already awake and making her life miserable.

SIXTEEN

"Albion Court Security. Doyle speaking."

"Don't you *ever* sleep?" For the first time, Marti used her phone to make a call rather than fake a call. It felt a little strange to hear Dmitri's voice coming from the thing instead of Grandma's or The Judge's coming from beside or behind her.

"Hi, Marti. I took last night off. Which is more than I heard you did."

"I went for a drive. To clear my head."

"Uh-huh. What's up? Something wrong?"

"Nothing that wasn't wrong yesterday. I need to run into town. Can I get by the vultures? RachelAnne said they swarmed her in the alley yesterday."

"They're all over the place. Not only have they made the connection between your dad and Sheila, they got ahold of a photo of your mother holding the alleged murder weapon."

"Mr. Stumpy?"

"Yeah. Even better. That fire last night? The McDonaghs' house. The story, as they say, has legs."

Like a freaking centipede. "So, if I run down one or two it would be a bad thing?"

"I'm thinking you should just stay in."

"I need to go to the store. It's an emergency. You know, wimminny-stuff." One more little white lie.

"You couldn't have done it last night?" He wasn't fazed.

"It wasn't an issue."

"Here's a hint. Next time you go for a drive to clear your head, do your yelling in the car where no one can hear you."

"Oh gosh, that wasn't recorded, was it?" She was so fed up with The Judge, she forgot the ever-present cameras.

"Just you leaving and coming back. No sound on the video."

"Then how . . . ?"

"Richie saw you pull into the garage and not come out, so he went to check on you. You about scared him to death."

"I'm sorry. It's been more than a little strange since I got back." Since before she left Franklinville, but that was on a need-to-know basis and Dmitri didn't need to know. "I needed to blow off some steam. I'm sorry I scared your baby guard."

"He's not as young as he looks. He's Rodney's brother."

"Of course he is."

"I told him your bark was worse than your bite."

"You're confusing me with my mother." Another lie. Mom's bark was delivered with a spoonful of honey. Her bite was vicious. "We are a lot alike."

"You could be twins."

Oh my gosh. He was flirting with her. Or insulting her. She was so bad at the game she found it hard to tell the difference. "We do have the same fashion sense."

"Let me guess. Today's sweatshirt has a DAR logo?"

"Exactly, because I'm going to town. One must set an example for the lesser life forms inhabiting our fair hamlet. Can I get out?"

"How about if I find someone to go to the store for you? Or you call the store if you're embarrassed at involving me in your *wimminny stuff*. Your parents have things delivered all the time. Your mom does."

"I need to take the donut receipt to Big. You said it was important."

"I can deliver it for you."

He *really* didn't want her going out. Maybe he thought she'd put on a show for the vultures like she put on for Richie, which was ridiculous. If she'd known Baby Guard was listening, she would have been louder and far more colorful.

"I have to stop at Peter's place. The car lot. The receipt was in the Taurus when they hauled it off. Besides, isn't there something about chain of evidence?"

"You watch too much TV. Big trusts me."

"But I'm not sure I do." Shopping was a lie. The receipt was an excuse. Time for some truth. At least part of it. "Look, I have to get out of this house. I'm going stir crazy. Mom doesn't need me. She's got Myrna. I am going out. I'm leaving in ten, fifteen minutes. Watch the cameras." As if he wasn't glued to them already. "You'll see me coming. Any vultures get in my way, I'm taking them out. It would be a shame to dent my mother's pretty little car." She cut the connection before he could reply. Dmitri was much more eloquent on the phone than in person.

"Come on, Grandma," she said. "Time for you to schmooze an old friend."

Grandma Bertie's grin made Marti think the old ghost was enjoying the detecting thing a little too much. She hoped that was where the grin came from.

It better not have anything to do with Dmitri Doyle.

HER FIRST STOP was Rudawski Motors, business base of her brother-in-law, the county's used-car king. Or maybe he was the crown prince. Marti didn't know if the nice old man she remembered from the car lot was still alive, and as long as he wasn't haunting her, she didn't care. When she was last a Bicklesburg resident, the car lot was isolated outside of town, a necessary evil. The elder Rudawski had a gentlemen's agreement with the powers-that-were not to sell anything too embarrassing. The plebs needed transportation, but that transportation needed to meet a certain standard. The beaters, like her Taurus, were purchased out of town and ended up ticketed and towed so often they weren't worth keeping.

Peter's long-ago attempt to commercialize the Avenue failed, but, according to RachelAnne, he had his fingers in a multitude of pots. Her sister was vague on what those pots held, "investments, real estate, that sort of thing," but said the car lot remained his base of operations. There was a good chance he'd be there. If not, someone would know the fate of her car.

The car lot hadn't moved, but the expanding town had engulfed it. She drove past the So-nutt-ee without stopping and turned at the red Hummer—she assumed it was the same one. After all, how many could there be? It sat in a choice location by the street, *SALE!* painted in florescent letters across its front window. And side windows. And back window. Peter must be having trouble unloading the beast.

She parked near the showroom building. Peter was on the lot. He stood by a late-model compact car, working a sweet young thing. He leaned forward and brushed the woman's arm. She giggled. He moved in closer. In a bar, his body language would take on a whole different meaning. He was old enough to be her father, but from the looks of things, she was buying whatever he was selling. For her sister's sake, Marti hoped it was the car.

"I'll just wait here," Grandma said.

"Don't want to say hello to your great-grandson-in-law?"

"Don't be a brat." Grandma shut her eyes and pretended to lean back and go to sleep.

Marti wasn't fooled. Ghosts didn't sleep. She got out of the TT, and a beaming young man in khakis and a pale-yellow button-down shirt hustled over.

"You must be Peter's sister-in-law. What can I help you with?" His name tag identified him as *JASON-SALES*. He took in her sweatshirt of the day.

Considering her reputation in Bicklesburg, "I have reason to believe the squirrels are mocking me" might not have been her wisest fashion choice. She thought it hilarious when she discovered it in the Franklinville Goodwill store looking like new.

"You must be one of Peter's minions. Nothing. I'll wait for the boss." She wondered how he knew who she was. She'd never met him. He didn't bear the mark of any Bicklesburg clan she remembered.

"If your mother ever wants to sell this baby, I'll take it off her hands." Jason caressed the hood of the TT, his expression not unlike a hyena salivating over a fresh kill—and not unlike the look Peter gave his little blonde customer.

He recognized Mom's car, not her—perfectly understandable. "Down, boy. I've got dibs." She'd steal the little roadster before she let Jason-Sales or anyone else but Mom behind the wheel. Unless Myrna was willing to give up the Camaro. Then, she might consider a trade.

"Well, if you or your mother find yourselves in need of cash . . ." Sales Boy didn't finish his sentence. He blushed and studied a far-off point somewhere over her shoulder.

It hadn't dawned on her The Judge's misdeeds could leave her mother broke. She wasn't worried about herself. She couldn't end up in much worse shape—financially, anyway—than she started, but the terms *Margaret Mickkleson* and *penniless*, used in tandem and made real, could prove cataclysmic. RachelAnne mentioned things already being in Mom's name when The Judge died. Out of character, considering how tightfisted he was with the purse strings when she was growing up, but maybe Mom was safe.

"He's a pro," Jason said.

"Who?" Marti said.

"The boss." Jason didn't add "he's my hero," but she heard it anyway.

"Marti!" Peter and his mark walked toward them.

The young woman was older than Marti first thought. Young, but not jailbait. It was a toss-up whether she or Peter looked more pleased with themselves.

"Let me take Megan here to my finance guy, and I'll be right with you." He patted Megan's arm and puffed up like a rooster when she giggled. He didn't appear to notice her slight cringe at the physical contact, but Marti did.

"This way, m'dear." Peter the Paragon of Courtly Manners made Marti's skin crawl.

Megan winked at Marti, who choked back a laugh. If the wink meant what she thought—and she was sure it did—Peter was the one who got played. She hoped Megan charmed a good deal out of her slime-ball brother-in-law.

Peter wasn't gone long. "So. Your heap is dead. Not even good for parts. Take a look around. I can set you up with something. Drive it off the lot today."

"I think I'll stick to the TT for a while." And when she had to give it up, she wasn't buying anything Peter was selling. "Where's my car? I need to get something from it." A movement inside the Hummer caught her eye.

"In the back. Tell me what you're after and I'll send someone."

"I'd rather get it myself." She stared across the lot at the red monster. Someone was inside. The question was, was that someone dead or alive?

Or was she imagining it?

"Are you okay? You seeing things? You're not going to flip out on me or anything?" Peter said.

"Do you lock the cars on the lot?" A better question than "So, did anybody die inside your red monstrosity?" She wasn't imagining anything. Unlike Ralph, whoever was inside the Hummer didn't disappear.

"What? I'm sure your car is locked. Although as far as I could tell, there was nothing in it but trash."

The side door swung open. Definitely an alive somebody. "No—there. Your Hummer."

Weasel Boy vaulted from the beast and waved. "Hi, Marti!"

"Hey!" Peter took off at a run. He was no match for Weasel Boy, who was younger, wearing sneakers as opposed to shiny loafers, and from the way Peter panted and wheezed when he returned, in much better shape. His beet-colored flush was probably 50 percent exertion and 50 percent pissed off.

"Friend of yours?" Peter croaked between gasps.

"No." Marti saw no need to elaborate. Weasel Boy wasn't her friend. He was shaping up to be her personal pain in the butt, but not her friend.

"We don't usually operate like this. Somebody's fired. You sure you don't know that guy? Sounded like he knew you."

Marti recalculated. Sixty percent pissed off.

"So, where's my car?" she said.

Peter went off to behead a serf or two. Apparently Jason-Sales wasn't in charge of locking the Hummer and still had his job. He accompanied her to the back lot.

Her poor Taurus sat hidden from street view, alone and dejected.

The salesman held out her key and a plastic bag plastered with Peter's grinning face. "If there's anything in the glove box or trunk or wherever you want, you can use this."

The inside of the Taurus was cleaner than when she bought it. Years of car trash, including the donut bag and empty coffee cup, were gone. The receipt was history.

She handed the empty bag back to Jason-Sales. "Junk it all." She had no attachment to the car or anything in it.

TELLING BIG THE receipt was no more was as good of an excuse to visit the station as giving it to him.

Weasel Boy was an even better excuse. He qualified as a reason. Not only was he possibly stalking her, he was around for two fires, the Franklinville Burger Buster and the McDonagh house. Probably nothing more than a coincidence. She was around for both too. If nothing else, maybe Big would send Rodney to question him, and an encounter with the police would send Weasel Boy and his mother running. She had enough to deal with without him popping up everywhere she turned.

One-Eye met them at the door. "Alberta! Welcome home!" No greeting for Marti. "That family of yours has been creating quite a stir around here—and it has nothing to do with that one." At least he acknowledged her presence.

"Eustace," Grandma said. "Still as dashing as ever."

Watching her great-grandmother flirt with the old crank made seeing Big look like fun. She headed for the front desk. "I need to speak with Chief Fysh."

"He's in a meeting. Can I get someone else to help you? What is this in reference to?"

The woman behind the counter was either adopted or a Bicklesburg newcomer. Marti didn't recognize her, and she didn't recognize Marti.

"I'm Marcile Mickkleson. I'd like to speak with Chief Fysh, please." She was a Mickkleson in a place where it meant something. She might as well use it. She'd watched her mother in action for enough years to know how to do it. Either that, or she'd absorbed some Mom Fu through the seats of the TT. Whichever, the Mickkleson command voice worked.

"Wait right here, Ms. Mickkleson. I will see if he has a minute." The worker bee scuttled off and returned with the police chief.

"Marti!" Somewhere along the line, the former football star added jovial to his repertoire. Bicklesburg hired their police chiefs, but if Big ever ran for county sheriff, glad-handing would take him further than Fysh Smash. "Would you like to step into my office?"

Said the spider to the fly, Marti thought.

"Go," Grandma said. "Give Eustace here and me time to catch up." She batted her eyes at Big's long-dead predecessor.

"Lead the way," Marti said.

Big unfolded a metal chair and placed it in front of his utilitarian desk.

"Have a seat," he said.

The desk's chipped green paint was popular in the last century but not old enough to fit the Bicklesburg style. News of the paperless revolution hadn't made it to the station. File cabinets lined two walls, making the small room even more cramped. Depressing gray enamel covered the cinderblock walls. Brown paper blocked the single window, and the fluorescent overhead light flickered. In a pinch, Big's office could double as a torture chamber.

Big took his seat in a cracked vinyl chair behind the desk. The cushion sighed.

"Nice digs," Marti said.

"The budget here goes for personnel, not interior decorating."

"Must need a lot of personnel."

"The town's changed since you left. More people means more crime. Most of it minor, until this week. Listen, Marti . . ." He squirmed. His chair squeaked. He picked up a pen and tapped it against the desk.

She steeled herself for bad news.

"I owe you an apology," he continued.

Not at all what she expected. "For what?"

"Saturday. When I called you . . . that name. It just came out. I should know better."

It was her turn to squirm. She accepted apologies with less grace than she accepted compliments. Not that she had a whole lot of experience with either. "Don't worry about it. It's Bicklesburg. I'm used to it."

Big eyed her sweatshirt. Her face burned. "Don't worry," she said. "I don't think you're a squirrel."

Big blinked. "Okay then." He put down the pen, picked it up again. "How's your mother holding up?"

"As well as can be expected." She was grateful for the change of subject but had no desire to discuss her mother with him if she could avoid it. "I came about the donut store receipt. It's gone. My car died. Peter had it towed to his garage, and someone there cleaned the inside. They thought it was trash. Because it was."

"I heard—about the towing, not the cleaning. From what I

understand, if you can get a few more years out of it, it'll qualify for classic car plates."

She was wrong. Big was a squirrel, but he didn't appear overly concerned about the receipt. "The Taurus appears to be terminal. It's headed off to the big car lot in the sky."

She waited for him to make a crack about it haunting her. He wanted to. She saw it. The battle between High School Big and Chief of Police Fysh played across his face. Chief Fysh won.

"The receipt's not important," he said. "It was a formality. We know the McDonaghs were at the So-nutt-ee, and what time they left. We know what time you arrived on Albion Court. Unless bending time and space is among your talents, you're off the hook."

"I had no reason to be on it."

A small earthquake, which Marti interpreted as a shrug, shook the chief's mountainous shoulders. He not only still lived up to his nickname, he'd acquired some padding. If he wasn't careful, he'd end up Extra Large Fysh. Maybe XXL. Marti smiled.

"Well. If that's all you came for, I guess we're finished. You could have called, you know," he said.

"I was in town anyway. Checking on my car. Looking for the receipt." No sign of Grandma yet. By now, she should have finished flirting and moved on to info extraction. Unless she and One-Eye were having such a grand time, she forgot why she was there. And that she was supposed to come retrieve Marti when her mission was accomplished. In which case, Marti would, well, do nothing. There wasn't much, if anything, she could do to a woman dead for thirty-two years.

"There is something else," she said.

The mountain didn't move. Maybe a twitch of the eyebrows, but she wouldn't swear to it.

"There's this kid. Well, young man, I guess." She proceeded to tell Big about Weasel Boy. He stayed quiet and let her talk. She spun the story out as long as she could. His expression went from skeptical to bored. "Oh yeah. He doesn't drive. His mother brought him here." She sounded lame, even to her own ears. "That's about it," she finished. Where was Grandma?

Big's eyes were glazed. She wondered if he was awake.

"What's this Weas—Darrell 'Something or other' look like?" Mount Fysh was awake and had listened.

"You remember Jughead from the *Archie* comics? Give him dirty-blond hair. And pimples. Shorten the nose—but not all that much. And get rid of the hat."

"Really. And you say he's in Bicklesburg?" Big was more than skeptical, he was downright condescending.

"Dmitri saw him." Their bromance ought to lend her credibility.

"And you say he has a history of setting fires?"

"I didn't say that."

"What are you saying?" Mister Apologetic was gone.

"I'm just saying he was there when the Franklinville Burger Buster caught fire, and he was here when the McDonagh house burned. And he's a little weird." *A little weird.* She waited for him to make a pot-kettle comment.

"How do you know he was at the Franklinville fire?" The pen was still in his hand. Instead of playing with it, he wrote on a small white pad.

"I saw him." She strained to see what he wrote. He was a pro. He wrote with one hand and blocked her view with the other.

"So you were there too."

This wasn't going at all like she planned.

"I was driving by and stopped to see what was going on."

"Why?"

"I worked there. I wanted to know if I still had a job or not."

"You worked there?" Big's smug smile sent Marti straight back to high school. Maybe he'd try to stuff her into a locker. Or one of the filing cabinets.

"Look. Forget about it. I should get going." Grandma must have gotten anything she was going to get out of One-Eye. They were probably floating around a jail cell making eyes at each other. Making eye, in Eustace's case.

"Why did you say this Darrell 'Something or other' is in Bicklesburg?"

She hadn't. She'd hoped to avoid that. "He has some sort of misguided crush on me. He followed me here."

Big leaned back in his chair and crossed his legs. Marti hoped he'd topple over. He'd bounce off the wall behind him before he hit the floor. The entertainment value would be high.

"Talk to my brother-in-law," she said. "Weasel Boy was at the car lot today. Inside the bright red Hummer."

"You think he's stalking you?" Big sat up straight. "He could be one of those damned reporters."

"That's possible, but not likely."

"Got the scoop," Grandma said. "Let's go."

Marti stood, a little too fast. The metal chair fell with a clatter.

"What's wrong?" Big said.

"Time to blow this popcorn stand," Grandma said. Edwards was rubbing off on her.

"Nothing," Marti said. "Talk to Dmitri. He got rid of Weasel—Darrell when he showed up at Bickle House. I need to go."

"I'll check into it," Big said. "You sure you're okay?"

"I'm good." The overhead light flickered. "You should get a decorator in here, or at least a handyman. That light's giving me a headache."

"I'll check into it."

"You should make a list. I need to get home. Check on my mother."

"I'm sure Myrna Ward has everything under control," he said.

"You haven't seen the state of the family parlor."

Big gave her a funny look, but he came around the desk and held the door open for her.

"Such a gentleman," Grandma said.

SEVENTEEN

SHE GOT INTO THE CAR AND TOOK OUT HER PHONE. INSTEAD of putting it to her ear, she held it, swiped at the screen a few times, and made her pretend call on pretend speakerphone. If the mobile phone company knew, they'd institute a special beyond-the-grave extra-long-distance fee.

"You look ridiculous," Grandma said.

"Somebody's always watching, especially when you don't want them to," Marti said. "Number four, maybe three, on the list of rules of small-town life." With all the security cameras on the Avenue, maybe she should promote it to rule one. "What did old One-Eye have to say?"

"His name is Eustace."

"He doesn't seem to mind One-Eye."

"Don't believe everything you hear."

"Okay. What did Ewww-staaaace have to say?"

Grandma gave her the don't-get-snotty-with-me-young-lady look. "I am as lovely and enchanting as ever. You, on the other hand, need to clean yourself up. In his day, Eustace would have pulled you in for vagrancy—or worse—and run you out of town. He says, by the way, that he's judging you by today's standard of dress, not the far higher standards of his own day."

"Everyone's a critic. Ralph? What did he say about Ralph?"

"Oh, there's been more than a bit of a fuss in the station about *that*." Grandma preened like a peacock.

Whatever Grandma Bertie heard from the late police chief, she thought it was good. After dealing with Big, Marti didn't have the patience or inclination to wheedle the story out of her bit by bit. "Spill it."

Grandma rolled her eyes and heaved her chest in an exaggerated sigh.

"You need to stop that. It's unbecoming. Talk," Marti said.

"You have no sense of drama."

"Grand-maaaa."

"Don't whine. *That's* unbecoming. Well. Let's see. First, Ralph McDonagh is the number-one suspect in Sheila's death. Just like in the movies. The spouse is always the first suspect."

"One-Eye's seen a lot of movies?"

"No, but thanks to you, I have. Do you want me to continue or not?"

"Sorry. Keep going."

"They have all sorts of bulletins or whatever out all over the state, but haven't found a trace of him. His credit cards haven't been used, but they were all at their limits anyway. They were maxed once this month, paid off, and used to the hilt again. No activity since Saturday."

So far, nothing Grandma said suggested Ralph was still alive, but if he killed his wife and took off, he could, despite The Judge's assessment of him, be smart enough not to leave a paper trail.

She was certain he was dead. She saw him sitting, stunned, in the SUV driver's seat as clearly as she saw her great-grandmother sitting next to her. The clarity might be memory enhancement, but it convinced her Dead Ralph wasn't her imagination. Or a hallucination. "What about the Escalade?"

"A pair of courting kids noticed tire tracks going into Billings Pond. You know which one that is?"

Marti nodded. She didn't want to get Grandma off track. She was on a roll. Billings Pond was at the end of a long road—dirt in her day and she doubted anyone bothered to pave it. Isolated and surrounded by woods, it was popular with generation after generation of local teenagers. "Courting kids" was a euphemism for any number of things. Whatever the kids were up to at Billings Pond, it was a wonder they noticed the tire tracks.

"They didn't do anything right away."

Probably doing something they didn't want to admit, Marti thought.

"But the next morning, the girl went to the station and reported it. The pond's not deep. In the sunshine, the Escalade was visible at the bottom."

Whoever put it there, whether it was Sheila's killer and maybe Ralph's—or Ralph himself—didn't care if it was found. Billings Pond didn't often draw a crowd in the daytime, but the SUV was bound to be discovered eventually.

"They hauled out the car, but found no sign of Ralph McDonagh." Grandma paused. "That's about it."

"Are they looking at anyone else? Or just looking for Ralph?"

"According to Eustace, the official suspect is Ralph, although there's still a contingent sure your mother did it."

"And she'll be eloping with him any day now," Marti said.

"That's the popular theory. Young Chief Fysh doesn't believe it, though."

Big earned back a point he'd lost during their talk.

"There is one more wrinkle," Grandma said. "Ralph McDonagh has a sister."

"Or had," Marti said.

"Whatever. She is definitely alive and well. She showed up at the station yesterday and delivered an envelope with a note from her brother. It said 'If anything happens to me, Thaddeus Mickkleson did it. Don't let him get away with it.'"

"Ralph's 'insurance policy.' That's all it said?"

"Yep. They verified Ralph's signature, but since your father passed before he disappeared they aren't taking it too seriously."

"*Too* seriously?"

"Some think it lends credence to the rumors about Ralph and your mother."

214 KAY CHARLES

The police didn't know about the blackmail.

"Did One—Eustace hear anything about The Judge's other mess?"

"The local police aren't allowed anywhere near *that* investigation. Eustace isn't happy at the good name of the Bicklesburg justice system being dragged through the mud. It's not what your father did or didn't do, mind you. It's because he got caught. Eustace never liked your father—he's very perceptive—and if he ever gets his hands on him, Thaddeus is in trouble."

"He can pop The Judge one for me." Marti checked the time. For all her messing around at Rudawski Motors and the police station, it wasn't as late as she thought. She could, as she'd told Big, head home and check in on her mother. Which would mean leaving again if she wanted to visit the pond, an action Dmitri or Richie or the vultures would note. Mom was in good hands with Myrna—she survived just dandy before Marti's return. Billings Road wasn't far out of her way.

"I think we'll take a little detour on the way home." Marti pretend hung up her pretend call.

"Let's roll," Grandma said.

They didn't roll far. Marti no sooner left the Municipal Center parking lot when she was forced to pull over for flashing lights and sirens. Four police cars, two fire trucks, and an ambulance flew past.

Sticking to the speed limit on the square wasn't a problem. Vulture vans tied up traffic in front of the courthouse. Baby Face Rodney leapt from a cruiser and started directing traffic. Marti decided against putting down her window and asking what was going on.

A vulture followed by a cameraman ran across the street. She recognized them, the same duo who rang the Bickle House doorbell. The excitement probably had something to do with the charges against The Judge. She'd hear about it soon enough.

Dirt roads weren't Mom's style, and Marti doubted the TT had ever seen one. It handled Billings Road well, but she hoped the dust wasn't a shock to its system. She should find a car wash before heading home. The grime was a dead giveaway she'd done more than run into town, and more important, she wasn't about to risk scratching the pretty paint job.

She took a sharp right off Billings onto a narrow access road. A few yards in, she stopped and cut the engine.

"We'll walk from here," she said. The gravel and dirt of the road was one thing, but the TT wasn't built for the glorified cow path leading to the pond.

"I remember this place," Grandma said with a hint of disapproval.

Back when Marti snuck out to meet Dmitri at Billings Pond, Grandma's disapproval was a full-on assault.

"It's a wonder those youngsters noticed anything," Grandma said.

Good point. Every few years, the adult contingent—all of whom had enjoyed their own youthful adventures in the land of teenage vice—made noises about putting a stop to the fun. It always blew over. Billings Pond was as much a Bicklesburg tradition as the Founders' Day Parade.

"There's Parson Morely." Grandma waved. The morose spirit in the black frock coat turned his back on them. "So sad," she said, unbothered by the lack of greeting.

Billings Pond was rumored to be haunted, and like most places, it was. The tales were half-right. The ghost was correct, but stories of Parson Morely drowning himself, heartbroken over his ladylove eloping with a salesman from the big city (which city remained unspecified) were the product of adolescent romantic yearnings. Morely died after a drunken fall from his horse. He'd lain undiscovered for days before dying.

Marti doubted he ever had a ladylove, but the reality of his death was sadder than the legend. Not ending up a modern version of Morely ranked high on her priority list.

"Maybe he saw something," Grandma said.

"We'll ask on our way out," Marti said. Parson Morely was one of the few, if not the only, of Bicklesburg's truly old-time residents not completely enamored with Grandma Bertie. Prying information from him wouldn't be easy. Talking to him was depressing.

The access road lead straight into the pond. Broken yellow police tape fluttered in the breeze, tied in bows on the temporary posts stuck in the ground to support it. Without a live cop guarding the scene, the plastic tape proved more temptation than deterrent to the kids. The number of empty cans on the ground suggested a recent party. Marti reckoned the place was hopping the night before, after word got out of the Escalade's discovery.

The churned mud where the road—such as it was—ran into the pond held boot prints, ruts from the vehicles used to retrieve the Escalade, and sneaker prints. She assumed the last were left by whomever emptied the cans. The tire tracks were gone.

No sign of Ralph McDonagh.

She and Grandma appeared to be the only ones there, but she couldn't be sure. Anyone could be lurking in the woods surrounding the pond. In fact, she hoped Ralph was lurking. As long as it was Dead Ralph. She hadn't considered what she would do if she came face to face with Live Ralph. Live Ralph was more than likely a murderer. The dead, she could deal with. She had practice. Dead murderers, she didn't know whether she had experience with them or not, but they didn't scare her. A real live murderer was a different matter.

If Ralph killed his wife, he was long gone by now.

Probably.

"Grandma, holler for Ralph," Marti said. A live Ralph wasn't her only problem. If anyone alive heard her shouting for him, it wouldn't do her reputation any good. Or her mother's. No one but the dead would hear her great-grandmother. No one other than her.

"Ralph! Ralph McDonagh!"

No answer. Marti squinted and studied the trees. She might have seen a flash of movement. She wasn't sure. "Again," she said. "Give it your best bellow. Wake the dead."

"*Ralph McDonagh*. Get your handsome self out here!" Grandma shouted. "A little flattery never hurt," she said to Marti, knocking off a few decibels.

"There!" Marti pointed to the tree line, sure she spotted their quarry.

"Where? I don't see him—Ralph!" Grandma looked wildly to her left and right.

"There, right in front of us. In the shadows—" Marti's phone went off. "I should have left the stupid thing in the car." She pulled it from her pocket.

Ralph disappeared.

"Crap. Did you see him?" Marti was positive she saw Sheila's husband, the departed version, but wanted confirmation.

"Maybe," Grandma Bertie said without much conviction. "Are you going to answer that thing?"

The iPhone stopped ringing. The words *Missed call from Dmitri* popped up on the screen.

"Double crap," Marti said. She could call him back now, but she'd end up lying about where she was. She could ignore it and pretend she was driving when he called. He'd approve of her not answering the phone when behind the wheel.

She couldn't come up with a single good reason for him to be calling, only bad reasons. Mom. Weasel Boy. Before she made up her mind what to do, the phone chirped, and *New Voice Mail from Dmitri* appeared above the first message.

Maybe he wanted to ask if she wanted lime with her next Corona.

She found the voice mail and hit play.

"Marti. Where are you? Big says you left ages ago. You need to get home. Now. Your mother's gone. Again."

Triple crap. "Come on, Grandma. We need to go."

"What about Ralph?"

"Later." Marti headed back for the car. She was 99 percent sure he was dead. Well, 98 percent. The other 2 percent was the lingering fear she really was Marti Cray-Cray. Her mother was alive and wandering. Who knew what she might get up to this time? At least she wasn't—contrary to the Bicklesburg gossip factory—running off with Sheila's husband. That match could only be made in the afterlife.

She stopped, chilled.

"I thought you were in a hurry?" Grandma said.

"I—" Marti's voice stuck in her throat. What if Mom saw the McDonaghs' killer? Nothing Mom said suggested she saw anything other than Mr. Stumpy. In her current cloud la-la land state, she didn't seem aware she'd been present at a crime scene. She hadn't mentioned Sheila since Saturday.

If the killer knew—or believed—Mom saw them, they wouldn't know she wasn't talking. A normal person would talk.

Even healthy, Margaret Dibble Mickkleson wasn't normal, or at least not average, but she would report witnessing a murder. Unless she was so out of it she didn't understand what she saw. Or unless she had something to do with it herself. Dmitri said the security tapes cleared her of actually *doing* it, but Mom excelled at delegation.

No. Marti didn't want to go there, but she couldn't deny her mother might well be in danger.

"Marti? Are you okay? You look like you've, well, seen a ghost."

"Mom's wandered off."

"I'm sure she is fine. Just took a little walk, like last time." Grandma waffled on the *fine*. Marti wasn't reassured.

"Let's hope this walk doesn't turn out like the last." Marti decided to concentrate on one thing at a time. The first thing was putting one foot in front of the other and making it back to the car without falling on her face. She wasn't made for cow-path country lanes any more than the TT was.

Focused on the road and keeping herself upright, she didn't realize how far they'd gone until Grandma spoke.

"Oh dear. It looks like you were right."

Ralph McDonagh stood next to the TT, dressed in the same clothes he wore the last time Marti saw him. He looked solid enough. His ghostly shimmer dimmed in the daylight, but Marti knew he was a goner. Somehow, she always knew.

"Who are you? Have you seen my truck? Where's Sheila?" Ralph's whine clashed with his manly-man posture.

Grandma giggled. Marti didn't. The man didn't know he was dead.

Her phone rang again. She checked the screen. Dmitri. She hit *Ignore*. He was either going to tell her Mom was found or urge her to get her butt home. A few minutes wouldn't matter. She'd found Ralph, and she had questions to ask before he disappeared again. She might not have another chance.

"Mr. McDonagh, I'm afraid I have some bad news."

THE LATE RALPH McDonagh took the news of his wife's death—and his own—stoically. As soon as he found out he was no longer a resident of the physical world, his ghostly glow grew stronger and he grew paler.

"Was it an accident? The Escalade? Sheila always said I drove too fast."

"I don't think it was an accident." Marti wondered how to tell him how intentional their deaths were.

"I always told her, 'Don't worry. I'm a professional.'" His voice grew thinner and his form, translucent.

"He's not going to be with us for long," Grandma said.

"Mr. McDonagh—"

"Call me Ralph."

"Ralph, what's the last thing you remember?"

"How did I get here? I haven't been to Billings Pond for years. Decades. I woke up in my Escalade—in town."

She *had* seen him in the SUV. Good for her peace of mind, but not much help overall.

"Then I was here," he continued. "I can't seem to leave. Every time I make it to the road, I end up back at the pond."

Which might mean he was buried somewhere close. Or he was killed there. If he was bound to the pond, there had to be a reason. She didn't have time to figure it out. Ralph was fading fast, and her phone was beeping.

"Before that," she said, "the last thing you remember. Before waking up in your car."

"It's not a car. It's a top-of-the-line, luxury SUV."

"Ralph. Think. The last thing you remember."

He closed his eyes and wrinkled his forehead. Dead Ralph didn't appear to be overly endowed with smarts. If Live Ralph was this dim, maybe it explained Sheila's attraction to The Judge.

"Think, Ralph. Think."

"He's fading," Grandma said.

"Donuts. We had donuts. One glazed for me. Two cream filled with sprinkles for Sheila."

"Good. After that." Marti didn't care what kind of donuts they had, but it was a start. "What did you do next?"

"We went home. Sheila wouldn't shut up. Travel plans. She was making travel plans. I stopped listening. I didn't care where we went as long as it was warm."

He'd gone from translucent to transparent. Marti needed usable info before he disappeared. "When you got home. What happened when you got home?"

"I let Sheila out in the driveway. She wouldn't get in and out of the Escalade in the garage. Said there wasn't enough room. She didn't want me to buy it in the first place. Wanted something small and fast. Like that Mickkleson woman's car. This car. Who did you say you are?" He opened his eyes and gaped at her. "Do I know you?"

"After you let Sheila out? Keep going, Ralph. Think."

GHOSTS IN GLASS HOUSES 221

He closed his eyes again. At least he followed orders well.

"I pulled into the garage. Put the door down. Shut off the Escalade." The strain of thinking showed. He dimmed and flickered.

"After that?"

"Nothing." His voice was a whisper. He opened his eyes. "Sheila?" His eyes went wide. He shut his eyes one last time, flickered, and disappeared.

"Grandma? Will he be back?"

"You never know, but I don't think so," Grandma said. "He may have crossed over."

"Over? Where—" Marti's phone chimed again. She pulled it out and looked at the screen.

Message from RachelAnne: Where are you? Why aren't you answering your phone? GET HOME.

Missed Call from RachelAnne.

Message from Dmitri. GET HOME.

Voice Mail from Dmitri.

Missed call from Dmitri.

Missed call from Albion Court Security Office.

The contact list in her phone held three numbers, and she'd received calls from each.

She needed to get home.

Parson Morely leaned against the TT looking morose.

She didn't know where RachelAnne was calling from, but couldn't imagine her sister not rushing to Bickle House to take charge of the situation. Dmitri was on the job. There wasn't a lot Marti could do that they weren't already doing.

One more tiny delay wouldn't hurt.

"Pastor Morely, a few minutes of your time." Marti employed Grandma's you-catch-more-flies-with-honey philosophy, threw in a dose of formality, and hoped the gloomy old coot would talk to her.

"Sin and vice. Hellfire and damnation." He drew himself up to his full height.

He was impressive—and a little frightening.

"That man. The one I was talking to. The dead one. Do you know how he got here?" Forget the honey, she went for the direct approach.

"Cain and Able," he intoned.

She wondered if he knew Billson. The two of them made a great pair.

"Oh, come off it," Grandma said. "Parson is your given name, not a title. You're no more a man of the cloth than I am. In fact, you're a bum and a reprobate. Always were. Always will be. Now, tell my great-granddaughter what you saw."

So much for honey. Parson Morely snarled and stalked away.

"Thanks a lot, Grandma."

"He wasn't going to tell you anything anyway."

Maybe he had. "Did Ralph have a brother?"

"Not that I know of," Grandma said, "but I'm hardly an expert on the McDonagh family tree."

Marti's phone went off again. She didn't bother to answer it or check to see who was calling.

"Come on, Grandma. We need to head home." No time for the car wash. She carefully backed the TT onto Billings Road, then let it rip.

There was absolutely no reason for Grandma to grab the holy cow handle and hang on for dear life. Aside from Grandma's no-life factor, the little car handled the corners beautifully. At any speed.

EIGHTEEN

Her phone rang twice during the drive home. She didn't answer it. She didn't want to deal with Dmitri or her sister on the phone, especially while driving. Who was she kidding? She didn't want to deal with them at all. What she wanted was to toss the phone out the window and keep driving. Forever.

She didn't bother to call and let security know she was coming. If the reporters in town were the ones from the Avenue, she hoped they were still at the courthouse. If not, the Avenue's ever present cameras had to be good for something. Whoever was in the ACS office should see her and come shepherd her though the horde.

In case they didn't, she and Grandma made contingency plans.

Grandma pooh-poohed Marti's plan to mow down a few vultures and suggested a more sensible strategy.

Worst case scenario, Marti would park the TT and walk to the house while Grandma worked crowd control. Any reporter who pressed too close would experience a deep and sudden chill. As a rule, Grandma avoided physical-metaphysical contact with the living. She claimed it was as unpleasant for her as it was for them, although she refused to explain why. For the press, she was more than willing to make an exception, if only to keep Marti from being charged with vehicular homicide. Any vulture who didn't back off would find themselves wishing they were at an Antarctic research station just to warm up.

"Here we go." Marti turned into the alley alongside Albion Court.

Not a vulture in sight.

"Wow," Grandma said.

"Whatever was going on in town must be huge." Marti's relief at not dealing with reporters was tempered by the fear whatever drew them away would send them scuttling back with renewed determination.

Her sister's Subaru and a police cruiser blocked her path to the garage. She left the TT behind the latter.

RachelAnne flung open the back door before Marti stuck her key in the lock. "Where have you been?"

"I went for a drive." Half-truths were, as always, her friend. "I came as soon as I got your message. And Dmitri's. Did you find Mom?" She talked fast and hoped it would distract RachelAnne from questioning her.

"No. Dmitri and his men are looking for her."

The last time Mom disappeared, RachelAnne was out the door in an instant. Her sister wasn't the wait-around type.

"Why are the cops here?"

RachelAnne clutched her phone in one hand and pulled Marti through the door with the other.

Baby Face Rodney sat in the breakfast nook. Myrna slumped across from him, dabbing her red and swollen eyes with a crumpled tissue, a mountain of soggy tissues in front of her. The waterworks had been flowing for a while.

"Oh, Marti, I'm so sorry!" The housekeeper screwed up her face, let loose with a dramatic wail, and burst into a fresh bout of tears. The sodden paper hankie wasn't up to the task. Rodney picked up a box of fresh tissues from the bench beside him and slid it across to the bawling woman.

Marti turned to her sister. "What's going on here?" Even taking recent events into consideration, Myrna's hysteria was totally out of proportion to the situation—unless there was more to the situation than Mom wandering away. "What's happened to Mom?" She couldn't keep the tremor from her voice.

"We don't know. Why weren't you here?"

Grandma disappeared. Marti hoped she was off to find Edwards and get his version of whatever was happening.

"Oh! I just remembered!" Myrna gulped and blew her nose. "Mrs. Mickkleson took a call this morning. Or made one. I don't know which—I found her talking on the phone."

"I told you to keep her away from the phone." RachelAnne, Ice Queen, was not pleased.

Myrna turned on the faucet again.

A knot formed in Marti's stomach.

Rodney grabbed the box of tissues and brandished it in Myrna's face. "Mrs. Ward, try to pull yourself together. Do you know who she was talking to?"

"No. I didn't hear a name." She sniffed and grabbed another tissue. "But I'm sure it was a man."

"Why's that?"

"She . . . she . . . she always sounded different when she spoke to men. I can't explain it. But she did."

Marti understood. The women of her mother's social crowd had a stockpile of voices. One for their children. One for the help. One for the general public. One for women considered their social equals. The one they used on the male of the species was special. Soft, low, exaggeratedly feminine and packed with flattery, spelled m-a-n-i-p-u-l-a-t-i-o-n. When deployed by an expert, the voice made men forget how to spell. Mom was an expert.

Myrna knew how to use that voice. She'd used it on the phone with RachelAnne's boss.

"Was she on the landline or her cell phone?" Rodney asked.

Myrna's eyes widened and her lower lip trembled. Instead of answering, she collapsed in sobs again.

"You need to tell me what's going on," Marti said to her sister.

"If you'd been here like you were supposed to be, this wouldn't have happened," RachelAnne snapped.

"I didn't know I was a prisoner. Myrna had things under

control." It wasn't like she was indispensable. Everyone survived perfectly fine without her for ages. "And if Mom wandered off again, why aren't *you* out looking for her?"

RachelAnne glared. Her cheeks flushed.

For all the sisterly bonding they'd done—well, come close to—in the past days, they were right back to their old pattern. Everything wrong with the world, up to and including climate change, was Marti's fault.

The urge to run overwhelmed her. She'd never come back. She tried Bickle House, and it didn't work out.

If she took off in Mom's TT RachelAnne would not only report it stolen, she'd jump ship to the prosecutor's office and press for the maximum penalty.

And despite her stormy relationship with her mother, Marti knew walking—running—away again would eat at her. Mom was not only missing, she was sick. As for the mess The Judge left behind, who knew how that would play out.

And the immediate problem—where was Mom? Marti assumed she'd gone walkabout like last time, but the last time didn't involve the police. At least not until Sheila turned up dead.

Sensible big sister was never Marti's family role, and she was a lousy actress. She decided to give it a go anyway. "Look, I don't know what the situation is, but I'm pretty sure us at each other's throats won't help. What *might* help is if someone, preferably you, tells me what exactly *is* going on."

"I think it was Ralph," Myrna said.

"*What?*" Marti and her sister spoke in unison. Marti knew their disbelief sprang from different roots.

"On the phone." The housekeeper cleared her throat and pulled herself together. "The man. I'll bet it was Ralph."

"Why do you say that?" Rodney asked.

"Well, it is what everybody is saying . . . but maybe I'm wrong. I'm sure Mrs. Micckleson had nothing to do with . . . well, you know . . . Sheila McDonagh . . ." Myrna backed up so fast Marti heard the beeping. "Look at the mess I made." She gathered her used tissues, stood up, burst into tears—again—and collapsed back into her seat.

"*Ralph?*" RachelAnne said. "Why would he call Mom? What is everybody saying?"

Marti wondered if her sister made a conscious effort at selective deafness. No one lived in that big of a bubble.

"It's not my fault." Myrna blew her nose and dabbed her eyes. "Mrs. Mickkleson does what she wants, and it's not my place to stop her."

"It was your job to stop her from wandering off!" RachelAnne said.

"Now ladies—" Baby Face Rodney looked like he'd rather be dealing with a hostage situation involving rabid tigers than where he was.

"Don't 'now ladies' me," RachelAnne said.

Myrna wailed.

Rodney quailed.

Marti wanted to slap them all.

"That's it. *Someone tell me what's happening.*" She heard The Judge in her voice and wanted to crawl into a hole, but it worked. Myrna sniveled in the corner, Baby Face Rodney sat at attention, and RachelAnne talked.

MYRNA HAD LEFT Mom in the kitchen with tea and cookies. An empty cup and saucer—bone china with blue roses—still sat on the counter, along with a plate holding a lone Oreo.

The cookie reminded Marti she hadn't eaten lunch. Eating the Oreo might be destroying evidence or something. She concentrated on RachelAnne. Once her sister started talking, the floodgates opened, and Marti barely kept up with the story.

Why Myrna left Mom alone in the kitchen was unclear, but it didn't matter. The power went out. Myrna went to check on Mom and found the door open and Mom gone.

"I thought she'd be okay. I wasn't gone for long." Myrna dabbed her eyes.

"Mrs. Ward, I'm sure it wasn't your fault," Baby Face said.

Maybe the housekeeper really was worried about Mom, but she also enjoyed the attention. She was overacting. She reached for another tissue, and Baby Face Rodney patted her hand.

"What about Harriet?" Every time Marti opened a door, Electro-Woman announced it to the world. "Didn't you hear her?"

Myrna blew her nose.

"Who is this Harriet?" Rodney perked up.

"The 'back door open' lady," Marti said.

"She means the alarm system," RachelAnne said. "According to Myrna, she didn't talk."

"I'm *sure* I would have heard her." Myrna sniveled and killed another tissue.

Even with the dramatics, Marti believed her. No matter how dulcet Harriet's tones, she was impossible to miss.

"What about the vultures—I mean, the reporters?"

"There was a bomb threat at the courthouse," Rodney said.

That explained the scene on the square.

"The caller—" He blushed. "Well, he mentioned your father . . . well, you know. All that stuff. When the press found out, they all headed into town."

Blushing and stammering couldn't be a good thing for a cop. Maybe that was what got Baby Face pulled off traffic detail and sent to Bickle House to hold Myrna's hand.

"So, the vultures left. That doesn't explain where Harriet went."

"Dmitri said the cameras shut down for a minute or two before the backup generator kicked in. He's checking to see if it was the whole alarm system. Including Harriet," RachelAnne said.

"I thought he was out looking for Mom?"

"That too."

A knock on the door was followed by a loud "It's me."

"Me" could be anyone. Marti checked the kitchen monitor. Dmitri stared into the camera.

She let him in.

"Back door open. Back door open." Harriet was in fine voice.

"Where were you? Big said you left his office hours ago," Dmitri said.

"Obviously, I wasn't here." Marti was fed up with this obsession over where she'd been. Sidestepping the question was wearing her out. *I went to look for Dead Ralph* wasn't a viable answer, and if there was a lifetime limit on little white lies, she was fast approaching it. "I thought you were looking for my mother. Who *is* looking for my mother?"

"My guys are on it. Big's sending out a couple of cars."

"If Big can send out men . . . more men . . ." Marti glanced apologetically at Baby Face Rodney. "Does that mean the brouhaha at the courthouse is over?"

"How did you know about that?" Dmitri said.

What was with everyone giving her the third degree? "*A*, it happened at the same time I left the police station. *B*, RachelAnne or Rodney, one of them, told me about the bomb threat. *C, what does it matter?*"

"Calm down," RachelAnne said.

"Don't tell me to calm down." The knot in Marti's stomach grew. "What happened to the security system? All these expensive cameras and crap—I'm assuming they are expensive, since The Judge installed them—and the power goes out and everything shuts down? Doesn't sound like much security to me."

Grandma appeared at the counter, Edwards and Amity in tow. Marti wished they'd learn to use the door.

"The power outage was only the Avenue. There's a backup power source. By the time it kicked in, your mother was gone." Dmitri said.

"How long was that?"

"Maybe five minutes. Long enough. There's a glitch in the system. Sometimes it reboots when it goes to generator power. Your father and I were discussing an upgrade when he died."

"Passed," Grandma said. "Why don't people say passed anymore? Died is *so* final."

"How about bit the big one?" Edwards said.

"Bought the farm," Amity said. "A farm with ponies. Real ones."

"Kicked the bucket," Edwards said.

"Went to eat some worms!" Amity twirled, all smiles.

"And you just dropped it? Why didn't you discuss this with me? Are you saying this could have been prevented?" RachelAnne needed someone to blame.

"You were busy. But you're right. I should have discussed it with you." Dmitri accepted responsibility without a blink. His shoulders were broad.

"Croaked. Went belly up. Gave up the ghost! Play with us, Marti!" Amity danced and sang.

"We will be discussing this, as well as your future with ACS, as soon as my mother is found," RachelAnne said.

"He didn't exactly *give up* the ghost," Edwards said, "'cause he is one!"

Marti put her hands to her head and pressed her temples. If she didn't know better, she'd think Amity and Edwards had caught whatever was wrong with Mom. The knot in her stomach was gone, but she felt like her head was about to explode. "Everybody, *shut up*!"

RachelAnne and Dmitri looked at her with concern, as did Grandma and Edwards. Amity pouted.

"Now see what you did?" Grandma said.

Marti took a deep breath. "So. There's a bomb threat at the courthouse, and the nosy-butt reporters, who've surrounded the house for days, disappear. The power goes out, and the expensive security system fails. And my mother, who appears to be suffering from dementia, chooses that exact moment to go for a stroll. Am I the only one who thinks this all sounds a little too coincidental?"

"Why do you think we called Big?" RachelAnne said.

"It wasn't a coincidence at all," Grandma said.

"The madam ran away with the man with poofy hair," Amity said.

"Elvis has left the building," Edwards said, "and your mother went with him."

All afternoon, cops wandered in and out of the house. Big put in an appearance, made soothing noises to RachelAnne, and questioned Marti on where she'd been after she left his office.

"I drove. I wanted to be alone, and . . . well . . . I had Mom's TT."

He seemed to accept her explanation, but the way he looked at her made her feel like a bug under a microscope.

The vultures returned to their roosts on the Avenue.

Peter showed up sans kids. He'd gotten a real babysitter. Winter Adams. The girl was a jack-of-all trades.

Her brother-in-law made sympathetic noises about Mom. Marti didn't believe him. She caught him examining the marks on the bottoms of Mom's china collection and saw a cash register in his eyes. The little dirtbag didn't protest when RachelAnne announced she would, once again, spend the night at Bickle House. Not a groan or a whine about babysitting his own kids. Maybe he hired Winter for the entire night.

By the time she and RachelAnne called it a day, Marti was so tired she couldn't see straight. She crawled into bed and expected to fall asleep as soon as she turned out the light.

Her body was willing, but her stupid head wouldn't shut up.

Both Amity and Edwards implied Mom left with someone. A man. She hadn't managed a moment alone with either ghost all afternoon. She could get up and go look for them, but Rachel-Anne was in the house. If she managed to search for the resident haunts without her sister waking up and questioning her, there was no guarantee she'd find them. Ghosts were like cats. If they didn't want to be found, they wouldn't be.

If she found them, and her sister caught her interrogating her invisible friends, things could get ugly. Uglier. RachelAnne spent the afternoon riding her high horse, blaming Mom's disappearance on Marti's absence. Which made no sense. If Marti was responsible, why was Myrna there? Responsible or not, her sister made her feel guilty. RachelAnne and Big were a fine pair.

Big promised he'd have men searching for Mom all night. Dmitri promised the same thing, even though he was off duty. Both said the sisters should stay home and wait for news—or for Mom to come wandering back.

Her phone was by the bed. RachelAnne no doubt had hers clutched to her chest. If there was any news, they'd hear. No news was good news, right?

No. No news was no news. Nothing more, nothing less.

She hated waiting. She wanted—needed—sleep. Rehashing the day was as exhausting as living it.

She counted sheep. Backward from two hundred. At fifty-seven, she heard Parson Morely shout, "Hellfire and damnation!" The old fraud was trying to tell her something, but she couldn't understand him.

She listed every spirit she knew by name, in chronological order of first meeting, starting with Grandma Bertie. She drifted off somewhere around Eeyore George and Just Call Me Joe. Her mother shouted her name, and she was wide awake. She tried to convince herself it was a dream. A worry-induced nightmare. Because if she did hear her mother, it meant only one thing. She refused to believe her mother had joined The Judge.

She tossed and turned and drifted off again and again. The same dream woke her each time. *Her mother—full strength Margaret Alberta Dibble Mickkleson, not the ditzy watered down version—stood before her. "Marcile. Get out of that bed now. You have potential. You're a Mickkleson and a Dibble. Think of what you could accomplish if you didn't spend so much time lying around. And do something about that hair!"*

In the twilight haze between waking and dozing, her mother's voice was clear and sharp. Marti felt her presence in the room. Fully awake, she sat up.

"Mom?"

No answer.

She was alone. Her mother wasn't in her room. She was somewhere, alive. She had to be. Not even Grandma Bertie lurked in the bedroom. She was probably off playing some version of ghostly pinochle with Edwards.

Although she'd spent most of her life longing for solitude, she felt abandoned.

She switched on the bedside lamp. Attempting to sleep was pointless. She'd get up and go to The Judge's study and find a book to read. Maybe grab a little refreshment from the stash inside the globe. And if she ran into Grandma, maybe she would come back to the bedroom for a little chat. Maybe Grandma learned something new from Edwards. Or Amity.

It wasn't like she missed Grandma Bertie's company or anything.

She retrieved her old bathrobe from the back of the closet door where it had hung for ten years. Her rubber-ducky pajama pants were the nicest piece of clothing she owned—a real score, brand new in the wrapper at Goodwill. There was no point in scandalizing the old-school male resident—residents, if The Judge was lurking—of the house with her skimpy tank top, even if they were dead.

She headed downstairs to the study.

Before she hit the first floor, a familiar and disgusting odor greeted her. The stench beckoned, like a foggy hand from an old cartoon, and led her straight to the kitchen.

"Mom?" Marti knew she sounded foolish, but who else drank the revolting concoction?

NINETEEN

"Where?" RachelAnne said. "Did you find her? Where is she? Is she okay?"

"No—the finding her, that is. I'm sure she's okay," Marti said. She wasn't sure Mom was okay, and she was less sure about her sister.

RachelAnne hunched over the counter, a delicate china teacup in hand. A bag of cookies and a teapot, the same blue lusterware Mom used the day Marti arrived, sat in front of her.

"How can you stomach that stuff? It smells like dirty sweat socks. And skunk. And something very, very rotten." Or dead.

"It's not bad after the first few sips." RachelAnne gave her a beatific smile. "And Mom's right. It's calming. Very, very calming." Her sister swayed on her stool.

"Are you sure you didn't add a little something from The Judge's stash of liquid refreshment?" Forget Mom's tea. No more *maybe* about it. Marti was raiding The Judge's stash. If the tea was all that calming, maybe she could wheedle the liquor cabinet key out of her sister, skip the globe stock, and go for the good stuff.

"Marti! This is no time for drinking. Mom is missing. We need to be alert. Responsible. I need to be responsible. You're never responsible."

"Whatever." Marti was too exhausted to bicker. Besides, RachelAnne didn't sound like she was trying to pick a fight. More like she was talking to herself. They'd both had a hard day.

"You should have some tea." RachelAnne pushed the teapot toward her. "You'll have to find your own cup. I'm not getting up."

"No thanks."

"Suit yourself." RachelAnne grabbed the pot, placed a silver strainer over her cup, and refilled it. Leave it to her sister to go the classic strainer route rather than the infuser route.

Marti wasn't interested in the foul-smelling brew, but Oreos were a different matter. She thought they were gone. Either RachelAnne made a cookie run, or Mom and Myrna kept a secret stash. Good thing she didn't know there were Oreos in the house. She would have scarfed them all by now. No way was RachelAnne hogging them all to herself.

"You've been holding out on me." Marti reached for the bag.

Her sister slapped her hand. "Keep your hands off my cookies." She all but growled and bared her teeth. Since she wasn't a bear and she had opposable thumbs, she grabbed the bag and hugged it to her chest.

"What the—" Marti stopped.

Something was wrong with her sister. Seriously wrong. New Mom-level wrong.

RachelAnne clung to the bag of cookies with enough ferocity to crush them, which would be a real crime. She closed her eyes and rocked and hummed. Softly at first, but as she got louder, Marti recognized the tune. The zoo song.

"RachelAnne?"

"One word, capital *A*, and don't forget the *e*." She opened her eyes. Tears rolled down her cheeks. "Mommy sang us that song."

"Are you all right? Are you *sure* you haven't been drinking?"

"Don't be ridiculous." RachelAnne loosened her grasp on the cookies. She opened the bag and gawked at its contents.

Marti watched her sister stare, entranced by Oreos. The cookies were heaven, but looking at them wasn't all that interesting. "RachelAnne?"

She tore herself away from the cookies. "Oh. Hi Marti. Do you know who invented Oreos? Whoever it was is a genius. They are a work of art."

Her sister was high. The only reason she hadn't worked it out sooner was—RachelAnne. Perfect, law abiding, angelic, RachelAnne.

"Did you take something? Smoke something?"

"Smoking is bad for you and everyone around you."

Marti laughed at her sister's exaggerated shock. RachelAnne high was funny. High-larious. The problem was she didn't seem aware of her condition, and that wasn't funny.

"Don't laugh at me. *You* probably smoke. *You* do all the bad stuff. *I* have to be the good sister, and *you* still get all the attention." RachelAnne stuffed an Oreo in her mouth whole and washed it down with a slug of tea. More than one slug. She drained the cup and went for a refill. A few drops trickled from pot to cup. "I need to make more. Are you sure you don't want some?"

"I don't think it's a good idea." Mom's tea. One small pot of the stuff and RachelAnne turned into an extra from a Cheech and Chong movie. Mom swilled the stuff. No wonder she'd taken up residence in la-la land. "Did you say Mom had blood work done?" Would anyone have thought to test Margaret Mickkleson, arbitrator of propriety and lifetime chair of the Drug Free Bicklesburg committee, for drugs?

"I think that's tomorrow. Do you think she'll be back in time? I should call and reschedule. Where's my phone? Have you seen my purse?"

RachelAnne's iPhone was on the counter in plain sight.

"It's eleven o'clock. At night. No one's there," Marti said. "Also, you're high."

"What?"

"High. Stoned."

"Don't be ridiculous. Did I say that already?"

"Under the influence. Wasted. Baked."

RachelAnne sat up straight. "Never," she said, pinched her lips, and wobbled on her stool.

Marti caught her sister and steadied her before she fell. "I think it's the tea. Mom's tea. Do you know what she puts in it?"

"Dried leaves."

"You're a big help."

"I'll make another pot. Maybe we can figure it out." RachelAnne reached for the teapot.

"Ohhh, I don't think so, Baby Sister. I think you've had enough." It was Marti's turn to slap her sister's hand.

"I do feel a little odd," RachelAnne said. "I kinda like it."

"That's the dangerous part," Marti said. Her sister was relaxed, happy. Maybe she should let RachelAnne make more tea—and share it with her. They could get all sensible and grown-up in the morning. "Where is the tea? The dried stuff, I mean."

"In the canister that says *Tea*. Duh." RachelAnne pointed at the blue ceramic canisters, the same set where the Oreos were kept.

Marti opened the smallest canister. The stench killed any desire to try Mom's special recipe. Which was just as well. There wasn't much left. She'd give it to Dmitri. He could use his pull with Big to have it tested, find out what Mom was doing to herself.

"Tea in the Tea canister, but Oreos in the Flour canister. What's in the Sugar canister?" Out of curiosity, Marti checked. It was empty.

"Housekeeping money," RachelAnne said. "Mom keeps a couple hundred in there, so Myrna doesn't have to bother her every time she needs something. If I can't have more tea, I can still have an Oreo, right?"

"Did anyone check this today?" If Mom left under her own steam, she had cash.

"I think I should to go to bed now," RachelAnne said. Her eyelids drooped, and her speech slurred. "I'll take these cookies with me."

"Go sleep it off. Tomorrow we're going to find out what's so special about this special recipe," Marti said.

"And we'll find Mom too. Right?"

"I hope so." If Mom was high, not ill, and the tea was the culprit, she hadn't had any for hours. If she'd wandered away under the effect of her concoction, she should have sobered up and found her way home by now.

Unless whatever was in the tea was addictive. Mom could be curled up in a dark corner suffering withdrawal.

"At least she's not barefoot," RachelAnne said.

"Huh?"

"Mom. She wore her shoes this time. Myrna said she had her leopard-print loafers on."

Maybe Mom was completely sober and healthy and didn't want to come back. Marti sympathized but couldn't imagine her mother willingly deserting everything she held dear, especially T3 and Maggie.

She could be completely sober and healthy, and something or someone prevented her from coming home.

Or she might be neither sober nor healthy and never coming home.

Marti didn't know which option frightened her the most. She was tempted to brew herself a pot of the odious concoction. Maybe once she got past the smell. . .

RachelAnne stood, Oreos in hand. "I'm going to bed."

"Leave me a cookie or two, okay?"

"Nope." Her sister left and took the whole bag with her.

Marti skipped raiding The Judge's bar. One of them had to keep their wits about them, at least until Mom was found, and at the moment, it certainly wasn't RachelAnne.

SHE TOSSED AND turned all night, worried. Mom. The tea. RachelAnne. The Judge's mess. The McDonaghs' murders. The sun came up and she finally dozed.

"Up and at 'em, sleepyhead. We've got places to go, people to see. Or to find. Let's ankle!" Grandma chirped.

"What?"

"Ankle. Skedaddle," Grandma said. "Edwards taught it to me. It means get your lazy butt out of bed and let's get moving."

"Drop dead." Marti pulled a pillow over her head. She regretted not breaking into The Judge's booze. Lack of sleep was worse than a hangover. She knew a dozen hangover cures, but only one for lack of sleep. "I need sleep."

"Rise and shine! Your sister's already up!"

Of course she was. Marti wondered if RachelAnne's foray into substance-enhanced relaxation left any effect on her. Probably not. Her sister was probably sitting downstairs, hair, makeup, and outfit perfect, ready to take on the day, whereas she felt like a slice of three-week-old leftover pizza.

She dragged herself out of bed, threw on her bathrobe, and debated running a brush through her hair. Too much trouble. She'd avoid mirrors until she had some coffee in her—a good plan on any day.

"Did Edwards have anything to say or did he just enhance your vocabulary? About Mom I mean."

"Not much. Amity said she left with a stuffed shirt. Edwards said he was a drugstore cowboy. Apparently the two descriptions are incompatible. They got into an argument."

"That's it?"

"They did agree they'd never seen him before, which means he'd never been to the house. You know those two check out everyone who walks through the door. Also, he had impressive hair, and Margaret left willingly."

If Mom was drugged, willingly didn't necessarily mean she wanted to leave—or even knew what was happening. If the man with the impressive hair told her they were going to visit the neon ponies, chances were she raced him for the door.

RACHELANNE WAS UP but didn't appear ready to take on the day. She didn't look ready to take on anything. She sat in the breakfast nook, elbows on the table, head in her hands. Her hair was unbrushed. Her pajamas were higher caliber than Marti's—a matching set of navy-blue silk with white piping. Other than her choice in sleeping attire, she wasn't in any better shape than Marti. Worse.

Her phone lay on the table, alone. No teapot or cup and saucer—at least she wasn't drinking Mom-tea. No toast or coffee or normal tea or anything.

"Are you okay?" Marti turned the fire on under the kettle and collected the French press and ground coffee.

"Just worried," RachelAnne said.

Marti was worried too, but it wasn't going to keep her from her coffee.

RachelAnne's phone rang. She tapped the screen without answering it and it shut up.

"Where's Myrna this morning?"

"She called at the crack o'dawn o'thirty. She says she's 'just too heartbroken' or guilt-ridden or whatever to come to work today." RachelAnne's attempt at Myrna's gravelly voice fell short, but her mocking impression of yesterday's overwrought performance was spot on. "I told her to take as much time as she needs. Frankly, I don't want her around."

"I wanted to ask her what she knows about Mom's tea recipe, but that can wait." If the housekeeper still had her undies in a twist, Marti didn't want to deal with her either. "Maybe I'll call her later."

RachelAnne picked up her phone and put it back down. Her hand shook. Red spots stood out against her pale cheeks. Marti wondered if her sister's condition was due to the tea or simply morning. She'd had worse mornings herself, most of them earned.

The kettle whistled. "Do you want coffee? Or tea—the safe, commercially packaged kind? You'll have to wait for coffee. First cup's mine. Then I'm calling Dmitri."

"Big would have called us if they found Mom."

"He would have called you. He's not my biggest fan. I'm giving Dmitri the rest of Mom's so-called tea. If Dmitri asks, maybe Big will get it analyzed. They're all buddy-buddy. If I take it to Big, he'll no doubt use it as an excuse to throw me in jail."

RachelAnne buried her face in her hands and mumbled.

"Speak up. I can't hear a word you're saying. Did that stuff give you a hangover?" It didn't appear to have that effect on Mom. The way she swilled it, she'd probably built up some kind of tolerance.

Her sister sat up straight and said, "No . . . I did . . . I guess I'll have tea. Lemon Lift, thank you."

Marti dug in the cupboard for the box of nice, sealed, not smelly tea. Safe tea. Real tea.

"I . . . was stupid," RachelAnne said.

"You didn't know," Marti said. Although now that she thought about it, why hadn't anyone checked into Mom's special recipe when she started to go off the deep end? "It could happen to anyone." That sounded lame even to her. Maybe RachelAnne had enough of a buzz left to fall for it. "How are you feeling this morning?"

"Not . . . last night . . . what you saw. I *did* something stupid. After you went to bed."

"The condition you were in, it's a good thing you were here and not someplace where you could do a whole bunch of stupid. Trust me. I know." Scooter's and Just Call Me Joe felt like a lifetime ago, not what, three, four days ago? "At least you remember your stupid."

"Marti. Shut up and let me talk. Do you really think the tea has something to do with what's wrong with Mom?"

"After what it did to you, I think it's possible. Probable, even."

"Do you think, well, she's doing it to herself? On purpose?"

"I don't know." Marti hadn't thought that far ahead. The possible discovery of the *what* of Mom's condition distracted her from the *why*.

Mom had a good knowledge of teas and herbalism. It was hard

to believe she'd accidentally poison herself. If she intended to get a nice buzz on and float through life in happy-happy land, she'd seriously miscalculated—also hard to believe, at least from Old Mom. New Mom might miscalculate, but that would mean the dementia wasn't the result of the tea.

Myrna had access to the tea, but despite their history, the housekeeper liked Mom. Marti doubted Myrna LaRue Ward was a good enough actress to pull off either her idolization of Mom or her hysteria at Mom's disappearance. Not to mention, the woman wasn't bright enough to cook up whatever the new tea recipe was on her own.

"Marti, I—" RachelAnne's phone rang again. This time she answered it.

Marti turned on the kitchen television. It was still set on the security channel. The front yard was empty. Two news vans, the call letters of local channels emblazoned on each, sat on the street. The vultures in the seats appeared to be asleep. She switched to a news channel.

RachelAnne argued with her caller. She kept her voice low, but she was no longer pathetic. She was businesslike. She wasn't talking to her husband.

The big news story of the day wasn't Bicklesburg. A young, blonde celebrity Marti'd never heard of crashed her car into a restaurant. Luckily, there were no casualties other than a few potted palms, but the actress was some sort of icon of family values and innocent girlhood. America was shocked and disillusioned. *Welcome to the club*, Marti thought.

The Mickkleson family troubles were reduced to a transition between more current and sensational stories. "Investigators report no new developments in the new Kids for Cash scandal. In a related story, Margaret Mickkleson, wife of the allegedly implicated late Judge Thaddeus A. Mickkleson, has been reported missing after wandering away from her home late yesterday afternoon."

Mom's official portrait, the one she used for the annual reports of charities whose boards she chaired, filled the screen. It was at least five years out of date, and the elegant woman in the photo bore little resemblance to the Margaret Mickkleson of the past few days.

"Wait—I have to watch this," RachelAnne said.

"Mrs. Mickkleson is possibly ill and disoriented. If you see her, please call one of the numbers at the bottom of the screen."

The numbers for both the Bicklesburg Police and the Battlesburough County Sheriff's Office scrolled beneath Mom's smiling face. Big took Mom's disappearance seriously if he got the county boys involved, but he must not believe it was kidnapping. That would mean federal investigators. Or were they just for kids?

Mom's photo disappeared, replaced by a smiling child holding a trophy bigger than she was. "National Spelling Bee champion—" Marti switched off the set.

"No. I *won't* be in today. In fact, I won't be in until my mother is found. Deal with it." RachelAnne slammed her phone on the counter, businesslike replaced by pissed.

"Everything okay?"

"Larry Brumble sees no reason why I shouldn't come in to work today. The professionals are searching for Mom, and all I can do is wait, so I might as well do it at the office."

"I thought you were on leave?"

"He says not anymore. He has a headache and wants to stay in bed. Poor baby."

"The Judge always said he was an idiot. Maybe he got too much sun on that bald dome of his." Husbands or bosses, RachelAnne's judgment in men left a lot to be desired.

"I used to think Daddy exaggerated. I'm beginning to think otherwise."

"Weren't you trying to tell me something? Before Bumbles called?" If nothing else, talking to Larry Brumble restored her sister's power of speech.

RachelAnne's expression came full circle. She slumped, once again a dishrag in expensive pajamas. The red spots on her cheeks disappeared, but only because her whole face was the color of a boiled lobster. Marti stuck a cup of harmless Lemon Lift in front of her and turned to pour her own coffee.

"Promise you won't be mad. I have enough people mad at me." RachelAnne's voice quavered, but she spoke in full sentences.

"Can't promise until you tell me." Marti took a gulp of coffee. She didn't like the sound of her sister's voice.

"Mom's tea. I couldn't sleep."

"And?"

"I got up. It was the tea. I wasn't thinking clearly. If I'd been myself, I would never have done it."

"Don't tell me you made more." The teapot, cup, and strainer from last night were upside down in the dish rack. Washed clean. Well, they'd been empty anyway. Except for the strainer.

Even spent, the used leaves might have told them something. "You didn't use it all, did you?"

"Worse."

Marti opened the tea canister. Empty. Not only empty but sparkly clean. "RachelAnne? What did you do with the tea?"

"I'm a lawyer. I should know better. I do know better."

"You haven't passed the bar yet. And if you want a chance to, you'd better tell me what you did." Throttling her sister was a bad idea, even if the cause was just.

"I flushed it."

"*WHAT?*"

"I couldn't sleep. I kept thinking about Mom. And drugs. She's the head of the Drug Free Bicklesburg committee you know, and don't we have enough scandal in our lives? And . . . I don't know. Maybe I was still high. It made sense last night."

"Maybe there's more stashed." Marti opened a cupboard and slammed it shut. "How could you *do* that?" With her luck, if she gave in to impulse and killed her sister, she'd end up with another ghost in her entourage. They could all go to prison together.

"The tea won't help us find Mom. Don't yell at me. I'm sorry. I *know* I shouldn't have done it." RachelAnne sniffled. Tears ran down her face.

Marti wasn't impressed with her sister's contrite act.

Act.

Maybe it was all an act. "What do you know about the tea? What's in it?"

"What are you talking about? How would I know?"

"Just how badly does Peter want this house? How far are the two of you willing to go to get it?" RachelAnne and Peter had unfettered access to the house, even before The Judge's death. If her sister poisoned their mother, what about The Judge? Was his final whiskey sour meant to be just that—final?

"*Marthile*. You're talking crathy."

"Don't call me that." Marti's head pounded. Her eyes burned. "Seeing red" was more than a figure of speech.

"You know I can't help it. I'm upthet."

"No. The other thing." She had to get away. "But I'd rather be crazy than stupid." She yanked open the back door.

"Back door open."

"Where are you going?"

"To look for Mom."

"Don't you think you should get drethed firtht?"

TWENTY

Marti pulled a Mickey Mouse sweatshirt over her Donald Duck tank top and changed her rubber-ducky pajama pants for jeans. Day three for the jeans, but no one would know. Grandma might, but she'd disappeared the moment Marti started throwing accusations at her sister.

Good riddance. She was fed up with her family. All of them.

She wasn't the responsible one. Responsible was RachelAnne's job. Her sister was built for it, groomed for it. Marti wasn't.

She didn't mean what she said. Anger removed the filter between her brain and her mouth, and she lashed out in fury. She didn't believe her sister had anything to do with her mother's condition or The Judge's death. Not really.

Peter was a different story. She found it easy—too easy—to imagine him as a conniving killer. She tried to convince herself he wasn't a different story, that she wanted to blame him because she didn't like him. Or trust him.

Her sister would never marry anyone capable of murder and kidnapping.

On the other hand, RachelAnne had proven herself awfully naive. Marti remembered her brother-in-law running his hand through his hair and putting on his aviator sunglasses. *A man with poofy hair*, Amity said. *Elvis*, Edwards called him. It was a stretch, but Peter's hair could be called *poofy*. Mom might willingly leave with Peter. Whatever else he was, he was the father of her grandchildren.

The ghosts knew him. They would have identified him.

Unless they didn't want to. Neither were fond of her parents.

That line of reasoning wasn't helping. It added to her confusion, which in turn fueled her anger. She had to get out of the house. Searching for Mom was as good of an excuse as any. Who knew, maybe she'd spot something that Dmitri and Big and their armies missed. She could bounce ideas off Grandma Bertie. Ask if she thought Peter was capable of more than simply being a lousy husband.

And if RachelAnne was capable of being his accomplice.

Wherever Grandma was, she'd show up before Marti went far. She had no choice.

If nothing else, she could walk off her mood—or at least find a suitable target for her anger. Where was Weasel Boy when she needed him?

She threw open her bedroom door.

"Your father needs to talk to you." Grandma and The Judge stood shoulder to shoulder and blocked her way.

No good could come of the two of them ganging up on her.

"You have to find your mother," The Judge said.

"Thanks for the news flash. I'll let everybody know. Bet nobody's thought of that." She couldn't get around them. Through them meant full-body freezer burn.

"Please," The Judge said.

He was thin. Translucent. His voice wavered. He reminded her of Ralph.

"What's wrong with you?" If she dove through him and dodged Grandma, whose presence was as strong as ever, maybe she could avoid internal frostbite, at least the worst of it.

"I don't have much time," he said.

"What are you talking about? You know you're dead, right? Well past your expiration date."

"Now listen to me young lady. We don't have time for your smart mouth." He flickered.

"Save your energy," Grandma said.

"What's wrong with you? You look like a low-budget special

effect in a lame movie," Marti said. If he thought otherworldly woo-woo scared her, he had another think coming.

"He crossed over," Grandma said. "Once you do that, you're not supposed to come back."

"Crossed over? Does that mean what I think it means?"

"Yes," Grandma said.

The Judge opened his mouth, but Marti didn't want to hear anything he had to say.

"You mean you guys can leave anytime you want?" The information didn't help Marti's current anger management issues.

"He could. And don't call us 'you guys.'" Grandma said.

"I went to find Sheila," The Judge said.

"Of course you did. Things get tough and you run to your girlfriend," Marti said.

"No. I wanted information. I needed to know." He was fading fast.

"Know what?"

"What they say. I did it, but not for the money. I did it to keep you safe."

"Don't give me that crap." Marti's anger flared. For all his lectures on responsibility, The Judge never accepted responsibility for his own actions.

"Your generation was out of control. School shootings. Gangs. I had to cut out the tumor. Keep Battlesburough County safe. Clean. It wasn't for the money. *He* did it for the money. Sheila knew."

The Judge was making about as much sense as Mom.

Marti heard footsteps on the stairs, but she no longer cared what RachelAnne thought of her. "Who did it for the money?"

"They're not talking about him. He did it for the money."

She barely heard him. "Dad? Who?"

"Your mother isn't there," he said and disappeared. Just blinked out. Not even a puff of smoke.

"He's gone," Grandma said. "He won't be back."

"Marti? Who are you talking to?" RachelAnne said.

"Myself."

"You're *sure* you're not hearing voices again?"

"Only yours. Quit asking me that. I'm going for a walk." She pushed past her sister and ran down the stairs.

"Marti? We may not be much, but we may be all we've got."

Marti didn't look back. She hated it when her sister was right.

"Back door open."

Harriet was the least annoying resident of Bickle House, even if she'd flaked out when she was needed. Marti slammed the door on her.

No one, vulture or security, stopped her in the alley. Grandma Bertie showed up before she made it to the street.

"Do you want to talk?" Grandma said.

"No. Yes. Maybe." She didn't know what she wanted.

Her father was gone. More than dead. Gone from her life. The reality sunk in. Grief added to her confusion, diluted her anger. He finally knew the truth. She saw—and heard and talked to—ghosts. They still didn't manage to make peace with each other. Or had they? He tried to tell her something before he evaporated. Maybe he'd made his peace with her, and she was too ornery to reciprocate. She was ornery.

With no destination in mind, she walked, turning left here, right there. As long as she stuck to the sidewalks, her chances of getting lost were slim. It was a small town.

With her father gone, she was technically an orphan. A half orphan. She didn't want to be a full orphan.

She should be searching for her mother, but she couldn't get her father out of her mind. She didn't fulfill her end of the bargain. Grandma Bertie insisted he died of natural causes. All the signs pointed in that direction. She refused to believe her mother had anything to do with his death.

Grandma knew things. Things about death and the dead Marti didn't understand and never wanted to understand.

"He's really gone?" she asked.

"Yes," Grandma said.

"What about Mom?"

"I honestly don't know."

They stopped in front of the McDonagh house. Yellow police tape cordoned off the yard. The front didn't look bad. The second story windows were blown out. Someone had nailed a large piece of plywood over the big window. The porch was undamaged. And ghost free. No Sheila. No Mom.

Your mother isn't there. If The Judge meant he hadn't found her mother on the other side, he should know it didn't mean anything. Even if the worst had happened, she could still be here. In this world. He'd stayed long enough.

If so, why didn't Mom find her? The Judge did.

She could be stuck somewhere, like Ralph.

A car approached, a cherry light on top. She might as well stay where she was. If she was lucky, they'd cruise past. If not, they'd stop and ask what she was doing loitering at the burned-out house. Gawking was as good an answer as any. If Baby Face Rodney was in the car, he would fall for it.

She wasn't lucky. The car cruised to a stop, and Big put down the window. Dmitri sat in the passenger seat.

"Thick as thieves, those two," Grandma said.

"Marti." Big dipped his head in greeting.

"Hey." Dmitri waved.

"Have you found my mother?"

"No. I've got every available officer out looking," the chief said.

"And how many is that?" It was a small force, and they had other things on their plate. Like Sheila's murder. And Ralph.

"I'm looking right now."

"Me too," she said.

"I wanted to speak to you, so this is convenient." The police chief was polite, formal. Quite a change from the last time she saw him. "Your friend. Darrell Schoenburg."

"Darrell Scho—you mean Weasel Boy? Is that his last name?" No wonder she couldn't remember it. "He's not my friend." She peeked around Big. Dmitri wasn't smirking. That was a plus.

"You seen him lately?"

"Not since the car lot," she said.

"If you do, give us a call."

"Why?"

"They want to talk to him in Franklinville. The Burger Buster fire was no more an accident than that one." He tipped his head toward the McDonagh house. He looked like a bobblehead. "I'd kinda like a word with him myself."

"If I see him, you'll be the first to know."

"When we find your mother—and we will—you'll be . . . among the first to know."

Big Chief Honest. "I'm sure RachelAnne will call me as soon as you call her."

Big flushed. "Be careful. You Mickklesons haven't been on a run of good luck lately." He put the window up and drove off.

There was no reason to take his warning as a threat. It was the truth. It still sent a shiver up her spine.

"HEY, KITTY." A fat marmalade cat sat at the end of a driveway. He answered her with a meow and twined himself around her legs. She squatted and scratched his chin.

"We need a cat," Marti said. When this was all over, when she and Grandma had a house in the middle of nowhere, a living companion might not be a bad idea. As long as it walked on four legs, wore a fur coat, and was in no way related to her.

"I'm not cleaning the litter box," Grandma said.

As if she could.

"I don't know what to do," Marti said.

"Don't you think you need to get that phone out if you're going to talk to me?" Grandma said.

"I forgot it. I'm talking to the cat." She didn't care if people thought she was talking to herself, the cat, or an imaginary friend. Odds were anyone who saw or heard her remembered her as Marti Cray-Cray anyway. "Got any idea where Mom might be?"

The cat meowed, rolled over on his back, and showed his belly.

"Not you," Marti said. She obliged him with a belly rub. He rewarded her by revving up his motor and letting loose with the purrs. She picked him up.

"Who do you belong to?" He was too well fed to be a stray, but he smelled of stale smoke and charred wood and something nasty. "You kind of stink, big guy." The first two odors were easily accounted for. He'd found his way into the McDonagh house. The third smell had to be her imagination. She swore the cat smelled like her mother's tea.

"*Marti,* watch out," Grandma cried.

A silver car barreled down the driveway. Marti jumped and landed with a thud on her rear end. The cat leapt from her arms.

The Prius scooted soundlessly by, hit the street, and took off. The driver didn't acknowledge her. She doubted he saw her, but she saw him.

"That's not possible," she said.

"It wasn't him," Grandma said, "but for a second there . . ."

"Yeah," Marti said. For a split second, she saw Ralph behind the wheel of the Prius.

"This fellow was bald," Grandma said, "or close to it. Might have had a bit of a comb-over, unless he was wearing a rug on his head."

"I know him," Marti said. The car moved so fast she didn't get a good look, but she was sure she'd seen the driver before. Recently.

"Or one of his no doubt numerous relatives," Grandma said. "Remember—Bicklesburg."

"Good point," Marti said.

At the other end of the driveway, the automatic garage door screeched and began its slow descent.

"I thought Myrna said she lived in Harrison Heights?" Grandma said.

GHOSTS IN GLASS HOUSES 253

The door jerked to a stop.

If the housekeeper was at home, prostrated by stress and guilt, what was the "CLN-QU3N" Camaro doing in a garage four doors away from the McDonagh house?

The garage door squealed and moved.

"That's what she said." It hit Marti who the Jeff Gordon in the Prius was. Maybe. She *had* seen him before, and someone—she couldn't remember who—mentioned he was related to Ralph McDonagh.

Maybe Myrna was hedging her bets. Making sure she had a job if Mom never came back. "Grandma? Why is Myrna at Bumbles McBrumble's house?"

Brumble could be at Myrna's house. She could have lied about Harrison Heights.

"Is that who it was? Maybe they're consoling each other," Grandma said.

"What do you think, Ginger Boy?" The cat didn't answer. He was gone.

The garage door caught on something, stopped, started, and finally quit altogether about six inches from the ground.

Enough room for a fat orange cat with a fluffy tail to duck underneath.

JUST BECAUSE THE cat went into the garage didn't mean he was Brumble's. Or Myrna's. Just because he reminded her of Mom's tea didn't mean—what? The tea did have an air of the litter box. It could all be coincidence.

There'd been an awful lot of coincidences in the past few days, starting with Mom and Mr. Stumpy and ending with Mom disappearing in the few minutes afforded by the flaw in The Judge's expensive security system.

It was entirely possible Myrna knew about the glitch.

If Marti called the police and said "A cat smelled like my mother's tea," what would they do? Dmitri might believe her, or at least humor her, but he was with Big. She couldn't picture Big believing or humoring her.

She needed to go home to call. She didn't have her phone.

"Nice cat," Grandma said. "Are you going to sit there all day?"

"He smelled like Mom's tea." Marti stood. "I don't suppose you'd be willing to go take a quick look around?" Grandma Bertie claimed to have scruples about spying on people—people who weren't her great-granddaughter—but those scruples were flexible. She was gone before Marti finished asking.

And back before Marti finished brushing the dried leaves off her butt.

"You'd better come. Your mother's in there."

"Is she okay?"

"Define okay."

She rang the doorbell and rang it again.

"Myrna's in there," Grandma said.

She didn't know what she would say if Myrna answered—*Hey, did you by any chance kidnap my mom?*—but she stuck her finger on the button and held it down.

Still no answer.

"Over here," Grandma said. "Your mother's in the basement. There's a window behind the hydrangea."

"And just how am I supposed to get to it?" The bush was huge.

"Don't be a baby. There's plenty of room."

Grandma's definition of *plenty* left a lot to be desired, but Marti got down on her stomach and squirmed behind the bush. Twigs pulled at her hair. At least hydrangeas didn't have thorns.

"Watch out for spiders," Grandma said.

"Thank you so much for that." As soon as Grandma mentioned eight-legged creepy-crawlies, Marti felt them crawling all over her. Inching down her arms. Skittering up her pant legs. Throwing a spider party in her hair.

Mom. Mom was inside. She told herself a few spiders were nothing.

"And snakes."

"Did you see something?" She stopped worrying about spiders.

"No, but it pays to be vigilant."

Years' worth of grime coated the small window. If this was Myrna's house, she wasn't much of a housekeeper when it came to her own home. If it was Brumble's house, he was paying her too much.

Marti brushed away the remains of an intricate web. Cobweb, not spiderweb, she told herself. Cobwebs held dead flies too, right? She tried not to think about it and peered through the dirty window.

Mom sat on a broken-down couch, watching a flat-screen TV. Nowhere near as big as the one at home but, from what Marti saw, the newest thing in the room. The furnishings were bad, even by her standards. Myrna's chair was either growing fluffy white fungus or the stuffing was coming out in tufts. It looked ready to swallow the pile of florescent yarn the housekeeper held in her lap. The project hadn't grown much since the last time Marti saw it.

Mom held out a mug. Myrna set aside the ghastly afghan-in-progress and grabbed the mug. She said something. Marti was no lip reader, but it didn't look like she called Mom "sweetie." The housekeeper left the room.

She needed to call for help. Big. Dmitri. RachelAnne. She didn't know how she'd explain, but explanations could wait. She'd found Mom. Alive.

She didn't have her phone. Was it safe to leave Mom alone while she went and found one?

Myrna returned and handed the mug to Mom.

The tea. Myrna was using the tea to keep Mom drugged.

Unless Mom was there willingly.

"Grandma," she whispered. "When you were inside—"

A snake wrapped itself around her ankles and hauled her from behind the hydrangea. It sunk its teeth into her butt. She yelped. The snake covered her face, clamped itself over her mouth.

"I'm not your grandma."

Snakes don't talk, she thought, and dark overtook her.

TWENTY-ONE

"I want to watch the ponies."

Mom. Mom was home. Silly television and stinky tea. All was right with the world. Or would be, if she could wake up, pull herself out of the fog . . . or maybe she'd go back to sleep. Sleep was good. She needed a nap. RachelAnne could take care of Mom. Her sister did a better job of looking after Mom anyway. Marti couldn't take care of herself.

"Shut that woman up."

She knew that voice. Not Myrna. Bumbles McBrumblehead. Was he giving another news conference? No wonder Mom wanted the ponies.

Snakes twisted around her ankles. She tried to get up and run. She couldn't move.

Brumble wasn't on television fumbling through a news conference. He was behind her . . . *I'm not your grandma.*

Mom wasn't home and neither was she.

Her butt hurt. She strained to stand. She was trapped. Quicksand. Her limbs were leaden. Concrete. She was Mr. Stumpy. Sleep was the best plan. Naps were good. She drifted off.

"Marti. Wake up." Why did Grandma never let her sleep?

Go away. She tried to voice the thought. Her mouth didn't work. She forced her eyes open.

"Wake up." Grandma shimmered in the dark. "I'm sorry. I didn't see him coming. I was inside, listening to your mother and Myrna."

Marti's "Where am I?" came out *"Memmeuhuh."* Her lips itched. Something clung to her face. Tape. She was allergic to adhesive.

She struggled. It wasn't all a dream. She was trapped, bound.

Her eyes adjusted to the dark. Not completely dark. Light filtered through a high, dingy window. She was in the basement. Not the room she'd seen. Not the room where Mom and Myrna watched television. This one was smaller than her mother's walk-in closet.

Stacked cardboard boxes lined the walls. Garbage bags filled the corners. A broken chair lay on the floor. A high table sat under the window, its contents in shadow.

"Drink this and shut up." Myrna's deep voice dripped with menace, the stuff of nightmares.

"They stuck you in the storage room," Grandma said. "Your mother never noticed that man hauling you in. I'm worried about her."

That man had to be Brumble. For a short, fat guy, he was stronger than he looked if he carried her in by himself.

"She'll be out like a light in a few minutes," Myrna said, the menace gone. From the sound of it, Myrna LaRue Ward did far more than clean house for the public defender.

"Yeah, but now we've got two of them to deal with," Brumble said.

"We'll figure it out," Myrna said, more confident than her partner in crime.

Partners in crime. Myrna the Maid and Bumbles McBrumble. The two of them had her mother. Myrna obviously did know about the glitch in the security system. One of them probably caused the power outage.

Marti wondered who was the mastermind. If it was Brumble, he wasn't as dense as The Judge claimed. If it was Myrna, Marti had underestimated her. Maybe it was a case of two heads being better than one. Or equaling one.

"You tied up Miss Crazy Pants, right? Gagged her? She wakes up, no problem?" Mastermind or not, Myrna was definitely the one in charge.

"How stupid do you think I am?"

Familiar snoring drowned out Myrna's soft answer. Mom was down for the count.

He hadn't blindfolded her. That might be good. That might be bad. If Myrna and Bumbles didn't care what she saw . . . she chose to believe they intended to be long gone before anybody found her. If anybody found her.

Marti's arms ached, and her shoulders burned. She had a cramp in her neck. Her fingers tingled and her wrists itched and pain shot up her arms.

"Since you got yourself duct taped to that chair, you're no help." Grandma said. "I'm going to go see what they're doing. Make sure your mother's all right. You seem fine, for the time being anyway."

Goody. Duct tape. If the itching on her wrists and face was any indication, she was as allergic to that as any other adhesive tape. She'd have red wrists and a big, red clown mouth when she got out of there.

If she got out of there.

She'd seen an online report showing how to escape if your wrists were taped together. Brumble must have seen the same video. Her wrists were bound behind her. She couldn't move her arms, let alone lift them over her head. She squirmed. Every movement made her shoulders hurt worse. She could, for a few seconds, take a little weight off her sore rear end. She hadn't had a butt shot since she was a kid. He must have used a huge, square, rusty needle, and he didn't reward her with a lollipop, sugar-free or otherwise, afterward.

Whatever Brumble—she assumed it was Brumble, since Myrna was with her mother—shot her with was wearing off. The fog in her head cleared.

Stupid silent hybrid car. She never heard him return.

He could have at least taped her to a padded chair. This one had to be a twin to the broken one in the corner. Hard wood from a cheap dining set. It rocked, but otherwise felt sturdy.

Her legs weren't bound together. Each ankle was strapped to a chair leg at an awkward angle. She couldn't plant her feet on the floor. No hopping around, although she had no clue where she'd hop to. For first-time kidnappers, Myrna and Brumble had their act together.

Maybe not. Maybe the table was a workbench. If she rocked the chair enough, maybe she could scoot to the bench, find something to—to what? Assuming she made it to the table without crashing to the floor and flopping like a beached fish and making enough noise to bring Brumble and Myrna running, what could she do?

Something caught her eye on the table. In the shadow. *A rat.* A big furry rodent. In her head, she let loose with a scream loud enough to bring all of Bicklesburg running. Thanks to the duct-tape gag, her muffled gurgle wasn't loud enough to let her captors know she was awake.

Which was probably a good thing.

Tape on her mouth. She'd watched more than one *Escape from Duct Tape* video. The Internet was educational, no matter what anyone said. Her face itched from ear to ear. One piece of tape. It wouldn't taste good, but it was an inefficient gag. She worked her tongue between her lips and loosened the tape.

"Maybe I should go check on the other one," Brumble said.

"Leave her alone. We need to decide what to do with her," Myrna said.

"We could just lock them both in and leave them here," Brumble said.

"We'll have to move them. Don't want them found too soon." Myrna didn't specify whether they would be found dead or alive. "We can leave them at the McDonaghs."

Marti stopped working on the tape. She'd wait. Getting the gag off wouldn't free her from the chair. Screaming and shouting would only anger her captors. If they checked on her, finding the gag gone wouldn't please them either. If they hadn't made a decision on the dead-or-alive thing, she saw no reason to push them into one.

Knowing she could work the gag off was comforting. Scant comfort but better than nothing.

The thing on the workbench was another matter. Was it in the same place? She couldn't tell. She told herself it wasn't a rat. She hoped it wasn't a rat.

"Are you okay?" Myrna said.

"W-W-Why's it s-s-so c-c-cold in h-h-here?"

Marti had an idea whatever was wrong with Brumble was Grandma Bertie's doing. If Grandma had a plan, she needed to fill her in on it.

"Don't you go getting sick on me. I'm outta here with or without you."

So much for the Larry and Myrna-Bonnie and Clyde love affair. When it came down to it, Myrna was all about number one—herself.

"I'm good. Don't think you'll get away without me. Remember, I've got the money." Brumble's chattering was replaced by smug.

The fur ball moved. No, it didn't. It was her imagination. Probably.

"Your mother's asleep," Grandma reported. "Frank and Jessica James out there are packed. I looked for tickets, but couldn't see anything. I think they're in Jessica's big ugly purse. What's your problem? You can get that tape off your mouth if you try, you know."

Marti didn't answer, but only because she couldn't.

"I should check on what's her name, Crazy Girl," Brumble said. "What if I gave her too much . . . you know. It wasn't like I had much time to think about it. I'm a lawyer, not a doctor."

"She's fine," Myrna said. "In the long run, it won't make a bit of difference."

She had bigger things to worry about than the big hairy thing sitting on the workbench, but she couldn't stop thinking about it. It was there, in the room with her, and Butch Cassidy and the

Sundance Kid were in the other room. Just because she hadn't seen teeth or little scrabbly claws didn't mean the hairball monster didn't have them.

She cocked her head and stuck her chin out toward the table.

"What?" Grandma said.

Marti turned her head and looked at the fur thing, looked back at Grandma, and back at the table.

Grandma Bertie wandered over to the workbench. "This thing? Oh! It's Ralph McDonagh's scalp."

Marti gagged.

"Don't be such a baby." Grandma said. "I don't see any blood or anything. It's a wig. A gray Elvis wig. A Ralph wig."

Marti's relief that Ralph hadn't been scalped and her roommate was a toupee rather than a rodent was short lived.

Myrna said she saw Ralph driving the Escalade out of town the morning of Sheila's death. So had the Walmart manager. No wonder Myrna was so anxious for the other woman to go to the police.

Lawrence "Bumbles" Brumble was Ralph McDonagh's cousin. Stick Ralph's hair on him, hide the protruding belly, and disguise the lack of height behind the wheel of an enormous honking SUV, and they would look an awful lot alike.

Enough to mistake one for the other when Brumble tore by in Ralph's Escalade.

Enough to look like brothers. *Cain and Abel.* Myrna and Brumble had killed not just once, but twice. If the first was the hardest, numbers three and four would be a breeze.

"Put the bags in the car," Myrna said. "Back seat. We're gonna need the trunk for other things."

She and Mom were in deep doo-doo.

THE DUCT TAPE tasted worse than she thought it would. What she was going to do once she got it loose, she didn't know. The only people to hear her shouts were Myrna and Brumble, the only ones she didn't want to hear. And Grandma, but she was no help.

She couldn't get her hands loose. Her legs were strapped to the chair. The gag was the only thing she could do anything about, and she would do it.

A shadow crossed the shaft of dim light from the basement window. Marti looked up, hoping the cavalry had arrived.

The big orange cat gazed at her. She couldn't catch a break.

A face appeared next to the cat.

"It's your boyfriend!" Grandma said. "I wonder how he knew you were here?"

Weasel Boy waved.

Marti didn't care how he found her. He was her new favorite person. Heck, she'd let him call himself her boyfriend for at least three minutes if he got her out of there.

She spat out the tape.

"Call the police," she mouthed and hoped he could read lips.

He cocked his head. So did the cat.

"Get help. Call the police." She exaggerated her silent plea. Honestly, she was tied up in a basement. He should be able to figure it out just by context.

The cat yawned. Weasel Boy blew her a kiss and disappeared.

Mom's steady snoring hiccoughed, stopped, and started up again.

"Tie her up. Gag her," Myrna said.

"Can't I just give her a shot?" Brumble said.

"Go see what Weasel Boy's doing," Marti whispered.

"Do it," Myrna said.

"As soon as I check on your mother." Grandma vanished and left her alone.

A YELP INTERRUPTED Mom's rhythmic snores.

"Did you give her enough?" Myrna said.

The snores resumed.

"Grab her feet," Brumble said.

They were moving Mom—probably to the car trunk. Where was Grandma? What was Weasel Boy doing?

A thud was followed by a string of curses from Brumble and a groan. Marti thought the last came from her mother.

"What is wrong with you?" Myrna said. "Grab her shoulders. We need to get moving."

"W-W-Why is it-t-t so f-freaking c cold in here?" Brumble said.

"Who cares. Get moving." Impatience deepened Myrna's voice. If she didn't scare Brumble, she scared Marti.

More grunts and groans, then silence.

"They took your mother to the garage and stuck her in the trunk of the Prius," Grandma said. "They're in the kitchen right now arguing about when they should leave. He's for waiting until dark. She wants to go now."

A clatter and an oath came from the other room.

"I know it's here someplace," Myrna said.

"Leave it. You can buy another," Brumble said.

"Idiot. Tickets? Passports? Traveling cash? All in my purse."

"Go see what Weasel Boy's doing," Marti whispered. This time, Grandma didn't argue.

"I don't know how you can misplace something that big and ugly," Brumble said.

"Do you smell something?" Myrna said.

"Just that swill you've been dosing Queen Margaret with," Brumble said.

Marti sniffed. She smelled something. Faint, but unmistakably smoke.

The smoke alarm shrieked. Marti jumped. Her chair wobbled and rocked, but all four legs settled onto the floor, and she remained upright. *Weebles wobble but they don't fall down,* she thought. She really was losing it. They wouldn't leave her in a burning building, would they?

"Found it. Go," Myrna said.

"What about the other one?" Brumble said.

"Leave her."

They would.

Sirens joined the screaming alarm. Not police, fire department. Dmitri was right. There was a difference. She didn't care. *Someone was coming.*

"Help!" she shouted.

The only answer was a crash and the awful sound of scraping metal.

Another siren joined the chorus. Police. Both sirens grew shriller and louder until they came to a stop.

"Help! I'm in here! Get me out!" Marti shouted.

She heard people yelling at each other but no sign they heard her. She gave up on words and screamed at the top of her lungs.

"What have we here?"

She stopped screaming. She hadn't heard Big come in.

"That's one way of making you stay put," Dmitri said.

"Get me out of here." Her voice was as hoarse and nasty as Myrna's.

The two men, one on each side, lifted her, chair and all, carried her outside, and set her in the driveway.

Two fire trucks and a police car were in the street. A hose snaked across the yard. Only two yellow-coated firemen stood in the garage.

The crowd was in the yard across the street. Brumble lay on his back and flailed his arms and legs like an upside-down turtle. Weasel Boy sat on his mountainous belly, his hands around the lawyer's neck. Baby Face Rodney bent over the two of them.

"H-H-H-Help-p-p m-me! I'm d-d-d-dying!" Myrna curled up on the ground. Grandma sat not on, but in the housekeeper. Two firemen knelt next to her.

"It serves her right," Marti said.

The Prius's nose was buried in shrubbery. It didn't look like it had crashed through the front walls of Dmitri's childhood home, but it was hard to tell from her angle. The driver's side was crumpled. It must have bounced off the big oak tree at the end of the Doyle driveway. The back end was intact.

"My mother. She's in the trunk."

Neither Big nor Dmitri questioned her. They raced to the car. Dmitri popped open the trunk.

Her mother sat up. "I don't want to go to Moldova," she said.

TWENTY-TWO

Marti sat by the hospital bed and watched her mother sleep.

They still didn't know what all was in the tea mixture found at Brumble's. It did contain actual tea, along with the valerian and chamomile Mom had used for years. The stench was likely due to eastern skunk cabbage, a modification Mom herself might have made. Its stench covered the smell of the marijuana, an addition Mom was unlikely to have made. The Ativan, Benadryl, and who knew what else were Myrna's additions. The police found a veritable pharmacy—full of medications that combined, could mimic the symptoms of dementia—stashed at Myrna's place in Harrison Heights. No wonder the dynamic duo grabbed her the day before she was scheduled for blood work.

The doctor said Mom had the constitution of an ox. Both RachelAnne and Marti suggested he not use those exact words to her face. Her prognosis was good, once she detoxed. The doctor wasn't making any promises. It was possible the poisoned tea had something to work with in the dementia department, and it looked like Myrna upped the dosage during Mom's captivity. Long-term effects were a possibility.

In the day and a half since her rescue, Marti and RachelAnne took shifts sitting at the hospital. They sat, a few hours at a time, either alone or together, hoping for signs Mom was recovering, returning to her old self. Mostly, they listened to her snore.

During Marti's shift, Dmitri dropped by for a visit and filled her in on the investigation. Investigations. There were more than one, all tangled into a Gordian knot.

"It'll be all over the news tomorrow," he said. "You might as well know now."

He talked. She listened.

The who of Sheila and Ralph's murders and Mom's abduction was obvious. The why was convoluted.

Myrna and Brumble were falling all over each other, each trying to lay the blame on the other.

When the knot was cut, The Judge was at the center. No surprise there.

When the new juvenile detention center in Franklinville was built, her father and the other two judges pulled strings to make sure the contract was awarded to ReAdaptive Systems Inc., a private, for-profit prison-management company. He, along with his cohorts, received a finder's fee for doing so. The two living conspirators maintained they'd done nothing illegal. The Judge wasn't available for comment.

Although The Judge did his part to keep the beds at Wayfair School filled and producing profit, there was no evidence he was paid. That was where Brumble came in. His finder's fees were paid on a head-by-head basis. He was a lousy attorney long before ReAdaptive Systems approached him. Getting paid for mounting defenses so ludicrous the judge—usually the Not-So-Honorable Thaddeus A. Mickkleson—had no choice but to send the youthful defendant away must have seemed like manna from heaven.

The Judge knew what Brumble was doing. Her father knew and turned a blind eye. As far as Marti was concerned, he might as well have taken the money himself.

Brumble knew The Judge knew, and somehow, it was unclear how, he also knew about The Judge's so-called finder's fee.

While The Judge was alive, the two of them had a standoff. They hated each other, but neither could rat out the other without landing themselves in the same manure pile.

Mom stirred. Marti leaned forward. Each time Mom woke, she

was a little more herself. RachelAnne said she'd asked to see her grandchildren. They would be good for her. Marti wasn't sure Dmitri's story would.

False alarm. Mom snored on. Dmitri lowered his voice and continued.

Both her father and Brumble got nervous when the Pennsylvania Kids for Cash news broke. The Judge moved the family fortune, both the old money and the new money, into his wife's name. Brumble didn't have that option.

Brumble's problems worsened when The Judge died. He got a whiff of an impending investigation into ReAdaptive Systems and decided it was time to step up his retirement plans. Plans that included a retreat to a country with no US extradition treaty and the company of his part-time housekeeper and full-time secret girlfriend. Plans that might have gone smoothly if it wasn't for The Judge's penchant for pillow talk.

Sheila knew everything. Whether the extortion was her idea or Ralph's, they didn't ask for peanuts.

Brumble claimed they went to the McDonagh house to "talk some sense into them," and things fell apart when Myrna killed Sheila. Anything he might have done after, she forced him to do. She threatened to go to the police and not only blame him for the murder but tell them about his deal with ReAdaptive. The Judge wasn't the only one with a fondness for pillow talk.

According to Myrna, she was in the house talking to Sheila when Brumble burst in and bashed the poor woman's head with the garden gnome. He'd already ambushed Ralph, shot him full of sedative—probably the same one he used on Marti—and stuffed him in the back of the Escalade.

Brumble said Ralph's murder was improvised by Myrna after she used Mr. Stumpy on Sheila.

Myrna said both murders were premeditated, planned by Brumble, who wore the Ralph wig when he drove the Escalade and Ralph away. He forced her to help him and tell the police she'd seen Ralph on the road that morning. She said he hoped for another witness, but she was insurance.

Mom showing up at the McDonaghs' that morning was sheer luck on their part. Sometimes, coincidences did happen.

Myrna told the police where to find Ralph's body, buried in the woods next to Billings Pond. The coroner said he was still breathing when they stuck him in the ground.

As for Mom, since Sheila knew about ReAdaptive, they worried she did too. Both Brumble and Myrna claimed their intention was to keep her doped up enough to discredit anything she said, at least until they were gone. Brumble claimed it was Myrna's idea. Myrna claimed it was Brumble's. When the investigation broke, Mom's kidnapping was supposed to be a distraction. They hoped the search for the Bicklesburg queen bee would keep Big and crew busy until they got out of town and out of the country and put the McDonagh murders behind them.

Myrna swore she would never do anything to hurt Margaret Mickkleson. She refused to explain why she had Mom's passport and a suitcase of Mom's clothes with her in the Prius. Brumble claimed he knew nothing about that.

Both denied any knowledge of the obscene robocalls. On that one point, Marti thought they might both be telling the truth. She didn't have any proof, but she suspected a Pernelli. Any Pernelli.

Federal investigators locked Brumble's financial accounts. Myrna had blown her life's savings on a perfectly restored metallic-blue 1967 Chevy Camaro. There was a good chance they'd both end up with public defenders. With any luck, their lawyers would be just as good at their jobs as Brumble had been at his.

As for Weasel Boy—Darrell—she needed to start using his name. He'd saved her life. She owed him that much. Why he called 911 and reported a fire then proceeded to set a fire instead of simply calling the police, no one knew—other than he liked to start fires. He was implicated in both the Burger Buster fire and the burning of the McDonagh house. He set both in some misguided attempt to impress her.

"He swears the fire was small and you weren't in any danger," Dmitri said. "He's right. If he hadn't called it in, it *might* have grown, but he knew what he was doing. When the fire department got there, it was just big enough to roast hot dogs over."

She wasn't impressed, but she hoped Darrell ended up with better lawyers than Myrna and Brumble and got the help he obviously needed. She was considering paying for his defense herself.

Before Dmitri left, she asked how he knew so much.

"Remember our agreement?" he said.

"That was the last ten years," she said. "This is current events."

"We'll add a corollary," he said. "Don't ask how I got my information, and I won't push for a better explanation of how you knew your mother was in Brumble's basement."

In her statement to the police, she'd stayed vague on that point. She mentioned the cat but omitted Grandma Bertie. Especially the part about Grandma applying the full-body ghost freeze to the driver of the getaway car.

Dmitri left her sitting by her sleeping mother, wondering what his big secret was. And if the peck on the cheek he gave her before he left meant anything more than . . . whatever a peck on the cheek meant.

"Marti? Are you ever going to do something with your hair? And get yourself some respectable clothes. I happen to know you can afford it."

"Welcome back, Mom. How are you feeling?"

"Tired. Has anyone made a list of these flowers and their senders? Thank-you notes need to be written." Once word got out that Margaret Mickkleson might be in full possession of her wits and able to retake her throne, the floral tributes poured in, each bigger than the last. "Make a list and get rid of them. Send them to the children's ward or something. The smell annoys me."

"Sure, Mom. Anything you say." If the nagging kept up, Marti's benevolence would wear off. Right then, she was grateful to have Old Mom back.

"Oh, Marti. One more thing," Mom said. "Make friends with little Maggie. I have a feeling she'll need a friend."

Marti was dumbfounded. Mom couldn't mean what she thought she meant—but what else could she mean?

"Nana!" T3 and Maggie charged into the room and leapt onto the bed.

"Kids! Go easy on your grandmother. She's had a rough time," RachelAnne said.

"Ohhh, leave them alone. Hugs, my pretties?" Mom gathered the kids into her arms.

"I brought you a pony," Maggie said. She handed her grandmother a neon-green vinyl horse and smiled at her great-great-grandmother's ghost, who stood quietly in the corner and watched the proceedings.

"Six months," Grandma Bertie said. "You can give them six months."

"So," RachelAnne said. "What are your plans?" She didn't specify long or short term.

Marti decided to go with the short.

"Well, I'm told I need a haircut. And I guess we need to go shopping. I'm also told I need to refurbish my wardrobe." Six months. She could do six months, then reassess the situation. She had a feeling Grandma would make her life miserable if she didn't. And the kids were cute.

"Please take her shopping," Mom said. "I've had enough of you two hovering over me every time I wake up."

RachelAnne's face lit up. "Tomorrow. We'll go tomorrow."

"Peter?" Marti said.

"I'll get a sitter. We'll make a day of it." She looked at Marti's sweatshirt. "Maybe two days."

"Promise me one thing," Marti said. "No Ann Taylor, please."

"How about Lilly Pulitzer?"

Marti couldn't tell if her sister was serious. "Maybe this isn't such a good idea," she said.

"Just kidding. I know just the place for you. I'll pick you up bright and early. Seven thirty? Eight?"

"Aunt Marti? Why is the yady yaughing?" Maggie said.

"Lllllady lllllaughing," RachelAnne said.

"Because your mommy thinks she's funny," Marti said. "Make it nine and bring coffee." Six months. They might even be fun. As long as nobody got themselves killed or kidnapped. Scratch that. The rest of the world could do whatever they wanted, as long as no one—dead or alive—asked her to investigate.

"Deal," RachelAnne said.

ACKNOWLEDGMENTS

A big thank you to V.M. Burns for her help and encouragement and for the multiple readings as I worked my way through both the writing and the revising of my first mystery.

Many thanks to the members of AWFUL and the NoName Crit Group for reading the early chapters.

My deepest appreciation goes to my beta readers—Doug Anderson, Jennifer Ryan, Laurie Sterbens, Dan Fiore, Sigal Gottlieb, and Mark Cooker—for reading drafts and offering their honest opinions.

Love and gratitude by the bucketful go to my cousin Jennifer for putting up with me while I finished the first and second drafts, and to Lana and Andy for providing me with a beautiful place to live and write.

Thank you all.

ABOUT THE AUTHOR

Kay Charles is the much nicer, mystery-writing alter ego of dark fiction writer Patricia Lillie (author of *The Ceiling Man*, a 2016 Kindle Scout selection). Like her evil twin, Kay grew up in a haunted house in a small town in Northeast Ohio, earned her MFA from Seton Hill University's Writing Popular Fiction program, and is addicted to coffee, chocolate, and cake. Both their lives would be much easier if one of them enjoyed housework.

Visit her on the web at KayCharles.com

Printed in Dunstable, United Kingdom